THE FIFTH KNIGHT

by

CLAIRE LUANA
&
J. Sundin

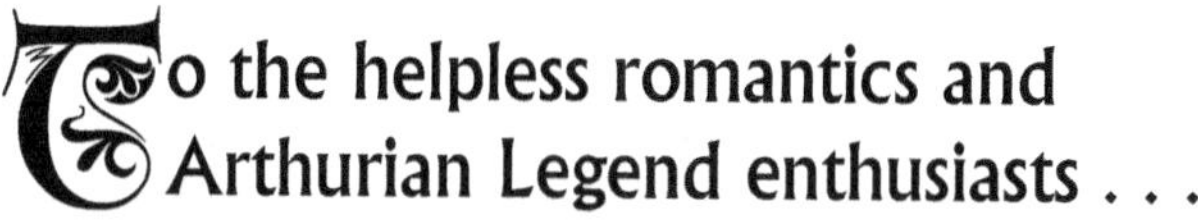

To the helpless romantics and
Arthurian Legend enthusiasts . . .

This swoony faerie tale is for you!

Glossary & Definitions

Adder Stone	(At-her stone) a stone from the Welsh *Mabinogion* that allows the beholder to see invisible magic. In Celtic beliefs at large, an adder stone (or magical snake egg) is created by the twining of serpent slime and saliva, especially on May Eve, so named after the European adder, and considered a highly esteemed talisman among Druids. But in reality, an adder stone is a naturally occurring glassy rock with a hole in it.
Afanc	(Ah-vank) a mythological lake/river monster of northwest Wales believed to have caused epic floods and held responsible for many small village deaths (also called an Addanc).
Aghanravel	(AH-gan-ra-vell) a fictional city in in the Glens of Antrim along Lough Neagh, province of Ulster, Northern Ireland. Home to the fictional Clann Allán.
Breton	(breh-tun) People from Brittany (a region in France) or who speak the Celtic language of Brittany (similar to Cornish).
Britannia	(breh-tan-knee-uh) A Roman province that incorporated all areas of the island of Britain south of Caledonia (what is mostly Scotland). This term is still used to this day.
Briton	(Bri-ten) the people who inhabited the island of Britain before the Anglo-Saxon invasion and who spoke Brittonic languages known today as Welsh, Cornish, and Breton. During the mid-medieval period, they inhabited most of the west coastline of Britain, even up into parts of Scotland.

Caerleon	(Car-LEE-un) A city in Southern Wales. Known as the mighty Roman "City of the Legion" and where King Arthur is historically believed to have held court.
Dál nAraidi	(Dahl-en-ah-ride-ee) a Cruithne kingdom, or possibly a confederation of Cruithne clanns in the medieval era, located in Northeastern Ireland around Lough Neagh.
Druid	(Drew-id) a person in ancient Celtic cultures who belonged to one of the highest-ranking professional classes. While some were religious leaders, many were also legal authorities, presided as judges, bards (aka lore keepers and historians), medical professionals, and political advisors. In neo-pagan circles, druids are considered nature magicians as well.
Fiann / Fianna	(FEE-an / FEE-an-uh) In Irish mythology, they were small war bands, typically semi-independent. In history, they were usually young warrior nobles / war bands who didn't own land of their own or hadn't yet come into their inheritance.
Fionnabhair	(FEE-oh-nuh-var) the Irish cognate of the Welsh name Gwenhwyfar or Gwenevere, meaning "white fay" or "white enchantress"
Fomorians (aka Fomhórach / Fomhóraigh)	(Foe-more-ee-ahn) They are known as the "people/tribes (children) of the goddess Domnu," a supernatural race and the enemies of the Túatha dé Danann, the first settlers of Ireland. Though many from both clanns intermarry. The Formorians are typically portrayed as orcish-like giants with water-monster features. Children born of Formorians and Túatha dé are considered extremely beautiful.
Grail	(Gr-ALE) From the Old French "graal" which means crater, dish. Grail's were common serving dishes. The idea of a "cup" or "chalice" is from the 13th-14th century.

Gwen	(Gwin) Welsh for a young woman who is so profoundly beautiful, you'll die if you gaze upon her for too long. A sacred and holy form of beauty tied to being a sun or moon demi-goddess, or a goddess of light.
Gwenevere	(Gwin-iv-eer) the English spelling of Gwenhwyfar, Welsh name for "white fay" or "white enchantress"
In-Between	The shadow "foggy" world in Celtic mythology that lies between the mortal and Otherworld realms. The place of "mist."
Lough Insholin	(Lock Inch-uh-oh-lin) means "Lake of the O'Lynn Island," for the Ó Fhloinn family, or O'Lynn, who hailed originally from Londonderry, Ulster, and eventually took over most of Antrim.
Lough Neagh	(Lock Nay) A large lake in the province of Ulster, Northern Ireland.
Ogham	(Ome) the ancient 20-letter rune alphabet of Britain and Ireland, used primarily by druids. Also used as divination runes in neo-pagan magic.
Otherworld	(Uh-thur-werld) also known as Tír na nÓg in Irish mythology, it is the realm of the gods and the dead
Pendragon	(Pen-drah-gun) the title given to the King of Briton during and after Roman occupation through the medieval period, primarily held by a king in Wales. Also known as the Head Dragon.
Sídhe	(Shay) The faerie people of Irish mythology (Túatha dé Danann) who lived beneath the hills (gateway to the Otherworld).
The Morrígan	(More-ree-ghon) the Celtic goddess of war and fate, the Great Phantom (Fay) Queen, often interpreted as a triple sister goddess. Also known as the "Crow of Battle" or the "Carrion Crow" and can shapeshift into a crow. Some scholars believe Morgan la Fay / Morgana stemmed from The Morrígan.

Tintagel (Tin-TAH-jell) City in North Cornwall, where Arthur was conceived.

Túatha dé Danann (Too-ah day don-an) is translated as "people/tribes (children) of the goddess Danu" and were a supernatural race in Irish mythology who lived in the Otherworld, but who interacted with humans in the mortal realms. They are also known as the first settlers of Ireland. Often called "faeries" and "elves." Though Irish, the mythological figures appear throughout the Celtic/Gaelic world.

Twrch Trwyth (Tork Troy-th) The Welsh re-telling of the mythological faerie boar of Ireland (Triath) as found in the Welsh romance prose *Culhwch and Olwen*, where King Arthur assists Cullwch in completing one of his impossible tasks by retrieving a magical razor and grooming kit from the bristles of a monstrous faerie boar for Olwen's father, a giant, who must shave his beard before his daughter's wedding.

Uí Tuírtri (Oo-EE tour-tree) A clann of Northern Ireland, descending from one of the three Collas, primarily ruled by the O'Lynn chiefs.

Ulster (Ohl-stir) Province in Northern Ireland

MORAY
ALBA
Caer-Benic
Castellum Puellarum
CASTLE OF MAIDENS
STRATHCLYDE
Lough Isholin
Aghanravel
ULSTER
ISLE OF MAN
Irish Sea
NORTHUMBRIA
Dublin
IRELAND
GWYNEDD
Brunanburh
Chester
Betws-y-Coed
Maesbury Marsh
MERCIA
Talgarth
SEISYLLWG
Caerleon
ARTHUR'S KEEP
EAST ANGLIA
Swansea
Severn Sea
ESSEX
Tintagel
WESSEX
CORNWALL
King Arthur's
Britain
1 BUELLT
2 BRYCHEINIOG
3 GWENT
4 MORGANNWG
5 DYFED
6 ANTRIM
7 LONDONBERRY
8 LOUGH NEAGH

"Then it is better, sir, to love

whom one cannot have?"

"Probably better," Lancelot said.

"Certainly safer."

John Steinbeck

The Acts of King Arthur and His Noble Knights

Chapter One

Arthur

The runestones clattered to a stop. Their long, Rounded forms remained shadowed in the cave's flickering light Arthur leaned forward to examine the carved marks on the wood, even though the Ogham language would elude him.

Merlin crouched down, sweeping his gray woolen robes out over the rough cave floor. The druid pressed two fingers to his lips and then grunted softly to himself.

Arthur stilled his hands at his side. The urge to test Excalibur once again was almost too powerful to resist. But no, a hundredth try wouldn't yield a different result. The sword wouldn't pull from its jeweled scabbard, no matter how hard he tried. Excalibur was stuck.

"Úath." Merlin touched the Ogham rune and peered up at Arthur. "Hawthorn. The faerie tree." He touched another wooden rune. "Straif."

"Blackthorn," Arthur said. "I do know that one."

Merlin dipped his head. "Then you probably already know that this rune is often associated with The Morrígan."

Arthur blew out a breath. "Morgana?" he asked.

A dark storm cloud crossed Merlin's ageless tan face at the mention of his wayward pupil. "This magic has the smell of fae all over it. If not Morgana, one of her older sisters. Perhaps Elaine."

Arthur swore under his breath. "So, there's a faerie curse on Excalibur?"

"Yes," the druid replied simply. The gold in his hazel eyes glinted from both torchlight and magic. Part mortal and part incubus, Merlin's cambion blood possessed a rare gift to divine glimpses into the future. Though not in a trance, Merlin's pupils narrowed with magic as the lines around his eyes relaxed. "Though," the druid said, blinking, "this curse is worse than I feared."

"We suspected a curse when the angry missive arrived, demanding Lancelot's head. But you say it's worse? I'm not sure what's worse than offending three unhinged sídhe heirs of the Túatha dé Danann."

"There's a second curse. I suspect a gift from the second sister, Morgause."

Arthur's blood turned cold within him. "Tell me."

"I fear Caerleon itself is also cursed."

"The keep?" Arthur asked, horror welling within him. He had claimed enemies a plenty in his four years on the throne without a stuck sword and a cursed fortress to contend with.

"Not the keep. The land itself. If you remain king, Briton will begin to wither as the land's lifeforce slowly drains away."

Arthur seized the tankard of ale Merlin had poured him and hurled it into the fireplace. The copper vessel ricocheted against the fireplace's back wall and then bounced across the floor before rolling to a stop against Merlin's booted foot.

Merlin was unmoved by Arthur's outburst. The tall druid simply bent over and picked up the dented tankard, setting it on a nearby table.

A flush of embarrassment flooded Arthur. He and Merlin had been through much during Arthur's rise to power, and the man knew all of him—every shining hope and shadowed fear. Still, it was no excuse. Arthur was king of Caerleon—the famed Roman "City of the Legion" of centuries past—and overking of the Kingdom of Gwent. Kings did not lose control over every piece of bad news.

"Finished?" Merlin asked, raising a dark eyebrow.

"Are you?" Arthur asked, raising one of his own.

Merlin barked a laugh. "Shall we move to the good news?"

"There's good news?" Arthur loosed a shaky breath. "Are you trying to kill me, druid? Tell me."

Crouching on his cave's stone floor once again, Merlin pointed to another rune. "Fearn—Alder, the warrior's shield." Touching another wooden rune, he said, "Úr. Heather, for healing and the Otherworld. Interesting . . ." Merlin indicated another rune with a side glance Arthur's way. "Ébhadh. It symbolizes conflict resolution. See how the Ébhadh partially lies atop Óir, the spindle tree?"

Arthur met the Merlin's inquisitive stare with a quick nod.

"The solution to your problem will come in the form of something small, perhaps delicate, but that wields an unexpected mighty strength."

Merlin left Arthur to ponder his revelations and crossed the room to a dark, smoky corner, where a set of shelves bore numerous items of questionable origin. Before the Lady of the Lake had declared Arthur the Pendragon and gifted him Excalibur—and, thus, sovereignty as king over Caerleon as well as all of Briton—he had been fascinated by Merlin's craft and spent many a wondrous hour flipping through cracking tomes, smelling bundles of dried sage, and peering into jars of pickled crickets. These days, he hardly had time to say hello to his old friend, let alone ponder the mysteries of the unknown.

The druid returned with a flat silver bowl, placing the common grail dish on the table between them. He filled the bowl with a pitcher of water and the droplets tinkled against the metal. "All magic can be undone. Every curse has a cure. It is just a matter of finding the right one."

"If you can't find a solution, no one can," Arthur said, watching as Merlin positioned crystals in a rainbow of colors around the bowl.

"How is Lancelot faring?" Merlin glided his hand over the bowl in sweeping passes. To Arthur's untrained eye, Merlin's movements seemed to match the tattoos carved onto the shaved sides of the druid's head.

"He's as ornery as a stallion with a pebble in his shoe," Arthur said. "It doesn't help that Percival and Galahad refuse to give him a moment's peace. Their jests have been merciless."

"They find a potential war with the sídhe fae to be humorous?" Merlin asked, leaning over the bowl.

"They're knights. And bored ones at that. So, the prospect of war may not be humorous, but they and their fellow soldiers find the prospect of battle exciting. And more so, they're men. The fact that Lancelot's betrothed caught him in bed with not one, but two kitchen maids . . ." Arthur sighed. He loved Lancelot like a brother, but he had half a mind to let Morgana and her sisters unleash their wrath upon him. How could the man have been so stupid?

"I blame myself," Merlin said. "I knew how dangerous it was to deal with the fae. But when Morgana came to me, wanting to be my apprentice as her older sisters had once been . . . Well, I let her flattery carry away my better judgment."

"We share the blame, my friend. Despite seeing Lancelot flirt his way into the beds of half the women in my court, I thought that his feelings for Morgana were different. He knows better than most not to trifle with the Túatha dé Danann. I should have trusted my instinct. Forbade their union."

"Morgana was desperately in love with that fool man and has been since before her magic manifested. And for a time, I believed Lancelot felt the same. If you had tried to keep them from each other, we'd be scrying for a cure to a different curse."

"Damned if we did. Damned if we didn't." Arthur ran his fingers through his short hair.

"That is the way of love, Your Majesty," Merlin said as the gold around his hazel eyes glowed unnaturally bright. "Ah, here we go. I found something. Give me a moment."

Arthur paced the length of the cave, eating up the distance across the plush carpet with his long strides. He wasn't sure why his friend preferred to live in this cave, deep beneath the grounds of Arthur's keep. But, at least, he had relented when Arthur offered to donate a few furnishings.

Growing even more restless, Arthur found his fingers straying to Excalibur's jeweled hilt. What kind of king couldn't draw his own sword? What kind of king was poison to his own kingdom? He shook his head, sending up a prayer to the gods that Merlin could find a way out of this.

"Yes, there is an answer!" Merlin shouted, his eyes wide. "I've seen something. More like, someone."

"Someone?" Arthur whirled around, hurrying back over to the bowl. The dish was empty, but for the still water and their own reflections. Once again, Merlin's magic eluded him.

"A knight. A fifth knight of Caerleon. He is the key to unlocking the curse." Natural light returned to Merlin's eyes as he pulled out of his trance and looked at Arthur. "The Alder rune now makes clearer sense to me. At first, I thought Fearn signified Lancelot, but no—"

"Who is this man?" Arthur asked, relief welling in him. His kingdom needed more noble-titled warriors anyway, but his other duties had prevented him from ordering a proper search. Perhaps this cure could be a solution to two different problems.

"I cannot see his face in my vision."

"How will we find him then? He could be anywhere in Briton."

"You must host a great tourney. Announce that you seek the strongest men in the land to fight for you. He will be there. And his blood will unlock the sword."

"A tourney. You're sure?" Arthur asked.

"The future is never certain. But I see this fate more clearly than most. If you hold the tourney, the warrior will come. Alder is not only the warrior shield but also unlocks the faerie realms."

"And this warrior's blood will heal the land as well? The second curse?"

Merlin frowned. "This is less clear to me. But I see that this fifth knight will help you find the Otherworld's Grail. And the fae's legendary bowl has the power to heal as well as break all enchantments."

Arthur groaned. "The fae's Grail? It's a legend. My father wasted years of his rule searching for it. If I must rely on finding the Blessed Grail, I fear all is lost."

"Excalibur was a legend as well, yet the Sword of Light *blessedly* hangs at your side," Merlin pointed out.

"Blessedly stuck in its scabbard," Arthur grumbled. Disappointment welled in him. He needed a solution, not a quest over a myth shrouded in mist.

"You will have something your father never had. This fifth knight is the key. Five is a sacred number, representing the elements of this world—air, water, fire, earth, and aether. Together, you will have a chance."

Arthur gnawed the inside of his lip, then gave a reluctant nod.

"Or, you can give up now and hand your kingdom over to Morgana and her sisters." Merlin's hazel eyes flashed.

Arthur bristled at Merlin's slight, drawing himself up to his full height. "A tourney and a fifth knight, you say. Very well. We will have both. We *will* restore my sword and my kingdom and show the sídhe faerie court that Arthur Pendragon is not so easily bested."

Chapter Two

Fionnabhair

I tossed a bag of gold at the man's mud-splattered boots, wishing I could knock his teeth out with the coins instead.

"Here is yer blood money."

Donal O'Lynn looked up from the apple he was cutting with a curved hunting knife, his dark eyes hinting at mirth. "Why Princess Fionnabhair Allán, in the flesh. To what do I owe this rare pleasure?"

Around the tent, Donal's warriors chuckled at their clann leader's slight. They all knew why I was here, and why I travelled alone. Though the men's laughter was light, their hands hadn't strayed from the hilts of their swords. They clearly viewed me as a threat, which was perfectly fine with me. I was one.

My fingers curled into fists when Donal tossed a delicate slice of apple into his worm-rotted mouth.

"Don't waste my time O'Lynn." I spat the name of the Uí Tuírtri Clann chieftain, the sworn enemy of my own family and clann. "I'm here for my father and sister. There's enough gold in here to ransom them twice over, just to ensure ye cooperate."

Donal took a huge bite from the uncut area of his apple, chewing slowly, savoring his ill-gotten victory over Clann Allán.

I didn't shy away from his gaze, taking in his long braid, the notch out of his left earlobe, the curving golden torc circling his throat. The slight twist in his proud posture that betrayed a pain—a wound to his right side or hip perhaps. I tucked all the information away. Details were what made a man. Details were how you found his weaknesses. And skies help me, I would find this man's weakness.

"Why don't ye sit and sup with me." Donal motioned to a small table nestled into the corner of his war tent. The hide walls reeked of sweat and blood, though far too clean to have seen battle. Donal tilted his head, a gesture meant to appear polite. But I knew otherwise. "Ye must have journeyed far," he said, "all the way from the glens of Antrim. Beautiful country. I'm partial to yer fertile land myself."

"I don't sup with snakes," I hissed. "Ye have yer money. I travelled alone. Now I want my family."

"So impatient." The corner of his lip curled in a smile that didn't reach his eyes. "Fine. We will negotiate yer way. Take yer money and go. Brin and Aideen Allán are not for sale today. Not for gold anyway."

I ground my teeth to keep my anger in check. I had spent the past month galloping through the province of Ulster and into Túatha de Londonderry, promising the moon to half the Dál nAraidi clanns, anything to raise sufficient funds to ransom my father and sister. I was sore, I was tired, and I had promised my sister or myself as a bride to a dozen different chieftain's sons. And now the fool man *didn't want gold*?

"Do not toy with me," I said. "I am not in the mood."

"Neither am I," Donal stood. "I'm afraid I enjoy having a king of Tara in my prison far too much. My men have not tired of yer sister's company, either. Keeping the men of Clann Uí Tuírtri happy is a matter of pride."

My sword was halfway out of its scabbard before I knew it. But O'Lynn's men were just as fast, and I found myself frozen, with the points of six swords leveled at me. Fury writhed in my veins, my blood deafening in my ears. For him to suggest that my sister had been defiled by his soldiers . . .

"Relax, Allán," he sneered. "I jest. No need to die today."

"What makes ye think I would be the one dying?" I countered.

"Ye've prowess in battle, I'll give ye that, lass. I saw yer little warrior band on the field at Ballymena, right before I took yer father. Impressive. But even ye cannot defeat seven men in hand-to-hand combat."

"I'll take my chances." I flexed my fingers on the hilt of my sword. I suspected he was right, though I would never admit it. I had sparred with four before, during endless drills with the warriors in my fiann—one of three female and male mixed war bands in Northern Ireland. But yes, seven was too many.

"Stand down," Donal snapped at his men, who quickly complied. "My men can't be killing ye today, because I have need of ye yet, lass. I told ye I would not take yer gold, but there is something I would trade for yer family."

I sheathed my sword, furrowing my brow. "I'm listening."

"Will ye sit?" He motioned to the table again.

My nerves gnawed at my gut, but I nodded stiffly. Perching on the edge of a wooden chair, I thunked my helm onto the crudely fashioned, hewn table. The bleached white antlers on my helm clawed toward Donal.

He pushed my helm aside, feigning disgust. "Ye're nothing like her, ye know."

"Who?" I asked.

"Yer sister. She's quite compelling." Donal speared a hunk of cheese with his knife, sliding the piece into his mouth.

I stifled a grimace. His praise of my sister was no surprise, nor his cutting comparison of us. Aideen's physical beauty—auburn curls, honey-gold skin, and brown doe-like eyes—paled in comparison to her compassionate heart and her clever wit. She was beloved throughout the clann territories by young and old. And where Aideen was the warmth of autumn, I was the ice of winter—white-blonde hair, silver eyes, skin smooth and white as fresh cream. My father, Brin, praised us both, boasting how a chieftain needed the warmth of his hearth and the cold of his steel. Some days, I believed him.

"Mistreat my sister and yer life will be forfeit," I finally replied as my fingers played against a point on one of my helm's antlers.

Donal flashed a toothy smile.

"Tell me of this deal ye speak of," I continued. "The hour grows late."

"There is a king across the Irish Sea—"

"In Briton?" I asked.

"Indeed. A king in Caerleon, Wales, by the name of Arthur Pendragon. And he has something I want. A sword."

"I fail to see how yer problem interests me." What was he on about? A sword in Briton? There were plenty of swords right here in Ireland. Was there no end to the greed of men?

"I have received word that Arthur Pendragon is hosting a tourney. To choose a new knight."

"I wish ye the best in earning the position." I knew I walked a dangerous line, but I couldn't help the bitter reply. O'Lynn thought to make light of my family's imprisonment, so I would make light of him.

"But it's ye, fair warrior, who will be winning the role. *Ye will* compete in the tourney. *Ye will* win. *Ye will* steal his sword and bring it to me. When I have the sword they call Excalibur in my hands, yer father and sister will go free."

I let out a disbelieving laugh. "Ye expect me to sail to Briton, win a tournament, *become a knight*, and steal a king's sword? I believe ye have taken too many hilts to the head, O'Lynn."

Donal leaned over the table, his smell of sweat and ale washing over her. "What I *have* is the upper hand. While ye have two choices. Do this for me, bring me Excalibur, and yer family goes free. Or refuse, and yer family becomes permanent guests here in Lough Insholin."

"And risk facing a king of Tara's warriors?"

"Clann Allán will be too busy fighting amongst themselves for a dead king's throne. Why do ye think my demand that ye attend me alone was an easy request?" He leaned forward and lowered his voice, as if we shared a knowing secret. "For how long did ye raise money? How many chieftains refused their sons in marriage to either princess of Allán?"

Blood drained from my face as the truth of his words sank in. Last winter a neighboring clann nearly vanished from the goddess's green earth in a battle over title and land. I was loathe to agree but, at this moment, Donal O'Lynn could set the terms. He could order me to steal the faerie queen's slippers, and I would have to do so to restore my father's rightful place in Aghanravel, home of Clann Allán. I supposed fighting in a tournament wasn't the worst task he could have set before me.

"And if I do this, ye will let my father and sister go free?"

"Yes."

"And while ye wait for yer precious sword, not a hair on their heads will be harmed?"

"Of course."

"They will be fed and clothed generously, protected as one of yer own clann?"

Donal put a hand on his leather breastplate, over his heart. "I swear it as Chieftain of Clann Uí Tuírtri. Their captivity will be as gentle as springtime."

I narrowed my eyes at him, my mind working the puzzle, turning each piece over to find a trick, an angle. "Why do ye want this sword?"

"Does my answer change yers?" Donal asked, stabbing another chunk of cheese. When I didn't answer, he continued, almost bored. "Suffice it to say, this sword, called Excalibur, has special value, both to me and a new acquaintance of mine."

I didn't like his demand . . . but what was to like about this situation? I sighed. It seemed I wouldn't be sleeping in my own bed for some time yet. Nor my family in theirs. "Ye will pay my expenses," I said. "My passage to Wales, entry in the tourney."

Donal stood, bending over to retrieve the bag of gold I had deposited before his great chair. He tossed the coins onto the table in front of me, as I had to him just minutes earlier. Large, calloused hands gripped the back of my chair as he leaned over my shoulder. "I would say ye have gold a plenty, lass."

My skin crawled at his nearness, his breath on my neck. It was all I could do not to pull a knife and slide the blade into his ribs.

"Now best get riding. The tournament starts in one week."

$\mathcal{I}$nterlude

Morgana

$\mathcal{T}$he crow soared above the war camp, a scatter of movement far below her. Cool spring air brushed against her dark feathers with every beat of her wings. Pregnant clouds gathered on the horizon, shadowing the moors of Ulster. She would need to find his tent before the storm rolled over the landscape. Her trained black eye peered past the numerous fires dotting the encampment, sliding over humans busy with their tasks. There it was. A large hide tent.

She released a loud caw and crows in nearby trees burst into flight, their wings like black leaves swirled by a furious Samhain wind. They circled around her, swarming in looping lines and knots in the sky. Distracted by the ominous sight, the guards failed to notice when she flew past and slipped into their chieftain's tent.

Donal O'Lynn's sharp gaze fell upon her as she landed with a flutter of wings before his crude blackthorn tree throne. A slow smile teased his cruel lips as he watched her magic summon the shadows of his makeshift court. Darkness and thousands of whispers—the desperate, greedy prayers of men at war—swirled around her, fueling her transformation from crow to a faerie queen and druid priestess.

"Morgana," Donal said, tipping his head in deference. His gaze crawled over her body as he lifted his eyes to finally meet hers.

"You have pleased me, mortal." She glided past him to a decanter of ale and poured herself a goblet. But rather than enjoy a sip, she turned and held the cup to his mouth. "Drink."

His hawk-eyes never left hers as he drank long and deep. His Adam's apple bobbed as he swallowed.

Morgana spoke. "The witch now sails the Irish Sea for Wales."

"Witch?" He laughed, as if she spoke lies. How fickle the mortal mind, quick to judge and quick to forget. She was fae. Lies never graced her tongue.

"Shhh . . ." Morgana caressed his stubbled cheek with one long, sharp nail. "Since the beginning of time, men have slaughtered their brethren in wars for what *she* offers. I have bathed in their bloodshed and fed on their fear. I know the signs."

Donal licked his lips. "I far prefer what *ye* offer."

"Of course you do." She leaned in and pressed her lips to his, satisfied when the hard lines of his muscles trembled beneath her touch. Men were weak. And Donal O'Lynn was weaker than most. "Mmm . . . you taste of power," she murmured. *My power*, she thought.

Donal's eyes riveted onto her once more, expectant. "Then tell me, why do ye desire to wrest power from this King Arthur?"

She pulled away—seductively—enjoying as the man before her fought his animal urges to claim her now before she flew away. A knowing smile curved her lips as she called once more to the shadows and whispered prayers, ignoring his question. Let him wonder. Let him yearn for the answer until he was driven mad with longing, as the weak often are. She had learned much in her time with Lancelot, most of all that when it came to human men, she would never again surrender her power.

Or her heart.

Darkness rushed around her. But, before she returned to her crow form, she said, "Do not fail me and you will be king."

"Of where?" Donal rasped. "Ulster or Briton?"

But she said nothing, for her powers of human speech were gone. The crow regarded the human male with one beady eye. He smelled of ambition, lust, and blood. It would do.

The magic welled up in her and she crowed, loud and triumphant. Then she took flight from the hide tent and joined the black-feathered murder darkening the sky.

Chapter Three

Lancelot

Lancelot had been taking his breakfast early this past month. Early meant enjoying his trout and stewed figs with a side of solitude. This morning, however, he would not be so lucky.

"Good morning crabapple," Percival said brightly from the end of the table, where he crouched over a heaping plate of food. The lad was trying and failing to keep the mischievous grin from his face. It seemed the only thing he was never without.

"I told you not to call me *that*," Lancelot growled as he sat down at the other end of the table. It was too early for Percival's shenanigans.

Galahad grunted from his seat next to Percival, where he was wiping his trencher clean with a chunk of honeyed rye bread. "At least he doesn't call you 'chipmunk.'"

Lancelot struggled to keep a smile off his face at that nickname. Of all Percival's ridiculous pet names for them, calling Galahad "chipmunk" had to be the best. The Norse man was built like a well-muscled oak tree. "I keep telling you to just crush his windpipe in your fist," Lancelot said to Galahad while waving down a servant for a goblet of ale and a trencher of food. "That'd teach the lad a lesson."

"I don't think our king would like that much," Galahad

retorted.

"I wouldn't like what?" Arthur asked, striding in, pulling his gloves off. It seemed their king had already visited the Round Table—the Roman amphitheater grounds—to prepare for this morning's tournament. Did the man ever sleep?

"Galahad crushing the life from me, ye ken," Percival said sweetly, batting his flaxen eyelashes. The knight was far too pretty for his own good, with straight chin-length copper hair that brushed at his pale square jaw. And he had only just turned eighteen. Lancelot sighed. Had he been so . . . obnoxiously cheerful at that age? He didn't think so.

Arthur stood with arms crossed and a sideways look directed at Percival. "Indeed, if Galahad ended you, it would deprive me the pleasure of doing so myself. Is there a reason you're in my chair?"

Galahad let out a deep booming laugh as Percival scrambled out of Arthur's chair and into one across from the large knight. "Wanted to see what it felt like, Yer Majesty," Percival said with a sheepish grin and clumsy half-bow from his chair.

"And?" Arthur asked, raising an eyebrow. His tone was light, but Lancelot could see the tension in the set of his king's muscular shoulders. He was worried about the tournament today. It was too important to go awry.

"A wee too serious," Percival remarked, stuffing his last piece of sausage into his mouth, adding, "Yer Majesty."

Arthur nodded sagely. "A serious ass needs a serious chair."

The knights burst out laughing, and even the servant who placed a trencher in front of Lancelot was struggling to keep a smile from his face.

Lancelot grinned at Arthur as he dug into his meal of venison sausage, trout, creamed barley, and stewed figs. When Arthur had become king, a part of Lancelot had worried that his ascension would change things between them, that his friend would become distant and unreachable. He was the only family Lancelot had, even if just sworn blood brothers. His concern hadn't been warranted, however. For the most part, Arthur was one of them—a fellow warrior noble. Or at least, he tried to be.

"Keeping your own counsel?" Arthur nodded toward Lancelot, who sat all the way at the other end of the table.

"Trying to keep away from those two." Lancelot nodded back at Percival and Galahad.

"All in good fun—" Percival began, but Arthur cut him off.

"The tourney grounds are readied," he said. "We've at least three dozen knights signed up to compete, some hailing from as far as Northern Ireland and Normandy."

Lancelot nodded, grateful for Arthur's change of subject. And then his mood soured as he thought of the last few weeks. He shouldn't need his king's protection from Percival and Galahad's barbs. Lancelot was Arthur's second-in-command, leader over all of Arthur's soldiers. But these past few days, he had not been himself.

Their king continued to speak about the tournament's details, but Lancelot only half listened, chewing his breakfast mechanically. How had things gone so wrong and so quickly? Lancelot had always loved the pleasures of men and women, and men and women loved to pleasure him. Dalliances had never felt like a curse.

Not until Morgana.

There had been something about Merlin's apprentice, Arthur's half-sister—from the first time Lancelot had laid eyes on her, she had fascinated him. Her beauty was ethereal and otherworldly, from the long ebony hair glinting auburn in the sun, to her discerning violet eyes, to the curve of her hips and breasts, arresting even in the simple gowns she wore while working in Merlin's cave. Raised by the Lady of the Lake, Lancelot was no stranger to magic. But Morgana's faerie power sang to him. A forbidden fruit that had to be tasted.

And taste her he did—all over the keep.

Heavens above, he grew hard just remembering the heat and desperation of their coupling. Nails raking down his back, teeth digging into the flesh of his shoulder. When she had suggested they marry, nuptials had seemed a novel idea. He was twenty-five after all, old enough to have sons several times over. And the passion—he couldn't imagine a time when he wouldn't want that fire in his life. Almost as soon as he had agreed, he realized his mistake. There was a wildness in her eyes that unsettled him more than he cared to admit, and she grew jealous, deeply jealous, like he was now a thing that she owned, not a man with a life and a path of his own. But he didn't know how to extricate himself from the match. Arthur seemed keen on the idea of strengthening his alliance with the Túatha dé Danann beyond his own blood ties; what king wouldn't want the might of faerie behind his reign?

And so, Lancelot indulged in what he knew best: a distraction from his coming nuptials. He hadn't sought out the two maids—he wasn't *that* fool a man—but when they had offered themselves to him . . . well, he hadn't said no either.

Morgana had torn into the room like a black thundercloud, and he feared for the girls, believing she would kill them in her rage. He had feared for himself too, if he were honest. Before him stood a black sídhe druidess, crackling with power and venom and vengeance. Pointing a finger at him, she spat a curse. A curse that sounded more like prophecy.

"If this is your wish," she had sneered, gesturing to the two girls. "Then this is your lot. Never again will you know the pureness of love that flows between one man and one woman. There will be a woman, a Gwenevere pure like the white of driven snow. You will long for her with all your heart. Perhaps she will love you too. But, if you join as man and woman, she will not only bring your downfall, but the downfall of all you love." Her violet eyes slitted in triumph. "Briton. And my half-brother, Arthur." And with those cruel words ringing in the air, she had vaporized into a crow and flown through the opened window and into the moonless night's chill.

The two girls had run sobbing from the room, clutching their clothes to their naked bodies. Lancelot sat, stunned, sheets draped around him as he digested Morgana's words, turning each one over in his mind while trying to find a way in which his life hadn't been irreparably changed. She had said he would love a "Gwenevere." The name was a legend in Wales, a nearly long-forgotten Cymry word for a white enchantress, a white sídhe fae. Well, he knew no such woman. Even when he had lived with his elemental foster mother, they had encountered no such creatures. He had heaved a shaky breath. Morgana's curse was meaningless.

"Lancelot?" Arthur was looking at him from the other end of the table. "You've paled as white as a ghost."

Lancelot shoved his thoughts away and summoned a carefree smile. "Just wondering if we'll indeed find a new knight today," he said, redirecting to a safer topic.

"Merlin seems certain of it," Arthur replied quickly. "We must all keep our eyes open. Amongst the competitors is a man who can break these wretched curses."

Lancelot nodded, guilt flooding through him. He had never been worthy of Arthur's friendship. He remembered clearly the day he had arrived in Caerleon at the age of fourteen, his foster mother, the Lady of the Lake, by his side. Uther was to foster and train him in the ways of war and men, as the prince Lancelot was born to become. He was old to begin such training, and Uther welcomed him with the same care he gave most of his subjects—thinly veiled interest. His foster mother departed in a misty vapor and left him to his own devices, and to the cruelty that followed for being fae-raised. The second time a mother figure had left him as an offering—or burden—for another to take in.

It was a time when Lancelot didn't understand the ways of men after being raised by faeries. His fellow soldiers had been quick to teach him—taking turns either ignoring his presence or picking on him until he bruised and bled. He was an exiled prince, a title with no power, a man with no living biological parents. No kin that he could claim as his own. He had drifted through Caerleon, desperate for connection and finding little.

Until Arthur. Until his friend made Lancelot his blood oath brother during a village feast and claimed him before all. Uther regarded Lancelot as another son soon after.

But how had Lancelot repaid him? With curses. Arthur's current struggles were all Lancelot's fault. After Morgana had left his room, she had flown to Arthur to demand Lancelot's head for his betrayal. Arthur's refusal to give in to her demands invited the wrath of Morgana's two fae sisters upon Briton. The kingdoms of Wales already questioned Arthur's claim to the Pendragon title without their suffering for his decision to defend Lancelot. And then there was the third curse. The one for Lancelot alone. He knew he should have told Arthur, but he couldn't bring himself to add to his friend's worries. Lancelot would handle this one himself. As long as he stayed away from any stray Gweneveres, everything would be fine.

Chapter Four

Fionna

My mood teetered between annoyance and awe as I surveyed the strangely round amphitheater from atop my mare. Wide grassy berms stepped down toward the enormous field below, where competitors swarmed like ants.

I squinted as the sun glinted off a particularly bright set of armor. I snorted. A set that clean had never seen battle.

I straightened my own leather armor, wishing the plates and guards didn't hang quite so loose. The ride across the Irish Sea and into the Severn Sea to the port of Cardiff, Wales had been nothing short of hell. Despite fair weather, my stomach had not taken kindly to the undulating waves or the rocking boat. I had passed a full three days at sea by spending equal times vomiting over the side and cursing Donal O'Lynn for setting me on this foolish quest. By the time I sighted land, I was weak from hunger and sick to my core. Two days of rest had restored my strength. Still, my agony had given birth to several creative ways to kill the man. I prayed to the sister goddesses that I would have every chance to use them.

But now I was here, and there was nowhere to go but forward. I clicked my tongue, urging my horse, Zephyr, down toward the field. The mare tossed her head, blowing out a snort that sounded skeptical. "I don't know why we're here either girl," I muttered, patting Zephy's dappled gray coat. I was grateful I had one ally here, at least.

Back home, clannsmen often snickered at my mount's Greco-Roman name. But when a cleric had visited from the Holy Roman Church and uttered the old god's name for the wind, I had known it fit her perfectly. My mare galloped light-footed, as though across clouds . . . the name was a far better moniker than the one my father had originally gifted her—Bolg Liath—Irish for "grey belly."

A riot of colorful pennants fluttered above a gathering crowd. The people were clothed in fine velvets and silks, the garments trimmed in pearls and threads of gold. Everything about this land spoke of plenty. I considered my own attire of rough hand-spun linens, animal furs and hides, and worn, oak gall-stained leather armor. They looked crude in comparison.

On my ride from Cardiff's seaport to Caerleon, my head had swiveled to take in the rolling green hills, golden fields, and tidy lime-washed villages bounded by neat stone hedgerows. A warm sun had shone down upon me from an azure sky, glittering off the crystal-clear rivers I had passed. Flocks of quail scattered before herds of red deer, who had hardly remarked my passage. My admiration made me feel slightly guilty, as I compared this verdant land to Northern Ulster's wind-swept shores and craggy mores. Of course, I still preferred my home. Perhaps the thought of stepping foot on that cursed boat once more had made Briton look so appealing.

As I neared the amphitheater's tourney green, I donned my stag helm. Few of the other competitors wore helmets yet, but I imagined those warriors were men. I doubted women could compete here. Briton was not as enlightened as her Celtic cousins across the Irish Sea when approving of female warriors—perhaps even women, regardless of station or occupation. Well, it was an easy problem to solve with my helm. Some men grew funny about fighting a woman. I would just as soon be treated like all the rest.

I slid off Zephyr and led her through a maze of swinging practice swords and chatting contestants, toward a bright tent slashed in the red and gold of Caerleon. Outside the tent, a wooden scoreboard towered above the crowd on tall legs. Painted placards, announcing the participants' colors and crests, hung from numerous wooden pegs. I tied up Zephyr and ducked inside.

Two men, clad in black leather armor and red cloaks, turned as I entered. I nearly stumbled, glad that my helm disguised the blush heating my cheeks. Perhaps it wasn't only the fair land of Wales that overflowed with abundance. Her men, it seemed, also put those of my homeland to shame.

The two before me couldn't have been more different. The man on the left possessed black chin-length hair curling about his head like a halo, and blue eyes as piercing as ice. Dark stubble shadowed his olive skin, framing a mouth with full pouting lips that didn't seem entirely fair on a man. Where the dark-haired man was tall and well-muscled, the man on the right towered over even him, with thickly muscled arms crossed over his well-sculpted chest. His blond hair was pulled into a messy top-knot, slightly darker than the honey-gold of his neatly-trimmed beard—a similar fashion to the Norse men in nearby Danish settlements.

I found myself wishing I had something to drink.

"Here for the tourney?" the dark-haired man asked. His voice was deep and smooth as silk, and he carried himself with an air of authority that was instantly recognizable. This man was in charge here. Perhaps only second to the king.

I nodded.

The taller man clapped his fellow on his shoulder. "Told you not to fret like a nursemaid. Things always turn out."

A look of annoyance crossed the other man's face. "You're in luck. A Northern Lord's son dropped out of the tourney. We're in need of another competitor."

"Good," I said, lowering my voice in a manner I hoped was convincing.

The big man walked behind the table and took up a quill. "Name?"

I thought fast. "Er, Finn Allán. Of Clann Allán. In Ulster, Ireland."

The man raised an eyebrow, turning his already handsome face truly devastating. *Steady Fionna*, I cautioned myself. I was here to get the sword and get out. I could ill afford any distractions, even such handsome ones.

"All the way from Ulster, eh?" He wrote my name down. "Nice to meet you Finn. I'm Sir Galijorheledanik of Swansea, but call me Galahad. And this is Sir Lancelot du Lac."

"Throwing out your long name now, are we?" the dark-haired man, Lancelot, dryly quipped.

"Fretting like a nursemaid *and* jealous." Galahad grinned and turned my way. "Sir Lancelot feels inadequate and needs to prove the size of his—"

"Don't we all," I interjected, hoping I sounded as ridiculous as these men. This earned me a large grin and a wink from the Norse man.

Lancelot placed hands on his narrow hips and was looking at me with his head cocked to the side. "Speaking of size, you're awfully small. You sure you're up to the task? The first bout is a four-man melee, followed by three more rounds of hand-to-hand combat. There are real warriors out there who've seen battle."

"I'm sure," I said, bristling. "I'm sure I've fought in more battles than many of yer so-called warriors."

Lancelot and Galahad exchanged an amused look. "Why don't you take off that helmet, so we can get a real look at you, boy," Lancelot said. "The tournament is to first blood only, but that doesn't mean men aren't injured. I would hate to send a green lad out there to be ripped apart."

I backed up a step, trying not to panic. "Ye wrote my name down. That means I'm in, doesn't it?"

Lancelot took a step toward me. "Yes, but the king's law—"

"Then I'll see ye on the field," I said and swiveled on my heel, striding from the tent with Galahad's booming laughter trailing behind me.

I stalked toward the practice ground, my heart hammering in my throat. I felt uneasy in this new place, surrounded by these strangers, like my skin was on too tight. I prayed to the sister goddesses of war and fate that I could shake off the feeling before my time to fight.

Aideen's heart-shaped face swam to my mind, and I let out a

deep breath, centering myself. I knew why I was here, and I knew what I had to do. I had held a sword from the age of four and had fought with a fiann since my first blood coursed. These pampered men wouldn't know what hit them.

Thirty-two men competed in the tournament that day. Well, thirty-one men and one woman. The first round was comprised of eight groups of four warriors, who would compete in a melee-style battle. I was in the last group and watched with interest as the other men fought before me, taking in the details, weapons, and fighting styles of each competitor. I would be pitted one-on-one with some of these men in future rounds. It would serve me to learn what I could.

Nevertheless, I found my eye wandering to the throne dais where King Arthur Pendragon surveyed the tourney. Even from a distance, I could see that the man was handsome—his short brown hair bounded by a circlet of gold oak leaves, his aquiline profile commanding in the morning sun. A sword hung from his narrow hips, decorated by a ruby atop the pommel. Excalibur. I set my jaw. That sword would be mine.

The two warrior nobles from the tent flanked Arthur in the stands, along with another I hadn't seen yet, a handsome young man with copper hair and an exuberant attitude. Arthur and his knights of Caerleon, the virile guardians of this realm.

The winner of the tournament, if deemed worthy, would join these proud men as the fifth knight to defend this land. The thought made me uneasy. Deceit wasn't in my nature. As far as I knew, these men had done nothing to warrant O'Lynn's ire, at least not to justify stealing a priceless relic like Excalibur.

I cast aside my sentimentality with a vicious shove. Excalibur was merely one sword. Little good the blade did while hanging on this pompous king's hip. In my hands, this blade would save my sister and father and keep our clann from civil war. I would take

Excalibur and flee this land. It mattered not whether these men were young or old, handsome or vile, honorable or cruel. I would take what was mine and never see them again.

It was with that thought that I stepped into the ring, saluting my three opponents with the blade of my sword. The pommel's worn grip soothed me, lulling my raging nerves.

As the first man came at me, a beast in brown armor trimmed in gold, a grim smile broke across my face. I was ready.

Galahad

Galahad liked rooting for an underdog, and so watching the little warrior in the stag helm thoroughly trounce the competition pleased him greatly. His good cheer only increased as Lancelot's eyes grew wider and more disbelieving. His brother-in-arms let out a muffled exclamation as the boy—Finn was his name—vaulted over his opponent and landed a blow on the man's undefended left flank. Sometimes he thought Lancelot forgot that others existed in the world who were also good with a sword. It didn't hurt for him to be reminded.

Arthur appeared impressed as well. His king leaned forward, forearms resting on the rail, his forehead wrinkled. "Where did you say that fighter was from?"

"Ulster, Ireland," Galahad said. "Seems your reputation is spreading far and wide."

Merlin had joined them atop the platform and watched with fingers tented before him, still as a statue. The druid unnerved Galahad, with his gold-ringed eyes and whispered words. But Arthur trusted him, and so by extension, Galahad did too.

"Do you sense anything about the competitors?" Arthur slid a glance to Merlin.

The druid nodded his head up and down slowly. "There is

something. A presence here that pulls to me . . . that is *other*. Hard to say where *it* comes from."

Galahad idly spun a ring on his right index finger, pondering what a strange twist of fate had brought him here to sup with kings and druids and the sídhe. He hadn't believed Excalibur was cursed, not until he tried to pull the sword from the scabbard himself. Infernal faeries. What did this mean for Arthur's sovereignty as king over the land?

Savoring the reminder of simpler times, Galahad ran his thumb along the smooth silver of the ring. His father, a blacksmith in Swansea, made each of his eight children such a ring, swearing this token would always lead them home. The ring's constant presence brought Galahad comfort, especially when his fate seemed too strange. Galahad spun the silver ring and gnawed the inside of his lip as he thought of his mother's incurable optimism, even when she served soup thinned with water and stale bread. Her happiness was infectious and he grew up never realizing how poor they were in a large Danish seaport town that boasted several blacksmiths.

Percival jogged up the steps to the platform, pulling Galahad from his thoughts. The young warrior's pale brow furrowed. "I'm back from the surgery tent. The chirurgeon says that Lord Iwan is bleeding profusely and won't be able to fight in the upcoming round."

The next moment, the crowd roared, drowning out what Arthur had opened his mouth to say.

Galahad looked down on the field below. Finn had drawn first blood with a slicing blow across his opponent's meaty thigh. Their match was over.

"He fights like a wee banshee," Percival remarked. "Watch out lads, we may soon be joined by the world's smallest warrior."

"Lord Iwan would have fought this man?" Arthur asked, nodding to where the stag-helmed warrior stood before taking a long drink of ale. "Could the loser of Lord Iwan's round fight instead?"

Percival shook his head. "He was injured in their bout as well."

"What about one of the other competitors?" Lancelot suggested.

"Someone already defeated?" Percival shook his head. "Nae,

that wouldn't be verra sporting."

There were supposed to be two more man-to-man matches before the victors of those would face off in a final battle. "I'll fight him," Galahad said. "His fighting style is unusual. It would be good practice."

Lancelot snorted, but Arthur nodded, gratitude flickering across his king's leaf-green gaze. Lancelot and Percival seemed to sometimes forget that a knight's job was to be of service to his king. That meant making your king's life easier, not more difficult.

Galahad stood and stretched, his back popping. He patted his stomach, now taut from the afternoon's meal, though still rippling with muscle. "Wish I would have eaten a bit less," he remarked.

Percival laughed. "Gives him a fighting chance, aye?"

"Get your armor on," Arthur said. "We'll delay by an hour."

Galahad hummed a jaunty tune as he walked onto the green grass of the tourney round. He enjoyed sparring with the other knights, but he knew each of their patterns by now. With Percival, the key was to be leisurely, fighting and striking until the lad grew impatient and opened himself up with a wild attack. Lancelot, who was a superior fighter when his heart was engaged, seemed so sure of his superiority that he often missed training. Often, after sparring for hours, he would begin to tire, his sword-arm growing heavy and his breath labored.

It was Arthur he enjoyed sparring with the most. Arthur was careful, disciplined, and skilled. His king watched and analyzed and executed. The only weakness of Arthur's he had discovered was caution. Openings that a more daring fighter would have seized passed Arthur by. His king needed to learn to take risks. Galahad tried to always be there with that painful yet cheerful reminder.

The little warrior Finn was waiting in the fighting ring, his helmet still on. He was swinging a sword in one hand and an axe in the other with a coordinated precision that often eluded even the most seasoned of fighters.

Finn turned and saw him approaching, his tenor voice muffled behind his helm. "I was hoping they'd send Lancelot."

Galahad chuckled, tightening his shield on his left arm. "I think he might be a touch afraid of you."

"Good," Finn said.

Galahad imagined his teeth bared in challenge.

"You sure are hungry, boy," Galahad said with a shake of his head. Had he been that eager for a fight, when he was growing into manhood? "Plenty of years to prove yourself."

"Why wait," Finn roared, and then lunged at Galahad.

Galahad brought his sword up in an instant and parried Finn's attack. The force of the boy's blow startled him. The fighter was strong, his thin short sword reverberating against Galahad's longsword. And fast. Galahad retreated against the force of Finn's assault. An axe and blade arced toward him in quick succession. The boy's style—to surge forward in a furious assault, and with unexpected strength—set his opponent on the defensive until he made an inevitable mistake. Well, that was enough of that.

Galahad roared and swung his shield at the boy, taking advantage of the significant height and weight he had on the other fighter.

Finn moved impossibly fast, rolling away from his blow. Galahad advanced with sword and shield. He then struck in fast succession much as Finn had, but with terrible force. The boy withstood the assault with quivering muscle. Each strike was met with a pounding of metal on metal, metal on wood.

Galahad found himself grinning. This boy was *good*. In the distance, a part of Galahad registered the cheers and hazzahs from the other knights, but his focus remained on Finn. It had to.

Finn came at him, throwing axe raised. With a loud cry, he buried the blade into Galahad's shield. Galahad's muscles bunched as he wrenched the shield back, pulling the axe handle from the boy's grip. Finn's silver eyes widened. A noticeable response despite his helm. Then the lad's gaze riveted to the weapon he had lost. Galahad tossed the axed shield across the ring, priming to battle with only his sword. This would remain a fair fight.

Finn rewarded Galahad's honorable act by lashing out with his boot and connecting with the side of Galahad's knee. Pain exploded up his leg. His knee buckled. But he wasn't going down without returning the favor. He toppled forward. Catching Finn around the waist, he dragged the fighter to the ground, half on top of the man.

Finn growled and jerked his sword's pommel toward Galahad's head.

Galahad's hand shot out and caught Finn's wrist. So small. Yet so deadly. He bashed the lad's hand against the ground again and again until the boy's grip loosened and the sword tumbled from his fingers.

Finn thrashed beneath Galahad like a wild thing. His small form remained enveloped by Galahad's bulk despite his efforts. The boy was skilled with a sword, but man-to-man, there was no way he could match Galahad in raw strength.

"Yield," Galahad growled, bringing his sword against Finn's throat.

"Ye yield," Finn replied, his voice as deadly as the grave.

A sharp prick nicked Galahad's neck. He peered sideways and blinked. Once. Twice. Finn had somehow managed to free a dagger, which was now leveled at the thick trunk of Galahad's neck.

Galahad started to laugh, the booming sound bubbling forth from deep within. "Good show Finn," he said, and then pushed off the ground to free the other warrior beneath him. He offered a hand to help the boy up, but Finn ignored it, scrambling to his feet.

Sweat dripped into Galahad's eyes as he shook his head. *What a strange man.* "A draw!" he called out, turning to the stands where Arthur gaped, eyes round and mouth parted. Galahad's booming voice carried over the crowd's low hum, spectators who were no doubt scandalized by how Sir Galahad had been nearly beaten by an upstart. Galahad didn't mind the prospect of losing so much. He had found his new sparring partner. "Your Majesty, the match should be declared a draw."

"A draw it is," Arthur announced as he stood and raised outstretched hands to quiet the crowd. "Finn Allán of Ulster will advance to the final round."

Galahad sheathed his sword and retrieved his shield, pulling

Finn's throwing axe from where the blade was buried in the surface. He flipped the axe over in his hand and offered the weapon to Finn, handle first. "Good fight," he said with a smile.

Finn took the offered weapon silently, staring at Galahad in seeming contemplation.

Without another word, Galahad turned and strode back toward the armory tent.

It was only when Galahad was past the crowds and peering faces that he let his smile slip. A strange feeling had arisen in him when he gazed into Finn's furious silver eyes. There was something strange about that warrior. Was this the *other* Merlin felt? Though Galahad didn't believe in premonitions, his skin prickled with gooseflesh as a sudden feeling came over him—a feeling that somehow, this tiny, stag-headed warrior was the key to all their futures.

Chapter Six

Arthur

Arthur had watched in disbelief as Galahad, the strongest man he had ever known, was was nearly bested by a fighter the size of a scrawny stable boy. He had declared the match a draw as his friend had requested, before turning to Merlin.

The druid leaned forward, his fingers tight on the rail. His gold-ringed gaze followed the fighter like a hawk watching a mouse. "My king, I think we have found him," Merlin said. "The fifth knight. The one I saw."

"Are you certain?" Arthur asked, his hand straying to Excalibur. He tamped down the tendrils of hope growing within him— what if Merlin was wrong? What if the tournament was a failure, if the knight who could break the curse wasn't here? But what if the druid was right?

How Arthur longed to draw his sword, to hear the clear ring of steel, to once again behold the faerie runes running down its length, urging the holder to "take me up, cast me away." He knew his loyal knights and friends did not question his right to rule, or his claim to the throne. But the sovereignty goddess' gift of Excalibur had made him, unquestionably, king of this land. If word of the sword's rebellion got out . . . Arthur wasn't sure how long he could fight off his challengers.

"I am never certain," Merlin replied, "but I do have a feeling. This is a path we must walk down longer."

"Then let us walk it," Arthur said. "Percival, will you summon the man of Ulster? I would like to speak to him."

Percival leaped from his seat and bounded down the stairs toward the man. Arthur suppressed a smile. Percival's youthful exuberance was equal parts endearing and annoying. Sometimes Arthur felt decades older than those around him. He tried to focus on the positive.

Arthur glanced at Lancelot beside him, whose blue eyes were narrowed. He didn't like how withdrawn his friend had been lately while he stewed in a world of his own thoughts.

"Ask him to take off his helm," Lancelot murmured for Arthur's ears alone.

"Why?" Arthur turned back toward the fighter who was summiting the stairs behind Percival. "We have never made such demands before."

"The king's law," Lancelot said.

"There is no such law."

"Sure there is," Lancelot said. "If you are king, your word *is* law."

"Finn Allán of Ulster," Percival said, announcing the warrior.

The short man bowed slightly, a fist over his heart. "Yer Majesty."

Not a low bow, Arthur noted. Some kings might be insulted by such a slight. Arthur was just amused. This fighter lacked respect for him. So why was he here?

"Take off your helm and let us see you," Arthur commanded.

Lancelot leaned forward slightly in interest.

Finn hesitated. "I would rather be judged for the skill of my blade than the look of my face," he said. His voice was slightly accented, but clear and hard.

"Are you refusing me?" Arthur slid a glance Lancelot's way. What was the boy hiding? Was he disfigured? And did Lancelot know something?

"I'm asking ye to let me win my final bout and prove myself worthy."

Arthur's eyebrows furrowed as he nibbled the inside of his lip. "Why do you want to be a knight of Caerleon?"

A split-second pause as Finn seemed to consider.

"The truth, not what you think I desire to hear."

"Becoming a knight is the best way to help my family," Finn said.

Arthur nodded. "An admirable reason. Very well Finn, you will have one last chance to prove yourself worthy of knighthood."

Merlin leaned over, grasping Arthur's wrist tightly. He whispered in Arthur's ear: "Fight him yourself."

Arthur looked at the druid sharply. "What?"

"Take his measure yourself," Merlin said quietly.

Arthur examined Merlin's face for some explanation, and found none. The druid was as enigmatic as ever. But, he had learned to trust the man.

Clearing his throat, Arthur stood. "I shall be your opponent for your last bout. Make yourself ready. The match shall begin within the next candle mark."

Finn seemed momentarily taken aback but covered his slip in reaction well. Then, he dipped his head in a slight bow and turned, stalking off the platform.

"You should have made him take his helmet off," Lancelot protested.

"What do I care?" Arthur snapped, his patience at Lancelot wearing thin. "He could have the head of a donkey and I will knight him, if doing so means saving this kingdom." He took a breath, steadying himself. "Besides, you're pretty enough for three knights." He gave Lancelot a playful slap on the cheek before heading off the platform to retrieve his armor.

Percival's laugh followed him down the steps.

t had been years since Arthur had fought in a tourney. Despite the dire circumstances, he found his steps light as a smile played across his face.

The little warrior was in the corner of the ring and turned toward Arthur as he strode into the round. Arthur found the lack of deference strangely refreshing. The man from Ulster didn't scrape and bow or even kneel to him. This was the part of being king he least liked—the endless parade of supplicants and nobles, trying either to win his favor or to gain a favor.

"Not going to fight with yer fancy sword?" Finn nodded from Excalibur, still strapped to Arthur's hip, toward the simple blade Arthur held in his hand. Arthur stifled a grimace as his mood dropped like an anchor. All right, maybe the man's impertinence wasn't entirely refreshing.

"Excalibur is an enchanted blade," he replied with a slight shrug. "Such a weapon wouldn't be fair for a tourney."

"Then why won't ye take your sacred blade off?"

"Why won't you take off your helm?" Arthur countered.

Finn nodded at that, as if to give the point to Arthur.

Galahad had returned to the raised dais, and now waved a flagon of ale, calling out in a cheerful voice, "Are you going to yammer all day like old women or are you going to fight?"

It was all the encouragement Finn needed, for the man came at Arthur with a shout.

Arthur had watched Finn fight in several bouts now, including the fight against Galahad. So, he was ready. He countered Finn's furious strokes with parries and blows of his own. Their feet shuffled around the ring in a warrior's dance.

The fighting stretched on, each of them trying and testing, fighting and falling back.

Arthur panted. Sweat poured down his face. His muscles burned and shook from the exertion. Still, he was surprised to find that he had meant his earlier comment. Finn could have the head of a donkey, and Arthur would still be happy to have him as a knight. Even if he wasn't the man foretold by Merlin to break the curse. He could always use another soldier. But, if Finn *was* the man who would free Excalibur . . . Arthur had to know. Time to end this fight.

And, so, he took a page out of Finn's book. The warrior came at him with a particularly vicious swing. Arthur met it with his own blade. The two swords locked together. Finn strained against his sword, gritting his teeth while struggling to shove Arthur off.

Arthur pulled out a wicked little dagger sheathed behind his back and, in one lithe motion, he sliced across Finn's forearm. "First blood," Arthur declared.

The fighter's eyes went wide. "Did ye just . . . steal my trick?" he asked, breaking away from Arthur, his sword tip drooping toward the ground.

"Never let history say how we're not adaptable here in the mighty City of the Legion." Arthur grinned and, with a surreptitious motion, wiped the dagger's blade across Excalibur's leather grip.

The effect was instantaneous. Searing light blasted from Excalibur, sending streaks of silver over the gathered crowd. Arthur threw up his arm to ward off the onslaught.

Finn stumbled away from him as the crowd shouted in surprise—many pointing, a few running from the stands in fear.

But as suddenly as the magic had begun, the light died, leaving Excalibur quiet and dim at Arthur's side. Hope bloomed in his chest and he gripped the sword with a murmured prayer to the old gods.

His sword yielded.

Arthur pulled Excalibur from its scabbard, the sword ringing out in a single pealing note. The Sword of Light was as beautiful and deadly as the first day the Lady of the Lake had bequeathed the blade to him. He wanted to fall to the grass and weep in relief.

Around him, the crowd stood in hushed awe.

But Finn stood back warily.

Arthur scrambled for an explanation for the sudden burst of magic. Only his knights and Merlin knew that anything had been wrong with Excalibur. And he intended to keep it that way.

"I held this tournament to find a fifth knight! A fighter worthy to join my inner-circle of warrior nobles." Arthur called out. His deep voice resounded throughout the amphitheater. "And now we have found one. Excalibur itself has recognized the divine calling of this man. You all were witness to its magic, blessing his service to our land. You have seen him fight bravely and valiantly today. Caerleon is fortunate indeed to have such a worthy warrior to defend her, as well as all of Briton." His path was clear now. Though from a foreign land, Finn was Caerleon's—and his—only hope.

"So kneel, Finn Allán," Arthur said.

Finn did as he was told, his stag helm lowering before Arthur.

"Do you, Finn Allán of Ulster, swear fealty to me as your king, to follow me into battle and protect the land I govern?"

The stag helm lifted and silver eyes met his. "I do swear my fealty and my sword arm, My King."

"Then I, Arthur Pendragon, son of Uther Pendragon, king of Caerleon, overking in the Kingdom of Gwent, and High King of Briton, hereby deem thee knight." Arthur tapped his sword on the man's shoulders. A thin tendril of violet light left Excalibur and touched Finn's shoulders with each tap, and Arthur relaxed. The sword recognized Finn as belonging to his inner circle.

"Now rise, Sir Finn Allán, knight of Caerleon," Arthur said with confidence. But deep within, he wondered what sort of man he had just yoked to his kingdom.

Chapter Seven

Fionna

King Arthur Pendragon was not what I had expected. I tried to shake my unease. His words—the phantom feeling of his enchanted blade—settled upon my shoulders like a stonweight.

The crowd stood around the amphitheater, clapping and stomping their feet in jubilee. This unsettled me too. I hadn't expected to be welcomed. To be celebrated. In truth, I didn't know what I had expected.

Arthur addressed the crowd. "Join us for a feast in the Great Hall! We will make merry and show our newest knight a true Caerleon welcome!"

The hazzahs and hollers grew deafening, most likely at the prospect of free food and ale.

The king laid a friendly hand on my shoulder. "I am eager to become acquainted with you Finn, and I know my men are too." His touch sent tingles down my spine, and I nodded, unable to resist eyeing him sideways through the slit in my helm. Even with sweat beading on his tan brow, his helmet under his arm, he looked every inch a king. A square jaw and proud nose sprinkled with a light dusting of freckles, vibrant green eyes that spoke of a man of both wisdom and kindness, despite his youth. He had to be no more than twenty-two, yet he carried himself with the confidence of a white-haired ruler. And his smile . . . which he was turning on me right now. Lush lips, straight white teeth. Happiness transformed his face from handsome to knee-wobbling. A hay-loft smile, Aideen would have called it.

"A man who was blessed with such a grin can expect to enjoy a trip to the hayloft," I could almost hear my younger sister explain with a sly giggle. I swallowed back the ache tightening my throat. Was my sister safe? My father?

It was as if Arthur could hear my thoughts. Well, thankfully not *all* of my thoughts. "You spoke of your family. I should like to hear of them, and your life in Ulster," the king said. "I suspect you have a story to tell."

You have no idea, I thought darkly. I managed another nod.

"Ah, Percival," Arthur said, as the copper-haired young man vaulted over the railing of their viewing platform and down onto the ground before us. "Sir Percival of Caer Benic, the newest of my knights. Well, not anymore," Arthur corrected himself with a rueful laugh.

"The role of newest knight comes with all the shit jobs, Finn," Percival said with a wide grin. "I for one, am pleased to pass the torch. Welcome to Caerleon, lad."

"There aren't any shit jobs," Arthur frowned, but his expression wasn't serious.

"Not for the king," Percival shot back.

To my surprise, Arthur just grinned. "One of the perks, my boy," he said, clapping the other man on the shoulder. Arthur's familiarity with his knights surprised me. Dál nAraidi clann chieftains were often close with their warriors, but I had expected a king of Briton to be aloof, to set himself apart. Arthur and his sword-brothers seemed—like friends.

"Will you show Finn to an extra room, so he can bathe and change? Then bring him to the feast?" Arthur asked Percival. "Hope that's not too much of a shit task for you."

"Nae, a job is far superior when there's ale at the end," Percival said, winking at me. "I think I can manage."

With a dip of his head, Arthur strode off, and I found myself walking beside Percival up to the wooden keep that was Arthur's main fortress.

Percival had the lanky build of youth, though his shoulders were broad under his leather jerkin, and he wore the sword on his hip with practiced ease. He'd fill out nicely in a year or two, I thought. His rich brown eyes were mirthful, framed by long copper lashes that would make any maiden jealous. I groaned inside, realizing that I was staring again. What was it about these men that addled my brain so?

The memory of Galahad's weight upon me set my cheeks flaming and a low heat coursing through my body. Never before in a fight had I ever seen a man as anything other than an opponent, a man to kill. But in that moment, my body had betrayed me. Every inch of me had wished that only night air separated us. My senses rebelled as if I could actually taste the salt and honey of his golden skin. The memory mortified me. A split second in battle made all the difference, and I had let the sweet daydream fill my mind. He had almost beaten me. Where would that leave my father? My sister? In my mind's eye, I seized myself by the scruff of my neck and shook—hard. No more slips.

From the amphitheater grounds, we followed a meandering path toward the keep, surrounded by chatting nobles and competitors. Arthur's fortress was a thing of beauty, hewn from dark timber that shone with brilliant red oak hues in the afternoon sun. I could almost envision the Romans establishing this military location, as I had been told by an overly-friendly warrior between bouts. The Pendragon banner—a red cloth trimmed in gold with an ornate dragon for the High King of Briton—fluttered from the keep's high timbered walls. The fortress sat atop a steep grass-covered hill, making the keep nicely defensible, and also a nuisance to climb toward.

The muscles in my legs burned as fatigue from the day's exertions settled bone deep. The high adrenaline from today was quickly draining from me, leaving a growing, empty pit within. I needed to eat, then sleep, then eat some more.

"I'll get ye a room in the East Wing, that's where Arthur and the rest of us knights sleep," Percival explained. "Ye can bathe and change before the feast."

My stomach clenched. I knew I was avoiding the inevitable, but I didn't want to face *that* moment—the very moment when my helmet came off and they all gaped slack-jawed as if I possessed three heads. Most men didn't take kindly to losing to a woman, and I didn't know enough about these four warriors to judge what their reaction would be. I would reveal my face after I had fortified myself with food. And ale. Lots of ale.

"I would like to go straight to the feast," I said, clearing my dry throat. "I'm starving."

A look of uncertainty crossed Percival's face, but then he shrugged. "If ye want to be covered in sweat and dirt. Yer choice, lad."

"Thanks," I said. "I'll bathe tonight," I added, finding that I didn't want him to think me a total savage. But then I caught myself. What did it matter what this man thought? I would bathe in blood if doing so meant I could steal the sword and escape alive. I had only one objective. Excalibur.

We crossed over the fortress's sparkling moat and into the keep's main courtyard, which brimmed with people in colorful dresses and coats. I craned my neck to take in three soaring towers and all the tidy rows of inner buildings constructed in cob and black timber fashion. Latticed windows scintillated in the warm sunlight and I squinted my eyes. I had never seen a structure so grand.

"Ye will like being a warrior noble here, Finn," Percival said with an air of infectious enthusiasm. "Food is excellent, the other knights are good men, and Arthur is a fair ruler. And women love braw knights," he said to me with a waggle of his ginger eyebrows. "If ye can steal one away from Lancelot, that is. The lot of them seem to be twisted around his cock, if ye ken my meaning."

"Yer meaning is quite plain," I said drolly. It didn't surprise me to hear that Lancelot was successful with women. The man was the most striking in the entire striking bunch. His blue eyes alone were remarkable, somehow filled with both fire and ice.

"Did I hear mention of my cock?" Lancelot jogged up behind them, falling into step beside me as we approached the Great Hall.

"No one is interested in yer cock," I retorted, prickling at his presence.

"You would be surprised." Lancelot slid me a smile and winked.

I focused on the ground moving beneath my feet. Did he just . . . flirt? Did he know I was a woman? Or did he sway toward men? Regardless, Lancelot made me uneasy, no matter how handsome he was. Several times during the tourney, I had caught his stare. While others on the throne dais appeared surprised by my show, the slight furrow of Lancelot's dark brows and the way his lips pinched suggested his disapproval. Of me personally or my prowess on the green? I knew not, and not knowing made him suspect as well.

The dark knight seemed more relaxed now, more at ease. I peered back up and wished I hadn't. He had loosened the buckles of his armor, revealing a glimpse of the broad plane of his chest through the low-cut neckline of his tunic. A finger of pale sunlight caressed his exposed olive skin and corded muscle. I swallowed thickly. Again. I really needed that ale.

We passed into the raucous Great Hall and I gawked at the sight. Two huge wrought iron chandeliers hung from arched vaulted ceilings, coated in wax drippings, while colored glass on the Hall's far end let in a kaleidoscope of rainbow hues. Dozens of long wooden tables flanked the room, their polished surfaces covered by an array of edibles. My entire clann could fit in this room. And be fed by this feast. I revised my assessment of Arthur's wealth and status. Caerleon was a rich city indeed.

I drew in a shaky breath and slowed my steps as my gaze locked onto the colored-glass windows once more. Windows could be stained? Or were they gems?

"A coronation gift for Arthur from the Túatha dé Danann," Lancelot said. "Presented by my foster mother."

"Beautiful," I breathed. "Faerie made, then?"

"The light glows more brightly in the presence of fae, so I was told."

I barely registered Lancelot's words. Rainbow beams of light held me captive as the air fairly vibrated with a magic that sang to my blood. For a moment, I was transported away from today and my troubles. It was as if I knew this place, though nothing could be further from the truth. My pulse thrummed loud in my chest, my lips parted with a wonder I could not explain. And I forgot—forgot about the knights at my side and the helmet upon my head until *he* shadowed my mood.

Lancelot stepped in front of my path—his ice-blue eyes flashing, his strong jaw set. "Do you wear that helmet to sleep Finn? Because you're a knight now, so the helm should be removed before standing before our king."

And before I could get my hands up to ward him off, he pounced, seizing an antler and jerking the helm from my head.

Cool air rushed in about me as my long white-blonde braids tumbled down over my shoulder. I took in a startled hiss of breath to smother the string of curses that threatened to bubble forth. Then, I squared my shoulders and drew myself up to full height, taking a perverse pleasure at the stunned expression on his face. Nothing for it. The deed was done. My secret was out.

Lancelot

ancelot wasn't sure what he had expected under the crown of Finn's antlers, but not this.

A woman. King Arthur Pendragon knighted a woman. Even Percival, never without a jest or a jab, was rendered mute, his mouth slackened in shock.

It was a peculiar sensation, the current of emotions flooding through him. Already the surprise was wearing off, bleeding into something deep and low and hot. For what a woman she was—this stranger they had tied their lives to.

As if carved from marble, she had a face hewn of elegant lines and angles. Faint brows formed the trails of two shooting stars. White-blonde hair, plaited with black-stained leather in a cord of braids, bunched and draped over her shoulders. Her eyes glimmered like waterfall mist, her skin as pure and unblemished as an untouched snowdrift. She shone with a cold fire that called to him, a wild song that kindled an answering blaze within him, startling in its intensity.

Fear seized his heart with a gauntleted grip as Morgana's words echoed loudly in his mind. *There will be a woman, a Gwenevere pure like the white of driven snow. You will long for her with all your heart. Perhaps she will love you too, but if you two join as man and woman, she will bring not only your downfall, but the downfall of all you love.*

Caerleon. And Arthur.

He had shrugged off the curse, dismissed her words as scorned nonsense. He knew no Gwenevere, no white enchantress pure as the driven snow. Or he hadn't . . . *then.*

"Sir Lancelot du Lac," she said, holding her chin at a haughty angle. "Is something amiss?"

Her words were a challenge, a dare. One he could not meet. For now, he saw the game she had played, saw how she had thoroughly out-maneuvered them. Arthur had made her a knight before the entire kingdom—an unmarried woman holding a noble title reserved only for men. No less, she had earned the spot. Gods help him, this woman outfought every competitor. She matched Galahad and Arthur blow for blow. Now they were too far down this road to turn back.

"Yer a lass!" Percival laughed, his arms akimbo. "A bonnie one at that too."

Perhaps Lancelot would have been delighted, too, had things been different. There were worse fates than to live and train beside a gorgeous woman. But Percival didn't know what this meant for Lancelot. For all of them. Didn't understand the danger she posed.

Arthur and Galahad chose that moment to stroll into the Great Hall. Arthur had removed his armor and once again donned his fine woolen tunic. His cheeks were flushed, a handsome smile on his face, almost boyish.

The smile disarmed Lancelot further, recalling memories of him and Arthur training with the soldiers, before Arthur's father had died at the hands of Saxons and Arthur's mother had declared never to remarry before disappearing into the Otherworld. When Arthur was a mere prince and not a King.

Seeing Arthur happy should warm the stone cockles of Lancelot's cursed heart. Especially as Morgana's vengeance had fallen over them all like a heavy cloak. At times, he felt as though he were drowning in his guilt and shame—but never as much so as right now.

Lancelot forced himself to watch when Arthur and Galahad noticed Finn—no, not Finn—who knew what her name really was. Arthur and Galahad saw her face first, for how could one not notice her ethereal beauty? Their eyes trailed down to the dull leather armor, the boots covered in dust, the sword at her hip. Brows scrunched, lips dipping into frowns, as they took in the helmet hanging limply in Lancelot's hand. And then the widening of eyes, the inhaled hiss of breath.

Arthur took a step back as though struck by an invisible blow.

Galahad, however, let out a bark of shocked laughter, one big hand slapping his thigh.

"Finn's a lass," Percival proclaimed, a giddy twinkle in the lad's eyes.

"Yer Majesty," the woman said, lowering her plaited head. "I meant no disrespect. I wished only to be treated as an equal. To be given a fair chance."

"And you thought deception the only way to get it?" Arthur's voice was cold.

Lancelot could see his mind working, the thoughts flying behind his carefully-schooled features. "You thought we would not treat you fairly as you were?"

"Would ye have?" Her head snapped up and she met his eyes with a challenge that burned bright and clean.

Arthur looked away with a muttered curse. Uncertainty was an unfamiliar look on their king.

Merlin chose that moment to stroll into the Great Hall, hands buried in his charcoal gray robe, his hood shadowing his rugged face. When he caught sight of the woman, he stilled. The golden-ring around his ageless hazel eyes glowed and his pupils appeared almost reptilian. The druid's incubus blood was reacting to something *other*—but only Lancelot knew the magic Merlin sensed, the magic the color windows sensed too. The unspoken confirmation was nearly Lancelot's undoing. His muscles tightened with the need to rage, to destroy, to know her cold fire intimately.

"We're drawing attention," Galahad rumbled. "Perhaps we should continue this discussion at our seats?"

Lancelot looked about, trying to calm his rapid pulse. It was true. The nobles, villagers, and warriors already seated were craning their necks to inspect the knot of knights.

Arthur nodded curtly and turned on his heel, stalking up toward the head table.

The woman marched after him, after grabbing her helm from Lancelot's grip.

He followed after her, head down to discreetly examine her armored form. She must be long and lean beneath the mass of buckles and leather but, with the benefit of his new knowledge, he could see a semblance of feminine curve there, waiting to be uncovered. How had he not seen her for what she was? Lancelot cursed under his breath as his cock began to stir beneath his breeches.

Arthur settled into the ornate chair in the center spot of honor, motioning for the woman to sit next to him. Lancelot took the spot to her right, forgiving Arthur for giving Lancelot's usual seat away. No doubt Arthur wished to question her. And Lancelot wished to listen.

Galahad and Percival filled in the chairs on Arthur's other side, Merlin settling in the empty seat next to Lancelot.

Arthur stood and hastily declared the feast begun, before dropping into his chair and turning to the woman with slitted eyes. "Who are you?"

"Fionnabhair Allán, oldest daughter of Brin Allán, chieftain of Aghanravel and a king of Tara," she said proudly, without flinching away from Arthur's fury. "Though call me Fionna." She leaned back in her seat and tilted her head toward Arthur. "I kept the truth of my sex hidden, but the rest is true. I hail from Ulster. I'm here to be yer knight."

"You will understand if it's hard for me to believe what you offer as truth," Arthur countered.

"Then believe the strength of my sword arm and the cut of my blade." Her cheeks flushed with Arthur's challenge, her eyes aglow.

Fionnabhair, Fionna. The name was honey sweet on Lancelot's tongue. His soul blazed hotter with her confession, as if recognizing the presence of a worthy conquest. An equal. Lancelot thought he might be sick.

Fionna continued, pointing a finger at Arthur like she possessed the audacity to poke the High King of Briton in the chest. "Ye said ye wanted the best in the land to be your fifth knight. Well, I am the best in two lands. So, which is it, King Arthur? Do ye want the best, or do ye want a *man?*"

The muscles of Arthur's jaw worked as he met Fionna's furious words, tension chilling the air like ice.

It was Percival who cracked the hoarfrost growing between them, the blessed fool boy. "We actually want the best *looking*, Fionna," he said, gesturing from his toes to his head with a crooked grin. "Obviously."

Arthur let out a strained burst of laughter, shaking his head.

Galahad reached out and mock-cuffed Percival across the ear, which Percival tried to avoid, resulting in a short tussle that found Percival's head locked under Galahad's sizable bicep.

But the challenge had passed, along with much of the tension. And when a servant appeared with a tray heavy-laden with wine goblets, everyone grabbed one gratefully.

Lancelot looked sideways at Merlin, who was watching Fionna with barefaced interest.

"You couldn't have foreseen this, druid?" Lancelot gave a false laugh, and reached for a golden-brown leg from a platter of chicken to appear natural.

"The Fates do seem to have a sense of humor," Merlin remarked, shifting the weight of his all-seeing gaze onto Lancelot. "Through I fear a dark one at that."

Lancelot tried not to shrink from the man, ignoring the feelings of unease that skittered like spiders across his skin. Merlin unnerved him when his cambion blood was at work. He saw too much. Sometimes Lancelot swore the druid saw the truth of his curse—knew the danger Lancelot now posed to Arthur and Caerleon—saw the damage he could yet do. Or perhaps he saw too little. Because he hadn't seen this—hadn't seen that their fifth knight would be a woman or the danger this revelation brought their brotherhood.

Doubt and fear warred inside Lancelot. He took a savage bite off the chicken leg, but the richly spiced meat tasted like sawdust in his mouth.

Should he tell Arthur the truth of Morgana's curse? No. He closed his eyes against the thought. He couldn't. Couldn't admit to letting him down one more time. What if Arthur sent him away, to keep his kingdom safe? Lancelot couldn't bear it. Arthur was his brother, this fortress his home. They grew up together when Uther agreed to foster him when he had reached the strange in-between age of boyhood and manhood. Perhaps he could try to convince Arthur to send her away, since a woman ranking within their knighthood was a terrible idea. But Arthur had already knighted her . . .

Another thought occurred to him. Perhaps he was overreacting. Certainly, he was attracted to Fionna. *But I don't love her*, he scolded himself. Perhaps Fionna wasn't the one Morgana had foretold. A Gwenevere was a creature of legend—a white fay, an enchantress from bardic tales and nothing more. Fionna was remarkable for her fighting prowess and beautiful, yes. But magic? He had seen no sign of magic beyond the glowing light streaming though the rainbow-hued windows. But that could have merely been a bright afternoon sun playing tricks on his mind. And he would recognize magic. After all, he was raised on the Isle of Man, among druid priestesses and sídhe fae.

Lancelot looked down to where Fionna sat, Arthur and Galahad and Percival all leaning into her like flowers tilting toward the morning sun.

"Are all women in Ulster such fierce warriors?" Galahad was asking.

"Many," Fionna replied, pausing. "But I am one of the best."

Perhaps she wasn't the woman. And even if so, the curse would only fall over Caerleon if he joined with her as man and woman. He could restrain himself. He shifted in his seat to hide evidence to the contrary. Relief welled in Lancelot, and he tore off a chunk of chicken with gusto. Yes, he would simply resist her. How hard could that be?

Chapter Nine

Percival

Percival always enjoyed a good feast, but that night's festivities were the best by far. Fionnabhair Allán was the most interesting thing to have happened to Caerleon for quite some time. She was akin to a maiden in a bardic faerie tale come to life, if that maiden could stick an axe through a man's eyeball without a second's thought. He hadn't even known that women came in this fierce and formidable variety. Was there no end to the surprising delights they possessed?

As the night wound on, the ale settled into Arthur and Galahad's blood. They appeared to have relaxed in Fionna's presence, chatting with her almost amiably. As it turned out, she was a princess, a king of Tara's daughter. No wonder she put Arthur to task so effortlessly.

Percival glanced to the head table's opposite end, where Lancelot sat brooding. Lancelot had a stick shoved firmly up his arse ever since Morgana. Percival resisted the urge to throw a grape at him. Before the disastrous business with Merlin's apprentice, Lancelot had been his favorite sword-brother, the most likely to join Percival in a prank or laugh. The most likely to flirt with him too. He never knew if those moments were in jest or earnest. Strangely, he found he hadn't minded either way. But those memories of Lancelot were fading. Each day, it grew harder to remember that carefree version of his friend.

With a bored sigh, Percival slouched over the table, resting his chin in one hand while the other picked at a splinter in the wood. The Great Hall had emptied hours earlier—or at least, it felt like hours—and he shivered in the night air. The fires in both grand hearths had cooled to barely glowing embers.

Galahad loosed a jaw-cracking yawn.

Fionna released an answering one, though she covered her mouth with leather-clad arm. "Perhaps I should retire," she said, before pausing. "Is there a particular room I should—"

"There's a spare room next to mine," Galahad leaned in, running a finger slowly around the rim of his empty goblet.

Percival narrowed his eyes. Galahad and Fionna were a ridiculously impractical match. Fionna was half his size. Galahad would probably crush the woman to death if he tried to bed her. Not to mention, Fionna seemed more inclined to crush a man's skull than lie with him.

"There's an available room in the North Wing," Arthur said. "I'll have the servants prepare the chamber for you."

Percival suppressed a groan. He saw what Arthur was doing—keeping Fionna far away from the knights' rooms in the East Wing. Where was the fun in that?

"I'll show her the way, lads," Percival offered, pushing his chair away from the scraps of food and empty goblets. Might as well find out exactly where her chamber was located.

Arthur hesitated.

"Ah, let him," Galahad crooned. "It's not like he's any danger to her, what with his vow and all." With a cheerful wink, he grinned at Percival and then raised his empty goblet in a mocking toast.

Fionna looked away from Percival's spitting glare and focused on Arthur, who was now pinching the bridge of his nose with his fingers. "I don't care one way or the other," she said. "Rest assured, no one is going in my room but me."

"Fine," Arthur muttered. His shoulders slumped as he leaned the back of his head onto his ebony wood chair, his glassy stare somehow burning holes through the rafters. After a few strained seconds, silent save the echoing clop of Fionna's boots, Arthur rolled his head toward Percival. "Stop by my study when you're done?"

Percival nodded before bouncing out of his chair after Fionna. Despite her shorter legs, she moved quite quickly. He had wanted to escort her, but now he found his nerves raw and ragged at the prospect. *Humor. Disarm her with humor*, he thought.

"I don't need a wet nurse to watch over me," Fionna snapped when Percival caught up.

"Good," Percival practically chirped in response. "Because ye would go awful hungry." He squeezed his pectorals, raising an eyebrow at her.

She rolled her eyes.

"I suppose ye dinnae need me to tell ye then . . ." Percival trailed off.

Fionna pursed her wine-flushed lips. "Tell me *what*?"

"That the North Wing is that way, lass." He cocked his thumb over his shoulder, toward a passageway they had breezed past just a few moments prior.

Fionna stopped in her tracks, whirling on him. Percival's blood thundered through his veins. Merciful gods, she was as intimidating as she was beautiful. And he couldn't stop looking at her mouth.

"Why are ye *now* telling me this?"

"Ye seemed so certain of yer course. I hated to correct you, is all."

She let out an exasperated hiss, before muttering under her breath, "Well, isn't that the story of my life." She pasted on a fake smile and inclined her head. "Sir Percival, please, do me the honor of leading the way."

Percival thrust out his elbow, offering her his arm. "Sir Fionnabhair, 'twould be my pleasure."

She ignored his gesture, and so he let his proffered arm drop, falling into step beside her instead.

"Sir Fionnabhair," she murmured. "Sounds odd."

"I'm actually not sure if there's a different name for a female knight. Madam Fionnabhair? Lady Fionnabhair?" he mused. "Maybe one of Arthur's books has an answer. What do they call women warriors in Ulster?"

"Warriors." Her face set like stone. Then the lines around her eyes softened slightly, like a bright afternoon fading to twilight. "What did Galahad mean? About yer vow?"

"Ye caught that, did ye?" Percival shoved his hands into his pockets. Well, he supposed his embarrassing secret would come out sooner or later. "I made a vow of chastity. Until I'm wed."

A surprised cough escaped Fionna's lips.

"Subtle," he said, willing his galloping heart to slow down to normal speed. She was just a woman. He talked to women all the time. When guttered after imbibing too much ale? Well, then he just talked endlessly.

"It's . . ." she searched for the words. "Not what most young men in Ulster would choose, anyway. Are things so different here?"

"Just for me."

She cocked an eyebrow at him, and when her silver eyes met his, a jolt of energy coursed through him. Faint, but unmistakable. He struggled to keep the shock from his face.

"Have ye not heard of the Blessed Grail?" he asked.

She shook her head.

"The land is fertile so long as the Grail serves a sovereign-blessed king. In the North, the Grail Maiden sups with the gods of Albion while she waits for the rightful king to arrive, using the fae bowl to serve her guests."

"Grail Maiden?"

"Yes, an earth goddess. Most men think the Grail is a myth, but it's not. My father, the last Fisher King, was the keeper of the Blessed Grail. When he died, the vessel disappeared." Percival slid her a half-smile.

"Do you know the location of this . . . sacred vessel?" she asked.

"No one knows for certain. Though it's possible the Grail Maiden guards the sacred vessel in the *in-between* until the Fisher King's heir can ask the Grail whom it serves. Ye see, my father died when I was young, when a neighboring clann lord lay siege to Caer Benic. But, because my father's blood flows through my veins, I have a connection to the Grail. I can sense . . . clues. Pieces of the puzzle that will help my king find the hidden location someday, even if partway to the Otherworld."

"Truly?" Fionna's face softened with his long-winded story, as if she cherished each word he uttered in his barely sober state. "What does the connection feel like?"

Like you, he wanted to say. *It feels like when you looked at me just now.* But he swallowed the words, not wanting to frighten her. "Hard to describe, really. A tingle. A knowing."

"Sure. But what does that have to do with you remaining . . . *chaste*?" She said the word as if it were a communicable disease.

"According to my father, the connection is lost if we dinnae remain pure of heart. And body. A holy virgin for a holy vessel. The bond of marriage purifies any coupling, of course."

"Oh, of course," she remarked tartly.

"Perhaps things are not so . . . proper in Ireland?" Percival grinned. He pointed left and they turned into a narrow hallway, heading toward a block of rooms in the North Wing.

"Perhaps," Fionna replied, arching an eyebrow. "This whole world feels strange to me."

"Wales was strange to me too, at first," Percival admitted. "When my father died in battle, my mother took me far from the world of men and raised me deep in Galloway Forest."

"You're Scoti?"

"Aye."

"I could tell you were Gael, though I considered ye a fellow Irishman until now."

"My family is of Pict heritage, long before the Kingdom of Alba formed." Percival flashed her a waggish smile. "Why else would I be so braw and fierce?" Fionna groaned and he laughed before continuing. "Arthur and Lancelot were the first men I ever remember seeing since I was a lad of six. I left at age fifteen against my mother's wishes, but Caerleon called to me."

"And yet now . . . this feels as true as home?"

"It's all of our home. Caerleon. Each other. Most of the knights had strange childhoods. Except Galahad that is, his father is a blacksmith, and he one of many mouths fed under their roof. That's pretty normal."

"He doesn't sound Norse."

Percival shrugged. "He was squired at a young age by a Welsh Lord in Gŵyr and raised in a manor."

"I see." Fionna tilted her head. "What do ye mean by strange upbringings?"

"Well, Lancelot was raised by a faerie." Percival lifted his shoulder in a slight shrug. "Vivien, Lady of the Lake, druid priestess on the Isle of Man. Have ye heard of her?"

Fionna's face remained blank.

"She provides protection over Briton. She's also the one who gifted Arthur with Excalibur, making him the Pendragon, High King of Briton. Though, the scattered kingdoms have yet to unite under his rule."

"Is Lancelot part fae, then?"

"No, Lancelot is the exiled Prince of Benoic, from the Kingdom of France. His father, King Ban, was murdered by his rival and his mother fled for her life. The Lady of the Lake fostered Lancelot when his mother left him as an offering to the goddess for safe keeping. He joined Uther's court for military training around the age of thirteen. He and Arthur have been inseparable ever since."

Fionna considered this, pausing. "Lancelot . . . a prince?" She turned to him, her brows knitted in a scowl. "He doesn't seem to like me very much."

Percival pasted a shocked look on his face, his hand to his breast. "Whatever do ye mean, lass . . ."

A half smile curved Fionna's lip, and Percival counted that a win. He thought of how to best explain the situation to Fionna. When the faerie sisters, Elaine and Morgause, had first cursed Arthur and Caerleon, Arthur had sworn the knights to secrecy, not wanting word of his weakness to reach his enemies. But Fionna was a knight. She was one of them now. Didn't that bring her within their circle of confidence? Percival chewed on his lip. Curse his ale-addled brain and tongue that acted as though attached to a bard.

What to do?

He had found out the hard way that kings were funny about secrets and their pride. It had been a *year* since Percival had joking-ly shared with several court ladies how Arthur didn't always wear small clothes under his breeches, and Arthur still turned scarlet at the mention of it. Best to receive Arthur's approval before airing all their dirty laundry to Fionna. But she was still waiting for an answer. Gods, he had been quiet too long! She must think him strange, especially after his rambling divulgences. He scrambled for an explanation.

"Lancelot had a bad experience with a woman," he practically blurted. "He's still recovering. Dinnae take his winning personality personally."

She nodded, her face unreadable. They were reaching the end of the hallway now.

"This is the biggest room in the North Wing. I hope it's to yer liking."

Fionna nodded her thanks and pushed through the door, closing it gently behind her.

Percival stood before her door, alone, with only her memory hanging in the torchlit hall. He found he meant it. He did hope she liked her time here. Because he wanted her to stay.

Chapter Ten

Arthur

Arthur didn't like being backed into a corner.

And Princess Fionnabhair Allán had thoroughly and completely put him in one.

The mood in his study was strangely subdued.

The knights should have been cheerful, even jubilant, after the day's excitement—tourney, feast, finding a fifth. But instead, each man seemed lost in thought. Lancelot stood by the hearth, staring into the flames; Galahad fixed on some distant point out the dark latticed window. Merlin was always enigmatic, so the look of quiet contemplation on his still form wasn't quite so unsettling to Arthur.

It was if something had shifted this night in the bedrock of their lives, tilting their course in an entirely new direction. Toward a path Arthur couldn't see down. And *that* made him most nervous of all.

Percival appeared in the doorway, a flush on his cheeks that seemed to breathe life into all of them. "Sorry I'm late, had to show our new knight all the perks of her new station, ye ken." He flashed his incorrigible Percival grin.

"She slammed the door in your face, didn't she?" Galahad asked.

"That she did, lads." Percival ducked his head in a nod before falling into an upholstered chair before the fire, one leg slung over the arm.

Arthur strode to the fireplace and leaned against the stone mantle, opposite of Lancelot, and sighed. His eyes were scratchy with fatigue and he had the start of a headache from all the ale, but he needed to talk this out, or he would never find peace tonight.

"What are we going to do about Fionna?" Arthur asked.

The room was silent, but for a pop of a log on the fire.

Arthur shifted uncomfortably. "I'll be the first to admit that her fighting skills are impressive. But we can't have a *female* knight. Caerleon will be the laughingstock of Briton!" The British kings from other chiefdoms and kingdoms already thought him strange enough, what with his kingship bestowed by a magic sword and a cambion druid for his chief advisor. Would anyone take him seriously if he fought with a woman by his side?

"Perhaps next time we shouldn't knight anyone before we see their face," Lancelot grumbled, not looking up from the flames.

Arthur's annoyance flared. "Thank you for that enlightening suggestion," he snapped. He needed his second-in-command back, not this moody shadow. A similar moody shadow he sported when he had first arrived in Caerleon a decade ago. Lately, it seemed like the man wasn't even here, his haunted gaze a thousand miles away. But where? What private hell was his friend lost in? And how could he bring him back?

"Female knights may be a novelty in Briton, but in Ulster, women warriors are commonplace," Merlin remarked.

"The Norse and Saxons too," Galahad rumbled. "Our shield-maidens fight alongside the men. They're just as good at killing as their husbands, brothers, and fathers."

Arthur frowned. That was true. Norse and Saxon war bands, his enemies to the east, were filled with men and women alike. But . . . asking women to fight was not done in Briton. Women were to be cared for, protected. They were the land's life-givers, the fair sex cherished for birthing strong warriors and kings for Britannia. Though Arthur had to relent. Fionna didn't need his physical protection.

"We all agree her fighting prowess isn't a concern, yes?" Galahad said.

The knights nodded.

"And perhaps the nobles will talk behind our backs, but we've never cared what those pompous arses thought," Galahad continued. "You've always done the unexpected, Your Majesty. Keep them guessing."

Arthur nodded in appreciation. That was true. But this cut to the heart of his concern, the one he was loathe to voice. It wasn't so much Fionna's femaleness that concerned him, it was her—Fionna-ness. The moment his gaze riveted onto her ethereal beauty and warrior's build, he had wanted her. She was a portrait of contrasts, hard against soft, dark against light. Even dirty and sweaty, wearing leather armor and a scowl upon her face, she had stolen the breath from his lungs, had set the blood racing through his veins. Sitting next to her at the feast had been like being in his body for the first time—newly aware of each sensation. His stomach, flipping nervously; his skin, feeling alive and energized as if by a lightning storm. His cock, hard and insistent. Fionna was a tonic far more potent than wine—the stubborn set of her jaw, her earthy scent of heather and moss, the lilting accent of her words challenging him as an equal. She had swept over him, sending his head spinning. He didn't know if he could focus with Fionna around, be dispassionate and fair and decisive. And that scared him more than even a faerie curse.

And then there were his other knights. He had seen their eyes following Fionna like drowning men seeking air. They all wanted her. Four stags—one doe—there was only one way this situation would end. The stags would tear each other apart trying to get to her. He had trouble enough with Morgana trying to destroy his inner circle and his kingdom, in some twisted effort to repair what Uther had done to her father and their mother. He didn't need the trouble Fionna brought, too. Fionna could tear them apart without even trying.

"She's very beautiful," Arthur finally said, realizing he had been standing in silent contemplation too long. "I fear she could come between us. We've already had trouble enough of the female variety."

Lancelot's face hardened, the firelight limning the hard set of his square jaw.

"Never a worry," Galahad said. "She'll choose me. It'll make it easy for the rest of you lads."

"I'm not sure walking tree trunks are her type," Percival quipped. "She seemed quite taken with me this evening."

"Too bad you took a vow of chastity then," Galahad retorted.

"Only until marriage, ye big oaf."

Arthur held up a hand and the two fell silent. "I'm not worried about you two. Lancelot?" He spoke his friend's name quietly, almost a warning hush.

Lancelot met his eyes, and a cold frost crackled in his gaze, one Arthur didn't understand. "I want nothing to do with her," Lancelot sneered. "She brings trouble."

"I'm not sure any of you have a choice," Merlin spoke, seeming to come back to life. The druid often fell still, his expression trance-like. Arthur had grown used to it, together with the wisdom that such a state would bring.

"What have you seen?"

"I have seen her drinking from the Blessed Grail," Merlin said. "Isn't that right, Percival?"

Arthur's head swiveled to look at Percival.

An apologetic look was written across the lad's face.

"What's this?" Arthur asked. Percival's connection to the Blessed Grail had not yet borne fruit, but his magical affinity to the vessel was one of the reasons Arthur had knighted him. That, and his indomitable good cheer and purity of heart.

"I thought I felt something," Percival admitted. "When I was walking with her. It was fleeting, but I dinnae think I was imagining it. She's connected to the Grail somehow. To the quest."

Merlin nodded. "She is the knight I had foreseen, though now her face has become clear. She is bound to you four, and you to her. The Fates did not make a mistake in sending her to you, Your Majesty."

Arthur crossed his arms, grappling with the excitement blooming within him. He knew he should send her away, that she would be trouble, but part of him was infinitely pleased that she had to stay. Arthur shoved that part down deep, locking the feeling within himself. He was king. He did not have the luxury of giving in to mindless infatuation, even if she were of noble blood.

"Seems we have little choice then," Arthur said. "Are we in agreement?"

"She's nice," Percival said. "I think we should keep her."

"She isn't a stray puppy," shot Lancelot darkly.

"Your vote?" Arthur asked Lancelot.

Lancelot gave a curt shake of his head, his unruly mop of dark curls swaying.

Arthur swallowed his surprise. Lancelot saying no to a woman. This business with Morgana had indeed shaken him deeply.

"I say yes," Galahad rumbled. "She earned her place."

"Very well," Arthur said. "But I will have a promise from each of you."

The knights looked to him.

"You are my brothers. I will not have a woman break the bonds between us. If she chooses one of us, or none of us, the others shall respect her choice, and bow out gracefully, and with honor."

"Maybe she'll want all of us," Percival said with sly grin.

Arthur massaged his temples. That headache had arrived in full force. "She will not tear us asunder. Do you so swear?"

His knights swore, and Arthur prayed that the vows from his sword-brothers would be enough to withstand the coming storm that was Fionna Allán.

Chapter Eleven

Fionna

ormally after battle, I slept like the dead. But last night, sleep's sweet embrace had eluded me completely.

With a groan, I sat up amongst a sweaty tangle of linen and woolen bedclothes. I longed for the single woven blanket from my bed at home, as well as my wolf pelt for unbearably cold nights. Aideen had made me the blanket gracing my cot. I picked the colors of red and orange and purple, and then Aideen wove the hemp yarns into a masterpiece of intricate intersecting lines. That was what Aideen did—beautify the world around her. That was her gift, to bring beauty and life, while my gift was to bring destruction and death.

It hadn't mattered how different Aideen and I were though, we had been inseparable since my little sister was born. We were inseparable still, or at least we had been before Donal O'Lynn had snatched Aideen off the battlefield at Ballymena, while our clanns fought with an expanding Norse settlement.

When we were girls, Aideen would sneak over from her own bed to mine more nights than I could count. And all to whisper stories and giggle beneath the rhythmic sound of our father's snores that crested and fell like waves on the rocky shores of Lough Ne-agh. Even when we grew too big to both fit in my narrow little bed, I would turn sideways, fitting my body around my sister's, stroking her rich auburn tresses as we murmured about lads from our village or fretted about our father's stiffening hip.

The last night we had bedfellowed, we had argued—Aideen insisting that she skirt the battlefield to heal our clann's fianna who returned injured and dying. I had argued about the danger, feeling like flint striking across the hard rock of Aideen's resolve. If there was one thing Aideen and I had in common, it was our stubbornness. And this was one time I took no joy in being right.

Sunlight streamed through a crack in the heavy wool curtains of my room, setting dust motes alive and dancing like flecks of gold. I stood, stretching my sore body, before leaning over to touch my toes. Wrinkling my nose, I lifted the lid to the chamber pot and relieved myself, and then enjoyed a deep drink from a pitcher of water a servant left the night prior on an ornately-carved sideboard. Those tasks complete, I looked around the lavish room helplessly, wondering what on earth to do next. Why, steal the sword of course. But how?

I looked about once more, taking closer stock of my surroundings. The plush woven carpet was softer beneath my toes than even the downiest pelt. Gold leaf and rich linen and wool fabrics decorated the room, from the large four-post bed, to the upholstered backs of chairs, to a vibrant tapestry covering one wall, depicting knights on unicorns battling dragons. Well, unless things were *very different* in Briton, more so than I realized, the mythical fight was mere fancy. Still, the amount of casual wealth in this fortress—in this room—was staggering. Bewitched, I fingered a silver candlestick inlaid with mother of pearl and calculated how much I could get by bartering the pair to the nearest Dál nAraidi clann. Maybe I could take a few things for my trouble when I departed.

A churning feeling returned to my stomach. The grinding anxiety nearly stole my breath.

The thought of stealing from these knights, from the king, unsettled me far too much. I wasn't sure why, but a part of me cared what Arthur Pendragon thought of me. His nearness felt right somehow. As if we were fated to be bound to one another. At first, I thought my draw was to how his smile invited my troublesome thoughts. Then, over supper, I noticed how the freckles sprayed across his nose were only the darker few. Faerie kisses touched every part of him that I could see, even the very tips of his ears. I was undone and drank two goblets full of wine, simply to forget the man's freckles, and smile, and the way he inclined his head just so when intently listening to another. Wanting to steal his good opinion of me would prove more unsafe than O'Lynn's demand.

So perhaps just the sword.

A knock sounded on the door and I flew to it, grateful for a distraction from my uneasy thoughts. I yanked on the door's iron ring to find a pretty brunette in a cornflower blue dress on the other side, teetering under the weight of several large bundles.

"Hello," the girl said, her voice sweet and tinkling. "I've brought you some things."

My breath caught. One of the bundles was my saddlebags. I pulled the heavy weight from the girl's shoulder, and then hugged the familiar leather bag to my chest. Hopefully Zephyr wasn't growing too fat and happy in the stables under Caerleon's rich care. She would never forgive me once we returned to Ireland.

The girl straightened, sighing with relief.

"Come in," I said, stepping aside.

The girl placed the other bundle on the little bench at the foot of my bed and turned to me, her eyes downcast. "His Majesty thought you might need more clothes. He wasn't sure . . . whether you would prefer dresses or breeches." The girl hurried through the words as if slightly scandalized. "So, he sent both."

I bit back a smile. "Give the king my thanks. What do they call ye, lass?"

The girl looked up, and I marveled at how her bright blue eyes matched her dress and envied the dimple in her chin. She was perhaps eighteen, just two years younger than me. "Margred, Your Ladyship."

"Simply call me Fionna, no need for formalities, please. May I ask for yer help?"

Margred nodded enthusiastically. "I've been assigned to attend you. Whatever you need, Lady . . . er, Fionna."

"A bath," I answered, hoping the blush I felt heating my neck didn't wend its way upward to blaze my cheeks. I had consciously avoided peering toward the looking glass on the far vanity table. For I was sure I looked a fright after a day fighting under my helm. "Some breakfast, and then I want ye to tell me everything ye know about the king's knights."

Margred grinned as if we had just shared a secret. "That I can do," she said.

After eating and bathing, I felt more like myself than I had since leaving Ulster. I was as clean as a newborn babe, my long hair now washed, combed and loosely braided. All the clothes from my saddlebag were ripe from the sea crossing, so I dressed in clothes that Arthur had sent—an emerald green linen tunic trimmed in silvered threads, and tight brown breeches beneath. After I laced up my worn leather boots and buckled on my sword belt, I had to admit, I didn't form an altogether displeasing picture.

Once finished, I desired to visit the stables and check on Zephyr before seeing to any other errands and duties this day. Margred walked with me part of the way through the maze of corridors, and then pointed down the stairs and out into the bright morning sunshine before returning to her own duties.

The lass had shared interesting tidbits about the knights, all of which kept with my own assessment. Arthur, proud and fair, with the weight of the world upon his shoulders. Percival—the jester of the group, his boasting and jokes hiding a sweetness and innocence that Margred hoped he would never lose. Galahad, a powerful warrior whose heart was as big as his stature.

Apparently, he had been nursing an injured fawn back to health in the stables for a week before the stable boys grew any the wiser. If the village ladies hadn't swooned for him before, that incident had seemed to cement him as one of their favorites.

And then there was Lancelot, a man who loved women and was equally beloved by them. The gossip about his engagement to a dark fae princess, together with the relationship's spectacular implosion, had been particularly juicy. Perhaps I could use this newly gained insight, somehow.

I was pleased to find Zephyr tucked in a cozy stall, munching contentedly on a full manger of hay. The mare looked up drowsily as I entered her stall, huffing gently against my face in greeting. I looked her up and down, nodding in approval when I noticed how Zephyr's hooves had been picked and oiled and how her coat had been brushed down to a sheen, not even a fleck of mud remaining from our voyage. Spoiled, indeed. My solid-treed saddle and bridle hung neatly from hooks on the wall, the leather padding and saddle cleaned and oiled as well. At least they treated horses right in Caerleon. And tack. My respect for the place increased.

Pondering what to do next, I laid my forehead against Zephyr's velvet neck. Margred had borne no message from Arthur other than the clothes; it would seem I had the day to myself. But how to use it? I needed to strategize, to plan my theft of Excalibur. Where to start?

The sound of clashing swords reached my ears through the quiet for the stable. Curiosity piqued, I gave Zephyr's forehead a last scratch before closing the stall door behind me.

I found Galahad and Lancelot in the stable yard's bright light, sparring in furious combat, their boots eating up the paddock's loose dirt, their swords flashing in the sun. I stilled in the stable's shadow, my cheeks growing hot at the sight. Both men fought shirtless, their rippling muscles glinting with the sweat of their exertions. Galahad was huge, his biceps bunching under tawny-gold skin, the peaks and furrows of his muscled back a foreign territory I desperately wanted to explore.

Lancelot was smaller in stature than Galahad, though still tall and incredibly strong. He had nary an ounce of body fat on him. His rippling stomach flexed and tensed with each stroke of his sword. Veins roped down his powerful arms, both of which were tattooed from his upper chest and shoulders down in indigo swirls and knots—symbols of my people, the Gaels. And the Túatha dé Danann. Warrior marks. Lancelot's dark hair hung in wet curls about his head, his expression deadly serious. He fought as though the Red Hounds of Cúalu were on his heel, his sword strikes as fast and deadly as a venomous snake.

My appreciation of his male form gave way to the appreciation of his skill—deep, intricate. He was better than me. My excitement flared. Years had passed since I had fought someone better. Or found someone to teach me more. There were lessons to learn from this man.

A ringing silence echoed in the wake of their battle—their weapons now tipped toward the earth. When had their fight ended? Had I truly given into reverie for so long? Lancelot glared at me from several paces away, his chest heaving.

Galahad, on the other hand, had a disarming grin stretched across his face.

I cleared my throat, disliking the feeling of being tongue-tied. But I shook it off and strode toward them. "Lancelot. Would ye spar with me?" I asked. Might as well get straight to it.

He shook his head, beads of his sweat flicking across my cheek. "Time to begin drills with my soldiers at the Round, *Lady*," he grunted, before turning on his heel and stalking across the stable yard.

My teeth ground together, fury lancing through me at the slight.

"Don't take his dismissal personally," Galahad remarked, sheathing his sword. He strode toward the stable and then dunked his whole head into the nearest water trough. He came up with a flick of golden-blond hair, sending rivulets down the planes of his chest, each droplet of water sparkling like a diamond.

"Isn't it personal?" I managed, my voice hoarse. Then I swallowed back the forming knot, unable to tear my eyes from the sight before me.

Galahad didn't answer, pulling his hair back into a messy knot, securing his long, wild strands with a piece of leather cord. "I'll spar with you," he said, setting one hand on his narrow waist. "If you're up for a rematch."

I attmpted to banish the memory of his weight upon me during our bout yesterday. "Goddess help me," I prayed under my breath. A sparring round was not at all the type of rematch I wanted.

Chapter Twelve

Fionna

The morning passed in a pleasant blur of sword strikes and parries, all the while surrounded by the steady moon of Galahad's grin, the sun on his bronzed skin, and the sparkle of his eyes. It surprised me how quickly I settled into an easy rapport with the man, joking and fighting, giving each other tips and taking them. Galahad clearly took great pride in his fighting prowess, yet he was eager for me to teach him the fighting style favored by my fiann. I had thought of my war band brothers and sisters with a pang, and then shoved the feeling down and away from my notice. I would see them before long.

When at last my muscles were quivering, my mind a soft haze, I yielded, holding up a hand, the other on my hip. "I think I've had enough for one day." I puffed in a few deep breaths, struggling to regain my wind after a particularly aerobatic sparring match.

"Thank the heavens." Galahad's muscled shoulders drooped. "Between you and Lancelot, I thought I might drop dead of exhaustion."

I pursed my lips into a fine line at the mention of Lancelot. The exiled prince clearly distrusted me, and I needed to gain trust from all the knights to accomplish my dark deed. "Should I confront Lancelot?" I asked. "Find out the cause of his great dislike for me?"

Galahad shook his head, sheathing his sword. "Lancelot doesn't like being pushed. I would wait. He'll warm to you, eventually. The man has never met a beautiful woman he didn't like."

The tips of my ears heated at the compliment. "Very well." I moved quickly past it. "I shall do as ye recommend."

"I take my leave," Galahad inclined his blond head toward me before bowing slightly at the waist. "I am off in search of a bath." And then he spun on his heel and swaggered into the stable's dark, leaving a heady scent of cedarwood and sweat and something else I couldn't name in his wake, addling my senses.

At a clean trough, I took a long drink and then splashed the cool water on my face, trying to chill the heat of desire rising through my body. *The sword. Focus on the sword, not on Galahad bathing.* I closed my eyes and huffed, trying in vain to rid the delicious mental image from my mind. *The sword.*

A distraction was needed. Something. Anything.

As far as I knew, I had the afternoon to roam or train or indulge as I pleased. Idleness was as foreign as to me as this land and my muscles, though fatigued, itched to move. But I remained where I stood and closed my eyes, hoping to hear the land's whispers. A breeze skipped over the grass and wildflowers in the paddock. I lifted my face to the warming sun. In a stall nearby, a horse nickered. Familiar sensations and sounds in an unfamiliar place. Perhaps exploring the grounds of Caerleon would prove diverting. I need to know the ins and outs of this fortress city for a quick escape anyway, including any back doors that led into the surrounding forests or to the River Usk.

A clanging rap faintly beat behind the other village sounds and I opened my eyes. A warrior should also make friends with a reliable smithy, I reasoned. Feeling a little lighter, I turned away from the stalls and surveyed the kingdom before me. First, I would wander the kitchen gardens adjacent to the stables. Perhaps next I would walk around the old Roman barracks the soldiers used, and then I would visit the blacksmith.

After an hour of exploring and an hour of watching several thousand soldiers spar in the Round under Lancelot's guidance, I found myself ducking out a side door cut into the wooden keep's wall, tucked behind the kitchen. A shadowed path led down from the hill, winding through the windswept grass toward the shimmering blue ribbon of the River Usk.

I stopped a moment and closed my eyes—I could not resist doing so all afternoon wherever I went—savoring the cool shade on my skin, the tang of wood smoke on the air, the chatter of crows gathered on tree limbs along the river or soaring high above. This country's verdant beauty soothed my soul in an unexpected way. The forests here were different from the craggy heaths of Antrim, weathered and beaten down as though by a fellow warring clann. Different than the forests of Southern Ulster and Londonderry. This place was peaceful. But somehow vulnerable too. As though the land needed protecting. I bent down and plucked a vibrant pink wildflower that grew alongside the earthen path, twirling the stem in my fingers. I had never seen a hue quite like it.

"Campion," a voice said, and I whipped my gaze up.

The druid, Merlin, stood farther down the path, his gray robes fastened with an intricately-engraved leather belt. I took his measure subconsciously, as was my habit. He was solidly built beneath those shapeless robes, probably just as fit and muscled as Arthur's other warriors. His face was handsome and rugged in a way I would normally not think as beautiful—as if Otherworldly blood ran in his veins—though much of his face was covered in a trimmed brown beard. It was hard to guess his age. Thirty? But other moments he seemed far older, a preternatural knowing in his hazel eyes. The aura of magic about him set me on edge. The clanns believed that druids who were acquainted with divination could see to the truth of a person. Arthur mentioned how his druid practiced magic. Would Merlin see the real reason behind my presence in Caerleon?

But all he did was walk closer, pointing at the flower. "Campion. The seeds, when ground, are useful for treating snakebites. Or cleansing the body from toxins."

"And the bloom?" I asked, studying the flower cradled in my

palm.

"Why, it's very lovely."

"So not useful at all." I let the flower fall.

Merlin shook his head, and I found my eye drawn to the strange marks tattooed on the sides of his shorn scalp. So odd. "Beauty can be very useful. How else would the bees know how to find the flowers?" He knelt and scooped up the bloom I had dropped, and then tucked the flower into a little leather pouch on his belt.

I considered his words. I hadn't found my beauty helpful in my world. At times, my fair colorings had felt a hindrance. But perhaps in this new one, my unusual looks could have its uses. I thought of Galahad's comment. Would I dare try to use my beauty to melt Lancelot's icy demeanor?

"Where are you wandering off to next?" Merlin asked. His tone was friendly, but the gold ringing his irises flashed.

"Oh, just exploring," I said. "Trying to get the lay of the land."

"Well, the only place down this path is my cave. I would be happy to give you a tour."

My desire for immediate space from the druid and his all-seeing eyes warred with my practical side, which insisted that I also needed to know my enemy. Plus, I didn't want to be rude and insult such a powerful man on my first official day.

"Very well."

I followed Merlin down the winding dirt and rock path, almost to the fern-lined river bank below. The forest enveloped my senses and I breathed deeply the surrounding greens and sky. Before we reached the River Usk, we turned, ducking into a very peculiar space. The cave mouth was low and wide, but upon entering, I was able to stand up straight and—

"Skies above," I whispered in awe.

Craning my neck, I gaped at the glittering ceiling, covered in tiny blue and white crystals. Merlin murmured a word under his breath and a torch flared to life in a wrought iron sconce fastened to the wall closest to where he stood. My feet forgot how to move as Merlin grasped the torch and began to move deeper into the cave.

"Come on," he said, with an amused expression on his face.

I stumbled after him. *That had been magic. Real live magic.* The first I had ever seen.

The main cavern was furnished like a disorderly study, covered in a jumble of items with a purpose I couldn't even guess. Merlin took the slightly-crushed campion bloom from his pouch and rested the bruised stem upon his carved wooden desk. "I admit, I had ulterior motives in bringing you here."

My head jerked up, my senses suddenly firing in alert.

Merlin chuckled, settling into a chair in front of a strange rocky fireplace, currently empty of flames. "All I meant is that you're a bit of a mystery to me. I would like to ask you a few questions. Would you care to sit?"

He gestured to the other chair, and I stiffly lowered myself onto the seat, albeit hesitantly. *Fool Fionna*, I scolded myself. I should never have agreed to come here or sit to answer his penetrating questions. But if I fled now, my departure would look too suspicious.

"You appeared so suddenly and have taken Caerleon by storm. Where again do you hail from?"

I relaxed slightly, reciting again the details of my heritage, my clann.

Merlin frowned. "Your father, Brin Allán you say? A chieftain. And your mother?"

I suppressed my own frown. Why did he want to know about my mother? "She was from my clann as well and died while giving birth to my wee sister, Aideen."

"Do either of your parents have any . . . magical heritage?"

I recoiled. "Magical? No, we're as plain as they come."

"I doubt that very much," Merlin murmured. "Any faerie blood?"

I shook my head. Faeries? What was this man on about?

"Do you take after your mother?"

I hesitated before replying, recalling my father doting on Aideen, stroking her auburn curls, telling her how much she looked like our mother. "No," I admitted. *Why?* I wanted to ask, but I swallowed the word, afraid of what he might tell me, of what he might suggest. I belonged to Brin and Catríona Allán, and no one else. They were my parents.

Merlin seemed to take in my discomfort, and blessedly changed the subject. "Whatever your heritage, I am glad you are here. This is a treacherous time for Arthur's rule. Your prowess and strength are a welcome addition to the court. Five is a sacred number, and Arthur needed a strong fifth for the days to come. I am confident he found this in you."

Guilt needled at me, its dark tendrils snaking around my stomach and clenching tight. I wouldn't be here long enough to help Arthur and his knights. Instead, I would be betraying them, leaving them even more vulnerable than when I had first arrived. But my loyalty didn't lie here in Caerleon, no matter what oath I had taken. My duty was to protect my family, my clann. First. Always.

"I am grateful to serve among such brave warriors," I managed when realizing he was waiting for a reply. "But I admit, I don't understand what dangers face Caerleon? Seems rather idyllic here."

Merlin sighed deeply. "This is Arthur's story to tell. I would ask him, if I were you."

"Perhaps I will," I sprang to my feet, grateful for an excuse to leave his prying eyes. "Do ye know where I can find him?"

"Likely the library," Merlin said, a weariness washing over him. "Always the library."

Chapter Thirteen

Arthur

rthur once loved the library. This room was a place of respite, where he could find whatever knowledge he sought, and much that he didn't know he needed. But that was *before*.

Now, he was growing to loathe this tranquil space. Arthur had spent every spare hour here since Merlin discovered the truth of Morgause and Elaine's curse.

The curse was about more than Lancelot's betrayal of his betrothed. His half-sisters wanted the line of Uther Pendragon removed from Caerleon's succession. Lancelot had only played into their plans.

If he hadn't known better, he would have suspected that Morgana's relationship with Lancelot was all a carefully-crafted plot. But he knew the truth. Morgana had loved Lancelot since she'd first met him as a young woman, when Arthur's mother, Igraine, had taken Arthur and his half-sisters to the Isle of Man for a solstice ceremony. Lancelot hadn't returned Morgana's infatuation until well after she had budded into womanhood. Lancelot had claimed his longing was love, but Arthur didn't think his friend knew what falling in love was truly like. He didn't bond easily with others as it was, and certainly not with any of his sexual partners. The ability to remain objective was a perfect quality in his military's commander.

Fighting for another's heart, however, wasn't the same as clashing swords on the battle field. Or maybe little differed between love and war and it was Arthur who knew little about falling for another.

They were both hopeless.

He sighed and ran a hand through his short strands. Arthur had been combing through a stack of crumbling books as high as his waist for days, and he now focused on the two leather-bound notebooks containing his father's neat notes. The pages were just beginning to reveal themselves to him after weeks of study and cross-reference. The Grail was crafted by the old gods of Albion for her protection against foreign kings and their poisonous gods. When the sacred vessel served a ruler, it also served his or her land. But the Blessed Grail only served a man or woman sovereign *blessed* by the Túatha dé Danann. In the wrong hands, the Grail could become a poison. The secrets of the Otherworld's Grail—both a blessing and a curse. It was like these books spoke a foreign tongue to their Welsh and Breton minds, and his father, after years of study, had only just begun speak it. What hope did Arthur have in a few weeks? Percival knew even less of his own heritage, thanks to his fool mother. Arthur slammed one of this father's notebooks shut with a huff, seeming to banish his father's watching spirit. He may resent his father's domineering ways, but he didn't want Uther Pendragon to see him fail either.

"What did that book do to ye?" a lilting feminine voice asked from the shadows of a tall bookshelf. Fionna stood there in a tunic of green, her pale-blonde hair freshly braided and corded with black leather. She looked softer this morning—hesitant. As if a new version of herself had emerged from the fierce warrior he had clashed wills with yesterday.

Arthur rubbed his scratchy eyes. "The book refused to yield its secrets to me," he admitted.

She approached, lingering across from him, her long slender fingers tracing the table's wood grain. Her hands were mesmerizing.

"Do most things yield to ye willingly, King Arthur?" she asked.

"A king does get used to having his way," Arthur managed. It's like her presence sucked all air from the room, leaving only Fionna.

He knew not whether she meant her words to sound so alluring, but his growing cock was quite insistent that he found them so. Without the dirt and sweat of a day's exertions, Fionna's beauty was even more startling, her scent of fresh herbs and heather smelling like freedom, like moors and cliffs and wild places. Even clad in a man's tunic and boots, he wanted to seize her narrow waist, to tangle his fingers in her hair and take her right there on the library table. He feared if she ever put on a dress he might implode where he stood.

But she was speaking. He tried to focus on her words, to banish his illicit daydream. She was asking him about the books.

Arthur cleared his throat. "They're books on the Blessed Grail legend. My father studied them in his youth. Discovering the Fisher King's castle became an obsession for him as he grew older."

"Ye sound disapproving." Fionna turned a book around until the title faced her. "Yet ye follow in his footsteps?"

"Not willingly," Arthur growled.

"Ye are compelled?" She raised one pale eyebrow.

"By necessity, My Lady. It's complicated."

Fionna pulled a chair out from the neighboring table, spinning it around and dropping into the seat. It was impertinent for her to sit without him giving her leave, but Arthur found he rather liked her defiance.

Her knee brushed into his as she adjusted her position while looking at him expectantly. "I think it's time I hear this story, Yer Majesty. I am now a knight of Caerleon, am I not?"

Arthur nodded reluctantly, trying to banish the tingle that a single touch of her knee sent up his leg while also ignoring his disappointment at her knee's absence. It was a *knee*, Cerridwen save him. What was he, a celibate monk from a secluded cloister, swooning at the touch of a woman's *knee*?

He shifted his attention to the more important task at hand. What should he share with Fionna? He had knighted her, but still, he didn't know her. Until she proved herself loyal, he didn't want to share the depth of Caerleon's vulnerability with her. The truth of the faerie sisters' curse.

He chose his words carefully, like a horse picking its way

down a shifting mountainside. "The Blessed Grail has the ability to break any enchantment, even fae magic, and heal all afflictions set upon a sovereign-blessed man and his land. I recently encountered some . . . difficulty with several sídhe fae. Having their Grail in my possession would provide Caerleon with protection against any retaliation they might further attempt."

"Does this have anything to do with Lancelot's disastrous engagement to Morgana, yer half-sister?" Fionna asked, a hint of a smile playing on her lips. "I hear she apprenticed under Merlin's instruction for a spell."

She had been in Caerleon less than twenty-four hours! How did she—

"Servants talk."

Her smile broke free and he became a man possessed, staring beyond rudeness and far beyond his good senses. Her radiance rivaled the first ray of sunshine that appeared over the horizon, bathing the landscape in golden light. The brilliance transformed her face, from one of cold, unapproachable elegance to something more. Something hard earned—and all the more precious for it.

Shifting in his chair, he broke the enthralling silence, his voice hoarse. "I'm not sure why you even needed to hear this story from me, then."

"I needed to know why the Grail is so important. Everywhere I turn, it's all I hear of."

"Merlin foresaw a fifth knight that would help us find this Grail. That's why we held the tourney."

She recoiled slightly, playing unconsciously with the end of one of her braids. "And ye think this fifth knight is me?"

"I wouldn't have knighted you if I didn't." Arthur smiled shyly.

"But I know nothing about this Grail. I'm sorry, but I don't see how I could be of help. Perhaps this honor was meant for someone else." Her silver eyes met his, and there was an apology there that he didn't fully understand.

"Do not worry so," he reassured her. "Even if I made a mistake, Excalibur didn't." He patted the sword hilt at his waist.

Fionna's focus shifted to his sword like a falcon catching sight of prey. "Ye wear Excalibur even here?" she asked softly. "Is it so dangerous for ye in yer own keep, surrounded by barracks and soldiers?"

Arthur shrugged. "No, princess. Habit, I suppose. It's more comfortable to have Excalibur with me than not."

"Please, call me Fionna."

"If it pleases you, Fionna."

"Yes, Yer Majesty. It pleases me." She flicked her gaze to his, held him there a beat, then returned focus to Excalibur. "Do ye never take your sword off?"

"Only to sleep," Arthur said, his cheeks heating, then added, "Naturally." Did her cheeks redden as well? Or was he imagining it?

"And the flash of violet light . . . that was magic? That was Excalibur . . . choosing *me*?"

He stood, pulling Excalibur from its scabbard, handing his sword to her. "See these runes carved into the blade? It's faerie made. My sword possesses a magic even I don't understand. But Excalibur responded to you, that was clear to see and how I knew, Fionnabhair Allán, that you were our needed knight."

Fionna held the blade reverently before setting the sword gently on her knees, and then she ran her fingers over the runes, the sheen of the blade. "A remarkable weapon." Her touch lingered on the sword for a moment before she handed Excalibur back to him, almost regretfully.

He sheathed Excalibur again, relaxing slightly as the familiar weight settled again at his side.

Silence fell upon them, and Arthur found himself biting his lower lip, anxious, wishing he could kiss her. Never feeling so awkward in his life, he struggled for another topic. Perhaps their previous one was safer than he originally thought. "We will leave to find the Grail as soon as I figure out where we're going," he said with a little laugh, turning back to the books and away from her. The desire to chase her lips with his was growing by the second. Did they taste of the wild strawberries they enjoyed mid-day in the Great Hall?

"Perhaps I could help ye look." She pulled one of the books closer.

He softly said, "I wouldn't accomplish much with you here, Fionna."

"Why?" She cocked her head.

Arthur realized his misstep and fumbled to cover it. "I . . . I work best alone, is all."

"And what am I to do in the meantime, Yer Majesty?" Fionna traced her finger along the spine of the book next to his hand. "Do I have duties as a knight? Tasks I must complete?"

"What do you mean?"

"What do I do all day?" Fionna asked, gesturing wide. "I'm not used to such free time."

"Oh." Arthur furrowed his brows. "The other knights never seem to complain. Your time is your own, to train, or study, or find leisure that suits you. Lancelot trains the soldiers, but he seems to have that well in hand. I will assign tasks, if I have them. I've received word of raids near the Kingdom of Gwent's northern border. Once my scouts return, I may dispatch several soldiers under the direction of my knights to secure our borders."

"So, in the meantime I . . . do whatever I fancy?"

Arthur nodded, slowly, his brows still furrowed. Why did she seem so put out? Lancelot, Galahad and Percival enjoyed running their own days. Though, perhaps, if he had given Lancelot more to keep busy, they wouldn't all be in their current predicament.

Fionna snatched a book off the table, and tucked the tome under her arm, standing. "Then I think I will learn about the Blessed Grail legend. If I am meant to help ye search, then I better know something about this sacred vessel."

With that pronouncement, Fionna spun and strode out of the library, leaving Arthur with one less book and the laces of his breeches strained tight.

Chapter Fourteen

Lancelot

Lancelot needed a hobby. Once, enjoying the company of women had been his unofficial hobby. But it seemed dalliances were yet another thing Morgana had ruined. There was always the company of men, he supposed. Though, engaging in relations with either gender didn't feel satisfying for once. He couldn't pretend away how his careless choices harmed the people—and the land—he cared about. A people and land he was willing to die for. Maybe that was why his mood felt as black as tar. When was the last time he had been celibate for a whole month? At least Percival didn't know what he was missing out on.

This morning, Lancelot visited the stable yard to clear his head from yesterday's fog, to exhaust his body until he had no energy left to remind him of how alluring he found their newest knight. The plan had worked for a time, but then *she* had appeared, like a specter from a dream. He was too spooked to remain in her company. He didn't trust himself around her.

Still, from the shadows, Lancelot had watched as Fionna sparred with Galahad, jealousy twisting in his gut. Fionna was the siren *and* the rocks, and Lancelot wanted nothing more than to bash himself against them, to be bludgeoned and torn apart by loving her. Needing to leave but unable to remain away, he drank in the sight of Fionna from afar. Every flash of her sword, every peal of her laughter ringing out bright and clear, the look of her cheeks flush with exhilaration from the fight. He drank long and deep before he finally made himself turn away, walking stiffly back toward his chambers.

He really did need a hobby. Double drills for the soldiers? Archery? Hunting, perhaps? A hunt might be good for him. Maybe he should talk to Percival. What did celibate knights do all day?

Lancelot had settled on a nap, and so was quite disoriented when a knock sounded on his door. He stumbled to open it, his eyes blurry with sleep.

On the other side stood a wide-eyed servant. "His Majesty asks that you attend him in the throne room. We have an ambassador from Tintagel."

Tintagel. The word struck him like an arrow, jolting him awake. "A moment," Lancelot said.

He flew about his chamber, grabbing his boots and hopping into them quickly, pulling a gray-blue tunic over his head. He retrieved his sword belt from where he'd abandoned his effects on the floor and buckled the leather and weapon around his waist while hurrying after the servant. Lancelot ran his hands through his hair, trying to tame his wild curls. An ambassador from Tintagel, where Morgana and her sisters lived. This couldn't be good. What fresh horrors had Morgana, Elaine, and Morgause decided to visit upon Caerleon now?

Arthur was sitting on his throne, the carved, high-backed chair gilded in gold. His king thought the throne too ostentatious, but for moments like this, it suited. Percival stood on Arthur's right, leaving a spot for Lancelot between them. And on Arthur's left stood Galahad and Fionna. The image of the three other knights startled him, and the reality of his predicament truly began to sink in. She was a part of their lives now—day in, day out. They were five. Gods help him.

"Nice of you to join us," Arthur murmured as Lancelot took up the position by his right hand.

"Do we know why they've come?" Lancelot asked.

"Regardless of their reasons, I ask that you *please* remain quiet."

"Even if you're in danger?"

"From an ambassador?" Arthur narrowed his eyes to slits. "Do not cause a scene. I need to mend relations not give Tintagel an excuse to declare war."

A muscle twitched in Lancelot's jaw as his king held his gaze. Their ambassador was still fae and, thus, still dangerous. *Still*, he ground out a simple, "Yes, Your Majesty."

Satisfied, Arthur nodded to the servants by the door, who opened the two large wooden doors.

The ambassador was strangely beautiful, typical of most sídhe males. Unnaturally tall and thin, though well-muscled, and pale as a stalk of winter grass, bleached by the cold. His nose, cheeks, and jaw cut at captivating angles, and his lips curved upward in a disdainful twist. Fae. Lancelot found his hand gravitating toward his sword hilt. Though the ambassador was the sort of male Lancelot once enjoyed when he roamed the sídhe courts for pleasure, he never forgot fae were predators and humans mere prey.

Arthur seemed to little mind the ambassador's strangeness. Or his rudeness. Or his king merely did a better job of hiding his sentiments than Lancelot. "Welcome to Caerleon," Arthur said warmly. "I hope your journey has treated you well."

"Well enough," the faerie male sniffed. His tunic glimmered a pale green with embroidery in a pattern of twisting leaves running up the sleeves. "My name is Alworn. My mistresses, the ladies Morgause, Elaine, and Morgana desire to express their congratulations to you for your joining of a fifth knight."

Arthur's brow wrinkled slightly at that. "Our new knight was only selected yesterday. But your journey must have taken a week at least . . ."

Alworn inclined his head to acknowledge the incongruity, a small smile twisting his arrogant mouth. Lancelot wanted to smack the insolence off his perfectly sculpted face. Bloody faerie magic.

"As you no doubt know, the mistresses of Tintagel are powerful priestesses. They had foreseen the knighthood of Fionnabhair Allán, and they celebrate her arrival." Alworn's eyes swiveled to Lancelot, and the man's shit-eating grin broadened. Lancelot's blood heated. Of course, Morgana knew Fionna would be joining them, and knew Lancelot could not help but love her. The cruelty of Morgana's curse took his breath away. Here was the woman Lancelot hadn't known he wanted—no simpering maiden swooning at his feet, but a woman fierce and bold as she was beautiful. An equal. And Morgana had made sure he could never have her—that he would live the rest of his days with an empty bed and aching balls. Gods, he wanted to break something.

The ambassador continued. "My mistresses relay their pleasure in how you have taken a fifth knight of such unusual skill and power, and a woman no less. For surely it could not have been easy for Lady Fionnabhair to overcome the prejudices of Briton to rise so far. They wish to give her a gift for her bravery and courage."

All eyes turned to Fionna. She held herself stiffly, her lean face betraying no hint of what she might think of the male's offer. Lancelot wanted to lean over to tell Arthur to reject the gift, but Arthur was already nodding. "Lady Fionna?" He gestured her forward.

Lancelot cursed inwardly. Faerie gifts came with strings attached. Strings tied to unforeseen dangers and tricks. He didn't know what the sisters had against Fionna, but this "gift" surely brought trouble.

Fionna glided down the stairs to stand before the ambassador, her eyes narrowed in such a way that made Lancelot wonder if she had ever met a fae in the flesh. If not, he hoped she well remembered all the faerie stories she had surely heard over the years, and would guard herself against tricks or unwittingly given favors.

Fionna's tunic and sword were odd for a lady in Arthur's throne room. Yet, she appeared every inch regal—an Irish warrior princess—looking Alworn straight into his unnatural aquamarine eyes, framed by white lashes. Seeing the two of them face each other gave Lancelot pause—it was like peering into the reflection of a looking glass. Fionna's pale coloring and white-blonde hair mirrored Alworn's. Though, Lancelot knew people of the North were fairer in coloring, even with hair so blond the strands shone white as Fionna's. He had traveled once to Northern Ireland and the Kingdom of Denmark. And he knew the Kingdoms of Strathclyde and Alba in Scotia as though his own hunting grounds. Still, the pair of them together unsettled him.

The ambassador presented a small wooden box carved with snaking vines and glistening dewdrops, and Fionna took it, opening the lid. Lancelot craned his neck to see while fighting his urge to rush down the steps and bat the box out of her hand.

"A necklace," Fionna said, holding up the gift. The silver chain held a pendant shaped like a budding lily, iridescent and sparkling and pure white. "Lovely," she said, bowing before the male.

Good, she didn't thank him.

Alworn inclined his head. Again. "It would please my mistresses greatly to see you wear their gift, I'm sure. May I?"

"Of course," she said after a moment's pause, handing him the necklace. She pulled her long cord of braids over one shoulder and turned her back to the man. "I fear this isn't proper attire for such a grand necklace," she added with a little laugh.

Warning bells rung in Lancelot's mind. "Don't—" he grit between clenched teeth, but Arthur grabbed his wrist in an iron grip, silencing him.

Lancelot ground his teeth together harder as Alworn clasped the necklace around Fionna's neck, letting the chain fall. "Lovely," he murmured, echoing her earlier sentiments.

"We must celebrate your visit here," Arthur said to the ambassador. "We will have a feast tonight in your honor. Perhaps we can convince Lady Fionna to wear something to better suit her new gift?"

Fionna glared daggers at Arthur as she stalked back up the stairs to resume her position at Galahad's side.

Arthur chuckled nervously. "Or perhaps not."

Alworn dipped his head. "I look forward to the feast, Little Dragon King." The ambassador turned and retreated from the throne room.

"Thank you for attending," Arthur said once the thick doors

closed behind him. "And Fionna, thank you for entertaining the ambassador so graciously."

She gave a curt nod while inspecting the necklace hanging around her swan's neck.

"Sir Lancelot, a word?" Arthur asked, and the others took his cue to disappear.

Arthur stood as the others filed out, stretching his back. "That chair is as hard as a rock," he complained.

"You shouldn't have let Alworn place *that* necklace on her," Lancelot said, gritting his teeth again. "We know not what the pendant does."

"Perhaps, but if we had refused the gift, it would have further alienated Morgana and her sisters from us. And we can ill afford more enmity between the Tintagel and Caerleon."

"Still—" Lancelot protested.

"I chose a risk of harm over a certain one. Sometimes that's the only choice before a king."

Lancelot studied his fingers, the muscles in his jaw clenching tighter. He decided not to mention how Arthur had chosen a risk to Fionna over a risk to his rule, which didn't seem very kingly at all. But he supposed Fionna was part of his rule now, so perhaps Arthur saw them all as one and the same.

"Lancelot," Arthur said. "Might be best if you skip the feast tonight. With your and Morgana's history . . . we should minimize your interaction with Tintagel for the time being."

"Very well," Lancelot said woodenly. How things had changed. A knight of Caerleon, banished from a feast in his king's own Great Hall. "But promise you will be careful, Arthur Pendragon. Do not thank the male, or you will be beholden to him or his mistresses. Remember, when you sup with sídhe faeries, you must be on your guard."

Chapter Fifteen

Galahad

The Great Hall looked resplendent, all dressed up for the feast. *And so do I, if I don't say so myself,* Galahad mused to himself. Candlelight flickered across the hall as though dancing will-ó-the wisps. Fern and wildflower garlands draped across rafters and festooned banquet tables. And fresh rushes released a soft, earthy scent with each step.

His thumbs hooked into his sword belt, Galahad whistled a bawdy tune as he strolled past clan lords who were clustered together for a hearty debate. Galahad wore his finest tunic—a rich woven linen fabric of maroon and gold, cinched with a leather belt stamped with interconnected lines and knots—a gift from his father when Galahad had left home for Caerleon. He had even bathed and trimmed his beard, wanting to look his best this evening, his hair brushed to a sheen and falling around his shoulders.

The moment he stepped past the visiting lords and their families, his eyes were searching for her. They found Percival instead, who popped into his line of sight, his expression eager. Percival grabbed Galahad's tunic and gave him a little shake.

"What is it man?" Galahad said with amusement, clapping his sword-brother on his shoulder.

"Wait 'till ye see her!" Percival said with unadulterated delight. "She's a beauty. An enchantress. Nae—a goddess!"

The youngest knight's tongue seemed to trip over itself while searching for the right word. The poor lad was akin to an awkward lamb trying to walk on shaking legs for the first time. And this, just by noticing a woman at a feast. Still, Galahad had no doubt of whom Percival spoke. And when he caught sight of her, his own legs grew shaky. She was all the things Percival had said—and none of them. Because no word could encompass the vision that was their fifth knight.

Fionna stood against the far wall amongst a gaggle of nobles from neighboring chiefdoms, a pewter goblet held daintily in her hand. Her white-blonde hair hung free, cascading in ripples to her waist but for a few pieces pulled back from her temples and braided around the crown of her head. She wore a dress of the deepest blue embroidered in silver, and the shimmering yards flowed over her form like a moonlit river. His eyes snaked up the same path, following her curving hips past her trim waist, leading to firm breasts that begged to be kissed. Her dress bared the milky skin above her plunging bodice line—as though a Roman goddess carved of marble—revealing the faerie necklace nestled atop her cleavage.

"Yer hurting me," Percival choked, and Galahad turned to him with a start.

"Sorry." Galahad released his crushing grip on Percival's shoulder.

The young man rubbed his neck with a grimace. "Not verra sporting to kill yer competition, arsehole."

"Competition?" Galahad raised an eyebrow. He slung his arm around Percival, leading him toward the head table, where a goblet of wine waited with Galahad's name on it. "With that little vow of celibacy, I'm not sure you're even allowed to play the game."

"There are plenty of ways to play without . . . taking the queen, ye ken," Percival said, nearly rolling his eyes.

Galahad guffawed. "Been skulking around, listening to the maid's gossip, have we?" he asked.

Percival was well on his way to becoming a powerful fighter, but in the ways of women, the lad was greener than a newly budding leaf. Stars shone bright in the young man's eyes, but Percival wasn't real competition. Not when it came to a woman like Fionna.

He'd known a few women like her before, though none so remarkable. She was capable and crafty and above all—in control. She needed a lover to ignite her passion until she blazed white hot, not as a warrior or noble, but as woman set on fire by the kind of searing, breathless pleasure that could only be given by a man. Galahad would be more than happy to fill that role.

"Hardly need to eavesdrop on the maids," Percival was saying when Galahad pulled out of his head. "Lancelot shares every intimate detail of his exploits. Or at least, he used to."

That was true. Lancelot had some most interesting conquests. And he was never shy about kissing and telling. Until Morgana that was. "Where is Lancelot?" Galahad craned his neck to take in the crowd, searching for a familiar mop of curly black hair. His sword-brother was conspicuously absent.

"He won't be joining us," Arthur said, approaching. The king shone like the high-noon sun in a tunic of gold and black thread, matching the auric tones of the oak-leaf crown resting on his brow.

Galahad frowned, but swallowed the question as Fionna joined them. "I kept waiting for someone to rescue me over there," she said, blowing out a slow, measured breath.

"Are you now the type of lady who needs rescuing?" Galahad winked.

"I would much rather face a Saxon horde than a grasping clann lord who's maneuvering for power."

"We share your sentiments," Arthur remarked.

Percival flashed Fionna a wicked grin. "Did Lord Tyrin tell ye about his goat breeding program?"

Fionna gaped. "How did ye—"

The knights laughed. "He can talk about his goats for hours," Galahad said. "Trust me, if he hadn't yet spouted poetry about the flavor profiles of Cheviot versus Snowdonian goats milk, you are lucky indeed."

"Isn't a goat a goat?"

"Nooo." Arthur shook his head in mock horror. "Never let him hear you say *that*."

Fionna heaved a withering sigh. "I do believe I need more wine."

"See? And ye lads were worried. Our Fionna is already familiar with our ways around here." Percival threaded his arm through hers, a waggish smile on his proud face. "Regardless of the question, the answer is usually 'more wine.'"

The feast now reveled in full swing. The musicians played a toe-tapping reel, the courses were plentiful, and the company was excellent.

Fionna had just finished regaling their group with a tale of one of her fiann mates tangling with an angry mother badger, which had sent them all into roars of laughter. *The woman was funny, too?* Galahad groaned inwardly. It was hardly fair.

The merry atmosphere between them dimmed slightly, however, when their guest of honor arrived. Alworn had fashioned his long silver hair in a braid, and he had changed into an even more elaborate tunic of white linen beaded in tiny pearls. Galahad stifled a snort. Never had he seen a more impractical garment in all his twenty-four years.

Tucked under his arm, the fae male carried a bottle that piqued Galahad's interest, though. The ambassador approached the head table where Arthur and the knights sat, inclining his head.

"Little Dragon King," Alworn began, preferring to use Arthur's nickname among the Túatha dé Danann. The male's voice was like snakeskin, smooth yet slithery. "Another gift, to add to tonight's festivities. Sweet woodruff wine, one of Tintagel's finest May vintages." He offered the bottle to Arthur, who took the gift from his outstretched hands.

Arthur dipped his head in answer. "Shall we have a toast?"

A servant hurried over with a tray of fresh goblets and wild strawberries. Alworn came around the table and settled into the empty seat on Fionna's right as the servant poured the wine, plunking in a wild strawberry or two per May wine tradition.

Galahad accepted a goblet and sniffed the libation with interest, savoring the ambrosial scents of vanilla and honey from the sweet woodruff. He hadn't much of a nose for wine, preferring ale. But this smelled tasty and brought him back to village days with the Manor Lord who squired him.

Arthur stood and raised his cup. "A toast, to our honored guest, Alworn of Tintagel. To a long and prosperous friendship between our two lands."

"Hear, hear," the revelers cried, raising their own cups in answer.

The wine's taste was even richer than the aroma—the sweet flavor was lush and full on Galahad's tongue. Utterly intoxicating.

Even Arthur regarded his goblet with an expression of pleasant surprise. "I've enjoyed May wine countless times, but I have never tasted one quite like your vintage."

"I brought a second bottle, Your Majesty." Alworn leaned in conspiratorially, a wide smile breaking across his pale features. "When you're ready."

On Arthur's other side, Fionna set her goblet down, her pink tongue flicking across her lower lip to capture a stray drop. Heat coursed through Galahad and pooled into a singular ache to know how good that tongue would feel. Would taste. Sharing more stories suddenly seemed a waste of an evening. Why weren't they dancing? He wanted to pull Fionna's lithe body against his, to feel the fit of her hipbones in his firm grip.

Galahad downed the rest of his May wine in one swallow, pushing back from the table. He strode behind Arthur and held out his hand. "Fionna, would you do me the honor of this dance?"

Fionna looked from his outstretched hand to his face, a flicker of indecision in her eyes. "I'm not sure I know the steps . . ."

"I've been told I'm an excellent teacher," he pressed, not willing to take no for an answer. He needed her in his arms. Yesterday. "And if this is to be your home now, learning a dance or two might come in handy."

She slinked out of her seat in a graceful arch, laying her hand in his. As soon as their palms touched, a buzz of energy—of awareness—coursed through Galahad and his chest tightened. He led her around the table onto the dance floor, feeling more alive than he had in years. Galahad took her into his arms, tucking her against him more tightly than was strictly necessary.

Her body fit perfectly against his, the warmth of her hands in his, the firm press of her breasts against his chest, her low neckline giving him an excellent view. And gods, the way she shifted against the bulging length of his throbbing cock. He couldn't breathe. He hissed in a breath when she shifted again. Without her armor on, she was softer, disarmed. A woman—a strong and fearless one, yes—but still tender too. Yielding. And impish. She knew what she was doing to him.

"I believe this is the part where we begin dancing," Fionna said, amusement sparkling in her eyes. He had been studying her, noticing every freckle, the silver of her eyelashes.

"I thought ye were teaching me," Galahad said, struggling not to growl the words. His longing for her was pulsing within him like a feral beast, roaring to be set free.

"I believe that's the opposite of what I was promised," Fionna pointed out, arching a single pale eyebrow.

"Well, I'm a man who delivers what he promised." Galahad pulled her tighter against him, running his thumb up the arrow of her spine. "Let's dance."

The musicians struck up a slower tune, the melody all the invitation Galahad needed. He pulled her into the steps, moving around the floor, weaving between the other nobles who spun around them. Heat flooded his wildly pounding pulse as they danced. Each time he spun her away, he pulled her back closer and, in such a way, she pressed against his length until he wished there was nothing between them but gasps and moans. The feel of her softness against his hard lines was maddening, her scent of heather and steel a headier concoction than he had ever known. The bodies around them seemed to fade away, and it was only him and her, and one possible end.

Galahad lowered his head to her ear, growling into it, made breathless by his need for her. "You have enchanted me, My Lady, leaving me utterly defenseless against your charms." He had planned to wait, to bide his time, to woo her as a man should. But his plans were but ash on the wind in the face of the power she had over him.

"Come to my chamber with me," he murmured. "And allow me do the same to you."

Chapter Sixteen

Fionna

Galahad surrounded me. The pressure of his fingers splayed against my back, the scratch of his beard against my cheek, the heat of his words in my ear. My senses galloped about like an unfettered wild horse. Dance. I needed to focus on dancing. My hand clutched the soft linen of my skirt and I moved to the drumbeat.

Clann wars and power plays by greedy kinsman perpetually decorated me in leather and shields. Not since we visited the High King of Ireland four years past had I worn an elegant dress such as this, or known the melodious footwork inspired by instruments instead of clanging metal on metal. Or received an offer that I hadn't responded to with a bawdy retort or knife blade to the man's throat. I can't remember when I had last received an offer I wanted to accept. And I wanted to accept Galahad's offer. Badly.

My lungs seemed to press against the ties of my dress. Was the large hearth stoked too hot?

My feet had a mind of their own, happily following Galahad across the dance floor.

"From your silence, I believe you're considering my invitation," Galahad said with a little laugh. A pleasant buzz tingled down to my slippers at the husky sound.

I really shouldn't. But oh, how I really should. I was wading through the argument in my heated, sluggish mind when the music stopped, breaking the spell. The crowd clapped politely while dance partners bowed to one another. I pulled back from Galahad, relieved as cool air flooded the space between us.

"I need to sit, Sir." I tore my hand from his grip and my gaze from the intense expression on his flushed face.

He was like a man possessed at the sight of me, and the aroused expression he wore both thrilled and frightened me in turn. I took a much-needed deep breath, trying to slow my heart's staccato beat. *Getting involved with Galahad romantically would be a terrible idea,* I told myself. *No matter how toe-curling our dalliance might be.* My body protested, however, refusing to relinquish its memory of his strength and vitality as he pressed his hard-muscled chest to mine. Goddess help me, I would need a cold bath tonight. But first, a chair.

I rounded the head table toward my blessed seat in a rush. My thoughts were so tangled that I didn't notice a body blocking my escape until I ran right into its solidity. "Percival!"

"Fionna . . ." Instead of flashing a smile and cracking a joke, as I was coming to learn was his way, he snaked a strong arm around my waist and threaded his other hand through my hair. Percival pulled me flush against him, tugging my hair so my head tilted back, my lips at the perfect angle for kissing.

The quick bite of pain in my scalp shocked me, but nothing surprised me so much as the expert way Percival seemed to fit me against his body. A bolt of desire coursed through me. Any other man might have received a knee to the groin for his impertinence, but I balked, trying to reconcile the smoldering heat in this man's brown eyes with the playful Percival I knew.

"Percival!" I pushed against his chest, pulling in a ragged breath. His scent of bergamot and sage washed over me, fresh and clear. "Have ye lost yer wits?"

"Ye have bewitched me, lass. There's only one way I will be free from yer spell."

Dread fluttered in my belly at his strange words. My heart thundered as though a mere yearling in battle, feet frozen to the blood-soaked ground. But I was a battle-hardened warrior who knew how to listen to the warnings in her gut.

I pushed harder against his chest. "What about yer vow? The Grail?"

"My vow means nothing. There is nae dish I would rather drink from than ye."

He wasn't talking sense. I shook my head, my heart sinking into my churning stomach. Something was definitely wrong. "Percival, no. I'm returning to my seat." I shoved my elbow against him, breaking his hold on me.

Thankfully, he released me, but not without a pained expression on his face. I hurried to my seat, crumpled onto the ebony wood, and then hid my shaking hands under my thighs. What was going on? Galahad had been forward, yes, but I knew he was attracted to me. I had seen his interest when we sparred. But Percival?

"Are you well, My Lady?" Alworn leaned over to me, concern written on his ageless face.

"No need for worry." I struggled to paste on a smile. "A friend is acting a wee bit strange, nothing more."

"Perhaps he can't hold his wine." Alworn touched a hand to his chest. "I hear tell it's a problem some mortals have."

I chanced a look to the dance floor, where Galahad and Percival now danced with new partners. The knights' flushed faces pressed close to the women's own, a preternatural gleam in their eyes.

A faintly predatory smile teased Alworn's lips. He hadn't touched the wine in his own goblet or the food on his plate.

"Remind me, what kind of wine did ye gift?" I asked.

"Sweet Woodruff. A special May blend."

I nodded slowly, my thoughts racing. Alworn was an emissary from Morgana and her sisters. Wasn't this the family Lancelot had offended by breaking his engagement to Morgana? What if this wasn't a diplomatic visit at all, but a veiled attack? The blood drained from me, the rich food roiling in my stomach. Had Arthur and his knights been poisoned? But no, Galahad and Percival didn't seem ill. They only acted strangely. And I had drank the wine, and I felt fine.

I needed to talk to Arthur and warn him that something might be amiss. But how, with the ambassador sitting next to us? I turned to Arthur, who watched the dancing, his chin resting on a fist. "Yer Majesty, would ye do me the honor of a dance?"

Arthur was on his feet in a blink, his hand out to me.

I started at his sudden movement, but stood cautiously, placing my hand in his long fingers. His hand felt warm—feverishly hot.

As we approached the dance floor, the other revelers began to clear for their king to claim the floor.

"Carry on!" Arthur called out, and then gestured to the musicians to take up a tune once again. As a lovely ballad began, Arthur wrapped his arm around my waist like a vise.

My breath hitched in surprise.

He leaned in, his voice low and purring in my ear. "Less prying eyes this way." His hard cock pressed into my stomach.

My whispered warning died on my lips. By the goddess, Arthur was infected too!

We began to dance, my mind racing for a solution.

"You are more beautiful than a starlit night," Arthur murmured, burying his face into the crook of my neck. "Your hair like the fall of moonlight on a snowy field."

Skies above, I couldn't concentrate with his whispered poetry. Still, I tried to remember what I had learned about faeries. All I recalled were children's stories and fireside myths. I had no idea how to break the spell of tainted faerie wine. And if I didn't, would my knights dance and dance until their feet fell off? Was that Morgana's plan?

And then two conflicting realizations struck me like bolts of lightning. First, I had thought of them as "my" knights. When had they become *mine*? Second, Arthur was addled beyond belief. Now would be a perfect time to steal Excalibur and get the hell out of Caerleon. Arthur and his knights wouldn't be able to pursue me for some time. Zephyr and I could be on the next boat for Ireland before Arthur even stopped dancing. If he stopped dancing. Guilt needled at me. I couldn't really leave him like this, could I? Leave all of them like this?

"Would your skin leave stardust on my lips?" he whispered hoarsely into my neck.

Arthur stroked my ear and pressed a kiss to the delicate flesh right beneath my lobe. I couldn't stop the shiver of pleasure that ran through me, all thoughts fleeing from my mind. Arthur smelled like the forest—oak and cypress and . . . home. My heart nearly stopped. Home? But I didn't have long to think of what *that* could mean when he trailed a line of kisses down my throat and over my collarbone. My head fell back, my breath trembling. I no longer thought of tainted wine or faerie swords or anything but Arthur. This close, he was magnificent. My fingers took on a mind of their own and roved over the hard lines of his muscles under his soft tunic, caressing each dip and valley, while my eyes took in the freckles across his nose, the gleam in the golden crown across his brow. This man was a king. This land, this fortress, these subjects belonged to him— he could have anything he desired. But he wanted me.

And I wanted him.

His mouth captured mine, and my eyelids fluttered closed as my world tilted on its axis. I melted against this strong, thoughtful man, the room around us fading away. There was only Arthur, and the velvet strokes of his tongue against mine, and the heat pooling between my legs. His lips were firm and soft, and he tasted of May wine. Of magic.

My eyes popped open. This wasn't Arthur. This was the wine. Arthur and his court were under attack. My heart grew sick. I would rob him and betray him, but the manner in which I would do so was of my choosing. Not like this. I would never leave him like this.

It took every ounce of my self-control, but I pulled back from Arthur's heady kiss.

His green eyes were hooded with longing, his breathing rapid.

"I'm sorry, Yer Majesty," I said. "But we must stop."

Arthur's brows creased before he dipped down for another taste of my swollen lips.

"I said *no*, Yer Majesty." I shoved off him and fled through the crowd toward the large hewn doors, feeling the crawling gaze of Alworn on my back.

I stumbled against the stone wall outside of the Great Hall, my hand on my chest as if the pressure from my palm was the only thing keeping my heart from beating out of my body. An errant tear broke free and rolled down my flushed cheek. Two days in Caerleon and I was a wreck. Galahad, Percival, Arthur . . . my emotions were ragged, my body desperate with need. Who was I—this gasping maiden in a hallway, so thoroughly disarmed by the knights of Caerleon? I needed Fionnabhair Allán back. I needed my fiann; I needed my armor; I needed someone to slap sense into me and tell me to do what needed to be done.

"Lancelot." I said his name like a prayer. Blessed goddess, I needed Lancelot.

Chapter Seventeen

Lancelot

Pounding on Lancelot's door startled him out of his bitter reverie. He unwound himself from his chair, where he had been staring morosely into the fire.

More pounding, followed by a muffled shout. His name.

He huffed, stalking to the door and yanking it open. "I thought I wasn't welcome—" The words died on his tongue. Fionna. And Fionna's breasts. His gaze traveled down her midnight blue dress that dipped low Roman style. A dress, he cursed silently, that hugged every curve of her firm, supple body. He thought he had a fighting chance of resisting her when she was dirty and sweaty and strapped into her armor. But like this? . . . Sweet merciful gods. Tamping down his desire, he snapped, "What do *you* want?"

Perhaps he did too good of a job, because Fionna recoiled slightly, her expression darkening. "I'm sorry to interrupt yer valuable time, but I thought ye would wish to know that yer king and fellow knights have fallen under a strange spell." She whirled to go, tossing over her shoulder, "I must have been wrong about ye."

He reached out and grabbed her wrist. "Wait."

She looked down at where his hand held her captive. Clenching his jaw, he released her more than a little reluctantly. It was the first time he had touched Fionna, and felt the heat of her. The realness.

"Tell me," he somehow managed.

"The ambassador offered a toast. May wine he brought from Tintagel. I think the bottle may have been laced with something."

"They drank faerie wine?" Lancelot asked, incredulous. He stabbed his fingers through his black curls with a furious groan. He never should have let Arthur banish him from that feast! His hand fell to his waist in angry defeat. Arthur was altogether too trusting sometimes.

Guilt wrinkled her smooth brow. "I do believe so, yes."

"Rule number one when dealing with faeries," Lancelot seethed, "don't eat any food or drink they offer. Idiots!"

When Lancelot was a young lad of twelve, a lord visited the Isle of Man. Drunk on faerie mead, he had grown so enchanted by Vivien, Lady of the Lake, that he cut off his own feet in order to become a merman and wed her. So drunk with magic was this visiting lord that he had failed to see Vivien's two feet planted in the wild grass and ferns. Lancelot had watched in horror as the noble bled out—the man grinning with the headiness of death. His foster mother knelt in a pool of the dying man's blood and kissed the final breaths from his lungs, then used his air to blow his limp body into the rippled surface her lake like a dandelion on the wind. Traumatized, Lancelot had refused any drop of alcohol until well past his eighteenth birthday. The memory sent a shudder down his spine.

"I think they didn't want to offend him," Fionna offered weakly.

"Of course," Lancelot sneered. "When someone offers you poisoned wine, of course you drink it, so as not to *offend them*!"

Fionna set her jaw, as if steeling herself against the buffeting force of Lancelot's anger.

He took a deep breath and exhaled slowly through gritted teeth. "What are they doing? Just dancing? Making merry?"

A blush colored Fionna's cheeks, the rosy hue softening her seemingly untouchable beauty. "They've grown . . . forward."

"Forward? Spit it out woman."

"Arthur kissed me," Fionna whispered, a hushed confession. She peered over her shoulder before settling a level gaze back onto Lancelot. "And Galahad asked me to come to his chamber. And

Percival . . ." she ran her hand over her eyes, as if attempting to banish the memory. "They're not themselves, Sir."

"Bloody hell," Lancelot muttered, pulling his door shut. "Let's go."

Fionna hurried after him down the hallway, the folds of her gown clutched in her fists. "How are ye going to fix them?"

"Damned if I know," Lancelot shot back. "This is magic wine. We need druid magic."

"Merlin!" Fionna's eyes lit up. "I forgot about him."

"Probably the first time that's happened," Lancelot said wryly. He looked at her sideways, trying to ignore the pleasant bounce of her breasts as she strode beside him. "When I get my hands on Alworn, I'm going to throttle that male. Like Morgana and her cursed sisters haven't wreaked enough havoc on Caerleon!"

Fionna looked at him with interest. "What do ye mean? What else have they done?"

Lancelot realized his mistake too late. Arthur hadn't told Fionna yet about the curse. He raced for an excuse as they rounded the corner into the main hallway that led to the Great Hall. "Morgana demanded that Arthur execute me for my . . . crimes against her. She didn't take it kindly when he refused, swearing vengeance."

"Execute ye! That's preposterous. Ye weren't even married yet." Fionna's lips formed a straight line. "Aren't faeries notoriously promiscuous? Ye would think Morgana would be a little more understanding."

"Morgana is wrath and ruin, not understanding. She's unlike any other faerie I've known," Lancelot admitted.

"Oh goddess," Fionna breathed as they passed through the wide-open doors into the Great Hall.

The scene was even worse than Lancelot could have imagined. Arthur, Galahad, and Percival were standing in the middle of the spacious room, shouting at each other—a circle of wary onlookers curving around them. Treacherous Alworn was nowhere to be found.

Percival pushed Galahad with an angry oath, who pushed the younger man in return, sending him stumbling back into a hapless lord standing nearby.

"I claim her," Arthur shouted, and the sound of steel echoed in the room as he drew Excalibur. "I am king and you will, therefore, desist all claims!"

The circle of onlookers stepped back. Gasps and worried whispers fell over the gathering like rain.

"Arthur!" Lancelot pushed through the crowd, Fionna close on his heel.

Arthur, Percival, and Galahad spun toward him, each of their blank faces homing in on Fionna like hungry predators catching the scent of prey.

Lancelot skidded to a stop, throwing up an arm to stop Fionna from approaching any closer.

At the sight of the clashing stags, Fionna blanched, burying her fist in the tunic at Lancelot's waist. She took a step behind him, shielding herself with his body. "It's worse than when I left," she said and, for the first time, Lancelot thought he heard a waver of fear in her voice.

"Fionna," Arthur strode toward them first, Excalibur swinging wildly in his hand, his green eyes glowing with need. A path parted between them as feast-goers scrambled away from his careening weapon.

Lancelot and Fionna backed up slowly toward the door, her other hand grasping his wrist, even as he held his arm out over her protectively.

"Feast is over," Lancelot bellowed to the other guests. "Time to retire to your chambers. The show is over."

"Where are you going?" Galahad rumbled angrily. Galahad and Percival were following like fish on a line, towed by an invisible current. Linked inextricably to Fionna.

"Fionna," Arthur begged. "Please—"

"Put away Excalibur, Yer Majesty," Fionna commanded, still backing away slowly into the hallway. "And come with me. Ye . . . ye shall have what ye w-wish." She stumbled over the words, the strain evident in her voice. "All of ye."

That well and truly hooked them. The three men followed like eager puppies, and Fionna turned to Lancelot, her eyes shining with angry tears. "It's awful," she said. "Their free will is gone.

How could someone do this to another human being?"

Lancelot squeezed her hand once before forcing himself to let her go. Her righteous anger for his sword-brothers touched something deeper within him than even her haunting beauty. He struggled to ignore it. "Faeries aren't human beings," he said. "We're pets to them. Playthings. You can't trust them."

She stared at him in horror—one beat of his thundering heart, then two—before they ducked out the door and into the cool of the night. The moon was full and low that night, illuminating the rocky path as they picked their way toward Merlin's cave.

Lancelot shivered, the skin on the back of his neck crawling with the feel of someone watching him. He took a steadying breath. The night's events were simply unsettling him. They weren't *actually* being watched.

"Where are we going?" Percival asked behind them. His voice was dreamy—false.

"Somewhere to be alone," Fionna said, her eyes fixed firmly on the ground, her hair shining like a halo around her.

They ducked into the darkness of Merlin's cave, their party silent but for the rushing of the River Usk over the mossy rocks below. The sharp tang of herbs and the cave's musty smell washed over him and, for once, Lancelot found the scents comforting.

"Merlin!" he called out, his deep voice echoing on the damp stones. A torch on their right sprang to life, and they all jumped back.

"I thought we were going to be alone," Arthur said suspiciously.

Fionna shushed him, then whispered, "Soon, My King."

From the flickering shadows, Merlin appeared, his gold-ringed eyes glowing in the dark. "All the knights of Caerleon at my door—I sense magic."

"Faerie wine," Lancelot said, disliking the pleading in his tone.

Merlin clucked his tongue but motioned them forward into the main cavern. "Come, fool lads."

Galahad cozied behind Fionna, snaking his arms around her waist and burying his face into her hair. "At last," he whispered. A hand roamed up her taut stomach toward her breasts; the other seized her chin and tilted her head back toward him.

Jealousy roiled hot in Lancelot at the sight of Galahad's hands where he wanted his own to be.

"A little help?" Fionna yelped, trying to squirm out of Galahad's iron grip. The knight was lowering his lips to the curve of her neck. "I don't want to hurt him. But I will—"

Merlin murmured under his breath and the three enchanted men swayed on their feet as their eyes fluttered shut. Lancelot lunged for Percival, catching the wiry lad before he toppled forward, while Merlin went for Arthur, catching him under the armpits and lowering him to the floor. Galahad, who was thoroughly twined about Fionna, crashed backwards like a felled tree, pulling her down onto him. With a muffled curse, Fionna rolled away and flopped onto the floor as Galahad's huge arms went limp.

Reclining on one elbow, she panted for breath. "A little warning next time, druid."

Merlin inclined his shorn head and walked to his shelves, pulling items into his arms.

"Can you fix them?" Lancelot asked.

"I can," Merlin said. "The magic in the wine was more whimsical than deadly. Lighthearted faerie fun. I can undo it."

"Remind me to never have fun with a faerie." Fionna pushed herself to her feet and straightened her dress, pulling her long, flowing locks and braids over her shoulder.

"It's lucky you two didn't drink the faerie wine." Merlin deposited his ingredients onto his carved desk, then looked at both he and Fionna.

"I wasn't there," Lancelot said. "Or I would have stopped the fools from drinking the wine too. But . . ." he turned to Fionna, his brows drawing together. "Why didn't you drink the wine?"

Fionna shrugged, an unreadable emotion playing across her face. "I simply didn't want any," she said. "Alworn left me far too unsettled."

Lancelot nodded slowly, studying her, trying to read the truth behind her silver eyes. And failing. There was something she wasn't saying. She may have clasped his hand that night, but he would do well to remember: their fifth knight kept her own counsel.

Interlude

Morgana

The crow watched from an oak branch as the fae male transformed into a white wolf and loped into the night-shadowed forest. She launched into the air, silently tailing him until he reached a safe distance from prying human eyes.

The crow flapped her moonlight dusted wings, swooping onto the deer trail the white wolf followed. She cawed as he approached.

The wolf's hackles rose, an answering snarl escaping his snout. The night provided ample darkness and whispered prayers and she transformed in a rush of wind and decaying leaves.

"Alworn," Morgana said simply, touching the wolf on his head.

Her ambassador vaporized into his male form, all slender lines and angles. His haughty gaze found hers before, remembering himself, he stumbled into a hasty bow—one knee to the forest floor, his head low.

"Your Highness," he intoned. "How may I serve you further this night."

"I require your confession."

He looked up then, graceful eyebrows drawn together. Under the moon's watchful eyes, his hair glinted silver and his eyes paled to their unnatural aquamarine shade. "Confession?"

"Do not play coy with me, Alworn. I observed the whole sordid affair from the rafters."

"Then surely you saw how your brother and his knights made fools of themselves with the witch."

Morgana laughed. Crows slumbering in the branches above awakened and joined their caws of laughter with hers.

A sliver of fear tightened the muscles of Alworn's beautiful face.

She stepped close and traced along his bottom lip, drawing blood with her sharp fingernail.

"Surely you witnessed how our May wine failed to enchant the witch. Why is this, dear Alworn?"

"I am as baffled as you."

Morgana bared her teeth as blood dripped from Alworn's mouth, then leaned toward his ear. "Convince me not to peck your eyes out," she whispered, her voice sultry and inviting.

"Must be her . . . m-magic protecting her. B-but the necklace," he stammered. His body shuddered under her touch and she smiled, satisfied. "She w-wears the n-necklace you enchanted, Your Highness."

"Yes," Morgana hissed, drawing out the sound until the word slithered from her tongue into his ear. "The necklace." Releasing him, she stepped back. "It is enough, for now. I will spare your eyes this time. Do not fail me again or you will wander blind until a pack of wolves scents your weakness and shreds you to ribbons."

"You are m-merciful, Your Highness." His eyes fixed onto the dirt beneath his feet.

"Go, Alworn." Morgana touched his forehead and he vaporized into his white wolf form once more. "Be swift. Return to Tintagel and keep my sisters company."

The white wolf tucked his tail and loped into the distance, disappearing between the inky silhouettes of tall, swaying trees.

A dark breeze ruffled Morgana's hair and she lifted her face to the sister moon. "Guide my journey . . ."

The rest of her whispered prayer was lost to the night as the crow appeared once more. She joined the twinkling stars and low-hanging clouds high above Caerleon, her mind filled with thoughts of freedom, and magic, and revenge.

Fionna

I pressed my forehead to the slick glass of the latticed windowpanes and tried, in vain, to cool my feverish skin. An hour had passed since Merlin's magic banished the strange echantment gripping Arthur, Galahad, and Percival, since the five of us walked in silence back up the path to the wooden keep.

We parted ways by the corridor's mouth that led to my room, the knights heading to theirs. I had never seen them so morose, or so quiet.

I didn't know if the men remembered what they had done while in the faerie wine's grip, but I did. My body burned with the memories. Arthur's velvet tongue in my mouth; Percival's hand gripped tightly in my hair; Galahad's massive arms locked around me. Their remembered words were flint striking in the dark of my mind, kindling a fire within me that burned so hot it frightened me. And then there was Lancelot—ornery as a penned stallion one moment, ready to protect me with his life the next.

Even I had my limits as a seasoned fighter. I could fight one—maybe two—men. But three strong, skilled warriors? A sick feeling twisted in my stomach once more. I both enjoyed and loathed their advances, for how the feelings forced me to question my morality and sense of honor, while also embracing how each man made me feel desirable. The nausea swirled stronger and I had to admit the real truth— my mind was drifting farther and farther away from my father and sister and the sacrifice I must make for their lives.

I pushed back from the window, heaving a sigh, before crossing the room to the sideboard. I poured water from a silver pitcher and splashed cool liquid onto my face, desperate to find myself again. My body no longer felt like my own. Nor my heart. Many a song declared the misery and ache of a stolen heart. Is this what I felt? My heart torn between two lands and two callings?

I blotted my face dry. I didn't understand this . . . this confusion. I had been with two men before—one, a lad from Aghanravel, another a warrior in a fiann I fought beside. Both had been pleasant enough experiences, though short and somewhat underwhelming. In truth, I had set thoughts of sex aside and dismissed intimacy with another as something that held little interest to me. Fighting and sparring and honing my skills as a warrior—these were the physical activities that inflamed the passion in my blood.

Until I came here.

I wondered if I knew myself at all. I thought of Lancelot's question about the faerie wine. I had hoped neither he nor Merlin would pick up on my sudden discomfort. I should have known I wouldn't be so lucky to escape their inspection. I didn't know why I had lied. I drank the faerie wine. So why wasn't I affected by the enchantment? Did the tainted May wine only affect men? Or could I have some other magical immunity?

The silver necklace dangling around my neck caught the firelight, and I lifted the pendant, examining the jeweled lily. Could the necklace be a form of protection? My skin crawled at the thought of anything from Alworn touching me. I grew overcome with the need to toss the gift far from me. I reached back to remove the necklace, but the clasp stuck. My fingers fumbled with the delicate mechanism. I grunted, spinning the chain around, trying to work the clasp from the front. The clasp's lever didn't budge. I tried to pull the chain off over my head, but the length was too short, too tight. Frustrated, I yanked on the chain and grimaced at the biting pain in my neck.

I let the necklace fall, huffing. I guessed Tintagel's gift was staying on. For now.

Between the excitement of Alworn's attack, the ache in my loins, and the guilt-tinged pang in my chest, sleep would elude me tonight. I slipped out my door into the dimly lit hallway, candle in hand. Perhaps I could find a book in the grand library to explain my immunity to the faerie wine. That would set my mind at ease.

My jittery mood settled as soon as I had a task before me. My shoulders sagged slightly in relief. Nothing like boring, dusty books to distract me from the tumbling confusion in my head and the yearning heat deep in my belly.

Or so I thought. The library was lit from within. Candlelight flickered gentle amber light onto the stone walls.

"Fionna . . ." Arthur whispered my name from behind a table. Shadows smudged the skin under his eyes.

I briefly contemplated excusing myself, but it was the look of him that convinced me to move forward. His short hair was tousled, his full lips pinched, his brow twisted with worry.

"Yer Majesty," I said, needing the formality to remain. I settled into the chair across from him, grateful for the expanse of wood and books that stretched between us like a barricade.

"Please Fionna, Arthur is fine," he said, his voice soft and shy. "Percival calls me 'pumpkin' behind my back. You may at least call me by my first name."

A smile tugged on the corner of my mouth. "Pumpkin?"

He closed his book and, in a single blink, met my gaze. "I don't understand his reasons. I'm sure it's only a matter of time before he crowns you with a mildly insulting moniker as well."

"Percival's terms of endearment?"

"Precisely." Arthur smiled weakly over one of his books, his eyes glossing red in the candlelight. "About tonight . . ." He rose from behind the table and knelt at my feet, bowing his head. I bit back a gasp, unable to process a king lowering himself before me as Arthur did so now, his shoulders slumped, dejection posturing the angle of his head. "I cannot express how utterly sorry I am for what happened, for my behavior. All of our behavior."

"Do ye . . . remember?" My cheeks flamed and I swallowed at the forming knot in my throat.

Arthur lifted his head and searched my eyes, almost pleading. "I wish I did not, but I do. Every wretched moment."

His confession stung. Wretched? He wished to forget our kiss? Or the different sort of magic that enveloped us as our lips touched and breath mixed? But even as the thought surfaced, I scolded myself. Of course he desired to forget. He had embarrassed himself in front of his entire court. Anyone would want to forget such a moment.

"I did not behave as a king should, nor a man of honor," Arthur continued, his voice shaking. "I deeply regret how you were subjected to my shameful actions. I shall never forgive myself nor will I ever forget."

I softened. "Ye were not yerself, Arthur."

"Matters not, for tonight still happened. Do not excuse how we—how I—treated you, and publicly no less. You're not an object to appease our carnal urges and deserve my utmost respect before my court." He rubbed his face, as if he could banish the memories. "My father . . ." Arthur trailed off, leaning his head back to gaze at the ceiling. I watched as his Adam's apple bobbed and his eyes blinked back growing emotion.

"My father and my mother," he began, almost a whisper. "Their union was not . . . consensual. He used magic to disguise himself as Gorlois—the Duke of Tintagel, a fae male from the Túatha dé Danann who gave up immortality for my mother, and my half-sisters' father—and then Uther bedded my mother. That same night I was conceived, my father placed Gorlois at the front lines in a battle against several Saxon clans and . . . and he died—violently. His body was returned the next morning to Tintagel, mutilated. I . . . I was eighteen when my father died after he drank from a spring the Saxons had poisoned in his war camp. The Lady of the Lake dissolved any gossip of my rightful claim to Caerleon's throne through Excalibur." Arthur's green eyes brimmed with anguish as he met my gaze. "I am born of rape and deceit, and I watched my mother live under Uther's obsessive claim over her for eighteen years, helpless. I swore that I would *never* condone that form of cruel behavior in my kingdom. To allow a woman to suffer such indignities where I had the power to stop it." His green eyes searched everywhere, landing anywhere but my face. "And then to find . . . it was I . . . who perpetrated them." His voice lowered to a near growl as he said, "Perhaps I'm more like him than I thought."

Grief flooded through me like a swollen river. How was it possible for a man in this dark world—a king no less—to have such a tender heart? In that moment, I would have done anything to soothe the guilt chafing at Arthur. Even, it seemed, tell the truth. "Our kiss was consensual," I managed, swallowing.

Arthur's eyes met mine as the words hung between us. "You forcefully had to tell me no and shoved me away."

"A surprise, certainly. The wrong venue, absolutely. But . . ." I closed my eyes, struggling against my embarrassment. What was I doing? Admitting to the king of Briton that I had wanted to kiss him! Was I a fool? I opened my eyes again, meeting his firmly. "Yes, I had told ye no, and I do not make excuses for ye. Simply, I knew ye were under a spell ye could not control. If I continued our kiss, is that not the same as taking advantage of ye?"

His chest rose and fell, though a hint of light chased away the shadows on his beautiful face.

"And, if I had truly felt unsafe," I continued, encouraged, "I would have knocked ye on yer arse, king or no."

A sad smile touched his lips, flushed from his sorrow. "I imagine that's experience talking?" he asked, softly.

"Men have a funny way of feeling entitled to something from a woman, especially when their blood is up. I've had to remind a few over the years that my body belongs to no one but me. And yer body belonged to ye, not the faerie wine."

He bowed his head toward me, the lines on his face relaxing. He whispered, "Thank you, Fionna."

"Ye're welcome, Arthur," I whispered in return, my heart squeezing in my chest.

He slowly rose to his feet and locked eyes with me before returning to his seat, saying, "Quick thinking, finding Lancelot. You're an asset to this kingdom. We're lucky to have you."

His praise warmed me like a hearth in winter. Who was the eager puppy now? I *wanted* this king's gratitude, his esteem. His view of me shouldn't matter, but skies, I found that I craved his good opinion. What would it do to him when I took the sword? The one granting him sovereignty over his land? Or when I fled from here? What would it do to me? How had I sank so deep so fast? The longer I stayed here, the greater my blood price would become. I needed to focus. I needed to remember my father and my sister, held prisoner by Donal O'Lynn. In danger.

It was in that moment that I saw what my muddled emotions had hid from me. My vision narrowed to a point. Arthur's hand rested on his thigh, where his fingers normally curled around the pommel of Excalibur. A pommel that was conspicuously absent.

I hissed in a breath, trying to keep the excitement from my face. He didn't have Excalibur with him. Now was my chance.

Then pain lanced through me. Blood drained from my face as I accepted my fate. I would deal with my treacherous heart later. First, I had to save my father and sister from certain death.

"Are you well?" Arthur asked. "You seem as if you've seen a ghost."

I scrambled for an excuse, standing. "My mind refused to tire after all of today's excitement, but exhaustion has finally found me. With yer leave, I will retire to bed."

"Of course," Arthur said, rising to his feet and bowing. "I should probably head to bed as well."

"No!" I nearly shouted, before realizing how unhinged I sounded. "I disrupted yer study. Please, stay and finish whatever ye were working on. Perhaps tonight will be the night ye will have yer breakthrough and find yer Grail."

"Your lips to the gods' ears," Arthur said, lowering himself back into his chair.

I relaxed—slightly.

"Good night Arthur," I whispered, my eyes tracing the planes of his handsome boyish face, memorizing every inch.

For what I really meant was *goodbye*.

Chapter Nineteen

Fionna

My footsteps thundered in my ears as I hurried toward the East Wing. My heart galloped in my chest like a wild stallion. Was I really doing this? I was really stealing Excalibur.

The fortress slumbered at this hour, and no one blocked my passage. Not that they would have any reason to, I reminded myself. I was a knight, after all. I could go anywhere I pleased. I straightened my shoulders and slowed my steps. I needn't skulk about like a common thief. *Though you are a thief*, my conscience whispered at me. *Curse you, Donal O'Lynn for putting me in this impossible situation!*

Perhaps I could leave a note. I dismissed that idea as soon as the thought surfaced. A note would be a clue to help them find me more quickly. Best that they not know why I've left or where I journey. A messenger then. When the deed was all said and done, I would send a messenger to explain everything, especially where to find O'Lynn. A grim smile crossed my face. That would be a worthy vengeance. As soon as I had my family free, my fiann would join with Arthur and his warriors in slaying O'Lynn and reclaiming Excalibur. Relief swelled in me. The very thought was enough to quiet the guilt gnawing at my gut.

The corridor leading to the knights' rooms was dark. It seemed a lifetime ago when I had pounded on Lancelot's door, demanding his aid. This night had felt like five nights, these last few days—a lifetime. I passed Galahad's door next and an ache of desire coiled deep within me. In other circumstances, I would have accepted Galahad's invitation gladly. And then I passed Percival's door, and whispered an apology. An image in my mind of his unflappable smile falling when he heard of my betrayal was almost too much to bear. I looked away, toward the staircase at the end of the hallway. Arthur's chamber tower. I could do this.

"For ye, Aideen. Papa. For ye, I'll do anything," I whispered to the shadows as I crept up the stairs.

Arthur's door was unlocked and I slipped inside silently. I let my eyes adjust to the dim space first, taking in my surroundings. His chambers were slightly larger than mine, but not by much. Nor were they gaudy and ostentatious as some kings favored. Rather, his personal space was neat and orderly, with simple, carved-oak furniture, and tidy stacks of books. A sad smile crossed my face at how very Arthur it all was. And then I went to work.

Knowing my time was short, I turned every inch of his chamber upside down as quickly and as delicately as I could. The four-post bed, the oak-hewn chest, the heavy desk, the bookshelves. Excalibur was large with an Otherworldly shine, incapable of hiding. Yet, the faerie sword was nowhere to be found. I rose to my feet after riffling under the bed for the second time. No, definitely not there. I brushed off my gown and huffed.

Slowly, I spun around again, taking in every nook and cranny. The coveted sword wasn't here. Excalibur wasn't with Arthur, but it also wasn't here.

My mind raced as I slipped down the stairs and back into the corridor. Chewing on my lip, my feet dragged as I twisted and untwisted possibilities. Perhaps Arthur had left the sword in Merlin's cave? I paused and closed my eyes, trying to replay the scene in my mind. Had Arthur removed Excalibur when Merlin administered the antidote to the faerie wine? If the sword was indeed with Merlin, I had no chance of stealing the blade tonight. But . . . if he had left Excalibur somewhere else—

"Fionna?"

A baritone voice startled me. My hand flew to my chest as I jumped as though a startled deer.

"Galahad . . ."

I pressed my body to the far wall as I willed myself to calm. I had been so lost in thought, I hadn't realized that I had stopped right in front of his doorway. Which he was now filling. Shirtless. His long blond hair tousled around his shoulders.

I swallowed as I took in his form, limned in torchlight—the flat planes of his pectorals, the rippling expanse of his abdomen. Behind me, I placed my palms flat against the cool stone wall. Without anchoring myself to something real, I feared I might float away. Had a man ever looked so devastating in firelight?

"What are you doing in the East Wing?" he leaned one muscled arm on the doorjamb.

I practically groaned at the way the movement displayed his muscles before me, my skin coming alive in his presence. "Couldn't sleep," I managed. "Simply enjoying a midnight walk."

"And your walk brought you to my door?"

His low chuckle rumbled through me, hardening my nipples against the fabric of my dress. I licked my dry lips.

Galahad shifted in the doorway, and I pressed myself harder to the far wall. With this space between us, I could retain some coherence of thought. If he came over here . . . I might grow weak, to my shame as a tested warrior.

Goddess, he moved toward me—was before me in a flash, his calloused hands taking one of mine. He loomed in my vision, a golden sight that I wanted to drink in until I drowned. Without a sword in my hand, without my armor on, I felt small compared to him. Distinctly female.

"Please forgive me for my ungallant behavior tonight," Galahad said. His dark blue eyes were earnest, sorrowful. "I would never think to impose myself on a woman who was not interested. My mother and sisters would have my hide, if they knew." A sad smile flitted across his lips. "If I offended you, I apologize profusely."

"I wasn't offended," I managed to say. My voice sounded hoarse to my ears. "I understood there were . . . extenuating circumstances."

He heaved a sigh of relief. "You are most gracious for understanding." The light in his eyes shifted, sending a trill of excitement up my spine. "Though, I would be false if I said I had not thought of my invitation before." His thumb drew lazy circles on the back of my hand. "Though I am naught but villager's son compared to other company you could keep, know that you are welcome in my chambers any time it pleases you." He winked at me before leaning forward and placing a soft kiss on my cheek, bracing one hand against the wall by my head. His lips were like a brand upon my skin, marking me his with one simple gesture. He lingered there, his lips hovering by my ear, the heat of his bare skin and his breath warming me like a Beltane fire. Allowing the choice to be mine.

I didn't want the choice to be mine. I wanted his passion to overcome my senses, my better judgment, so I could tell myself in the morning that I had been swept up in the madness of his offer. But that would be a lie. My emotions warred within me—wanting this man yet knowing my betrayal would hurt him even deeper should we become tangled up in each other's lives this way.

Galahad pulled back, sensing my hesitation, a sweet smile dimpling his cheek. Did he fear I judged him for his birth status? My heart spasmed painfully with the increased space between us, seizing my will. I had been teetering on the edge of a knife's blade, and I threw myself off it.

"What about tonight?" I heard myself whisper.

His smile turned sultry, and my pulse thrummed through my veins in response. He traced the line of my face, my ear, down to my chin, which he gently held between his fingers. "You're sure?"

I gave a little nod, as sure that this was a terrible idea as I was that I wanted him more than I had wanted anything in a very long time.

In one lithe motion, he scooped me up in his arms. His smell of cedarwood and leather teased my senses.

"Tonight," he murmured as he pushed back through his door, closing it with a bare foot, "you are a queen, and I your humble servant."

A spasm of need jolted through me with his words, and my breath grew shallow.

Wanton.

In one playful motion, he tossed me down upon the cover-let. I scrambled back as he pounced on top of me, finding myself giggling like a maid. My fevered grin was matched by one on Galahad's handsome face. And when he kissed me, his lips tasted as sweet as honey. All thoughts of O'Lynn and Excalibur and tomorrow fled from my mind, leaving only Galahad.

Chapter Twenty

Galahad

Fionna was in *his* chambers. Beneath him on *his* bed. In a dress sewn from folds of the night sky by Freya herself. Stars above, what delicious madness was this?

Two princes and a king slept on either side of his walls. He flirted and teased, but he didn't expect her to choose him. Especially not choose him over Arthur. As the son of a blacksmith—in a home of ten—as the one who was squired at a young age to help provide food for his sisters and brothers, he could not fathom why a princess would choose him.

Galahad nibbled on her lower lip before pulling away to confirm that he was not lost in a dream. He stilled at the sight before him.

A wicked gleam glimmered in her silver eyes—one that disarmed his hold on her waist and puddled every thought at her feet. And then she rolled out from underneath him as though they sparred in the paddock.

Galahad boomed with laughter, ready to pounce again.

But Fionna's lips, the ones he had just tasted, curved into a flirtatious smile as she rose onto her knees—and he stared, beguiled by the toned muscles of her arms, her long, graceful neck, and the way her gown dipped low between her breasts. Lifting an elegant arm, she pulled a few pins from atop her head. A waterfall of braids joined the moonlit tresses spilling to her waist.

His breath caught. Just to feel the fall of her hair about his face, her breasts pressed to his bare skin—it would be heaven and hell rolled into one. And she wasn't done tormenting him yet.

Tilting her head, Fionna trailed the tips of her fingers down his broad chest in a feathered touch, down his stomach ribbed in muscle, lower still. Galahad's muscles jumped and flexed. She was killing him. When her fingers reached the drawstrings of his breeches, she dipped forward and kissed the broad expanse of his pectorals.

"Gods," he whispered as his head fell back against his shoulders.

Her tongue explored his skin, roaming southward to his abdomen. His chest heaved as he watched her, mesmerized by every little movement, every languid sensation. Silver eyes locked onto his hungry gaze and she grinned, right before her pink tongue flicked below his navel, where a thin patch of hair traveled below his breeches.

A white-hot flame blazed through his groin and Galahad growled her name. He was unraveling by the second. Fionna laughed at the sound, as if taunting another warrior in the round. If a fight was what she wanted, a fight was what he'd give her. And this time, there would be no tie.

Tangling his fingers into her hair, Galahad lifted her cruel mouth to his. Their lips crashed in a bruising kiss, drinking each other in. Desperate for more. Longing for release. His hands slid up her waist until his thumbs brushed along her pebbled nipples. She moaned into their kiss and sagged against the hard planes of his body.

But only for a moment.

As if remembering herself, Fionna pushed away and narrowed her eyes. She thought she could take him. Do with him as she wanted. But he had other plans. Tonight was about *her* pleasure. Control, he knew, was a climax all its own. The corner of her mouth lifted in a challenge—come and get her—if he could.

Fionna tried to scramble off the bed, but he curled an arm around her waist and then flipped her onto her back in an easy motion. She thrashed beneath him, laughing, feigning a struggle. She wanted a chase. He wanted to win.

Nudging her legs open with his knee, his hand slipped under the folds of her skirt and caressed her calf, behind her knee, her thigh. She drew in a ragged breath of anticipation. The curve of her hip fit perfectly into the palm of his hand. Her eyes fluttered closed and her lips parted.

Galahad lowered his weight onto her and ground his throbbing cock between her thighs. Fionna arched, moaning, her breasts offered to his lips. He rolled his hips into hers again, sucking her breast into his mouth through her bodice. Her nails dug into his back as she bit back a cry.

He was dying. Heat curled violently in his blood. Vicious tendrils that burned and consumed. His muscles tightened and shook with need. And, Odin save him, he wanted her to know the same torture a tongue could inflict. A fair fight. Not that she fought fair, not even once since arriving. She didn't take kindly to losing either, a thought that billowed his determination.

Biting the edge of her bodice with his teeth, he tugged the fabric away until her breast sprang free. Fionna was perfect, ample and soft, cold moonlight caressing her skin. Her curves rose dangerously near his lips and then falling away. He wanted her rendered immobile. Unable to escape his returned attack.

Gently, Galahad grasped her wrist, freeing the nails that dug into the flesh of his back. He placed one hand above her head, then the other. She was now pinned down, but he knew she submitted willingly—for a moment, at least. Finding her heated gaze, he held it, allowed a wolfish grin to form, and then he licked her nipple with the tip of his tongue—flicking, toying, drawing circles—as his hardened length pressed against her once more.

A moan escaped her mouth, rumbling through him. He moved against her again and again, desperate for every sound. She melted into the sheets and bucked her hips to increase their friction. He dragged his lips to her mouth to silence her heavy breaths and hums of pleasure. And stars, his pulse was drunk, intoxicated by the feel of her body, the taste of her lips, the way she moved beneath him. Especially when her hips danced to his in a rhythm that grew frantic.

"Tell me what you want, My Lady," he whispered in her ear, breathless. "Command me and I will obey."

"Taste me," she sighed in answer.

He nipped the skin beneath her earlobe and whispered back, "Only if you remain silent."

"If I—"

"Silent," he repeated. "Do you accept my challenge?"

Fionna lifted herself up onto her elbows to glare at him. "Am I not in command?"

"Command comes with a price. Self-control." A devious smile curved on his lips.

"I have plenty of discipline," she parried. "Or have ye forgotten how I matched ye during the tourney?"

Galahad winked, rubbing the rough edge of his thumb against her exposed nipple. "Then what are you afraid of?"

Her eyes narrowed farther, and she tried—unsuccessfully—to suppress the shudder his motion was sending through her.

"Fear you will lose to me?" He pressed his cock to her sex next, grinding—lazily, erotically—his gaze never leaving hers.

Fionna's eyes widened in a flash of sensual anger and some-thing else—*want*. The liquid heat in her gaze almost unraveled him. Almost.

"Fine," she said. The reply was meant to be sharp, he knew. But the single word came out in a quivering breath. "I'll be silent."

"Good," Galahad breathed into her ear. Then he kissed her jaw, her neck, her breasts, down to her stomach. "I want to drink my fill and not be interrupted." He smiled into her gown, bunched at her waist, when her hands fisted his coverlet, white-knuckled with frustration.

But her legs willingly opened for him as he pushed the skirt of her dress up, running his hands up the smooth expanse of her thigh. Her scent enveloped him and his arms nearly weakened at how beautiful she was while spread out before him. . . and how beautifully wet with arousal. To test the waters, he kissed the inside of her thigh and waited. Fionna sucked in a quiet gasp.

"Silent," he purred from between her legs.

His hot breath on her skin sent a tremor across her body—both in frustration and desire. He knew she was ready to raze him to the ground and it took everything in him to not laugh. Instead, he kissed the inside of her other thigh. Happy when she didn't make a sound, he flicked her swollen nub with the tip of his tongue. Her entire body tensed as she gripped the coverlet tighter, sinking her other hand in the long strands of his hair.

It was the sight Galahad desired, and he buried himself in her. Her thighs shook with the effort to not cry out in deep-sated moans as he lapped and drank, as his lips slid between her seam. The taste of salt, honey, and sex danced in his mouth as she writhed against his tongue.

Now he was truly dying. Never had a woman tasted so divine nor felt so right in his battle-worn hands. It drove him deeper, made him more desperate to earn his name on her lips. Especially when her hips began grinding against him. When her fingers clawed his shoulders, fisted in his hair. Her back arched, her breasts swelled, nipples taut as she climaxed under his torment. Every part of her trembled and he was heady with the power she granted him over her.

A wild heartbeat later, Fionna's fingers released. Her thighs no longer straining under his pleasure. Still, he wasn't quite done with her yet and licked her one last time right as her body seemed to fully relax. Her reddened lips, swollen from his kisses, parted as a faint moan escaped before closing into a furious line.

She had lost.

And she knew it.

A surprise attack to repay hers on the tourney green.

Amused, he sat back on his knees, his cock hard and his balls tightening with need. But not tonight. He would make her wait for victory against him. Perhaps even beg. A bout he looked forward to fighting in, if he was lucky enough to receive a second match. He prayed he was.

"I think I won that round," he said, a triumphant grin on his face. "Perhaps you need another lesson in self-control."

Fionna sat up, emotions warring on her beautiful face. Her eyes blazed and he stole a quick kiss, wanting her to taste herself on his lips. She struggled to appear unmoved, though he knew she was affected when her eyelids began to droop in a drowsy blink. He pulled back from her and she straightened, head thrown back, shoulders squared. To a warrior as fierce as Fionna, defeat was un-acceptable. Galahad flashed his most cherubic grin in reply, almost challenging her to a second duel.

"I shouldn't linger here," Fionna forced out to cover for her slip in reaction. "I will sleep well now, thank ye." In a proud huff, she extricated herself from his bed and marched toward the door, a little wobbly on her feet. Pride rushed through him. He had weak-ened the mighty Fionnabhair Allán, knocked her off balance.

Before pulling on the iron ring of his chamber door, she peered over her shoulder at him, her face imperious, the plunging seams of her bodice pulled closed in her fist. "Actually, I have won Sir Galahad. For it seems I'm the only one who will depart satisfied this night."

And, with that, she left his chambers in a rush of skirts and wild, white-blonde hair.

Galahad released a thunderous laugh, one that rumbled clear to his toes. He hoped she heard his humor too.

Chapter Twenty-One

Percival

Percival pulled a pillow over his head to muffle the banging on his door. The stuff of nightmares. The day wasn't even light yet! Perhaps if he didn't answer, the offender would just skulk away.

The knock sounded again—louder this time.

"Go away!" he shouted, instantly regretting his movement. He felt like he had been trampled by a pair of cart-horses. His head pounded; his mouth tasted as if a small rodent had crawled behind his tongue and died; and his balls ached with unmet need.

Bloody faeries.

Percival let out a groan when his door opened.

"Good, you're up," Arthur said, pushing farther inside the room.

"Am I being punished?" Percival asked as Arthur crossed the room and threw open the heavy drapes. Dim, watery moonlight pooled through the windows, laying shadowed diamonds on the large rug beneath his bed.

"It's not even dawn." Percival had hardly slept an hour last night, tossing and tangling in his covers, thinking about Fionna. He was torn between embarrassment and longing, remembering the feel of her body against his as the faerie wine stole his better judgment. His behavior had been wrong, yet . . . touching her had felt so very right. Her scent of heather and moss, the catch in her breath as he seized her. Gods, he wanted this Grail business to be over, so he could be a real contender in the race for her heart. So, he could give up this ridiculous vow of chastity.

"I was in the library all night," Arthur said, plopping down on Percival's bed with a bounce.

Percival pushed himself up gingerly, trying not to jostle his pounding head. Arthur looked wild-eyed, stubble shadowing the cut of his jaw. A far cry from his normally immaculate self. "Is everything all right?"

Arthur waved a hand. "Besides the Túatha dé Danann meddling in my court and making us all fall like idiots over our newest knight? Things are fine."

"About that . . ." Percival said, trailing off. He didn't know what to say. None of them should have drank that wine. He remembered the ominous shrill ring of metal as Arthur pulled Excalibur from its sheath. Percival shivered. They were lucky Fionna and Lancelot had arrived when they did.

"I talked to Fionna, she understands. We're all forgiven for our impertinence."

"Good." Percival heaved a sigh of relief. "It's her own fault for being so beautiful. She had to know something like this would happen. If she were ugly, this would be so much less complicated."

"You cannot blame a woman for your own behavior, Percival, regardless of her fairness of form and face."

"Och, I know, forgive me. My brain is still addled. I speak more of my own ability to resist my attraction to her."

Arthur pursed his lips, holding back a smile. "Perhaps we should demand that she wear her stag helm each day, to make things easier on you."

"That's the first good idea I've heard in days," Percival said. "Ye're king. Make it happen. Though . . ." he paused. "Her figure is quite distracting. Anything you can do about that?"

"Shapeless sackcloth shift? Will that do?"

"Perfect," Percival said, grinning. "Make sure the sackcloth hangs down to her toes though. I'm not sure I can resist a flash of ankle. A man can only endure so much."

Arthur shook his head, a laugh escaping from him. He seized the pillow from Percival's hands and smacked him with it. "You're an idiot."

"Yes, well, I'm yer idiot. So, what does that make ye?"

"King of idiots, I suppose." Arthur tossed back the pillow to Percival, who tucked it behind his head while leaning back against the headboard, his hands interlocked behind his neck. "Now, I assume this isn't a social call. If it is, we need to talk about yer timing."

The mad gleam in Arthur's eye flared back to life. "Like I was saying . . . I found something." He pulled out a folded piece of parchment from his tunic's pocket and held it out.

Percival took the aged, wrinkled parchment, unfolding it. He blinked his eyes to clear them, to make out the cramped scrawl. "A letter?" Percival asked.

"To your father," Arthur replied. "And not just a letter. The missive references a secret."

Percival blinked at that, scooting up. "The note is from a Lord Bronn."

"Do you remember him?" Arthur asked eagerly. "Is the name familiar?"

Percival nodded slowly, searching his memories. "Aye. He was an old friend of my father's. If I recall, he helped my father when he was ill."

"Yes, that's what the letter says. He tells your father that he could not leave a wounded man to die on his manor lands."

Percival nodded, barely. Gods, his head. Drawing in a long, deep breath, he exhaled slowly, then said, "Nae, not an illness. He was injured. Lance to the thigh or some such thing. When he was hunting. I think Bronn lived nearby. He found my father bleeding and took him in." Percival scanned the letter. Lord Bronn did mention a secret. He read the note aloud. "*Lay your fears to rest that I will spill your secrets, or usurp the knowledge for my own uses. The things you said while you were wracked with fever are yours to keep. I understand the heavy burden resting upon you as Keeper of the Grail. I would be a man without honor were I not to respect your noble task.*"

Arthur's face was alight with excitement. "Don't you see? Your father said something when he was beside himself with fever. Details about the Grail. This man, Lord Bronn, promised to keep your father's secrets. He could know the location of the Grail!"

"Where did ye find this?" Percival asked, his mind racing. Arthur was right. This could be a clue. A real clue. It seemed like a lifetime ago, when he had lived with his parents in his father's grand manor at Caer Benic. Before his father died. Before his mother had gone half-mad, stealing him away to the darkest woods of Strathclyde in Alba, where they lived like hermits, away from the prying eyes she thought were searching for them. Before the Otherworld shrouded Caer Benic from mortal eyes to protect the Grail in the absence of a Fisher King. Before the sun had broken through the dark clouds of his life in the form of Arthur Pendragon. His way out of the gloom.

"The note was tucked inside a book in the library," Arthur answered, unaware of Percival's thoughts. "A dusty tome with your father's name scrawled on the front page. I think the book was from his personal library."

Percival stilled. "My father's books are in the library here?"

Arthur's brow softened. "When your father died, and you and your mother disappeared, I believe my father visited your father's known holdings in Northumbria. He must have brought a few of your father's personal books back with him. It's the type of thing Uther would do. He always took what he wanted, regardless of whom the property belonged to."

Percival frowned. He knew Arthur spoke not of books, but of his mother. Married to another man, until Uther Pendragon cast his eyes on her, and coveted her for himself, using fae charm to disguise him as the Duke of Tintagel. He supposed Arthur had ghosts enough of his own to haunt his past.

"You can have them, if you so desire," Arthur continued. "The books. I didn't know they were here. But they're yours by right."

Percival shrugged. "They can stay in the library with their bookish brethren. The Grail quest is more than enough legacy for me."

"Do you know where Lord Bronn lives?" Arthur asked hopefully.

"It's been a long time. But I think he lived in Chester, North of

Wales in the Kingdom of Mercia. I think . . . I think we visited him once." Percival closed his eyes, trying to focus. "I have a memory of his manor. There was a statue shaped like a gryphon, and a huge oak tree that I played in. A brook I fell into. An old Roman fort is nearby. Aye, I believe I could find my way back there."

"That's not far. Perhaps a three days' ride, if we stick to the Roman roads."

Percival raised an eyebrow. "Do I sense an outing in our future?"

"After the messiness of last night, a journey will do us all good. Plus, there's been raiding near Ewloe, not far from Chester."

"What, the Kingdom of Gwynedd dinnae fight raiders now? I always did think the Northern Lords were all bark and no bite, a bunch of self-important arseholes. King of the Britons, ha! Does their king still claim this ridiculous notion despite the Lady of the Lake's pronouncement that ye are the rightful Pendragon?"

Arthur played with a worn corner of the leather-bound book in his lap. "There was a call for aid to all the Kingdoms of Wales, be they king or peasant. The raiders have left a trail of wreckages down the River Dee. Perhaps we can speak with the townsfolk of Ewloe to ask if they know of Lord Bronn as well as see if we can take care of whoever has been terrorizing them. We can kill two birds with one stone."

"Count me in. Let us Southern lads show those pompous Northern Lords who the real Head Dragon of Wales is." Percival threw his covers off, springing to his feet. The thought of a trip out of the keep—a real chance to find the Grail—had invigorated him, banishing his headache.

Arthur groaned, shielding his eyes with a hand as he stood. "Give a man a little warning next time."

Percival looked down at his naked form. "I could say the same for ye. Ye're the one who barged into my chamber unannounced."

"I'll consider myself reprimanded." Arthur strode toward the hallway.

"Arthur," Percival said, and this king paused at the door. "When do we leave?"

"No time like the present. I'll tell the servants and have Lancelot ready the soldiers to stand guard. This morning."

"Excellent," Percival said, hands on his hips.

"And Percival?"

"Hmm?"

"Wear pants."

Chapter Twenty-Two

Fionna

Back in my armor, I felt more like myself than I had in days. My knives were strapped into their vambraces on my forearms, my sword on my hip. Now if only I had armor to surround my heart. And this damn faerie necklace off. The thing was clasped tight, refusing to yield. I had even tried to cut the chain free with one of my knives, to no success. I supposed the necklace was staying, for the time being.

Zephyr plucked an apple from my hand. This was our tradition before I cinched her saddle tight and loaded her up with my bedroll and saddle bags. She pawed the hay in her stall until I offered her another freshly plucked apple from the neighboring orchard. She could smell her favorite treat in the pouch hanging from my sword belt and I smiled.

Only an hour earlier, Percival had shown up at my door, bright eyed and bouncing, announcing how we were leaving on a mission. I had nodded cheerfully, hiding my discomfort the best I could. But when I had closed the door, I sagged against the rough wood with a shaky breath. I wasn't sure what I feared most. To be alone with all four knights? To find an opportunity to steal Excalibur? Or afraid that the others would see how something had happened between me and Galahad? My skin flushed as I thought of last night.

Zephyr curved her head back toward me, lipping my hair with her soft mouth. I leaned my forehead into her velvet neck, breathing in her comforting scent of hay and leather. My pulse became a wild, unfettered creature as the scent of leather reminded me of another. To distract myself, I braided a piece of Zephyr's mane, an occupation to banish the tempest of sensations flooding over me of where Galahad's fingers had marked me like woad. I didn't think I would ever be the same.

I had told myself I was going into Galahad's room last night only to keep him from suspecting the real reason behind my presence in their hallway. But that wasn't true. I entered his private chamber because I had wanted to, because I had desperately longed to forget myself for a while, yearned to feel the earth beneath me and the heavens before me when man moved both while loving a woman. And goddess, I received more than what I had bargained for, and then some.

Galahad's touch—his expert tongue—had me burning and quivering in an explosion that swept me away, obliterating my universe into nothing but a sweet ache and pleasant haze. And beyond his devilish smile, his playful banter, had been an earnestness and care that shook me more than my climax had. Galahad cared for me. Truly. And when I took Excalibur and ran, it would ruin him. My deceit would ruin them all. I feared O'Lynn's task would ruin *me*.

"You're looking well this morning, Fionna," a man's voice purred from beyond the stall. I turned and hid my surprise when my eyes locked onto the source.

Lancelot.

"Ye as well," I said, forcing a smile on my face. It was true, the man did look beyond handsome, with his ebony hair tousled from sleep, his leathers partially unbuckled to reveal the broad plane of his chest. A peek of indigo ink brushed along his upper chest, near his shoulder, in vined swirls and lines. I forced my eyes back to his and said, "Fair morning for a journey."

"Indeed. A fine spring day."

It seemed that some of Lancelot's ice had thawed, and I felt I should not let this moment pass, even if we had little more to discuss than the weather. "Thank ye for yer assistance last night. I am in yer debt."

Lancelot waved a hand. "Think little of it. If someone was indebted to me each time I saved these animals from a tight spot, I would be staggering under the weight."

"Isn't it a touch early to be stroking your ego, Lancelot?" Galahad chose that moment to swagger up, clapping the other knight on his shoulder.

Lancelot pursed his lips, but his blue eyes were mirthful. "It's never too early to stroke anything, that's what I say."

Galahad boomed a laugh. "I would have to agree. What about you, Fionna?"

I busied myself with tightening my saddlebags, but I could hear the grin in his words. "I'll leave the stroking to ye men." I pushed out of the stall and pulled Zephyr's substantial body between myself and the two men. The heat in Galahad's expression as I passed by made my body clench with need. Skies, this would be a long few days.

"Glad to see you're back to your old self, crabapple," I heard Galahad say behind me.

"You and me both, chipmunk," Lancelot replied.

I pressed my lips together to keep from smiling.

The day grew warm and bright, and Arthur and his knights were in even brighter spirits. Galahad seemed able to talk to me without filling very sentence with sexual innuendo and, after a few miles, I relaxed into Zephyr's rocking gait, laughing and jesting with the other knights. Even Arthur seemed to have forgotten the mess of the faerie wine, his cheeks flushed with life, his green eyes as rich as the forests surrounding us. I felt comfortable with these men, as comfortable as I was with my fiann, though I had only known these knights for a few days, and I had fought in my fiann for years.

The realization snuffed out my good mood. My eyes flicked to Excalibur hanging at Arthur's side, the rubies in the pommel winking in the sunlight. The sword suited Arthur—a beautiful blade for a beautiful man. To see such Otherworldly beauty hanging on Donal O'Lynn's hip would pain me to no end. The man deserved nothing so fine. The man deserved a knife in the gut.

Arthur slowed Llamrei, his black mare, to match Zephyr, and smiled at me. He didn't wear his golden oak-leaf crown today. Without it, he looked lighter. Freer. I said as much, and he smiled ruefully. "It pinches."

A startled laugh escaped my lips. "Ye're not what I expected, King Arthur of Caerleon."

"What did you expect?"

"I am really not sure." It was the truth. "For a man who's supposed to conquer all of Briton, ye seem remarkably content just riding through the countryside."

He snorted. "Conquer? No. The only reason I even accept Excalibur's charge to wear the coveted title Pendragon is to hopefully prevent even more war. Briton has bled enough since the Romans. And I like to think I am a decent enough king. I would do what I could to rule Briton justly."

"Ye're a wonderful king." My voice grew soft. "All of Briton will be lucky to have ye, once united."

"Thank you Fionna. I'm sure life is quite different here than the home of your father and clansman you've left behind. I hope you've found your time pleasant."

"Most pleasant." I swallowed, trying not to think of Galahad's honey-blond head between my legs. "In truth, I enjoy not being a princess—with the eyes of everyone constantly upon me."

"I doubt they're looking just because you're a princess," Arthur said, rubbing the stubble on his jaw.

I looked at him in mock confusion. "Why King Arthur, whatever could ye mean?"

He blushed and, for a shy heartbeat, appeared a young man and not a battle-worn king. A small smile flitted across his lips with the amusement on my face. "I promised Percival I would make you wear your helm all the time, so as not to distract us."

"And a sackcloth shift!" Percival called out from behind us. The young man was eavesdropping. I swiveled in my saddle to stick my tongue out at him, and he grinned, giving a little bow in his saddle while Galahad laughed beside him.

"Very well," I said. "Though my helm pinches, I'll wear it, so long as ye all wear yers too."

"Why Fionna . . ." Lancelot and his mount took the spot on my left, flanking me and Arthur. "Does this mean you find us distracting too?"

A smile twitched on my lips. "I think there's a reason why Arthur's feasts are attended by two women to every one man."

"Hmm," Lancelot seemed to ponder. "I hadn't noticed."

"That's because when ye bed one, she becomes invisible to ye!" Percival called.

"Percival." Lancelot turned back toward the other man. "I'm in need of a sparring session tonight. I think you are too."

Percival groaned so loud a flock of birds alighted from a nearby copse of trees. "There's no healer for miles!"

"I'll spar with ye, Lancelot," I offered. The man's skill with a blade impressed me, and I wanted to try myself against him.

The playfulness slipped from Lancelot's face, leaving an emotion I couldn't quite read.

"Unless ye're scared."

Lancelot inclined his head, accepting my challenge. "Saved by a woman, Percival," he called back to the other knight.

"Saved by a *knight*," Percival replied. "And a gallant one at that. Fionna can carry me off into the sunset any time."

We made camp in a meadow nestled between a grove of beech trees and a winding stream. The evening was warm, and I laid my bed-roll down beside a scattering of wildflowers. The knights made quick work collecting firewood, watering the horses, and arranging bedrolls. Arthur did his chores as cheerfully as any of the knights, reminding me yet again he was no ordinary king. No ordinary man.

After a meal of cured sausage, rye bread, and goat's cheese, Lancelot stood, stretched, and gestured to me. We tramped through the wildflowers together, our swords in hand, and squared off against each other while the setting sun gilded our landscape.

And then, as easily as if he were tying his boots, he came at me.

Lancelot's movements were as smooth as water over the stones of a river—each one flowing into the next. His footing was firm, his stance unshakable. He kept twisting his attacks, working his way around me until the sun glared in my eyes.

"Quit it," I panted, feinting at him and finding only air.

He chuckled. "A smart warrior uses the terrain around them." He attacked, his flashing sword coming at me with one, two, three blows in quick succession.

I bared my teeth, my frustration growing. He was winning. My sword arm felt like a ton of bricks, and sweat poured down my forehead, stinging my eyes. But I was too proud to yield, to admit defeat. I caught sight of a discarded tree branch on the ground and stifled a smile. I danced around him and redoubled my attack, driving him back toward the branch. Closer—closer—our blades met and locked, and we grappled against each other, the veins in his arms straining. I pushed with all my might, and his feet tangled in the branch. My eyes narrowed with victory, only to widen in surprise as he hooked his hand in my sword belt, pulling me down after him.

We hit the ground in a tumble, the meadow's tall grass a screen of golden-green around us. My heart hammered in my chest as his weight settled half atop me; as I realized, this close, his blue eyes were flecked with silver, that he smelled of mint and fresh soap.

Lancelot was looking at me, examining my face, my eyes, my mouth. He brushed a long, white-blonde tendril off my neck, his fingers grazing the soft skin there. For a moment, I thought he was going to kiss me.

But then he pushed himself up, offering me his hand once he stood. "Good fight."

I took his hand, pulling myself to my feet and trying, terribly, to ignore the feel of his calluses against my palm. "Someone once told me that a smart warrior uses the terrain around them."

He snorted, before turning back toward the camp.

I headed to the stream, needing a moment to compose myself, to pull the pieces of myself back together. I splashed cold water on my face, my neck, my chest. I walked back to camp on wobbly legs, knowing that it wasn't the night's exertion that was shaking me. It was this place. This land of caramel sun and sweeping verdant meadows. It was these men. Charming and arresting and playful and kind.

I walked past where the others chatted around the fire, to my bedroll. Tears were prickling my eyes. As I reached my bedroll, I stopped in my tracks. There where my head would lay down to rest, sat a bouquet of bluebells and violets. I didn't know which of the men had left them for me. It didn't matter. I fell to my knees, lifting them up in my shaking fingers. The dam burst within me, and I shattered.

Chapter Twenty-Three

Lancelot

The melodious chirps of robins and goldfinches pulled Lancelot from the cold, rocky ground beneath his bedroll. Upon opening his eyes, his gaze flitted across the campfire's ring of stones and onto Fionna's angelic sleeping form. The white tendrils and corded braids of her hair seemed to glow in the dim light of dawn, her skin smooth and milky as marble. One hand clutched a dagger, tucked neatly under her bedroll, beneath her cheek. The image was so very Fionna. How could a single sight fill him with so much joy and equal parts despair? He heaved a sigh and pushed up, running a hand through his bedmussed hair.

"Not you too, brother."

Lancelot shifted to look at Arthur. The man pulled his scarlet cloak tighter around his shoulders, then clasped hands around his drawn-up knees. Arthur was studying her too, his eyes drinking her in.

"I wish I could say otherwise," Lancelot admitted.

"Tell me we're not lost," Arthur said, his voice quiet and tender.

"You're not." A stone dropped in Lancelot's gut. Still, he quirked an eyebrow playfully. "The king usually gets the girl."

"Even if that's true, how could I enjoy my life knowing my

pursuit deprived my dearest friends of their happiness?”

“I do not know. But these sentiments are why you will remain our dearest friend. No matter what happens.”

Arthur squinted up at the lavender and gold brushed sky, a wistful smile crossing his face.

Feeling restless, Lancelot rose to his feet and dusted off his breeches. “Now, let’s talk of more pleasant things. Faerie curses and vengeful half-sisters and ex-betrotheds.”

Arthur laughed. “As you wish.”

The Roman road to Chester was a well-worn route through fertile green farmland and peaceful woods. As their band rode by, deer scattered in their path and herds of sheep watched with placid black eyes. Lancelot reveled in the sun’s warm caress on his skin while the cool spring air kissed his cheeks.

He almost felt like himself again.

Here, he could almost forget.

They passed through the shade of beech and maple trees. The filtered light dappled shadows across the mossy, leaf-littered forest floor and craggy stones. This was a place where the fae might govern, but the passing greenery felt friendly, almost welcoming. Lancelot flitted a veiled glance Fionna’s way. Not for the first time, he wondered about her. There was something “otherly” about her that reminded him too often of Vivien, his foster mother. Fionna said she didn’t possess any sídhe blood, yet she rode through the trees like a faerie queen. Perhaps he only noticed her noble heritage and bearing and nothing more.

The sunlight brightened as the trees thinned. His horse danced for a moment, most likely from the shadows elongating up ahead in the clearing. He shushed his stallion gently and nudged him along. His stallion’s ears flattened and his muscles from head to tail quivered, but he obeyed Lancelot. They were just passing out of the forest and into a meadow when Lancelot noticed that Arthur had fallen behind, his horse now pulled to a stop.

Lancelot slowed his horse and turned toward his king. "Arthur?"

Arthur was staring between his horse's ears as if he'd seen a ghost. "I . . . I'm not sure. I just have a strange, unpleasant feeling." He met Lancelot's intense stare and lifted a faint, shaky smile. "I'm fine. Let's go."

Lancelot placed a comforting hand on his skittish horse and considered Arthur's odd premonition. Some believed that moving from the woods and into the meadow was like leaving the Otherworld. Maybe they had crossed through a forest the fae governed.

He and Arthur rejoined the others, who were waiting a few hundred yards ahead, where they had stopped.

"Everything all right?" Galahad asked.

Arthur nodded, his face still pale.

It wasn't until they crested the next hill that it became clear that everything was most definitely *not* all right. His king—and Lancelot's stallion, for that matter—sensed true.

"My gods," Lancelot said as he surveyed the landscape before him. A river snaked through a checkerboard of farmland below. But everything the river touched seemed to have—*withered*. Dry and cracked crops shaded into the brighter green health of adjacent fields around them. As if the river carried poison, killing everything the tainted water touched. But only in this area. Was the disease spreading?

"What could do this?" Fionna breathed out, her mouth pinched in sorrow.

"Reminds me of old faerie tales about the Formorians," Lancelot said, unable to hide the disgust in his voice while mentioning the ancient enemy of the Túatha dé Danann.

"The Fomhóraigh?" Fionna asked, eyes growing wide.

Arthur didn't answer, kicking his horse into a canter.

The knights followed not too far behind, riding after him toward the blighted fields. As they neared, the destruction became more evident. Dead fish lay on the riverbank, their carcasses bloated and white. The bodies of birds and even a deer who had the misfortune of approaching for a drink littered the affected land.

"The water's been poisoned," Percival said, his eyes wide with horror. "Who would do such a thing?"

But Lancelot knew exactly who. And if Percival thought for a moment, he would too. Morgana. Elaine. Morgause. And their bloody curse. A curse on the building elements of Caerleon. A curse of destruction.

Lancelot swallowed the bile rising in his throat. This destruction was a result of his recklessness. His choice. He memorized it, taking in each withered blade of grass, each dead, glassy eye rotting on the bank. This was the cost of betraying a fae. This was the cost of a faerie curse. This is what would happen—and worse—if he gave in to his weakness and slept with Fionna. This. This. *This*. He beat himself with the word, with the images, an intentional self-flagellation. He wanted the wounds, the memories, to dig deep. So deep that he wouldn't forget the next time his cock stirred in Fionna's presence.

Arthur had dismounted and was kneeling at the edge of the blighted line, his fingers brushing the stalks of spring wheat that still lived.

A crow cawed loudly in the trees behind them and Lancelot jumped. He swiveled in his saddle and regarded the bird, its black-feathered head cocked to one side, seeming to watch him through one glassy eye. Icy fingers of fear crawled up his spine as he remembered Morgana fleeing from his chamber, leaping out the window and into the night air, borne aloft on dark crow wings. He shook himself. Crows were commonplace. The bird was just here for the carrion below, a decaying feast along the riverbank.

"What did this?" Fionna asked, summoning his attention back toward the group. Her voice was hard and angry. "We will kill them for it."

Arthur stood slowly. "I don't know," he said, turning back toward them. Lancelot hid his surprise when the king sent a knowing look toward him, Percival, and Galahad. He didn't want to share the truth of the curse with Fionna. Why? The other knights seemed to understand Arthur's silent admonition and stayed quiet.

Arthur pulled himself back into the saddle and nudged his

horse forward with his heels. "But rest assured, we'll find out."

They rode in silence the rest of the day, each knight in quiet contemplation. Sorrow warred with anger and guilt within Lancelot. And somewhere, deep down, a kernel of hope. Merlin had seen a way out. With Fionna's help, they could find the Blessed Grail. And, if they found the Grail, they could fix this. They had all grown distracted by her beauty, by the light she infused in their little brotherhood. The river was the clear reminder they had all needed. This wasn't a game. It wasn't fantasy. This was life and death, and their enemies were playing for keeps.

The village of Ewloe which, according to Percival, bordered Lord Bronn's manor house, appeared first as a smudge of smoke on the horizon two days later. Three days in the saddle with the earth for a bed and stars for a blanket. But as they approached, the smoke proved black and oily, not the cheerful puffing of wood-burning hearths.

"Something's wrong here," Galahad rumbled.

Arthur pulled Excalibur from its sheath and the others followed suit.

They rode into the village at a slow walk, their horses shying from the strange smells. As soon as they saw the first body, Lancelot's spirits sank. This village had been attacked.

"Skies," he hissed under his breath.

No building was spared and, it seemed, no villager either. The thatched homes had burned to ash and rubble, many with their inhabitants still inside.

Fionna swung down from the saddle, her arm thrown over her nose to ward off the smell. "A day ago, perhaps?" she said. "The fires would be out by now, if the attacked had happened before then. And these bodies aren't too ripe yet."

"They seem pretty ripe to me," Percival said, his face white as snow.

Fionna knelt in a patch of charred grass, pulling an axe from the back of a woman's body, and then examined the wood-carved handle and blade marks. "Flaming hells," she swore, standing.

"What is it?" Arthur asked, dismounting and striding over.

She held out the axe to him. "See this detailing on the handle? It's Dál nAraidi. And this symbol? The blackthorn tree? I know this clann. It's the Uí Tuírtri."

"Who are they?" Arthur asked.

Fionna bit her lip, seeming to hesitate. "They're a rival clann in Lough Insholin who wants to rule in Antrim, including the lands of Allán. I know the leader, Donal O'Lynn. He's a bastard. But . . . I don't know why his fianna are raiding here. I didn't even know they'd been to Briton."

Lancelot narrowed his eyes. Fionna's explanation rang false. Did she know more than she was letting on? Yet, Arthur knew more than he was telling Fionna. Perhaps there was a good reason for her to keep her own secrets.

Arthur threw the axe into the ground, where the blade stuck, quivering. "They picked a fight with the wrong king. The Kingdom of Gwynedd cannot rid themselves of these pests, but I will. If they're only a day's ride, we'll take them." His words rolled and boomed like thunder.

"Arthur," Percival said. "If the raiders came here . . . they might have visited Bronn's manor. Spoils to be had, in a house like that, ye ken."

Arthur's skin sickened to a greenish pallor. "Do you think . . ." He looked at the body by his feet, pale and unmoving.

Percival grimaced. "I think we better find out."

Chapter Twenty-Four

Arthur

Lord Bronn's house was a large, sturdy lime-washed cob and black timber manor with thatched roof, surrounded by stone walls, even as they approached, Arthur's senses rang in alarm. Adrenaline coursed through his body. The grounds were too quiet.

Fionna's hand rested on a dagger at her side; Percival rode with a sword in his hand.

A bird burst into flight from a nearby bush, swooping low across the dirt trail before them. Arthur jumped in his saddle, spooking his horse, Llamrei.

Galahad's horse danced in reply. "We're a cheerful bunch, aren't we?" the big warrior muttered.

They rounded the last curve and the manor's front came into view. Arthur let out a muffled curse. The wide oak door hung off its hinges, splintered and cracked.

The knights dismounted and pulled their swords from their scabbards. They crept into the manor.

Signs of raiders were everywhere. Mud trekked onto the plush woven carpets, dishes smashed to the floor, the lime-washed walls singed with smoke.

Up the stairs they went, one at a time, with Arthur leading the way. Then he saw it. A booted foot, poking out from around the corner.

His heart sank.

The man was broad and well-muscled, with thick dark hair and a neatly-trimmed beard. His brown eyes stared wide and vacant, frozen in death. A dark bloom of dried blood colored his white shirt.

"Lord Bronn is dead," Arthur said, his voice dull. The first lead he had received in years, and the man was dead.

Percival knelt by Lord Bronn's face and gently closed his eyes.

"Damn it!" Arthur cursed, swooping a hand across a nearby bookshelf. Papers and books scattered amongst the raid's detritus.

Fionna recoiled slightly at his outburst but, in that moment, he didn't care. He leaned his forehead against the bookshelf, closing his eyes. They had seemed so close. First Fionna, next finding the letter from Lord Bronn—a clue to the Grail mystery that had haunted his family for decades. Veiled hope had blossomed inside him, too powerful a feeling for him to remain guarded. And now that hope was dead, cut down as easily as poor Lord Bronn.

"We'll find another way to reach the Grail," Percival said softly.

Arthur heaved a sigh. "The first lead we have had in years. We can't wait years to find another. Caerleon can't." His frustration and disappointment kindled into rage within him like sparks striking dry tinder. These Dál nAraidi, this clan, had sailed into Wales and England and killed and maimed and took. He was supposed to protect these people as their High King. To defend this land, regardless of whether the Kingdoms recognized him as their Head Dragon. But he had failed. The people of Ewloe had died, and who knew where these Dál nAraidi snakes were slithering to next.

Arthur spun to the others, who stood mutely around the room. "We ride," he said. "We find the men who did this and we make them pay. I will not have these Irish bastards returning to their shores and gloating that Wales is ripe for the picking. Mount up." He wanted to rage and thunder and plunge Excalibur deep into the gut of whatever raider did this. Those men had taken something precious from him and they would pay for it. With their lives.

"No," Fionna said, her voice sharp as steel.

"What?" Arthur growled.

"Not until ye tell me why this Grail is so important. There's something unspoken between ye, and it's thick as sap. As much as I want to kill Uí Tuírtri, I'm not plunging into battle without knowing why."

"Isn't it enough that these Irish slaughtered my people?" Arthur asked.

"It would be, if that's the only reason we're here. But it's not. If I am to fight at yer side, Arthur Pendragon, if I am yer knight, I deserve to know the truth."

The other knights exchanged wide-eyed, pregnant gazes.

"She's right, Yer Majesty," Percival said. Arthur opened his mouth to tell Percival to shut it, but the fool man kept talking, his words coming faster. "Either we trust her or we dinnae. The Fates brought her to us so she could help with this quest. Let her help us."

Arthur ground his teeth in frustration. He didn't know exactly why he had been keeping the secret of Morgana's curse from Fionna. No, that wasn't true. The reason was his pride. He didn't want to admit to this beautiful stranger that he was fallible. That his kingdom was cursed and, by extension, so was he. But Percival was right. He had knighted Fionna. Excalibur had shown her to be the one. He couldn't keep her on the outside anymore.

"Fine, Percival." Arthur's shoulders sagged. "You tell her. But on the way. I'm not letting these dogs get one more minute on us."

"Should we bury him?" Galahad asked as they trampled down the stairs and out into the fresh air.

Arthur took in a shuddering breath, letting the cool air fill his lungs—banishing the oppressive stench of death. "Yes. On the way back. We can't risk losing the raiders."

The knights mounted, and Arthur kicked Llamrei into a gallop. Sometimes he felt that his horse was his oldest and truest friend. She sensed his mood better than most. And, right now, he wanted to be borne away by Llamrei's powerful strides, to let the whip of the wind wipe away his worries and fears and failures.

If only resolving matters were that easy.

Behind him, he knew Percival was shouting at Fionna, explaining to her the messy sordid tale of Arthur's failure as a diplomat. His half-sister's wrath and her sisters' cruel magic. Lancelot's fool mistake, falling in love with a faerie, and then his even worse mistake of falling out of love with one. He kicked Llamrei's heaving flanks with his boots, urging her forward, the landscape bleeding into a blur of green grass and golden fields and blue sky.

And then she was beside him, her white-blonde braid trailing behind her like a pennant, her dappled grey mare matching Llamrei stride for stride.

"How could ye not tell me?" she shouted at him. The wind's pull almost stole her words from his ears. "Did ye not think I needed to know?"

"You know now," he said, not able to confess to her the real reason, to admit that sometimes he wasn't an infallible king, but just a man.

"Percival had to convince ye," she said accusingly. "Ye should have told me yerself. Ye should have chosen to trust me."

"And do you not keep your own counsel, knight?" He needed to sting her back, push her away, keep her from getting too close.

She recoiled as if struck. Nor did she shout back a clever retort.

"Tell me of this clan. What do I need to know?"

"They bleed as red as any men. Seems that's all ye care to know," she said, before reigning in her mare and falling behind him.

Arthur slowed Llamrei as well, though he stayed before the other knights. The raiders' trail wasn't hard to follow, with a dozen men on horseback heavy laden with treasures but, in his haste, he didn't want to miss a turn or change in the trail. His mind was a whirlwind of three thoughts—Lord Bronn and the Grail, the crimson need to cut down these Irish for what they had done, and Fionna. Always Fionna. Had he driven her away by keeping the secret of the faerie curses from her? Would she forgive him? And what would he do, if she didn't? The very thought of being without her felt crippling. Felt like a cloud passing before the sun. She had become a firm fixture of his court. He didn't know why she had fought in his tourney, but he knew this: she belonged here. With them. He would convince her of that.

The whicker of horses was his first warning that they were coming upon the raiders' camp. The smell of campfire smoke was the second. A small, cautious part of him knew that he should reign in Llamrei and survey the camp with a measured, dispassionate eye. But that part of him was an ant compared to the lion of his anger. A need roared within him to rip apart these men for what they had done to that village, for killing Lord Bronn and murdering Arthur's chance at finding the Grail.

And so, he urged Llamrei forward and ignored the muffled curses from his knights behind him. He pulled Excalibur from its sheath and rode toward the Uí Tuírtri clan, a savage smile on his face.

Chapter Twenty-Five

Fionna

I had a ritual I always followed before battle. I would wash my face and hands, and carefully paint on lines with blue woad in the runic pattern that marked my clann—Beith, the silver birch. With blue stained onto my fingertips, I would then pray to The Morrígan, sister goddesses of war and fate, that my sword would swing true, that my shield would hold fast, marking each weapon with Beith runes as well. Afterward, I would sit in silence, if even for a few moments, feeling what it was to be inside my body, fully aware of the breath in my lungs and the blood in my veins. These were gifts that were fleeting, and I never felt that lesson so keenly as before battle. Small and fragile and mortal. After battle, I thrummed with power like the sister goddesses themselves, invincible and terrible.

But not today.

Today there wasn't woad or prayers or quiet contemplation. There wasn't even a plan. Today there was a wild gallop into a force of men three times our size. If this is how these knights fought, I had a thing or two to teach them.

And, today, there was a whirlwind of anger and emotion, hurt and betrayal, gut-twisting guilt. Arthur had lied to me from the moment I had arrived here. But I had done the same. Who was one liar to judge another? I needed time to think. To scream and shout into the uncaring breeze and pound a sparring strawman with my sword until my shoulder ached from the force of it.

I would have no chance to do any of it. Caerleon was cursed. And if Merlin and Percival were to be believed, I was a key to undoing that curse and finding the Grail—the one item that could stop the creeping elf-shot sickness that was overtaking this lush land. And I was leaving. Stealing Arthur's most prized possession, his sovereign-blessed connection to this land, and running with my tail between my legs back to Ireland.

Was I really willing to do that?

Could I truly abandon these men and leave Arthur's entire kingdom to its fate? Was that worthy punishment for a lie? Only the goddesses knew. I had told myself I would pay any price to ransom my father and sister back. But now I grasped for another way. How had things become so twisted so quickly?

All these thoughts spun in my head, a blizzard of emotions where the quiet calm before battle should be. I tried to focus on the force before me, to absorb the details that might save my life.

The Uí Tuírtri were camped in a sparse wooded bluff overlooking the River Dee. Their left side was flanked by a trickling stream that poured over the bluff in a waterfall down to the river's banks, while the right was guarded by a pile of large boulders that were arranged as if they had been tossed there a thousand years ago by a Fomhórach, an Underworld giant. This area was a smart and defensible position and, in the end, Arthur's mad dash was a fairly effective strategy.

We were amongst them—swords swinging and hooves trampling—before the sixteen raiders were hardly up from around the fires, scrambling for their weapons. I recognized one warrior, a tall burly bear of a man with long hair tightly braided down his back. I registered all this in the instant before Excalibur speared him through. The blade's scintillating length blazed in the afternoon sun like a sacred relic.

Then the clannsmen seemed all the same with sneering faces and flashing teeth and eyes shining manically with the frenzy of sudden battle.

I sliced one man across the back as he went for his weapons.

I whirled in my saddle and stabbed another through his throat before he slashed at Zephyr's belly. I vaulted off my charger and then whacked her flank with the flat of my blade to send her running. She'd linger nearby for me when the battle was done. The quarters were too small to fight on horseback, and I wouldn't risk her.

Arthur and the other knights had dismounted too. They now fought like the Danish berserkers I had seen in Aghanravel's neighboring Norse settlements. Their swords swung so fast that I could hardly see them. Drops of red arced through the air as Dál nAraidi clannsmen fell, their leather armor soaked through, their lifeblood spilling into disbelieving fingers.

And as quickly as that, we had cut down half the clannsmen, leaving eight. These men were the best of their clann, grizzled warriors with years of fighting seasons under their belt. Professional killers who lived for the sword and died for glory. They faced the knights with a ferocity that I think startled even Arthur out of his battle haze.

A big man came at me with a Danish axe and a blood-curdling shout in Irish, "Bua nó bás!" I recognized his words as the Uí Tuírtri clann motto, meaning "victory or death."

I screamed back at him as I brought my sword up to meet the fury of his blow, wishing I had my sturdy wooden shield. His shout was every warrior's motto, in a way. I would win today, or I would die.

I lashed out with a vicious kick to the man's gut. He stumbled back, providing me a moment to take stock. Lancelot was across the camp by the boulders, fighting two men. The dark knight's sword struck fast and deadly, slashing the men on arms and thighs, bleeding them from a dozen different places. Arthur fought two men as well; Galahad was grappling with one over the fire. And Percival had the last man—they slipped and splashed on the slick, mossy stones of the river.

No, not the last man. That was seven.

I rolled out of the way as my opponent swung at me again. His huge Danish axe's blade sliced into the ground until buried. My eyes fixed on the man creeping around behind Percival, raising his axe to throw.

"Percival!" I screamed, and then pulled one of my throwing daggers from its sheath along my forearm. The small blade loosed in an instant, borne aloft by muscle and whispered prayers. I watched as the dagger plunged into the man's chest. A relieved smile crossed my face when the raider stumbled backward. But there was no time for relieved smiles in battle. I realized a split second too late that I had lost sight of my opponent—that I couldn't account for the position of his battle axe's blade. Instinct possessed me and I jerked sharp to the right, knowing I needed to move somewhere, any-where.

It was that instinct that saved me. Had I waited a mere second more, the axe blade would have severed my spine rather than glance off my shoulder's muscle. Still, pain exploded through my side as the blade rent leather and flesh. A tangled scream escaped from my mouth, so high and animal I hardly recognized it.

I rolled to see the clannsman's eyes gleaming with the light of his killing blow, his certainty that he had me beat. But all I could think was how I couldn't let them all down. My father and sister, Arthur and the knights. If I lived, I would have to choose, but if I died, I failed them all.

I was on the ground, the Uí Tuírtri warrior looming above me. So, I did the only thing I could think of. I pulled out the wicked little dagger from my boot, and lunged forward, burying the blade into the meat of his groin. He bellowed with rage and pain as I yanked down in a jagged slice, seeking the lifeblood of his artery. Warm blood gushed over my hands and his axe thunked to the ground beside him. I shoved him away from me and he toppled backward, writhing in pain and shock.

I looked about for my knights, wild with fear. Had I missed an attack? Had something befallen any of the four while I was too distracted to help? One by one, my eyes drank in the sight of them. Percival, his chest heaving as he wiped his sword on the grass and moss, his opponent now face down in the river below him. Lance-lot, pulling his sword out of a man's chest. Arthur, running a shak-ing hand over his short hair. Galahad. Where was Galahad? The world seemed to tilt and I blinked through the fog as Galahad ran toward me. Wisps of honey-gold hair that escaped from their tie floated about his head like a halo. Relief welled in me.

They were all safe.

They were all alive.

"Fionna," Galahad's hand was beneath my head, cradling my neck. The other roamed over my body, checking for wounds. "There's so much blood—" he breathed. His voice sounded distant and thin.

"Not mine," I croaked. Everything felt faint and far away.

His hand was roaming over my back now, and came away wet with red. "And this?" he asked.

"Oh. That's . . . mine," I managed. My tongue was thick in my mouth, heavy with fatigue.

The other knights were by my side now. My vision blurred and swirled until all I saw was their colors. The colors I knew by heart. The blue ice of Lancelot's eyes, the grass-green of Arthur's. The copper of Percival's hair, the tawny warmth of Galahad's skin.

"Fionna, stay with us," Arthur said.

I wanted to do as he asked. I wanted to honor them, please them, protect them. I wanted to love them. But I couldn't. I felt consciousness slipping from me. Their colors draining into darkness. Then darkness carried me away.

Chapter Twenty-Six

Galahad

Fionna was bleeding. Fionna was injured. These were the words sounding in a loop in Galahad's head. This could not be.

He cradled her body to his chest as they moved away from the Uí Tuírtri camp, a few hundred yards up the river. They didn't want to move her far, but none of them were eager to stay amongst the dead.

"Here," Galahad called as they reached a sun dappled clearing next to a flat expanse of slow-moving river. "Lay out a bedroll."

It was Arthur himself who pulled his bedroll off his black mare, unfurling the hide layers at Galahad's feet. The other knights' faces were pinched with worry and fear, but none more so than Arthur.

Good, Galahad thought savagely. It was Arthur's furious dash into the enemy camp that placed Fionna into this mess. Let him feel the guilt keenly.

Fionna moaned as Galahad lay her down as gently as he could on the bedroll. She looked ghostly, her skin pale and flecked with blood. As if all the color had drained from her. Except crimson.

"Someone fetch water, someone start a fire so we can boil it, and someone retrieve my medical kit from my saddlebag," Galahad ordered, not looking up from his administrations to see who was jumping to which task. He was no healer, but his mother hadn't had eight children or a farm full of animals without some meager medical skill, and Galahad had always watched by her side, soaking up her instruction. As a page boy, he learned even more animal husbandry tricks.

There were times his limited medical and sewing skills and easy way with people of lower classes singled him out among the nobles of Arthur's court. From birth, they had the privilege of coin to hire tailors, apothecaries, and men of medicine. But right now, Galahad was grateful for his low-born knowledge.

Percival dropped to his knees at Fionna's side and delivered Galahad's meager kit of medical supplies. "Will she fare well?"

"Don't know yet," Galahad replied, keeping his voice impassive. She would be all right. She had to be. Fionna was the fiercest woman he had ever known. It would take more than a nick with an axe to end her.

Galahad unbuckled her leather armor, gently pulling the plates and guards from around her arms. "Help me turn her?" he asked Percival.

Together, they gently rolled Fionna onto her stomach, revealing the bloom of red blood on her white shirt.

Percival bit his lip, his eyes wild. "Looks bad," he said in a hushed whisper.

"Percival," Galahad said. He needed the lad out of here, distracted. "Fionna's horse is missing. The mare should be around here. She'll be beside herself, if she wakes and we haven't found her. Could you—"

Percival sprang to his feet, eager for a task. "I'll find her."

"Fionna will be in your debt," Galahad said, but the young man was already bounding toward his own charger.

Galahad ripped Fionna's shirt in two, revealing the slender arrow of her spine, the smooth stretch of pale skin as well as the muscles of her back.

Arthur had the fire going now and Lancelot had set a pot of water on a stand above it.

Galahad used his knife to cut strips from Fionna's shirt, silently apologizing for mangling her tunic so. They'd buy her a hundred new tunics when this was over. He folded a scrap neatly and pressed the linen to the wound, not wanting to examine the injury until he had washed his hands.

Lancelot knelt at Galahad's side and reached out with inquisitive fingers toward Fionna's wound, then let his hand fall. "Your assessment?"

"The wound is deep, but the location was lucky. The blade cut into muscle, but muscle will heal. The biggest risk will be infection. If I clean the laceration well and stitch the skin up, she should be fine."

"The slice isn't deep enough to pack with moss first?"

"No, I don't believe so. But if she continues to bleed after stitching, we will pack her wound."

Lancelot nodded, relaxing perceptibly.

It was almost painful, the way Galahad's heart twisted in his chest when he looked at her, the longing he felt, this unquestionable need for her. The exquisite taste he'd known the other night had only kindled his need all the brighter.

"She looks like an angel when she's like this, doesn't she?" Galahad asked.

"An angel of death," Lancelot whispered.

Arthur appeared with the pot of water, and Lancelot's odd response was forgotten. The three men went to work—washing and sterilizing the strips of cloth, cleansing Fionna's back, and finally, with clean, lye-scrubbed hands, Galahad bent over Fionna's back with a needle and gut and began to sew.

As he pierced Fionna's skin with the needle, she exploded awake with an anguished scream, struggling beneath Galahad. He pushed one forearm to her back to hold her still. "A little help!"

Arthur sat on her legs and Lancelot grabbed her shoulders as she cried out with a moan of pain.

"Fionnabhair . . ." Lancelot crouched low while still holding her, peering into Fionna's eyes, just inches from her. "Be still, warrior. Galahad is stitching your wound."

Her muscles relaxed and unclenched as Lancelot's words seemed to sink in. She let out a hiss of pain as Galahad pulled the needle and string through her skin, but held still.

"It will be all right," Lancelot murmured to her, stroking his fingers down her face before tucking a small braid behind her ear. "You will be fine."

Arthur shifted his weight off her to sit in the hard dirt, his face buried in his hands.

Galahad continued to sew, while Lancelot whispered soothing words to Fionna, and while Arthur buried himself deep into the despair of his own thoughts.

alahad was wrapping Fionna's wound when Percival reappeared in the clearing, leading Fionna's dappled mare by the reins. Percival swung down and led the horses toward the river to drink. "How is she?"

"Good," Galahad murmured, tying off the bandage. Finished, he pulled a blanket over her sleeping form and then strode over to the river beside Percival to wash his hands. "She'll be fine."

"When I saw all the blood on her . . ." Percival trailed off with a shaky smile. For once, the lad seemed lost for words. He tied the two horses to a nearby tree, before both he and Percival walked to join Arthur and Lancelot around the fire.

Percival, as usual, talked as if unaware of the tension brewing between the men. "The Kingdom of Gwynedd has plenty of warriors and enough ego to slay thousands of invaders. If they requested aid to defend the River Dee from raiders, why were the villages left unprotected?"

Arthur peered up from his perch beside the fire but remained silent.

"Perhaps these were not the raiders spoken of in the missive." Galahad volunteered. "Could be the Northern Lords and their warriors were already caring for the problem, not expecting a second set of raiders."

Lancelot tossed a twig into the flame. "Or the note was false."

"A fake request for help?" Percival asked, head angled in confusion. "Not verra sporting of Gwynedd."

"Not from Gwynedd," Lancelot drawled in irritation. "Obviously."

Arthur cleared his throat and nervously chanced a look their way. "You believe Tintagel is behind the Irish raiders?"

"They did ask for my head in a box and they knew of Fionna only one day after her knighting."

Their king closed his eyes tight as his face reddened.

Galahad's ire rose at the sight. "Arthur—"

"You don't need to say anything." Arthur held up a hand. "I know. I put us all at risk today. I was angry and I let reason give way to emotion. And, for that, I am truly sorry."

But Galahad didn't want to let his king off so easily. Fionna almost died. This reality wasn't something a simple apology could wipe away. "You can't risk her like that."

A strange look came over Arthur's face. "I value each of your lives over even my own. But I am king and you are my knights. Fionna included. Sometimes I will have to risk her."

"But she isn't *just* a knight," Galahad rumbled, his fingers curling into a fist.

"What are you saying?" Arthur asked.

"He's saying he's in love with her." Lancelot threw up his hands. "The whole lot of you are."

"That's the pot calling the kettle black, don't you think?" Galahad retorted. "I've never seen you push a woman away the way you've done to Fionna. That can only mean one thing. You're afraid to let her get close."

Lancelot was as mysterious as his fae foster mother when it came to some things, but not women. When it came to women, the man was as simple as a strawman. He wanted them, he bedded them, he left them. And since Lancelot hadn't bedded Fionna yet, he must still be in stage one.

"Or, maybe I learned my lesson with Morgana." Lancelot threw a small stick into the fire and then glared at Galahad.

"Is that why you were whispering to her while Galahad stitched her up?" Arthur pointed out.

Lancelot rolled his eyes. "I was calming her down. I would have done that for any of you."

"I dinnae recall Lancelot ever murmuring sweet nothings in my ear," Percival said. "What about ye, Galahad? Arthur?"

"Nope," Galahad said, unable to hide his victory from his icy sword-brother. His grin grew wider when a muscle pulsed in the other man's jaw.

Lancelot stood, his expression dark.

"No," Arthur commanded. "Sit. You're not walking away from this conversation. Any form of attraction to Fionna concerns all of us."

Lancelot dropped back down, crossing his arms before him, and then stared into the crackling fire.

"Well, I'm definitely in love with the lass," Percival said, chipper as usual. "I'm not ashamed to admit my feelings. I'll gladly wipe the floor with all of ye in the contest for her heart."

Arthur sighed. "She's captured my heart as well, despite my better judgment."

Galahad took a breath, his thoughts warring within him. Normally, he would keep the truth of what had happened with he and Fionna to himself—he wasn't a man like Lancelot, who liked to kiss and tell. But if the other men thought they had a fair claim to Fionna, it was only right to tell them that they had missed their chance.

"I'm afraid to break the news to you lads, but Fionna has already made her choice. She came to my room the night before we left Caerleon," Galahad said.

The other knights fell silent, shocked expressions on their faces.

Galahad struggled to keep another grin off his face. He would be lying to himself if he didn't admit that some part of him was pleased to stun them into silence.

"Did you—" Arthur tripped over his words, his mouth open and closing like a fish gasping for water.

Galahad shook his head. "No, but I made sure the lass enjoyed herself, if you catch my drift."

Percival apparently did not. "What do ye mean?" He leaned forward, his eyes wide.

Lancelot cuffed Percival over the head, but the gesture was gentle. "We'll tell you later."

Arthur furrowed his brows, seeming to pull his kingly mantle around himself. "She kissed me too. We don't know . . . what her attentions mean. What she wants. We vowed we wouldn't let her come between us. We let her choose. Maybe she'll choose Galahad and maybe she won't." Arthur's eyes met Galahad's, and there was a challenge there so powerful that Galahad recoiled slightly.

Arthur wanted Fionna, that much was clear. And who was he, the son of a Danish blacksmith, to stand between a king and what he wanted? Galahad knew that he should back down and step aside. But didn't he deserve to be happy too? If Fionna preferred Galahad, why should Arthur have her, just because he was born with noble blood and crowned King of all Briton?

"We let her choose," Galahad said.

The other men nodded.

"Trouble," Lancelot mumbled under his breath. "The lot of them."

The four knights turned and looked at Fionna's quiet sleeping form, her white-blonde hair peeking out from beneath the blanket. Galahad didn't envy her the choice. Or the fallout.

Chapter Twenty-Seven

Fionna

ot pain rippled through my shoulder as my eyelids fluttered open. I gulped in a startled breath before the pain stole the air from my lungs. Darkness filled my space. As did a strange, unnatural silence. Not even the low crackle of embers drifted to my pricked ears. Where was I? Unsure, I remained still, not wanting to alert anyone nearby to my return to consciousness. I glimpsed a sliver of light in the corner of my eye and turned toward it, achingly slow, gritting my teeth until I locked onto the source. A narrow band of moonlight crept through large, heavy drapes and across the wooden floor, illuminating timber-constructed walls. Mentally, I took stock of my surroundings. I was in a spacious room atop a luxurious feathered bed. My armor was on the floor beside me, and a man slept in a separate bed across from me.

My heart thundered at the many possibilities. Our ambush defeated O'Lynn's men. Why wasn't I under the stars on a bedroll beside my fellow knights? Was I still with my knights?

The word "my" twisted my insides. I had no right to claim those I would destroy. And, yet, I found the treacherous organ in my chest equally as treacherous as the woman I would become.

Memories flashed in my mind as the last thought spurred my rapid pulse—of Galahad sewing my wound shut, of Lancelot cupping my face and whispering words of encouragement, of Arthur burying his face in his knees, as if ashamed. The only face I couldn't remember was Percival's. Did he live? He must. I would know.

And then I felt the knowing ache, the sharp pang bleating behind my ribs. Not for Percival, but for them all. These men had wedged their way into an unknown chamber of my heart and this occupation, this residency was almost more than I could bear. Pushing up with my good arm, I clenched my jaw and rolled to a seated position. My breath came quick and heavy after such a simple task. But the pain was welcome compared to the breaking of my heart. How was I to do this? I forced myself to turn from my haunting thoughts to the body in the bed across from me.

Pale silvered fingers of light caressed the planes of the man's face, and I relaxed. Even dusted in moonlight, Arthur appeared boyish, all freckles and muscle, hair cut short but long enough to be disheveled by sleep. Such a contrast to the large presence he commanded when awake. My gaze trailed the length of him, uncovered and still fully armored. Except Excalibur, which no longer hung from his hip, but rested upright against the bed near his head.

"Goddess no," I whispered under my breath. I wasn't ready, not while injured. But when would I find a better opportunity? If my instincts proved true, we were back in Lord Bronn's fortress, which meant the Irish Sea was only a few hours up the River Dee from the port in Chester. I could hire a sailing vessel and be on my way long before the men awoke from their battle and travel fatigue.

Inching from the bed, I crept over my armor and tip-toed toward Arthur. My hands shook as hard as an untested warrior facing her first blood-stained field. This was all wrong; I should have prepared, gone through my ritual before I faced battle—even a fight with myself. My injured shoulder screamed similar sentiments with each step. Too late. I could brush the faerie sword with my fingertips this very moment. Just one more step and . . . cold metal branded my palm with guilt. Arthur would lose his gifted sovereignty as king. His land and people would suffer until a new king was appointed by the Otherworld.

And, yet, my father's land and people suffered *now*, and for similar reasons. Brin Allán's sovereignty was in question, for what king is taken from battle? Better to fall on his own sword than become paraded, tortured, and demeaned by his enemy.

Excalibur glinted in a pocket of moonlight as I used every breadth of control to lift the steel and jeweled scabbard. A shudder dragged long, jagged nails down my spine and I fell to my knees as gracefully as possible, my face contorted in a grimace. Pain seared down my arm and I nearly dropped the sword. Excalibur was too heavy for me to carry. Or perhaps the weight was in my mind—the weight of power over kings and men and land.

"Fionna?"

I whipped my gaze toward Arthur and stilled.

His face was mere inches from mine. Sleep softened the lines around his mouth and eyes, and he appeared so young without the weight of duty on him. So vulnerable. So incredibly beautiful, as if each feature were hand carved by the gods.

"Mmm, you smell of heaven and earth," he murmured, his eyes fluttering closed. Then, to my horror, he adjusted closer to the bed's edge and reached out. With eyes still closed, his fingers touched my cheek and slid to my mouth—as if he had touched me a thousand times. As if he always found me, even when separated by darkness. "With your permission, a kiss?" His voice held the same moonlight illuminating the hard lines of his armored body.

My thoughts tumbled like racing leaves in a black wind as a whirlpool of dread formed in my already soured gut. I wasn't sure how to respond, how to fight the shiver of desire coursing through me. His hand cradled my cheek and pulled me closer. His breath pulsed on my lips.

My mouth parted in anticipation, eyes closing, body leaning forward, wanting to feel the soft warmth of his lips on mine.

Tipped off balance, I dropped the sword. Metal clanked on the wooden floor and I bit back a curse.

Arthur's eyes flew open and he instinctually grasped for the sword no longer by his side. Not finding Excalibur, he jolted upright, his attention snapping wildly onto me.

My heart galloped through my veins as I knelt before him, hands now empty. At least I didn't wear my armor, an oversight that was now a blessing. Forcing myself to breathe, I pulled my gaze up to his and prayed that the guilt wasn't plain in my eyes.

A worried expression flitted across his face while he picked up and then rested his blade against the timber wall. "Did you tear your stitches?"

"I don't think so."

He scrubbed calloused hands over his handsome face before they fell to his lap. "Are you in . . . pain?"

"A little."

Even in the shadows I could see a blush color his stubbled cheeks. Did he think I approached his bed for pleasures? The sharp pang returned to my chest as I held my king's humbled gaze. I would steal away his inheritance and he looked at me as if I were his very salvation.

"Where are we?" I somehow managed to ask.

"Lord Bronn's estate." Arthur swallowed and blinked back shyness. "We buried him this afternoon."

"Ye stayed by my side . . . "

"Yes," he breathed. "I caused your injury with my foolish anger." He looked like he wanted to say more but didn't. Instead, he took my hand in his and bowed his head. "I am so sorry, Fionna. Please forgive me."

The vise in my chest ratcheted even tighter. "I am a warrior and I swore upon my life to follow ye into battle, King Arthur Pendragon."

A sad smile played across his lips as he stared at my hand in his.

"In Ireland, men do not fuss over women so," I continued when he didn't offer a reply. "We are their equals, not a delicate object to protect from harm's way. Not unless that is what the lass desires."

Arthur bashfully met my gaze once more. "I fuss for other reasons." Then his gaze dipped to my lips before he looked away, whispering, "I dreamed of you consenting to a kiss just now and I awake to find you real and near as if . . . as if you—"

"Almost kissed ye?"

"This guilt I carry over your pain is mine to bear." The voice of a king returned and I almost flinched. "You may be my sworn warrior, but I am responsible for you, for all of my knights." His shoulders slumped and his fingers gripped mine tighter, then he lowered his voice to an intimate whisper. "If I could, I would take your pain as my own, Princess Fionnabhair Allán. I would have you know only pleasure and happiness."

Tears burned the back of my eyes. Though the gesture seared hot across my shoulder, I rested my head against his leg. Never, in all my years, had I yielded myself before a man in such a way. But, as I knelt before my king, before a piece of my heart, I only wanted him to know pleasure and happiness too.

I blinked as the tears threatened to roll down my cheeks. My shoulders began to shake. Gently, Arthur lifted my face until our gazes touched.

"You *are* in pain," he said simply.

I was, but not in the way he believed. I couldn't confess my dilemma or how the very thought shattered me. Nor how my sister and father held captive by O'Lynn already tormented me until I wanted to double over in agony. I didn't want to think of it. I didn't want to think of anything.

Raising my hand, I cupped his face and whispered, "Help me to know only pleasure and happiness."

He sucked in a quiet breath.

"I give ye permission, Arthur."

Our breaths mingled as we held each other's faces. Vulnerability pooled in Arthur's gaze and I understood. He didn't give himself easily to another, not intimately at least. The realization lanced me anew.

Taking great care to not aggravate my wound, he tenderly scooped beneath my knees and lifted me to his chest before laying me upon the covers. I rolled to a seat before he could protest or join me on the bed. Then, unable to resist the temptation, I reached for his side and unbuckled a strap. And another. Arthur stood before me, his gaze unwavering, as I removed his armor piece by piece. Until only a loose tunic and breeches remained. My shoulder throbbed, but still I continued until I tugged up on his tunic. Arthur pulled the soft linen over his head, tossing the garment to the floor.

Goddess above, he was beautiful. A king forged from grace and battle. And as I had often secretly hoped, faint freckles covered his chest and muscled abdomen like a spill of stars. I wanted to kiss each one, to touch every mark and scar—to know every part of this incredible man.

Arthur leaned down until his hands settled on either side of my hips and then he brushed his lips across mine. He pulled back just enough to catch my gaze and gauge my reaction.

I smiled to encourage him. Where Galahad was all fire and fight, Arthur was sweet wine and the simmering warmth of home.

Home.

It wasn't the first time Arthur birthed this feeling in me. But I didn't have long to question why or ponder the strange emotions the word conjured.

His lips had returned to mine as he tipped my head back, reverently lowering me to the pillows below. My injury jolted with sparks of fire as my shoulder pressed into the bed. Breath fluttered free from my tightened chest, and I held back a grimace. But every ounce of pain dissolved when Arthur slowly crawled over the length my body, his skin practically glowing in the dusty moonlight. I watched, bewitched by the play of muscle and sinew across his chest, arms, and shoulders as he trailed soft kisses up my legs, around my navel, then between and under my breasts, before he buried his face into my neck.

"I feel as if my body knows yours already," he whispered across my skin. "As if I were made for you and you were made for me. Do you feel it?"

Pain tightened my chest once again as I whispered the word. One word that fully sealed my betrayal. "Yes."

I did feel this connection, and strongly. The pleasure was unlike any I had known before, slow and languid and devastating. He seemed content to explore the expanse of my skin with lips and soft caresses, ever careful of my wound. And yet my body reacted as though he were making love to me.

Perhaps he was, emotionally. And perhaps I wished him to.

We couldn't get enough of one another, memorizing each other's bodies in reverence, tasting passion's sweetness with one kiss after another. His affections were one of the most fulfilling experiences of my life. Every touch felt as though we joined completely, even though he remained respectful of my injury. We continued our exploration until the moon shifted from the window and the room shadowed into blissful darkness, a stillness broken only by our ragged breathing.

Until Arthur fell asleep, lips flushed and skin salted with sweat.

I stared at the ceiling, listening to the rise and fall of his peaceful slumber. This time I let the tears fall as my heart withered into brittle leaves and crumbled beneath the weight of my guilt. My choice was made, however.

My toes touched the cold floor and I crept back to the other bed where I gathered my armor, sword, and daggers. In the quiet hallway, I dressed, the tears still slipping down my flushed cheeks. When finished, I strode into the room, giving Arthur every opportunity to wake and stop me. But he remained sprawled across the bed, lost to pleasant dreams.

"Ye're a beautiful man, Arthur Pendragon," I whispered to his shadowed form. "It is I who asks for yer forgiveness."

My breath shuddered. Then, I pushed past the pain in my shoulder and in my chest and grabbed Excalibur.

I expected a knight to call out, "Traitor!" as I barreled out of the building and across the field. Yet, the only sound I heard when I reached the stables was a crow on a nearby branch, cawing. Strange for a crow to be active before dawn. I shook off the omen and threw Zephyr's saddle over her back.

The last sound I heard before Zephyr and I thundered onto the road that would carry us to the river port was that same crow. But this time the bird sounded as if it laughed.

Interlude

Morgana

The crow swooped low and trailed behind the witch's shadowed side unseen. Hooves turned up clods of dirt and grass. Her beast heaved and the charger's coat glistened with sweat. Occasionally, the crow could hear the witch hiccup with pathetic sobs. The task had broken her fierce spirit and weakened her focus. Good. The smell of her sickened grief was delightfully bitter and fed the crow more power to remain aloft.

Soaring on the wings of Arthur's destruction, the crow cawed with laughter. And if the witch heard? The better. Let the crowed triumph settle in the witch's bones. Let the mocking sound turn her blood to ice as she raced against the night and dawn and her failed destiny.

Arthur would spurn the witch now and, thus, his salvation. The crow laughed again, her caws growing louder when swollen silver eyes peered over an injured shoulder.

The witch pulled on her reins, and the horse slowed to a canter. The beast huffed large, hot puffs of vapor from her nostrils before shaking her head and flattening her ears.

The acrid smell of smoke still hung in the air. Crude wooden structures lay splintered in charred heaps. Bodies of villagers littered the dirt streets and soaked the ground with their innocent blood.

And their boats—the ones the witch needed—rested half-sunk, still tied to posts in the River Dee.

The witch kicked her beast in the flanks, turning her away from the ruined village. Ghostly white strands of hair streamed after her in a macabre dance as she galloped along the river bank toward the Irish Sea.

O'Lynn's men were idiots. How did they plan to sail away? Or was this a suicide mission from the onslaught?

The crow no longer laughed. Plans that were firmly within her claws now loosened and slipped. When Arthur and his knights gave chase, they might catch their little white whore. No, she couldn't allow Excalibur to touch the Little Dragon King's fingers ever again.

With a furious beat of her wings, the crow soared past the witch and her heaving beast toward the next big port town.

Chapter Twenty-Eight

Arthur

Arthur awoke to a honeyed kiss of morning light streaming through the drapes. He stretched slow and deep, his body alive and humming with the pleasure of last night's exertions. Fionna. Even her name tasted sweet on his lips. He closed his eyes, letting the memories wash over him.

It had been like a dreamscape—Fionna an enchantress, spinning his world into a string of miracles and wonders. The heat of her lips on his, the silken feel of her skin beneath his hands, the exquisite press of her lithe body against his. Arthur shivered at the memories, unable to keep the smile from breaking across his face. Every touch, every movement was careful, with her injured shoulder. But Arthur hadn't minded taking things slow or waiting for their coupling. The kisses and caresses they had shared last night had been gentle and deliberate and perfect.

Arthur heaved a soft sigh. He couldn't remain floating in a pleasant haze of daydreams all day. They needed to return to Caerleon and start the hunt for the Grail all over again. They had turned every inch of Lord Bronn's house upside down last night while Fionna slept, and found nothing that even mentioned the Grail, let alone contained a clue to the vessel's whereabouts. Arthur sighed, pushing himself up and out of bed. The bed where Fionna had lain was empty. He frowned. Perhaps she had already left for breakfast. Had he lingered abed so late?

Arthur pulled on his tunic and pants, sitting on the edge of the bed to lace up his boots. Once finished, he reached for Excalibur's familiar weight. And froze.

The sword wasn't there.

Arthur spun in a circle, his panicked gaze searching the room. He remembered setting his sword by his bedside last night. And . . . he wracked his mind, trying to recall details through the fog of sleep. Yes, Fionna had knocked Excalibur over. And he had set his blade against the wall. He stared at the empty spot where the sword should be. It was gone. His eyes swung to Fionna's bed. Fionna was gone. His heart seized in his chest. Panic charged through his veins. Perhaps she had taken Excalibur downstairs with her?

Arthur flew down the stairs and swung around a stone doorway leading into the dining room.

Lancelot, Galahad, and Percival sat at a long wooden table with trenchers of food and goblets of ale before them.

"Morning sleepyhead," Percival said cheerfully.

"Fionna . . ." Arthur breathed, his mind racing almost too quickly for words. "Where is Fionna?"

"*You* were the one who insisted that *you* stay with her." Galahad wrinkled his brows in a scowl. "And now *you've* lost her?"

"Excalibur is gone," Arthur rushed out, ignoring Galahad's impertinence. He couldn't believe it. This couldn't be happening. "And so is Fionna."

Lancelot was on his feet in an instant. "You sure?"

"It's a big bloody sword, I'm pretty damn sure," Arthur snapped. "None of you have seen her?"

The knights shook their heads.

"Could there be more Irishmen about?" Percival asked. "Could they have taken her? And the sword?"

Arthur bit the inside of his cheek. "I don't know how they could have moved past without me waking. I suppose stealing her out from underneath me is possible." As horrible as that would be—an injured Fionna being captured by a hostile clan—the thought was far preferable to the other one that seized him.

Of course, it was Lancelot who voiced his real concern. "Or she took your sword."

"Fionna wouldn't have stolen Excalibur," Galahad protested, pushing up from the table. "She swore an oath to serve Arthur. She's loyal."

"Stop thinking with your cocks for one minute," Lancelot said. "We've known her for less than a week. She showed up out of nowhere and disguised who she was to win the tourney. She seduced Galahad—"

"I seduced her, man," Galahad rumbled. "Get your facts straight."

"I thought you said she showed up at your room?" Lancelot pointed out.

"Well, she was . . . in the hallway. She didn't exactly knock on the door."

"You know who else's room is down in that hallway?" Lancelot lifted one dark brow. "Arthur's. Perhaps she went to seduce *him*, and you got in the way."

Lancelot looked from Arthur to Galahad, his blue eyes sharp as daggers. It took all of Arthur's self-control not to look away from his knight's accusatory gaze. If what Lancelot was suggesting was true . . . Arthur's mouth went dry. Last night's stolen kisses and heated caresses jumped into stark relief, exposed under the piercing light of Lancelot's suggestion. Had Fionna only kissed him last night to lull him into a false sense of security, so she could take his sword? His mind rebelled at the notion. The thought was too terrible.

"What night was it that you and Fionna . . ." Arthur trailed off.

"The night of the faerie wine," Galahad said.

Arthur wracked his brain again, recalling. "I wasn't in my room that night. I was at the library."

Galahad crossed arms over his chest, and Lancelot frowned, dragging angry fingers through his hair.

"Disna matter," Percival cut in. The young man had been staring forlornly at his plate, and now stood. "She's our fifth knight. Excalibur chose her. And she's the key to finding the Grail. I feel this as surely as I breathe. Perhaps she was taken, or perhaps she took the sword herself. If she did, I'm sure she has a good reason."

Lancelot sighed. "The world doesn't work that way, lad."

Percival jutted his chin out stubbornly. "Just because ye betrayed Morgana disna mean Fionna will betray us." The other knights flinched at that, but Percival pushed on. "Wherever she is, Excalibur is with her. We need to find them both. Every minute we waste here is another minute between us."

"Percival speaks sense," Arthur relented. At this moment, it didn't really matter who had taken his sword. They just needed to get Excalibur back. "Be ready to ride in five minutes."

The knights flew from the room, gathering belongings, and then dashed toward the stable to saddle their mounts.

Arthur was glad that his body knew by heart the familiar motions of saddling and bridling Llamrei. For his mind was useless to him, trapped in a spinning loop of fear and sorrow and self-loathing. Excalibur was his most precious possession, the gift that marked him as sovereign over Caerleon, the Kingdom of Gwent's overking, and the High King of all Briton. First, Morgause had cursed his blade, and now, he'd lost it, all in a span of a month. Were the gods testing him?

Perhaps he didn't deserve to rule Briton, if the promise of one night with a beautiful woman was all it took for him to abandon his charge to rule this land. Fionna. Bewitching and fierce . . . and duplicitous? He didn't want to believe this version of Fionna possible, but Lancelot was right. They knew little about their fifth knight, despite how deep the connection he felt with her. Perhaps she was a spider, carefully spinning a web of illusion and lies—a trap for a king. His face burned with shame at the thought that what he and Fionna had shared may have only been a clever ruse. Is this what his half-sister felt, he mused, when Lancelot had betrayed her? Embarrassed her before the entire kingdom? Arthur felt a newfound surge of kinship.

Llamrei stamped her hoof and Arthur started, realizing he was pulling the girth too tight. "Sorry girl," Arthur murmured, slipping the buckle into the correct notch in the leather. He led Llamrei into the open and swung onto her back.

Arthur's shame burned into anger and he let roiling feelings spark into a blaze within him. He welcomed the searing heat, a purifying fire burning away the softness of his emotions. The weakness of his desires. Until only rage remained.

A grim smile split his face. They would track and capture whoever had Excalibur. Perhaps Fionna was guilty, perhaps not. Whoever the thief, when he found them, he would make them pay.

Chapter Twenty-Nine

Lancelot

A small part of Lancelot refused to believe that Fionna would betray them. Lancelot saw the dim hope in Arthur's eyes. The rigid set of his shoulders spoke of Arthur's desperate prayer that Fionna had been taken somehow—that she wasn't the treacherous snake she now apeared to be.

But, sometimes, the simplest explanation was the right one.

The wind streamed through Lancelot's hair, his horse's rocking gait smooth beneath him. They were eating up the ground in their pursuit of her, or whomever had the sword.

"Arthur!" Galahad's booming shout sounded behind them, almost stolen by the wind and the distance. But their king heard and turned his mount, galloping past Lancelot, to where Galahad had stopped and pointed to a patch of mud on the road. "Tracks. A single horse."

Galahad and Lancelot exchanged a grim look. One horse meant just Fionna. She hadn't been taken. She had stolen the sword and run. All on her own. Sometimes Lancelot hated being right.

Arthur straightened in his saddle. "This is a well-traveled road, we don't know—"

Galahad cut in gently. "Possibly. I think it's safe to assume the tracks belong to Fionna's mount."

Percival was shaking his head, as if he didn't want to believe it either. A surge of compassion for the lad overcame him. True, perhaps Lancelot was more jaded than most, but there came a point in every man's life when he realized that life and love wasn't all courtly romance and fair maidens. Men were moths and women the devouring flame—they kept a man warm at a distance, but if he were foolish enough to get too close, they would burn him up in an instant.

Arthur was nodding woodenly, processing Galahad's unwelcome words, before saying, "Good. If we only face her, then Excalibur will be easier to recover. We ride." He kicked his horse's flanks. Llamrei spun about and then launched back into a gallop.

Lancelot sighed, urging his charger forward to match Arthur's pace.

It didn't make sense. Morgana's curse had said the Gwenevere would tear them apart. Would ruin Caerleon. And Fionna was certainly doing that, by taking Arthur's sovereign blade. But . . . Lancelot hadn't slept with her. He had exercised superhuman restraint against the most fascinating woman he had ever met. So . . . why was the curse coming true? Could Morgana have lied to him somehow about the nature of this curse? He didn't think that was possible. Fae couldn't lie. But they could omit details. He wished he had his foster mother to talk to about this situation. Vivin would know a thing or two about curses.

Should he tell Arthur? He looked at his king's back a few paces before him. No. Lancelot didn't think he had ever seen Arthur so unmoored. Now wouldn't be a good time to tell him. Besides, he didn't even know if his curse had anything to do with the current situation. He had stayed away from Fionna. He had done his part, regardless of how hard his heart and loins pulled him toward her with a ceaseless tug.

They continued to ride, past the raided village of Ewloe down the River Dee. Countryside blurred in greens and smoke. The stench of death carried on the wind and followed their trail.

Perhaps only a half hour later, they approached a crossroads and Arthur held up a hand as he reigned his horse in. Both he and Arthur slowed to a stop. Galahad and Percival were close behind and quickly came clattering to a stop as well. Their horses huffed and heaved for breath while anxiously pawing the ground. Each poor mount was caked in dust and sweat.

"I think I should have done without breakfast," Percival muttered, twisting in the saddle to relieve a crick in his side.

"That way leads to another port on the River Dee a touch southeast of where we stand," Arthur said. "The village there would be the fastest way for her to sail north to the Irish Sea since Ewloe's destruction."

"There's smoke on the horizon that way," Galahad pointed out. "It's the nearest port outside of Brunanburh. The raiders would be fools to land in a Danish sea town, though. If the Uí Tuírtri visited this shore, the village southeast of here would have been ravaged before Ewloe. There might not be any boats there either."

"Or anyone to man them," Arthur agreed. "North we go, then. To Brunanburh. The river port is less than two hour's ride that way."

"If she made straight for Brunanburh, she could already be on a boat," Lancelot offered apologetically. "She likely has at least a few hours on us."

Arthur's face blackened.

"If she tried for the River Dee, she would have lost a few hours," Galahad pointed out.

"She isnae on a boat," Percival said. He was staring into the distance, a strange expression on his face. "She's coming up that road." He pointed to the left, from the direction of the river village. Lancelot stilled, the hairs on the back of his arms raising. He'd been around magic long enough to know the tell-tale mental tug and intuitive heightened awareness, and magic was definitely dancing in the air.

"How do you know?" Arthur asked. "Makes little sense that we would catch up with her so soon."

Percival shook his head, his copper hair flashing in the sun. "I just know."

"So, we take her." Arthur's fists tightened on his reins. "And whoever she's with."

"Arthur, are you mad?" Galahad protested. "Do you want to

get killed? If we get into an all-out chase with her then someone will break their neck. Or end up on the point of a sword. And I don't know if you remember, but Fionna isn't bad with a sword. It might be one of us."

"What do *you* propose, then?"

The words were tight, clipped. The strain of this was breaking Arthur. Lancelot could visibly see his struggle. Gods, his king really loved Fionna. How could she have spit in his face like this? Especially after the tear of village raids and the loss of Lord Bronn? After their small band had made her one of them? Welcomed her into Caerleon with open arms?

"We lay a trap," Galahad suggested, pulling Lancelot from his ranting thoughts. "Perhaps Percival was right. Maybe she had a good reason for taking the sword. If she did, I for one would like to hear her tale before we come to blows. Let us not strike first and ask questions later."

"What kind of a trap?" Arthur asked.

"I will wait here for her. You three sneak around and hide—someone beside the road where we came, the others on the River Dee side. She'll slow when she sees me blocking the path. I'll find out what I can. If she tries to run, she'll be surrounded. We capture her, hopefully without killing her," Galahad looked meaningfully at Lancelot, "and get back the sword."

Lancelot grunted. It's not like he wanted to kill the woman! He was just apparently the only one of them who hadn't completely lost his mind for her.

"She comes soon," Percival added, his voice faint.

"Hurry," Galahad ordered. "To positions."

Arthur didn't seem to mind being commanded in that moment.

"I'll cut through the woods and circle back around to her," Lancelot said, trying to be kind by giving his grieving king the easier route. "Arthur, you take the road from Chester. Percival, wherever you would like."

Arthur nodded and Lancelot wheeled his horse, plunging into the sparse forest bordering the road. He looked behind him and didn't see Percival following. The knight must have decided to go with Arthur. Fine. It would be good for his friend to have moral support, if he had to do the worst.

Lancelot slowed his horse to a walk when he got far enough from the road to be hidden from sight. Then he turned to cut parallel to the path Fionna would emerge from. He wouldn't have to go far to be able to circle around and pen her in.

Trepidation filled him as the sound of stilted hoofbeats reached his ears. Whatever came next, it wouldn't be pretty.

Chapter Thirty

Galahad

Galahad sat at the crossroads, his heart in his hands. A small plume of dust rose in the distance as a rider limped up the road from the River Dee. How could the rider be Fionna? How could it not?

It's strange how much had shifted for him in the past few days. As effortlessly as a thread on a loom, Fionna had fit into the fabric of their lives as if she had always been there. Had there ever been a time when she wasn't supposed to be their fifth? It felt hazy and distant—her presence in their lives a given. And then this morning, everything shifted again. But now, instead of feeling comfortable and right, things felt strange and chaffing, like putting one's boots on the wrong feet. Fionna wasn't their enemy. Galahad didn't know why she had taken the sword, but he knew this much at least: she wasn't their enemy.

The white of her hair and the foam-flecked flanks of her limping horse came into view first. Had Zephyr thrown a shoe? Or gone lame? His eyes traveled back to Fionna and his pulse stuttered at the sight of her, each wounded beat of his heart panging with confusion.

Galahad took a steadying breath, clicking his tongue to turn his large charger sideways, to block most of the road. With Zephyr's injury, he knew she couldn't gallop away. This was more for show, to gain Fionna's full attention. He kept his sword in its scabbard, though he rested his hand on the big pommel. He prayed he didn't have to use his blade. Might as well cut off his own arm, as cut down Fionna. Still, through his trepidation, he marveled at how quickly he had come to love her. And love her he did.

Fionna caught sight of him and hauled on her gray mare's reins. Spooked from the pain, her horse slid to an agitated stop in a clatter of hooves just feet from Galahad. Fionna's lovely face was covered in a sheen of sweat, her white braids a wild tangle behind her. Her expression—he recognized it. Grief and heartbreak thinned her pink lips into a tight line, weariness drooped her proud shoulders. And over those shoulders, strapped to her back, the glittering pommel of a sword that winked in the morning sunlight.

Excalibur.

"Good morning, Fionna," Galahad said, grateful that his voice was clear and strong.

She let out a strangled laugh. "That's all ye have to say to me?"

"A few other things come to mind, but I thought we could skip those and be civil. Give us the sword, Fionna." He held out his hand toward her, like one might toward a wild animal, to let the beast test the stranger's scent on the air. "Excalibur doesn't belong to you."

"I know," Fionna choked out. "I'm sorry. I'm sorry for everything. But I need this sword more than Arthur does." Her mare danced beneath her, seeming to sense her rider's anxiety.

Galahad tensed, in case she was about to bolt. Though, her mare wouldn't travel far, if she did. And Zephyr could become permanently damaged too. He decided to keep her talking.

"He needs Excalibur most of all. Without this sword, his claim to the kingship of Caerleon, the Kingdom of Gwent, and all of Briton is lost. You swore an oath to protect him, to serve as his knight. Did that mean *nothing* to you?" He didn't ask the question that was ringing loud in his mind. *Did* we *mean nothing to you? Did I?*

Fionna looked up at the heavens, her mouth twisting as if she was fighting back tears. "Of course, my vows meant something. But I made another oath. As a daughter. And a sister. And that means more. It has to."

Galahad frowned. What was she talking about?

"Galahad—I'm sorry for what I did to ye. Our time together, every moment meant something to me. But we can never be."

"It doesn't have to be this way," he said tenderly. How was he to show her how much their moment had meant to him too?

She plunged on, choking on her apparent anguish. "And tell Arthur . . . tell Arthur I'm sorry. That I appreciated all he did for me. All . . . that passed between us."

"Tell him yourself," Galahad suggested. "Come back with us. Return the sword. Our fellowship can be as it once was."

She shook her head, her braid whirling. "That's impossible Galahad, and ye know it. I've ruined everything. The only chance I have now is returning home with this sword."

"You're not leaving Briton with Excalibur. Do you think Arthur would not come for you? That he would not ride to the ends of the earth to take back what is his?"

"I just need Excalibur for a time. After that, he can have his sword back. I'll even help him get his blade back."

"I don't understand."

Fionna licked her lips nervously, her gaze darting around as tears rolled down her cheeks. "I'm sorry Galahad, I've tarried too long. Tell the others . . . I don't know. Something to make the betrayal softer."

Even knowing an attempt to flee might happen, despite her horse's injury, Fionna's sudden motion to spur her mount into action startled him. The little mare was fast as the wind, whickering in pain. And, then, they were thundering past him on an uneven gait down the road to Brunanburh, the one direction they hadn't placed a trap.

Galahad swore, kicking his mount to follow. He hadn't thought she'd be able to get past him so nimbly!

Fionna was already putting distance between them. Galahad narrowed his eyes against the grit her horse kicked up, his focus on her form before him. But then, seemingly out of nowhere, a black steed and rider appeared directly in Fionna's path.

Zephyr screamed in surprise, rearing and pawing the air. Fionna tumbled off her back and landed with a thud on the hard-packed road. She hissed in pain as her shoulder smacked the earth, rolling to her side to protect her own injury.

Arthur. How had his king known?

Galahad had little time to wonder. Arthur threw himself off his mount onto the ground and grabbed Fionna by the buckles of her leather armor, hauling her up to her feet. Blotches of red blossomed from Fionna's wound.

"Arthur!" Galahad shouted, fearing what his king might do in his rage.

Lancelot's mount skittered to a stop behind him and he was off his horse in a flash, his sword drawn. He leveled his weapon at Fionna, laying the sharp edge against the nape of her neck. Where was Percival? Galahad thought briefly, but his attention was pulled back to his two murder-bent fellows.

Galahad pulled his sword from its sheath too, not sure if he would have to use his blade on Fionna or to scare sense into the other men. "Easy all," he bellowed.

Fionna was blinking away her confusion from the fall, one half of her coated in dust from the road. She held up her hands in surrender to the men surrounding her, gritting back in pain.

Arthur pulled a knife from his belt, leveling the razor-sharp edge at the other side of her pale throat, his other hand still twisted in the buckles of her leather armor. And his face contorted with thunderous wrath.

"I yield," she said with a cough. She closed her eyes, and said with what almost seemed like relief, "I am outmaneuvered. Take the sword. Excalibur is yers."

Chapter Thirty-One

Percival

Percival felt strange. In his mind, he knew his other knights needed him—that there was no more important place to be than at the crossroads waiting for Fionna. He needed to see her again, to gauge the look on her face and try to understand why she had left. But there was an invisible tether pulling him away. The unseen line tied a fisherman's knot to his stomach, or so it seemed. The tether tugged at him, making the contents of his breakfast lurch skyward. Giving in to the stronger sensation, he spurred his chestnut horse, Kit, to the east—away from Arthur and his brothers and Fionna.

They plunged through silver birch and hemlock trees and soft ferns, the feeling growing ever stronger. He had thought Fionna was the most powerful pull he had ever felt, and he felt her still, but this was more urgent. The sensation commanded him to hurry. It was always unsettling when his Fisher King heritage asserted itself. Years would go by without so much as a twinge, making him question whether hiding in the forest wasn't all a dreadful joke played by his mother to ruin his childhood, and his adulthood at that. But then the magic would seize him, and he would remember long-lost words from his father. The pull was true. Undeniable. That's how the invisible tether felt now.

Percival cursed under his breath. He didn't want to be thinking about the Grail, or his father, or magic. He wanted to be think-ing about Fionna, to be there to stop Arthur and Lancelot from do-ing something they would regret. When Galahad had pointed out the single set of hoof prints in the mud, Percival had felt his heart splinter. Not because he thought Fionna had betrayed them. Some-how, deep down, despite all evidence to the contrary, he knew she hadn't. He felt the truth in his bones. But he knew what her flight would do to Arthur. What her absence would mean for their fu-ture. Everything would change. And Percival wanted nothing to change. For the first time in a long time, with Fionna as their fifth, the world felt right. All of them together. Their quintet band of warriors was how their group was supposed to be.

Kit pushed through a dense patch of underbrush into a circle of trees. Percival reined him in. The hackles rose on the back of his neck, the breath stolen from his lungs.

It was a faerie circle. A single beam of light pierced through the dense tree canopy, spilling like liquid gold across a single pil-lar of ancient mossy stone. Excitement churned in his veins as he swung down onto the soft loamy soil.

Percival looked about, but he was alone, just him and the stone. He walked toward the large granite boulder slowly. The tumult of forest growth held no dominion here, the ground clear but for a carpet of tiny white flowers. A ring of mushrooms bounded the circle, their creamy white heads glowing in the ethereal light cast from above.

The circle looked as if the magic had not been disturbed in generations. Did anyone alive know that this relic existed? The stone was as tall as him, an oblong of dark gray granite. Though the stone's venerable form was covered in moss, Percival could see that something was etched onto the surface.

Slowly, with a shaking hand, Percival peeled the moss from the stone's face, baring the words written there. It was in Ogham, the runic language of the druids. And the faeries. Percival's mother had made him learn how to read the runes—just another part of her unconventional education. Half the time he believed her touched in the head.

He wiped away a wee bit of moss and squinted his eyes to better read the Ogham marks. His eyes then widened, a disbelieving laugh escaping him as he realized the rune's meaning.

"Across the wall and atop the rock hill, the blessed five shall drink their fill."

A riddle. But more than that. The runes were directions. To the Grail. Directions meant for five. Finally, the sídhe took pity on their mortal souls!

Chapter Thirty-Two

Fionna

I had never felt so broken as I did in that moment. The anger and hurt in the eyes of my knights tore at me with savage claws. Ripping away my resolve. Cutting to my core and draining the fight from me. Part of me was relieved they had found me. Excalibur belonged with Arthur. The thought of giving the sword to O'Lynn turned my stomach, no matter the reason.

And my reason—what would become of them now, after Arthur took out his rightful vengeance on me? The thought of my father's face when O'Lynn gloated about sending me to my death was too much to bear.

"Just kill me," I said, voice hoarse. Closing my eyes, I leaned forward incrementally, feeling the bite of Arthur's and Lancelot's blades against my neck. I relished the feeling. The sting brought me back to myself in some small way, returned my power to me.

"Unstrap the sword from her, Galahad." Arthur's tone was foreign—cold. It belonged to a cruel man, a bitter and twisted man. To think this was what I had done to my sweet and sincere king filled me with the hot flush of shame.

I opened my eyes as Galahad stepped in close, reaching around me to unstrap Excalibur from my back. I drank in the sight of his chiseled face so close to mine. I then breathed in his scent of cedarwood and leather, holding back a whimper at the comfort his nearness brought me. Never again. Never again would I feel the burning passion he ignited, nor the bright burst of laughter Percival chiseled out from my hard resolve. Never would I feel the warm sunshine of Arthur's favor that bolstered my confidence, or the sharp bite of Lancelot's edge drawing sparks against my own. I had told myself I would be strong, but I was nothing without them. These knights were like my limbs. How I had functioned so well before them, I knew not. But after them, without them, I was no longer whole.

Galahad stepped back, Excalibur held tightly to his chest. I felt the space between us as though it were a physical thing.

"Why?" Lancelot asked. I turned my head slightly in surprise. Of all of them, I expected least from him. But in his face, through the careful shield of his piercing eyes, I saw a hurt just as deep as Arthur's or Galahad's. Dear goddess. Was there no bottom to the depths of my betrayal?

"Where is Percival? Is he all right?" I asked, finding myself desperate to know that he was well. I felt his absence keenly. The five of us should all be present, when the five of us ended.

"You have lost your privilege to ask questions." The ice of Arthur's tone frosted my bleeding heart. "Or to care about my knights."

I chanced a glance at Galahad, who gave me a quiet encouraging nod. Relief welled in me. Percival was all right at least.

"I believe Lancelot asked you a question. I would know the reason for your betrayal, before the end," Arthur said.

Before the end. Before they killed me. I sighed, weariness settling into every aching bone.

"I was sent here by Donal O'Lynn, chieftain of the Uí Tuírtri clann. The very same clann who raided yer shores and killed Lord Bronn," I began. I saw the anger blackening their faces and hurried on. "He is my enemy. His clann and mine have fought for generations. In our last battle, he captured my father and sister. I paid him a generous ransom, but he refused any coin. The only price he would accept in exchange for my family's freedom was the sword of a Welsh king. Excalibur. So, I sailed to Wales to take yer blade. I didn't know . . ." I stumbled over the words, tears threatening to fall anew. "Didn't know what I would find here. How I would come to feel for ye."

The men were silent, the muscles in Arthur's jaw working furiously.

"How do we know you speak truth?" Arthur asked.

I shrugged helplessly. Lancelot and Arthur's blades had slackened slightly, but still rested on my collarbones. "Ye could verify my story if ye went to Ulster, but I have no proof on my person."

"Why does this chieftain want Excalibur?" Lancelot asked, his eyes narrowed to slitted chips of ice.

"I don't know," I answered. "He shared that he had a new acquaintance who had told him about the sword's power, that is all. Not even a name of the acquaintance . . ."

The men exchanged glances. "Could be Morgana, or the Saxons, or another Briton king," Lancelot said. "You have no shortage of enemies."

Arthur nodded.

A desperate piece of me wanted to beg for my life, but I didn't know how I could go on, torn between love and duty. Between my knights and my family. So, I settled for trying to tell them what they had meant to me.

"I know ye have no reason to believe me, but I will say the words anyway. These days with ye have been the strangest and best of my life. I didn't know when I came to Caerleon how I would come to feel for each of ye. I have never experienced such a powerful connection to any man, let alone . . ."

Let alone four. The confession sounded insane, even in my tumbling thoughts. I plunged ahead, anyway.

"Let . . . Let alone each of ye." I paused as a tight sob broke free, then choked out, "Taking Excalibur broke my heart. If ye believe nothing else, believe that. The sword belongs with ye, Arthur. The sword belongs in Caerleon. And I think, somehow, I do too. I know I've ruined every opportunity, though." I closed my eyes as more tears squeezed through. Disbelieving. How did it all come to this? "I just couldn't abandon my family. Without the sword, they'll be tortured and killed. My sister..." I struggled to keep my voice even. Opening my eyes, I swallowed against the knot in my throat and half-whispered, "Who knows what O'Lynn's men will do to her. I couldn't abandon them, no matter what my heart was telling me."

"Why didn't you tell us?" Arthur asked. The anguish in his green eyes twisted me like a knife in my gut. "We could have helped you."

I let out a hollow laugh. "Tell ye that the only reason I had come to Caerleon was to betray ye? I know ye are a generous king, Arthur, but I think even yer generosity doesn't extend that far."

"I might have surprised you," he said softly. "For you, my generosity would have extended to the ends of the earth."

I closed my eyes again at that. I didn't want to know that there could have been another way. I didn't want to hear his heart in his words.

"And now?" I asked, opening them, looking at my knights though blurry, tear-stained eyes. "What now?" Perhaps I asked the question to make the decision easier on them. Because I knew they were stalling. I could sense they didn't want to do what they must.

Arthur stepped back abruptly, turning from me, sheathing his knife. Lancelot stepped in closer, his blade still strong and sure against my neck. Our eyes met. In some ways, I think Lancelot and I understood each other the best. We knew what it was to make a fool decision, to betray your king. Yet, he was still standing here at Arthur's side. And I would pay for my mistake with my life.

Arthur turned, nodding, taking Excalibur from Galahad. The big knight laid a hand on Arthur's shoulder and squeezed.

My heart thundered in my chest as Arthur buckled Excalibur's scabbard around his waist, as he drew the blade. His movements seemed as slow as a dream, a nightmare that would not end—I wasn't sure if he was stalling further, or whether the last few moments at one's end moved more slowly.

I fought the weakness in my knees, the roiling of my gut, drawing myself up proudly. Arthur bowed his head at me, and I dipped mine in return, as much as Lancelot's blade would allow. I knew Arthur would strike clean and true.

The moment stilled as we all seemed to take in a breath. Centering ourselves. Preparing. It was then that the thundering roll of hoofbeats came into my awareness—so deafening I was shocked I hadn't noticed the clattering sound before. I supposed facing one's own death was like that—the moment drowned out all else.

"Arthur!" Percival crashed through the nearby trees, emerging onto the road, reigning his horse to a stop. He launched himself off his chestnut horse, running toward our strange little standoff, pushing away Lancelot's blade to pull me into a fierce hug.

I collapsed into him, weakened by my freshly bleeding wound. His warmth and smell of sunshine and sage infused me with comfort, soothing the terror and sorrow within me. "I missed ye, dove," he murmured into my ear, burying his nose into my neck.

I let out an incredulous, sorrow-filled laugh. Percival had returned. And he had brought me a nickname.

Chapter Thirty-Three

Arthur

Arthur was never so relieved for Percival to ruin his plans. His terror had felt like rid-ing for a cliff, able to see the horror but unable to pull away, until the young knight startled them out of sure disaster.

The thought of killing Fionna was too much to bear, but Arthur couldn't see another way, no matter how hard he longed for one. When a subject betrays their king, the pun-ishment is death. Great ancestors, how he longed for a better world between kings and men, where mercy was valued over blood sacrifices.

Fionna was crying now, shaking against Percival like a leaf in a gale. Percival was shushing her, stroking her hair.

Arthur turned away. It was one thing when Fionna was stand-ing strong and tall. A warrior. But that facade crumbled to reveal the frightened woman beneath. The woman he loved. And it was he who had caused her such terror. What was wrong with him? Even knowing what she had done, that she had tried to ruin him, he didn't want to live without her. Her reason for taking Excali-bur had been noble—understandable even. His heart told him she wasn't being false. That she hadn't wanted to take the sword. That there *was* something between them, and she felt the connection too. But could his heart be trusted?

"Percival, where in the gods' name have you been?" Lancelot asked, his sword still hanging loosely in his hand. His knight was on edge, and the guarded tone was a good reminder for him. Fionna may seem harmless right now, but their fifth knight was anything but.

Percival pulled back gently from Fionna, who wiped her eyes and her nose, a rosy blush of embarrassment coloring her cheeks. Then the lad's face grew alive with excitement. "I found a clue to the Grail."

That startled Arthur back to himself. "What?"

"I was going to go with ye, Arthur, to lay in wait for Fionna. But I felt the tug of magic—so strong I couldn't ignore the tethering pull. I followed the urge into the wood. Magic led me to a faerie circle where an ancient rock sat, carved with words in Ogham. A clue to the Grail!"

Lancelot narrowed his eyes. "A clue? Here? Why on the Mother Goddess's green Earth would a fae stone possess a clue to the Grail along the River Dee?"

"Ye doubt magic, crabapple?" Percival shot back, a cheeky grin in place. "Have ye forgotten yerself, oh wise foster son of the faeries?" The young knight tilted his head toward Arthur and added, "Obviously, some fae still favor our king."

"What did the stone say?" Arthur asked, trying not to let hope overtake him. He could use a little good news right now, and a touch of favor by the Túatha dé Danann would qualify. But he'd been disappointed before.

Percival cleared his throat and winked at Lancelot. "Across the wall and atop the hill, the blessed five shall drink their fill."

Arthur processed the words, disbelieving. "Five?" he asked.

Percival nodded meaningfully at him, gently squeezing Fionna's shoulder. She was still tucked against him. "Five."

Arthur exchanged glances with Galahad and Lancelot. Galahad looked hopeful, and Lancelot sighed, shoving his sword into his scabbard.

"Can you show us this faerie circle Percival?" Arthur asked.

"Of course!"

They rode through the woods after Percival, Fionna on Galahad's horse, leaning against the man. They tied her hands to be safe and had hobbled her lame horse. A stitch or two had snapped open and dark crimson bloomed down the exposed areas of her arm and shoulder where her armor didn't cover. The wound appeared to have stopped bleeding, thankfully. By bringing her along, she would have no chance of outrunning them, injury and lame horse or no. Arthur didn't want to take any chances.

The circle was just as Percival shared. The feel of magic was thick in the air like a humid summer day.

Arthur dismounted, nodding to Galahad, who helped Fionna off his horse.

Together they walked to stand before the stone as light streamed from above to illuminate the rough-hewn letters.

Percival pointed to each rune and explained their meaning, since neither Arthur or any other present could read Ogham. Very few could, the runic language of the gods was used only by the druids and the Túatha dé Danann. For all the wrong Percival's mother wrought—a former druidess in training before she married the Fisher King—at least she served the lad right in this way.

"Across the wall," Galahad said, repeating the riddle. "Could be Hadrian's Wall, no? So, the Grail is to the north, in the Scoti kingdom of Alba?"

Arthur nodded, gnawing the inside of his lip. "Atop a rock hill."

"The city of Castellum Puellarum is built atop a rock hill," Percival suggested. "That's where I would start."

"If Castellum Puellarum is good enough for the heir to the Fisher King," Arthur replied, "Then it is good enough for me."

They fell silent, none wanting to broach the next subject. None knowing how. Once again, Arthur was grateful when Percival barreled ahead with youthful tactlessness, giving little heed for the sensitivity of the situation.

"Fionna has to come with us. I dinnae care what she did. She's one of us. She's our fifth."

Arthur risked a glance at Fionna. She was staring vacantly at the stone, lost in her own thoughts.

"You're certain of this?" he asked carefully.

"We won't find the Grail without her," Percival said. "I know it in my bones. Just look at this." He motioned to the stone and the circle around them. "We never would have found this if Fionna hadn't fled. She led us right here."

"You led us here," Lancelot corrected.

"But we wouldn't have been close enough to feel the magic's pull without her, ye ken."

"Excalibur *did* choose her," Galahad pointed out.

"Yes, before she tried to steal it," Lancelot countered again.

Arthur tried to set aside his feelings, to view the situation dispassionately. Merlin had foreseen that a fifth knight would join them, whose blood would be the key to breaking the faerie curse on Excalibur and over all Caerleon. Fionna had broken the curse on Excalibur. There was no denying that. And now the stone suggested they needed her as well. He would welcome the devil himself under his roof, it meant healing Caerleon. Would it be so bad to allow Fionna to stay with them?

"Lancelot, a word," Arthur said, pulling his sword brother aside and away from the circle's bright, cloying feel. Arthur took a steadying breath. "I do not trust my judgment when it comes to her. What would your counsel be?"

Lancelot let out a dark laugh. "You're trusting *my* judgment when it comes to women?"

"As a fellow son of a king, as my second-in-command, as my *friend*, I'm trusting your judgment when it comes to my kingdom. I think we need her, if we have any hope of freeing Caerleon from this dark curse. But . . . I fear this idea is just my heart telling me so."

Lancelot closed his eyes, as if warring with something, though what, Arthur couldn't say. His eyelids snapped open and he leveled a gaze at Arthur. "Your judgment isn't worth shit when it comes to her, but you're right this time. Percival is right. Merlin is right. The bloody rock is right. We need her. The Fates have a funny way of bringing souls together, and for better or worse, Fionna *is ours* now."

"And we are hers," Arthur replied softly.

Lancelot nodded and clapped Arthur on the shoulder.

"But the punishment for betraying a king must be death. How could I deviate from that law? And what kind of precedent would I set, if I pardoned her?"

"As for the punishment, don't forget you *are* king. *You* make the rules. You could make her shine your boots every day for the rest of your life, if you wished."

Arthur frowned. "That wouldn't be very fitting for a lady."

Lancelot rolled his eyes. "You know what I mean. As for precedent, no one knows about Fionna's little misadventure but us five. Let's keep it that way."

"You're right." Lancelot spoke sense. For the first time in weeks, Lancelot seemed himself again—his eyes clear and bright, his shoulders pulled back proudly.

Arthur's mouth twisted as he tried to hold in a smile. "You're really loving not being the fuck up anymore, aren't you?"

Lancelot grinned, letting out a delighted laugh. "You have no idea."

Arthur laughed too, and they moved back toward the circle.

"But Arthur," Lancelot slowed him, his voice lowering. "We watch her. All of us. We must stay on our guard."

Arthur gave a curt nod. Wise counsel. Fionna would need to earn their trust, if she wanted their good opinion back. He didn't know what would pass between them now, if anything could. She had lied about so much. But not everything, he thought. He believed that what he and Fionna had shared the night before was real. Their connection had felt real—more real than anything he had ever experienced. He stabbed fingers through his hair in disbelief. Had their time together only been last night? It now seemed a lifetime ago.

The tension was thick as Arthur and Lancelot rejoined the other knights around the standing stone. Arthur took the moment to drink in the sight of Fionna—regal and lovely and fierce. Her tears had left trails through the dust on her face, but she stood proud, once again composed, ready to face his decision. His heart and soul longed for her still, despite her betrayal, perhaps stronger than ever. He couldn't let her pass from his life like nothing more than a surreal dream. He couldn't be the one to rob this world of her. He wouldn't. The worried expressions on Percival and Galahad's faces showed they prayed that he wouldn't either.

"Well," Arthur began. "Seems the Fates have bound us together with bonds so tight that even treachery cannot tear them asunder. For what it's worth, I believe your story, Fionna, about why you stole Excalibur. They do not justify theft, but I understand. I will pardon you for your crime, on one condition." He paused a beat and met her silver eyes. "Help us find the Grail."

Chapter Thirty-Four

Fionna

Arthur's words rang in my ears, foreign and strange. Hope surged in me like a tempest. Surely . . . surely, he couldn't be saying what I thought he was.

"Fionna?" Arthur asked, the warm green of his eyes filled with concern. His merciful gaze stunned me. Battle I understood. Strength, and competition, and kill or be killed. But forgiveness?—it took my breath away. A gift as tender and delicate as a newborn lamb. And one freely given. I wondered again, for the hundredth time, about what a strange manner of man King Arthur Pendragon was. Strange and unexpected and wonderful.

They were waiting for me to speak. I struggled to find my voice. I was still shaky after having stared into the dark of the abyss. "Ye would forgive me?" I asked, still not daring to believe his pardon could be true. That everything could go back to how it was . . . surely, this was a cruel dream and I would awake with Aideen in my arms and my father snoring like an old, grizzled bear nearby. And my knights? They would remain pure and whole and I would be spotless in their eyes, as before. The possibility of such a gift, of forgiveness, carved a gaping hole in my chest and I peered up, afraid to see truth.

Arthur blinked shyly at me, in that boyish way of his, before standing tall as king once more. "I believe you were acting under duress from one of my enemies. You cannot be entirely faulted for your actions." He swallowed and I watched as his Adam's apple bobbed. "And . . . and we need you. You've seen the curse. How the dark magic is poisoning Caerleon. We need your help to find the Grail. Help us find this fae relic and you're forgiven."

"But—" I began, wanting to foolishly protest that I knew nothing that could help them find the mythical bowl.

"Just yer presence will aid us lass," Percival said. "Trust me."

"Will you stay?" Galahad asked, his words breathless with hope.

I looked between them, my heart squeezing painfully as I took in each of their wary faces. Arthur, the sweet verdant warmth of summer; Percival, the playful swirl of ochre leaves in autumn; Lancelot, hard and cold as ice, but with a promise of a thaw. And Galahad. The explosion of life in the spring, exuberant and sensual. How had they so quickly worked their way into the marrow of my bones, the aether of my soul? They were my sun and night and stars, my seasons turning. I could no sooner leave these men than I could leave my own body.

"I will help ye find the Grail. I'll stay." I nodded heartily, all pretenses of a stoic warrior gone. I found I no longer cared. They had seen the real me—raw and imperfect and flawed. And still they welcomed me with open arms. My knees gave out beneath me, but Galahad was there on one side, Percival on the other.

Lancelot stepped forward and pulled a knife from his sheath, slicing the bonds at my wrists. And Arthur. He stepped close and I reached for him, unsure, afraid he would shy from me. But he didn't. He stepped into my arms and I clung to him—breathed in his scent of grass and summer that I feared I would never smell again.

There, in the deep of the forest, with my knights around me, I was overcome by a certainty stronger than anything I had ever felt. Whatever came next, we'd be able to face it.

Together.

Epilogue

Morgana

Perched atop a mossy stone, the crow burned with anger as she watched the Little Dragon King kiss the witch's forehead. The fool human man reeked of cloying pheromones and bruising shame. Did the man even realize he was enchanted still? Compelled by the lily dangling from her throat? Two other weak human men shared turns pulling the witch into an embrace, and the crow nearly cawed with disgust.

Almost, but . . .

A pulse thundered, singing to hers. The crow angled her head in search of the mortal heartbeat she knew intimately. There. The fourth man, who stood apart from the others to emotionally parry the witch's and necklace's charms. The one with glacial eyes and hair as black as her feathers. The one who had made a mockery of her love.

Clíodna be cursed!

Calling upon the forest's dark shadows and the prayers of warmongering men, the crow vaporized into a woman's form. A cool summer breeze swirled around Morgana in a fury of leaves and twigs. Her hair danced like obsidian snakes as her dark magic faded into the rotting forest floor and tree shadows.

"You are weakest of all," she whispered for the breeze's ears alone.

With a flutter of her hand she pushed the wind, warmed with guilt, toward Lancelot. The wildflowers and grass shuddered as her breath passed by. And when her words found their target, they caressed his face and toyed with the curls in his hair.

A muscle in his jaw worked as a flush colored his cheeks, his gaze chilled to ice. Lancelot turned stiffly from her half-brother and his idiots and strode over to his horse. He leaned his forehead against the beast's sleek withers.

A smile twisted her lips as his pulse changed tunes and began thundering with fear instead of desire. The war drums in his chest would demand a fight soon enough. Or some other drastic reaction. She cared not. She was not cowed by him. He deserved to know this torture. She would have loved him for all eternity. Morgana would have traded her immortality to rule a kingdom of man, if Lancelot remained by her side. Or she would have carried him into the Otherworld when his mortal days ended. Now he could rot like the farmlands and the forest beneath her slippers.

The witch may be in Arthur's good graces again, but he hadn't won. Caerleon was her and her sisters' birthright. The honor price for their father's death and mother's defiling. And for their mother's disappearance when Uther Pendragon died at the hands of his enemies—the Saxons. The very tribes who had slain her own father.

She dug her sharp nails into a maple tree until it wept sap. Excalibur would be hers, even if the witch failed in her blind mission. What did the Romans once say? A kingdom divided is easily conquered?

Lancelot tightened the straps on his saddlebag and then looked out into the forest near where she stood. Morgana stepped into golden light, revealing herself to him. They locked eyes.

Her lips curled back in wicked promise and his lips sneered into a cold vow of his own. She laughed, and leaves rustled and fluttered. *I am not done with you yet, little knight,* she thought. Then, the breeze glittered into swollen darkness filled with the sounds of wailing and gnashing of teeth.

The crow flew from the moss-covered stone into the dank shadows of the forest. In a sharp swoop, she turned toward the Irish

Sea to hunt for a vessel pushed by Lir's currents to his misty green Isle and the shores of Ulster.

The Dark Fates had a new course.

Historical Notes

Once upon a time, a starry-eyed college student majoring in geophysics, with high aspirations of becoming a technical writer for the National Oceanic and Atmospheric Administration (NOAA), decided to take classes that fed her equal love of the humanities. And so, she enrolled in an Arthurian Legend class and instantly fell in love with Arthurian Cycle stories and fairy tales (even more than she already had).

Hey there. This is Jesikah, one half of the Wonder-Twin duo known as MoonTree Books (aka Claire Luana & Jesikah Sundin). With our powers combined, we became badass mistresses of fairy tale fiction. Okay, we already were . . . *winks* But, we each have strengths that beautifully meld together in our partnership. Claire is truly magical when it comes to zero drafting and micro-outlining. And my powers manifest best in macro-outlining and research. We both write in ways that border on the poetic and pay hawk-eye attention to characterization. But I digress. Back to the title of this post: Historical Notes.

I. Love. Research. And I love historical factoids.

I also have a love for origin stories. And the Arthurian Legend is a tale with origins as

misty and mysterious as the gateway to the Otherworld. Most of the Arthurian narratives we know today stem from *The History of British Kings* by Geoffrey of Monmouth, a 12th century Welsh cleric who was obsessed with King Arthur and Merlin stories. Medieval tales aside, history buffs do know this: the Arthurian Legend is of Celtic origins and was hijacked by the French courts after the Norman invasion. The Normans, like the

Romans (ha! They kinda rhyme), knew the key to assimilating people groups was to kill their gods. So, they killed their gods by re-writing and assimilating their fables and myths first. King Arthur began as a Bran the Blessed archetype (from the Welsh *Mabinogion*) and was transformed into a biblical King David archetype by the Christian Normans. The Normans even changed the grail from a cauldron-like serving dish, common in Celtic homes, to the cup of Christ.

As I dug deeper into myth origins, I grew frustrated with the druids and medieval monks. The druids were historians and lore keepers for the Celts, whether Gaels or Britons. But—a big BUT—the druids and Celts were orators. It was against their religion to write things down. There were a few heretics in the bunch and so we do have Ogham runes carved into standing stones and a few stone tablets. But not many and certainly not enough to piece together historical details we can confirm absolutely. And with nothing written down, it was easy for medieval monasteries to re-write Celtic history as a propaganda campaign for the Holy Roman Church. And, thus, paganism dissolved into the Otherworld's mist and Christianity became the new state religion.

Despite these unfortunate drawbacks, I did learn a few interesting things about Celtic culture (from the continent and the Isles). The majority of their gods were water born (more on this in a bit). And they were branched out in Star Wars fashion. You either followed the Light side or the Dark side. The Light side were known as the Children of Danu (aka the Túatha dé Danann) and the Dark side were the Children of Domnu (aka the Formorians), as illustrated in *The Ulster Cycle* from Ireland.

The first mention of a "King Arthur" is in the *Historia Brittonum* dated 826 A.D., often attributed to Nennius, a 9th century Celtic monk and historian, who mentioned a "King Arthur" of Caerleon, Wales, also known as the Roman City of the Legion. Camelot is fantasy, which is why dozens of cities throughout Great Britain claim to be Camelot. Some historians even believe Arthur was Ambrosius Aurelianus, a Roman-British war leader from the 5th century who is famed for winning a major battle against the Anglo-Saxons. Me? I don't think Arthur existed. Not as an actual person in history. Rather, he was the equivalent of a super hero to deliver hope and rally the masses. We have The Avengers and they had Arthur Pendragon. That age was fraught with never-ending wars, invasions, territory expansion and border re-assignments, and old gods vs new gods. The people needed a hero to believe in, someone who would unite the masses and bring peace. Arthur was the post-Roman British mythological man for the job.

Another interesting factoid I learned about Celtic culture was their obsession with water sacrifices. When we modern people think of human sacrifices, we often think of a stone table and a bloody mess. But, actually, human sacrifices for the Celts were drownings. Their gods were born from and dwelled in water. And humans weren't the only things sacrificed to the water. Archeologists have found hoards of swords, shields, helmets, spears, and daggers in lakes, ponds, river beds, and even in the oceans around Celtic regions. Lady of the Lake anyone? Why a goddess would lift a sword out of the water makes sense when put in the context of Celtic culture. And Excalibur's inscription? Even more so. "Take me up, cast me away."

But my favorite part of the research? Learning how the Celts were more progressive than modern society with regard to certain social issues. They believed that women were 100% equal to the men, legally and socially. Women in Celtic cultures didn't need a man's approval or permission for . . . *anything*. And, the women practiced polyandry (multiple husbands). So, for those who are trying to piece together how an Arthurian Legend story works with Reverse Harem? This is how. Polyandry was a fairly common practice from what historians are beginning to uncover.

We set our tale in the mid-11th century. By this time, druids had appeared to have died out for nearly 800 years. Forgive our creative license, but Arthurian Legend just wouldn't be the same without Merlin. Also, the official term "knight" was first noted in the late 11th century, after the Norman invasion. Until then, they were just known as noble-titled warriors. And, finally, castles didn't appear until the 12th century, also thanks in part to the Normans. Wooden fortresses and manors were all that existed until then. Still, we used the term "Castle of the Maidens" as that is integral to Arthurian lore and even has Celtic ties.

There's far more, which I will delve into after book two. Especially information on who "Gwenevere" actually was in the myth origins of Arthurian Legend.

If you've read *The Biodome Chronicles*, then you'll recognize my ending: all errors that may exist while trying to represent Celtic and Welsh culture, mythology, geography, and Arthurian Legend elements are entirely mine. I am a storyteller, weaving together information that builds and forms worlds in our imaginations. In the famous words of Nennius, a ninth-century Celtic monk, "I have made a heap of all that I could find."

Your *Knights of Caerleon* lore keeper,

THE THIRD CURSE

by

CLAIRE LUANA
&
Jesikah Sundin

"...there is more to a king than a crown, and far more to a knight than a sword."

The Acts of King Arthur and His Noble Knights

Prologue

Morgana

Briny air ruffled the crow's feathers as a westerly wind skipped across the fathomless blue sky. Below, war tents and craggy moors dotted the landscape. The male who smelled of bitter lust and greed was nearby. Even now, high above the human clamor, she could smell his heart's whispered prayers.

The crow swooped low, gliding past sweat- and dirt-covered males and females and smoke-clouded cook fires. There. The hide tent with the ornate wooden frame. A caw rumbled from the crow and a nearby murder darkened the clear sky. Black feathers rained down, falling upon the encampment like dark, silent omens. With mortal eyes now fastened above, the crow soared low to the ground and slipped into the power-hungry male's tent, landing on his throne of black thorns.

A sharp gasp caught the crow's attention and she hopped on her feet until she faced the back corner. In the bed, crouched in a thin shift and surrounded by furs and blankets, lay a young woman with hair like tumbling autumn leaves and eyes the color of freshly-tilled earth.

Delighted, the crow cawed and the girl startled back, unable to move far. A metallic scent filled the air and the crow fluffed her feathers at the blissful fragrance. A drop of blood fell from the girl's knotted wrists, which now tugged hard on the short rope that was tied to the tent's center beam.

"Please . . ." the young woman rasped. "Do not harm me, I beg of ye. D-D-Donal threatened that . . . that ye would peck my eyes out, if I . . . I did not please him."

Shadows and the desperate prayers of vengeful men at war wrapped around the crow in spectral ribbons. Brittle leaves on the tent's earthen floor caught flight and swirled about in a macabre dance. The small, young woman bit back a shriek and curled into herself to become even smaller at the sight.

Morgana relished Aideen's fright, settling into O'Lynn's black throne as a heady sigh left her chest. Her claw-tipped fingers gripped the arms for show, her black feathered dress fanning over her legs and ruffling as though a thousand birds in flight. "Now, now . . ." Morgana cooed in a saccharin voice. "What would your brave warrior sister think of you this moment?" She lifted from the throne gracefully and moved toward the witch's kin slowly, each step calculated. "Does she know you are a coward? That you sold your pathetic life to a ruthless man to buy your father a few more days on this goddess-forsaken land?"

Tears gathered in Aideen's soft brown eyes and Morgana tilted her head and blinked. "You poor lamb." Reaching the bed, she slid a sharp nail down the girl's cheek, across the throbbing pulse in her neck, down farther to where the young woman's thunderous heart told Morgana everything she needed to know. A hidden strength lay beneath the fearful overtures.

She bared her fangs and Aideen stilled, a catatonic animal attempting to hide her trembling adrenaline. "I will not peck out your eyes today, for I have use of you yet. But you have given me an idea. How to torment your dear sister."

She spun away from Aideen and sauntered back toward the throne, saying, "If only you could see your sister now, writhing naked in the arms of various men, laughing, flirting, indulging in sensual pleasures, while you quake at the thought of the single touch of your husband. So unfair."

Aideen pushed against her restraints and spat, "Fionnabhair would never abandon me or Father! Ye lie! Ye're a queen of lies!"

"Do I now?" A faint smile played at the corners of her mouth. "We shall see."

Just as the words left her lips, the tent's flaps opened and Donal O'Lynn marched in, halting mid-stride. His gaze raked over Morgana and she twisted sideways, allowing him a better view of her breasts and narrow hips. O'Lynn was weak, easy to manipulate. A soft female body was all it took to stir his blood into submissive obedience. Morgana tilted her gaze toward Aideen, a cruel smile curling her lips, before turning back toward O'Lynn.

"You wed the girl, I see," she began.

"Aye, two eves past." O'Lynn strode toward Morgana.

She licked her bottom lip at his approach and his eyes shuttered. "I have visited the port towns of Ulster and spoken to several ship makers."

"Oh?" Donal slowed before her, his eyes taking in her curves, the ones practically spilling out of her slitted bodice. "And what do ye want with ships? I married the younger Allán princess to punish her whore sister and seize the Allán lands as my own. Do ye plan to parade my bride across the sea now?"

Morgana hissed at the mentioned of the witch and O'Lynn's eyebrows shot up.

"Ye promised me power," he practically growled. "Ye promised me kingship. I followed yer directions and the only thing I have at my hip is this wee slip of a girl." He leaned in close to Morgana and whispered, "A man of power craves more to keep him warm at night than this." He flung his arm out in Aideen's direction and the small, young woman sucked in a sharp breath.

"A man of power also craves war." Morgana trailed her nail across his bottom lip, before leaning down and nibbling the soft flesh with the points of her fangs, until he yielded to her with a moan. Satisfied, she flicked her tongue out to soothe the pain, then whispered, "Why let a female knight gain you a kingdom with a stolen sword when you can conquer a high king and steal the crown for yourself."

Donal separated enough to trace the curves of her breasts with the tips of his fingers, his voice ragged with need as he murmured, "Why indeed?"

"You want me?" she purred.

"Ye know I do."

"Bring war to Briton and defeat Arthur Pendragon and . . ." His eyes lifted to meet hers, his chest rising and falling in an alluring rhythm. The panting tempo of a stupid man. She blinked slowly at him. "And I will fulfill your every fantasy."

"I would die happy in your arms, Morgana," he growled.

She smiled as the shadows and whispers returned, swirling about her body. "Of course, you would."

The crow cocked her head and stared at the delicate young woman on the bed.

A tiny smile of challenge crossed her dirt-smudged face. A hidden strength, indeed.

With a flap of her wings and a loud caw, the crow leaped into flight and left the hide tent to join her dark sisters in the sky.

Chapter One

Arthur

rthur slumped into a chair before the fireplace in his chamber, toeing off his muddy boots. Seven moons and seven suns had passed since he lost Excalibur and then regained his sovereign-blessed sword again.

Seven days since he had almost executed the woman he loved. Seven bloody awkward days.

Never had he been happier to see his fortress—to be blessedly alone. The sheer force of will needed to maintain a demeanor of regal aloofness on the ride back to Caerleon had been exhausting. He had wanted to rage and scream and weep at how close he came to losing everything—his kingdom, his kingship. Fionna. But he couldn't let his knights see—these men who were as close to him as brothers—how much nearly executing Fionna had shaken him. Because no matter how close they were, he was still their king and, therefore, he needed to stand apart. And they were competitors for Fionna's heart. Even now. He made his knights swear that Fionna would never come between them. But he could feel the rip and tear already. In his own heart.

Arthur nodded his thanks absentmindedly as a set of maids hurried in, carrying buckets of hot water to a big copper bathing basin. His mind was filled with Fionna. He was all sensation and torment when it came to her. The sweet ache of the night they had spent together, the sharp cut of her betrayal. The staggering relief as she stepped in to embrace him, to accept his forgiveness.

Was it a mistake to forgive her? His heart shouted a vehement, "No!" But his heart wasn't particularly trustworthy as of late.

Fionna had tried to corner him time and again, from the very first day of their ride back. To explain or thank him, he wasn't sure. He just knew he couldn't face her. Not yet. He felt unsettled and raw, and the sight of her—the sorrow in her silver eyes—seemed to tilt his world farther. He had avoided her, attending to his horse, the fire, his fingernails, anything in the immediate vicinity that wasn't Fionna. Eventually, Lancelot had taken her aside and spoken quietly to her. And though her lovely face had darkened, she took whatever advice Lancelot had offered, and blessedly let Arthur be.

Arthur closed his eyes as the splashing sound of water being poured into the tub soothed his tension. Now, if only he could leave her alone.

Arthur lingered in his bath for far too long, until the water cooled to lukewarm and colored gray from the grit of his journey. He had asked the others, including Merlin, to gather in his study after bathing and filling their bellies with food.

His chest tightened, and then a ragged breath fluttered free. "You can't avoid her forever," he muttered to himself. He had nursed his wounded heart and pride long enough. It was time to put the events of the past week behind him.

Time to be a king again.

Arthur was feeling more like his old self when he strode into his study. He wore a linen tunic in a rich burgundy shade, black breeches, and polished black leather boots. The gold oak leaf circlet rested on his head and Excalibur swung at his hip. The sword would never leave his side again. Not while he lived.

He was the last to arrive, from all appearances; the other knights were arrayed in various chairs around the room. Lancelot, in a blue tunic that set off the black of his hair and the sky-blue of his eyes; Percival, sitting behind Arthur's desk, his feet up with a book in his lap; Galahad, dwarfing one of the two armchairs by the fire, polishing a dagger. And Fionna, in the other armchair, her hands in her lap, her head tilted down in a look of contrition that fit her about as well as a jester's motley on a yuletide goose. Her white-blonde hair was now washed and rebraided. But rather than a dress that would set off her curves and softness—a dress like the one she had worn for the faerie ambassador's visit—she wore a simple tunic and breeches like a man. At least, dressing for practicality suited her. And helped him to see her as a fellow knight—not as a woman.

Merlin strode up to Arthur and clapped him on the shoulder, pulling Arthur from his rambling thoughts. "I sense that you've endured an eventful week," the druid said. The gold rings of his eyes flashed with magic and compassion.

"That would be the understatement of the century," Arthur murmured, forcing a laugh. "Good to see you, my friend."

"Likewise." Merlin's hands disappeared back into the pockets of his coarse, gray robes.

Arthur marched to the front of the room by the fireplace and turned, crossing his arms across his still too-tight chest. "Have the knights filled you in on our journey?" Arthur asked Merlin.

"Yes. Though I suspect I received the . . . abridged version."

Arthur nodded. "Good. All the details of our trip to find Lord Bronn are not important. There is only one focus we must concern ourselves with now. Finding the Grail and curing this unnatural curse that has befallen Caerleon."

"Lancelot said the land's curse affected the river?" Merlin asked. "Caerleon's waters are poisoned?"

"That's what we saw," Galahad volunteered. "Everything the river touched withered and died, whether flora or fauna."

"We haven't yet received reports of any human deaths," Merlin said. "But this poison will spread quickly, now that the curse has fully begun."

"I will send word to the villages, instructing them to test the water before drinking from their wells, streams, or river," Arthur said. "This sickness . . . it is unnatural. Reminded me of old tales of Fomorian magic."

Merlin narrowed his eyes. "Indeed. They have not emerged from the sea's abyss in decades."

"Not the same as permanently banished, druid," Lancelot tossed out.

"True. And if they have emerged, we have much to fear."

Arthur pressed his lips together. "We must find the Grail soon or there won't be anyone in Caerleon left to warn."

Merlin turned to Percival. "Tell me of this stone you found. You are certain of the runic message?"

Percival sat up, pulling his feet off the desk. The copper-haired lad looked older, more world-weary. Perhaps he felt the weight of their quest settled squarely upon his shoulders. "Aye, I'm certain. The stone revealed a riddle to me. *Across the wall and atop the rock hill, the blessed five shall drink their fill.*"

"And you've interpreted this to mean that Caer Benic is in the Kingdom of Alba, located near the Strathclyde city of Castellum Puellarum?" Merlin tilted his head, considering. "I concur."

"We must leave at once," Arthur said. "Caerleon grows sicker with each passing candle mark."

"Don't leave in undue haste," Merlin said. "Knowing the location of the Grail is not enough. There are powerful magics that protect the vessel of the old gods. You must be prepared to face each defensive measure."

Arthur grimaced, though he knew Merlin offered wise counsel. "Very well. Tell us. How can we prepare?"

Merlin paced across the room, his gaze sharpening as his pupils narrowed. "Legends speak of three sacred relics that will aid the seeker in finding the Grail. The key, the stone, and the sword."

A tiny smile tugged the corner of Galahad's lips. They all recognized the patterned cue of Merlin's bardic nature as a lore keeper. A story was about to unfold.

"The Otherworld," Merlin began, "is comprised of three realms. The spirit lands of the Mother Goddess, the Underworld, and the *In-Between.* These realms are woven into the fabric of Earth and are as natural to her lands as they are unnatural. Three realms with three ways to enter but only two ways to leave, three ways to see what human eye cannot but five ways to unsee, and three ways to defend your mortal soul from immortal blood but only one way to truly lose your soul."

"Faerie riddles," Lancelot practically moaned. "Druid, our patience runs thin."

"Impatience," he hissed, his pupil's growing narrower, "is a fool's temptress. She will only lead you to ruin and shame. The real object of your affection is worth every wait, wouldn't you agree, Faerie Prince?"

Lancelot clenched his jaw.

"Where was I? Oh yes. The Story of Three's. Three sacred relics tied to the Grail, each object won with a test. One to prove what a man will sacrifice himself for. One to prove the true measure of strength. The last to prove whom he will serve."

"The key, the stone, and the sword," Percival murmured.

"The key to unlock the Otherworld," Merlin *finally* began to explain. "The stone to see invisible magic. And the sword to slay lies for truth."

"Do you know the location of any of these relics?" Arthur asked, his stomach churning in endless knots. He had to agree with Lancelot. Merlin's words set his mind spinning.

Merlin shook his head.

"So, we have *four* quests now, instead of one?" Lancelot asked, incredulous.

"Perhaps not," Merlin said. "I know of a woman who might be able to locate the key for you. She is a Bone Carver in Maesbury Marsh. If I were you, I would inquire with her first."

"And if she cannot help us?" Galahad asked. "What then?"

Arthur felt the air in his lungs grow hot as panic began to boil in his blood. "You must accompany us, Merlin. I will fall on my knees and beg of you, if I must. I can ill afford to fail this quest. My people do not deserve to suffer for my half-sister's thirst for war and death. You are best equipped to interpret any clues we may find. And to neutralize any hostile magic we encounter."

Merlin leveled his all-seeing gaze at Arthur as his lips pressed into a straight line. "I am sorry, Your Majesty, but I cannot go."

"And if I demand it of you, as your king?"

"The standing stone spoke of the blessed five. Not the blessed six," Merlin countered, but Arthur understood the underlying message. Merlin was not his to command, for he belonged to the gods, not man.

Gritting his teeth, Arthur turned away, nearly flinching when Merlin continued. "And unless my counting skills have fled me, you are the blessed five. Isn't that right, Percival?"

"He speaks truth," Percival said with certainty. It was strange to see the lad without a jest on his lips. Unsettling.

"And if I might say," Merlin turned his keen gaze to Fionna, "your fifth knight is strangely quiet. Are you well, My Lady?"

Fionna had been sitting silently, staring into the fire for the duration of the meeting. At Merlin's address, she looked up. "I am well. I will go where my king commands, of course. I had nothing of import to add to yer comments, druid."

Merlin's eyebrows nearly met his hairline as he turned to Arthur.

Arthur shifted uncomfortably. He understood what Fionna was doing. Acting contrite to prove her loyalty in the face of her betrayal. But this pale, meek version of Fionna wouldn't do. No, this wouldn't do at all. It pained him to see her so—the fight snuffed out of her, the fire doused. The Fionna he knew was a force of nature—a shooting star of passion and power. He thought he would rather lose her again than keep this caged, dim copy of the woman he loved. A woman he had pushed away in his anger and grief. And in his fear. She knew the beating rhythm of his heart, knew him in ways unlike any woman before her. As a bastard-born prince—and now a king—he had guarded himself from intimacy . . . until her. Another rip tore through his chest, the bleeding gap growing deeper. Wider. Perhaps the water around Caerleon wasn't the only thing poisoned.

Arthur gave Merlin a little shake of his head, shoving down his troubled thoughts. Caerleon needed to be his priority. Not Fionna. After they found the Grail, he could deal with the mess his life had become. Not before.

Chapter Two

Fionnabhair

I couldn't bring myself to meet Arthur's eyes. My gaze darted everywhere else—the floor, the fire, the nick in my leather belt—but I couldn't bear the look in his eyes. Arthur may have forgiven me, but he hadn't forgotten. He probably never would.

The weight of what I had done pulled at me like a stone dropped in a pool. True, I did have my reasons for stealing Excalibur—and good ones at that. But now I knew not what would become of my father, Brin, and my sister, Aideen, while held prisoner by our enemies, Clann Uí Tuírtri. Surely their chieftain, Donal O'Lynn, would realize soon how I had failed in my mission, if he didn't know already. What would he do to my family in his anger? The very thought of how they may suffer for my weakness, for my inability to finish the one task O'Lynn set before me as ransom for their lives, tormented my tattered heart.

Nor could I live with how my knights suffered for my duplicity. I knew they did, each one, even the aloof Lancelot, who seemed to relish in my betrayal with black satisfaction.

Perhaps the weight I felt wasn't my guilt. Perhaps I am the millstone, dragging down those I love into the dark abyss where even worse monsters dwell. I held in a ragged sigh and chanced a look around the room.

The knights were leaving Arthur's study, filing out one-by-one. Galahad and Percival each slipped me an encouraging smile, one I tried my best to return. I thought I could find my way back into the blessed good graces of those two. Arthur and Lancelot? . . . Another story.

My body ached, more so as I pushed myself up from the chair. Only Arthur and I now remained in his study. He had partially turned away from me and fidgeted with a book on a shelf to appear busy. Pain from my shoulder injury throbbed, a pain I could account for. The rest? It was like my body manifested the sorrow of my soul—my heart. I felt old and worn. He appeared similarly. Gone was the boyish smile and the summer light in his earthen gaze. Now, dark circles bruised the delicate skin beneath his eyes; his beautiful lips pulled tight into a thin line. Still, I wanted to reach out, to do something to bridge the chasm of our brokenness. Our wound screamed silent between us, a jagged sensation that rippled the air.

"Yer Majesty," I said, not yet ready to leave. There was so much I wanted to say to him. The unsaid words burned within me. But he didn't acknowledge my request for his attention, though the sudden rigidness of his posture suggested that he heard me. I drew in a shaky breath and blew it out slowly.

"That night—" I began and stopped. A knot in my throat tightened but I pushed forward. "That night meant something to me. Ye mean something to me—"

"I have been thinking on the matter of your honor price," Arthur said in reply, cutting me off. He twisted toward my direction and snapped shut the book in his hand.

I blinked in flushed surprise at the harshness of his rebuke, of his dismissal of my heartfelt confession. The memories of our reunion on the road to Brunanburh—of Arthur's hands running down my back in soothing lines, his strong arms circling my waist protectively, me sobbing into his chest—now seemed a distant dream. He placed a carefully built wall between us and meant to keep each stone intact. Well, if that was how he wished our relationship to be, then I suppose that was how we would have it.

"An honor price . . ." I hadn't been expecting this, though I should have offered one myself. An honor price was a sum paid to the kinsmen of an injured clannsman as recompense for the injury. Was there any price that would make right what I had done?

"Of course," I managed. "Whatever ye think is fair . . ."

"I think your assistance in locating the Blessed Grail is sufficient payment for breaking your oath," Arthur said. "I realize what you sacrifice by remaining here." His face was impassive, but there was sympathy in his grass-green eyes that twisted my heart anew. How very Arthur, to worry for me despite what I had done. This gave me hope. If he worried for me, if he understood what was at stake, perhaps he could find room for me in his heart once again. But even as the fevered hope surfaced, I dashed it. Things would never be as they once were. I needed to hold myself apart. For all our sakes.

My heart most of all.

"If ye think this price is sufficient," I said, "I will devote myself to helping ye find the Grail and heal Caerleon. Yer land and people don't deserve to suffer such a cruel fate." The poison I had seen seeping through the lifeblood of Caerleon, of all of Briton, chilled me. I knew faeries could be fickle vindictive creatures, but to force such suffering on innocents was unjust.

And I had to admit, a part of me was curious. Percival and Merlin both had named me as an integral player in the quest for the Grail. Why? I thought of when Merlin asked me about my mother, his strange gold-rimmed eyes blinking in the dark. Why had he seemed so certain there was something unusual about my heritage? Perhaps I would find answers on this journey.

"If you join our Grail quest," Arthur said, "your help will repay this honor price and more."

I wanted to swear to him that I would never hurt him again, but I knew this promise was one I couldn't keep. After all, I hadn't foreseen how the goddess would set our fates against each other last time. How could I be certain heartbreak wouldn't happen again?

"I hope there is never more to repay," I said softly.

Arthur gave me a terse nod. "On that we can agree."

I wanted to reach out to him, to run my hands through his hair, to feel the firmness of his muscles beneath my fingers. But I stilled my hands at my sides. I had lost such privileges.

"I was also thinking on your family's situation," Arthur continued. "It doesn't sit well with me that they might suffer while you aid me here in Caerleon."

The air burned in my lungs as I held my breath.

"With your permission, I would like to ransom your family."

A faint gasp escaped my knotted throat, too overcome by his kindness, his generosity. Arthur attempted to hide a blush by pretending to inspect the spine of the book in his hands. "Of course," I whispered with relief. "I would be most grateful for yer aid. But I fear nothing short of Excalibur would be payment enough."

Arthur's mouth set in a thin line once more. "Every man has his price," he murmured. "Even this O'Lynn. Besides, my motives are not entirely selfless. Perhaps my envoy can discover the identity of this friend of O'Lynn's who set us all down this wretched path."

"Yes, please, if ye can save my father and sister . . . I would be forever in your debt." I let out a hollow laugh. "Even more so than I already am."

"Very well." He flit his gaze my way for a single shuttered heartbeat, before pivoting toward the bookshelf once again. "I will send my man, and keep you apprised of his progress."

"Thank you," I said, sensing I was being dismissed. I suppose this was a better conversation than I could have hoped for, far better than I deserved. I would take it.

I wandered into the hall, my surroundings dissolving into the roiling tempest within me. When my thoughts resurfaced to the present, I found myself ambling through the fortress toward the stable to check on my mare, Zephyr. Another loved one I had wounded with my foolish flight. Galahad had promised to send for the farrier, but I feared what the doctor might find. What if her tendon was permanently damaged? If I lost Zephyr too . . . I shoved the thought away. No. That would be too cruel a hand for the goddess to deal me.

When I entered the stable, I found a wizened man in Zephyr's stall, a puff of white hair at his temples. He seemed to be mumbling to himself as he examined her, disappearing behind the stable door as he leaned down to examine the cannon of her leg.

I started as another head popped up in exchange, this one a mess of black curly hair. Lancelot. I must have said his name out loud because he turned to me, his expression darkening.

"How is she," I asked, pressing myself against the stall door, then reaching my hand out to stroke Zephyr's nose.

"A strain," the little man stood. Despite his small stature and advanced age, he looked fit and strong. His rolled-up tunic sleeves revealed wiry forearms, his brown eyes clear and sharp. "She should stay off this leg for two weeks at least, no hard riding for a month. But she'll recover. She's strong."

I sagged against the stall in relief. "Thank ye."

The farrier pushed out through the door, brushing the hay and horse hair off his hands. He turned to Lancelot. "I'll send His Majesty my bill."

"You always do," Lancelot said with a laugh.

I watched as the little man strolled out of the stable before turning to Lancelot.

He gave Zephyr a pat, and she lipped his curly hair in response, nickering.

I narrowed my eyes. When had they become so friendly? "What are ye doing here?" I asked. My tone came out more accusatory than intended.

"I see no need to take your treachery out on the mare," Lancelot practically sneered. "She's a fine beast."

"I know," I said. "I raised her from a foal."

"Guess that's one thing you did right," Lancelot replied, shouldering past me.

I narrowed my eyes farther and marched after him, grabbing his arm and spinning him around. I might be contrite around the other knights, but Lancelot . . . Lancelot infuriated me. And it felt good to feel something other than guilt for a change.

"If we're going on this quest together, we better find a way to get along," I practically spat. "Ye've been cold from the start. So, tell me, Sir Lancelot, what in the bloody hell did I ever do to ye?"

Chapter Three

Lancelot

ionna was a biting winter wind and the scorching summer sun when angry, a true sight to behold. But Lancelot knew this dark, all-consuming emotion intimately—he was a master of icy fury himself. He was angry at her, angry at Morgana, angry at himself, angry at the whole damn situation.

He took a step closer to her, leaned in, then grit between clenched teeth, "What did *you* ever do to *me*? Besides cheat your way into our knighthood, lie to us about your reasons here, steal my king and friend's most precious possession, and make the knights of Caerleon fawn all over you like lovesick idiots?" Lancelot threw out his hands. "It's so hard to pick just one!"

"I didn't cheat my way into the tournament." Fionna pointed her finger in his face.

He let out a harsh laugh. Of all her numerated wrongs, that's the one that bothered her?

"I just made sure I had a fair shot. And yes, I lied and took Excalibur, but ye dismissed me the moment my sex was revealed! Why?"

Lancelot looked at the timbered ceiling, a muscle in his jaw pulsing as he searched for any explanation but the truth. That Morgana had cursed him. That she had foretold how he would love a

Gwenevere, and that their coupling would destroy Arthur and all of Caerleon. And that he was growing more and more certain that the white enchantress foretold was indeed Fionna.

"The truth, Lancelot," Fionna spat. The way she hurled his name, the way her Irish brogue danced across the syllables, full of passion and fire . . . it nearly undid him. She stood just inches from his rigid body, hands firmly planted on her slender hips, waiting. He tried not to look at her lips, not react to the warm breath pulsing on his skin. It was nearly impossible. Her silver eyes glittered like diamonds amongst the drab brown of the stable.

"Why do *you* deserve truth when you've told us nothing but lies?"

"I haven't lied," Fionna said, her voice thickening. "Not about the things that mattered."

Lancelot heaved a sigh and flyaway strands around her face fluttered. "Your presence changes everything. We were a brotherhood. Allies, friends, kin. Now? I don't know what we are. Perhaps we haven't come to blows yet, but it's only a matter of time." His gaze caressed the curve of her blushing cheeks, her flushed lips, and drank in how her breasts rose and fell in a furious rhythm, before he continued in clipped tones. "We're . . . *competitors*. Rivals. Arthur thinks a promise is enough to keep us from turning on each other, but he's naïve." Lancelot's eyes snapped to hers once more. "I *know* human nature. We're heading for a fall. It's inevitable."

"Rivals?" Fionna asked quietly.

"For your heart, Fionna," Lancelot derided, rolling his eyes. Fool woman would make him spell it out?

She reared back a few steps, as if struck.

"Ye said *we* . . ." she whispered, her lips trembling. "*We're* . . . competitors."

"Would you like a prize?" Lancelot nearly spat at her. "Congratulations. You're beautiful and I desire you, like the rest of my besotted brothers. Are you happy now?"

"No." Tears were gathering on her pale lashes.

Lancelot closed his eyes, steadying himself, trying to rein in the wild fury galloping through his veins. He took in a deep, shuddering breath. "I made a mistake with Morgana and it cost us all dearly. Me, Arthur—Caerleon is still paying for my weakness." His lids blinked open and his gaze captured hers. "When I look at you, I see another mistake waiting to happen. So, I must hold myself aside. Do you understand?"

Fionna's shoulders raised a notch higher. "I understand. But believe that I would never ruin what ye and the other knights have. I wouldn't allow ye to turn against each other.

Oh Fionna, Lancelot thought. *Don't you see that you already have?*

She continued, "I would leave before that happened."

He struggled to keep his voice even, calm. "Then why didn't you leave?!"

"I—I tried."

"You let yourself get caught."

"Let myself?" her brows furrowed. "Zephyr injured herself, and the boats in the harbor were cinders . . ."

He stepped toward her again, their bodies nearly touching. Wanting her to breathe in every spiteful word, he lowered his face toward hers, and darkly whispered, "You are one of the smartest and craftiest warriors I have ever met. Yet you chose to take Excalibur without a clear exit strategy, in strange territory, on a black night, when you were weak from an injury. Fionna," he breathed her name, bitter, pleading, "if you had wanted Excalibur, *really* wanted that damn sword, you would be in Ulster by now."

Her mouth opened and then slowly closed as she took in his meaning. The whole scenario was clear as day to him. She hadn't wanted to succeed in stealing Arthur's sword. She hadn't really wanted to leave.

"So, you see," he said, taking a few steps back, wanting her to feel the sudden cold of his distance. "You've chosen to stay, even if you don't truly know it yet. But that means there can be a happy ending for only one man. Once you choose, perhaps the tension between us will ease. Still, for the unchosen . . ." Watching Fionna with whoever won her heart would be torture.

Fionna twisted a braid in her hand, her eyes fixed on the hay-strewn floor of the stable. "Why can't . . ." she seemed to draw her courage around herself, looking up. "Why can't I choose all of ye?"

Lancelot snorted. "That's a bit greedy of you, isn't it?"

She set her jaw. "Is it such an outlandish desire?"

By the gods, she was serious! "Perhaps not among the faerie folk, but humans generally seem to gravitate toward one mate."

"Perhaps in Briton, but not always in Ireland," Fionna said. "There are women in my clann and other Dál nAraidi who have more than one husband."

Lancelot raised an eyebrow, temporarily lost for words. The idea was intriguing. He had always enjoyed the company of both men and women, and society's prudish insistence on traditional modes of virtue and chastity had always annoyed him. But despite his modern proclivities, he had never considered such an arrangement could be possible in Briton.

"I admit, I have not heard of such marital relations existing in other Gaelic lands."

"There are plenty of reasons to take more than one husband. To increase warriors for one's clann, for political alliances, to keep the gene pool varied. Women are equal to the men in Ireland. If a man wants multiple wives to bear him sons to farm and daughters to gain him bride prices, then a woman can have multiple husbands for a stronger homestead and financial prestige among her clanns-men." Fionna softened her voice and said, "Least of all reasons? That ye love yer men."

"And here, when I was with two women, I got a whole king-dom cursed," Lancelot remarked dryly.

"I always thought Morgana's reaction too harsh . . ." Fionna's words trailed off as she shifted on her feet and cleared her throat, her gaze darting around the stables. "I am not suggesting such an arrangement between us. I don't even know if such a relationship would be possible here, or if the other men would desire or toler-ate this solution. All I know is that I feel a tie between each of us, a kinship that I cannot deny. My heart belongs to each of ye. The sacred five Merlin speaks of? Perhaps we are more than our simple number of knights."

Lancelot nodded begrudgingly. He felt this connection too. There was something that tied them together. This tether had al-ways existed. Though, he had previously thought those intimate feelings just the mere bonds of brotherhood, his affection and re-gard for the warriors whom he had grown up with and respected. But Fionna's addition had completed the circle somehow. No, not a circle. A pentacle. With each point inextricably linked to the other.

"Perhaps ye do not trust me yet," she continued in his silence. "But ye have my word, Lancelot. I will not tear yer brotherhood apart. Perhaps we can find a way . . . where no one needs to choose. And no one is left in the cold."

The silvered ice of her eyes bore into the glacial blue of his, challenging him to see the possibility. The very thought that each of them could find love in Fionna's arms, and she in theirs? A beau-tiful dream.

But only a dream. For Lancelot would be left in the cold, no matter what happiness the other knights found. Morgana ensured that cold, aching loneliness would be the only future in store for him.

Percival

Percival was a fount of nervous energy as he bounded across the keep toward the stable yard. He could hardly believe this day was truly here. They were riding out to find the Blessed Grail. Years he had been waiting, learning, chaffing under the weight of his father's legacy, his Fisher King heritage. Yet now someone had smiled upon him. The Mother Goddess? The sídhe, perhaps? Who the hell really knew? Whoever they were, they had shown him something that could save Caerleon, save his king's rule.

Finally, Percival would have a chance to prove his worth to his king and his fellow knights. Not to mention relieve himself of this cursed vow of chastity. Good riddance there.

Their fifth knight was in Zephyr's stall, a wistful smile on her face as she brushed down her mare.

"Fionna!" Percival said, and then winced at how his greeting came out—far too eager and excited, like a little boy before a giant rain puddle. If he were to compete for Fionna's heart, she needed to see him as more than a green lad. He was a man. A warrior. A sídhe-blessed Grail prince. He cleared his throat, lowering his voice a touch. "How is she?" he asked.

"On the mend," Fionna said, giving Zephyr a final pat. "Feels wrong to journey without her, ye know?"

"She'll be fat and happy when we return, ye'll see." Percival smiled. "Do ye need a mount for the trek?"

"Already handled," Galahad boomed in his deep baritone, leading a saddled white mare from her stall.

Percival pursed his lips. Of course, Galahad was already here, seeing to Fionna's every need. He was a worthy opponent for their lady knight's heart, and Percival's excitement over their departure dimmed.

"Aster is a fine mount," Percival murmured in quiet reassurance. Fionna quirked an eyebrow at his apparent shift in mood, so he quickly added, "Swift and surefooted. She'll treat ye well until ye get back to Zephyr."

"Thank ye both." A touch of a wry smile flitted across Fionna's face.

Percival pushed into Kit's stall, pulling his tack off the hooks on the wall. When he turned, he was surprised to find Fionna lingering there by the door, watching him work. She rested her elbows over the stall door, gnawing the inside of her bottom lip, her eyes darting around Kit's stall, looking everywhere but him. Uncertainty was an uncommon look on her, and he furrowed his brows.

"Percival," she said, hesitating. "I haven't had a chance to thank ye."

"Och, lass. Fer what?" he asked innocently, though he knew of what she spoke.

Fionna rolled her eyes. How did she make an eyeroll look so lovely? "Ye know what, ye wily fox. For riding to my rescue at the last moment. For vouching for me. For stopping Arthur from . . ." she swallowed.

"Nae, he wouldn't have," Percival said.

"He seemed fairly intent upon his course," Fionna countered.

"I helped remind him, sure. But Arthur would have stayed his hand, ye ken? It's not in his nature. He sees the truth in people, and judges them thusly. And ye, dove, are a good person."

"Am I, now?" she let out a harsh laugh, examining her fingernails. "I feel I hardly know myself anymore. Ever since I came to Caerleon, I've felt . . ."

"Confused? Overwhelmed?" Percival suggested, throwing his

saddle over Kit's withers. He knew what she was experiencing. The first couple of months had been much the same for him when he had first come here. "Arthur is like . . . a lodestone. I don't know if the attraction is because of Excalibur, or this place, or the Pendragon lineage, but he pulls people to him—he shapes the course of their lives by his very presence. It's easier if ye dinnae resist."

A smile quirked on her lips. "When did ye become so wise?"

"Stick with me dove, I'm full of surprises." Percival winked at her.

Fionna laughed, the sound bright as a babbling brook yet soft like snowfall on leaves. It warmed him. She had been too quiet and withdrawn since they had returned from Ewloe.

"I almost feel normal with ye," Fionna said. "Though I know that's not possible."

Percival gave an experimental tug on Kit's girth. The gelding liked to hold his breath to keep Percival from buckling his saddle as tightly has he should. *Clever beast.* Percival pulled the strap another notch tighter. Then he pushed open the stall door, and Fionna backed up, holding the door open for him. "Ye can feel normal with me," Percival said, as Fionna fell into step beside him. "I know ye may not believe me for a time, lass. But I forgive ye."

"I'm grateful to have one of ye on my side," she said.

"They'll come around," Percival said. "We understand yer reasons. I might have stolen Excalibur myself, were I in yer position. Well, except for the part about kissing the daylights out of Arthur. He's not my type."

Fionna's face turned scarlet. "Ye know about . . . our night together?" she whispered.

"Our rooms shared a wall. I've heard Arthur snore, and the sounds coming from his room were certainly not the snoring kinds."

Fionna buried her face into her hands.

"Never fear, My Lady," Percival said cheerfully. "I consider ye kissing the king a mere setback in my plans to convince ye that I am the knight most deserving of yer affection."

His tone was lighthearted, to put her at ease and numb her embarrassment. But he meant every word. Fionna had neither declared that her heart belonged to Arthur nor Galahad, despite having shared intimate moments with each. That meant Percival still had a chance.

Fionna placed a hand on his shoulder and smiled. "Percival, ye wonderful, foolish man."

"We usually leave off the 'wonderful' part," Galahad said, swaggering over, looking as big and as brash as ever. Percival swallowed a moment of envy. It wasn't fair to have to compete with muscles like those. But, he reminded himself, what Galahad offered in brawn, Percival more than made up for in wit. And what woman didn't like to laugh?

Arthur and Lancelot were standing across the stable yard, speaking quietly, as servants affixed heavy saddlebags to their mounts, laden with provisions for the journey.

A look of quiet thunder crossed Arthur's face as he saw Fionna standing between Percival and Galahad. His hand strayed to Excalibur at his side, as if checking that the sword was still there. Percival stifled a sigh. He *did* believe that the easy peace they had once enjoyed between the five of them would return. But healing took time.

Arthur and Lancelot strode into the stables, their boots crunching over the dried meadow grasses strewn across the yard. Lancelot caught Percival's eye, a dark look on the man's handsome face as he darted quick look at Fionna before seeking Percival's attention once more. Percival cocked his head and arched an eyebrow, a gesture that seemed to calm their dark knight a smidgeon. A reaction that also made Percival's pulse secretly blush. For some odd reason, the man seemed to quietly seek Percival's comfort, and often. Lancelot answered Percival's silent questions with a faint shake of his head, before crossing muscular arms over his chest and returning his focus back on Arthur.

Percival studied the way Lancelot's soft black curls fell across the frosty blue of his eyes and how a light shadow of stubble covered the firm set of his jaw. A strange tingle brewed in his chest, one Percival didn't quite understand. Or had ever when around him.

Blinking back the direction of his thoughts, Percival offered

Arthur a nod and asked, "Are we ready, My King?"

"As ready as we can be for a journey into the unknown." Arthur's voice was clear and strong. Percival recognized the tone—the one he used for kingly speeches and formal occasions. A tone that hardly seemed appropriate for just the five of them.

Percival opened his mouth to make a quip, but a black look from Lancelot shut it again. Percival narrowed his eyes playfully in reply, resisting the urge to stick his tongue out instead. Fine. If Arthur needed to hold himself apart, then so be it.

Arthur continued. "We all heard Merlin. We may face trials and tests, strange and foreign magics. The guardians of the Grail will not yield their sacred vessel willingly. First, we must find this relic, and then we must prove ourselves worthy."

Fionna paled, though her jaw was set with determination. She had faced trials aplenty the last few days. Percival didn't blame her for not wanting to forge ahead so soon.

"Should any of you encounter or feel anything strange, no matter how seemingly inconsequential, you share it. Especially you, Percival," Arthur said. "We can't afford to miss a clue. Or a warning."

The knights nodded.

"Then we ride to Castellum Puellarum," Arthur said. "To hunt a Grail."

"Your Majesty!" A servant in Arthur's red and gold livery was running from the direction of the keep, his round face red. He blew out a breath as he skittered to a stop before them, giving a hasty bow. "Your Majesty, a messenger."

"What is it?" Arthur asked, his eyebrows drawing together.

"There's been an attack near Talgarth," the man panted.

"What kind of an attack?"

"The Twrch Trwyth."

Arthur recoiled, and Lancelot let out a string of curses under his breath.

"The Twrch Trwyth in the Kingdom of Gwent?" Arthur's hand tightened on Excalibur's hilt.

"What is this . . ." Galahad stumbled over the name. "Twrch Trwyth?"

Fionna's lips thinned to a straight line. "A legendary faerie boar from Ireland."

"Though, this is not the first time Twrch Trwyth has visited Wales," Arthur added. To Galahad, he said, "I grew up on stories of this faerie boar. The monster was responsible for the destruction of many villages, leaving a path of ravaged homes, crops, and livestock across several neighboring kingdoms nearly a century ago."

"I thought the faerie boar was killed during Culhwch's impossible tasks?" Fionna asked.

Arthur considered her, as if forgetting that she was in their company. "I was under the same impression. I was told the faerie boar fell off a cliff into the sea."

Fionna's eyes widened. "To the realm of the Fomorians."

"This could be another of Morgana's schemes," Lancelot practically spat. "Designed to keep us from the Grail and, thus, the cure for her curse. The curse is the more pressing threat."

"Perhaps," Arthur said to Lancelot. "But the Twrch Trwyth rampaging through my lands will leave a trail of carnage behind even more quickly than the curse. Talgarth is on the way to Conwy, if we continue this path as you and I had discussed in the war room." Arthur turned to the servant. "Tell whoever brought these dark tidings that King Arthur and his knights will ride to their aid."

"So, we ride fer Talgarth," Percival said, offering Arthur an encouraging grin. "To hunt a faerie boar."

"And *then* to Castellum Puellarum to hunt the Grail," Galahad added.

"This quest is going to shit already," Lancelot muttered under his breath.

Galahad

Galahad rode through the thick forest behind Fionna, watching closely as she swayed with her horse's easy rhythm. She held herself stiffly, as if even the gentle gait pained her.

"Fionna," he called out.

She turned to peer back at him, and a grimace of pain lined the set of her mouth.

Trotting up beside her, he asked, "How fares your wound?"

"Fine," she clipped.

"You're a horrible liar," he remarked. "I'm amazed you were able to keep your true goal from us for so long."

"The wound pains me still. There. Are ye happy?"

"No, not at all. I don't wish you pain. Did you have the chirurgeon look at your shoulder?"

"Aye, I did. He complimented yer stitching. There's nothing the wound needs but time."

Galahad frowned. "Arthur shouldn't have made us leave on this quest so soon."

Fionna let out a hollow laugh. "Yes, well, it isn't my place to tell him otherwise."

"I see what you're doing," Galahad quietly replied. "But by trying to appease him, to be agreeable and cooperative, is just another form of being false."

Fionna opened her mouth to protest, but he held up a hand. "This quest doesn't need your placating. Our mission, our very lives need your fire and your fight. Your wisdom."

"I don't know how to be around him," she admitted with a sigh. "I don't know how to be around any of ye."

"Just be who you are, Fionna. That's all we ever wanted."

"I fear I don't know myself anymore."

"You do." Galahad offered her a kind smile. "You didn't spend so many years on this earth without learning a thing or two about who you are. Just because a man holds your family for ransom—and forced your hand—doesn't change this truth."

Fionna nodded, but he could still see the uncertainty in her eyes.

"There's more . . ." Galahad cocked his head, studying her.

"Must ye all see so much?" Fionna said ruefully. "I never—" she started, faltered, and took a breath. "I never thought of myself as a woman who would marry. I watched as my friends and fellow warriors fell to love's fickle embrace, and I swore matrimony would never catch me."

"Why?" Galahad asked. "Why would you not want something so wonderful?"

"Is marriage wonderful? Does not love cause many more troubles than it cures? The husband with the wandering eye? The chieftain who desires someone else's bride? The young maiden who ends up pregnant and shunned by her tribe? Or shackled to some oaf who never wanted more than a roll in the hay?"

"Rather cynical," Galahad said. "Was there no one in your life who was happy in love? What about your parents?"

Fionna's silver eyes grew wistful, distant as the fog on the moor, and Galahad realized his misstep.

"My mother died when I was young. My father mourned her. He mourns her still."

"But he has you, and your sister. He never would have, if not for love."

Fionna snorted and gave him a playful push. "Must ye insist upon finding a positive angle for every one of my thoughts? Can a woman not wallow for a while in her own morose feelings?"

"Perhaps for a while," Galahad said with a wink. "But I'm afraid if you wallow much more, I'll have to unleash Percival on you. And he is far more annoyingly positive than I."

"Ye dare not." Fionna laughed.

"Oh, I dare." Galahad raised an eyebrow. The sight of her smile warmed him. Around her, his thoughts were peaceful, though he knew how her betrayal should trouble him. He couldn't bring himself to hate himself for enjoying the pleasure of her company, or worry for her loyalty. Perhaps Lancelot and Arthur doubted her but, somehow, he knew. He saw her soul—deep down where she hid herself—and she was as pure as a mountain stream, and as soft as the breath of a butterfly's wings.

"Galahad . . ." she said. "I kissed Arthur."

"Yes, the night of the faerie wine. Arthur told me."

"No." She shook her head. Her features were twisted, sorrowful. "The night I took Excalibur."

He stilled as details came into focus. Fionna kissed Arthur . . . and then took his sword? "Perhaps," Galahad began, slowly, "I now understand his upset more than I did before."

"Yer not angry with me? After what we . . . shared?"

He tested the feelings within him, like taking the temperature of water, or feeling for the direction of the wind. No, he didn't think he was angry at her. He could see that each of the knights meant something to Fionna, and her to them.

"Do you want me to be mad at you?" he asked softly.

"No," she admitted, squeezing her eyes shut. "If ye were angry with me . . ." her voice wavered. "I don't know how I could bear it."

"Peace Fionna." Galahad reached between them and rested a gentle hand on her thigh. Her leg was warm and firm, and the simple feel of her filled his veins with fire. "Thank you for telling me."

She seemed surprised, but looked down at his hand, and rested hers on top. Her fingers were gentle, tentative. They held none of the sureness of their games in his chamber. That woman seemed a distant memory. But he would find her again.

"Yer welcome," Fionna whispered.

"But don't think I don't know what you're doing."

"What am I doing?"

"Trying to prove yourself right. That love brings only pain. Don't involve me in those schemes. I'll have no part of them."

"I'm trying to tell ye the truth. There have been too many secrets between us. I never want it to be so again."

"Nor I, My Lady," Galahad said, and then twined his fingers briefly through hers, squeezing.

"There's a stream ahead," Arthur called out. "We'll stop to sup and to water the horses."

Fionna pulled her hand from Galahad's, perhaps a touch reluctantly, wrapping her fingers back around her reins. Her simple touch had buoyed him, filled him with light and energy.

But when they reached the river, Galahad's spirits sank.

Lancelot threw an arm over his face, burying his nose into his tunic.

The smells of rot and death were powerful.

"The curse," Percival said in dismay, running a hand through his copper hair. "The poison has traveled so far and so quickly."

Arthur's face hardened with fury. "We're less than a day's ride from Caerleon. Another few days, and the sickness will reach the keep."

"Might there be any nearby rivers that are not yet compromised?" Galahad asked.

Arthur shrugged, the lines around his eyes deepening. "I can only hope. For without clean water . . ." he trailed off.

The knights looked at the brackish water, the bodies of fish and squirrels strewn along the bank. Summer was around the corner. There would be little rain in the coming months. Without these rivers . . . Galahad shook off the thought. They would find the Grail. They had a lead. The sídhe had smiled upon them and revealed the location to Percival. Surely, they must desire the curse to be broken as much as Arthur and the knights.

"We knew the urgency of this quest," Lancelot said. "This revelation changes nothing. We must continue."

Arthur nodded. "Indeed." And with that, he urged Llamrei forward into a gallop, plunging through the leafy underbrush.

They followed Arthur for a time, slowing to a canter. Fionna's jaw clenched as her shoulder jostled with each step of her horse. Galahad prayed that the wound wouldn't reopen on the trip.

Several candle marks passed as they rode in silence. Several candle marks since they passed Talgarth, the village still in shambles after the faerie boar. Galahad fixed his gaze on the horizon while the sun began to sit low in the sleepy sky. Around them, the shadows of trees lengthened to spindly fingers in the twilight.

"Shall we stop for the night?" Percival asked.

"We ride on," Arthur said. "The small village of Maesbury Marsh is close, if memory serves me. There should be an inn we can stay at."

Galahad peered into the forest, his mind playing tricks in the low light. The thick bed of pine needles blanketing the loamy soil muffled the clop of their horses' hooves. A flash of movement to his right drew his gaze into the dark shadows there. He squinted, slowing his horse, peering through the crisscross of branches and leaves. Something shone white in the dark. Arcing like a bow.

His horse shied beneath him, catching scent of something and dancing away. Something dangerous and deadly. Stalking them. Galahad pulled his sword from its scabbard as the apparition pushed forward through the blackness, emerging into the dim twilight.

The beast was as big as a horse, with white matted fur, grayed with dirt and blood. A spine of protruding ridges arched across the monster's humped back. Black beady eyes gleamed with preternatural intelligence between two wickedly curved tusks as long as a man's forearm.

This animal was nothing mortal. It was nothing he had ever seen before.

And Galahad could have sworn he saw the beast smile before it charged him.

Chapter Six

Fionna

I heard Galahad's bellow first, his horse's panicked whinny second. And then . . . an inhuman squeal that raised my hackles like sharp nails dragging down my spine.

I spun Aster around and the mount danced beneath me, far too sluggish of a response for a war horse. A pang of longing for Zephyr lanced through me but was immediately forgotten when I glimpsed, in the distance, what barreled toward Galahad.

A beast of nightmares—huge and deadly.

"By the goddess," I breathed, my blood surging in my veins. "Arthur!" I called out, shouting to the other knights. I didn't know how far ahead they were, only that Galahad needed help, and soon I would too. I kicked Aster into a gallop. My mind went curiously blank as my honed battle training took over. With my sword in hand, Aster and I charged the huge white boar.

Aster shied from the unnatural beast as we passed, dancing and bucking beneath me. I struggled to hold her steady as I leaned out with my sword and slashed across the boar's broad backside.

The creature—it could only be Twrch Trwyth—let out a scream of pain as a line of blood welled along its ridged back. The faerie monster rounded on me with impossible speed, regarding me with feral intent—its new target. But a grim smile crept onto my face. For if the boar bled, it could die.

Twrch Trwyth charged.

Panic seized me at the sight—white flesh and coarse hair, dust and leaves kicked up into the air, tusks lowered to impale my mount. In all my training as a warrior, I had never fought anything like this. But instinct is a powerful force. Intuition possessed me within a wild heartbeat, and I dug my heels into Aster's flanks. She leaped away from the passing boar by a hair's breadth, huffing her displeasure. My braids blew about my face in the beast's wake. The monster's smell was overpowering—a musk of death and decay that made the bile rise in my throat.

"Over here!" Galahad hollered to the creature, who spun on cloven hooves, digging furrows into the black soil.

The thunderous sound of hoofbeats cut through the pounding pulse in my ears, and I allowed myself a split second to glance over my shoulder. A blur of three horses and riders bolted down the leaf-littered trail and I nearly sagged in relief.

Twrch Trwyth charged Galahad, and the knight spurred his mount out of the way, just inches from the boar's wicked tusks.

Arthur galloped past me like a man possessed, his face set and furious. Clearly my king had tired of curses and was ready to fight something flesh and blood. Something that could be killed. He stabbed his sword into the Twrch Trwyth's flank, burying his sword to the hilt. With a roar, the boar twisted away. Excalibur yanked out of Arthur's hands with the beast's jerky movements. Then the faerie monster rammed into Llamrei with its burly shoulder.

Horror welled in me as Llamrei reared and toppled sideways, taking Arthur down with her.

The boar's eyes went wild as the creature spotted its prey laying vulnerable and prone.

Large muscles bunched as the beast prepared to charge Llamrei and Arthur, who was struggling to pull himself out from beneath his horse. They would be gutted, for sure. I gauged the distance even as I spurred Aster into action, but I knew I would be too late. Arthur was too far away.

An arrow with white and black fletching zipped past me and

buried itself—quivering and deep—into the eye of Twrch Trwyth.

The creature roared with pain, shaking its massive tusks while pawing at its face.

I whirled to see Percival on Kit, pulling another arrow from the quiver that hung behind his saddle. But I had no time to marvel at his incredible shot.

Twrch Trwyth was frantic with anger and pain. Terrified, Llamrei clamored to her feet, gaining the boar's attention. Arthur managed to remount, his eyes on the skittish mare beneath him and not their enemy. The boar noticed too. With a monstrous grunt, it ran at Arthur anew.

"Arthur!" I cried out in warning.

His head shot up just as Lancelot and his horse barreled into the boar's side, toppling the huge creature off its feet. Dust exploded in a yellow cloud as the boar crashed to the ground in a rippling heap of muscle and vengeance.

Lancelot angled off his saddle, his charger holding steady. Then, he pulled Excalibur from the creature's side. A stream of black blood cascaded over the faerie creature's dirty white flank.

Cheval—Lancelot's horse—danced back a few steps. Still, Lancelot spun in his stirrups and tossed the sword to Arthur, who nimbly caught the blade sailing through the air.

Twrch Trwyth stumbled to its feet, rounding warily on the five of us, seeming to reevaluate its prey. The beast looked even more hideous with an arrow protruding from its eye, black blood dripping down its snout. Hot breath panted from the boar's maw as the monster tossed its head to taunt us with those wicked tusks.

"We tire the beast," Arthur said, his chest heaving. His crown had fallen to the ground somewhere, but he seemed unconcerned as he surveyed their enemy with cold calculation. "No taking risks or playing heroic. Percival, keep the arrows coming. We bleed it; we all leave here today."

Another arrow whizzed through the air. The pointed head disappeared into the side of the beast's neck with a sickening *thwump*. The boar released a guttural squeal and charged.

At me.

Arthur's calm words rang in my head. I held Aster steady as the beast came for us, my sword slick with sweat in my hand. Then I dug in my heels. Aster sidestepped as the boar passed by, giving me an opening for another blow.

Or, at least, that was my idea. The boar pivoted at the last moment, moving with us—smarter and faster than I imagined from a mere beast.

Aster let out a wild whinny of pain as the boar's tusks tore into her side. The world tilted as the force of Twrch Trwyth's blow threw us both to the ground. My sword whirled through the air from the impact, and away from me. Then pain flamed across my upper body as I hit the ground hard with my wounded shoulder, stealing the breath from my lungs. The boar's screams of triumph mingled with Aster's shrill cries of pain and terror, creating a cacophony of animal sounds.

I drew breath into my lungs and scrambled from beneath her. Blood covered Aster's white coat, dripping to the decaying leaves below. I wanted to vomit. I staggered back on unsteady feet as the boar rooted and dug into her flesh and bone with bestial cruelty.

My sword. I lunged for my sword and then jumped to my feet as Galahad rode up behind Twrch Trwyth and stabbed his blade deep into its spine.

The creature screamed in agony. The crimson-stained head whipped up from poor Aster's exposed belly, spraying droplets of blood across me.

From the ground, Twrch Trwyth was huge. Taller than me. I could feel the heat of its unnatural magic from here. My stomach twisted painfully, and my mouth parched as dry as a rainless summer.

Galahad had scored a good shot. The creature moved sluggishly now. A hind leg wobbled with a meaty step. But even the death throes of a creature such as this could be deadly; warnings rang in my mind as the boar fixed its one-eyed stare upon me.

I held my sword angled before my body, and the scene seemed to slow. My eyes narrowed at the foul monster. The beast who had just horribly maimed an innocent creature. This thing, this faerie monster, didn't belong on this earth. And I would be the one to send it back to whatever abyss it crawled out from. A strategy crystalized in my mind, and calm lapped at my pulse. Twrch Trwyth would charge me, and I would roll, before coming up and stabbing the boar's throat or stomach. Or both. It wouldn't survive another blow to its vital underbelly.

The beast leaped over Aster's prone body and came at me, but I was ready. I tensed my legs, primed to move when the mass of muscle and death drew close enough.

But another body barreled into me from the side, shoving me out of the way. A blur of black hair and brown leather and strong arms.

"Lancelot!" I cried out. The fool man had pushed me out of the way. And now stood directly in the path of Twrch Trwyth.

The boar hit Lancelot with an audible crash, tossing his body across the clearing like a rag doll. Lancelot hit the ground and rolled to a stop against a tree trunk, his arms and legs splayed like a dead man's.

Oh goddess . . . a gut-wrenching scream clawed viciously at my throat. My mind rebelled against the reality before me. Lancelot . . .

But there was no time for grief's heart-stabbing pain, only reaction. The boar was rounding on me again. And where I had felt calm certainty before, I was now frozen with fear and desperation. Lancelot had to be all right. He had to be alive.

The boar pawed the ground, appearing to delight in the scent of my fear. It was all the time Arthur needed. Seemingly out of nowhere, my king appeared on his black steed. A warrior's cry left his mouth right as he plunged his shining sword between the beast's shoulder blades, severing the spine.

The blow was instantaneous. Twrch Trwyth gave a weak mewling cry and stumbled to its knees before landing in the dirt with a teeth-rattling crash.

Eerie silence hung in the forest around us. Twrch Trwyth was dead. And goddess help me, Lancelot might be too.

Chapter Seven

Arthur

Arthur's heart hammered in his throat. Lancelot was tough. But to survive a blow like that? His thoughts stuttered and stopped.

Behind him, Galahad and Percival launched off their horses. Then all three knights—running and scrambling—converged on Lancelot in a blur of action.

Fionna's pale hands fluttered by his head, feeling for his pulse. A breath.

Lancelot quietly groaned. Stars above, he was alive!

Arthur released a ragged sigh, pushing back his surfacing emotions. He couldn't lose Lancelot. He needed his dearest friend, far more than Lancelot probably realized. While Arthur had his other knights, Lancelot was his foster brother—truly the only real family Arthur had left. His half-sisters made their position clear, their familial titles more tradition than truth.

"Give the man some room," Galahad said, pulling Arthur from his thoughts. But no one moved. They all needed to see. They needed to watch as Galahad probed Lancelot's chest, his abdomen, felt upon his arms and legs for breaks or rends in the flesh.

Lancelot's eyes fluttered open, his head tilting toward Fionna.

Galahad sat back on his heels, brushing a lock of blond hair from his eyes. "You have Hel's own luck, brother. I can't find a single scratch on you."

Lancelot reached out a hand and Arthur grasped it, pulling Lancelot to a seat. Another groan escaped Lancelot's lips as one of his hands flew to his back, his mouth tightening in pain.

Galahad was there in a moment, probing with strong fingers. "Can you move your legs?"

"I'm moving them right now," Lancelot griped.

It was true. His booted feet were stirring.

"Nice to see the fall didn't injure your sunny disposition." Galahad smirked.

"Ye fool man," Fionna said. "I had the faerie boar."

"You're welcome," Lancelot muttered, and then slowly, with Arthur's help, he climbed to his feet, his back hunched.

Arthur wrapped Lancelot's arm around his shoulders, holding his weight, and helped him walk.

After hobbling over to his horse, Lancelot sagged against the saddle, beads of sweat breaking out on his pale face. "I'm not sure I can mount," he admitted.

But luckily, the horses of Caerleon were well trained animals. Arthur tapped behind Cheval's knee, signaling for the stallion to kneel.

Galahad and Percival came around the other side and, between the three of them, they maneuvered Lancelot onto the horse.

Fionna stood back, her face a painted mask of anger and worry.

A crow's shrill caw broke through the silence, startling Arthur. He looked up and spotted a large black bird sitting atop Twrch Trwyth's corpse, regarding them with a beady eye.

A shiver ran up Arthur's spine as he studied the crow. There was something about it—the body was too big, the eye too sharp. The bird's caw too much like mocking laughter.

"A carrion crow has already arrived," Galahad mumbled. "Strange. The beast's foul blood is still warm. Are animals growing *that* hungry?"

"Make for Maesbury Marsh," Arthur said, ignoring Galahad. "Find the nearest inn. I'll meet you there."

"Meet us—" Fionna wrinkled her smooth brow. "Why won't ye come with us?"

"Someone needs to retrieve the tusks." Arthur nodded to the body of the great boar. "Merlin gave us directions to a bone carver. Well, now we have a bone to carve."

"Ye shouldn't stay alone," Fionna protested, hesitating. The others had already mounted and were now waiting at the edge of a copse. "Twrch Trwyth should have traveled south to Caerleon, not north of Talgarth. The faerie monster knew where to find us."

"I'll not be far behind," Arthur said. "See to Lancelot's comfort. Ride with him, and make sure he doesn't fall off. He doesn't look too stable." A stab of jealousy shot through Arthur at the thought of Fionna doting on Lancelot, soothing his hurt and comforting him. He shoved the feelings down viciously. His friend had nearly died. Was Arthur truly so petty to begrudge him a tender hand or a kind word?

Fionna nodded, uncertain, but followed his command. "Don't tarry long, My King," she said, looking back at the great white body and the black bird perched atop the muscular flesh. Then, she crossed over to Lancelot—who sagged forward while astride his horse—and pulled herself up behind him, reaching around his slumped frame to take the reins.

Arthur turned to the task at hand as they left. The boar. And the crow.

He picked up a rock, testing the weight in his hand. And then he hurled the stone right at the bird.

The crow launched into the air with a raucous laugh as the rock sailed by without a hit.

"Get out of here!" he shouted, picking up another rock and throwing it.

The crow flapped its wings, hopping off the corpse and onto the ground.

Arthur leaned over to retrieve another rock and faltered as the sound of hushed whispers reached his ears. The air around him grew cold for a moment and he straightened, his hand on Excalibur. There was magic afoot.

Dark shadows swirled around the crow, stirring the leaves and pine needles beneath its black talons. And then those talons became black boots, feathers became fabric—and the swirl of magic became

Morgana. In the flesh. Standing before him.

She wasn't natural—his half-sister. Her face too wan, her movements too sinuous, her form too sleek and curved to be human. She wore a black dress slashed with deep violet, and her black hair hung over one shoulder in loose curls. How Lancelot had ever felt safe to court this faerie, he knew not. She was desirable, that was plain for any man to see. But she was also *terrifying*.

"Brother," she said, a secret smile on her face. "Did you have to kill my pet?" She leaned down and dipped one delicate finger into the cooling blood on Twrch Trwyth's coat, before drawing a black line from her collarbone to down between her breasts.

Arthur kept his eyes fixed on her face. If she was here to unnerve him, he wouldn't give her the satisfaction. "I'm afraid your *pet*"—he spit the word—"escaped from its yard and strayed into my lands."

Morgana sulked, looking at the boar. "You were always far too serious. Do you never have fun?"

"None of this is fun, Morgana," Arthur grit slowly, his jaw clenched as anger surged within him. "People's lives are at stake."

"Human lives."

"Yes, human lives." He opened his hands before her, pleading. "Sister, what Lancelot did to you was unforgivable. But don't punish the people of Caerleon. You punished me. You played your jest on me by locking Excalibur in its sheath. You cursed Caerleon, poisoning her waters. Now you send this faerie boar? *Enough*, Morgana. Your grief is acknowledged. Two curses is enough." He hadn't been able to speak to her since the night of Lancelot's betrayal. Perhaps she had calmed down. Perhaps he could reason with her . . . get her to remove the curse—

"Two curses?" She threw her head back and laughed, her shriek sounding eerily like the crow's caw.

Arthur frowned, his hand straying back toward Excalibur. Was she mad?

"Two curses." Her lips curled in a wicked grin as she sauntered toward him, every sway of her hips calculated. "My poor foolish brother. You don't even know about the third curse, do you?" Her violet-hued eyes flashed with humor.

Arthur froze. "Do not mock me. What is this third curse of which you speak?"

"King of Caerleon, overking of Gwent, the Pendragon of Briton." She cocked her head, as if a bird angling to better see their prey. "So many titles, yet still you cannot inspire the loyalty of even those closest to you."

"You lie." Though, her words stung like salt in a wound.

"Do I?" She traced a fingernail down the drying line of boar's blood on her chest. "I do not think so. Whether kings or paupers, mortals are squabbling idiots. They are not fit to rule."

Morgana leaned over in a graceful arc and picked up an object from the dirt of the forest floor that glinted in the low light of dusk.

His crown.

He swallowed, stilling his hand at his side, refusing to touch his brow like he wanted.

"You and your treacherous father may have fooled Vivien, but the faeries of Tintagel see the truth of you, Arthur Pendragon. You are weak. You are failing. And soon enough, you will be *nothing*." She tossed the crown at his feet with a contemptuous motion. And then the whispers and dark enveloped her, and she was a crow once again.

The great bird cawed in delight, swooping toward him.

Arthur threw an arm up and ducked as Morgana's crow dove where his head had just been, before winging toward the dipping sun in the darkening sky.

He took in a deep shuddering breath as he watched her disappear, the ebony of her form melding into the black shadows of the forest.

Arthur leaned over slowly and picked up his crown, turning the gold circlet in his hands. A clod of dirt was caught between two prongs. He brushed it off and buffed it on his tunic. There.

He placed Gwent's crown back onto his head with shaking hands before pulling Excalibur from its sheath. He turned to the boar and began cutting, trying with all his power not to think upon the words now echoing in his mind.

A third curse.

Chapter Eight

Lancelot

Lancelot wanted to weep with relief when the first lantern light of Maesbury Marsh came into view. Every swaying step of Cheval's walk was torture. Shooting pain seared up his spine and down into his legs.

He hadn't been thinking. When he had seen Fionna standing there, so small compared to the might of the boar . . . his mind had fled completely. He would have done anything in that moment to keep her from harm. Even, it appeared, sacrifice himself.

It was a surprising feeling, this gallantry that had come over him. Surprising and bloody dangerous. The type of foolhardy action he would expect from Percival or Galahad. Not from himself.

The only good thing to have come out of this whole debacle was how Fionna was now sitting behind him, her arms wrapped around his waist.

Lancelot ground his teeth through the pain, trying to focus his mind instead of the feel of her breasts pressed into his back, the way her strong thighs moved beside his, the sweet yet herbaceous smell of her. Fionna's hot breath tickled his neck and his cock stirred painfully against his breeches. He muttered a muffled curse. So much for distracting himself.

"An inn," Galahad called out, pointing at the swinging sign that hung from a sturdy two-story timber and white-washed structure ahead. He let out a boom of laughter. "You'll love this. 'The Dancing Boar.'"

Lancelot hissed. "If I never saw another boar, it would be too soon."

"Are ye in pain?" Fionna's words were knitted with concern.

"What do you think?" he snapped.

He felt her stiffen behind him, and he closed his eyes against his stupidity. No need to take his frustration out on her.

"Serves ye right," he heard her mutter under her breath.

"What?" Lancelot asked incredulously, trying to turn to regard her with disbelief. But the pain exploded through his back and radiated through his legs, stealing his breath. A groan escaped his lips when his chest loosened, and he tilted in the saddle, suddenly dizzy and unsteady.

Fionna caught him, her arms circling him like a ship's rail, keeping him from plunging to his doom below. She reined Cheval to a stop before The Dancing Boar. "Can you hold yerself while I dismount?"

Lancelot grunted a nod.

Fionna swung down from his horse. "Galahad, Percival, will ye help?"

Embarrassment warmed Lancelot's face as the knights helped him off Cheval and into the inn. The Dancing Boar's common room was a cheerful, tidy wood-paneled room filled with chatting and laughing townsfolk. A lute player sat by the hearth, plucking out a jaunty tune, and several couples spun and danced in the space before the yawning fireplace.

Lancelot tried to ignore the curious faces who peered at him as he sucked the breath in and out through his clenched teeth. The room felt too hot, and then too cold.

"All right," Percival said, appearing in front of Lancelot's line of vision. When had the lad left his side? "I secured us two rooms on the ground floor. Let's go."

Lancelot shuffled through the common room, much of his weight leaning on Galahad on one side, Percival on the other. In some corner of his consciousness, he saw the looks cast Fionna's way—appreciative . . . predatory. He wanted to face them down, to tell each man to place their eyes elsewhere lest they have them plucked out. But he was in no shape to intimidate anyone.

They pushed into the small room, just large enough for a two-person bed, a storage chest, and a little cupboard. Galahad and Percival lowered him down as gently as they could, but still the jostling sent stabbing pain through his body. "Easy," Lancelot panted, finally letting his head collapse back on the pillow. The bed was hard and lumpy, but it was blessedly still.

Lancelot opened his eyes and saw the other knights standing in a line, regarding him with worried eyes. "He shouldn't ride," Galahad was murmuring. "He likely bruised his spine or the muscles in his back."

"We need him," Percival said. "The standing stone said the blessed five."

Galahad frowned. "We'll have to wait."

"Arthur won't be happy about that," Percival murmured.

"Arthur can stuff it," Fionna said. Her voice grew soft. "But can Caerleon wait?"

"Quit talking about me like I'm not here," Lancelot practically barked. "I had a fall, I'm not dead. Give me more than five minutes to shake off the injury."

Galahad squinted his eyes. "His head seems in working order."

"And his attitude," Percival added.

"Should we find a chirurgeon?" Fionna asked. "Perhaps he could supply a tonic for the pain and swelling."

"Excellent idea," Galahad said. "I'll see if I can locate one. Percival, you see to the horses, and keep an eye out for Arthur?"

"Fine," Percival sighed. "But then I'm having an ale."

"Get me one of those too," Lancelot demanded hoarsely. A cold ale sounded heavenly.

Fionna pressed her lips together. "I'll stay here and make sure he doesn't do anything heroic."

"Little chance of that with the frosty reception I received last time," Lancelot shot back. "You're welcome, *Your Highness*."

"Oooh . . ." Percival's eyes grew wide.

"Let's leave them to it," Galahad said, pulling Percival from the room.

Fionna closed the door behind them, rounding on Lancelot, her hands on her hips. It wasn't fair to face her like this—her standing strong and proud—while he lay prone like an invalid.

"What do ye have to say for yerself?" she asked, crossing her arms beneath her breasts.

"I saved your life!" he shouted. "And nearly died in the process. I suppose it's too much to expect a little gratitude from the great and might Fionnabhair Allán."

"Ye didn't save my life, ye arrogant donkey!" Fionna shouted back. "I had the boar in my sights. I had a plan. I was ready for the beast."

"Apologies for not reading your mind, My Lady. What I saw was an eight-stone woman about to be trampled by a supernatural beast the size of two war horses!"

Fionna reared back, her smooth face darkening with fury. "That's all ye see when ye look at me? A frail woman who needs protecting?"

"No—" he protested, but she cut him off.

"Would you have pushed Galahad out of the way? Arthur?"

Lancelot bit his tongue. No, he wouldn't have. He would have trusted his fellow knights' training. But they knew the risks. They had trained for years. But so *had* Fionna, though not under his tutelage. So why had he felt the need to dive between her and the faerie boar?

"Curse it Lancelot, I'm a knight first, a woman second! When will ye get it through yer thick skull that I don't need ye to save me?"

Lancelot warred with himself, refusing to meet her sparking gaze. Bloody hell, he knew why. Hissing through the pain, he struggled to push himself to a seat. Some words shouldn't be spoken while lying down—this moment no different.

But Fionna was at his side in an instant. Her angry words were all but forgotten, gentleness and care taking resentment's place as she pushed him back down onto the bed. "Don't move," she said softly. "Ye could injure yerself worse."

Lancelot squeezed his eyes closed for a several heartbeats before meeting her piercing, silver-hued eyes. "I didn't push you out of the boar's path because I thought you weak, or female, or unable to defend yourself. I did it because . . . the thought of losing you terrified me beyond reason. I acted on instinct."

Fionna licked her lips as she processed his words. When she spoke, her voice wavered. "And do ye not think it terrified me to see ye lying there? To know not if ye were still alive? I have fought beside my brothers and sisters countless times, yet never did I know the fear I experienced today. If ye were dead . . ." A tear glistened at the corner of her eye, clinging to her white lashes.

Gods, she was beautiful like this. Raw and real, even more formidable in her vulnerability. Lancelot drew a hand up and cupped her cheek, wiping the tear with the pad of his thumb. Her skin was as soft as silk, as smooth as he had imagined.

She tilted her head into his palm, her eyes fluttering closed.

And then she opened them and reached out to brush a stray curl from his forehead. Her touch burned like sweet cinnamon, and their eyes locked. Sensations, as dark and sensual as a new moon, doused their fiery pulses with even darker desires. Fionna leaned forward, and awareness surged within him anew as her curtain of white braids swept around him, and then her lips caressed his.

Though the kiss was tender and sweet, almost chaste, her touch set his blood racing like he was a lad of sixteen, like this was his first taste of a woman. Energy and warmth surged through him, dulling the pain, banishing each wince and pang from his thoughts, from his body. For what other sensation could compete with the feel of her? *Goddess, take me now.*

"Fionna," he murmured against her lips.

"I do not mean to lose ye, Lancelot du Lac," she whispered back. Fionna pulled away a few inches, her lips and cheeks flushed. "Not now, not ever."

Her soft words wrapped around his lonely heart, and he nearly started at the foreign feel of genuine devotion. Acceptance. Brushing her lips across his once more, she smiled before nestling gently against him, her head tucked against his shoulder.

Lancelot stared at the shadowed ceiling and stroked her silken hair. No, she would never lose him. For Morgana had ensured that he would never be hers in the first place.

Chapter Nine

Fionna

I woke to Lancelot stirring beside me. His warm presence was a comfort I was unused to enjoying; I had never slept beside anyone but Aideen. My heart spasmed painfully as I thought of my sister. Surely Arthur's messenger was already on his way to Lough Insholin to treat with Donal O'Lynn. I prayed Arthur's coffers were deep enough to secure my family's safety.

Lancelot's blue eyes blinked open beside me, and I banished thoughts of home. If I was to help my family, I needed to see this quest through. And to do that, we needed Lancelot well again.

"How are ye feeling?" I asked, laying a feather-light hand on his arm. I felt strange—touching him. As though I wasn't sure I could do so, that I wouldn't be scorned or have my head bitten off per his usual response toward me. But after last night's kiss, surely laying a hand on him was allowed, if not welcome.

Lancelot pushed himself to a seat gingerly. One hand strayed to his back, and he straightened his spine, twisting one way and then the other. "Better," Lancelot said, the word a sigh of relief. "Much better."

Galahad had found a doctor last night, but the man had been attending a woman in labor and promised to come when he was free. Apparently, it was a long labor, the poor woman.

Lancelot swung his feet off the bed and stood. He stretched, lifting his arms above his head until his back popped. "I feel like a new man."

Healing so quickly seemed a peculiar thing. How could he be so injured yesterday, yet be fine this morning? But, this miracle wasn't the strangest magic I had encountered since arriving in Briton. Not even this week.

A knock sounded on the door.

"Come," Lancelot barked. His eyes were bright, his color high. He seemed back to his old self. I shoved down a bubble of remorse for the loss of the sweet, quiet Lancelot I had lain beside during the night. *It was good that he was healed*, I admonished myself. We could now continue the quest.

The door opened to Arthur in a fresh tunic, his short hair ruffled as though finger-combed through with water. Shadows beneath his eyes spoke of a sleepless night, but his voice was cheerful. "You're up. From Galahad and Percival's description, I feared we would have to leave you."

"Fit as ever," Lancelot said, slapping himself on his broad chest.

Arthur narrowed his eyes, but there was a smile on his face as he said, "I suppose we have Fionna's tender ministrations to thank for your miraculous recovery? For surely you wouldn't have exaggerated your symptoms . . ."

I covered my chuckle with a hand. "I assure ye, Yer Majesty, if I ever catch the faintest whiff of any of ye trying to milk an injury for sympathy, ye'll be receiving a not-too-tender kick to the arse."

Arthur threw back his head and laughed, and the sound warmed me, making up for the icy daggers Lancelot was now shooting my way.

"Ye should have seen him last night. He could hardly dismount his horse. Lancelot is far too proud a man to fake an injury so severe."

"Are we done speaking of me as if I'm an invalid?" Lancelot asked.

"I don't know, what do you think, Fionna? Seems there are a few more jokes to be made."

"We don't want to hog them all though," I countered, sliding our dark knight a sly grin. "Percival would be beyond cross with us."

Lancelot threw up his hands, then began buckling on his sword belt. "What's the plan today."

"We're near Maesbury Marsh, where the bone carver lives," Arthur said. "We should pay her a visit before we head back to the main road."

"Who is this bone carver person?" I asked.

"I am not sure exactly," Arthur said. "She is a legend. But if Merlin thinks she can help us, it's worth the trip."

"The Bone Carver is as mysterious as the Otherworld's mist," Lancelot volunteered, darting a glance Arthur's way. "Some say she walked the Earth before man was born. Some even believe humans are made from her very bones and that she still carves life into existence from the bones she gathers. Maybe Merlin believed she could carve us a talisman."

"Made from her own bones?" I asked, mouth agape.

Percival's ginger head popped around the corner. "How's crabapple doing? Feeling sour this morning? Though, not sure how you could be with such a lovely bedmate."

Lancelot scowled, and a blush rose on my cheeks.

"Has anyone thought of securing me a horse?" I asked, changing the subject. "Poor Aster didn't last long." I realized then how lucky it was that I wasn't riding Zephyr. I mourned any animal's death, but Zephyr would have been a blow to my very soul.

"We'll find one in the village before we head out," Arthur said.

The road north of Maesbury Marsh wound through thick forest, gnarled and old. The ground grew soggy beneath our horse's hooves, and the foliage began to change from the beech and ferns of the forest to the reeds and wildflowers of the marshland. Frogs croaked their warnings with every hoofbeat. Fireflies danced around the rushes and reflected off the blackened water—almost pretty, but they reminded me too much of will-ó-the-wisps, leading us to our doom.

"Not sure why anyone would want to live way out here," Galahad muttered, his eyes darting around the marsh and moss-draped tree cover.

"I suppose if you're a creepy old woman who likes to carve bones, a stinky marsh might just be the perfect location," Percival added, chipper as usual. How the lad wasn't nonplussed by the sights around him was beyond me. Then again, he grew up isolated in a forest with an eccentric mother.

"Shhh . . ." Arthur peered over his shoulder, then furrowed his brows. "She might hear you."

"Who is she, the Mother Goddess?" Percival quirked an eyebrow.

"We don't know how much farther," Arthur practically whispered. "We might be on her doorstep even now."

The knights fell into an uneasy silence at that, their heads swiveling back and forth, eyes peering into the marsh and to the shadows beyond. The smells of rot and brine tickled my nose.

I didn't see the moss-greened structure at first. The bone carver's cottage blended into the forest, so overgrown with roots and vines that the home seemed a living thing itself. A faded red door and the puff of wood smoke from the chimney were the only signs that this place belonged in the mortal realms.

Arthur dismounted first and the rest of us followed, a bit reluctant to make this woman's acquaintance. There was something ancient about the cottage—something *other*. The horses nickered nervously, stamping the ground as we tied them to a gnarled fencepost. An animal awareness shivered down my skin.

The door opened slowly, and within I could see only darkness, like peering into the throat of a great beast.

"Greetings," the woman said. Her voice was not that of an old crone like I had expected, but smooth and melodious. The lilting sound perked my curiosity to see her.

"Not often I receive visitors out this way. Please, come in."

One by one, we filed into the cabin, exchanging uneasy glances. Galahad placed a protective hand on the small of my back, as if to steady me. His touch stoked the fire within me instead. I missed Galahad. His strong hands, his honeyed kisses. I wanted to feel again what had passed between us—that and more. I stifled a sigh, trying to tear my thoughts from the emotion this man's simple touch could garner from me.

The cabin was much larger than it appeared from the outside, boasting one large circular room and holding all a person might need. A bed, a washbasin, a desk cluttered with papers and quills. Surprisingly mundane furnishings crowded one half of the space. But then there was the rest. Shelves of oddities—desiccated bodies of insects and small rodents and snakes. Jars of powders and liquids, whose purpose I couldn't dare imagine. And bones. Shelves and shelves of bones and teeth and skulls. The smell of the place was cloying, thick with smoke and a sweet odor that swirled about in my head.

"My name is Arthur Pendragon," Arthur began. "Overking of Gwent. I have come to request your aid in our quest to find the Blessed Grail."

I could see her now, and was surprised by the woman's beauty, despite her age. Her sleek, gray hair was roped into a thick braid over one shoulder, her fine features delicate and elfin. She must have been extraordinarily beautiful in her youth. And now in her current age? She produced a feeling of wisdom and power. So much so, my hand strayed toward the sword at my hip.

"And what makes you think I can help, Little Dragon King?" the woman asked.

"My druid, Merlin," Arthur answered.

"Merlin?" she repeated, raising an eyebrow.

She had heard of him. Although I supposed most in this part of the world had.

"Who else have you brought?" she asked, turning her deep black gaze to each of us in turn.

"These are my knights. Galjorheledanik of Swansea, Lancelot du Lac, Percival of Caer Benic."

"Ah. A Fisher King. Perhaps you do not need my aid with him by your side."

"Och, I fear ye overestimate me, My Lady," Percival said.

"Though . . . what should we call ye?"

"The Bone Carver." A smile played on her lips as she regarded Percival. "Or the Mother Goddess. Whatever you prefer, Grail prince."

Percival's Adam's apple bobbed as he swallowed thickly. "I meant no disrespect," he whispered, his brown eyes wide.

The Bone Carver turned toward me, and I could see Percival sag with relief from the corner of my eye as the weight of her attention passed from him. Icy fear crystalized in my veins. The woman stared as if she could see to my very core. My fears and doubts and shortcomings. All of them, laid bare.

"This is Fionnabhair Allán," Arthur said, "Princess of Clann Allán and the newest knight in my court."

The woman drifted toward me. Reaching out a hand out, she lifted one of my braids from my shoulder and examined my hair. I struggled to hold myself still, not wanting to insult the woman, but wanting desperately to be away from her. "An unusual knight," she mused to herself. "Very unusual indeed. You have power, fair Fionnabhair. Yet you do not use your magic. Why?"

My skin crawled beneath her scrutiny, and I buried my hands in the fabric of my tunic. "I don't know to what ye refer," I managed. "I'm a warrior. And a knight. I use those skills plenty."

The Bone Carver regarded me with an expression that I thought might be patronizing amusement. The searing gaze rankled me. What was this mad woman on about?

"Very well. You may keep your secrets. For now." She whirled to Arthur, and it was my turn to sag with relief. "You have brought me something. I can taste its magic in the air."

Arthur reached out to Galahad, who handed him a satchel. Our king then pulled one of the boar's tusks out and handed the ivory to her.

"These are from Twrch Trwyth. The faerie boar."

The Bone Carver took the tusk with reverence. "Oh yes, Arthur Pendragon. I will fashion you something from this, an object unlike anything in the mortal world."

"And this . . . object will aid us in our quest?" Arthur asked, his voice nearly breathless with excitement.

The Bone Carver nodded. "Do you have the other tusk as well?"

Galahad handed the ivory over to Arthur.

She regarded the two tusks with a wild gleam in her eye. "The second tusk will serve as payment. Are we agreed?"

"Agreed," Arthur said.

"You have come to the right place, dear knights. Wait and see what I shall carve you."

Chapter Ten

Galahad

Rain splattered across Galahad's unbound hair and shoulders as he stomped through the mud toward The Dancing Boar, the horses now bedded down for the night. The Bone Carver needed one more day to carve her object from the boar tusk. "Return tomorrow before the noon meal," she had said from her moss-draped doorway.

They had ridden into the yard behind the inn after the sun had set, a nightfall that was far too young. The strangeness was only confirmed when the innkeeper shared how they had departed five hours earlier. Yet the Bone Carver was only a thirty-minute trot from the inn.

Lightning flashed through the night air followed by a rumble of thunder. After kicking the mud from his boots, Galahad entered the inn and wiped the trailing raindrops from his face. If only he could shake his unease at the strange afternoon as easily.

Fionna peered up from a table near the hearth. Firelight flickered in her gaze as she studied how his dampened tunic clung to his chest and stomach. Heat curled in his groin and flushed to his limbs. Their eyes touched for the briefest moment before she returned to her flagon of ale. He was glad to see how her spark and confidence had returned, especially when their king wasn't around. Arthur and Lancelot must have turned in for the evening.

Percival, noting his and Fionna's exchange, practically rolled his eyes.

Galahad slapped the backside of Percival's head and then fell into a seat right before the fire. "Fetch me an ale, lad."

"Fetch yer own, ye big oaf—"

"Need a drink?" A serving woman asked, leaning onto the table.

Her tightly-laced bodice fell forward, and gods. Large, soft breasts rose and fell in front of Percival's ale-flushed face. The kind of breasts a man could happily bury himself into and forget to breathe. Apparently, Percival had a similar thought. Galahad tugged on the back Percival's tunic to reel the younger knight back against his seat. Percival shot a look like daggers at Galahad, making him grin.

"Ale," Galahad said, pushing a copper across the table.

The barmaid pushed it back. "Free with a kiss." Her rouge-painted lips tilted in a seductive smile. Loose blonde curls fell over her shoulder as she eyed Galahad, her delicate eyebrow arched. "Or ale and a meal on the house, if you would like me to help you into dry clothes."

"I'll take a free ale," Percival chirped. Galahad still had a grip on the lad's tunic and held him in place.

Fionna cleared her throat and pretended to inspect her dagger, now in her hands.

"Just an ale," Galahad said with an appreciative wink. The barmaid pouted and then pushed off the table toward the barrels and caskets in the back. When she disappeared, Galahad released Percival's tunic.

"I'm not a wee lad." Percival scowled and shoved to his feet. To Fionna, he softened his voice, as if embarrassed, and said, "See ye in the morning, dove." And to him, "Ye get the floor tonight."

With that, Percival's lanky form marched from their table and down the hallway to the private two-bed room they shared with Fionna. Arthur preferred his second-in-command to keep guard when he traveled and rested in public places such as this. Though, Galahad thought it might be more from habit—the two had shared rooms since they were lads.

The barmaid returned and placed a large mug of ale before Galahad, gifting him another glimpse of her bouncing cleavage. Even he had to resist the pull toward falling into her bodice. Mayhap he was too harsh on his sword brother. Still, Percival was a strange dichotomy. Percival the warrior knight and Percival the sheltered young man from the forest. Odin's blessing, Galahad was well acquainted with maids by Percival's age. The young man should be allowed to play too. Sighing, Galahad eyed the half-empty mug of ale Percival had left behind and grabbed it, taking a long swig before gulping a few swigs from his own cup. Finished, he tipped back in his chair, resting his head, eyes closed, and enjoyed the warmth of the hearth.

"Ye're certainly pleased with yerself."

He cracked open one eye and focused on Fionna. "Not pleased. Warming up."

"Perhaps ye should change into dry clothes. Ye reek of horse."

A grin stretched across his face. "Strange how getting me out of these wet clothes seems of utmost concern to the fair maidens of this inn."

Fionna sheathed her dagger and then leaned forward on the table. A mischievous glint glimmered in her gaze. "I think I'll go keep Percival company."

His chair screeched as the front two legs slid back onto the floor. "And what do you plan to do with him?"

"Wouldn't ye like to know." Fionna downed the remaining dregs and slammed her mug onto the table. "See ye in the morning, *chipmunk*."

As she angled through the crowd of men and barmaids, he watched her narrow hips sway with each angry step—hips that fit perfectly in the palms of his hands. Hips that had once moved in rhythm to his. Galahad practically groaned as his cock stirred to life with the mere memory.

A man, deep in his cups, reached out and slapped Fionna across the arse. She whirled on him fast. The man didn't have a chance to blink before she slammed his head to the table, spitting next to his face.

"The next time, I'll cut off yer balls," Fionna hissed.

Men roared with laughter, a few cheered. Fionna slid Galahad a satisfied smirk and then waltzed away, down the hallway. To Percival.

Wait. Was that an invitation to join?

Oh gods.

In a flash, Galahad was on his feet and pushing through the crowd, his ale forgotten.

Fionna lingered outside his and Percival's door, and so Galahad stepped away from the lantern light and into the hallway's shadows. A few seconds later, Percival appeared, his mouth open with surprise. Before disappearing into their room, Fionna shot Galahad an impish smile.

The damn woman. Still picking a fight with him.

His long strides ate up the distance to his room in seconds. Without knocking, he pushed open the door and found Fionna and Percival in the center of their shared chamber, her lips pressed to the young man's, his arms practically limp on her waist. Was this Percival's first kiss? He didn't know. Nor was Galahad sure how he felt seeing Fionna kiss another. Jealous . . . or aroused?

Unaware of his presence in the doorway, Percival gripped Fionna's hips tight in his hands and tugged her against him. Fionna gasped and pulled back, her eyes wide, uncertain.

They stared at one another for a few erratic heartbeats, unspoken words passing between them. And then Galahad saw the shift, the moment Fionna looked at Percival, not with pity and surprise, but as a man who aroused her interest. Her fingers sank into his copper hair as her lips returned to his. And Percival deepened their kiss, as if he were a seasoned expert.

Galahad quirked a brow, resisting the urge to grin. But then Fionna's hands dipped to Percival's waist and begun unbuckling his belt and Galahad knew he needed to step in. She probably didn't know the rules of his vow.

"He might have a heart attack, if you go too fast," Galahad said, shutting the door.

"Come to chastise me, have ye? Not my fault yer ego can't handle that Fionna regards me as more than a chaste weakling." Percival glared at him once more. A strange look for their incurably happy knight.

Galahad smiled at him, not to mock, but in understanding. This was the challenge of a *man*, not a boy. And, if he were honest with himself, Fionna wasn't too much older than Percival. And he fully considered her a woman.

Fionna finished unbuckling Percival's belt and let it drop to the floor. The clanking sound filled the tense silence between them, until she asked Percival, "What do *ye* want?"

"Ye lass," he answered, breathless. "I want ye. But I fear I will want all of ye and I can't. Not yet." A flush colored Percival's cheeks and he twisted away, but she caught his face.

"Ye possess a strength the other men have not. There is no shame in yer sacrifice."

She leaned forward and delicately traced Percival's bottom lip with her tongue until he opened for her. Their kiss grew hungry and Percival moaned. A sound that pricked Galahad with guilt.

Her words shamed *him*, for she was right. All this time, they had flaunted their freedoms in front of Percival and mocked his vow and the younger knight took it in stride, all smiles and laughter. Until this moment, Galahad hadn't realized that was a front. That a serious nature brewed beneath the cheerfulness. Because of the Fisher King's son, they might save Caerleon and Briton. Because of Percival, Fionna was alive and in this room.

Perhaps Percival was more of a man than any of them.

Chapter Eleven

Fionna

Percival's lips were soft and warm and beautifully reverent on mine. This other side of him, a serious side I had not expected, ripped the seals from my eyes. There was more to him than wit and boyish charm.

I had never quite payed attention to the deep timbre of his voice or the play of muscles along his jaw. Now, touching him, I realized he was far from soft and scrawny. Muscle and sinew stretched firm beneath my fingertips—formed from years of drills and fighting. And his eyes, gods his eyes. Up close, I could see every long coppery lash framing the rich, earthen tones. Eyes so brown, they were nearly black—sinful even. And his kiss? His mouth dancing across mine was akin to laughter and sunshine and . . . bliss.

His affections didn't hold the earnestness of Arthur's lips or the danger of Lancelot's kiss or even the seduction of Galahad's embrace. Percival was his own. Joyful.

A shadow of warmth sidled up behind me and my breath caught as I recognized Galahad, approaching even as my arms were twined about Percival. Galahad softly lifted my braids and kissed my injured shoulder. I shuddered beneath Galahad's touch and Percival gently pulled away at my reaction. Moons above, I had missed the honey-sweet of Galahad's touch, how he melted me to my core.

"Maybe," Galahad whispered, "we should show Percival the

pleasures between a man and a woman."

"Ye mean—" Percival began but Galahad cut him off.

"You can't have sex, but you can watch."

Galahad's hands moved up my stomach and then cupped my breasts. His fingers were chilled from the cold of the night, a refreshing coolness on along my heated skin. My senses blazed into awareness as my head arched back against his chest, my gaze locked with Percival's. "What can ye do?"

"Kiss, touch ye." Percival swallowed as Galahad began rubbing the hardened tip of one my nipples with his thumb. "But I cannot be touched by another, ye ken?"

"Aye." My eyes fluttered shut. "Then watch for a spell and touch yerself. Join in when ye're ready. I won't allow ye to go too far."

"Two men?" Percival's breath came in quick. "Yer sure?"

"Does that bother ye?" I turned in Galahad's arms, nipping at his lower lip before peering over my shoulder at Percival.

"Nae lass." His eyes were bright.

"Then enjoy."

Percival sauntered over to his bed and fell back against the pillows, unlacing his breeches and pushing up his tunic. Each nerve-ending I possessed ignited as I appreciated the ripple of stomach muscles under the candlelight, his eyes never leaving mine.

So many firsts flooded this space. The first time a man watched as I was pleasured by another man—a thrilling, daring prospect. The first time I would enjoy not one man, but two.

Wanting to arouse Percival farther, and eager for the forgotten taste of Galahad, I pushed up Galahad's tunic and licked at the raindrops still gathered on his pectorals. I wanted my tongue to carve fire across his damp skin. To sear his chest, his abdomen. From the corner of my eye, I could see Percival begin to stroke himself. At least the man wasn't shy.

I grinned up at Galahad, a predatory smile that I hoped relayed my message: I remembered last time. And I was going to make him pay. Galahad's dark blue eyes sparkled, silently accepting the gauntlet I threw down.

"How far do I have permission for?" Galahad asked.

"As far as ye like," I whispered back, gently biting his nipple.

A heady rush whipped through me as he flinched with the intended pain. Goddess save me, I wanted to bring this man to his knees. But not yet. No, the torment had only begun.

In one fluid motion, Galahad yanked his tunic over his head and then shook the water from his hair. I slitted my eyes when droplets hit my face.

"You're not wet enough," Galahad said with a grin. Lightning forked across the night sky outside, lining the sultry angles of his face with streaks of white light. Thunder rumbled through our room. "Even the gods agree."

My fingers played with the laces of his breeches. "How do ye plan to appease the gods?"

He whispered, "I only want to please one," then lifted my tunic slowly over my head, tossing the garment to the floor. "A goddess."

Rain slipped down the latticed window panes and cast warbled candlelight across his already honey-toned skin. His chest was hard, everything about him was hard. I drowned in the feel of him, every line, every dip, the way his nipples rubbed against my palm, my fingertips, the way his muscles danced under my feather-light touch.

"Beautiful," Percival moaned from the bed. "So beautiful."

I glanced over my shoulder at the man, before turning to give him a better view . . . pressing my arse to Galahad's cock and slithering over his bulge. Galahad gripped my hips and moved me against him, achingly slow. Wanting to feel the anguish of every caress, I knew.

Percival watched, lips parted, his chest rising and falling with every flushed breath. Then the man's eyes dipped low and Galahad sucked in a breath as I slipped out of my breeches.

With Percival's eyes riveted to me, Galahad snaked an arm around my waist and trailed his finger down to my sex. I arched my back with a delicious moan. And so, he increased the friction, his finger moving back and forth. Percival shifted to sit on the edge of his bed, his own hand moving to the same rhythm. Galahad trailed kisses down my neck, to my shoulder, then he slipped his finger inside me.

"Oh gods," Percival whispered. His eyes watched Galahad move his finger in and out as his other hand played with my breast. The younger man's muscles flexed and tightened, his expression caught somewhere between ecstasy and lust. His lips parting farther when Galahad slipped in another finger deep within me.

Heat roared through my body and my knees grew limp.

I pressed harder against Galahad's cock, rolling my hips with each pump of his fingers. Wanting more. Needing more. Galahad turned my head toward his and he lowered himself until our lips crashed. My entire body sparked into a wild blaze. Every heightened sensation pulsed hot, a searing, liquifying pain I craved. Enough. I needed him on the bed beneath me. Now.

Apparently, Galahad felt the same.

He maneuvered to nudge me toward the bed, but I was faster. In a single move, I twisted him around and kicked under his calves until he fell on top of the covers. Galahad released a booming laugh. I knew he let me win. Just this once. And only because Percival was watching. Still, satisfied with myself, I crawled onto the bed with a wicked smile and tugged on his breeches until they slipped down his hips, down his thighs, and off onto the floor.

My heart stuttered to a halt. Galahad was surely the most god-like built man I had ever beheld. Every inch of his body was sculpted to wondrous perfection. And he was mine for the taking. To destroy and torment and tease.

To love. And stars above, I loved him. I loved him and Percival both.

But part of me still wanted to win this round.

The length of Galahad's cock throbbed, and he nearly roared with release when I lowered myself down and swirled my tongue across his crown. He gasped my name, his chest heaving. My tongue would be the end of him, I was determined. Until he couldn't breathe. Until he clawed at the bed and tightened with building need. Then and only then would I pull away and give him what he needed. What I needed. Our eyes connected, and I flashed a taunting smile. Then my mouth slid down his length. Sweet agony burned each nerve-ending anew as he fisted my braids in his hands. Warm pleasure spread through my belly with his passionate response. My head moved up and down as he rocked his hips, groaning languidly. I could hear Percival's quivering breaths increasing nearby. The man's moans, too, as my tongue licked down Galahad's cock and back up, only to swallow him once more.

"Fionna . . ." Galahad choked out. "I am not sure I will la—"

He didn't need to finish. I crawled up his body, my hair brushing along the tightened muscles of his stomach and chest. And then I waited. Galahad's eyes snapped open as he adjusted his position on the bed. Fidgeting with desire for me. His hands running down the length of my back and settling, firmly, on my arse. Still, I didn't move, not until the glimmer in his eyes grew desperate, almost begging.

"Not a sound," I said right before I sank down onto him, until I felt his hips touch mine. Air hissed from his clenched teeth as he filled me completely. My head fell back with the intense feel of him, my eyes closing momentarily. My head buzzed and spun, dizzy with every hazy, soul-melting sensation. Then, with an impish smile in place, I lifted my hips up and hovered just above him. "No. Sound."

He reached up and curled a single finger around the infernal silver chain and lily pendant dangling from my neck. Then gently yanked until my lips collided with his. I could get lost and never recover in just his kiss alone. Releasing me, he closed his eyes and nodded his head in agreement to my terms.

Hot breath rushed from his lungs when I sank onto him again. With his nails digging into my arse and mine digging into his pectorals, I began to move. And not just move, I writhed as if I possessed him and knew it. One hand fell behind his head as the other moved from the soft flesh of my arse to cup my hip, pulling me back and forth to our fevered rhythm.

Galahad bit down on his bottom lip, hard, as if to keep from making a sound with each thrust. After several long, glorious heartbeats, he opened his eyes. I could tell he was watching me—the way my breasts bounced, the way my white-blond braids fell over my shoulders. The way the muscles in my arms and stomach flexed. His open appreciation and silent worship of my body brought me nearly to the edge. But not as much as when Percival approached our bed.

Gods, these men made me feel so beautiful, so incredibly desirable.

I lifted my head toward Percival's, welcoming the heat of his kiss. Our lips danced to a soft, erotic melody. Then I arched my back, increasing the rolling motions of my hips. Percival knelt, taking my offered breast in his heated mouth. The most toe-curling moan I had ever heard left Galahad's parted lips. And I didn't know I could be anymore aroused. Percival blinked up drowsily from my breast before turning his attention to Galahad, brushing his fingertips along Galahad's ribbed stomach. Feeling how the man moved and rocked beneath me. Galahad stared at Percival, as if to warn the man that he wasn't interested. But Percival didn't notice, too taken with Galahad's body as well as mine. Then Percival returned his attention to exploring my breasts, cupping one in his hand while meeting my eyes.

"I want ye to be my first," Percival whispered between ragged breaths. "Once the Grail Quest is over."

I replied with a bruising kiss before whispering back, "I am yers." My eyes flitted back to Galahad's, and I whispered, "And I am yers."

Galahad gripped my hip, grinding me against him, hard, frantic, saying, "I am yours. Always."

I didn't care if I lost control of this bout. Gods, I could lose every fight, if they destroyed me like this. Heat rolled between my thighs as my body clenched then rippled with a sensation so earth-shattering, I cried out.

Lightning flashed white in our candlelit room, illuminating our naked bodies. Then thunder cracked across the black sky, as if in reply to my release. The rain pounded on the glass. Percival continued to explore my body and kiss my swollen lips. Galahad lost himself to the delirium of my every touch and sigh. But me? I couldn't imagine feeling headier and more complete than I did now—to claim my knights and be claimed in return.

I was undone. And I never wanted to be put back together so long as I breathed.

Chapter Twelve

Arthur

Arthur awoke to the steady pitter-patter of rain on the window and the cold pebbling of his skin. Lancelot hogged the covers. He had practically the whole coverlet bunched onto his side, wrapped around him tightly. Arthur pushed himself to a seat, elbowing Lancelot.

"Another few minutes, pumpkin," Lancelot murmured, and Arthur gave him another sharp elbow in the side.

Lancelot's eyes snapped open as a grin crossed his face.

"Awake you lump," Arthur said. "Bad enough for a king to share a bed with an unwashed man rather than a fair maiden. But you add insult to injury by stealing all the blankets!"

Lancelot stood, stretching over to touch his toes. "You have only yourself to blame, Your Majesty." How come when Lancelot said those words, it sounded a trifle mocking? "The innkeeper offered to turn someone out, so you could have your own room. But you are too damn gallant for your own good and didn't want to pull rank."

"Yes, well, with the storm . . ." Arthur murmured.

"They would have put them up with the horses. No one would have been caught in the rain. And as for the fair maiden, our fifth knight would likely leap into bed with you, if you would only start talking to her again." Lancelot slid him a mock-flirtatious smile. "That's an easy conquest, even for you."

Arthur rubbed his face to clear the sleep, ignoring the tightening in his breeches. "Yes, well, if the sounds coming from the other room had anything to say about her interests, I'm too late." The rumble and clap of thunder had deafened most of the noises emanating from the other knights' room, but there were a few telltale moments that Arthur couldn't argue away as his imagination. It had to be Fionna and Galahad. The damn Dane was far too brawny and handsome. Arthur combed his fingers through his hair. "God knows what poor Percival did to drown out the sound. Perhaps he put a pillow over his head."

"Or perhaps he partook," Lancelot raised an eyebrow, lacing his boots.

Arthur raised an answering eyebrow, pausing as he reached for his sword belt. "Partook? But the Grail Quest—"

"I'm not saying he bedded her, but there are . . . *things* a man can do short of the full deed."

Arthur's face flushed at the possibilities. He knew Lancelot was relaxed about his own sexuality as well as sexual experiences— from his youth with the faeries. But the very thought of one woman with two men was new to Arthur. And alarming. Though, if he were honest, a touch arousing. He cleared his throat, pulling on his boots. "And you think Fionna would be willing to enjoy the company of two men?"

Lancelot shrugged. "She mentioned how women in her clann often take two or more husbands. And that she feels something for several of us. *Definitely you.* She has been beside herself since she betrayed you. And she'll do anything to win back your favor."

Arthur furrowed his brows, buckling Excalibur around his waist. "I don't like the thought of Fionna laying with me simply to win back my favor. I would have her choose me freely, not to appease some sense of obligation or duty."

Lancelot rolled his eyes, letting out an exasperated breath. "Will you stop being so noble, man? All I'm saying is that *she cares for you.*" He pushed a finger into Arthur's shoulder. "*You,* Arthur Pendragon. She's holding back because she fears *you* are still angry with her. If *you* show her that you're not, she'll come to your bed-side gladly."

Perhaps Lancelot was right. He had been holding himself back from Fionna since she had stolen Excalibur. But was he truly ready to open his heart to her again? He wasn't sure. But if he didn't now, perhaps he would lose her—Galahad would stake his claim—and then when Arthur finally came around, he would be too late. "Wise counsel, my friend. But, I thought you possessed no favor for Fion-na. Now you think we can trust her?"

Lancelot buckled on his cloak. Something foreign flashed through his eyes—something shadowed that Arthur couldn't quite place. What was it about the two of them? "Fionna . . . she's not for me. That doesn't mean she's not for you." He clapped Arthur on the shoulder. "Now let's go get whatever creepy-as-hell bone thing the witch carved for you."

Arthur laughed. "Can't wait."

The road back to the Bone Carver's cottage was much as it was before. The rain had mostly stopped. Fat drops slid off the leaves above them, finding their way onto foreheads and down tunic fronts not protected by their cloaks. Arthur liked the smell of the air after a storm—as if the whole world was fresh and rejuvenated. If only the curse could be vanquished as easily.

Arthur rode by Lancelot and Fionna rode behind with Per-cival and Galahad. Those three warriors were gleeful as maidens around a Maypole, chattering and laughing, the color high on their cheeks. Envy snaked through him, its green fingers grasping at his heart. He wanted to make Fionna laugh like that, to put that sultry, knowing smile on her face.

Lancelot cast a sideways smirk his way. "You keep sighing like that, you're going to run out of breath. Just go talk to her. Tell her you forgive her. Fully this time, and not just because you need her on the quest."

Arthur stifled another sigh. "I hadn't realized my thoughts were so plain."

"A goat is better at keeping secrets than you."

"I don't know, a goat can be sly. They steal the washing off the line and eat it . . ." Arthur said, frowning.

"Fine." Lancelot threw up his hands. "A chicken. A chicken could lie better than you."

Arthur chuckled. "A king needn't do everything himself. Perhaps you can serve the roll. Be my royal deceiver. Whenever I need a lie told, I'll send you in—" He fell silent as Lancelot's face grew blacker and blacker.

"As you wish, Your Majesty," Lancelot said stiffly, before kicking his horse into a trot and pulling ahead.

"Lance—" Arthur called out, cursing his unthoughtful jest. Lancelot must still be sensitive over the business with Morgana and the two serving-wenches. Would he never be rid of his half-sister's foreboding presence?

Arthur went in alone to retrieve the item the Bone Carver had created for them. Curiosity warred with wariness as he entered her house again while the others awaited him outside.

"Little Dragon King," the woman said, a smile curving her face as he entered. "I have something quite magnificent for you."

"I could hardly sleep last night from the suspense," he admitted.

"You sure it wasn't the pounding?" the Bone Carver said, the smile growing wider.

How could she possibly . . . "What?" he asked, his mouth going dry.

"Of the weather," she clarified. "The storm was a loud one."

"Yes, the storm. Perhaps thunder and rain contributed."

She pulled a box off a shelf—the size of his two palms together—then she handed the plain, carved wood over to him. "Open the lid."

Arthur swallowed as the hinges creaked. Inside lay a key. Milky white, carved of bone. The craftsmanship was exquisite, the key's bow an intricate triskelion knot of intersecting lines. "A key," he said. He fought disappointment. He didn't know why, but he had expected a dagger, or a staff, or something that wasn't . . . a key. "What does it open?"

"The door will reveal itself to you when the time is right," the Bone Carver said.

Of course. Another faerie riddle. Anything to do with the Grail was full to the brim with intrigues. He nodded. "I thank you for your aid. The craftsmanship is superb." He closed the lid and bowed. "Now, if I may beg your leave, we must be on our way. The journey is long, and time is of the essence." He turned toward the door.

"Don't you want to ask me your question?" she asked after him.

Arthur spun on his heel. "What question . . ." he trailed off. But he knew what question and straightened. "You said my knight Fionna had power. What power do you speak of?"

"I know not. The truth of her is shielded from my sight, for a reason I cannot discern. But this hidden magic is a mystery worth exploring."

His shoulders drooped slightly. He didn't know why he had thought this strange woman could tell him something about Fionna. And he didn't know exactly why he thought there was something to tell. Only what he already knew: there was indeed something unique about his fifth knight. And as the woman said, a mystery worth solving.

"I will offer you this advice, Arthur Pendragon, free of charge. Keep her close to your side. For she is the other key you need on this quest."

Arthur ducked his head in thanks. The Bone Carver's words followed him out the door. Another key. But to unlock what?

Chapter Thirteen

Percival

Nothing ruined a ride through the countryside like coming upon a dead body. Percival's mood that day had been buoyant, to say the least. Ecstatic might be a fairer description. He couldn't stop thinking of Fionna—the look of her taut stomach in the candlelight, the feel of her bare breasts . . . his cock grew hard with each lingering thought. The way her eyes had fluttered shut in pleasure as Galahad took her. As soon as this quest was over, he would show her such pleasure. He was surprised at how little he had minded sharing the experience with Galahad, though part of him wanted a woman all to himself. Wanted a night with *Fionna*—all to himself.

As the latter thought ignited him once more, his horse danced to the side beneath him—the movement so sudden, he was nearly thrown.

"Och," Percival groaned as he caught sight of what Kit had avoided. "Arthur!" he called back. "Ye need to see this." They were deep in the territory of Gwynedd. Though, not technically Arthur's kingdom, his role as the Pendragon together with his generally honorable nature meant the problems of other Welsh lands still weighed heavy upon his king's conscience.

The knights gathered around the poor fellow, who had been horribly mauled from the looks of it. Must have been a gruesome way to die.

"This just happened," Fionna said, a pale hand before her mouth. "Less than a few hours ago, I would say."

"What manner of creature did this? A wolf? A boar?" Percival asked, looking about.

Lancelot muttered, "Not another bloody boar."

"Look at these tracks," Galahad said, kneeling in the crushed grass, just beyond the man. "They don't look like wolf or boar." He frowned, placing a hand down next to the prints. "There are almost—fingers. I mean, clawed fingers. Five on this print . . ." he rolled in his bottom lip while thinking. "Four on this one. I've never seen anything like these marks." He stood.

"The tracks seem to lead in the direction of that lake," Fionna pointed. "Could the creature live in the lake?"

"But why didn't the creature take the man with it? Or eat him?" Lancelot asked. "Could this mysterious beast kill for sport?"

"There's a village round the other side of the lake." Arthur pointed just ahead of their trail. "The poor fellow likely belongs to someone there. Let's take him back for burial, and then find out what they know about the beast behind this vicious attack."

Betws-y-Coed was a quaint town much like one would find in Gwent. Squat, lime-washed houses topped with thatched roofs and bounded by tidy vegetable gardens. As they rode slowly through the main thoroughfare into the cobblestone circle at the center of town, the faces of townsfolk followed them with curiosity, rather than hostility. Even when they dismounted.

A man strode out of the only large building in town, which professed itself to be the village inn. "We welcome you," the man said. He was barrel-chested and tall, nearly bald, but with strong features and a confident way about him. "I'm Willum, the Manor Lord of this village. What brings you to us?"

"Arthur Pendragon, Overking of Gwent," Arthur said, and Willum bowed hurriedly, his brown eyes going wide. Those eyes flicked over each of the knights in turn, settling on Fionna with startling intensity. Percival frowned.

"My humble apologies, Your Majesty. I did not see a king's banner or I might have graced you with better manners befitting your crown."

"At ease, Willum," Arthur held out a kind hand. "We were traveling nearby and came across a man who had been slain. We feared he may be a man from Betws-y-Coed and thought only to deliver him back to his family." Arthur motioned to Galahad, who gently pulled the man's body off the back of his horse, lowering him to the ground. They had wrapped him in a spare cloak, but blood was seeping through the fabric.

Willum's hand strayed to his bare head in an unconscious gesture. "Another one? Bloody hell." He winced, seeming to realize his words. "Pardon, Your Majesty."

"Another one?" Percival asked, stepping up. "He isn't the first?"

Galahad knelt and pulled the cloak back, revealing the man's identity.

Willum's face fell. "Yes, he's one of ours." A semi-circle of townsfolk had grown around them, and Willum turned to a lad who was hanging back. "Jon, go fetch Roselyn, will you? Tell her to bring her sister. Be gentle about it."

The boy nodded and dashed off down the road.

"I'm afraid he isn't the first. A monster lives in our lake and stalks the good people of our town. And I fear within the month, a town won't be left to find."

"A monster?" Percival asked. "What nature of creature? Have you seen this beast?"

Arthur cast him an annoyed look, but he couldn't help his curiosity. Wasn't it every knight's duty to slay the beasts preying on innocent Welshmen and women like this?

"The beast is called the Afanc," a lilting female voice answered.

They all turned to where the voice had come from and Percival's eyes widened at the sight. On the fringe of the circle stood two women—unlike women he had ever seen. Their hair shone black as midnight, their skin tawny and bronzed. With tilting eyes framed by dark lashes and full, voluptuous lips, the two women were some of the most beautiful creatures he had ever laid eyes on. Excluding Fionna perhaps—though the beauty of these women was of a different type altogether. Sultry and foreign. Their attire was stranger still, colorful silken fabrics flowing around them, tied about their tiny waists. Curved swords rested at their hips and gold glinted in their ears and . . . even in a woman's nose!

"And who are you?" Lancelot asked, lifting his piercing blue eyes her way. Percival suppressed a snort. Nothing drew Lancelot out of his black mood like a beautiful woman.

"I am Cyra," said the one with the nose ring. She was shorter, fuller of hip and bosom. "And this is my sister, Lelah."

The other sister had long silken hair that cascaded down to the small of her back; she wore a necklace with a ruby the size of a robin's egg. The women must know how to use those swords, if they felt safe to ride about alone with such jewels on their person.

"We have traveled from our home of Constantinople, tracking the Afanc," Cyra added. "The creature was born of dark magic in our land and, therefore, it is our duty to kill this monster."

Cyra knelt by the man who had died, and placed a hand on his chest, closing her eyes. Then she looked up at Willum and shook her head. "I'm too late."

Too late? Percival thought. It was plain to see the man was dead, but Willum seemed crushed. His face fell even more until deep lines crinkled his eyes and around his mouth.

Lelah spoke, her voice soft as a rose's petals, "We are grieved how the creature made it so far, killing so many. The Afanc has taken to this land's cold climate, and so we have bound it to this place, to keep the monster from moving on. If we have any chance of ending this beast, it will be here."

"Your cause is noble," Arthur said, nodding. "But it's only a beast. Surely with all of you together, you could make quick work of it?"

"This is no ordinary beast," Willum said. "It has magic and controls the river somehow, making the water overflow beyond the banks with devastating results. Our farms have been flooded time and again. We'll have nothing for winter."

"Even magical creatures can be slain," Galahad said.

"Not this one." Willum's grief-stricken gaze met Galahad's. "All the Afanc does is kill. Again, and again."

"What do ye mean?" Fionna asked.

Lelah spoke, laying a gentle hand on Willum's drooping shoulder. The man suddenly looked exhausted, as though he had never known a day of sleep in his life. "To keep the creature sated, each day Willum and his son and daughter go down to the pool where it lays in wait and sacrifice their lives to the monster."

Percival recoiled, and the other knights exchanged shocked glances.

Arthur spoke first. "How do you still live? And what do you mean, each day?"

"The creature isn't hungry," Willum said. "It just wants to kill mortals. So, we give it something to kill. And then Cyra and Lelah bring us back to life."

Lancelot's brows furrowed over his darkening eyes. "What sorcery is this?"

"Our magic is similar to the type that crafted the Afanc," Lelah said. "The connection between this place, the creature, and these people—it enables us to do what no man or woman should be able to do. Bring back the dead. It was a solution for a time, but we cannot continue indefinitely. We haven't been able to end this cycle."

Excitement was building in Percival. This was a perfect opportunity to prove his worth—to Arthur, to Fionna. He knew last night had been a step toward her seeing him not as a mere lad anymore, but as the man he was. But slaying this beast would cement this truth in all their minds. Plus, these poor townspeople needed relief. A hero.

Percival straightened, lifting his chin. "The monster must die. And I will help ye slay the Afanc."

Lelah's face softened. "We thank you for your offer, brave knight, but I am afraid it would be a death sentence. For the Afanc cannot be killed by any mortal weapon."

Arthur cast Percival an exasperated look. "If that is the case, then I believe we can help. For my blade is not forged by a man."

Chapter Fourteen

Fionna

I couldn't help but think of what a strange world I had tangled myself up into by joining Arthur and his knights. In Ulster, there were goddesses to honor before battle and whispers of faerie tales around the hearth fire.

But here, in Wales, the extraordinary seemed an everyday occurrence.

I noticed the stiff set of Arthur's shoulders as Percival boldly announced how he would valiantly slay the Afanc. Then how the frown on Arthur's shadow-lined face deepened as he reluctantly agreed to Percival's heroics. But I knew my king's bleeding heart, and we would not have ridden from this hidden village without helping her suffering people first. It wasn't in his nature to be calloused or indifferent.

"There are rooms enough in the inn for each of you," Willum said, tugging me from my internal ramblings. "Don't have a lot of visitors these days. Get settled, Your Majesty, and then we can talk further at dinner."

I turned to lead my new horse to the stables—a dark earthen brown gelding named Acorn—when Galahad strode my way, intent upon me. My breath hitched in my chest as I beheld him, as the heat of memories billowed in my blazing pulse and curled throughout my body. The exquisite feel of him inside me, all around me. Skies above, he was a singular pleasure unlike any I had ever known. And with Percival there beside us, his hands and his lips upon me . . . I was more daring than I had ever been, but our shared intimacy still felt so very right. Even now, I reveled in the sensations of my body, the sweet soreness between my legs.

All these thoughts flashed in the space of a second. But Galahad pushed past me gently, laying a hand on my shoulder before he leaned down to lift Acorn's hoof.

I craned my head around the bulk of his torso and pressed my lips into a thin line. The shoe was loose.

Galahad clucked his tongue in disapproval, straightening. He patted Acorn's sleek shoulder. "He was favoring this foot during the latter part of the ride," Galahad said. "Willum! You have a farrier?"

Willum nodded, pointing toward a wattle and daub structure at the end of the village. "Blacksmith can shoe a horse."

Embarrassment prickled at my flushing face. "I should have noticed." I prided myself on paying expert attention to my mounts. They were partners and friends. But apparently, I had been too wrapped up in my thoughts over my knights to notice. Once again, I found these men were changing me. Some of my new differences I liked, but other alterations I found quite unwelcome.

"Don't worry." Galahad shrugged and leaned in, his body heat and sandalwood scent threatening to destroy what was left of my good sense. "I only noticed," he whispered in my ear, "because I was admiring how nice your arse looks in a saddle."

I replied with a snort of outrage, but my heart wasn't in it.

Galahad gave my chin a little tap with his knuckles before sauntering away to join Arthur and the others who conversed with the eastern mystics. The beautiful, seductive, compelling magical mystics with hair as black as onyx and skin as smooth as buttermilk.

I shoved down a tendril of jealousy as I led Acorn toward the forge. What was I afraid of? That Arthur or his knights would fall for one of the women? They were free men, I had no claim to them. But even as I said those words to myself, they rang hollow. I had laid claim to each of them, and them to me. Even the-ever-in-sulating Lancelot, who seemed inexplicably determined to resist the dark, passionate bond that was germinating between us. Already, the building steam began escaping his tamped-down control. My lip curled in disgust, and I kicked a pebble with the toe of my boot. I would not be one of those women who schemed to keep a man through tricks or jealousy. If I wasn't compelling enough for the likes of them, then I was better off without their fair-weather hearts.

The blacksmith was a rugged man with arms as large as Galahad's. He kept his black hair cropped close to his scalp, and his thick beard neatly trimmed. His eyes widened at my and Acorn's approach, and he laid down his hammer to straighten his apron.

"My Lady," he said, inclining his head. He had a pleasant voice, deep and honest. "How may I assist you?"

"My horse's shoe is loose," I said. "Left front. Do ye have time to re-shoe?"

"It would be my honor, Lady." He took Acorn's reins and then felt down his fetlock toward the shoe. "I am called Colwyn. What brings you to Betws-y-Coed?"

"I am Fionna," I replied in kind. "We were passing through when we found . . . one of the Afanc's victims. I believe my fellow knight is going to try to help."

"Help?" Colwyn lay a hand on Acorn's neck, stepping closer to me. His eyes darted to the necklace around my neck and then, slowly, his gaze traveled back to mine. "Are you the maiden?"

I wrinkled my brow. "I'm not sure what ye mean."

He took another step closer and I stilled my hand's twitch toward my sword. I didn't think he was being threatening. If anything, the glint in his dark eyes as he regarded me was—reverent? He smelled of sweat and woodsmoke, iron and musk. Honest smells.

"You've met the mystics?"

I nodded.

"Well then surely they've shared that there is only one way to lure the Afanc out into the open. The creature is partial to fair maidens. And you, My Lady, may be the fairest of all."

My mouth opened and then closed in surprise. Men had complimented me before, but few were so forward. "I thank ye," I managed. "If a maiden is needed to lure the Afanc out to be killed, then I suppose I can volunteer. Now I'll leave ye to your work and return when ye're finished with Acorn's shoe."

I unbuckled and pulled my saddlebags off Acorn's rump quickly, grateful for their bulk before me.

"Fair Fionna . . ." Colwyn's voice caressed my name and a chill clawed its icy fingers up my spine. "I am a man of few means, and surely you could sup with gods and kings, but if you would have me—"

"I thank ye for yer kindness, sir."

I backed up hastily out of the forge's heat. Then I spun on my heel, my mind working furiously as I hurried toward the inn. The man offered me his hand in marriage! What manner of madness was this? This town was growing stranger by the minute.

Night fell quickly over the little village. Willum had served us a mouth-watering stew flavored by spiced rabbit and carrots and turnips, the remnants sopped up with warm, hearty rye bread. The farm ale was naturally chilled by the elements and light, just as I preferred my hard drinks. I was now feeling comfortable and drowsy as I leaned back in my chair, my mind drifting comfortably in the way only a good meal can inspire.

Willum was blowing out the candles in the far corner of the common room while sweeping the floor.

"We should retire," I said. When had the hour bloomed so late?

"Indeed," Arthur said, pushing to his feet. "Lord Willum, thank you for the fine meal. Please give your daughter my esteemed regards for her culinary skills."

The innkeeper and Manor Lord paused from his tasks. "If you can rid us of the Afanc, you've free meals here for life, Your—"

Galahad stood. "I accept your generous offer."

"Not you, good Sir." Willum grinned, an odd look on his sorrow-lined face. "You look as though you could eat a wagonload each meal."

Galahad guffawed at the man's audacity, and the rest of us laughed as well. I wanted to help these people. They had spirit, despite their current circumstances.

Lelah, the woman with the long flowing tresses, appeared in the stairwell's doorway. She had changed into a dress of cobalt silk that left little to the imagination. "My sister and I desire your company. To share more about the creature. Will you come?"

Arthur nodded and followed Lelah up the stairs, followed quickly by the others. I pursed my lips before joining the invitation.

And stars, the sisters' chambers were unlike any I had ever seen.

"Remarkable." Percival goggled, his head swiveling back-and-forth to take in all the extravagance.

The familiar-styled furniture I knew lined the side walls to make room for a dozen large, colorful pillows, each cushion carefully positioned over a vibrant-patterned rug. Tapestries stitched with gold thread hung on the walls, and brightly-hued lanterns in octagonal shapes cast strange symbols all around the warmly illuminated room.

"Welcome," Cyra said, kneeling on a pillow before a roaring fireplace.

"You brought all of this with you?" Lancelot surveyed the room, wrinkles appearing on his forehead, his mouth tilted halfway between a sneer and a frown.

"Home is so far away. The endless distance is difficult at times. So, we thought to bring a bit of home with us," Lelah said, as if carrying all of one's home furnishings across the known world was perfectly common.

"Pity the mule who had to carry your treasures," Lancelot muttered, and I stifled a laugh, grateful for Lancelot's cynicism to break the spell of this bewitching place.

"This is cozy." Galahad plopped onto a pillow by the fire across from Cyra, toeing off his boots.

"No, beautiful . . ." Percival whispered. But his eyes weren't fixed on the room. They were fixed solely on Lelah.

I started to sigh but stopped when I caught Lancelot watching me. A calculating look glittered in his icy-blue gaze—a shadow of a smile on his sensual lips. With just a single look, I felt naked before him—I knew he had undressed my thoughts—could see my petty jealousy. Arthur, Galahad, Percival, Lancelot—these incredible men were mine. But I hadn't claimed them. Not truly. Not in a way that was binding.

The smile broke across Lancelot's face in earnest as he strode forward, dropping onto a cerulean-hued cushion beside Cyra. "We thank you for your hospitality, dear sisters," Lancelot practically purred at her, each sultry-spoken word frothing my blood into action.

I narrowed my eyes at him and his smile grew wider, his scintillating eyes locked with mine. Oh, so that's how he wanted to play?

My good sense fled me as I slinked onto a beaded cushion between Arthur and Galahad. Closer to Arthur than was strictly required. Let the games begin.

Chapter Fifteen

Fionna

"May we offer you refreshments?" Lelah peered up through her lashes at the men—a look both demure and coy. In one hand, she held a blue glass bottle that I assumed contained some sort of alcohol and, in the other, a finely carved bowl.

Lelah settled onto a cushion between Percival and Arthur as Cyra stretched back and retrieved a tray with glasses from a low bookshelf.

Lancelot examined her arched form with unveiled interest, and I rolled my eyes.

The sisters poured a clear liquid into the tiny glasses and passed them round. I studied mine, marveling in the glass's beveling and the gold inlay. They were chalices a queen might drink from. I couldn't fathom how these beautiful vessels traveled unimaginable leagues and remained intact.

"My gods!" Galahad exclaimed, regarding his empty glass—he had already downed the contents. He blinked rapidly. "That tastes of . . . anise."

"Anise?" I asked, sniffing my drink. "What is anise?"

Cyra laughed, a light, carefree sound. "Pace yourself, good Sir. Even a man such as yourself will feel the effects of Arak, if you drink so quickly. Arak is strong." Cyra turned her gaze onto me. "Anise is a spice native to Constantinople, where we are from. Sultans and Pharaohs, even the Greeks and Romans, have enjoyed drinks and candies made from anise seeds and licorice root for ages."

"The Welsh Lord who squired me would travel to Rome every so often," Galahad shared. "He returned with licorice and anise candies for his household each time."

Lelah was attending to the bowl now, lighting the end of a little wrapped herb bundle in the fire. "Breathing in the vapors of the dried cannabis plant is tradition in our land. Before battle. This medicinal herb will help you relax and sleep deeply. This is the least we can do to honor and prepare you for tomorrow."

"We thank you, My Ladies," Arthur said, taking a sip from his glass. "But what would also help prepare us is more information about the Afanc. You said this creature comes from your land. What else can you share?"

"The blacksmith shared how the Afanc is only lured out of its lair by a fair maiden. Then the creature begins to kill," I added. "I offered to serve."

All the knights' heads swiveled my way. I shrugged.

"I am only being logical. I can defend myself." Though a horrible thought struck me. Hopefully by maiden he meant young woman and not . . . an actual maiden, as in virgin. After what Galahad and Percival and I had done last night, I certainly didn't qualify in the latter sense. Remembered pleasure shivered over my skin, and I took a gulp of the drink to down the memory. The liquid burned my throat, the powerful taste of anise filing my nostrils. I coughed. "Arak is . . . interesting," I managed, hoarsely.

Galahad laughed.

"Arak isn't for everyone," Cyra said sweetly.

Lelah was waving a graceful hand through the pungent smelling smoke now, wafting ribboned tendrils in lazy curlicues.

"Lady Fionna speaks truth," Lelah said, setting the bowl on the carpet between us. "The Afanc requires a fair woman to bring the creature out into the open. But there is something else you must know. The Afanc is invisible."

Lancelot froze mid-sip and coughed. "I'm sorry, is that a joke?"

"We're afraid not, Sir. But," Cyra said hastily, "we have a talisman to help."

She reached across Lancelot's lap, flashing him a flirtatious smile, and then retrieved a little box by the fireplace. The lid was carved in geometric designs and inlaid with mother of pearl. Here in Wales, a treasure such as this box would fetch a king's ransom. Or in Ulster. The latter thought burrowed deep into my mind. And, with a painful pang, images of Father and Aideen tormented my grief. Surely Arthur's messenger was drawing near the shores of Ulster by now. My stomach heaved at the memory of my own voyage across the Irish Sea. A sailor I was not.

Cyra opened the intricately-carved box to reveal a small, green, rough-cut gemstone. "This is an adder stone." She offered the talisman to Percival. "If you are the warrior who will face the beast tomorrow, then this stone is yours to carry."

Percival took the gem, turning the stone over and examining the colors in the light. "I would like to remain the warrior, lass. But . . . His Majesty's sword possesses the power to slay the beast, ye ken? Perhaps . . ." He turned to Arthur, hope in his brown eyes. "Perhaps I could borrow your blade, My King?"

Arthur frowned, his hand straying to Excalibur's hilt. He seemed to consider, wearing the face of a king, rather than the boyish one I preferred. Finally, he nodded. "I will lend you Excalibur to complete this task. Just don't run off with my sword." I froze as Arthur slid a sideways look my way. Relief flooded me when a hint of a smile appeared at one corner of his fine mouth.

I let out a shaky laugh. "Indeed. For what kind of knight runs off with their king's sword?"

"A treacherous one," Lancelot muttered, robbing the moment of all its levity. I resisted making a lewd gesture at him as he scooted closer to Cyra.

"May I have more of that liquor?" Galahad held his glass out as I took an experimental breath from the bundled herbs.

"So, tell us of this Afanc's creation, My Ladies," Lancelot said, his voice smooth and sweet. "You mentioned how the creature's magic mirrors your own? How can that possibly be true?"

Lelah wound her thick hair into a braid as she began to regale us with stories of how their mentor, a great mystic in Constantinople, explored dark magics. Her voice was melodious and mesmerizing, the story hanging in the air before me as if a moving tapestry. I could feel the heat from the desert's beating sun—though, I knew not of what a desert truly was or looked like. A land of endless, golden earth and sparse vegetation? It boggled the mind. I could smell her mentor's bubbling cauldrons as Lelah spoke them into life in the room, and I could also see the glint of gold and scarlet of their master's turban, which Lelah demonstrated by using a scarf. So many wonderous new words and images. I was riveted.

Sweat trickled down my back and I pulled at my thick tunic. I was so hot—my limbs heavy and pleasantly numb. The sweet-smelling smoke seemed to fill my head, dulling my senses. I unbuckled my sword belt and pulled off my boots. Against the backdrop of the story, I was dimly aware of the movement in the room—Galahad pouring himself another glass; Percival's fingers trailing up Lelah's arm and around her swan's neck; Lancelot pulling Cyra onto his lap, his strong hand tangling in her black tresses, his lips brushing along her collarbone as she arched her head back in delight.

Jealousy coiled in my stomach, until I noticed Arthur next to me. He had removed his crown and his boots, though not Excalibur. He was gazing at me with such a look of plaintive longing that his ardor, his open desire lanced through the fog in my head and pierced straight to my heart. My king . . . my king still *wanted me.* Even after all I had done—the treachery, the betrayal. I knew what that sleepy, dreamy look meant in a man's eye. And seeing Arthur's face softened so? An answer to a prayer I dared not express even in the shadows of my heart.

The room faded away as Lelah finished her story, and I grabbed a fistful of Arthur's tunic and pulled him to me with more strength than I realized. He toppled forward and we both tumbled back onto the pillows with a surprised laugh and soft, pleasurable exhales of breath.

The others peered our way in surprise at the sudden motion— Percival's lips plump from kissing Lelah, Lancelot turning from the half-untied laces of Cyra's gown. Galahad—well Galahad was snoring softly, passed out in a pile of cushions, his arms and limbs spread out.

Arthur pushed himself back up and tugged me to my feet. "I thank you for your hospitality this evening, My Ladies. I fear I must retire."

"I am tired as well," I managed, though I'm not sure who I was trying to fool.

Lancelot's eyes darkened before he turned back to Cyra, burying his face between the curves of her full breasts.

I shoved aside my unease at the sight and grabbed my boots and sword belt. Then, I allowed Arthur to tow me by the hand to his chamber two doors down.

Once inside, he pushed the door shut, walking me back with the bulk of his body until my spine pressed to the door. My breath hitched as his lips met mine, strong and sure and *Arthur*.

". . . My Lady . . ."

"Arthur—"

"—Do you—"

I couldn't give my consent fast enough. "Kiss me. Touch me. I give ye permission to do as ye please."

Arthur pulled away just enough to meet my eyes. "I do not wish for you to think I only long for you after imbibing in tonight's exotic offerings. Nor as a guilt offering." He cupped my face with a sweet, chaste kiss. "I have behaved the fool," he whispered hoarsely. "I ache to bridge the distance I selfishly created between us."

I traced my fingertips over his lips and whispered back, "I wish for you to only know pleasure and happiness, Arthur Pendragon."

His eyes fluttered shut as an appreciative shudder wended down his body. "I need you, Fionnabhair Allán."

"I am yers, My King. My heart, my mind, my body, I give it all to ye this night. Whatever ye need of me."

His lips were upon mine, this time slow and reverent. The back of his fingers caressed the curve of my cheek and down my neck. Light touches that betrayed his trembling hands and his quivering breaths. As if he were holding back an enormity of emotion. As if he knew apologies and requests for forgiveness were trite compared to the words his heart wished to express instead. No man had ever touched me with such veneration and my knees grew weak at the beauty he made me feel with just the tips of his fingers and the soft stroke of his lips.

Pulling back, Arthur took my hand in his and led me toward the bed. Candlelight flickered across the walls and glinted in a night-blackened latticed window. A blush colored his fair skin as he glanced at me shyly over his shoulder. The authority of a king had melted away to reveal a vulnerable young man, a boyishness I couldn't resist. Longing pooled deep in his gaze as he cherished the very sight of me, and I found myself flushing as well, as though a bashful maiden instead of a fierce warrior. Our awareness of one another charged the air between us. An energy both bright and beautiful. A deep connection I could not explain yet felt all the same, as sure as I breathed.

At his bed, Arthur leaned in and pressed his lips to mine once more. This time with building urgency. A firestorm burst between us and my hands roamed the broad expanse of his chest, shoulders, and back, needing to explore the searing flames licking our bodies. The heat was utterly delicious, the headiness more blissful than the finest wine. We fell to the covers and tangled into each other's embrace, our clothing and armor tossed about the floor.

His breath shuddered as I began kissing the freckles across his chest and down the ribbed muscles of his abdomen. Hard muscle formed a tantalizing V down his hips to his groin and my mouth needed to savor every dip and curve of his masculinity. The soft caress of his fingers on my face, the feel of his skin on my lips, the moans of pleasure escaping his mouth, the way every sculpted line of his body flexed when the tip of my tongue tasted the salt of his excitement—they were a far more intoxicating drug than the one we had enjoyed earlier this evening.

I licked the length of him, my core burning for release as he breathed my name . . . as though a prayer, as though a plea. As though my name formed the very breath in his lungs. To draw out each sensation intensely, my mouth slid down the shaft of his cock achingly slow while my tongue swirled across the sensitive skin. His hands left my face to grip the headboard and his hips rolled beneath my ministrations. And then they rocked again, slow at first, but quickly gaining rhythm as his breaths grew more ragged.

"Fionna . . ." he called out as his body stiffened until the veins in his forearms stood in stark relief. I leaned back to watch him cli-max, a smile on my lips as he groaned, muscles tightening and then relaxing. He was the most beautiful man I had ever known, even more so when he peaked.

I crawled up the bed to his mouth, wanting him to taste him-self on my lips. His kiss was deep, erotic, and breathless. More sen-sual than I expected of Arthur. Then he rolled me onto my back and, with a grin, cherished me in return. And gods, the feel of him as the hard planes of his body brushed along the soft curves of mine, as his tongue played with my nipples before dipping to my thighs. The fire blazing hot and licking our bodies now pooled between my legs, and I burned with each sizzling flick of his tongue. I want-ed to turn to ash in his fingers, to feel the earth quake beneath me. The pleasure built and billowed as he lapped at my arousal until I cried out, clutching his hair, then the covers, then the headboard behind me.

Arthur moved up my body and buried his face into my neck. He trailed light kisses down to my collarbone, then to my shoulder. "We are fated for each other," he whispered into my skin. "My body belongs to yours. I am your servant and gladly kneel before you."

He grazed his nose along my jaw, his hot breath branding my skin. With a sigh, my head fell back, and my eyes closed while the moon kissed my pulse and glittering stars danced in my veins.

"I love ye, Arthur Pendragon."

"I love you, Fionnabhair Allán."

Chapter Sixteen

Percival

Percival felt different with Excalibur on his hip. Stronger. Invincible. Was this how Arthur felt like all the time? He didn't think so. Perhaps the weight of Arthur's crown balanced out whatever joy he might gain from this faerie blade. Lately, his king walked with a mantle of worry about him that seemed to grow heavier by the day.

With a sigh, he squinted his eyes and peered down the trail.

According to Lelah and Cyra, the Afanc slept in a slow-moving stretch of river just past the village, where the water rippled in lazy circles against an expanse of flat stones.

The thought of Lelah set Percival's blood racing. His head still felt filled with wool from last night's spicy drink and strange ceremonial smoke. His memories were etched in hazy images that were as slippery as eels. He knew he hadn't broken his vow last night. Indeed, he thought he had only put the skills he had gained with Fionna to good use. Glimpsed memories of Lelah's caramel skin and the sound of her soft moans as he saw to her pleasure tantalized him. She was an exquisite woman. But . . . Percival glanced at their fifth knight out of the corner of his eye, walking beside him through the forest, her face peaceful. Lelah had been like a pleasant dream, but only a dream. Elusive as their herbal smoke. Fionna was real. What he had felt when he had touched her—when her lips had burned across his skin—the solid presence of her at his side and in his life. His night with the mystic had confirmed one detail in his mind. For him, there was only Fionna.

"Ye have the stone?" Fionna asked, for the third time.

"Aye, dove. I didn't lose it between the village and here." Percival pulled the stone from his belt pouch and tossed the talisman into the air, watching as the rough-hewn facets sparkled in the morning light.

"I just want ye to be prepared. This beast has taken down many men. And the mystics can't bring us back, like they do the villagers."

"Ye know, lass, if I didn't know better, I would say ye were worried for me." A smile quirked at the corner of his mouth.

Fionna looked at him with a mixture of care and exasperation. She reached out and grabbed a fistful of his tunic, pulling him sideways against her. She then tucked herself under his arm in a way that Percival found extremely pleasant. "Of course, I'm worried for ye. I am fond of ye, Percy. Ye must promise ye'll be careful. No heroics."

"Percy?" he asked, a grin forming.

She arched a white brow. "What, ye think yer the only one who can hand out nicknames?"

"Fair point, lass."

"So, ye just have to hold the stone?" Fionna asked. "And the invisible and secret will be revealed to ye?"

"According to Cyra, it really is that simple." He felt Fionna stiffen beneath him at the mention of the mystic.

Percival softened. "Ye know . . . last night meant nothing, right? Just idle fun. For Lancelot too."

"It's none of my business who ye bed with." Fionna focused on the ground, a muscle in her jaw jumping.

"If ye say so." Was Fionna jealous? The thought filled him with a bolt of gleeful excitement. "Ye know there's only one lass I want to be with . . ."

Fionna remained silent.

"It's ye," he added.

She rolled her eyes, pushing him away from her. "Yes, I gathered that, ye goat."

Percival laughed, but as he did, his eyes caught something strange about Fionna. He blinked, then squinted in case the streaming sunlight was playing tricks with his eyes. But the strangeness was still there. A web of delicate silver filaments covered her from head to toe—as though Fionna had walked through the gossamer strands of a bejeweled spiderweb.

"What?" Fionna asked. "Ye're gaping at me like a fish."

"There's . . ." he hesitated. Did Fionna know she was covered in a web of magic? Why had he never seen the signs before? A sudden thought occurred to him and Percival shoved the stone back into his belt pouch. As soon as his fingers broke contact, the shimmering lines disappeared. He pushed out a shaky breath.

"Fion—" he began, but she shushed him.

"There's the pool." She pointed. "Hide yerself. I will go from here alone."

Percival retrieved the stone again from his pouch, ignoring the strange lines resting over Fionna's fair form. He would deal with that mysterious magic later. Now, the Afanc needed to be his sole focus. He slowly pulled Excalibur out of its sheath, reveling in the surge of energy flooding up his arm.

"Be careful, dove," he hissed in warning as she crept toward the riverbank. She held a dagger near her hip, but her sword wasn't out. She didn't want to frighten the Afanc.

Percival crept closer, pushing through the trees to find a better vantage point.

Fionna reached a large flat rock on the riverbed, its granite face dappled by the sun. She settled upon the top, her dagger gripped beneath her bent knee. And then she began to sing.

Percival's mouth fell open as the first notes of her melody reached his ears, borne gently on the spring breeze. Her voice was as clear and pure as the rushing waters beneath her, sweet as honey mead. A lullaby. Perhaps one that was sung to her when she was wee bairn . . .

O sleep my wee babe, under the rowan,
With the sun repairing

With the moon in her silver chair in
Watches with your mother
Too-ra-la-la, Tra-la-lo…

He closed his eyes, allowing the sound of Fionna's voice to wash over him, to permeate his very soul. He hadn't thought their knight could be any more magnificent a woman than she already was. But this new gentle facet of her only made him love her all the more.

A tear dripped from the corner of his eye and crawled down his flushed cheek. He wiped away the moisture hastily as he opened his eyes, sniffing.

And then he recoiled, only just keeping himself from crying out in alarm. For resting its monstrous head in Fionna's lap was a creature more hideous than he had ever encountered before. Long and sinuous, covered in dark gray scales, the Afanc's long flat snout brimmed with sharp white fangs. Its eyes, set on either side of its grotesque head, were closed.

Fionna continued singing but was gesturing wildly, pointing to her lap, her eyes white with fright. Percival nodded, creeping out of the trees. What a sensation it must be for Fionna, feeling the weight in her lap but not being able to see the creature's form. Or perhaps cradling an aggressive monster was easier this way.

Her voice wavered but she cleared her throat quickly, taking a deep breath before launching into another verse. The creature stirred briefly but settled again as the notes rang out, flicking its meaty tail in contentment.

Percival leaped onto the rock where Fionna sat, landing as gently as he could. He froze, watching the creature with predatory grace. The Afanc didn't move, lulled to sleep by Fionna's sweet tune.

Fionna made a stabbing motion at the beast, followed by one that could only translate as: *get on with it.*

Percival felt a pang of regret as he crept closer. Seemed a shame to end a creature that enjoyed Fionna's song as much as he . . . but the Afanc had killed and would kill again.

When he stood mere inches from the beast's outstretched

claws, he raised Excalibur's shining form, aimed at the beast's spine, and plunged the sword point down.

The Afanc exploded in a fury of pain and gnashing teeth. Fionna rolled out of the way, launching herself off the rock and into the shallow river below.

Percival pulled Excalibur free and swung it in a deadly arc, slicing through the creature's neck to the spine. Black foul-smelling blood welled from the monster's dismembered parts. The Afanc's violent death throes—its scaly tail whipping across the rock—knocked Percival's legs out from under him. He tumbled backwards, rolling awkwardly down the side of the rock and into the stream next to Fionna.

With a spluttering shake of his head, he righted himself, pushing to his feet.

The monster had fallen still—dead.

Fionna grinned, splashing water at him. "Percy, Briton's most graceful monster slayer."

"Och, ye're going to pay for that, ye goose." Percival shoved the stone back into his pocket and Excalibur in its sheath. And then he ran for her, tackling her back into the pool over her shriek of protest.

"Percival!" Fionna sputtered, pushing her braids out of her eyes. "I'm soaked!" She narrowed her eyes at him before splashing him full in the face.

Percival laughed, opening his arms wide. "Go ahead, lass. Hit me with yer best shot!"

Fionna cupped her hands in the river and doused him.

"Nice to see you two are enjoying yourselves," a dry voice came from the riverbank.

Percival and Fionna froze, then slowly turned toward Arthur. The other knights were emerging from the trees, followed by the mystics and Lord Willum.

"All in a day's work," Percival said cheerfully, quickly adding, "Yer Majesty."

"That blade better not get any rust on it," Arthur called out.

"Faerie blades can't rust," Percival said.   "Right?"

"You sure about that?" Arthur arched a brow, crossing his arms before him.

"The Afanc is really dead." Lord Willum stepped out onto the rock, regarding the bloodstained rock with an expression of shocked delight. "You did it! You killed the beast!"

"Well done, brave knights," Lelah said, her beautiful face beaming at them. "You have freed this village, as well as me and my sister, from this creature's terrible hold. How can we thank you?"

Percival stepped up onto the rock, pulling Fionna up after him. "As knights of King Arthur Pendragon, High King of Briton, it is our call to help those in need. No thanks necessary, My Lady."

"Please," Cyra said. "We must give you something."

Percival unbuckled Excalibur and passed the sword back to Arthur, relieved as the weight left his side. He pulled the adder stone from his pouch and offered the talisman back to Cyra. "This relic was invaluable. Thank ye."

"Keep the adder stone." Cyra pushed his hand back. "I have a feeling our talisman may aid you on your journey."

Percival looked at the glittering facets, thinking of the strange lines over Fionna's features. "If ye're sure."

"Where do you travel next, fair knights?" Lelah asked.

"To Castellum Puellarum," Arthur answered. "Traveling along the River Conwy will be the fastest route to the Irish Sea. There, we'll sail to the Port of Ayr, journeying across Strathclyde and into Alba. We need to avoid Anglo-Saxon territory as much as possible, save Castellum Puellarum, of course."

Fionna blanched. "Wait . . . did you say sail?"

"Would you rather face Anglo-Saxon armies by crossing through most of Mercia and Northumbria?" Arthur tilted his head, his eyes studying her face.

She grimaced. "A battle I can fight. But my stomach doesn't care much for boats."

Chapter Seventeen

Lancelot

ancelot trailed behind the others as they rode toward the port town of Conwy. Arthur and the other knights were in high spirits since leaving Betws-y-Coed, after enjoying the hospitality of the mystics and slaying the Afanc. They had freed a village of a monster and Percival had secured for them an invaluable relic.

He glanced over at the handsome young man, his heart faltering a beat at the impish smile pulling on Percival's lips. The lips he sometimes found himself thinking about kissing. Maybe one day he would work up the nerve.

Lancelot heaved a shaky sigh and returned his attention to the river trail. He should feel as celebratory as the rest. But a black cloud hung over his mood, one he failed to banish.

The frosty look Fionna had been leveling at him all morning didn't help, either. Well fine. If she was offended, then he could be upset at her too. He wasn't the only one who enjoyed the comfort of another last night. Fionna hadn't claimed him personally. He didn't belong to her beyond mutual duty to their king and land.

He had wanted to believe that a night with Cyra was exactly what he needed to rid Fionna from his mind. The mystic was beautiful, intriguing, and powerful—and talented in the art of lovemaking. But as he lost himself in the caramel skin of her neck, her dark obsidian eyes, the shimmer of gold from her nose ring—the colors had been all wrong. His traitorous mind kept sliding to thoughts of silver and white—the silver of beech bark on a still winter's day, the soft gray of a dove's feather. And as he laid beside Cyra after their lovemaking ended, Lancelot had stared at the ceiling, wondering what Arthur and Fionna were doing in that very moment.

It was good, he told himself. Good for Arthur and Fionna to be together. If she was Arthur's lover . . . she moved one step farther from Lancelot. Yet another reason why she was untouchable. Never mind that she had apparently ruined him for all other women. That was his burden to bear.

"So, let me see this adder stone," Galahad said, interrupting Lancelot's internal rants. "This talisman will make the magical visible?"

"That's what the mystics said," Percival said. "Certainly worked on the Afanc."

"That beast was hideous." Galahad shuddered.

Lancelot privately agreed. The beast had become visible to all upon its death. The creature was an unnatural horror.

"Ye didn't have that monster laying its bulbous, scaly head in yer lap!" Fionna said as Percival handed over the stone to Galahad. The copper-haired knight seemed hesitant to part with the stone.

"I can't blame the creature," Galahad murmured, holding the adder stone up to the light. "You have such an appealing lap."

"That doesn't mean my lap is open for any man or beast who would like to nap!"

Arthur laughed. "The Afanc certainly had not heard that edict."

"I don't know, Percival," Galahad said. "I'm not seeing anything magical."

"Oh?" Percival asked. There was a hint of strain in his voice that Lancelot couldn't account for. "Perhaps we are in a distinctly un-magical area."

"Ah, here's a sign for Conwy," Arthur said.

They had reached a junction in the road, and a sturdy wooden post announced the directions and mileage to several nearby villages. "We're just a league away."

"What language is *that*?" Galahad asked, squinting at the sign.

"I've never seen the likes before."

The others looked at him.

"Which sign?" Fionna asked.

"The bottom one. With all the squiggles."

Lancelot exchanged a look with Arthur.

"The bottom one announces the distance to Llandudno," Arthur said.

Percival shot Galahad an impish smirk. "Perhaps that licorice potion guttered yer mind."

"Or the cannabis smoke." Fionna blew out a breath. "That stuff was especially strong."

"I'm not addled." Galahad pointed. "Right there. Under the marker for Llandudno. There's another sign." He looked incredulously at the others as they shook their heads and shrugged.

"Give me the stone," Percival said.

Galahad handed the relic over.

Percival's eyes widened. "I see it too! Nae, he wasn't addled, he was addered!" He hoisted the stone for all to see with a cheeky grin.

"Wow," Lancelot muttered as Arthur pinched the bridge of his nose. "That was terrible."

"Clever," Fionna offered weakly.

Galahad playfully glared at Fionna. "Don't encourage the man."

"Can you read the language, Percy?" Fionna asked.

"Percy?" Galahad cackled so loud a flock of birds roosting in a nearby tree burst into flight.

"Yes well," Percival cooed, "just because ye don't warrant a Fionna nickname isn't a reason to be jealous, chipmunk."

Galahad opened his mouth to retort, but Arthur silenced him. "Can we get back to the magical sign, please?"

"Right. I can't read the language," Percival said, handing the stone to Arthur.

"Appears to be a form of faerie script," Arthur said. "Lancelot?"

Lancelot took the stone from Arthur. The talisman was warm and heavy in his hand. When he looked up at the sign-post, he saw what the others were referring to. Below the placard for Llandudno was another sign etched onto what looked like hammered silver.

Lancelot urged his horse closer and peered at the writing. "Faerie runes. The language of the Túatha dé Danann. The sign says . . . 'Percival is an idiot.' Huh, I guess this unfortunate truth is becoming common knowledge." Lancelot raised an eyebrow at their mischievous knight.

"Har har," Percival said, throwing a lewd gesture at him.

"Can you read faerie runes?" Arthur asked Lancelot.

"It says, 'Caer Benic, 95 leagues north and 31 leagues east.' I think they're coordinates."

Arthur's eyes lit up. "Truly? Directions to Caer Benic? Here?"

"Must be another message from the Grail Maiden!" Percival said, practically falling off his horse in his excitement. "Like the stone circle! She is leaving clues for us to follow."

"Appears so," Lancelot said, handing the stone back to Percival. As their fingers touched, warmth traveled up Lancelot's arm. Percival's eyes snapped to his and he drew in a quiet breath. Aware of other eyes upon them, Lancelot retracted his hand and busied himself by chipping away at a piece of dried mud on his saddle. Then he remembered. The instant before he handed over the stone, he thought he had seen something shimmering around Fionna. But then the stone passed from his fingers, and Percival's touch stirred him, and now he wasn't sure if he had imagined the vision around Fionna.

"But we're going by sea," Fionna said, tugging Lancelot's focus back to the present. He slid Percival a furtive glance before resting his attention onto Fionna. "So, how will this distance help us?" she asked. "Perhaps we'll have to go overland from Conwy?"

"No such luck, My Lady," Arthur said softly. "We travel north to the Kingdom of Strathclyde, across from Ulster, actually. The Anglo-Saxons would revel in my captivity, if we port farther south or travel by horse across the isle."

"If we can find a map and estimate the distance from Ayr to Castellum Puellarum," Galahad reasoned, "we could then use those figures to determine how far Caer Benic is from our eastern Strathclyde destination."

Arthur nodded. "I thought the same thing myself. Perhaps our search will still be a needle in a haystack, but this should narrow our quest down to the right haystack, and keep our party safe. Let's keep riding while the sun is in our favor." Arthur kicked Llamrei into a trot.

They reached the port village of Conwy in no time.

Lancelot reigned Cheval behind Fionna's mount as they walked onto the crowded wharf, full of fishmongers selling their latest catch and merchants loading or unloading vessels.

"My steward has arranged a vessel to take us to Ayr," Arthur said, nudging Llamrei forward. "We're looking for the Scarlet Selkie."

"Sounds like a fun ship," Galahad said with a soft laugh.

"No ship is a fun ship," Fionna countered. She was looking even paler than normal.

Galahad quirked an eyebrow. "Am I to understand that our fair Fionna isn't a sailor?"

"If the goddess intended for me to float on water, she would have made me a swan," Fionna muttered.

"Ye would be a very handsome swan," Percival said.

Fionna wrinkled her nose. "No one looks handsome while retching over the side of a boat."

Lancelot tried to hide a smirk.

"What are ye looking at?" Fionna asked him, her eyes flashing in challenge.

"It gives me comfort to finally discover one thing that you are *not* good at."

"There are plenty of things I'm not good at," Fionna shot back.

"Such as?"

"Understanding brooding French princes."

"I share a similar weakness in trying to understand the whims of murderous Irish princesses—"

"There she is," Arthur said, interrupting them. He pointed to a sturdy vessel with a hull painted in red ochre.

Fionna turned from Lancelot and closed her eyes. She seemed to be muttering a prayer. Whether it was for an iron stomach or patience, Lancelot wasn't sure. He could use the same divine aid.

Chapter Eighteen

Arthur

rthur had never really trusted the sea. The land was firm and solid and reliable. But the sea? Ever-changing and unpredictable. Always moving. Even on a calm day, unfathomable life teemed beneath the surface. Creatures of this world and unnatural monsters. An entire underwater realm he didn't understand and would never see. It didn't help that in a single blink of the eye, that strange life could turn on you, swallowing you into its abyssal depths.

Perhaps the sea was akin to loving a woman. Though with Fionna, he had glimpsed beneath her surface—or so he thought. Regardless, she was a woman he dearly wanted to understand. Like a sailor takes to the sea, learning Fionna might take him a lifetime of trying and failing, learning and exploring. With Fionna, it would be a life well lived.

The captain of the Scarlet Selkie was a short stocky Welshman with a brown shaggy hair and a weathered face so furrowed you could plant crops in the wrinkles. Davies ran a tight ship—his crew was tidy, respectful, and hardworking. On this clinker-built cog and the two others carrying their horses and supplies, Davies was king. And Arthur could respect a man who fairly ruled his domain.

For three days now, they had been at sea and would port this day. Fionna spent the better part of these three days with her head over the side. The warrior hadn't been jesting. She truly was seasick.

They took turns sitting beside her in a nook the five of them shared at the longboat's stern, regaling her with tales when the ship's bard wasn't on duty. They shared stories of brave deeds or foolish ones.

Except Lancelot.

Lancelot had taken up a position on the longboat's bow and appeared as fixed and as firm as the ship's selkie masthead. He stared out over the sea, watching the endless waves, the soaring gulls, and the craggy coastline of Wales and Strathclyde pass by. Arthur had thought Lancelot was surfacing from his black cloud, but his mood seemed to be declining further instead. Arthur sighed. He had resisted talking to Lancelot, knowing his friend was just as likely to bite his head off when he got like this. But . . . maybe he could help, nonetheless.

Arthur walked across the boat, past coiled ropes and sailors, to stand by Lancelot's side. "You aiming for a record?"

Without turning Arthur's way, Lancelot grunted, the sound more like a question.

"How long a man can stand and look at the sea?"

Lancelot shot him a sideways look. The gray of the sea reflected in his light eyes, turning them a smoky hue.

"Oh no, you broke your streak." Arthur flashed him a crooked grin.

Lancelot rumbled out a dark laugh. "Not much else to do on this vessel."

"You could help us keep Fionna company. She's asked after you."

Silence.

"Did something happen between the two of you?" Arthur asked. "I thought . . . I don't know. I thought things were better."

"Don't you ever miss how things were? When it was just the four of us?" Lancelot asked.

"I—I don't know. Things can't stay the same forever, Lancelot. We were always going to add more knights."

"More knights, yes. But with Fionna . . . nothing is the same." A gust of frigid wind teased Lancelot's curls and Arthur wrapped his cloak more tightly about himself.

"We're still the same, Lance," Arthur said, using his nickname from when they were younger men. "You and I? We are brothers."

Lancelot turned to him, and the pain in his friend's eyes nearly stole Arthur's breath. "We'll never be the same again. Not since Morgana. And certainly not after Fionna. My friendship with you is the one possession I treasured most in this world. And now our brotherhood is the one thing I fear will never be the same again."

Arthur set his jaw. "Different, yes. But let us make our friend-ship stronger, then. Allow these adversities to bring us closer. I feel like you are giving up, and I don't know why. If this is about Fion-na, my friend, my *brother*, I have been thinking much on what you shared. The time she spent with Galahad and Percival doesn't both-er me so much as I thought it might. Perhaps . . . there is room for all of us in her heart. Even you."

"And in her bed?" Lancelot's lip curled, his dark eyebrows knitting together.

"Even in her bed. If that is what she wishes . . . I think . . . I think I might be warming to the very idea."

"You mean, *brother*, that you will put up with anything be-cause you are so desperately in love with her?"

Arthur's pulse darkened. "I *mean*, each of you is dear to me in a way I cannot express. Our fellowship is precious to me, and even more so now that Fionna has joined our brotherhood. Somehow, she has completed us. But this completion doesn't feel right with you on the outside like this. And I don't understand why you insist upon separation when I am insisting that you are welcome. And needed."

Lancelot buried his face in his hands, scrubbing at the morose, haunted shadows lining his face. "You deserve happiness Arthur Pendragon, more than any man I have known. With me in the mix . . . things could only implode spectacularly. It is because I love you, and I love her, and I love Caerleon that I will hold myself apart."

Arthur whispered, "I do not understand . . ."

"Someday you will. And you will thank me." Lancelot twisted

away from Arthur and resumed his post as before—his mind lost at sea.

Arthur waited several heartbeats before walking stiffly back to the ship's stern, ducking his head and studying the planked floor beneath his boots. Emotions roiled within him. His friend had proved an enigma even since they were lads. But lately . . . Arthur heaved a tight breath as heavy and chilled as the North Wind. Perhaps being raised by the cursed faeries darkened Lancelot's tongue. He had learned their ability to speak truth without saying anything decipherable whatsoever.

As Arthur pushed past a sailor to his party's corner nook, the smell of sick hit him like a top wave, turning his already soured stomach. Fionna lay on the sea-drenched floor, shivering, her head resting on Percival's thigh—the lad asleep—with an extra cloak draped over her weakened body. She hardly looked up when he lowered himself against the rail boards. Her face was pale and coated in a sheen of sweat, and her arms wrapped around a wooden slop bucket.

Galahad stood, giving Arthur a little more room. "Going to stretch my legs," the big knight said. Arthur didn't blame him. This ship was oppressive.

"Thank you, friend," Arthur said. "And you, Fionna? Would you like to try and stretch your legs a bit too? Might help you."

She moaned, her eyes fluttering. "The only thing helping me," she rasped, "is this strange little root Lelah gave me." She held up a piece of gnarled brown root in her hand. "Chewing on this actually soothes my stomach."

"What did she call it again?" Arthur reached out to examine the root, but Fionna snatched the strange plant back, as if it were the most precious possession in the world.

"Ginger," Fionna managed. "Oh boy," she shoved herself up onto the rail, jostling Percival awake while positioning herself over the sea.

Arthur stood and pulled her long tresses and braids off her sweaty neck and out of the way. Then he placed a comforting hand on her back and drew soft, soothing circles. With his head, he gestured for Percival to go stretch and walk with Galahad. The young man complied, but only after a hesitant look Fionna's way.

She breathed out slowly, sagging in relief. "False alarm, I think."

"Do you desire another story?" Arthur asked, settling back onto planked floor beside her.

"You have any left? I think Percival has exhausted all the Scoti tales he knows, and Galahad the Norse ones."

"I have a few left to share. Do you want the one about the knight and the green man or the knight who befriends a lion?" Arthur asked

"Do all your stories revolve around knights?"

"Obviously, they have the best adventures."

A ghost of a smile flickered across Fionna's face. "You choose."

"All right. Once, a king was hosting a feast. A huge green giant showed up and offered to let someone cut off his head with an axe, so long as he could do the same to them one year and a day later—"

"That doesn't make any sense," Fionna countered, her eyes closed. "The giant would be dead."

"They're legends Fionna. Details don't need to be plausible."

"Right," she whispered.

"Are you going to listen?" Arthur asked. "Or are you going to argue?

"Argue . . ." she whispered faintly in reply once more, but her body had grown still.

Arthur brushed loosened strands of hair from her cheek. Her pale, waxen face finally appeared relaxed, the lines of tension around her eyes and mouth now peaceful, her breathing even.

Arthur gently pulled the bucket from her grasp, wincing when she stirred. But the motion had not awakened her, and she settled back into much-needed slumber.

He placed the bucket on the other side of where he sat and then pulled an extra wool blanket slowly up over her, softly kissing her clammy brow. "Rest fair Fionna. Dream of green giants and solid shores."

Chapter Nineteen

Galahad

Nearly five days had passed since arriving in the Kingdom of Strathclyde. One day of rest in the grand port city of Ayr, followed by four days of hunger and growing weakness while skirting around musty peat bogs and crossing through endless birch, pine, and oak lined woodlands. Forests and marshes that should be teaming with game, but strangely remained shrouded in pale, misty silence. The trees and grasses had withered into shades of brown and gold, odd colors for this rain-soaked land. Black sap oozed from trunks and limbs and oiled the surface of every bog they passed. Galahad's horse, without grass or grain for leagues now, dragged each hoof over yet another hill.

So many hills and rock formations. He didn't know the land rose to such heights and so willingly until he had ventured into Scoti territory.

But nothing compared to the hunger gnawing at Galahad's stomach, like a wolf that slowly chipped away at the bones of its last kill. His fellow sword-brothers fared no better, and Fionna even worse. The poor woman was but a husk of her former self. After three days of purging all nourishment from her body, she was barely present at times. Her silver eyes frosted over from a dull, persistent ache he knew she felt in the deepest recesses of her gut.

Her skin shimmered in the chill as though ice crystals. Yet, she held herself aloft in the saddle with nary a complaint. A warrior even when flirting with the delusions of hunger, even when shivering from the never-ending mist.

A moving, almost living mist that appeared deep in the forest, several leagues east of Ayr.

He thought back to the day they had reached port. Striding across solid ground had warmed Galahad's dampened spirits after so long at sea—strange for a Norseman, he knew. Still, the earth had felt strange beneath his boots, his legs unsure of how to walk without a deck tilting beneath his feet.

Fionna looked about ready to weep with relief as she led her horse off the livestock ship and onto the docks of Ayr. She had lost significant weight from her already thin frame.

"We need to fatten you up," Galahad had remarked, falling into step beside her.

"Your lips to the goddess's ears," Fionna murmured. "Give me another ten minutes and I'll be so hungry I could eat a whole cow in one sitting."

Galahad chuckled to himself at the memory before reaching into his saddlebag. His fingers searched around for something, anything, and made contact with a strip of dried venison. He had only two strips left, the only food stores he possessed untouched by the finger of death and rot in this goddess-forsaken land. Steering his horse beside Fionna's, he reached out and gently pressed the dried venison into her cold-stiffened fingers. "Until you get a whole cow to eat in one sitting."   They were out of rations after the voyage. Though they had restocked in Ayr, the foul—almost preternatural—weather quickly spoiled most of their newly gathered supplies. They would need to find provisions in Castellum Puellarum—and desperately—before embarking to Caer Benic. Galahad was lucky he had even scrounged up this piece.

"Thank ye," Fionna smiled sleepily, as though the act took the energy of a full day's practice on the tourney round. And then she woodenly nibbled a tiny bite between her front teeth.

Galahad swung his gaze up ahead onto the narrow trail for a glimpse of the emerging village beneath the dormant volcano of

Castle Rock.

High on a hill above them, just visible through the sheet of white, a ghostly timber and stone fortress dominated the landscape, like something made by Odin himself. Winding, compacted-earth streets snaked up the hill throughout the tidy turf-sided buildings. They had made it. But Castellum Puellarum was not what he had expected. Even the name differed here. A post outside of the village read "Eiden's Burgh"—Anglo-Saxon rather than Roman. From the stories that had reached his ears from his time as a squire, he expect-ed a large, bustling city. But there was not a soul in sight.

Arthur pulled Llamrei to a stop next to Galahad, surveying the village, a troubled look on his face. "It's so quiet."

"Where is everyone?" Percival asked. "When I came here with my father as a wee lad, these streets were full to the brim."

"Is it still early?" Fionna asked, her voice slurred and drowsy. "I've lost all sense of time."

Galahad frowned as an uneasy feeling twisted his stomach. "Just past mid-day. There should be fishermen stringing up their early morning catch, people tending to their gardens . . ." His voice trailed off as he spotted a couple of small croft plots, now barren.

"Perhaps there's a festival, drawing people into the village cen-ter?" Fionna murmured weakly. But Galahad could tell by the tight set of her jaw that even she didn't believe her own words.

"Or perhaps, there's foul magic afoot," Lancelot said. "Could this be Morgana's doing?"

"My half-sister dogs our journey," Arthur replied, his voice hesitant. "But I'm not sure even she is capable of making the people within an entire village disappear." Arthur squared his shoulders. "Whatever is going on here, this changes nothing. We need pro-visions and then we need to find our way to Caer Benic. Percival, I think this would be a good time to keep the adder stone handy. Everyone else, swords at the ready. I agree with Lancelot. Some-thing strange has bewitched Eiden's Burgh. We must be on alert."

The knights rode up the narrow streets single file, their swords out, save Fionna. She was still too weak and her body slumped slightly, as if talking had consumed what remained of her strength.

A thick, wet fog mixed with the bluish mist, blanketing the

buildings and glistening along thatched roofs. Haar or sea fret, if Galahad remembered the term correctly. The kind of sea mist that clung to fur and eyelashes and seeped cold fingers into a man's bones until he rattled and his teeth chattered hard enough to fall out. A different kind of cruel cold than the mist they had traveled through for days.

Though the hour had reached mid-day, an oppressive gray sky hung low overhead. They saw not a single soul in the houses or shops they passed by, nor on the street. Not even a rat scurrying in the gutter or a bird soaring overhead. Had a vile plague darkened their doors? Though, the smell of death didn't linger in the air.

The knights remained as silent as the ghostly village around them. Somehow, speaking seemed wrong, even if a hushed whisper. Galahad had experienced magic before, even black magic, like Morgana and her sisters' curse on Caerleon. But this . . . this was something altogether different. This was Otherworldly.

When Fionna broke the silence, her warbled words were deafening. "Should we check that inn for food?" She pointed to a nearby longhouse with a sign dangling from the roof's beam: "The Glæd Bard."

Lancelot cocked his head. "I do not speak barbarian." He looked at Galahad, a faint smirk playing on his lips. "Translate?"

"Anglo-Saxon for 'happy.'" Galahad smirked back at Lancelot, refusing to give in to the man's jibe.

"I doubt crabapple is feeling verra jolly right now," Percival muttered under his breath, completely unaware of Galahad and Lancelot's silent poke at one another. But Galahad couldn't help but grin at their mopey, dark knight as the last word left Percival's mouth.

"I bet you're right, Percy," Galahad said. "He probably doesn't even know the meaning of the word."

Lancelot rolled his eyes.

Galahad dismounted first and assisted Fionna while Percival tied up their horses.

The inside of the inn's common room was even more eerie. Tables and benches sat neatly throughout the room, and a row of clay pitchers lined the wall behind a large serving table, beside stacks of oak barrels. But the center fire pit and candles were dark. And the place was completely empty.

"What happened to all the people?" Arthur asked, seemingly to no one.

"Everything is neat, just as they left it," Lancelot said. "A raid hasn't killed or driven off the townsfolk. This is magic."

"Percival, do you see anything strange?" Arthur asked.

Percival shook his head, drawing his cloak tighter around himself. "Nae. Everything appears . . . as though a macabre tapestry."

Fionna's stomach rumbled audibly. She pressed her hands to her midsection, as if to keep her hunger quiet. "Perhaps we could see if they left anything to eat?"

"I'm feeling quite peckish myself," Galahad said. "I'm sure even this empty village of ghouls will look better after a good meal and a fire."

Without another word, the knights settled Fionna into a chair and then dispersed through the inn, into every alcove and walled-off space, poking about every cooking utensil.

Percival stood up from where he had been peering into a storage chest with a look of dismay. "Empty."

Lancelot and Arthur appeared out of a back room. "The pots and barrels are empty," Arthur said, almost apologetically at Fionna. "Not a crumb."

Galahad nodded, holding up a log. "I found nothing but firewood."

"Water?" Arthur asked.

"Perhaps in a nearby well," Lancelot suggested.

"All right," Arthur said. "We're going to bed down here for the night. Percival and Lancelot, get the horses set up properly and see if there's water to boil. Galahad, make us the biggest fire you can manage. Fionna, your job is to eat every scrap bit of food we can rummage from our saddlebags."

"But—" she began to protest, but Arthur held up a hand.

"You haven't had a full meal in a week. The rest of us will live. You *need* to eat."

Her stomach rumbled again, and she nodded.

Interlude

Morgana

Perched on a window ledge, the crow angled her head to track the mortals with her beady eye. She could see the spectral ribbons of fears dancing wildly before their vision, those same threads building cobwebs in their minds.

Swords half-drawn, the males circled around the witch, who appeared sickly and weak. The crow almost cawed in laughter. They were more skittish than a field mouse scurrying away from an owl. But then the large male with golden hair strode by the window and gained her attention. His deep voice rumbled even the fog blanketing the *In-Between*. Then another voice, one more familiar, pierced through the shadows and illusions.

Him.

The male with tumbling darkness for hair and the Other-world's veiled mist for eyes. He belonged to her. He was *her* possession, not the Little Dragon King's. And certainly not the witch's or the other male's, the one with magic in his blood. Unable to resist the lure of his scent, the call of his voice, the crow fluttered to the ground and transformed.

Morgana crept to the sill and peered inside from the shadows. The magic of the *In-Between* made her invisible until she granted the powers here permission to help her fully materialize. Still, she used caution, not wishing to disturb the trap.

She could see, even now, the mortals' unease. The landscape around them unsettled them in its emptiness and quiet. How little they understood the Otherworld was laughable. Not even the witch or the Fisher whelp, who had magic singing in their blood, possessed The Sight. Rather, they saw only darkness and space, uncomprehending how the bone key they carried had allowed them to pass through the mortal realm and into the *In-Between*—the thin veil between the human world and the faerie Otherworld—where even more dangerous monsters tread.

True, the key would unlock the gate to Caer Benic and their precious Grail. But it also unlocked other doors. And so, earlier in the week, while the party traversed Strathclyde, she had used the morning's fog to weave with the *In-Between*'s mist to funnel them into the hushed shadows of this place. Conjuration was magic she particularly enjoyed—perfect for implanting ideas in dreams or to terrorize through nightmares. Or to lure warriors to their deaths through visions of a beautiful maiden. Perhaps one by a streamside, collecting berries. The red stains on her lips the blood she thirsts to drink from their veins as they lay dying.

And lure a warrior she would. Fogging the window with her breath, she wrote runes onto the glass. As her fingertip formed the last line, Lancelot snapped his intense gaze to where she stood. But he couldn't see her. Rather, he would feel a longing to peer out the window and search for whom his heart desired. Slowly, he ambled across the creaking floor to the fogged glass and cupped his eyes to peer outside, looking right through her.

Morgana traced the outline of his face with her finger. "You do not belong here, prince," she whispered to each beloved, cursed feature. "You are of no value to this quest. Forsake my brother and his witch and I will forgive you. Together, as a mortal son from the Isle of Man and a fae daughter from the Otherworld, we will reign this wretched land. The people will finally accept you. Finally *love* you."

Lancelot stepped back from the window, his dark brows furrowed, his beautiful lips tipped down in a frown. With a sigh, long and slow, he twisted away from her and moved beside the fire, his shoulders slumped.

Cackling with delighted laughter, Morgana's body faded into the swirling fog until she was born aloft by the unnatural wind. The crow glided across the false city of Castellum Puellarum to the *In-Between*'s Castle of the Maidens. Time to alert her sisters and fellow sídhe priestesses that their guests were soon to arrive.

Chapter Twenty

Fionna

I shivered under the thin blankets, praying for sleep. We had used up all the firewood we could find in the common room, but none of us had wanted to brave the rain or the unsettling quiet of the city to venture out and look for more. So, the center fire pit was now dark and cold.

I had experienced worse, I reminded myself as I tried to unclench my frigid muscles enough to let sleep take me. One fighting season, when cattle raids were especially bad, the snow had come early. With nowhere to properly hide, I had slept under the boughs of an oak tree with only my cloak above me and a fellow fiann mate at my back. I worried endlessly about losing fingers and toes those two days, rubbing my limbs and digits regularly. The cold hard bed below me now was luxury compared to that near misadventure. Grasping at gratitude, I finally drifted to sleep.

But my sleep was as restless and as troubled as the hours leading up to the moment we huddled up for the night. I found myself back on the Scarlet Selkie, the swaying and undulating of the sea stealing my equilibrium and my dignity once more. The sky above the dream state Welsh longboat was roiling with storm clouds. A streak of lightning danced across the sky, followed by a crack of bellowing thunder. I stood and ducked out from beneath the protective burlap cloth. The rain slashed against my face, plastering my hair to my scalp. But I was alone. The crew, the captain, Arthur and the other knights, they were nowhere to be found. The sails cracked wildly in the wind, ropes like thrashing snakes twisting against my feet. I ran for a set of oars near the stern, plunging the paddles into the swirling ocean, trying to slow the ship's wild movement. But I couldn't. As lightning split the sky, whitening the deadly sea in my vision momentarily, my breath caught in my throat. A wave stood before me, tall as Arthur's keep, impossible to avoid. I dove for the mast, rapping my arms around the solid oak post. Clinging to the wood and ropes with all my strength. But when the wave hit me, the momentum was too powerful. The water hit with the force of a hundred tonnes, ripping my fingers from the mast and tossing me into the frigid, uncaring sea. Up was down, right was left. I fell into darkness. My chest screaming for air.

I bolted upright, my lungs gasping, as if they had truly been straining for their last breath. In the still blackness, my hand strayed to my forehead, where clammy sweat beaded on my brow. Ten frantic heartbeats passed before my eyes adjusted to the darkness and I realized where I was. No longer was I in Eiden's Burgh. I was back home. In Aghanravel. I was in the bed that I shared with Aideen. I threw off the covers and biting cold air gnashed at the exposed skin of my face, neck, and hands.

"Father? Aideen?" I called out, my mind struggling to make sense.

How had I returned here? What in the hell was going on? I threw open the front door and ran into a hazy dawn. The landscape looked like my home. The crooked, wattle fence post, the trough for the horses and pigs, the little stretch of garden beneath the eaves that Aideen tended to daily. But everything was wrong.

The lush land surrounding my father's home was barren—blackened like the black of the rivers in Caerleon. The tall birch trees were stark, bare skeletons, Aideen's garden shriveled and dead. *What happened here?* I turned slowly in a circle, horror permeating every fiber of my body. *Not here too.* How had Morgana known? Was this the work of the fae? Had Aghanravel been torched? But no—the house was untouched.

I saw a figure in the distance with chestnut hair flowing in the wind, a dress of cornflower blue and gray wrapped onto her thin frame. "Aideen?" I cried out, excitement warring with alarm within me. I took a few tentative steps toward her and then broke into a run, flying at my sister. "Aideen!"

I spun her around. But when I saw her face, a ragged gasp broke from me. I recoiled, a sob prickling the back of my throat. Aideen's eyes were lifeless, her skin a patchwork of black spiderwebs. The curse . . . the dark magic had taken her too. I caressed Aideen's hair, her arms, taking her face between my hands.

"Aideen. Wake up, *mo chroí*. Fight the curse. I'll find a way to fix this. I'll find a way to heal you."

Aideen opened her mouth to say something.

Relief welled in me. My sister was still in there somewhere.

"Yes, Aideen?" I asked.

But out of my sister's mouth came a singular sound. Foreign and grating.

The single caw of a crow.

I jerked awake, tangled in my blankets. I was in the inn in Eiden's Burgh. I flopped back into my bed, trying to slow my racing heartbeat. Goddess above, they had only been dreams. Horrible, horrible dreams. I threw off the tangle of blankets, moving toward a window, trying to gather my wits about me. The rain had let up and was now just a misty drizzle on the windowpanes. The night was still dark though. Unnaturally so.

I heard a caw in the distance and whirled toward the source, my eyes going wide. Was the bird inside the inn?

Grabbing my sword, I tip-toed back toward our circle around the fire pit, searching for Arthur in the dark. I didn't want to wake him, if I were going mad. Arthur's bedroll was empty. What? Where was he?

I moved quietly to Percival's bedroll. Empty as well.

Galahad's. Empty.

The caw sounded again. I froze. It had emanated from down the hallway, near the back door. Lancelot's post. I lifted my sword and crept toward the back end of the inn. I rounded a corner, letting my eyes adjust to the dim light inside. I sighed audibly when I saw Lancelot's form curled up within his bedroll.

But my relief was short-lived. Something was wrong. I crept closer and when I saw him—truly—I couldn't stop the garbled scream from escaping my throat.

He lay on the bed, his form limp. His eyes—his eyes . . . "No, no, no!" I cried, pressing against a wall. His eyes had been pecked out.

A deafening caw from behind chilled my blood and I leaped, spinning. A huge crow perched at the window. As soon as my eyes met the beast's, the bird launched from the windowsill and flew out into the rainy night.

I sat up. A sob escaped me. I was in bed—disoriented and terrified. Was this a dream? Another dream within a dream? Or goddess . . . Lancelot . . .

I threw my covers off and ran down the hallway toward where Lancelot lay before the back door. I burst around the corner. "Lancelot!" I crossed the back room in a blink, falling at his side.

He startled awake as my fingers found his face, the soft unbroken skin of his eyelids. I felt across his stubbled jaw, the peaks of his cheekbones, the smooth expanse of his temple. Relief uncoiled within me, my body nearly toppling over limp and spent. He was alive. And he was whole.

"Fionna?" He asked groggily. His voice was low and rasping with sleep. "What's going on?"

"I had a dream," I managed, my fingers still straying over his face of their own volition. "Ye were . . ." embarrassment prickled me as my voice caught in my throat, thick with threatening tears.

"Shhh," he whispered, wrapping an arm around me and pulling me into the crook beneath his shoulder. "It's all right. I'm fine. Gods, woman, you're frigid!" He pulled open the blankets to usher me inside. "Get in here before you die of cold."

I let him wrap me in the comfort of his blankets and his arms, breathing in the scent of mint and moonlight that was all Lancelot. I shivered against him—whether from the cold of the night or my fright at the dream, I wasn't sure. I couldn't get the image out of my mind—the dark bloody wounds where his eyes had once been.

"What happened? You had a bad dream?"

"The images were so real," I said, suddenly feeling like a foolish child, and wanting to explain myself. "I was having another dream, and I woke up in my bed here, but everyone was gone. Everyone but ye. And ye . . . yer eyes had been pecked out. There was a massive crow." My shivers wracked me against the hard muscle of Lancelot's body.

"All is well," he murmured into my hair, pulling me tighter against him. His warmth was beginning to leech into me, to soothe my nerves. "Morgana's shadow hangs over all of us. Especially in this place. I don't know why, but fae magic is strong here. I'm not surprised foul thoughts invaded your dreams. But rest assured, I am alive and whole. I would put up quite a fight before I would allow anyone to peck out my eyes."

"And quite a racket?" I asked, cracking a small smile. I imagined muttered curses and crashing about, if Lancelot truly went to battle with a giant crow inside the tiny end room of this inn.

"I'll make a huge racket. There would be no way you could sleep through my annoyance."

"Promise?" I asked, looking up at him in the dark. My eyes drank in the sight of him so close—the tangle of his hair, the smooth expanse of his skin beneath me. My hands itched to rove freely over the muscles of his chest and shoulders. But I held myself still, not knowing how far our truce extended. Not wanting to ruin this moment.

"I promise, Fi," Lancelot whispered, and gently kissed my brow.

My heart squeezed at the nickname. Fi was what Aideen called me since girlhood. But Fi sounded especially sweet on Lancelot's lips. Thoughts of Aideen sent my stomach churning again—the memory of the horrible dream version of her and the real woman, who was perhaps just as doomed.

"You were so worried," Lancelot looked down at me, his light eyes shining in the dark. "When you feared me dead . . ." he trailed off. His words were tentative, as if he couldn't quite dare believe. Fool man. Of course, I cared for him!

"Does it truly surprise ye that the thought of finding ye wounded and bleeding terrifies me? Did I not make clear to ye after Twrch Trwyth that I would like ye whole and intact?"

"I recall the angry lecture . . . the rest is a little blurry. I could use a refresher."

I snorted. "Oh, could ye? Well let me put it more plainly, Lancelot du Luc. I want ye alive. The only way ye're dying is if I stab ye myself, ye infuriating goat."

Lancelot softly laughed. "Consider the feeling mutual." He tucked a stray braid behind my ear, gazing down at me. His look unarmed me. There was a raw tenderness there I had never seen until this moment. How could he hide his vulnerability so well?

"I care for ye, Lancelot," I whispered as I traced the curved shell of his ear. "And I always will."

Lancelot closed his eyes briefly, shuddering under my ministrations. And when they fluttered back open, the glinting steel of his eyes were alight with a fire. A cool heat that thrilled me deep down to my core. He seized my arms and then rolled me beneath him in one swift movement, the shock of the cold air mingling with the heat of his lips on mine.

Chapter Twenty-One

Lancelot

Fionna's kiss was the most bewitching sensation Lancelot had ever known. Her touch a magic unparalleled. A hot chill stole its way down his spine, igniting every dark and lonely corner of his soul. His heart drank greedily, desperately. To him, there was nothing more alluring than a woman who asserted herself—confident and comfortable with her own body. With her own mind.

Fionna's tongue thrust between his lips and his chest heaved with desire. *Claim me*, he wanted to shout. *Make me yours.* Lancelot had little fight left in him and he yielded to the warrior's body pressed firmly to his. A warrior who was his equal.

"Fi . . ." Lancelot pulled away just far enough for his breath to tangle with hers. He cupped her face and whispered, "I want to know your . . . love."

"Then allow me to love ye."

Those words unlocked a hidden flood of grief within him. A gnawing hunger took over—a desperate need to be loved, to be wanted, dousing all reason within him.

With practiced grace, Lancelot rolled Fionna over to top him. Whispered warnings clamored in his racing mind. But when she fisted his tunic and yanked him up to meet her lips, the whispers silenced. His heartbeat knew only hers.

Lancelot, now sitting up, gripped her hips and positioned her across his lap.

Fionna's legs curled around his lower back, her fingers tracing the indigo knots and swirls peeking out from his tunic. Then she leaned forward and her tongue flicked out, to lick along the lines of his tattoos.

He groaned softly, his head falling back. A breath fluttered free from his chest. *More.* He needed *more.*

Their lips collided in a thrilling rush, a wildness breaking through their carefully built walls. She clawed at his back, her nails raking his skin even through the wool tunic. Narrow hips and flexing stomach muscle ground into his, her rhythm fast and urgent. His hands roamed the expanse of her shoulders, her arms, wanting to feel the flex and pull of her strength. Wanting to know both her softness and hardness simultaneously. And her fight. Gods, her fight. He snaked his hands up her back, until his fingers grasped her braids and yanked her head back. A wicked smile played across her swollen lips. Skies above, she would ruin any lingering self-control he possessed.

Skin, as breathtaking as a first snow, called to him. Her neck lay bared to the night, the same expanse he had once held a sword to. The memory shuddered through him. His foolishness. His anger. As he lowered his lips to her submissive stretch of skin, he breathed deeply her scent of heathered moors, of moss-covered rocks, and the biting cold of a Northern sea breeze. His tongue flicked out and tasted her sweetness first before he scraped the edge of his teeth along the tender skin.

Fionna moaned, and his cock hardened tight at her pleasure. And so, he bit her—hard—where her shoulder met her neck.

"Lance . . ." she breathed, deepening the grind of her hips, the tight grip of her fist in his tunic. The sound twisted his heart until he bled out, his treacherous organ aching to die in her arms. But a thought battled against his arousal, a thought that blazed hot as a refining fire. The only person who ever called him Lance was Arthur.

Arthur.

Lancelot wrenched back, shoving himself out of her embrace. "Gods, I'm a bloody idiot!"

Fionna fell on her arse and gaped at him, shock and hurt glittering in her silver eyes. A gaze he could perfectly see from the sliver of moonlight breaking through the storm clouds and fog outside.

"Done with me already, are ye?"

"No, nothing like that." Lancelot huffed out an irritated breath and a dark curl floated away from his eyes. "I . . . I can't . . . this . . . . goddess save me." He stood and began pacing the short stretch of the hallway, back and forth. His pulse galloped loud in his ears. His breath came quick and hard, almost matching the shaking in his hands. In a moment of weakness, he had almost unleashed another curse on Arthur, on Caerleon. "Sorry," he muttered before turning his back to her.

"Sorry?" she spat. "I'm not some trifling maiden to conquest and discard." Lancelot winced, a muscle pulsing in his clenched jaw. Fionna shuffled to her feet behind him and then grabbed his arm, spinning him toward her. "Nor is my body available for whenever the mood fancies yer famous cock."

He remained silent, his gaze unyielding.

"Do ye still love her?"

"Morgana?" Lancelot reared back, as if slapped. "Hell no."

"Is there something wrong with me, then?"

Lancelot relaxed his body further into an aloof posture and derisively said one word—the one he knew would seal his betrayal in her mind. But would save Arthur.

"Yes."

Fionna stumbled back a step. The pain in her gaze ripped through him, but he remained steady, staring her down. The angrier she was with him, the better. For everyone.

"I don't believe ye, Lancelot du Lac. Ye wanted me, *begged* to know my love." Fionna stepped into his space and pushed on his shoulder with two, strong fingers. "Fight me until yer last breath, but I will still care for ye, no matter what. But do *not* touch me again until yer sure of yer heart."

She swiveled on her heel, hair whipping through the shadows, before fading down the hallway and into the nightmare that had become his life.

When he was certain she was gone, he breathed again. But

it hurt—to breathe. Every draw of air ached hot between his ribs. Every exhale chilled his tattered soul.

Lancelot fell to his knees and buried his face into his hands, slowly lowering his forehead to the bitter cold floor. The icy shock on his skin rippled through him. His body began to shake, but not from the unnatural wintered air or the frozen floors. Tears, long buried, surfaced with a vengeance. A sob loosened in his chest as his heart continued to bleed out.

It would kill him anew each time he rejected Fionna's gift of love. A love he had desperately wanted to know for so long. Every day he would have to hold himself apart, to be cruel to her—the most magnificent woman he had ever known. He was useless to Arthur now, to his sword-brothers, to himself.

Perhaps he should have just given his head to Morgana. Perhaps they would all be better off without him.

Chapter Twenty-Two

Arthur

Arthur peered through the window. The storm from last night had moved on, leaving only the Haar fog that had greeted them when first arriving in this cursed place. His eyes narrowed as he caught sight of something. Craning his neck, he moved closer, squinting his eyes at the foreboding fortress high on the hill above them.

Was that? . . . It was! A light in the castle window.

Excitement surged Arthur's pulse into a gallop. Light meant people. And people meant food. And perhaps an explanation for the madness behind this ghostly village.

Arthur woke Galahad, Percival, and Lancelot quickly, and they rose without much complaint. Though, it was evident that a good night's sleep had also eluded his sword-brothers.

He paused before Fionna's bedroll, inhaling a breath. When he knelt beside her, the splay of her white braids across the pillow seized his heart. A sight he wanted to wake to each morning.

Lost to his fevered thoughts, he bent over her to softly press a kiss to her cheek, forgetting about the knights behind him. But then he froze, his animal instincts kicking in and snapping him back to reality. Something cold and sharp nicked his neck.

Her eyes were wild, her teeth bared. A dagger was clutched in her fist, the naked blade held steady against his exposed throat.

"Arthur," she breathed, and then her hand dropped as the confusion in her face cleared.

"Remind me not to surprise you in bed," Arthur joked as he straightened. His hand strayed to his throat and his fingers came away with a tiny drop of blood.

"Waking to yer face each morning would be a welcome surprise," she said, standing. "If not for this place, that is. Eiden's Burgh sets me on edge."

Fionna's words warmed him and he fought a creeping flush. "You're not the only one," he said. "I want to be gone from here as quickly as I can."

She pulled on her boots and then trailed Arthur to where the other knights were gathering their saddlebags and donning cloaks. Dark shadows lined their faces, as if the cold and hunger of last night had aged them beyond their years.

"I saw a light in the castle," Arthur announced. "I think we should investigate before we leave the village."

"A light could mean people," Galahad said.

"Could mean food," Percival added.

"My thoughts exactly." Arthur nodded.

"Aye, what are we waiting fer?" Percival asked.

The knights quickly saddled their horses and set off into the empty streets.

Arthur had visited Castellum Puellarum once before, when he was a boy. He remembered how impressive the keep had seemed—what a feat of engineering and construction—how many men and beasts it must have taken to get those stones so high upon the hill. He was struck by a similar sense of awe today, but the wonder warred with the trepidation this empty village stirred within him. He prayed the castle would provide much-needed answers.

They remained silent until they finally summited the high hill. Though worry etched lines into each face, it seemed like no one wanted to express their hesitation.

They rode through the castle's gaping front gates to find a courtyard as lifeless as everything else in Eiden's Burgh.

"Perhaps they're inside?" Percival finally asked. The absence of his kinsmen had seemed to dim even Percival's unflappable good mood.

"Perhaps," Arthur concurred. Despite the light he had seen, he knew not what they would find within the castle walls.

Inside the huge oaken front door, the fortress resembled the village. Empty hallways furnished for invisible inhabitants. But the air inside the castle was warmer and grew even warmer the farther they walked.

"Do I feel a hearth fire?" Fionna asked, her face lifted to the shadows as though the very sun.

They were towed down the hallway by the blissful heat, the walls they passed ornamented with dark tapestries and crossed swords and impressive antlers.

"In here," Percival said, turning a corner.

Percival was right. Around the corner, two open doors welcomed their party. Light and heat emanated from inside.

Arthur held his breath, not sure of what to expect, for nothing here was as it should be. But here—here was an even bigger surprise.

Percival laughed in delight, and Fionna clapped her hands over her mouth.

"I think I'm dreaming," she said.

"I'm in the same dream," Lancelot agreed. "Because I see a feast before me, set for a king."

"Well, we have a king here. Two if ye count me," Percival said with a sly smirk at Arthur. "So, let's feast!"

The room was warm and cheerful and brightly lit. Sconces flickered on the wall, candelabras graced each table, and a wooden chandelier spilled amber light from above. Near the banquet, two half-wall hearths roared merrily ablaze. And set before them on a table, as long as a jousting tiltyard, was a cornucopia unlike anything Arthur had ever seen.

Glistening roast quail and duck; crisp, lovely apples as green as a spring field; loaves of bread, fresh and warm. Pies—of what type he didn't know—but with crusts so flakey, his mouth watered as he imagined each bite melting on his tongue. The smells wafted together in a heady perfume—warm spices and cool mint and the yeasty smell of fresh bread.

"Is that—" Fionna began to ask, gravitating toward the table, her eyes wide. "This can't be!" She retrieved a sliced pastry reverently, turning the morsel toward them. "These are like the caraway seed cake Aideen makes." And without another word, she bit into the dessert, her eyes fluttering closed. "Ohmuhgahddess," she murmured around a full bite. She swallowed thickly. "Perhaps sacrilege to say, but I think this caraway seed cake is even better than Aideen's."

Percival floated toward the table, too, his fingers snagging a glistening sausage. "They made these cured meats back home," he said and took a bite, the juice dripping down his chin. His eyes closed as he shuddered in delight. "Lamb, just as I remembered . . ."

Arthur found his feet moving. There were drinks calling to him—pitchers of ale so cold condensation dripped down the side—a rare treat—plus a half-dozen carafes of sweet wine. He picked up a pomegranate, and he could feel his mouth soften into a sad smile. "My mother used to feed these to me when I was a child," Arthur said. "I always felt like a little heathen with the red juice all over my fingers."

"What a beautiful fruit," Fionna said, tilting her head in wonder.

"And delicious," Lancelot added. "I remember those. Traders would bring pomegranates to our shores with tales of a new god from the East."

"How is this possible?" Arthur asked.

Fionna polished off the pastry with a last bite. "I am too hungry to care. Are not ye?"

Galahad was the only one hanging back, Arthur noticed, his knight's face grave. "Something is wrong. This smells of magic."

"Nae, it smells of minced meat pie!" Percival had retrieved a slice of pie and was biting into the dense fruited filling.

"Lancelot?" Galahad asked. "Think of the faerie wine Morgana sent us. This could be a trap, don't you think?"

"I tend to agree," Lancelot said. "But, Fionna and Percival have already eaten. Do you feel anything?"

"I feel like I'm going to eat someone's arm off, if they don't let me eat this food," Fionna snapped, picking up a cluster of grapes and popping one into her mouth.

"I don't feel any different," Percival said. "Except fuller than I've been in days."

"Perhaps this was left for us by someone who is on our side," Arthur said. "Like the standing stones and faerie-scribed plaque. Not all magic has harmed us. We desired food, did we not? This may very well be a gift that we shouldn't squander."

"Ye're a smart man, Yer Majesty," Percival said, pointing a caramelized duck leg at him with a hasty bow before taking a large bite. He still held a half-eaten pie in the other hand.

"What about the adder stone," Galahad suggested. "Perhaps the talisman will reveal a warning?"

Percival gestured toward the pocket of his tunic with his head, raising his pie and duck leg. "Grab it, ye fussy old woman."

"Fool Scot," Galahad grumbled, but crossed to Percival and riffled around in his pocket, seizing the stone.

"That tickles," Percival laughed, and Galahad mock cuffed him.

"Anything?" Arthur asked.

Galahad surveyed the table from one end to the other. "I don't see any sign of enchantment. The food looks . . . normal."

"Thank the gods," Lancelot said, falling upon a dripping slice of roast beef like a dying man while pouring himself a goblet of wine.

Arthur pulled up a chair, retrieving a silver trencher, and then carefully began to select perfectly prepared food from various platters and bowls.

Galahad frowned, shaking his head. "Still doesn't feel right. If this food isn't enchanted, then servants should be bustling about. Where are they? Why did their Lord abandon this feast?"

The questions swirled in Arthur's mind, filling him with disquiet. Galahad was right. Something was going on here that baffled the mind. But, if they were to solve this mystery, at least they could do so on a full stomach. So, he took a bite.

Chapter Twenty-Three

Fionna

I leaned back in a pleasant haze. My belly was taut with the delicious meal, my head buzzing with the heady wine I had guzzled. I had eaten my fill, my stomach blessedly cooperating for the first time since leaving Wales.

Percival sat in a chair beside me. Lancelot watched below lowered lashes, I noticed, as their cheerful knight, with drooping eyelids, licked the sticky sugar off his fingers from his third pear tart. "Och, I've never had such wonderful fare." Percival patted his belly happily, pouring himself another goblet of wine.

"Galahad, any luck?" Arthur asked drowsily from the head of the table, before he downed the dregs from his jug of ale.

Galahad prowled the far edge of the long room, his fists clenching and unclenching at his sides. "Nothing. Not hide nor hair of whoever cooked this feast, nor even scraps of ingredients. The food is magic, I'm telling you."

"The only magic I feel is the delightful headiness of wine," I said, pouring myself another goblet full. "Nothing more, nothing less."

While the rest of us gorged ourselves, Galahad had refused to eat even the tiniest crumb. I frowned, remembering the sparse provisions he had shared with me the night before. His longing for the food was plain, and his stomach grumbled noisily several times. The poor man had to be beyond starving at this point. Perhaps the delusions of hunger had altered his good sense. Instead of partaking among his friends, he stormed from the room to explore the castle, vowing to discover every secret. Seemed like the secrets had eluded him, though.

"We aren't disputing that magic could be at work here," Lancelot said.

He waggled his fingers toward the wine nestled near me, and I passed the pitcher over.

"What the charming prince said." Percival gave Lancelot an official-looking head nod. "We just don't care at this particular moment." He then released an appreciative belch. "'Scuse me," he added, looking at me apologetically.

Like I hadn't heard ten times worse living with my fiann. I let loose a belch of my own, even louder than Percival's. All the knights' heads swiveled my way, their eyes wide with shock.

"Princess Fionnabhair Allán!" Arthur whistled appreciatively as I started to laugh. The wine was filling me with a drowsy warmth and silliness I hadn't felt in so long.

"My father only had girls," I gushed out. "But he raised me to be his heir. So, naturally, I had to hold my own with the boys. I could drink any of ye under the table." I wiggled my eyebrows at them.

"That sounds like a challenge, My Lady," Lancelot leaned forward, a wicked gleam in his eye and a flirty smile on his lips.

"Even Galahad?" Percival arched a copper brow. "He drinks as much as a war horse. Don't ye, chipmunk?"

"Our dear Galahji . . ." I tried to say his full Norse name but garbled each foreign sound terribly as my tongue tripped over itself.

"I'll go under the table with ye," Percival said to me with a rascally grin and a wink.

I snorted with laughter as I continued. "Our Gally has been replaced by a boring, serious old man." I lowered my voice to sound like Galahad and said, "I am Galahad the Gallant." The knights all burst into laughter, encouraging me on. "For fun, I like to wear the color green, skip across meadows, and ruin my friends' happiness at finally filling their empty bellies."

Galahad glowered at me from his position by the far fireplace, ignoring our laughter. "Someone has to keep you fools from getting harmed. Or am I the only one who remembers the incident with the faerie wine?"

Memories of the night with the faerie wine heated my blood as images flashed by my mind's eye—of Arthur's passionate kiss, Galahad's sultry moves, and Percival's grip on my hips. I wouldn't mind a repeat of Alworn's enchanted vintage just now. Need coiled deep within me, low and hot, as my eyes flitted from Lancelot to Percival to Arthur. I wasn't sure what I wanted in this moment—who I wanted—only that going to bed alone would be an unnecessary shame.

"You've had enough." Galahad strode across the room to the table, prying the goblet from my fingers gently but firmly. "Bed is in order."

The others protested, their words twining together.

"Now see here—" Arthur began.

"—what makes you—" Lancelot pushed to his feet unsteadily.

"Let the lady stay!" Percival protested.

"All of you fools are going to bed," Galahad snapped, the dark blue of his eyes roiling like a furious sea. "I will be depositing Fionna in a room where she can sleep off this wine. *Alone.*" The threat in his tone seemed to mollify the others.

"Oh fine." Arthur heaved a sigh. "A good night's sleep would do us all good. We have a long journey in the morning." He stood and then leaned heavily against the table. I hadn't seen Arthur this relaxed in so long. Perhaps ever. And now I truly didn't want the night to end.

I pouted, shoving against Galahad's bulk. I might as well as have tried to pull a great oak from the ground by its tangled roots. Completely useless.

The world tilted beneath me wonderfully, all heady, every sensation a swirling wave of bliss. Several giddy heartbeats later, I registered that Galahad had picked me up in his arms, as easily as a child. "Put me down," I said. "I'm not a hapless maiden!" But my head lolled against his strong shoulder even as I spoke, dizziness overtaking me once more. Had I drank so much? Apparently I had.

"I found rooms for us," Galahad said, peering over his shoulder.

Through drooping eyes, I watched as Lancelot plopped into his seat, leaning back with his boots atop the table, while Arthur poured himself another drink. Percival had retrieved a fourth pastry and was chewing with a look of rapture softening his face, his eyes closed.

"Now you animals!" Galahad barked, and Arthur, Percival, and Lancelot jumped to their feet guiltily, staggering along behind him toward the hallway.

"Fionna," Percival murmured, stumbling behind Galahad.

"Mmm?" I replied, tilting my head back over Galahad's meaty bicep to survey Percival upside down.

"I need to let ye down easy, lass. This tart has claimed my heart, and there's no room for another, ye ken?"

Lancelot snorted and then broke into hysterical laughter. "A fine wedding, if ever there was one. Huzzah!" He tripped, halfway falling onto the stairway Galahad was now climbing. I had never heard such a genuine laugh from Lancelot. And such a glorious sound it was.

"Think we'll offend your fair bride by eating the rest of her brethren at the reception?" Arthur asked, laughter sputtering through pressed lips as he hauled Lancelot up by his armpits.

"Surrounded by drunken idiots," Galahad grumbled to himself as he summited the stairs.

"Oh Galahad . . ." I murmured to him, stroking his beard as though petting a loyal hound. "No need to be so serious."

"Silly me," he said. "What's so serious about a deadly quest to find an ancient faerie artifact to end a devastating plague now destroying our land?"

I stuck my tongue out at him and then blew out a crude noise.

Arthur, Lancelot, and Percival roared with laughter—Percival stumbling against the wall, holding his stomach and gasping for breath. Lancelot bumped into him and they tangled together, their eyes locked. A current of something powerful passed between them, and I bit back a smile. Crabapple and eternal sunshine? I started to giggle when Lancelot leaned down and affixed his mouth firmly to

Percival's.

Arthur's eyebrows shot up before a grin stretched across his face.

"To make your tart jealous," Lancelot murmured as he pushed off the wall, winking at Percival before continuing up the stairs.

Percival watched Lancelot, a silly smile on his blushing face.

I snorted, which caused the knights to erupt into laughter once more.

"Gods help me," Galahad said with a groan as he kicked open a door. "Arthur, Lancelot. This suite of rooms is yours."

I squirmed in his arms as he crossed the hallway and kicked open another door. "Percival. You and I will take this one." While balancing my weight, he shoved Percival inside and pointed at him—"Stay!"

Galahad walked farther down the hall and opened a third door. A dark chamber lay inside, surrounding a large bed cast in shadows. He lay me down gently upon the coverlet. "Rest, Fionna," he said, trying to stand.

But I didn't want to rest. My body was alive with sensation, my blood surging through my veins. I locked my hands around his neck and pulled him back down to me, locking his lips with mine.

My kiss met an impenetrable wall—Galahad's lips were pressed firmly together, unwilling to be swayed by my own. "Fionnabhair—" he said, trying to extricate himself from my ensnaring arms.

"Stay," I pleaded, trying a new tactic by pressing kisses across his jaw line, then up and around the curve of his ear. I snaked my tongue deftly against his earlobe and I felt him shiver above me. Now we were getting somewhere.

"My Lady, no," Galahad snapped. He pried my hands apart, twisting them up above my head where he pressed them into the pillow above me. I struggled briefly against his strong grip, discovering myself well and truly caught. My pulse quickened, and my nipples hardened as desire coursed through me. Perhaps this was a fine tact after all. I surged up to try to capture his mouth with mine, but he shied back.

His handsome face hovered above mine in the dark, his breathing labored. "You are not yourself. If you wish for me tomorrow, I will give you pleasure until the Grail Maiden herself hears you screaming my name all the way from Caer Benic. But tonight, you sleep."

He shoved back from me and crossed the room quickly, closing the door with a decisive click.

I sat up on my elbows, watching the dark door with a pout, before flopping back on the bed with a heavy sigh. How could I sleep? My head was heavy, but my body was alive with desire that flamed through me, the fire pooling insistently between my legs.

Should I go to one of the other knights? I blew out a breath. No, Galahad was right. We needed to sleep. But memories burned bright—the sweet agony of Galahad's length deep within me; Arthur's deft tongue between my legs and his boyish freckles, gods his freckles; Lancelot's weight atop me as his lips spoke what his heart could not; and Percival's hot breath on the crook of my neck as my fingers trailed over his beautiful heart. I squirmed. Perhaps I didn't need a man to reach some satisfaction this night.

My hand was drifting southward when a click sounded across the room—the quiet sound of my door opening. "Who's there?" I looked up, my hand flying to the hilt of my dagger.

"Shh, only me." Arthur's voice reached me as he moved quietly toward the bed.

My heart trilled at the sight of his chiseled jaw, his strong form. His green eyes seemed to flash with preternatural light in the dark. But the thought fled my mind as his weight settled atop me and as his heated lips found mine.

Surely, the flash was merely a trick of moonlight, nothing more.

Chapter Twenty-Four

Galahad

alahad sagged against the wall outside of Fionna's room, pushing a stray strand of hair from his eyes. By Odin's beard, did the woman have to be so compelling? Did she understand the amount of supernatural strength needed to resist her advances? Yet, he knew he had made the right choice. None of the others were themselves after eating the fare banqueting the large table. To take advantage of her flushed state would have been wrong. No matter how tempting Fionna was, even while intoxicated.

Galahad's empty stomach yowled within him. He was chilled to the marrow of his bones, growing weak from endless hunger, and his balls now ached something fierce. Still, he was strangely proud of himself. As frustrating as the antics were of his king and fellow knights, he was glad to allow them the gift of this night. The curses and Blessed Grail quest consumed their every breath and had for weeks—no, months. Each second was wrapped tight in numerous apprehensions. And these tensions had only grown worse since journeying to Alba. Hearing their genuine laughter, even if summoned forth by an unnatural spell, had done Galahad's heart good. And seeing Lancelot kiss Percival? Well, that was strange. But perhaps not. They would be an interesting pair, if anything moved forward beyond their drunken moment. And less competition for

Fionna, that way. That could work in his favor.

His head rolled to the side along the stone wall, and he blinked back images of Fionna in his arms, giggling.

A shadow moved down the hallway toward the staircase they had just summitted.

Galahad froze a single heartbeat before his hand flew to his sword's hilt. He held his breath, his eyes searching in the dark. Slowly, he pulled his sword from its scabbard, the telltale ring of metal-on-metal breaking the corridor's silence.

A flash of white moved quickly, disappearing down the stairs.

"Halt!" Galahad yelled, bolting down the corridor after the apparition. His boots hammered down the stairs until skidding to a stop on the main floor, his head swiveling back and forth wildly as he searched for whoever—or whatever—he had seen.

The hallway remained empty. Torches burned low on the walls and illuminated the space before him. No other soul was here. Galahad's pulse thundered in his ears as he crept forward, sword held aloft. He burst into each room lining the hallway, ready to face whatever beast or man he might find. But each room only held furniture, tapestries, draped windows, and cobwebs. Nothing living.

Toe-to-heel, he prowled into the great hall where the other knights had dined. Panic-stricken shock chilled his blood to ice. The table, heavy-laden with food mere minutes prior, now sat desolate in a room as dark and quiet as the grave. Gone were the dishes, the pitchers of wine and ale, and the roaring hearth that had lured them in from the haar fog.

Galahad whirled around in a circle, his senses firing in alarm. They weren't alone here. Someone was moving. Someone had cleared the feast.

His skin crawled with disquiet as he hurried back up the stairs, sword clutched in his clammy fist. He needed to tell Arthur. They should leave this place. Immediately.

Galahad pushed into the sitting room of Arthur and Lancelot's suite, relieved to find the space empty. He opened the door to the larger of the two attached rooms next, hoping he would find his king within.

"Arth—" Galahad began but stopped. His eyes widened at the

vision before him. Then his gaze narrowed in anger. Arthur wasn't alone. His king's muscular back blocked much of the form beneath him, but little imagination was needed to guess whom he entertained. Apparently, Fionna hadn't intended to take no for an answer this night.

Wrapped into each other and oblivious to Galahad's presence, Arthur rolled over in the bed with a satisfied moan. Fionna's white-blonde braids trailed across her bare back as she maneuvered on top of him. Then her body began to move, much as she had moved against Galahad as Percival pleasured her beside him.

He pressed his lips into a thin line, a strange, bleating ache pounding within his heart at the sight. Softly, he let himself out of the room, closing the door behind him. Emotions ignited into a war between his heart and mind, and his hand curled into a fist. Still, as much as he wanted to break up his king and Fionna's coupling out of spite, he wasn't that petty. His brows knitted together. His lips dipping into a frown.

What was he doing? This territorial jealousy wasn't like him. Not really. She could bed and love each of them. Why not? He and Percival were able to share her without ruffled feelings toward one another. And, sharing Fionna with one of his sword-brothers was a pleasure unlike any other—more arousing than he expected. Feeling a bit lighter, Galahad decided he would leave Arthur to his moment and, instead, tell Lancelot and Percival of what he had seen.

Galahad crossed the sitting room and opened the door to the other bedroom, slipping inside. And then sucked in a sharp breath.

No—it wasn't possible. Galahad closed his eyes, rubbing his temple and clearing his thoughts, then snapped his eyes back open. But the vision didn't clear.

In the dim light, Galahad took in the white-blonde of Fionna's braids, the slender curve of her bare waist. She sat astride Lancelot naked as the day she was borne, her hips grinding against Lancelot's in a tantalizing, sensual rhythm as Lancelot's fingers dug into the soft flesh of her arse.

Their moans filled Galahad's ears as he looked uncertainly back at the closed door of Arthur's room. Was *he* going mad? But he hadn't eaten or drank a thing!

Fionna threw back her head with a gasp as Lancelot reached up to cup one perfect breast. The waterfall of her hair fell across her shoulder as she arched, baring her back.

Galahad's breath hitched. His vision narrowed in on her shoulder blades. Her back was far too smooth—no puckered red skin from the healing wound he had stitched up himself. This wasn't Fionna.

The hair on his arms stood on end.

Panic surged through his veins.

He was a humble blacksmith's son and knew not what to do in the face of such strange enchantments. If he confronted this false Fionna, would she turn on him? Would this being hurt Lancelot?

A thought blazed through him as clear and bright as a shooting star. He shoved his hand into his pocket and pulled out the adder stone.

His fingers closed around the talisman, and the shadowy vision before him changed. The white-blonde of Fionna's braids disappeared, along with her familiar form. In her place writhed a curvaceous woman with hair as red as a Beltane fire.

"Get off him!" Galahad surged forward, seizing the faerie by the shoulder and yanking her off Lancelot. She tumbled backwards, but twisted nimbly, coming to her feet with lithe grace. Her exquisite face was twisted in a snarl of rage, her lush lips bared, revealing teeth topped with savage points.

She screamed and leaped at Galahad, moving faster than he would have thought possible. Galahad barely managed to lift his sword in time. But he did—spearing the faerie through her naked abdomen.

"What in the gods' name did you do?!" Lancelot's eyes were wild and unhinged. He leaped off the bed with a growl and then barreled toward Galahad, crashing into him with a powerful fist to Galahad's gut.

"It . . . wasn't . . . her!" Galahad coughed out.

The faerie slid off his sword to crumple on the floor, blood bubbling through her sharp teeth.

Lancelot threw another blow, this time straight at Galahad's head. But Galahad managed to deflect Lancelot's punch with his forearm. He caught his sword-brother's hand in his own, crushing the adder stone into the man's fingers. "Look at her!"

Lancelot did so and then staggered into Galahad. The man blinked, his eyes adjusting in the darkness while his mind was no doubt trying to reconcile what he now saw.

"But—" Lancelot stumbled back, falling to the ground, his hands gripping his tangled hair.

Galahad sagged with relief as Lancelot came back to himself.

"A glamour," Lancelot said as the horror of the situation washed over him.

"Someone is with Arthur," Galahad said, pulling Lancelot to his feet. "I don't know if she's the real Fionna."

"You saved me before our king?" Lancelot grabbed his scabbard and then pulled his sword free, not bothering with clothes. Galahad bit back a sharp reply and followed the infuriating man.

He crossed the sitting room once again and then Galahad opened the door. Lancelot burst in and wrapped one arm around Fionna's waist, pulling her body from Arthur's. And with the adder stone grasped in Galahad's hand, he now saw that she wasn't Fionna. A different faerie had violated their king, this one plump with long golden tresses.

The faerie struggled against Lancelot's grip, shoving free of him as Arthur stood. "Unhand her!" their king barked.

"She's not Fionna," Galahad shouted back, leveling his sword at the sneering creature.

Lancelot did the same.

The faerie tensed to move, her dark eyes flicking between Lancelot and Galahad.

"Stand down!" Arthur cried out, trying to throw an arm across the creature in protection. "Have you two gone frothing mad?"

"Your Majesty, if you have ever trusted me, then listen," Lancelot said, his voice low and hard. "You need to move away from her and toward safety."

"I will not—" Arthur began, but the word was cut off by a garbled cry.

The faerie moved with impossible speed. A spear had materialized in her hand and, in one fluid motion, she had turned on

Arthur, stabbing the spearhead into his gut while screaming indecipherable words in the sídhe tongue.

"No!" Lancelot released a war cry and surged forward, stabbing the faerie through the breast with his own blade.

She crumpled backwards, the wicked spear falling from her grip and clattering to the floor. Lancelot stabbed again with another roar of fury, this time driving his sword through the faerie's throat.

She fell still.

Arthur staggered backwards, his hands covering his side where the faerie's weapon had pierced him. A look of incredulity crossed his face as crimson blood seeped through his fingers.

Galahad grabbed the coverlet off the bed as Lancelot helped Arthur sit.

"Easy," Galahad said.

"The others," Arthur coughed. "Fionna is undefended."

"She can hold her own for a moment," Lancelot said as Galahad pressed the bunched cloth to the wound.

"Percival," Arthur coughed. "His vow . . . the Grail . . ."

Galahad and Lancelot looked at each other in horror. If one of these vile faeries successfully seduced Percival, he would lose his connection to the Grail.

The two knights sprang to their feet.

"Go to them," Arthur said, grimacing in pain. And when he saw the hesitation on their face at the prospect of leaving him, he shouted, "That's an order!"

Chapter Twenty-Five

Fionna

My desire for Arthur was an all-consuming blaze, and I was slowly becoming ash beneath his touch. I didn't know if it was the food or the wine or this strange unfamiliar castle, but I found myself unmoored—overcome by the magic that always stirred between us. A connection even more heady with magic this moment. His weight on top of me was an exquisite thrill; his kisses burned hot as fire. I wanted to be destroyed by loving him—to let our passion devour me until we were nothing but skin and moans and soft whispers—no walls, no secrets.

Arthur's freckled face was tucked between my legs, making me writhe in pleasure, when the door to my chamber burst open.

A huge silhouetted form, holding a torch and a sword, appeared in the darkness. And instinct took over to protect my king, pleasure forgotten. I scrambled off the bed for my sword, seizing the hilt and pulling my blade from its scabbard.

But the beast didn't come at me. It went for Arthur, who rolled off the other side of the bed just in time to avoid a deadly sword strike.

I ran at the monster and crashed into its hulking body as it tried to lunge for Arthur once more, knocking the beast sideways off its feet. I fell sideways, too, my own equilibrium unsteady and tilting.

"Fionna!" I heard a familiar voice say.

I sprang back to my feet, sword at the ready, blinking. Then, my eyes came into focus. I knew the huge beast who had invaded my room.

"Galahad?" I asked, stepping back with confusion.

"This isn't Arthur," Galahad shouted, surging toward Arthur, the sharp edge of his sword glinting in the torchlight.

Galahad had gone mad. He was going to kill his king!

"No!" I threw my arms around his huge waist, and my sword tumbled from my grip. With every ounce of strength in my body, I heaved sideways, trying to unbalance Galahad enough to slow him. It worked. We fell sideways into the wall in a thunderous crash. The torch slipped from Galahad's fingers and rolled across the floor where the crackling flame stopped beside a pooled set of curtains. *Oh goddess.*

Flames burst into light with a *whoosh* and then quickly began licking up the woolen curtains.

But I had no time to douse the fire, for Galahad was already leaping to his feet with a cry.

Arthur had taken advantage of our temporary incapacity and was now dashing across the room for the door. But he didn't get far. Another figure appeared in the doorway, blocking his exit.

A sharp breath seized my lungs. Goosebumps fleshed over my body in a violent shiver.

"Who are . . ." I couldn't even finish. My mind rebelled at the sight before me.

Standing in the doorway was . . . *Arthur.* He held Excalibur in one hand and the other clutched a bundle of fabric to his abdomen. No glow around him, either.

The Arthur in the room hissed and recoiled, backing into the center of the room.

Galahad wasted no time and plunged his sword into our king's back.

A scream ripped from my throat and my hands flew over my mouth. My knees went weak and I staggered against the bed. *Arthur. My Arthur.* Goddess, no. I couldn't tear my eyes from the blood seeping from his back, from his strong muscled form now crumpled on the ornate carpet. In some corner of my mind, I registered that something foul was afoot, that there was another Arthur I needed to concern myself with—whether he the true or false Arthur. But I was riveted with terror at the sight of my king, my love, dead before me.

And then he changed. A garbled gasp escaped me as Arthur's body shimmered and twisted, transforming into something else. A naked woman, her hair short and dark.

I shook my head as horror paralyzed me. My body grew numb and my sluggish mind fought a raging current of grief and confusion and terror. It was like my horrible dream within a dream—blurring my sense of reality.

"What the fuck is going on here?" I croaked, ripping a sheet from the bed and covering myself up.

But no one answered. We were wrapped in our own worlds: Arthur sagged against the door jamb, his face twisted in pain, while Galahad stared at the sword in his hand, as if he had never seen this particular blade before.

Lancelot and Percival appeared in the doorway, naked from head to toe. Their bare skin registered dimly in my mind. Galahad was the only one present who was clothed.

Lancelot threw up an arm, his blue eyes widening.

Oh yes. The fire.

Arthur turned toward his knights. "Percival?" he asked.

"Got to him in time," Lancelot said. "Galahad?"

"Killed another. Not sure if this faerie is the last."

Lancelot coughed, stumbling forward. The flames were licking from floor to ceiling now, the heat of the blaze warming my cheeks. "Let's get the hell out of here!"

No one moved. I couldn't seem to summon my limbs. Or banish from my mind the image of Galahad's sword piercing through Arthur. But that hadn't been Arthur. *This* was Arthur. And he was injured.

"Now!" barked Lancelot, and then he clapped his hands. The loud noise startled me back to myself and I scrambled around the bed to retrieve my clothes and armor. Then I collected the spear, in case it was poisoned and a remedy was needed.

Galahad sheathed his sword and crossed to Arthur's side, throwing Arthur's arm around him.

Arthur cried out, but let Galahad help him into the hallway.

We retrieved clothes and armor and boots and saddlebags and then carried them all downstairs in messy bundles, the oily black smoke from the fire stinging our eyes and filling our nostrils.

In the hallway, we took a moment to dress. As Galahad helped Arthur into his tunic, I caught sight of Arthur's wound. Blood leaked freely from a puncture wound in his lower abdomen. Fear gripped me with iron fingers, ripping at my already ragged nerves. If the weapon had pierced an internal organ—the injury could be fatal.

"Ye need to stitch the wound," I said. "He's losing too much blood."

Sweat beaded Arthur's pale face.

"I can't do it here or he'll die in the blaze before he has time to bleed out," Galahad countered.

"The blacksmith's," I said, an idea seizing me. "The forge was just a few streets down. We passed it on the way here. A smithy will have water and fire to sterilize your needle."

Galahad nodded and tried to help Arthur back to his feet.

But Arthur's knees buckled beneath him.

Galahad swooped our king up in his huge arms as though cradling a child.

Arthur grunted in protest, but then his eyelids fluttered shut as blessed unconsciousness took him.

"Get the horses and meet me there," Galahad said.

My thoughts roiled like a tempest as we hurried across the dark courtyard toward the stable where we had left our mounts. The sky was still pitch black above us, without even a sliver of moon. Strange. A moon was present earlier. I looked back at the forbidding castle. An orange glow shone from the upper windows. The fire was spreading, though the flames would likely just eat up the contents of the castle and scorch the thick stones. We should be safe in the village.

"Does anyone know what in the hell happened back there?" Percival finally asked.

I let out a desperate laugh of relief as tears prickled at the corners of my eyes. My ragged nerves felt like wool pulled thin for spinning. One stiff tug and the threads would part forever.

"Faeries attacked us," Lancelot said, striding into the dim stable. His face was thunderous, his dark brows scrunched. "I can only assume that Morgana had something to do with this night."

"Or perhaps someone else doesn't want us to get the Grail?" Percival asked.

"Possible. In the end, I'm not sure it matters. They disguised themselves with glamour. Only the adder stone could see through the magic. That's how Galahad knew . . . that a faerie was atop me."

"Who did the faerie impersonate?" I asked. It had been Arthur for me, but who did the other knights think was lying with them?

Percival and Lancelot both quickly looked away from me, their cheeks noticeably reddening in the dark.

"Oh." A blush rose on my own face as well.

Percival kicked Kit's stall, causing his horse to toss his head. "Idiot! I almost ruined everything! I should have been stronger, should have pushed her away. But she was so . . . convincing." Percival closed his eyes briefly. "Lancelot, if ye hadn't come in . . . I was ready to break my vow."

"Hurry," Lancelot said gruffly to Percival, before pushing into his own horse's stall. "Don't blame yourself, Percival. Stronger men than you have been fooled by the sídhe." A dark look flashed across his eyes. "Even ones who know better."

We tacked our horses quickly and then Lancelot saw to Llamrei while I saddled Galahad's huge charger. The familiar motions soothed me, providing something else to focus on besides the memories flashing before me. I had fought in battles that stayed with me for a time, my mind replaying images of a memorable face—perhaps a kill, sometimes a fiann mate—as the light faded from the warrior's eyes. But this night would haunt me for all my days.

We found Galahad at the empty blacksmith's shop, an unconscious Arthur laid out on a table.

Lancelot handed Galahad his medical kit, and then we stepped back to let him work. I grabbed Percival's hand, who grabbed Lancelot's. Despite the oppressive heat Galahad had stoked from the forge, no one seemed willing to leave the presence of the others, to venture out into the darkness of the night. I didn't think I would ever let my knights out of my sight.

When Galahad was done, he covered Arthur with a spare tunic and then plunged his hands into a bucket of water before collapsing onto a stool.

He shoved his blond locks out of his face. At some point, numerous strands had fallen from the leather tie he normally wore them in. "I told you all not to eat the food," he said quietly.

"The food wasn't enchanted," Lancelot snipped. "The lot of us were just drunk. Still, we can all agree this night falls firmly into the Galahad-told-us-so category."

"Will he . . . live?" I let go of Percival's hand and crossed the room to take in Arthur's sleeping form. I couldn't help myself and reached out to push the hair off his sweaty brow.

"I don't think the spear hit any organs," Galahad said. "He needs time to rest. But knowing Arthur, he'll want to move as soon as he's awake."

"The spear continues to weep blood," I said. I held the spear up and we watched as a drip fell from the head's tip down the rowan wood shaft. "Is it poisoned?"

"Just bloody faerie magic," Lancelot muttered. "Literally."

"Can he travel?" Percival asked, looking at Arthur once more. "I'm not eager to linger here any longer."

"If we take it slow," Galahad said. "He'll need food, and we don't have any here."

"Then," Lancelot said. "When Arthur wakes, we ride for Caer Benic."

I trailed my fingers along Arthur's temple, his jaw. I didn't want to stop touching him—assuring myself that he was real and alive. That is, alive for now. I sent up a prayer to the Mother Goddess and tried to infuse my strength with Arthur's. *Heal, My King*, I thought over and over and over again.

"At least there's one small silver lining," Galahad said.

"Aye? What's that?" Percival asked.

Galahad pulled his sword from its scabbard and held the blade up for us to see. The metal seemed to catch the light in a way that caused the sword to glow, and I squinted. Then blinked. This new sword was gorgeous. The slick sheen of the metal blade and cross-guard was covered in intricate knots and swirls, like the tattoos gracing Lancelot's shoulders and arms. And, set in the pommel was a violet stone the size of a quail's egg.

Percival's eyes went wide, and he crept toward the sword in awe. "Where did ye find this?"

Galahad shrugged. "When I killed the last faerie, the one in Fionna's room, my sword just . . . transformed."

A delighted laugh escaped from Percival. "We were due for a little good news, and this is good news indeed. For this isn't any ordinary sword, ye ken? This is the Grail Sword."

Chapter Twenty-Six

Lancelot

Lancelot stared at the smithy's ceiling from his bedroll. The third curse loomed heavy in his thoughts, a relentless weight pressing him down. He had one bloody job on this bloody quest—to not sleep with Fionna. And he had bloody gone and done it. True, by some twisted miracle of dark magic, the Fionna he had slept with hadn't been Fionna. And no, he hadn't been in his right mind, addled with enchanted food and wine instead. But none of that mattered. What mattered is that *he had thought the woman was Fionna*. And he had bedded her *anyway*. He didn't care about Arthur or Caerleon or anything that moment, only the overpowering urge within him to claim her for his own. All his weaknesses, all his fears had come home to roost. And now he knew one thing, as sure as the sun rose and set each day.

He couldn't be trusted.

The reality of what he had to do slammed into him, robbing the breath from his lungs. Arthur was wounded, they were about to complete the final leg of their journey . . . and Lancelot needed to leave. He had turned the problem over a dozen ways in his mind, and each time the calculations spit out the same result. He needed to go far away from Fionna. For if he remained here, sooner or later he would give in to his weakness—again—and doom them all.

The other knights had fallen into an uneasy sleep, their bedrolls splayed about the blacksmith's forge. The fire had burned down, but still pleasantly warmed the space. Now was his chance. If he were truly going to do this, he needed to do it now.

Quiet as a mouse, Lancelot gathered his belongings, hoisting his saddlebags onto his shoulder. The door creaked in the unnatural silence and he cringed. He glanced over his shoulder, relaxing a notch when he saw that the other knights hadn't stirred, not even a little.

The cold air kissed his face, a chill wind tousling the locks of his hair. His steps dragged, as if his boots were mired in mud. Gods, he didn't want to do this. Arthur would think Lancelot had betrayed him. And so soon after Fionna's own betrayal . . . and while weakened from injury and from Morgana and her sisters' machinations. Lancelot cursed himself, cursed his weakness, cursed the third curse. He hung his saddlebags over the stall door and grabbed his horse's bridle. Cheval flicked his ears towards him.

"If only I were stronger," Lancelot murmured. *None of this would have happened,* Lancelot finished internally. His weakness had set all of this into motion. But no more. He refused to let his weakness drive the final nail into Caerleon's coffin. Or Arthur's.

Where would he go? Lancelot chewed on his bottom lip, indecision washing over him and churning in his gut. Caerleon—and Arthur—was the only home he had ever known. Perhaps he could come back some day, if he found a way to break the curse. An idea struck him like a bolt of lightning. His foster mother. Her home on the Isle of Man was a different form of misery, her care of him best described as detached aloofness. But she was wise and ancient and skilled in the ways of magic. Perhaps she knew a way to break this wretched curse. Then he could return to Caerleon and beg his king's forgiveness.

His relief was like a sudden sunburst. This didn't have to be exile. A quest of his own. To protect Arthur and his kingdom. Lancelot buckled his horse's girth and secured his saddlebags.

He led Cheval out of the stall, closing the gate behind him.

"Where do ye think ye're skulking off to?" A quiet female voice asked from the stable door.

Lancelot whirled to find Fionna, arms crossed and eyes narrowed.

"I need to take care of something," Lancelot said gruffly, trying to walk past her.

She took a step to the side and blocked his path. "Yer king lies injured, we're a day from the Grail, and *you need to take care of something?*" Her voice grew shrill. "What, ye forgot ye left the washing hanging out in the yard?"

"It's personal," Lancelot said, glaring at her. Didn't she understand this was hard enough without her trying to convince him to stay? Even as she stood before him, furious and fierce, he felt his resolve growing soft while his cock grew hard. He clenched his jaw and toed the stable floor with his boot. This was exactly why he needed to leave—he couldn't be trusted around her.

"Arthur will try to find ye." Fionna grasped his elbow with an iron grip. Gods, she was beautiful when she was angry. "It'll derail the quest. Caerleon will suffer days more. Is this what ye want?"

"Of course not," Lancelot said. "That's why I need to go."

"What of Percival?" She asked, arching an eyebrow.

"What of him?" He snapped back.

"Do not pretend yer feelings for him are false too."

Lancelot looked out into the night, his heart pounding hard against his ribs. "They're not."

"Please . . ." Her voice softened. "I don't want ye to go."

Lancelot's fingers fisted around the reins to keep them from straying to her face, her hair, to pull her lush form hard against his. His voice was hoarse when he responded. "And that is even more of a reason to go."

She stiffened, hurt flaring in her eyes.

He held his tongue against the apology struggling to break free. It was better if he hurt her than be with her. For then he would hurt them all.

"I thought . . ." she cleared her throat, looking at her boots. "I thought ye desired my love. That we had moved past whatever distaste ye had for me. But now . . . have I done something to offend ye? To earn yer ire?"

Her words twisted his heart. Didn't she see how she was perfect for him—for them? That everything she did, who she was . . . It was as if she were custom-crafted to become the final piece of their puzzle. Fitting perfectly between them, linking them all together in bonds stronger than oaths or duty.

Bonds of love.

"You did nothing wrong," Lancelot whispered. "The fault is mine, a burden I must bear."

"Then tell me. Let me share this burden." She reached up and cupped his face. And he felt his head tilting in an unconscious motion, longing to melt against the comfort of her fingers. They were as soft as velvet yet calloused from years of fighting—just a small glimpse of the dichotomy that was their Fionna.

The need to share the truth of Morgana's curse roared within him. The secret was an animal that desperately wanted to be free of its barbed cage. He ached for Fionna to understand why he pushed her away, to see that he never meant to hurt her—not then, not now.

Fionna seemed to sense his weakening and soldiered on. "At least, tell me where ye go and why. Let me explain yer decision to our king, to keep him from doubting yer loyalty. Whatever is troubling ye so, ye need not carry this weight alone any longer."

Lancelot's throat tightened. Carrying this secret made him weary to his bones. He didn't want to carry this burden this alone anymore either.

"There's another curse." The words exploded out of him, tumbling from his mouth as if they had been waiting to do so all his life.

Fionna drew herself up, her silver brows scrunching together.

"When Morgana learned of my infidelity, her sisters cursed Excalibur and Caerleon, but Morgana cursed me."

"What curse?"

Lancelot recited Morgana's cruel words, the words branded on his heart. "Never again will you know the pureness of love that flows between one man and one woman. There will be a woman, a Gwenevere pure like the white of driven snow." He paused a beat, softening his voice as tears began to gather. "You will long for her with all your heart. Perhaps she will love you too. But, if you join as man and woman, she will not only bring your downfall, but the downfall of all you love."

Fionna's mouth set in a grim line. "I don't understand."

"Don't you see?" Lancelot struggled to slow his ragged breathing, to keep the tears from falling. "*You* are the Gwenevere pure like the white of driven snow. I long for you with all my heart. But if I join with you as one man and one woman, it will bring the downfall of all I love."

Fionna shook her head. "A Gwenevere is a sorceress. A fae enchantress. I am not a Gwenevere. I'm the daughter of Brin and Catríona Allán. Princess of Clann Allán." She tilted her head and then whispered, "Ye are mistaken, Lance."

"It's you, Fi. It has to be you. There is power dormant within you that even I don't understand. Your connection to us, the Grail, the sídhe . . . you're the foretold Gwenevere."

"Then we will not lie together," Fionna said, nodding to herself. "A simple solution."

Lancelot ran a trembling hand through his hair, his eyes darting about wildly. "I've thought of every option, every possibility, I've even tried it all! Why did you think I pushed you away, and then kept you at arm's length? But I'm weak." He drew in a quivering breath and choked out, "I long for you with all my heart. So much so, I laid with you!"

Fionna's brows pushed together. "I would remember such a beautiful moment with ye."

"I didn't join with *you*, but a dark faerie glamoured as you in that . . . that castle of maidens!" He thrust out his arm and pointed to the smoldering castle up on the hill. "But I didn't know that then! And I didn't care. As far as I knew, last night, by making love to someone I thought was you, I was bringing the downfall of myself, Arthur, Caerleon, all of us. I was triggering the third curse."

"Did you say *a third curse*?" A new voice rasped from the darkness outside the stable door. A voice he recognized. Their king's voice.

Chapter Twenty-Seven

Arthur

A third curse. Morgana had mentioned this, but Arthur had ignored her taunting babble. He didn't want to believe his half-sister, for he had curses enough to contend with.

His side throbbed as though the Norse fires of Hel pulsed within him, every movement blistering agony. But when his eyes had fluttered open to see Fionna slipping out the door, he had to follow. After what happened with Excalibur . . . a cynical part of him feared she was still not trustworthy. And then he discovered that it was Lancelot—his brother, his second-in-command—who was leaving.

"My King, you shouldn't be up without assistance." Fionna hurried to his side and wedged her shoulder under his arm to support his weight. But he ignored her. He didn't need to sit down. He needed answers.

"How could you not tell me?" Arthur asked Lancelot. "If there was a danger to my kingdom, I had the right to know. I am king!" The sudden surge of blood to his face left him lightheaded and woozy. Fionna's small frame staggered under his weight, and she steadied herself.

"Arthur—" she murmured, but it was Lancelot who filled Arthur's vision.

Guilt twisted Lancelot's face. "In a hundred years, I still could not atone for how sorry I am, Arthur. You took me in, you were a brother to me—the only family I have, really—and I repaid your kinship with ruin and destruction to your land. The other curses weighed so heavily upon your shoulders. I simply didn't want to burden you with something more to worry about."

"Bullshit," Arthur snapped. "You didn't want to admit that you failed again."

"I'm trying to make this right," Lancelot shot back. "It's why I'm leaving. I'm separating myself from Fionna, so I'm no longer a danger. I plan to visit Vivien and see if there's a way to break this curse upon me."

"*You* are *my* knight, and *you* are sworn to obey *me*," Arthur grit between clenched teeth. "And *you* do not leave without *my* permission"—he pointed a finger at Lancelot's chest—"The standing stone said the *blessed five* would find the Grail, which Merlin confirmed. Remember? That's why we forgave Fionna, even when she betrayed us."

Lancelot's face paled and he felt Fionna suck in a sharp breath at his cutting words. But Arthur's anger was too powerful a tide to be concerned for how his words affected others just now. The fury writhed within him, the betrayal a monster waking to life, sweeping him away.

"But you didn't think of that, did you?" He hurled at Lancelot's feet. "Your vision is consistently so narrow, so myopic, that you rarely consider how your actions will cost others." Arthur grimaced at a stab of pain while Lancelot's gaze hardened, as if each word fell upon him like whipped lashes. Drawing in a slow, steadying breath, Arthur continued. "You're supposed to be a leader of men, but leadership takes sacrifice. And to sacrifice, you must care for something other than yourself!"

"I love you, Arthur," Lancelot softly spoke. "And Caerleon, and our sword-brothers, and Fionna. And *that* is why I was leaving tonight."

"You can't leave until we complete the quest. I forbid it. After we drink from the Grail, your life is yours to ruin as you please. But not a minute before!"

Lancelot's hands curled into fists at his side, his jaw working. "As you command, Your Majesty."

"Now will you sit down?" Fionna asked in an exasperated voice.

"Fine," Arthur answered stiffly, and Fionna helped him to a bench in the corner of the stable, where he sat with a groan. "Wake Galahad . . . and Percival . . . We ride for . . . Caer Benic," Arthur managed through pain-laced breaths.

"Now?" Fionna asked. "Is that such a—"

"Now!" Arthur barked. It was time to finish this.

As they passed through the old city wall of Eiden's Burgh, the land around them transformed. Gone were the fog and darkness that had shrouded the city, and instead, countryside as bright and fair as Caerleon unfolded before them. Before Caerleon's curse, that was. They rode through green fields as flocks of sparrows swooped overhead. A rabbit with a bushy white tail darted in front of them in a zig-zag pattern.

Arthur held himself woodenly against the rocking movement of Llamrei's gait. A trickle of blood seeped from his wound and pooled on his breeches. But he said nothing. He couldn't stop now. Not when they were so close. He feared that if he stopped, he would never arrive at Caer Benic.

They had mapped out a distance and direction from Castellum Puellarum based on the enchanted signpost near Betws-y-Coed. But in the end, they hadn't needed the coordinates. For the beautiful blade—the one that had magically replaced Galahad's—possessed a mind of its own. Galahad held the Grail Sword loosely in his hand as they rode, and if they roamed off course, the sword tugged at him insistently, directing them onto the correct path.

"Don't know where the in hell this blade came from," Galahad said, "but I'm glad it's here."

Arthur let out a wheeze of a laugh, which sent pain shooting through his abdomen. The pain was so powerful, it took his breath away. He prayed they were almost there.

They rode up into craggy, boulder-strewn foothills of Alba. The shining expanse of the sea stretched far in the distance.

Lancelot hadn't uttered a single word since their exchange in the stable. Arthur knew his words were harsh to his friend, even cruel. But anger still burned within him. Lancelot should have trusted Arthur to handle the truth of this third curse. How weak must Lancelot think him?

A shiver wracked Arthur and he gripped his saddle, struggling to stay upright on Llamrei's back. He had been tricked by the faerie maidens in the castle too. But of all in their party, only he had been injured. So, maybe he really was the weak one.

The horses were puffing when they reached a plateau atop a hill. Galahad's sword pointed straight down as though drawn to a lodestone. He reined his horse in and peered over his shoulder.

"Is the Grail Sword broken?" Fionna asked. "Confused?"

Percival shook his head. "Nae, lass. I feel the pull here too. I think . . . we're here."

"There is no 'here,'" Arthur said. "The sword can't be right."

Galahad turned his horse in a circle, pointing the blade's tip in every direction. The sword rebelled against him, continuing to point down. As if they were supposed to come this far and no farther. "Any brilliant ideas?" Galahad asked.

Fionna furrowed her brow. "Haven't we learned that things aren't always as they seem? Especially when it comes to this quest? Percival, do you have the adder stone?"

Percival pulled the talisman out of his tunic and moved to hand the gem over. But as he did, he stilled.

"Fionna is right," he said. "Look."

Fionna took the stone from him and her eyes grew owlish. "My goddess!"

She handed the relic next to Arthur. His jaw dropped. For before him was something more extraordinary than he had ever seen in his life. A castle that floated upon the air. Huge and tall, with soaring white stone spires. No mortal had formed this keep. Relief rushed through him. They had made it—finally.

Galahad dismounted and crossed over the grass to Arthur and took the stone. He blew out a whistle and then tossed the stone to Lancelot. The giant of a knight moved to help Arthur off his horse and Arthur toppled sideways, the earth spinning beneath him.

"Bloody hell," Galahad said as he caught Arthur and helped him to the ground. "Your stitches have failed? Have you been bleeding all this time? You should have told us! We would have stopped."

"We finish this," Arthur rasped.

Galahad grumbled.

Fionna dismounted and knelt at Arthur's side, her hands fluttering over the wound. "Arthur," she said, his name soft and tender on her lips. "Ye need to take care of yerself."

"I have to take care of Caerleon," Arthur said. "If we get the Grail, the sacred vessel will heal me. So, let's get the fucking Grail."

Percival nodded. "The Blessed Grail is rumored to have healing powers."

"There's only one problem. How do we get up there?" Fionna asked.

Galahad pulled Arthur up in his arms and they walked forward.

Fionna took the stone once more from Lancelot. "There's a doorway. Here on the ground. But . . . I don't understand. It's a door to . . . nothing." She passed the talisman to Arthur and he squinted to focus.

She was right. A single door stood on the Scoti moor, with nothing behind the entryway but air and heather. The door made little sense. But they had passed beyond the realm of the logical, and into the fantastical. "We go through the door," Arthur said. "It's not the strangest thing we've seen on this quest."

The knights walked forward in a tight clump. When they reached the door, they paused. No one seemed to want to be the first to open the entry to the Grail Castle.

"You go first, Fisher heir," Galahad gestured with his head toward the large, carved oaken door.

"Great," Percival said. "I always wanted to be blasted by dragon fire or some other trap first in our party." But he wrapped his fingers around the doorknob and turned. Then he jiggled the handle and pushed. But the door didn't budge. "Locked," Percival said with a shrug.

Lancelot groaned and spun in an angry circle, but thankfully said nothing. Especially weakened how he was, Arthur had little patience for Lancelot's pessimism.

Percival was throwing his shoulder against the door now, but the entry held firm.

Arthur looked at the space where the door was, wishing his mind was more lucid, wishing he could burn through this fevered haze that was swallowing him whole. A locked door. They needed a key. Arthur let out an incredulous laugh that quickly turned into a cough.

"Easy," Galahad said.

"Could it be that simple?" Arthur said. "Put me down."

"But Your Majesty—" Galahad protested.

"Put. Me. Down," Arthur commanded. For whatever the Grail Quest had taken from him, he wouldn't let it take his dignity. He would walk through that door on his own two feet and face whatever he found there.

Arthur reached into his belt pouch and withdrew the bone key.

"Ye think . . ." Fionna trailed off.

"All I know is here lies a locked door and we have a key."

Leaning heavily on Galahad, Arthur limped to the door. Percival handed him the adder stone and the smooth wood finish of the door materialized before him, carved with faerie runes.

With a shaking hand, Arthur slid the ivory key into the lock. The knob turned with a click, and then the door swung open.

Chapter Twenty-Eight

Percival

The Grail Castle was empty, but not the haunted emptiness of the castle they had fled in Eiden's Burgh. This emptiness felt hushed and right. A quiet anticipation. As if the place was waiting for the rightful master's return. Percival's stomach clenched and unclenched. He wiped his clammy palms on his tunic. Part of him couldn't believe that they were actually here. That he now walked the quiet halls his father had once walked. That Percival had also once gamboled through, a cheerful and tumbling boy with a shock of red hair.

Memories flashed within him as they passed through the long corridor to the Great Hall, where his father had entertained nobles and dignitaries, human and fae alike.

His feet moved of their own volition, towing him forward.

"You know the way?" Galahad asked. The Grail Sword was in his hand—that same strange glittering thing with the violet pommel. Percival knew the sword was important. He knew the Grail Sword was tied to this place, the Blessed Grail, the whole sordid legacy. The same way he was.

"Aye," Percival said. "We should find the vessel up here."

Arthur was leaning heavily on Galahad, his pallor ashen and his face beaded with sweat.

Percival prayed what they found within the Great Hall was

friendly, for Arthur couldn't take another setback. He feared his king wouldn't last much longer.

Down the long hallway stretched an arching set of double doors. "There," Percival said. "The Grail should be behind those doors."

The knights' footsteps sounded ominous on the polished stone floors.

Percival's breath was tight in his chest as he reached the entry, and paused. "Are we ready?" He asked with a crooked grin.

"On with it," Lancelot barked. "We need to get Arthur healed."

Percival pushed the door open, his mouth parting. At the sight before them, they let out a collective groan.

"Another feast?" Fionna asked, her hand flying to her stomach.

A glittering array of food and drink, much like they had just left the day before, adorned a large banqueting table. But for one notable difference. A woman. Tall, lithe and fair, the woman's golden-blonde hair fell in soft waves down to her narrow waist. She wore a dress of a deep violet hue, her waist cinched with a belted girdle of golden links encrusted with amethysts. And her brow was crowned with a gold diadem boasting an amethyst stone that perfectly matched the gem on the pommel of Galahad's sword.

This, Percival was certain, was the Grail Maiden.

Percival scrambled into a bow and the others followed suit, Arthur with an audible groan.

"Fair knights. Kind king," she said. Her voice was soft and melodious, like the bubble of a fountain. "Welcome to Caer Benic. I have been waiting for you."

"We have been waiting to get here," Percival said. "Thank ye fer yer service in guarding the Blessed Grail."

"The honor is mine. I know these are dark times, and I felt it right to do what little I could to assist your righteous cause."

"The standing stone?" Percival asked. "Ye left that for us, didn't ye?"

She inclined her head in an affirmative.

"And the sign-post?" Fionna asked.

She nodded again. "This castle has been too long without her rightful king. Welcome home Percival of Caer Benic, Fisher King."

"It's good to be home," Percival said, his voice catching in his throat. However bloody and unpleasant his past had been, at least he had lived up to his father's legacy in this small way. He had done it. He had found the castle. And the Grail.

"Keeper of the Grail," Fionna began. "Our king is grievously wounded. I do not mean to be forward, but may we see the Grail and heal him? I fear he grows weaker with each passing candle mark."

The Maiden turned to survey Fionna with an appraising eye. Did her violet eyes widen as she took Fionna in? "I did not expect a Gwenevere, though perhaps I should have," the Maiden said.

Fionna winced at the title, but soldiered on. "He was pierced through with this spear, which has continued to weep blood ever since. Is the tip poisoned?"

"No. This is the sacred spear of Lleu, which weeps blood. A blessed relic of the fae to harm sovereign-blessed kings." She took the spear from Fionna's hands and the magical weapon disappeared. "We thank you for the spear's safe return. And, I am afraid the Grail does not heal mortal flesh, but I do have something that will help. Go to the table and fetch one of the red apples. They hail from the Isle of Man, from Manannán mac Lir's orchard, and possess healing properties. One bite should be enough to save the Little Dragon King."

"The sea god who delivers souls to the afterlife?" Fionna asked, mouth parted in horror.

"Yes, Princess." The Grail Maiden tilted her head prettily. "He may care for the dead, but he does not usher in death like The Morrígan. I assure you, his tree of life shall heal your king. The Lady of the Lake ferried his apples to me, should you have need of them."

Fionna studied the Grail Maiden a few wary heartbeats and then did as instructed, hurrying down the long table, her eyes searching for an apple amongst the arrayed bounty. She found one and grabbed the fruit, jogging back to Arthur.

His head was nodding now as consciousness slipped from him. "Arthur," she said, her hand stroking his sweaty brow. "Wake up, my love." She patted his face.

He jerked to alertness, but his eyes were unfocused. "Fionnabhair?"

"Eat Arthur, the apple will heal you."

She held the apple up to his mouth and he took a tiny bite.

"Chew," she encouraged, as if to a young child. "Swallow yer bite completely."

He did as instructed—a cooperative patient.

The effect was instantaneous. Arthur's color flushed and turned to the rosy pink of health. His back straightened and he let out a shuddering breath, shaking his head as if to clear the fog. He took another bite, chewing. His green eyes flew open, clear and verdant as the rolling grassy hills on a summer's day.

Gratitude and relief washed over Percival.

"Thank ye so much," Fionna said, tears glimmering in her eyes.

The Maiden nodded. "The least I can do for the sovereign-blessed king. Today is not his time. He has much left to do. Now, let us discuss your quest at Caer Benic." She looked meaningfully at Percival.

"Och!" Percival said. "The Grail." That's right. There were words he needed to speak. The very ones drilled into him as a young child. In his excitement of being here, he had completely forgotten. He cleared his throat. "What is the Grail and whom does it serve?"

The Maiden nodded approvingly. "The Blessed Grail is a sacred bowl, a vessel to grant life, and the Grail serves Arthur Pendragon of Caerleon, the rightful King over all of Briton." She waved her hand across the table, and a pile of fruit disappeared, revealing a silver bowl with engraved mythical creatures who danced around an orchard. She lifted the dish with both hands, and then offered the vessel to Percival. "I gift you the Blessed Grail."

Arthur's eyes were gleaming. "We must drink. To heal the wicked curse that has befallen Caerleon by Morgana and her sisters."

The Maiden peered kindly at Arthur. "To heal the land, you must drink from the land's life source, the land's blood. Drinking from the Grail would not be enough. There is a Chalice Well at the foot of Glastonbury Tor. If you dip the Grail into the holy waters of Avalon, and drink from her Red Spring, the Blessed Grail will do what you seek."

"Glastonbury Tor?" Arthur said with dismay. For the Tor was days' travel from here.

A shadow fell over her face. "But I cannot allow the Blessed Grail to leave Caer Benic. For the sacred vessel may fall into the wrong hands and I would be unprotected. Especially now that the Fisher King has returned and the way to the castle is unlocked."

The knights exchanged troubled glances.

"Perhaps you could come with us?" Lancelot asked.

"No, my charge is over the castle and the Grail."

"Perhaps I could offer you this," Galahad said, stepping forward. He held the sword out to her. "Would this be sufficient to protect you?"

"The Grail Sword." Her eyes glittered with a dancing light. "How did you come upon my blade, kind Sir?"

He shrugged. "The sword kind of just appeared."

She took the blade from him reverently, stroking the handle's leather. "Yes, I think this would be sufficient enough. I can lend you the Grail for a time. Though the vessel belongs here, in Caer Benic. As does the Fisher King," she said, looking meaningfully at Percival.

"Och, lass. Well, I still have duties to attend to with His Majesty," Percival said. "But I'll return. Never fear, fair Maiden."

A smile flashed across her face. "As long as you know your place is here, Your Highness."

"Of course."

"We must depart post haste," Arthur said. "Glastonbury Tor is in Wessex. A week's journey to be sure, and a dangerous one at that since we'll have no choice but to travel through Anglo-Saxon lands. Who knows how bad the curse in Caerleon will be by then."

"Perhaps I can help," the Grail Maiden said. "The paths across the Otherworld are often shorter than their mortal counterparts. I see you are familiar with walking the immortal realms already."

The knights looked at each other in mutual confusion. "What do you mean?" Arthur asked.

"The mist clings to you. You have just arrived from the Otherworld, have you not?" She stepped toward Arthur, a soft smile on her lips. "The ivory you carry? The Bone Key allows you to move in and out of the Otherworld at will, including the *In-Between*."

Percival wanted to smack himself for not thinking of this sooner. "Castellum Puellarum, Eiden's Burgh. This village wasn't empty—drained of people. Nae, we weren't in the real village. We were in its Otherworld shadow."

Arthur huffed an irritated sigh. "That explains quite a lot, actually." To the Grail Maiden, he said, "We are not eager to enter that shadow realm again. However, if the Otherworld shortens our journey, then show us the way, Maiden."

She nodded. "I believe I can open a door directly to Avalon. You will hardly need to step foot in the Otherworld."

"Avalon?" Arthur asked.

"Yes, Little Dragon King. Glastonbury Tor is the gateway to Avalon, where the Mother Goddess herself dwells."

"Our gratitude to you, Maiden," Arthur said with a sweeping bow.

The Grail Maiden crossed to the other side of the room, to a bare stretch of stone wall. She passed her hand across the stones and the wall shimmered into a door.

Percival's mouth fell open. He wasn't sure he would ever grow familiar with magical sightings every day. As if the unnatural were as common as stewed figs.

Arthur stepped up first, opening the door before them. Through the opening lay a dim field of dead, brown grass. Oh gods. Was that Wessex?

"Once more, I thank you for your aid," Arthur said. "Caerleon is in your debt."

"You are welcome, Arthur Pendragon. I had wondered if you were indeed the king that Briton needs. But now I know that Excalibur is in capable hands."

He dipped his head into a bow and then stepped through.

Galahad was next. She patted the scabbard, which she buckled around her waist. "Thank you, fair knight. You surely must be brave and selfless, if the sword appeared to you."

Galahad stepped through.

Fionna was next. "Whatever did ye mean? Ye called me a

Gwenevere. But I possess no magic. And a Gwenevere is but a faerie tale."

The Grail Maiden laid a gentle hand on Fionna's shoulder. "You have an additional quest to complete, Fionnabhair Allán. You must discover who you are. For I fear without you in all your strength, the Little Dragon King will not be able to do what must be done."

"How do I even begin such a quest?"

"Look into your past. Across the Irish Sea. It is time to look to your home, Princess."

Fionna drew in a quiet breath and then stepped through.

Lancelot was next. A dark look shadowed each handsome feature, an expression Percival knew well. His friend was angry, through Percival wasn't sure why. Perhaps he was angry over this third curse.

"Lancelot du Lac," the Maiden said. "It is time you forgive yourself."

Lancelot's jaw worked back-and-forth and, for a moment, Percival thought he might snap at her. But he curtly nodded and then stepped through.

"Sir Percival," she said. She looked at him and reached up to caress his face with a tender touch. "You remind me so much of your father. But you have the best of your mother as well."

A hollow laugh escaped him.

"I know life has been hard on you, and much of the blame lies with her. But there was indeed good in her, before the loss of your father drove her mad."

Percival couldn't stop himself from springing at the golden-haired faerie and pulling her into an embrace. "Thank ye, Grail Maiden, for standing vigil all these years."

"It is my great pleasure. But I shall relish the return of company around here, Your Majesty."

He let out another laugh. "I will return, lass. Promise. But first there are things that I must do."

Chapter Twenty-Nine

Fionna

I stumbled out of the Otherworld's doorway, my stomach heaving. I thought I might vomit. It felt as if my soul had been wrenched from within me.

I looked back as Lancelot staggered out through the doorway after me, his hands falling to his knees as he let out a hacking cough. Behind him, Percival grew visible within the doorframe, the image like a moving tapestry. He embraced the Grail Maiden before stepping through to join us.

"Och, that was fun," Percival said through gritted teeth, stumbling sideways.

The door winked shut behind us and we surveyed the surrounding land—a sorry sight. The grass had withered and died, the trees grasping skeletons, dry and shriveled leaves piled around their trunks as though fallen Samhain wraiths. Even the sky overhead hung pallid and brown, as if the smoke from a bonfire enveloped us.

"The curse has progressed so quickly," Arthur choked out, turning slowly in a circle, his keen eyes absorbing every nightmarish detail.

It grieved me deeply to see what had become of this beautiful territory. If this is how the Anglo-Saxon lands of Wessex now suffered, I shuddered to think of Caerleon and Briton. I thought fondly of the fertile, green rolling hills and lush, moss-draped forests that had first greeted me when I stepped off the boat from Ulster.

"How could Morgana do this?" I whispered to myself. "I thought the fae were creatures of earth."

Arthur heard me. "What my father did to my half-sisters . . . perverting any goodness they once held. I fear they are only creatures of wrath now. Creatures who desire to bring the downfall of man and whatever land supports him."

"I am beyond grieved," I said, finding his eyes. We held each other's gaze, the sadness in his tearing through my heart.

"Let us show them then," Percival said, pulling me from Arthur's intensity, "show them that mortals are no easy adversaries and not easily bested."

We stood at the foot of a massive terraced hill seeming to rise out of a desiccated marshland. Before the hill, a stone circle peeked out at us, the afternoon sun hitting a central stone in bronzed spears of dingy light. We made our way toward the large menhirs—the ancient stones—unsure of exactly where to locate the waters of Avalon. As we neared the first slope, the sound of a bubbling spring reached our ears.

Healthy, green yew trees swayed in a gentle breeze. The wind's fingers cooled my warmed skin and refreshed my spirit. For beyond the lacy boughs, a verdant garden sprawled around the reddest water I had ever seen. So red, in fact, it was as though the land were bleeding out. In a few steps, my feet stepped from golden brown death into a living wildness that rippled through my body in calming waves.

Arthur halted before what appeared to be a well and wrinkled his brow in distaste. The springs beyond were not just red, but thick. Like blood.

A chill wended down my spine as I remembered the Grail Maiden's words. *To heal the land, you must drink from the land's life source, the land's blood.*

"These are the waters of Avalon?" Lancelot said in dismay, a grimace on his face. He stood to the side, as if he were still in the Otherworld, as if he had never passed through. He was a specter, a mere shadow, his feelings transparent yet distant from us simultaneously. Since the stable in Eiden's Burgh, he had barely uttered a word. Since Arthur had dressed him down and commanded him as a soldier rather than as a friend.

The third curse offered two versions of death. Presently, he and Arthur's withering bonds of brotherhood suffered the same fate as these dying lands. I ached to show Lancelot how he was still welcome here. To show him that he was forgiven, no matter the mistakes or wrongs made. We were five. We were one. Hadn't these beautiful men shown this very care to me when I had stolen Excalibur? Now it was our turn to rise above betrayal for Lancelot. But first, we needed to absolve another curse.

Percival was surveying the spring, his brow furrowed. "Hand me the Grail, Yer Majesty?" He said to Arthur, who handed over the ornate bowl. Percival knelt before a stone lion that was carved into an ancient stone, the creature's mouth wide open. Thick, dark-red water trickled between the beast's fangs to a small pool below, as though blood dripped from its maw after a kill.

A delighted laugh escaped from him that was all Percival—joy. His heritage may be tied to the Fisher King line, but the true magic coursing through his veins was a happiness akin to the bluest of skies, sun-drenched meadows, and wildflowers dancing merrily in a melodic breeze. He stood, rays of sunshine on his lips as he brought the Grail back to us reverently. "Look!"

The water within was crystal clear, as though cupped from a mountain spring. And before any of us could stop him, he downed every last drop. And, as he did so, the land below us, down the hill, shimmered and changed. A sweet-scented wind played with Percival's copper strands affectionately before ripping through the skeletal trees, arousing the white and pink buds of spring to adorn each naked branch. The marsh grass—brown and dead—dotted with blades of green as new patches speared out from the cracked, earthen crust.

Arthur whooped like a boy and grabbed the Grail from Percival. He hurried to the spring and knelt, scooping rusted water into the vessel. Eagerly he downed the contents, clear water dribbling over his chin and onto his tunic.

The land glimmered with change once more. New leaves unfurled along the blossomed branches—bright yellowed-greens—

and the blackened bark warmed to umber hues. The glinting green of Arthur's eyes deepened as he stared about in wonder. A flock of birds alighted from nearby trees—birds, I was certain, that were not roosting there before. Patches of green grass sprang forth, as if emerging from winter's slumber to the dizzying heights of spring within a few erratic beats of my heart. In the garden around the spring, the ground gently quaked and split. Arthur anchored his feet, though the rest of us cautiously stepped back. Then, to my thundering pulse's surprise, a mighty oak grew from the small fissure in the enchanted garden. Knotted branches sprawled out in protection over the well, long limbs leafing out in seemingly endless shades of green. Arthur peered over his shoulder with a boyish grin, though his back remained straight as a king, his legs firmly planted as a warrior.

Galahad drank from the spring next and, again, the land transformed. Spring dawned much lighter now. Wildflowers in a rainbow of colors bloomed around the stone circle and carpeted the paths snaking around the marsh. Golden light pierced through the dingy sky and spilled honeyed rays across the land. And, I swore, the sun painted the very landscape from the palette of gold brushing Galahad's mane of wavy hair and skin. Even the deep blues saturating the sky reflected in Galahad's eyes.

Galahad handed the sacred dish to Lancelot, who hesitated.

"Go on," Arthur encouraged.

"You're one of us," I said softly.

Lancelot shot me a dark look, but he obeyed.

As he drank from the Blessed Grail, the land came alive as fireflies burst from the reeds as though cooling their wings in the gentle caress of an evening breeze. The flickering green and purple lights frolicked from stone to stone, sponging velvety moss in cracks and crevices. Yellow and sea-green lichen flowered on trunks, limbs, and dotted rocks. Ferns curled out from the ground and shadowed the newly sprouted grass as though a mother hen protecting her chicks. When the land rested once more, he lifted his granite-carved eyes to mine, his posture as rigid as the menhirs guarding his back.

"Fionna, you're next." Lancelot handed me the bowl. Our fingers touched, and a muscle along his jaw jumped.

"Thank ye," I whispered in reply, but he ignored me.

Drawing in a shaky breath, I knelt beside the spring, dipping the Grail into the red-tinged water. I drank deeply, the surprisingly sweet water sliding down my throat. When I lowered the bowl, I looked below us, ready to see the last patches of grass and brittle trees healed, the land surrounding the Tor as green and bright as ever.

But nothing happened. Not even the wind stirred. The land appeared the same as before I drank.

"Did I do something wrong?" I asked, looking from the spring to the bowl. "Should I try again?"

"Yes, try again," Arthur said.

So, I did, and though the water was pure on my tongue, the land was unaffected.

Arthur spun in a slow circle, running his hands through his hair. "I don't understand. The blessed five . . . should have healed the land. Right Percival?"

"Aye, that's what the standing stone declared and Merlin confirmed." Percival frowned, a strange look on the lad's face.

"As much as it pains me to say this," Arthur began, slowly, meeting each of our expectant gazes. "Let us return to Caerleon when dawn breaks. We have accomplished much. The land has begun to heal, and we now have the Grail. Perhaps Merlin can explain what went wrong and how to completely break the curse."

The thought of returning to Caerleon warmed me. I prayed news of my father and sister awaited me there.

The other knights nodded to Arthur's suggestion and I handed the bowl back to Arthur, no longer feeling as if I deserved to touch such a sacred relic.

Unease bubbled up within me, as dark as the bloody water of the spring. Why had I failed them? If I were truly one of the blessed five, then why did the curse over Caerleon and her neighboring lands remain?

Facing Merlin's gold-ringed cambion eyes unnerved me too. *Do you have any faerie blood?* The druid's question, from the day I had visited his cave, rang loud in my mind.

More memories surfaced. Drinking the faerie wine with no ill effects. The Bone Carver grasping a lock of my hair and asking me about my power. The Grail Maiden, just moments before, voicing a strange comment about unwittingly entertaining a Gwenevere at Caer Benic. Lancelot's certainty that I was the one tied to the prophesied third curse.

Suddenly, I was sure of nothing. Even, it seemed, who I was.

Chapter Thirty

Lancelot

ightfall's dew blanketed the magical garden around the Chalice Well and Red Spring. The droplets glistened in the fading moonlight as though a dusting of black diamonds. Lancelot welcomed the remaining darkness. Atop his bedroll, he allowed his unflappable mask to drop—the one he had held before him by sheer will alone.

Now he wanted to weep. For he knew what he must do before the sun finally rose to greet the new day.

They had made camp by the gurgling spring, beneath the boughs of the giant guardian oak and beside blackthorn trees. Soon after, their horses appeared from the northern side of the garden, nickering, vapor puffing angrily from their flaring nostrils. How had they forgotten about their horses? Even more baffling, how did the horses know where to find them and arrive so soon? Faerie magic, Lancelot knew. Another debt owed to the beautiful Grail Maiden of Caer Benic. Still, the excitement of the Grail had wiped away all reason and thought, it seemed.

Despite much coaxing, they had not been able to convince their horses to drink from the Tor's bloody waters. So, they took turns offering their mounts clear water from the ornate silver bowl, each knight cringing at the sacrilege.

Lancelot, then, laid out his bedroll far from the others. He didn't deserve to be near the fire now that his king regarded him with ice-frosted disapproval. It was fitting that Lancelot's body grew as numb as his spirit felt. Part of him wanted to rail at the unfairness of Morgana's vengeance and Arthur's judgment. He had made one mistake with Morgana. *One mistake*, and his life, all he had toiled so hard to obtain—family, recognized prestige, restoring a piece of his birthright by becoming second to the king—had been ripped from him. But he couldn't ignore the quiet voice whispering from the black corner of his mind that he hadn't made just *one* mistake. This was simply the "one mistake" exposed to the sunlight. There had been mistakes aplenty before, careless dalliances with nobles' wives and sons, or virgin maids. He had lived each day as though he were untouchable, following a path of self-indulgence and pleasure—whatever numbed his doubts over his own worthiness. But he had no more lingering doubts. This quest had shown him first-hand how unworthy he truly was.

Lancelot drank from the Grail and his act had healed the land. But that gift to his king, to the mortal lands he called home, was a thin consolation. He had never felt so useless as he did today in Caer Benic. Percival—the Fisher King—had known the phrase to summon forth the Grail's acceptance. Fionna, with her strange secrets, gave Arthur Manannán mac Lir's apple to heal his stab wound and returned Lleu's spear to the Grail Maiden. Even Galahad, a lowborn Norseman, had gained the Grail Sword through noble and valiant deeds, allowing them to take the Grail from its rightful home.

What had Lancelot offered? Nothing. *Blessed five, my arse,* he thought.

He knew that Arthur was most concerned, and rightfully so, with the remaining tendrils of poison clinging to Caerleon's waters and earth. But Lancelot's mind was consumed with the curse on him alone. Whatever good they achieved at Glastonbury Tor, he could undo it all if he gave into his weakness and lay with Fionna. And whether through trickery or magic or weakness, he couldn't guarantee their joining wouldn't happen. Not if they remained together.

Arthur had forbidden him to leave before they secured the Grail. Lancelot had honored this part of the quest. They had the

Grail. He drank from the spring. Arthur Pendragon and the Knights of Caerleon didn't need him anymore.

And now there was only one solution: he must leave.

The sound of soft snores and even breathing drifted past the fire's smoldering embers to his ears—sounds he had listened to for hours while he wobbled with indecision. But now he was resolved. Lancelot's heart sank, heavy with festering grief, as he crept out of his bedroll, rolling the furs and woolen blankets up quietly. He tiptoed through the trees to where they had tied their horses and, as silently as an overgrown grave, he saddled and bridled his mount.

He knew where he should go, though he shivered at the very thought. Home. Castle Peel on the Isle of Man—the main residence of Vivien, Lady of the Lake—hadn't been much of a home compared to his time in Wales. Though distant and fickle, his foster mother was kinder than most—as far as faeries went—understanding that humans had souls and destinies and hearts. She had never once comforted him, and she sometimes forgot he even existed for days on end. But she had taught him how to fit into a world he couldn't understand. A skill that had seen him through many trials, even today's.

Vivien also possessed unnatural wisdom. She was part of the strange tangle of threads that tied Arthur to Excalibur, the Grail, and the Túatha dé Danann. Perhaps she would lend a remnant of knowledge to help Lancelot break this foul curse. Perhaps she would even take pity upon him, if he prostrated himself before her. Maybe she would favor him with help to seize back his wretched life.

Dread pooled in his stomach as the Isle of Man haunted his bruised memories. Particularly one. His first hunt with his mother's court. As a lad of ten, Lancelot had begged Vivien for weeks to attend the Great Hunt on Beltane's eve. Finally, she relented. And when a gorgeous buck came into view, his herd in tow, his foster mother's faerie retinue had crowed at Lancelot to take the shot. He plucked an arrow from his quiver, drew back the string—and missed. Instead, he hit a mother deer in the flank, wounding her grievously. The faeries, including one named Grastin, a particularly cruel sídhe male, had dragged him forward to finish his kill.

Tears had brimmed in Lancelot's eyes as he regarded the spotted fawn hovering in the distance, bleating for her mother, afraid of the strange scents of man and fae. Grastin had handed a wicked hunting knife to Lancelot and demanded he kill both mother and fawn. For no baby could live without its mother.

Mocking words, Lancelot knew—even then—that were aimed at more than just the wildlife before them. The faerie courts found his mortal presence unnatural and believed Vivien should have left him for dead rather than accept his life as an offering from a weak woman who had chosen her husband's killer over her own flesh and blood.

An exiled prince he remained—not really belonging to anyone but himself.

Lancelot shook off the memory, thickly swallowing. He wasn't that boy anymore. He had only ever told one person that story. Arthur. "It was a mercy," Lancelot had said, still trying to convince himself.

"A mercy would have been the fae male killing the fawn himself," Arthur had said softly, those green eyes full of understanding. Arthur was like that. He saw a man's weakness, his vulnerability, and through a rare beauty only Arthur could possess, counted those failings as strength. And then, by his faith in those who kept his company, those perceived strengths became so. But . . . in Lancelot's case, Arthur's faith had been misplaced.

Lancelot swung into the saddle and then drank in the sight of his companions' sleeping forms beneath the giant oak, their bodies illuminated by a sliver of moonlight.

Percival, the male lover he had always wanted, yet never felt he deserved. Headstrong and impetuous and eager. His eternal, cheerful playfulness and ridiculous humor a balm to Lancelot's shadowed, insecure heart. Lancelot touched his lips in wonderment, closing his eyes and re-imagining the feel of Percival smile as he claimed Lancelot's mouth in return. The feel of stubble brushing against his lower lip. The magic dancing between Percival's breath and his. Lancelot opened his eyes and forced his gaze to move on before his decision faltered once more.

Galahad. Simple yet kind and honorable to a fault, and always ready to nurture a hurting soul through his gentle compassion. Protective and rascally like a brother too. The giant of a man was more secure in himself and his abilities than the wealthiest of nobles from the finest breeding. Around Galahad's strength, Lancelot often felt invincible. So much so, if ever Lancelot was lucky enough to know sons of his own, he wanted to name one Galahad in honor of his valiant sword-brother. Lancelot blinked back the building emotion and focused on a snowfall of swirling braids and flyaway strands strewn across a bed of furs.

Fionna. His very heart; his soul's true mate; his equal. Stronger and more beautiful than any woman he had ever known. Formidable in battle, and who loved even more fiercely—a tenacity so enduring, she would be willing to lay down her very life for those her heart claimed. Somehow, despite all his unkind acts to push her away, she still cared for him. And fought for him too. Longing for him to know the completeness of her love, even if their bodies never joined as lovers. Yearning for him to always belong—to her, to them. He thought that final truth might break him the most.

If not for Arthur.

His brother.

Arthur, who had been through more betrayal and sorrow and cruelty in his twenty-two years than most men did in their lifetimes, and yet, still managed to believe the best of people and the world. Arthur was the man that men wished to be. The man Lancelot aspired to be. And the king Lancelot would always fail. His foster brother was truly the most beautiful man Lancelot had ever known and leaving him felt like death. For how could Lancelot live without his dearest friend?

And yet, he must. If he possessed any love for Arthur, he would leave and not return until he was worthy of the honor and love his brother readily bestowed upon him.

Lancelot tapped his horse's flanks and whispered, "Farewell," as he cantered forward into the gray twilight of dawn.

This time, there was no fierce Fionna or angry Arthur to stop him.

This time, there was only the last vestiges of night and the lone caw of a crow.

Interlude

Morgana

The crow watched the dark, feather-haired male's retreating form from the swirling cloud banks rolling over the green land. The rising sun gilded the terraced grass slopes as the first rays peeked over the sacred hill of Avalon. This land belonged to the Mother Goddess and formed a gateway to the Túatha dé Danann courts. Mist began to shroud the surrounding area and the crow sank farther into the streams of both natural and unnatural fog. The crow hopped onto the ground and summoned the shadows and whispers around her, transforming.

Anger burned within Morgana. Despite staying ten steps ahead of these bumbling mortals, they had almost ruined everything today. All her carefully laid plans, her time grooming that fool O'Lynn, flying back and forth across the Irish Sea. She faulted the Grail Maiden and the old gods. Those meddling creatures had all but delivered the Blessed Grail into her half-brother's unworthy hands. But despite that unexpected downturn of fortune, two delightful events had taken place. Inexplicable even to her, the Grail had failed, and her sister's curse over Caerleon remained. And even better, her curse on Lancelot had driven him from the embrace of his sword-brothers and the witch.

To her faerie ears, she could hear the faint sound of hoofbeats echoing in the air. She smiled in triumph. Lancelot thought he did what was best for his king by abandoning him. How wrong he was. Lancelot's honor was his downfall; his loyalty sealed his betrayal.

Morgana observed Arthur's camp through black unblinking lashes. She pondered the puzzle before her, turning the strange circumstances over in her mind with distaste. She had never liked puzzles or riddles. Wastes of time, childrens' games. She treasured *results*.

But she needed to solve the riddle the witch presented. Could she be wrong, and the white-haired witch wasn't the foretold Gwenevere whispered among the sídhe? A demi moon goddess of centuries past? It had seemed evident that this witch was a "gwen," a specimen so beautiful, to look upon her was a form of torture. And, yet, Lancelot had not bedded the witch, even when charmed by the necklace's enchantment. He had never resisted a beautiful man or woman before.

A dark tortured thought spasmed within her and kindled a spark of hope. Did he miss his dark fae lover? Did he miss being with a female who understood the black pain he carried deep inside his mortal heart? Who was willing to rage and war beside him until his pain empowered her to greatness? She shoved the thought aside ruthlessly. Lancelot did not deserve one such as her.

Morgana focused upon the woman curled up in a nest of furs by the flickering embers of last night's fire. There was something *other* that replied to Morgana's test of magic. A mortal woman did not carry such strength, prowess, or steeled beauty. Nor did she reflect moonshine in her silver gaze. Only fae-born held such elemental traits. But the Blessed Grail had failed to dissolve all curses upon her half-brother and his land. Even fae who drank from the Grail were absolved from their curses and received the Mother Goddess's blessing.

The only way the Grail could fail fae or mortal alike is if they were under the protection of a more powerful magic. But what was mightier than the Grail? Perhaps . . . a géis, a powerful spell of protection or prohibition. Could this *gwen* be protected by such an enchantment? Hidden in plain sight until a Gwenevere was needed?

If so, then the witch truly did not know of her powers and, thus, did not have access to them. It meant Morgana and her sisters still had free reign to soak in the land's death and the people's too. And it gave her time to do all she could to prevent the witch from unlocking her powers as an earth- and sovereignty-goddess.

Or . . . she could end her right now. The feathers of Morgana's dress whispered across the grass as she crept toward where the witch slept. Curls of mist clawed the ground where she knelt and unsheathed an obsidian dagger to plunge into the witch's heart, a heart as pure as the driven snow.

"Morgana?" a voice slurred from a bedroll across the cold fire. The golden-haired knight sat up and rubbed at his eyes while cracking a roar of a yawn. A sound loud enough to wake the dead, and the remaining warriors around the fire. In a single drawn breath, shadows and the greedy prayers of men tumbled around her in a dark blur.

The crow hopped away from the witch and met the golden male's confused stare. Then, she flapped her wings with a warning caw and flew into the mists of Avalon. She would allow the witch to live. For now. She would discover who sired her and the terms of the géis, before joining O'Lynn.

Satisfied with her new course, the crow cawed once more and then slipped through the mortal veil into the Otherworld.

Chapter Thirty-One

Arthur

Arthur woke with the dawn, feeling stronger and more optimistic than he had in weeks. True, the curse over Caerleon wasn't completely broken, but *they had found the Blessed Grail*. A feat his father had strived to achieve for decades but never accomplished. But *Arthur* had done it. He had found the sacred vessel.

As he stretched, he felt none of the stiffness he normally did after a night of sleeping on the hard ground. The enchanted apple must have healed even the smallest of ailments. He rolled his shoulders, then covered a yawn as his eyes fell onto Fionna's stirring form.

The past few weeks felt akin to a lifetime. They had endured so much. But they had overcome every hardship. Together.

Arthur swept an appreciative gaze around the fire circle and paused. His brows furrowed. One bedroll was missing. Lancelot. Perhaps he had risen early. Maybe practicing with his blade as he sometimes did when he couldn't sleep.

Arthur stood and wove between the trees to where they had tied the horses, his heart in his throat. Lancelot's charger was gone.

"Fool man," Arthur spat.

"Mmm?" Fionna called out. She pulled on her boots and pushed loose strands of hair out of her eyes.

Arthur spun and stalked back to their fire pit.

"What troubles ye?" she asked. When he didn't reply, she tried again. "Ye seem upset."

"Lancelot is gone."

The blood drained from her face, each delicate feature paling more than her already fair skin. "Fool man!"

Arthur loosed a dark laugh. "That's what I said."

"I considered how we needed to talk to him just yesterday. We shouldn't have let offenses remain as strong as they were in the stables."

"You think this my fault?" Arthur asked, the words sounding more defensive than he intended. In truth, Lancelot's absence probably was his fault. He had let his anger get the better of him. Though he had meant every word he said in the stable, he also understood that Lancelot's lies were a misguided attempt to protect Arthur. Lancelot may be foolish and headstrong and impulsive at times, but he was always loyal.

"I don't blame ye, My King," Fionna said. "Lancelot is a grown man. He makes his own choices. But I know this quest wore on him differently than the rest of us. He bore a dissimilar burden. And we needed to show him that, despite his failings, he was still welcome."

Percival and Galahad began to stir and were now sitting up in their bedrolls.

Galahad let out a jaw-cracking yawn, then murmured, "Do you see a pesky crow?"

"Dreaming of birds, chipmunk?" Percival asked, a puckish look on his sleepy face.

"Wait." Galahad's visage scrunched up as he looked at the sky, as if he could see into his head this way. "No, I thought I saw Morgana earlier. But then I realized it was just a crow, so I went back to sleep."

"Shit." Arthur rubbed his brow. "Lancelot is gone. We need to go after him."

"Bloody crabapple," Percival swore. A dark expression flitted across the lad's eyes before brightening to their normal earthen hue, as though a flickering lightning strike of hurt. Arthur narrowed his eyes curiously. Was his and Lancelot's kiss more than drunken games?

Fionna cut through Arthur's wandering thoughts. "Do ye have any idea where he's heading?"

"I suspect north," Arthur said with a sigh. "Toward the Isle of Man. Perhaps he seeks a way to break the curse."

"I thought ye wanted to journey to Caerleon and speak with Merlin?" Fionna countered.

"I did. But we've bought ourselves a little time." Arthur combed fingers through his short strands. "Perhaps if we are quick, we can catch him and convince him to return home with us. I'm still not certain we won't need all five of us in the end."

"Uh, I'm not sure we'll need to return to speak with Merlin," Galahad said, standing. "Isn't that him right there?"

"Or maybe another bird," Percival practically chirped. "Are ye even awake, ye big oaf?"

Arthur blinked, not sure if the sight he beheld was a mirage or some strange trick of the mystical garden. For it did appear as though his chief advisor was indeed riding up the hillside toward their camp, the morning sun shining on the bald sides of his head.

"How in the name of the goddess did he know?" Fionna gnawed the inside of her lip.

"Maybe a little bird told him," Percival said, sliding another mischievous look Galahad's way.

Galahad groaned and wacked the younger man on the backside of his head. "It's not natural to be so cheerful first thing in the morn."

"Having a druid in your court is convenient at times," Arthur said to Fionna with a hollow chuckle, ignoring the antics of his other two knights. Gods, he was glad to see Merlin. Perhaps the druid would have answers to the riddles eluding their party.

"Good morning," Merlin said, reining his panting horse to a stop. Sweat and caked mud coated his brown and white dappled stallion. The horse heaved for breath as foam gathered around the charger's mouth. How hard had he ridden his horse? And for how long? Before Arthur could ask, Merlin swung down and wrapped Arthur into an embrace.

Galahad stepped forward and led the fatigued stallion to a freshly-filled Grail.

"Good morning yourself," Arthur replied, patting Merlin's shoulder. "Not often do I have the pleasure of seeing you outside of Caerleon's grounds. To what do I owe this honor?"

"Grave tidings, My King," Merlin said. "I wish that I could allow you this moment to celebrate, for the transformation around me tells that you have indeed found the Blessed Grail."

"Yes. Though the healing is not complete. We have questions."

"All in due time," Merlin said. "First, I must give you this." He handed over a crinkled letter.

Arthur studied the missive, his eyebrows knitting together. A stone grated along the pit of his stomach. For Merlin to journey so far to deliver a message personally . . .

The other knights crowded round.

Arthur opened the letter and scanned the contents quickly. As he took in the words, his spirits sank further. "A letter from Donal O'Lynn." He looked meaningfully at Fionna. "Respectfully rejecting our offer of ransoming anything less than Excalibur. And he says for the insult of such a minuscule offer, now the price for your father has increased. Not just Excalibur. But my crown as well."

Fionna's expression pinched into rage and she spat, "That snake!" Then she faltered, a deathly calm glazing her narrowed gaze. "Wait. My father? What about Aideen?"

Arthur met her silver eyes with pity. "The letter is signed Chieftain Donal and Aideen O'Lynn."

A cold wind whipped at Arthur's cloak, tugging the heavy wool into a swirl around his body. For a moment, Arthur believed he glimpsed thunderclouds gathering in Fionna's eyes before she spun away from their group and stalked into the trees.

"Should we go after her?" Galahad asked.

"Ye first," Percival said with a shaky laugh.

Arthur watched her retreating form until she disappeared into the foliage and dusky light. "Let her be."

From the dense shield of trees, a ragged scream rent the morning chill, followed by another. Her fury seeming to billow a bitter gust of icy wind that gnashed at their exposed skin. Percival's copper hair lashed about his face like licking flames while Galahad's golden waves floated in the air.

Merlin, however, simply pulled his cloak's hood over his head, shadowing his features, save the gold-rimmed light flashing from his Otherworldly hazel eyes.

Fionna's raw grief continued, clawing at Arthur's heart, shredding what remained of his strength. His hands curled into fists, his nails digging into the flesh of his palms as her battering ram of emotions beat down his walled fortress of anger and anguish and fear.

He began to turn toward her when a sudden burst of frigid rain erupted above them from a nearly cloudless sky, splattering on Arthur's upturned forehead. Rivulets of water dripped down his cheeks and down his neck.

Quickly, he folded the letter, tucking the missive away and out of this strange, furious weather. "I should have done far more," he grit between clenched, chattering teeth. Then he released his own fury to the wind and rain, shouting, "I shouldn't have laid all my focus on the Grail! Selfish! Now, Lancelot is gone and Fionna's sister is shackled to a monster!"

Merlin pulled his cloak tighter around his gray robes. "I'm afraid, Your Majesty, there is more. The messenger returned with other tidings. O'Lynn and his new bride have been sighted with a dark-haired fae at their side. A female."

"Morgana?"

"I believe so. He spotted them last in the port of Dublin, eight days prior, where Dál nAraidi ships are massing."

Arthur grew dizzy as his heart galloped into a feral rhythm. "What are you saying?" He barely spoke above a whisper. But he already knew the answer, the stone in his gut grinding his nerves to dust.

"Your Majesty," Merlin began, holding Arthur's gaze steady. "Your stray knight will have to wait. For you must return to Caerleon and prepare for war."

Historical Notes

ey there. This is your *Knights of Caerleon* lore keeper, Jesikah Sundin. And . . . whew! This was a doozy of a book to write, and for so many twisty-turny reasons. But for the sake of historical notes, I'm mainly going to focus on two topics: the Grail Quest and who Gwenevere was in Arthurian Legend mythos. And, because it's me, I might wander about to get there. So, hold tight.

First, if you missed the *Historical Notes* from book one, you can read all about the origins of Arthur Pendragon and Arthurian Celtic pagan lore on my blog.

Now to book two . . .

The Grail Quest. There are hundreds and hundreds of stories that make up the larger bulk of Arthurian Cycle stories. Tales that have inspired spin-off literature for centuries (just type "grail" into Amazon and you'll see what I mean). And tales that have given story fodder to Hollywood since the dawn of the silver screen. I just want you to know that it is REALLY hard to not spam this feature with Monty Python and Indiana Jones memes. Heh. I said spam. If you're not sure of why that's funny, then I suggest you look up Grail Quest inspired Broadway musicals.

And with the Grail Quest comes the equally as legendary "tests"—ones I certainly felt as I rifled through odd—mostly humorous in cringy "Go home, you're drunk Middle Ages"—story after story after story. My lore keeper's eagle eye was hunting for very specific tales, though. Ones as old as the Arthurian Legend itself. And I found three suitable candidates.

1. The Great Boar Hunt

A Celtic mythology staple. I encourage you to read this short Cliff's Notes version of the Twrch Trwyth story because it's hilarious (linked above). The Middle Ages are ripe with beard stories. No, seriously. But this beard story takes the hipster micro-craft beer . . . er, I mean cake. Alas, while I contemplated magical razor kits for Galahad, our gentle giant, both Claire and I kept our tale basic: faerie boar does bad things. Kill the boar!

The Bone Carver is my faerytale twist to this cornerstone Celtic mythological story. Though Bone Carvers do exist in folktales, as far as I could tell, they're not present in Arthurian lore. Boo. Well, now one certainly is *winks*.

2. The Afanc of Betws-y-Coed

Also known as the Addanc, this legend is another strange Celtic myth origin story that has actually shaped the history and tourist appeal of a real town nestled in the Snowdonia region of northwest Wales. Though this isn't a beard story, it is a monster beaver story. Yes. A giant, flood-inducing, people-killing beaver. *side-eyes the Middles Ages* Click on the link above for a quick pre-Arthurian *Mabinogion* read about this monstrous beaver and the lullaby-singing maiden. But, when Arthurian adventures rolled around, the original folktale was dressed up in *Peredur son of Efrawg*, a romance found within the *Mabinogion* (Peredur is Welsh for Percival). This Welsh folktale, blinged out by The Crusades, introduced a maiden who gives Peredur a "stone of invisibility" to aid in his slay-the-monster hero's feat. A monster that was no longer a giant killer beaver, but more reptilian and demonic in nature. Turns out, to Peredur's delight, that this maiden is none other than the Queen of Constantinople who is accompanied by two female mystics—sexy maidens who can raise the dead.

And, yes, in case you're curious, cannabis was really what most of the ancient world smoked until tobacco was introduced in the late Medieval period and early Renaissance. (Probably explains all the beard and monster beaver stories).

3. Castle of the Maidens

Ahhh, where do I even begin with this one? Perhaps the most famous of all the Grail Quest "tests" and present in every Grail cycle story. So much so, even *Monty Python and the Holy Grail* had to mock this trope with desperate young women trying to take Galahad's virginity.

Oh, I am afraid our life must seem very dull and quiet compared to yours. We are but eight score young blondes and brunettes, all between sixteen and nineteen and a half, cut off in this castle with no one to protect us! Oh, it is a lonely life -- bathing, dressing, undressing, making exciting underwear.... We are just not used to handsome knights. Nay, nay, come, come, you may lie here

(Read the rest of the Castle Anthrax scene with a simple Google search)

As a side note, Galahad the Chaste and Percival the Chaste are oscillating tropes as well. We chose Percival for our tale, as he seemed to have the most "holy virgin" stories of all the knights.

Soooo, originally . . . the Castle of the Maidens is the Celtic tale about The Nine Sorceresses, which is also from *Peredur son of Efrawg* in the *Mabinogion*. In this tale, these sorceresses are the armed witches of Caer Lyow. By-the-way, "The Nine Maidens" is a reoccurring trope in British/Celtic mythology. Which is how this Welsh tale ended up in Scotland. And, interestingly enough, the "Castel of the Maidens" in Scotland influenced the Welsh tale of The Nine Sorceresses. Savvy? Good. So, what was the actual Castle of the Maidens?

Edinburgh Castle. Until the 1500's, this castle was known throughout as the Maidens' Castle (Latin: *Castellum Puellarum*). Castle Rock, where the present-day castle dwells, was a site often mentioned throughout ancient texts. The problem? No one can confirm, absolutely, the historical origins of why "maidens" are truly associated with this place. Though, they do believe that young women of Picti royal heritage were kept in a structure of sorts atop Castle Rock at some point (When? The details are murky and, thus, chronicled as "the old time"—for reals, "the old times"). But this castle is most famous for St. Margaret's Chapel, the oldest surviving building in Edinburgh. This is a stone structure built by King David I of Scotland in the 12th century for his mother, Princess Margaret, who was eventually canonized by the Catholic church.

Did they make exciting underwear there, though? Well, the verdict is still out . . . BUT, it is interesting to note that a hill near Edinburgh Castle is named Arthur's Seat.

And Glastonbury Tor? Steeped in Arthurian Legend. This location in Wessex, England is considered the origins for the Isle of Avalon. The Tor was originally surrounded by marshlands, making this sacred hill an island. Tor is an Old English word for "hill." But the Celts referred to the Tor as *Ynys Wydryn*, aka the Isle of Glass. And the famous mists of Avalon? A fog bank rolls in often and cloaks the marshlands and surrounding areas until only the peak of Glastonbury Tor can be seen. In the 12th century, Gerald of Wales, a writer, alleged that he had discovered the tombs of Arthur and Gwenevere in 1191 atop the Tor. But the Tor is famous for something else: the Red Spring. And the descriptions of looking and feeling like blood? All true. This spring is a geological wonder and tied to Grail lore and Celtic mythology.

And, lastly, the Spear of Lleu that weeps blood is a must in Grail lore. But more on this in book three's *Historical Notes*.

Well, now for the part I know you're all really waiting for. Gwenevere.

Who was she really? As our story hints at, she's not some simpering fair maiden who is sold off for political alliances. My progressive, feminist sensibilities won't endlessly wax poetic the Gwenevere (or Guinevere) stuffed down our post-Victorian throats. Why? This barren, damsel-in-distress Queen isn't historical anyway, just part of the late Medieval, Victorian, and post-Victorian romance glamour that perfectly mirrored their ideal "Lady": gentle, fair, blonde, submissive to men, but who is easily led astray by her feeble, romantic heart. An "Eve" archetype character. So, ladies take note, do not end up like Gwenevere and become a homewrecker. Be a happy kept woman, instead.

Ick.

The *real* Gwenevere of legends is more powerful than Arthur and doesn't need a man. Rather, a man needs her to become king—which is Celtic pagan beliefs at its core. The woman is the life giver, the spring from which all creation and power stems. But first, we need to break down a few words.

"Gwen" is an old Cymry (Welsh) word for a young woman who was so profoundly beautiful that you would die if you gazed upon her for too long. It was a sacred or holy form of beauty tied to being a sun or moon demi-goddess, or perhaps even a goddess of light. When I look at the beauty of the sun directly, I want to die. I get it. *shrugs*

Gwenevere (Welsh: Gwenhwyfar) is a direct cognate of the Irish name Findabair (or Fionnabhair). Yup, the idea of a "Gwenevere" first came from 1st century Ireland and mentioned in The Ulster Cycle as the daughter of Queen Medb of Connacht, who later inspired Shakespeare's Queen Mab—a faerie queen. Findabair / Gwenhwyfar came from a line of earth- and-sovereignty goddesses—sídhe faeries who married a king to his land either through matrimony, sex, or the offering of sacred relics. A Celtic king was not truly king unless he was "sovereign blessed."

The first mention of a Gwenevere in Arthurian lore is Arthur's faerie bride. And, sadly, they weren't in love. In fact, Gwenhwyfar runs away and Arthur hunts her down and brings her back to his land, not because of love, but because he couldn't be King without her. The Celts believed that the land reflected the health of their King. If he were maimed, injured, or terminally ill, the people would demand a new king to ensure their land remained bountiful as his injury would demonstrate that he was clearly out of favor with the earth goddess who married him to the land.

Not a very romantic origin story for one of the most romanticized female characters and relationships in the history of literature. The irony is sadly delightful.

Historical inaccuracies: Medieval Inns weren't a thing until the 14th century. But, since this is also fantasy, we bent the timeline a bit to suit our storytelling needs.

Well, that's it for this segment. Stay tuned for book three, THE FIRST GWENEVERE, where I'll discuss the mythological origins of Morgana, Merlin, Galahad, Percival, and Lancelot, as well as share about the Four Ancient Artifacts of Ireland and how they inspired the Welsh Arthurian Legend tales.

All errors that may exist while trying to represent Celtic and Welsh culture, mythology, geography, and Arthurian Legend elements are entirely mine. I am a storyteller, weaving together information that builds and forms worlds in our imaginations. In the famous words of Nennius, a 9th century Celtic monk, "I have made a heap of all that I could find."

Your *Knights of Caerleon* lore keeper,

Jesikah Sundin

THE FIRST GWENEVERE

by

CLAIRE LUANA
&
Jesikah Sundin

"Like many cruel and evil women, Morgan le Fay knew men's weaknesses and discounted their strengths. And she knew also that most improbable actions may be successful so long as they are undertaken boldly and without hesitation, for men believe beyond proof to the contrary that blood is thicker than water and that a beautiful woman cannot be evil."

John Steinbeck
The Acts of King Arthur and His Noble Knights

Prologue

Morgana

Ships lined the harbor in Dublin as far as the crow's dark, beady eye could see. The salty air brimmed with the scents of impending war. The crow cawed in delight and swooped low, skimming along the shimmering Irish Sea. Then a certain scent hit her—one she craved and knew anywhere. Weakness. Greed. *Him.* The man with a heart as shadowed as her own. Stupid mortal.

In a swirl of sea mist, the crow dipped to land on a makeshift dock and transformed into her female form. A fae queen.

Morgana's lips curled into a wicked smile at O'Lynn's widened eyes as he took in her sudden appearance. "Expecting someone else?" she asked casually while stepping toward the Irish king.

"I never look at crows the same now." He blew out a slow breath and then shuffled his feet to a sturdier posture. "Especially carrion crows."

Her smile grew wider for several quick beats of the mortal's heart before she switched her focus to the ships and warriors. Men and women moved past them on the dock, oak chests and barrels filled with weapons and food in tow. Farther down the harbor, warriors wrapped strips of dark wool around their horses' eyes and led them onto longboats with stabling posts to tie them up. Others forked hay and grains onto the boats to help ease the spooked chargers.

"You have done well, mortal," she cooed, returning her gaze to O'Lynn. "I am pleased with you. Arthur Pendragon is ours for the plucking. Even though the Fisher whelp found the Blessed Grail, King Arthur's land still withers. Even now his people grow sick and their bellies roar with hunger."

O'Lynn's body softened at her words and his eyes drank her in—her cleavage rising and falling atop her bodice, her slim waist, the way her hair draped about her shoulders in a waterfall of raven-feathered black strands.

"Our plan is to depart tomorrow," he said. "Our druids predict fair weather to Wales."

"I plan to travel with you. Release the caged crows."

"No, they're necessary should we need to find the closest land point." O'Lynn crossed his arms over his chest. The gold torc around his neck glinted in the afternoon sun. A hint of a sneer curved the corner of his mouth up. "The crows will stay with their masters if released, anyway."

Morgana cocked her head and slitted her eyes. "The crows only stay with their tormentors to feast on their flesh once they die."

O'Lynn's Adam's apple bobbed as the flirtation and challenge in his eyes faded to trepidation.

"I will fly about to each ship to inform the captains, if necessary. Now, release the caged crows. I shall not ask again."

Heaving a resigned breath to cover his fear—a fear that filled Morgana's nostrils with a heady scent that lightened her head with pleasure—O'Lynn grabbed the arm of a warrior passing by. "Tell each captain who sails to release their navigation crows."

"Yer Majesty?" the young man asked, uncertain.

Morgana slid up to the younger man and leaned in close, trailing her sharp fingernail down his cheek. His brown eyes blinked a few times in surprise, though he remained still. "You are a beautiful specimen," she purred. Her nail trailed down his neck to his chest. "Now, be a good lad and do as you're told."

"Yes, Lady," the young man said softly.

Morgana smiled sweetly at him, biting down on her lower lip, a canine bared.

"Anything ye ask of me," he added in an affected whisper before darting away.

O'Lynn glowered at Morgana. Good. He needed a reminder that she was in charge, not him. In a dismissive motion, she turned her back on the older man. She could feel his heated stare before he walked away to finish preparing for their departure at dawn.

Morgana remained on the dock, whispering incantations over the boats for a swift travel, until the sun began to set and a crescent moon began to rise. Only breaking her focus to greet her sister and brother crows who launched into the starry night. Their black wings cut through the air with a song of vengeance. A melody she hummed to the wind.

Sea mist and the whispered prayers of greedy men preparing for war swirled around her. The crow hopped on the dock and peered at the humans who gawked at the sky, mouths agape, fear icing the blood in their veins. The crow then flapped her wings with a loud caw and joined the dark celebration swooping before the goddess moon.

There was nothing that alighted her soul more than impending war and death.

 Chapter One

Fionnabhair

I was back in Caerleon. I was home.

The thought struck me like a lightning bolt as we rode through the gates of Arthur's proud keep. I tested the feeling, trying the idea on for size. Yes, this place was the harmony to the joyous song in my heart. Caerleon, and King Arthur Pendragon, and my knights. Strong Galahad, laughing Percival, and infuriating Lancelot. Though Lancelot was as moody as an Irish winter, I missed him like the summer sun. I felt his absence keenly.

Our return to Caerleon should have been a triumphant thing—proclaimed from the hillsides with horns and witnessed by a parade of grateful citizens who tossed flower petals before our horses' hooves. We had done the impossible and found the Blessed Grail. The feat was no small miracle—and yet—I didn't think the enormity of what we had accomplished had truly sank in among our small group. For all we could think of was the dark, grasping curse still seeping through Caerleon's clear waters and flaxen fields.

And the army sailing for our shores.

Arthur had depended on the Grail to breathe new life into his dying lands. A black, creeping death courtesy of his sídhe half-sisters—Morgana, Morgause, and Elaine. The Blessed faerie bowl had almost absolved the dark curse.

Almost, if not for me.

Merlin foresaw how the Grail would heal the land when our group of five each drank from the enchanted bowl. The mystical Grail Maiden confirmed Merlin's theory, the same sovereignty-goddess who had aided us on our quest. She also helped us travel to Avalon, located at the foot of Glastonbury Tor, where we drank from the sacred spring.

Lancelot, Percival, Galahad, and Arthur each drank from Avalon's Red Spring and the land flushed incrementally back to life after each bowlful. But when I drank—the last of us to do so—nothing happened. Not even the wisp of a warm spring breeze or the melodic twitter of birdsong.

I promised myself weeks prior that I would never let Arthur down again. But despite all attempts to prove my worthiness, I had failed him. And, in this misdeed, I felt worse. For I didn't understand why the Grail rejected me. Now, because of my apparent brokenness, innocents would continue to suffer under this wretched curse.

I drew in a deep breath and squared my shoulders against the rocking gait of my horse.

The mood through Caerleon proper was tangibly strained as we approached Arthur's keep. The wary faces of his nobles and common folk alike watched on silently as we dismounted, the jagged look in their eyes a none too subtle reproach for failing to amend the foul magic crippling the kingdom's outlying villages. We had born witness to the curse's dark veins spreading all the way to Caerleon. If something wasn't done, and quickly, people would begin to perish with the poisoned land.

"To my study," Arthur barked, and we hurried after him, leaving our horses with the grooms.

I was eager to visit Zephyr, my beloved mare I had been forced to leave behind while she healed from an injury. But she would have to wait. I knew what Arthur was going to ask me—what we would talk about—and I didn't want to face the truth. My mind spun horrors with every turn of thought. And each possible scenario weakened my resolve to remain mentally and emotionally present.

Why hadn't the Blessed Grail worked on me? What was this strange power thrumming through my body that others seemed to sense but me?

But more so—Arthur would ask about Donal O'Lynn. And this thought was one I couldn't face, not without the red haze of fury covering my vision, setting my fingers itching for a knife.

Donal O'Lynn, Chieftain of the Uí Tuírtri clann, the sworn enemy of my own clann. The man who held my father and sister for ransom and who now sailed for Caerleon with a fleet of ships laden with Dál nAraidi warriors to claim Arthur's crown. With a dark fae priestess on one side. And a new wife on the other. I choked on the latter thought, unable to shove that hellish reality away far enough. At least, far enough away for me to properly focus.

We reached Arthur's study and filed into his room, but no one sat. We were too uneasy, too unsettled. Too lost in our own troubles. I hardly registered Galahad's hulking presence, or Percival's lean, pacing form behind me. Or Merlin's gold-ringed eyes that watched us all with the intensity of a hawk tracking a bevy of field mice.

Arthur rounded on me and I met his fierceness with my own. I knew the anger in his grass-green eyes was not directed at me. But his anger called to me, to the fury pounding through my veins. "O'Lynn," Arthur practically growled, his voice low and deep. "Tell me of him. How many men? Allies? With his new union, could he claim the support of Clann Allán as well?"

His new union. I wanted to retch. *Aideen.* My soul keened my sister's name. I saw her waves of chestnut hair, her kind eyes, her sweet laugh. I knew there was a strength hiding beneath her gentleness, but I feared her courage wouldn't be enough against a man like O'Lynn. How he had managed to claim her as wife haunted me too. Irish women were free to choose their own husband. They could not be forced to marry. So, what could have made Aideen take such a drastic step and agree to marry him? My imagination filled in a parade of nightmares, most of which featured my father. Aideen was tender hearted and loved our father more than any. If O'Lynn demanded Aideen's hand as the price of sparing our father . . . I had no doubt that her consent was a price she would pay without hesitation.

"He will never claim the loyalty of Clann Allán," I said, sure of *that* at least. "There are several strong warriors who would declare leadership over my clann if . . ." I stumbled over the words. "If my father was lost. None of them would side with a snake like O'Lynn. Our clanns have fought and slaughtered each other for generations."

"That's a relief. How many warriors does he have?"

"A thousand, perhaps? But all strong and fierce. Seasoned fighters. They will not be easy to defeat." My hand strayed to my sword, aching to bury the sharp blade into a Uí Tuírtri body.

"How long before they reach Caerleon?" Arthur looked to Merlin, who had relayed the message of the massing ships in Dublin.

"It is unknown," Merlin said calmly.

I wished I could face word of an approaching army with such serenity. It wasn't that I feared O'Lynn and his men. To the contrary, I welcomed a fight with them. But I feared for Caerleon—this soft, gentle land would break under the weight of a war like this. And I feared for my knights and my king. For what I had found in Wales, with them . . . the very thought of losing any part of my life here terrified me.

The druid continued. "It is a three-day passage by boat from Dublin to the Usk River here in Caerleon. Or three days overland to Caerleon on horseback, if they traveled one to two days by boat to Conwy, up north. If they left today, we might have four or five days, a week at best. But I think it is safe to believe they are already en route."

"The messenger who observed the ships in Dublin didn't know when they were leaving?" Arthur asked.

"He couldn't tell. Though he did not think they were leaving for several days. The ships were not manned yet, and provisions were still being secured."

"We must assume arrival is as you say, then—a few days at best." Arthur shook his head in disbelief, gritting his teeth. "There is no way we can withstand a siege with poisoned water and food."

"Ah yes," Merlin said. "The curse. Tell me of what happened

at Glastonbury Tor."

"There's something wrong with me," I blurted out.

"Lass, that's not—" Percival began, but I held up a hand, and he fell silent.

"There's no need to protect my feelings. Not at the expense of Caerleon," I said. "We were all there. We all saw. The curse lifted when each of ye drank. Except me."

"Do you know why, Merlin?" Arthur asked. "What went wrong?"

The druid examined me, and I squirmed under the weight of his piercing gaze, as if the man could see right through me. Right into the darkest recesses. Well, he wasn't a man, was he? Only half a man. Half an immortal incubus.

"Alas, I have no answers for you," Merlin said. "But I will cast my runes and see what I can learn. Perhaps there is something that can be done."

"Before the army reaches our gate would be preferable," Arthur muttered.

"And what of Lancelot?" Galahad rumbled. "Apologies, Arthur, but who is to lead your forces while Lancelot is absent?"

Arthur winced at the mention of Lancelot's name. I think we all did.

Lancelot had grown more and more withdrawn from us as our Grail quest continued. And, in the last days leading up to quest's end, we learned why. Morgana had placed a special curse on him alone—a curse that would destroy all Lancelot held dear, but only if he slept with a Gwenevere. A legendary white enchantress that he proclaimed was me.

I let out a hissing sigh as I thought of him. Why had the fool knight carried his burden all on his own? If he had only told me, I would have known why he pulled back from me, why it was important that he did. If by some strange twist of fate I was indeed this Gwenevere, which I believed untrue, I would have resisted the growing connection between us. It's not as though we were animals. We could have resisted our attraction. Though, if I were honest, I hadn't done a very good job at resisting my animal impulses as of late. One glance at the impossibly handsome forms of my king and the two knights surrounding me was all the confirmation I needed, and I cursed the shiver of desire pulsing hot through my body.

Arthur slipped a quiet look my way before finally cutting through the tension and speaking. "Lancelot made his choice. As much as it grieves me, his choice is one we all must accept. With all the trouble bearing upon my kingdom, I do not have time to chase down stray knights. Even if they are ones who are like brothers to me." Arthur loosed a quavering breath, running a hand through his hair. "Galahad." He turned to the brawny Norseman. "Until Lancelot returns, and perhaps even after, I deem you my second-in-command and charge you with the forces of Caerleon. I hope you don't mind the promotion, because things are about to get messy around here."

Chapter Two

Galahad

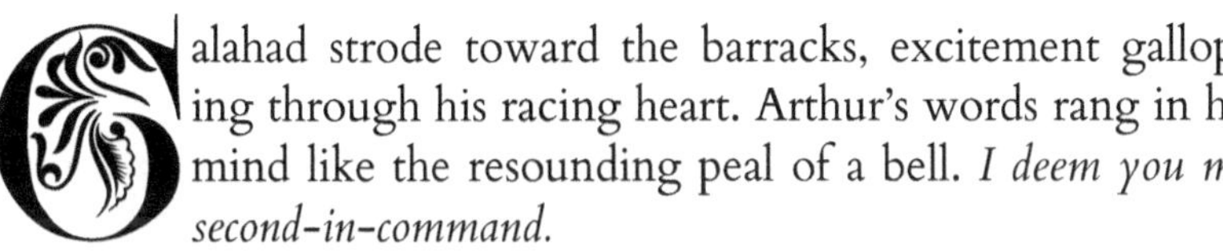

alahad strode toward the barracks, excitement galloping through his racing heart. Arthur's words rang in his mind like the resounding peal of a bell. *I deem you my second-in-command.*

Was it opportunistic to step into Lancelot's shoes in his absence? His sword-brother had been gone less than a day, and Galahad had already seized his role. But no. Arthur had chosen him—it wasn't as if Galahad vied for the position. And Caerleon needed someone to defend her lands and people after Lancelot abandoned his post. Galahad worked his entire life for a chance like this. He wasn't going to let this opportunity pass him by.

The soldiers in the barracks snapped to attention when Galahad entered.

"Sir," one soldier said, stepping forward. The man was short but well-muscled, a dark brown beard covering his round face.

Galahad wracked his memories for the man's name. "Clive," he said.

The man gave a little nod and Galahad relaxed slightly. It had been a while since he had trained with the soldiers. But now he would need to know them each, especially as he would spend more time among their ranks.

"What can we do for you, Sir?" Clive asked, redirecting Galahad's thoughts. "I was not aware the king's knights had returned."

"Just a few hours ago," Galahad replied.

Other soldiers gathered around, and Galahad swept a calculating eye over each man. They were a well-fed lot, their red linen uniforms clean, their weapons well cared for. Arthur was a kind employer. But still, did these men have the raw power and bloodthirst that Galahad had witnessed among the Uí Tuírtri he had fought near Lord Bronn's manor? Even if so, that detail mattered not. These men were what they had. And they would have to be enough.

Galahad cleared his throat and dozens of eyes snapped to his. "We've received word that a fleet of Irish ships bearing Dál nAraidi warriors is bound for our shores, if they have not already landed."

Murmurs of dismay rippled through the group.

"We must warn the neighboring villages to take shelter within the keep," Galahad continued. "There's no telling what horrors might be visited upon them, if they stay where they are."

"Of course, Sir," Clive replied, dipping his head. "Consider it done."

"Sir," one of the other men, a red-head with a puckered scar traversing his jaw, began hesitantly. "Has Sir Lancelot not returned with you?"

"No," Galahad said simply. "He had other business to attend to. The Pendragon has appointed me as his second-in-command in Lancelot's absence."

Another man stepped forward. They seemed to be growing bolder. "Is the king aware of the strange blackness befouling Caerleon's waters?"

The other men nodded, eyes wide.

"My brother said his entire crop rotted," the red-headed soldier chimed in. "Whatever it is, the black is spreading."

"Rest assured," Galahad said, "the king is aware and doing everything he can to cure this strange sickness. He is consulting with the druid Merlin as we speak. In these difficult times, we must band together and hold fast."

A mutter of affirmations warmed Galahad's core.

"The people should be assured as well," Clive said. "Fear is creeping through the villages. A fear just as vile as the sickness that's infecting our land. The people speak against His Majesty, saying the land has rebelled against him, that his kingship is illegitimate."

Galahad's heart stilled. "You have heard these sentiments spoken?"

"By more than one," Clive said, an apologetic frown pulling on his face.

A sour lurch tightened Galahad's stomach. Likely, the news of an encroaching army would only lower Arthur's popularity farther.

Galahad chewed on his bottom lip, his gaze darting from one man to another. "I will ride with you. Perhaps the presence of a knight carrying the Pendragon's banner will assure the people that their sovereign is doing everything within his power to save them."

It was another hour before Galahad and the soldiers saddled their horses, rode through the keep's gates, and reached the first outlying village. The land, though not as fouled as it had been, still showed signs of Morgana curse. The row of fruit trees along the village's dirt path were speckled with black spots. The cheerful stream bordering the tiny village showed flecks of darkness as well.

"It's not safe to drink," Clive said. He rode beside Galahad. "The water doesn't kill you, but you'll ail. The villagers have stuck to ciders and ale, but their stores are growing low."

Galahad's spirits sank deeper. After all they had endured to find the Grail¬—fighting the Twrch Trwyth and the Afanc, facing off against the evil faeries in Eiden's Burgh, journeying through the Otherworld's mist . . . it still had not been enough. What if they couldn't find the final piece of the puzzle before Caerleon starved? The people probably wouldn't wait that long before demanding Arthur's head. And the heads of all his knights.

As Galahad and a half-dozen soldiers rode into a quaint village square, the lime-washed facades bright in the afternoon sun, he did his best to focus on solutions. Arthur and Merlin would find a way to pull this problem out of the fire. They always did.

Galahad swung off his charger and strode toward the largest building in the square, what appeared to be the town's tavern and inn. Taking the steps, he called out in a booming voice, "Gather around, kind people. I have an announcement from your king, Arthur Pendragon!"

Townsfolk sat their burdens before their feet as others came out of the houses—men with wary expressions who should be tending the fields, and women leading grubby-faced toddlers.

"A force of men from Ulster make their way here even now," Galahad called out once more. "Their sights are set on Caerleon, but they will burn, pillage, and raid on their way. We urge every man, woman, and child to come within the keep's walls, where you will be safe until the threat has passed." Another thought occurred to him, and he added, "Bring whatever assures your comfort. Food, ale. If you have herbs or medical supplies, bring them as well. We will set up a makeshift hospital in the keep's Great Hall. Able-bodied women who can help are welcome. Able-bodied men who can fight are welcome as well. Rest assured, your king has the forces and might to defeat these invaders. We only wish to keep you safe until he does."

"And what of the plague on our land, Sir Knight?" someone shouted from the back of the crowd. "Our crops wither. We can't drink the water."

"The king is aware of this blight and has traveled through the Otherworld to fix it. Surely you saw how, just yesterday, the condition of the land greatly improved?"

"Sir, we still can't eat or drink from the land. We'll starve!" someone else shouted.

"It's a sign of the gods' disfavor," someone else yelled. "Arthur isn't the rightful king over Caerleon!"

"Aye!" Another voice. "Uther's bastard shouldn't be our king any longer. He'll drive us all to ruin. The land herself rebels against him. Why shouldn't we?"

Galahad pulled his sword from its scabbard with an ominous ring. When he spoke, his voice boomed. "King Arthur Pendragon is the noblest, mightiest, most honorable man that I have ever known, and who has ever presided over Caerleon. The Lady of the Lake, blessed of the Túatha dé Danann, gifted him the sword Excalibur, confirming his kingship over Caerleon, the Kingdom of Gwent, and over all of Briton. Yes, King Arthur has heavy burdens on his shoulders. Would you wish to be in his shoes? Would you?" Galahad asked, pointing his sword at the men who had spoken. "To defend your people from an army? And defeat a strange magical wasting sickness? No. None of you would have the fortitude it takes to face these grave challenges and defeat them. No other man would either. There is no king for Caerleon but Arthur. And anyone who says otherwise should not hide behind a crowd but should face me man to man. "

The crowd hushed into a tense silence for several beats of Galahad's heart. Then, the ruffle of uncomfortably shifting feet and bodies filled the deafening emptiness at the force of his rebuke.

"Very well," Galahad said. "Then I suggest that you gather your things. And prepare for war."

Chapter Three

Arthur

Arthur enjoyed the snug warmth of Merlin's cave. This place of mystery and magic brought him a strange comfort. And today, he prayed this crystal-lined cave would bring him answers.

Merlin approached the wide fireplace, stoking the embers with a poker before adding another log. "Ale?" his friend asked.

"Absolutely." At Arthur's reply, the druid disappeared into the chill recesses of his cave where he stored his food and drink. His friend might be able to light a fire with his thought or travel the currents of time and space with a spell, but he wasn't a show off. Despite having every right to be. That was one of the many virtues Arthur appreciated about Merlin.

The man returned with two horns of ale clasped between his body and forearm while balancing a tray of bread and cheese in his other hand. "You look hungry," Merlin said as Arthur carefully retrieved the ale from its precarious perch. Arthur took a long drink and sighed in delight at the malty flavor. "Gods that's good."

Merlin set the food on a table between them and sat down in the other chair before the fire.

"I am hungry," Arthur admitted. "There wasn't much to eat on the quest, no thanks to the curse. Nor here, it seems."

"Your stores are well equipped enough for a few more weeks," Merlin said. "But before we speak of this . . . do you have the faerie relic?" Firelight flickered in Merlin's eyes, highlighting the gold rings around his irises.

There was no doubt as to what Merlin spoke. Arthur reached into the satchel he had brought and pulled out the Blessed Grail.

Merlin took the bowl reverently with two hands, turning the dish over, gently stroking the embossed, polished surface. "Magnificent," Merlin murmured with awe.

"It's defective," Arthur replied darkly.

Merlin's eyes jerked up, as if Arthur had spoken sacrilege.

"I mean, yes, the Grail is impressive. But this . . . *this* faerie relic didn't break the curse," he practically spat. "And I did everything I was instructed to do. I found the Blessed Grail, battled monsters and shape-changing faeries, and even got *stabbed* by Lleu's spear. . . but it was all for nothing."

"Lleu's spear?" Merlin dropped the Grail to his lap and gaped at Arthur. "Why don't you start at the beginning. Leave nothing out."

So, Arthur told him. He recounted every detail of their quest, going through two more horns of ale and all the bread and cheese Merlin had brought him. And when he was finally finished, Merlin merely let out a long, "Hmmm . . ."

"What do you think?" Arthur asked. He felt a bit light headed from the fire's heat and the ale's strength.

"Fionna is the key. She has always been the key."

"The key to *what*?" Arthur asked.

"Everything," Merlin replied, now pacing before the fire, his long woolen robes billowing with his movements.

Just everything? Illuminating, Merlin.

"You were magically tied to the land through Excalibur when the Lady of the Lake granted you a sovereign-blessed kingship, Your Majesty. But how you described the land healing incrementally when each of you drank from the Grail . . ." Merlin turned to Arthur, his face alit with excitement. "I think when you knighted each of your knights, laying Excalibur upon them, you tied them to your kingship. Your sovereignty over the land."

"Right," Arthur muttered, furrowing his brow. "That's what

knighting is, friend."

"No. Not just by feudal law or duty. *Magically.*"

"I'm not sure I follow," Arthur admitted.

"Imagine . . . when you laid Excalibur on their shoulders, a piece of your sovereignty transferred to each of their care. That's why the standing stone spoke of the blessed five. And that's why, though Morgana and her sisters cursed Caerleon and you as the land's king, it took all five of you to drink from the Grail to heal the land. Each knight holds a piece of your kingship. And by extension, each one of you holds a piece of the curse."

Arthur nodded, wishing he had drank one less cup of ale, so his head wasn't quite so foggy. "I believe I understand. So, the Grail healed the portion of the curse held by me, Galahad, Lancelot, and Percival. But not Fionna? Why couldn't the Grail heal her portion of the curse?"

"I have no idea," Merlin said simply.

Arthur threw up his hands up in exasperation.

"I have theories," Merlin continued. "But . . . Caerleon needs better than theories. There is something strange about Fionna. I sensed the Otherworld from the moment I saw her in the arena. She assuredly holds a dormant power."

"Lancelot believes she is a Gwenevere."

"How does Fionna respond to his claim?"

"She says it's madness," Arthur replied. Was Lancelot's belief madness? There was something Otherworldly about Fionna's beauty, as well as her strength and prowess in battle. But Fionna insisted, often, that she didn't possess a magical ability.

"You believe her?"

"I do." And though she had lied to him before about Excalibur, he found he did believe her. Over the past few weeks, she had regained his trust. And had captured his heart well and truly.

"The land has not known a Gwenevere for many generations." Merlin crossed the cave to his desk, where he retrieved a leather bag that held a set of old divination rune stones. "But we live in trying times," his friend offered quietly. "Perhaps it is time for such an enchantress to arise. Give me a moment."

Merlin strode to the empty space before the fire and knelt,

closing his eyes.

Arthur watched the druid as he centered himself and called to whatever forces would aid him. The fine hairs on Arthur's arms stood on end, as they sometimes did in the presence of magic. A disconcerting feeling, to know there was something on the air but not able to trust one's senses. Still, if Merlin's magic could discover an answer, Arthur would tolerate just about any strangeness.

Merlin threw the stones and then they both leaned forward to inspect the runes laying face up.

"Interesting," Merlin said, placing a single finger on a rune. One that lay atop all other front-facing stones. "This is *Ur*, or heather."

"What about it?"

"The reading is hazy, but one piece comes through clearly. Heather is used as protection against the evil eye."

Arthur frowned. "The evil eye . . ."

"Yes, indeed. Heather brings only good luck, even symbolizing unselfish love in some Gaelic circles. For heather is immensely infused with faerie magic. Surely you have had heather beer?"

"Well, yes, but—"

"Then you understand the effects of heather. This herb is connected to the Otherworld." Merlin leaned back and met Arthur's eyes.

"Fionna smells of heather, soft and sweet," Arthur said, hoping the flush creeping up his neck didn't reach his face.

Merlin smiled. "You will find the answers you seek in the Otherworld. In the halls of the Túatha dé Danann."

Arthur groaned, his hand straying to his side, where his lifeblood flowed out just days before. "We have only now returned from the Otherworld, and we didn't find the realm of mist particularly friendly."

"The Castle of Maidens was a trap for you within the *In-Between*, not the Otherworld's courts. But, this time, you will know to be on guard. I can better prepare you."

"What makes you think the Túatha dé Danann will even be friendly toward us? Or give us the answers we seek? They've had no qualms about letting Morgana, Elaine, and Morgause wreak all sorts of havoc upon my kingdom. Perhaps they support these wretched curses."

Merlin shook his head. "Vivien gifted you Excalibur and your kingship. She speaks for them more than the ladies of Tintagel do. I am confident these curses were not sanctioned by the Túatha dé Danann leadership or the goddess Danu."

"I don't have time for another quest, Merlin," Arthur insisted. "A fleet of ships is headed our way. This army could reach my keep at any moment. A king cannot abandon his people on the eve of war. Not if he wishes to remain king. The people are already grumbling. Hungry and scared. If I leave now, O'Lynn won't need to take my kingdom from me. My own people will."

Merlin's lined face pinched in thought. "Perhaps there is a second reason to visit the Otherworld then. The Túatha dé Danann are keepers of another magical relic. The Cauldron of Plenty."

"You wish for us to retrieve a . . . *cauldron?*" Arthur asked.

"Yes, for this *cauldron* is one of the four objects of power in Ireland, where the Túatha dé Danann dwell. And, this *cauldron* is rumored to have healing powers, like the Grail. Even the ability to raise a man from the dead. But importantly—with this magical relic, you can create whatever food and drink you need. Enough to feed all within the walls of Caerleon until the curse is dealt with. Enough to withstand a siege easily."

Arthur considered Merlin's explanation. The Cauldron of Plenty did sound helpful. Though curse its faerie-made iron. The Grail was also supposed to be his kingdom's salvation, and *that* magical relic had proven a disappointment. Could he really go off on a wild goose chase after another mythical object? He had real problems to face here.

Merlin seemed to sense Arthur's thoughts. "What if I found a way for you to travel to the Otherworld quickly. A portal, such as the one the Grail Maiden created for you?"

"You have such magic?" Arthur asked, his eyebrows raising. He hadn't known Merlin to conjure such things before. If his druid could indeed create a portal . . . then perhaps there was time to make a fast trip.

"I have never done such a thing, but now that I know a portal can be made . . . it is only a matter of study. I am certain I could cobble the spell together." Excitement lit Merlin's face, and a ghost of a smile tugged at Arthur's lips. Merlin was man of magic, but he was a scholar too, much like Arthur. A chance to solve a puzzle like this? Merlin had to be dancing with anticipation, despite his calm composure.

Arthur stood, ignoring how his head spun briefly. He needed a good night's sleep. "Then I will leave you to it. If you find me a way into the Otherworld from Caerleon, I will undertake the journey. Seems my questing days are not yet behind me."

Chapter Four

Fionna

My racing mind wouldn't settle that night. Everything felt wrong. Caerleon still cursed. Lancelot gone. My sister married to O'Lynn. My father . . . he must still be alive. There was no way Aideen would have married O'Lynn, if the bastard wasn't holding my father's life as the alternative. I felt as if the solution to all these hardships should lie with me. Like a brilliant shining moment of insight would occur and loop the disparate threads of my life together in a perfect, victorious tapestry. But Aideen had always had the skill with weaving. All I was good for was killing.

Helplessness squeezed at the air in my lungs. The sensation was like battling in an ill-fitting set of armor. I paced my room for half a candle mark before I decided that I held onto a small remnant of control: I was still keeping secrets. And, at this point, I wasn't sure why. It was time I bared the whole truth to the one person who might know what these burdens meant. I needed to see Merlin.

I made my way down the familiar earth and rock path and into the warm spring night. The once-soothing sound of the river now only served as a reminder of my failure. Black poison churned through those crystal waters, destroying whatever it touched.

I was so lost in my thoughts that I didn't notice another shadowed form coming my way until the figure was almost upon me. When I saw the hooded man, my heart took flight like a startled bird, my hand flying to the knife at my belt.

"Peace Fionna, it's only I, Arthur," he said in the dark.

I sagged with relief.

"Most days you're not so easy to sneak up on," he remarked with a chuckle.

"Most days my mind isn't twisted into *Dara* knots," I admitted.

"I'm distracted as well," he replied softly. "How could we not be, with all that has happened?"

I nodded, peering out into the darkened forest across the river. "I can't stop thinking about Aideen. Tied to that man. His hands on her . . ." I closed my eyes against the horror roiling in my stomach. My beautiful, vibrant sister shouldn't be forced to subject herself to such violations.

"What has happened to your family grieves me deeply. I can't help but wonder if I could have done more."

"And me," I said.

Arthur sighed. "But then I cannot see what I could have done. Even with the benefit of hindsight, the needs of Caerleon came first."

"Ye are the land's king. But I shouldn't have joined the quest," I said. "I should have returned to Ulster and rescued my father and sister."

"No—"

"All I did was drive Lancelot away and fail to break the curse—any curse."

"No, My Lady. You couldn't have freed them single-handedly. And if you hadn't been on the quest, we wouldn't have defeated the Twrch Trwyth or the Afanc. We wouldn't have obtained the key or the stone or the Blessed Grail."

"But—" I began to protest and stopped. Arthur stepped close to me and then stroked the side of my face, enveloping me with his summer scent of green grass and apples. Of home.

The words I had previously spoken had fallen like fallow seeds from my lips. How could I be anywhere but here? Never mind that the price for keeping my head was to join the Grail quest. This is where I had wanted to be. Where I still wanted to be. Arthur was the Caerleon that should be—strong and just and healthy. I cursed the world that punished me for following my heart with Aideen's slavery.

My hand strayed to Arthur's side, where the wound had been. "Ye fare well? No lingering effects from yer injury?"

"I am as healthy as I've ever been."

"Good." My voice tightened. "We couldn't do this without ye. I couldn't—"

Arthur cut off my words with a kiss then, wrapping one arm around my waist, the other around my shoulders. His lips danced across mine—his body an anchor, grounding me to the earth. He was warmth and comfort, and I drank greedily, savoring the taste of him, the feel of being folded within his arms.

It was he who pulled away, but to lay feather-light kisses on the tip of my nose and forehead before pressing me close to him once more.

I leaned my head against the hard planes of his chest with a sigh.

"You go to see Merlin?" he asked, his deep voice rumbling pleasantly against me.

"Aye. I thought . . . I need to talk to him about my past. Perhaps we can discover something."

"He thinks I need to return to the Otherworld."

I pulled back, gaping at him in the dark. "Now? With an army sailing for Caerleon?"

"Yes, that's what he advised. I don't know. I must think on it. Now, you should not tarry any longer. Perhaps Merlin can discover all your secrets this night." He touched his lips softly to mine.

"Can't wait," I said dryly as I pushed away, letting his fingers trail mine as I continued down the hill toward the Usk River and Merlin's cave.

My gaze remained on the windy footpath, but I could feel the caress of Arthur's eyes upon my back. I sighed, reveling in the sensations fluttering through me, even as I approached the cave's entrance. One kiss from Arthur was enough to turn my legs weak with need. From any of my knights, really. But for now, I *needed* to focus.

"Merlin?" I picked my way carefully over the rocky ground and moved deeper into his cave. "It's Fionna."

The druid appeared suddenly in front of me and I halted my steps with a sharp inhale.

"There ye are," I said, shoving down my annoyance. I swear, sometimes he popped out like that just to seem more mysterious!

"To what do I owe this rare honor?" Merlin asked, ushering me into the main cavern with a welcoming hand.

"I need to tell ye something," I admitted.

"Very well," Merlin said, crossing to sit in one of the chairs in front of the fire. I took the other.

"The night of the faerie wine," I began, words tumbling forth before my nerves got the better of me, "I drank the wine. But it didn't affect me. Not like it did the others."

Merlin studied at me, blinking, his eyes glowing with magic. "Interesting," he finally said.

"I thought perhaps this necklace affected how I felt the wine," I said, picking up the delicate lily pendant that hung from my neck. "A gift from Morgana and her sisters, from the night of the feast."

Merlin leaned forward and picked the pendant up off my breastbone, leaning in to examine the details. This close, he smelled of spices—clove and dried sage and . . . ale? An unexpected scent that was strangely comforting.

He dropped the necklace and leaned back. "There is an enchantment of sorts on the necklace. But I do not think the magic is harmful. It's . . ." he furrowed his brow. "As if the magic is outward facing, rather than affecting the wearer. I will research the origins of such a necklace. But I do not think this piece of enchanted jewelry is what protected you from the faerie wine's effects."

"All right, sure," I said. "Do ye know what did, then?"

Merlin tilted his head and considered me a moment. "I think you have fae heritage somewhere in your family tree," he said. "But the power is blocked somehow. Suppressed."

"So, I'm . . . defective?" I whispered, examining my fingernails instead of acknowledging the piteous look in Merlin's hawk-eyed gaze. I had always been different than my father and Aideen, but

I had found my place within my family, the clann. Made my way as a warrior. It was all I had needed. But now, that reality seemed lacking.

"No," Merlin said kindly. "Your magic was suppressed on purpose."

I looked up sharply. "What do ye mean?"

"I sense there is an enchantment over you. Of a kind I cannot see or recognize. And that makes me think the magic is fae born."

"There is a faerie enchantment on me?" I jumped to my feet, my heart in my throat. "Well, get it off!"

"It's not that simple. The one who put the géis on you is also the one who will need to remove it. And do not be so alarmed. If the enchantment protected you from the wine, then perhaps this magic is benevolent." He paused a beat, the gold ring around his eyes flashing. "A ward against the evil eye."

"Benevolent, evil eye, or no, I want this géis removed. This magic has something to do with why I couldn't use the Grail, doesn't it?"

"We must assume so," Merlin said.

"So how in the hell do I find out who put a faerie charm on me?"

"I think this enchantment has been with you for many years. Perhaps since you were a babe. Your best chance of unraveling this mystery is to speak to the only other human who might have been there."

"Ye mean my father."

"I believe you are not the only Allán with secrets."

"But my father is in enemy hands," I protested. It was ironic. I spent years living under the same roof as my father, and never thought to ask him why I looked so different from Aideen. In truth, I had never wanted to know the answer. And now, when I was desperate for the truth, he was out of my reach.

"I suppose it is luck that the enemy is bringing him to us, then," Merlin countered, bending to pick an *Ur* rune up off the rug before the hearth—a rune mark for heather.

"Yes," I said slowly, a kernel of an idea blooming to life inside me. "Yes, luck indeed."

Chapter Five

Lancelot

ancelot led Cheval onto the ferry, his stomach bobbing with the longboat. He was a man of one-and-twenty the last time he had set foot on the Isle of Man. Following that visit, he had sworn never to return. Now here he was, four years later, coming back with his tail tucked between his legs. A man of twenty-five years, crying to his foster mother for help.

The ferryman, a gruff little man—with a face covered in sharp, gray stubble, and a short reed sticking out from between yellowed teeth—secured the rope behind him. The ferry was an old, less-than-sturdy-looking clinker with red ochre paint, now chipped and faded from years of exposure. Luckily, the passage was short, and the craft was faerie enchanted to keep the boat from swamping—the only way Lancelot would even think to climb aboard this rotting pile of heap.

The night was dark and strangely cloying. A sickening sweet scent he normally associated with magic. Low clouds crowded out the sliver of moon while grasping fog swirled around the boat. It was always misty on the approach to Man. He wondered if the weather phenomena was just some strange quirk of geography, or if it was a spell cast by his foster mother to disquiet anyone who approached. Probably the latter. There was no such thing as coincidence when it came to the fae.

Lancelot stood by Cheval's head, idly stroking his velvety neck, savoring the connection to something real. The mist seemed alive. And Lancelot swore he could see shapes materialize and dissipate. Figures. He left his horse and strode the short distance to the edge of the ferry and then peered out into the darkness.

"Careful," the man said. "Folks always see strangeness in the fog. Don't think the Lady likes visitors."

"I'll consider myself warned," Lancelot murmured.

He pulled his black, woolen cloak tight against the wind, when a flicker of an image coalesced before him. He drew in a sharp breath as he beheld a vision of himself as a lad of eighteen, writhing atop a maiden behind a hay wagon during a Beltane feast. Shame heated his neck and face as he remembered ducking around the keep for weeks to avoid that same girl until she finally understood his disinterest. What was her name?

The shape changed again, flashing images of him whispering into a lady's ear in the Great Hall; his face pressed into a woman's bosom in a dark hallway. That knight from Morganwgg whom he had shared a wild night with. Lancelot's mouth went dry as he saw the man beneath him, Lancelot's hand fisted in the knight's blond locks. The images flashed faster now, and he wanted to turn away, to close his eyes against the assault. All he had ever done—those he had hurt—laid bare before him. The mist was accounting for his every misguided attempt to find connection. To numb the emptiness within him.

The fog flashed Fionna's ethereal face now, sorrowful and tender. Even she could not fill this void, the gaping hole created by the two mothers who had abandoned him. He was a burden from his very first breath, even as he breathed now. On his ride north from Glastonbury Tor, Lancelot had thought long and hard. Picking apart his psyche piece by twisted piece, turning toward the darkness he normally shied away from. A shadow self he normally tried to hide. But he would do anything to be worthy of Fionna.

Even face his own demons.

And he thought he finally understood. This mist, it too understood. The enchanted fog showed him exactly who he had been.

Perhaps the price to return to Vivien's kingdom was nothing less than brutal honesty as to the man he became, the people he hurt. He had been living a half-life—seeking comfort by filling his days with training and sex and even his friendship with Arthur. Being Arthur's second-in-command had made him feel worthy—finally—but not deep down, where it mattered most. The twisted part of him knew, from the beginning, how he didn't deserve such an esteemed responsibility over others. And so, he had sabotaged the honor, tarnishing his reputation and reliability time and again. But no more. He would find his way out of this dark place, no matter the cost. No matter how long it took. This was his new mission.

The ferry bumped against the dock and Lancelot blinked in surprise. They had already made the crossing?

He tossed the ferryman a coin and then led Cheval onto the creaking, log-hewn dock. The cool smell of the Isle of Man greeted him—the brine of the sea mingled with the sweet scent of gorse and blaeberry. He swung onto his horse, riding the familiar path through rocky outcroppings and tough, wild grasses to Vivien's stone keep.

Two guards in Vivien's blue and silver livery snapped to attention at the open gate, their delicate pointed ears and pale skin marking them fae. "Sir Lancelot here to see the Lady of the Lake," Lancelot announced.

They nodded him through and Lancelot urged Cheval forward, his horse's hooves resounding on the cobbled stones beneath his feet. At the keep's entrance, Lancelot swung down and then strode inside, shivering from the dank, cold journey, all-the-while surveying the castle where he had grown up. He suppressed his nervousness as he walked toward the gathering hall where he suspected Vivien entertained.

Her main residence looked no different from his memories—fantastical trees and beasts adorning the stone walls in ornate carvings and tapestries, faerie nobles in strange finery who were wrapped around each other in dark alcoves, their cups of sweet wine forgotten. Human servants moving about, as if invisible—cringing when a faerie passed by. His mother didn't mistreat her servants, but a faerie court still wasn't the safest place to serve as a mortal. The fae turned from whimsical and lighthearted to cruel and manipulative in the blink of an eye. It was part of what made growing up here such a holy terror.

Music and light emanated from the end of the hallway—the sounds of laughter and chattering hanging on the air. Lancelot took a deep breath and then walked into the room, squinting at the brightness.

"Lancelot!" Vivien cried out when she sighted him, launching from her throne before flowing down the stairs toward him like a rushing river. Her dark brunette hair was arranged beneath a jeweled headdress he hadn't seen until now, and her cerulean gown was also new. But everything else about her was just as he remembered. She was as smooth and cool as ice, lovely as a spring's thaw—as unpredictable and deadly as one too.

"My son!" she reached him and placed one chilled hand upon his cheek, a rare smile gracing her lips. He almost flinched at her bright display of happiness. "To what do I owe this rare pleasure? I thought perhaps you were so secure in Caerleon, you would never again grace your poor foster mother with your presence."

Lancelot's eyes narrowed. She rarely used the word "mother" around him, let alone in front of an entire gathering. He peered over her shoulder and glimpsed a handsome man of obvious stature sitting near her throne, looking on. Men often crawled out of their gilded hovels for political favors from the legendary Lady of the Lake. Though, by her buoyant behavior, Lancelot guessed Vivien sought this man's patronage. To increase her status and wealth among the human nobility and, thus, more influence and power within the faerie courts. Always scheming and maneuvering, his foster mother.

"I'm sorry I haven't visited in several years," Lancelot replied with all the pleasantness he could muster. It was good to see her, in a strange way. She was familiar, if not exactly comforting.

"You are forgiven," she said sweetly—too sweetly. "You must be hungry from your journey! Thirsty?" She gestured at a servant, who materialized at their side, a cup of wine on a tray before him.

Lancelot eyed the goblet. He was parched, but not parched enough for faerie wine, even from Vivien's cellar. He waved away the cup and returned his focus back to his foster mother.

"I have a few questions for you."

He looked around at the glittering nobles of Vivien's court. Though they continued to chat and dance as if nothing had changed, he could feel their eyes on him. As a human foster son to a faerie, he had been an aberration when a boy—especially when titled "faerie prince." But now, as the second-in-command to the High King of Briton . . . he garnered even more interest. Like the man who awaited Vivien's company to negotiate political alliances with the Túatha dé Danann.

"Could we speak privately?"

"Of course," Vivien said, threading her arm into his. "Come."

They walked back up the steps of her raised dais and then through a door leading to Vivien's private meeting room.

She settled herself behind a desk, one situated by an open window.

Lancelot shivered. "Mind if we sit by the fire?"

She let out a little annoyed laugh. "I forget how sensitive to hot and cold you mortals are," she practically grumbled. Still, she stood and crossed to a chair beside the fire.

Lancelot stoked the low-burning flames, throwing on another log. "Just one of the many inconveniences of humanity."

"Ask me your questions, dearest Lancelot. I'm *dying* to know why my princeling is here."

"For court gossip, *Mother*?"

"I will not spill a word of what you share without your permission, I swear it."

Lancelot took a deep breath and plunged forward. "Do you know what has transpired between Morgana and Arthur? And . . . me?"

"I know I received a wedding invitation, and then another card soon after, expressing regrets for the cancellation."

Lancelot grimaced. "Yes. Morgana didn't . . . take the cancellation well. She and her sisters cursed Caerleon. And me."

Vivien clucked her tongue. "Such children they are, those three, playing with curses and retribution. If you wronged her somehow, she should have just killed you."

"Thanks," he muttered dryly.

"Well, she obviously didn't." Vivien waved her hand. "You're here for assistance to break the curse, I imagine?"

Lancelot nodded.

"Tell me of the magic's nature."

"The spell was more like a prophecy. Morgana declared that I would fall in love with a Gwenevere—"

"A Gwenevere?" Vivien's head whipped up, her dark blue eyes widening.

"Yes. But if I lay with her, our joining would ruin all I love."

Vivien laughed, full of innocent humor and black wickedness. "And do you deserve this . . . prophecy?"

He scowled. "Will you help or not?"

One delicate brow raised. "If you are here to break this curse, then it must also mean that you have found this 'Gwenevere.'" She cocked her head in an inhuman, predatory way. "You honestly believe you have, don't you dearest Lancelot?"

He clenched his jaw but remained silent.

"If this is so, then I'm afraid you have an even bigger problem."

"What do you mean?" His heart sank into the churning, bubbling cauldron of his sickened stomach. They were already battling several fairly large problems.

"A Gwenevere, a white enchantress, only arises when the High King of Briton faces powerful, Otherworldly challengers to his throne, and thus needs more than a relic, like Excalibur, to claim and maintain his sovereignty. He needs a blessing from Danu herself, Mother Goddess and queen of the Túatha dé Danann. A Gwenevere is a direct conduit of power from Danu to physically marry a king to his land."

"And the Gwenevere is this . . . blessing?"

Vivien leaned forward and placed her hands on either side of Lancelot's face, gently cradling his face. And ignoring his question. Typical faerie. She closed her eyes, murmuring quietly in a language he didn't understand.

Lancelot held his breath.

She opened her eyes, leaning back. "Whatever curse was upon you has lifted. You are clean of enchantments."

"Truly?" Lancelot's pulse leaped within his chest. Drinking from the Blessed Grail must have cleansed him of Morgana's curse!

His foster mother dipped her head in a dignified nod. But he didn't care about decorum. Instead, he whooped and then pulled her into an embrace, spinning her around, shouting, "Thank you!"

Vivien laughed, her head thrown back. Lancelot stared at the points of her canines as he set her gently down on her feet. As her giggles tapered, she ironed out invisible wrinkles over her gown with fluttering hands. Then she squared her shoulders and leveled a cool gaze—girlish whimsy out and scheming, maneuvering Vivien back in control. "Shall I take this to mean that you are in love with this woman? The one you suspect is the Gwenevere?"

"More than anything." Lancelot ran a hand through his tussled curls. "But . . . how do I know if she really is an enchantress? She insists that she has no magical ability."

"That is odd." Vivien frowned, her dark blue eyes sparkling with mischief. "Well, there is only one way to know for sure."

"Which is?"

"I shall have to meet her."

Chapter Six

Fionna

I was in Zephyr's stall, explaining my absence to her very accusing black eyes, when I felt a pair of strong arms encircle my waist.

I whirled, a dagger in hand, the sharp point laid deliberately along the interloper's jugular.

Galahad quirked a brow. "If you can't tell my touch from that of a foe, then I didn't leave enough of an impression." His words ended in a laugh, a deep rumble in his barreled chest.

I snorted as I lowered my dagger, flipping the small blade in my hand before sheathing it at my side. "Didn't anyone ever tell ye not to sneak up on a woman?"

"Yes, but where's the fun in that?" he asked, his broad hands re-circling my waist and tugging me to his hard, chiseled body.

I knew I should scold him, or ask him about his ride through the villages, but his wild, blond hair was down, tumbling about his shoulders, and his eyes were fixed on my mouth. The urge to taste him simmered hot within me, smothering all higher thought. I rose on my tiptoes and claimed his mouth with mine, melting into his warmth as his arms pressed me even closer to him, one hand roving up to tangle in my hair, the other roaming down to grip my arse.

The Grail quest's final days were a blur. Had it really been since Betws-y-Coed that we kissed like this? The night he and Percival and I—the thought of our shared intimacy sent a curl of heat through me. I shuddered at the memory. With a knowing smile, Galahad's mouth angled against mine expertly, his tongue darting playfully between my lips. Goddess above, he tasted divinely of honey and adventure and sex. I reached up to grab his head and pull him closer when a huge, velvet head butted against my back.

I pulled back and looked over my shoulder, shooting Zephyr a dark look. "Do ye mind?" I asked, to which Zephyr gave a whinny and a stamp of her hoof in reply.

Galahad chuckled. "Seems I'm not the only one starved for a little attention." He reached out and scratched Zephyr's forehead. Zephyr shook her head in delight and I resisted the urge to roll my eyes.

"Ye do have a way with the lasses," I muttered dryly. Reluctantly, I extricated myself from Galahad's embrace.

"Is that jealousy I hear?" Galahad grinned, and it was like the whole stall brightened. He rested his hands on my hips and placed a kiss on the tip of my nose. "Once we trounce O'Lynn and these faeries, we'll have all the time in the world for me to demonstrate how you have nothing to fear. There's no woman for me but you."

I opened my mouth to reply and the words stalled on my tongue. I couldn't say the same, could I? Guilt reared its ugly head. An unwelcomed and far too frequent a visitor as of late. True, Galahad hadn't appeared to object to sharing my affections in the past, but our feelings were all so hopelessly tangled. Could I really think that my love for these four men wouldn't end in broken hearts and a broken fellowship? As Lancelot shared? I quieted the ache in my chest. We needed to focus on the task before us. So, I seized the distraction eagerly.

"How was yer visit to the villages?" I asked.

A shadow fell across Galahad's handsome face, dimming the light his earlier smile had cast around the stable. As though the sun had suddenly set.

"The people are unhappy. They speak out against their king." He folded his arms across his chest. "I don't think we have much time."

"Rebellion?" I asked in rising horror. "At such a time? Don't they realize Arthur is their only hope against Morgana and the Uí Tuírtri?"

"I fear logic and reason are not the going currency in such a time. Fear seems the champion today."

I huffed in frustration. "Have ye told Arthur?"

Galahad nodded.

"Where is he?" I asked. "I should go to him . . ." I trailed off. I didn't know what I could do, only that Arthur had to be suffering, and I wanted to be at his side.

"He's inspecting the fortifications," Galahad said.

I hesitated.

"Go," Galahad encouraged. "If anyone can help Arthur right now, it's you."

I smiled at him, grateful for his understanding.

"Zephyr and I will keep each other company," he said, patting my mare once again.

"No moping in my absence," I replied, my smile twisting wider.

"No promises." Galahad smushed his face next to Zephyr's and then angled a long, mopey frown and big, puppy dog eyes my way.

I shook my head with a laugh as I hurried out of the stable.

I found Arthur walking the walls of the keep, speaking quietly with soldiers and tradesmen alike. I watched him for a few moments from the shadow of the wall. I think he was trying to convince every inhabitant of Caerleon individually of his worth as king. My heart softened at the sight. Sometimes I worried—could a man in Arthur's position care so deeply and so genuinely? Surely the cruelties of this world would break him by now. My fists tightened at my side. That's what we knights were for. I would not let this world destroy the man he was, while I still had breath in my body to stop it. I would protect him and his kingdom.

I felt the wrongness first—the faint lift of hairs on the back of my neck. An awareness that I couldn't account for. My hand flew to my sword and the newly sharpened blade was out of its sheath before I even knew why.

But then I saw the reason. A smoky whiteness, filtered by slanting afternoon light, billowed up from the earth like steam rising from a great cauldron.

Magic.

My first instinct was Arthur. In just four paces, I was between him and the strange growing cloud, the mist pouring into the space where only air and grass and sunshine should be.

"What?" I heard Arthur pounding down the stairs behind me from the wall, the ring of Excalibur's steel. My eyes stayed fixed on that unnatural mist. "Stay back," I called, throwing my arm out.

A figure stepped through. Tall, wearing a tunic of blue . . . with dark hair . . .

My mouth fell open. "Lancelot?" My sword drooped in my hand, my pulse still not sure if he were real or an apparition. His hair was tousled, and he wore a look of contrition on his face that was as unfamiliar to me as the mist that had delivered him.

Arthur stepped up beside me, sheathing his sword. "I take it you found your foster mother," Arthur said. His voice was hard—wary. I knew Arthur regretted what had passed between him and Lancelot when they last spoke, but the pride of men and kings especially was a funny thing.

The thought fled my mind as another stepped through the mist. A faerie female, tall and willowy as a reed. She was like a black alder tree in winter, her dark hair was the rich hue of bark, her pale skin milky as new-fallen snow. Long dark lashes fringed eyes wide and granite gray-blue as Lancelot's, though I knew they were not related. For this had to be Vivien, his foster mother. Lady of the Lake. She was a legend brought to life.

Arthur gave a slight bow. "Welcome to Caerleon, My Lady," he said. "To what do we owe this pleasure?"

The Otherworld evaporated behind the two mist-born wayfarers.

"Lancelot shared your unfortunate predicament with me," she said, gliding nearer, moving with preternatural grace.

"Are you here to assist?" Arthur asked, a hopeful ring to his question.

She blinked, then cocked her head, her fangs bared as she seemed to examine the mortal standing before her. "I'm afraid there is little I can do that the Grail did not, Little Dragon King. But . . ."

Her gaze flicked to me, pinning me where I stood. "When Lancelot told me how Morgana spoke of a Gwenevere, I had to see this mythological creature for myself."

She approached me and, without asking, placed ice-cold fingertips on either side of my face, then closed her eyes. I froze in shock, standing stock still as a shiver passed through me from my toes upward to my head, leaving a tingling in its wake. I tried to quiet my thundering pulse, to shake the feeling that I was being weighed and judged by this female, that she was turning me inside out. Did she find me wanting?

Her eyes snapped back open and she withdrew her hands.

"Well?" Lancelot asked.

Vivien cocked her head at me—similar to how she had with Arthur—as if I were a five-fold knot her ancient faerie mind couldn't untangle. "She appears mortal. Yet . . . there *is* something. Something magical that lies deep, a power that is more than human. Waiting."

"Is she the Gwenevere?" Lancelot asked. "Can you tell?"

I opened my mouth to object to being discussed as if I wasn't right before them, but Vivien spoke first. "There is only one way to tell. Ask her parents."

"What do ye mean?" I asked, finding my voice.

"A Gwenevere is a great enchantress, yes. But she is more than that. She is the daughter of the goddess Danu, conceived when she lays with a mortal king on Beltane. Is your father a king?"

"Aye," I whispered, my throat a pile of dry, brittle leaves. *Daughter of the goddess Danu?* My mouth fell open, again, and my eyes widened.

"And your birthday?" Vivien asked, heaving a dramatic sigh. She fluttered a look of longsuffering patience at Lancelot. When I continued to gape at her, she huffed, "Well, when is it, so-called White Enchantress?"

"Fe-February third . . ." I trailed off, doing the math in my head. Nine months after the new spring. Everything in me wanted to look at Arthur, to see if he figured the math out as well. But I didn't. Instead, I continued to stare at the Lady of the Lake in fear and in wonderment.

Vivien lifted a single eyebrow. "I cannot account for your appearance. Though you are pretty-ish for a mortal, I suppose."

"How can we know for sure?" Lancelot asked.

"If she is pretty-ish?" Vivien asked with a girlish, baiting smile, and cool, glittering mischief twinkling in her unnatural eyes. "What say you, Sir Knight?"

Lancelot groaned. "No faerie tricks. You know of what I ask, *Mother*. Is she the Gwenevere?"

I glared at him, my idiotic fish-gape quickly turning into a scowl. Why did the fool man need to know so badly if I was a bloody Gwenevere? Was this still about the third curse? I had no compulsion to sleep with him right now, that's for damn certain. Did any other thing ever cross the man's irritatingly obsessed mind?

"Like I said, dearest *Lancelot du Lac*." Vivien punctuated each word. "Ask her parents." Then she shifted toward me. "Your father."

I swallowed thickly. "My father is held captive by my clann's enemy." This faerie was the second individual today to proclaim my father as the one who held the answers I sought. I longed to see him again, to talk to him, to storm into that bastard O'Lynn's camp and fight my way to him. To take my family and leave only a path of destruction in my wake.

"A shame," Vivien replied with an elegant shrug of her slender shoulder. Then, as if bored with the conversation, she slid a glance my way and said, "Danu would be the only one who could tell you for certain, then. Too bad she hasn't been seen in twenty years."

"What?" Arthur exploded. "I thought she held court in the Otherworld?"

Vivien shook her head, then lifted a hand to fuss with a loose curl. "It's not common knowledge among mortals." She hissed the last word with sizzling disgust over our kind. "But a regent presides over her court. In her absence, obviously."

The earth goddess was missing? The earth goddess . . . and possibly . . . my mother?

It was madness.

This was all madness.

Life made sense before Caerleon. Now it was all curses and

faerie relics and magic beasts and mists that transported people. Madness.

Chapter Seven

Percival

Percival strode through the hallway, his mind racing with the events of the past weeks. They had found the Blessed Grail. Part of him had never thought they would do it, even as fevered as Arthur was about finding this relic . . . and as hopeful as he had been when Fionna joined them. Percival still had doubted. Until signs from the Grail Maiden began to appear, he thought that the legend of the Grail—the legend of the Fisher King—was just one more cruel twist of fate in the long line of tragedies shadowing the noble lines of Pendragon and Caer Benic. But they had found it. And now he was free.

True, the Grail Maiden had bid him return to Caer Benic and take up his place as the Fisher King. And perhaps one day he would. When he wasn't needed here. But, for now, he was needed. And he was wanted. And gods, did *he* want.

Images of Fionna filled his mind and tightened his breeches. Her features, delicate and soft as a feather—so incongruous with the skill of her blade—combined with the fire in her eyes. Compelling yet kind. Hard and soft—yielding as butter in his hands yet strong as stone when she faced monsters the likes of which he had never seen. Fionna was the most powerful woman he had ever known. She would strip his chastity from him with a power and gentleness that was all her—and the thought exhilarated and terrified him in turns. He wanted to please her. To make her moan the way she had for Galahad—

"Fionna!" he said as she ran full into him.

"Percival," she said at the same time, stumbling back. Her hand pressed to her breast as she breathed out. "My mind was elsewhere, my apologies."

"The fault was mine, dove," Percival said, studying her. Her silver eyes darted about, her breathing was shallow. "Is everything all right, lass?"

"Aye." She shook her head, closing her eyes. "No. I don't know. Lancelot is back."

"Well that's good," Percival said with a whoop.

"Indeed," Fionna agreed. "He brought Vivien. Arthur invited her to dinner."

"Vivien." Percival's elation dimmed, and he peered over his shoulder. "Is it just me," he whispered, "or have ye had enough of faeries for a spell?"

She let out a hard laugh. "Nay, not just ye. She brings riddles. I don't know. I need to change and put on something more suitable for evening's feast."

"I'll walk ye," Percival said, falling into step beside her. "Did Lancelot get any answers about the third curse?"

Fionna shrugged. "He didn't say. Vivien just put her hands all over me to discern if I was 'the Gwenevere.'" Fionna made marks in the air with her fingers. "I'm starting to hate the word."

"I know the feeling," Percival agreed. "Being the "Fisher King's son,' 'heir to the Grail' isnae any more fun."

She looked at him softly. "I don't think I realized how hard it was on ye."

"Och, we'll get this sorted, ye'll see," Percival said.

"How can ye be so optimistic?" she asked.

Percival tucked strands of hair behind his ear and shrugged. "I dinnae ken. The feeling is just more pleasant than the alternative."

"That simple?"

"Not everything has to be complicated." They had reached Fionna's door, and she turned to face him.

"Tell that to the possible mortal/immortal daughter of a goddess, who or may or may not be a Gwenevere, yet very certainly screwed up the Grail's healing of Caerleon."

Percival fought a smile. "That is a mouthful. I think I'll just stick to 'dove.'"

Fionna grinned at him, giving a playful roll of her eyes. "What would I do without ye?"

Percival took her hands in his and kissed the backs of each one. "Ye shall never have to know, fair Lady." He dropped his hands but didn't let hers go. Even her hands were so Fionna—pale and slender and soft on the backs, yet with hard callouses covering her palms. His thumbs traced two circles on the backs of them. "Fionna—" he began, finding himself suddenly tripping over each sound and syllable in just her name.

"I must dress for dinner," she said, pulling back her hands, clearly impatient. "What do you need?"

He cleared his throat, banging a fist softly against her door-frame. *Out with it, Percival!* "My vow—" he murmured, silently cursing his stupid tongue.

"I'm not sure I heard you?" Fionna asked.

He looked up then, meeting her eyes. If he wanted her, he needed to claim her. No longer a boy. He was a man. He was the Fisher King. Percival cleared his tightened throat again. "We have found the Grail, ye ken? I am now released of my vow. And the thought of my newfound freedom, it burns within me, lass."

Fionna's mouth opened in a little O as she realized what he meant. Then she closed her eyes, letting out a little sigh. "Percival, my head is in knots over everything that has happened right now. The curses, and Vivien, and my sister."

"Of course." Percival swallowed thickly, fighting his disappointment. "I didn't mean to come off as insensitive, or meant this very moment . . . I just . . ." his face heated.

He didn't know what he had been thinking. Coming here, asking her like a hound begging for a treat, then allowing his needs to have a voice after he knew she was upset. Sometimes he wanted to hide in a hole over his own awkward ignorance.

"Percy," she began, almost as though a big sister rather than a lover. He stilled. Did she only see him as a friend, then? The other men were handsome and virile and strong. But he? Was he only good for cheering up his friends? Fionna reached for him, but he stepped back. "It's not a no. It's just . . . not now."

He nodded stiffly at the tone of her voice. He wasn't a wee bairn, nor did he need her sympathy. Had he misread what they had shared in Betws-y-Coed? These past weeks? No, she cared for him. He was sure of it. Though, perhaps Fionna still saw him as a lad. A little brother to laugh with. Her tone certainly suggested so. But he wasn't that boy anymore. He had earned the adder stone and pleasured a witch of Byzantium and claimed the Blessed Grail for himself. He was capable, a man among men. But he just needed to prove it to her.

An idea bloomed to life inside of him.

"I wonder," he said, "If there is something I can do for ye . . ."

Fionna's cheeks reddened. "Oh Percival, that's very gener-ous—"

"Nae, not *that*," he said hastily. "Though, I would happily serve ye in such a way, whenever ye wish for pleasures between a man and woman. Rather, I meant . . . I would like to make a gesture of my favor. Prove to ye the depth of my regard for ye, and my wor-thiness. To lie with ye and . . . to love ye."

"Ye don't need to earn my favor," Fionna said, threading her fingers through the ends of her braids. "Ye already have my affec-tions."

"Please, I want to, dove," Percival said. "There must be some-thing I can do for ye."

Fionna's expression grew thoughtful, and then a conspiratorial smile crept over her face. "I've half a mind to do something danger-ous," she quietly confessed. "Something that rides the borderland between bravery and stupidity."

Percival's heart soared, and a mischievous smile crested on his own face. "Go on . . ."

Chapter Eight

Arthur

ntertaining a faerie always proved disconcerting. Arthur had felt uneasy around the Túatha dé Danann since boyhood. For he was the product of a vile act against the children of Danu when his conniving father, Uther, had arranged others in the front lines of war to slaughter Gorlois—Arthur's mother's first fae husband. His half-sisters never forgot or forgave. And with Uther now dead, their vengeful attentions turned Arthur's way.

His steps dragged as he made his way to the Great Hall from his room. Freshly bathed and wearing a tunic of emerald green, Arthur was physically clean. But nothing could wash away the worry that clouded him. A fog swirled about in his mind, thick as the Otherworldly mist of Castellum Puellarum, paralyzing his reason and quick wit. Everything was spinning out of control. The curse, the broken Grail, war, rebellion, his errant knight come home. His love, the daughter of a goddess? Half fae? Certainly, Fionna was no ordinary woman. It was as plain as day. But he had always attributed her unique grace, beauty, and battle prowess to the wonder that was Fionna herself, not some undeserved gift of divine parentage.

"That look can't be good," a deep voice called out.

He looked up and found Lancelot striding toward him. His knight and sword-brother met him in the hallway outside of the

Great Hall, wearing a tunic of grey trimmed in silver.

Arthur forced a laugh. "I admit, there is much on my mind as of late."

"A large piece of the blame lies with me," Lancelot said. "And for all the pain I have caused you and Caerleon, I am deeply sorry." Lancelot dropped to one knee, his head bowed.

"Lance—" Arthur began, but Lancelot interrupted him.

"You must let me make amends, Your Majesty. I wronged you. I wronged you all, by keeping the secret of the third curse. Though my motives were to keep the burden from you . . . my desires were selfish too. I wounded you a second time when I left. But I have returned with aid from my foster mother, and glad tidings. The Blessed Grail's magic washed the third curse from me. Morgana's prophecy hangs over our head no longer. I wish nothing more than for you to give me another chance. To be your second-in-command once again. To earn your trust again." Lancelot peered up at him, his eyes red and glossy with building emotion. His voice grew thick. "Arthur, I will do *anything*."

Lancelot's words warmed Arthur like a roaring hearth on the coldest of winter nights. Yes, part of him remained angry. But he no longer desired to be at odds with his dearest and oldest friend. His brother. He needed Lancelot, now more than ever.

"Stand, Sir Lancelot du Lac," Arthur said, and Lancelot did. "I'm afraid you've underestimated the depths of my feelings on this subject."

The anxious thoughts racing behind his friend's ice-blue eyes flashed bright with grief, the muscles in his jaw working. "I understand," Lancelot whispered, gritting back the tears. "It's nothing less than I deserve, Your Majesty."

Arthur laid a hand on Lancelot's shoulder, his friend's body a tense, coiled spring. "I love you far too much, brother, to let your fool-headedness tear us apart."

Lancelot let out a gasp of disbelieving laughter, his head curling down. He nodded, and a hand strayed to cover his eyes as his shoulders began to shake. Arthur pulled him into an embrace, and Lancelot shuddered against him, before he wrapped his arms around Arthur, his hands fisting in Arthur's tunic. Arthur clapped his friend's back, his relief at Lancelot's safe return forming into something harder. Something strong and unyielding as granite. His enemies could take his sword, the health of his land, even his kingship. But they could never take the *loyalty* of those Arthur loved. Lancelot and Galahad and Percival and now Fionna—he would lay down his life for any of them. And he knew in the marrow of his bones that they would each do the same for him. For each other. The Celts believed that a cord of three strands was not easily broken. *Well, Morgana,* he thought, the fire stoked within him—*try five.*

Lancelot pulled back, wiping his eyes.

"Do you fare well?" Arthur asked. "For I have need of my second. One who is clear-headed. No more doubts. No more letting faeries play upon our weaknesses. Each of us must be ready to do what needs to be done, if we are to get through the days to come."

Lancelot's smile was grim and his voice hard. "Let them come. We'll be ready."

"Do I sense a spring thaw in the ice of yer fated brotherhood?" Fionna asked, striding up the corridor in a stunning gown the color of plum. The dress dipped low, revealing the slender curve of her neck, the spill of her cleavage where the lily necklace gifted by Morgana's ambassador still nestled. Her hair was freshly braided at the crown of her hair, the rest falling free down her back in a waterfall of white. Lancelot slid him a questioning look and Arthur smiled his assent.

"A man can do naught but burn inside in the face of your beauty," Lancelot said with a grin, taking Fionna's hand and bowing over her fingers with a kiss.

She quirked a brow. "Just returned and ye're already back to full form I see."

Arthur motioned them inside. "You have no idea Fionna. You've been stuck with crabapple. If the old Lancelot is back, get ready for interesting times ahead."

Lancelot offered Fionna his arm, which she accepted, and then they all moved into the candlelight-warmed Great Hall.

"Back with a vengeance and ready to kick some faerie arse," Lancelot said with a laugh, before realizing his foster mother and Merlin stood inside the dining hall. "Er, sorry Mother," he said.

Vivien patted him on the cheek, grinning in such a way that her canines appeared. "Perhaps it best you stick to *kicking faerie arse* for a spell, rather than doing anything else with it."

A booming laugh sounded behind them, and Arthur turned to see Galahad and Percival joining their circle.

"Too right, My Lady." Galahad greeted the Lady of the Lake with a bow and a kiss on her delicate hand.

"Fair Galahad." Vivien studied him with a gleam in her eyes before she caressed one of his sizable biceps. "My son has spoken of you. Time has treated you well. And Percival! Our very own Fisher King, in the flesh."

"Welcome, Lady," Percival said, with a wide smile.

Arthur couldn't help the grin that now stretched across his face. Gods, it was good to have them all back together, here in his keep. Despite all that faced them outside these walls, inside, things were finally as they were supposed to be.

"Shall we sit?" Arthur asked, gesturing to the head table.

Murmurs of affirmation rounded the group and they made their way to their seats. Until Vivien grabbed Fionna's wrist, her glittering blue eyes growing wide. "What is this you wear?" Vivian half-whispered, her hand straying to the necklace at Fionna's throat.

Arthur halted all movement, his instincts on alert.

Fionna shot him a wild look as the Lady of the Lake picked up the pendant hanging from Fionna's neck and inspected the lily.

"How did you come upon this necklace, child?" Vivien asked.

"The ambassador Alworn delivered this gift from Tintagel," Arthur said. "When we knighted Fionna."

"The chain won't come off," Fionna admitted. "No matter what I try."

"You did not mention this during our discussion," Merlin quietly said.

"Nor me," Arthur added. "I wish I had known, so I could have sought your relief sooner."

Fionna gnawed the inside of her lip. "There were far more important matters at hand than troubles with a silly necklace."

"This *silly* necklace was stolen from me," Vivien hissed. Her eyes darted about the room, resting on each person in turn. "And missing for months from my keep on the Isle of Man."

Horror flickered across Fionna's face. "I'm so sorry, I didn't know, My Lady. Please, take the necklace back." Fionna fumbled with the clasp, letting out a growl of frustration.

"Relax child, I care not that my property was here in *your* safe-keeping. Tintagel, however . . . I shall deal with the dark sisters." Vivien grasped the necklace, closing her eyes and murmuring under her breath.

The clasp of the necklace sprang apart, and then the silver chain slithered down from around Fionna's neck and into Vivien's hand.

Fionna released a gasp, feeling her bare neck. "Thank ye!"

"Little Dragon King, your half-sister's meddling was more than just idle," Vivien said. She loosed a laugh, but her blue eyes held little mirth. There was something foreign in her gaze that made Arthur's stomach clench in fear. Pity. She looked upon him with pity. "Rather clever, actually. A curse on my dearest Lancelot, declaring ruin if he fell in love. And a necklace enchanted to ensure he did."

Silence blanketed the room, thick and heavy.

"What do ye mean?" Fionna whispered, her hand still on her throat.

"This necklace is enchanted with a love charm. Whoever wears this pendant and corded chain will be irresistible to the opposite sex. Whatever men cross her path will have no choice but to fall madly in love with her."

 Chapter Nine

Lancelot

ivien's words settled over them like a drenched wool cloak, heavy and stifling.

Lancelot looked at Arthur, and saw his own shock mirrored on his king's face. The necklace made a man fall in love with the wearer? So . . . were their feelings for Fionna . . . false? Lies spun of faerie enchantments? Had the last weeks, the fire that had burned hot within him—

"I think it's bollocks," Percival cut in, marching across the room. He took Fionna's hand and began walking toward the head table, saying, "A man need no enchantment to fall for our fifth knight. If her beauty and wit weren't enough, the might of her sword arm would capture him completely." Fionna followed Percival to her seat like an obedient child. "I for one am certain that my feelings are my own."

Fionna shot Percival a grateful look as she sank heavily into her chair.

For once, Lancelot envied Percival's quick thinking. While he stood stock-still, processing his doubts and shock, Percival had proven his loyalty.

"Agreed," Galahad said, sinking into his chair as well. "No faerie trinket can confuse my heart."

His foster mother was watching this all with a twinkle of impish amusement in her eyes.

"Thank you, Vivien," Arthur said quietly, "for removing the necklace. Perhaps now we are almost rid of Morgana and her sisters' magical meddling."

"But not quite." Vivien sank gracefully into her chair between Merlin and Arthur, and then cocked her head at Arthur in that inhuman, animalistic way of hers. "The Blessed Grail failed to eradicate the curse upon your land."

"A mystery, that," Merlin murmured, leaning in toward Vivien eagerly as his pupils narrowed into reptilian slits. "I would relish your ancient wisdom on the matter, My Lady. When each of them drank from the Grail, the land healed. Except Fionna's portion."

Fionna's face remained downturned, her eyes fixed on her empty trencher.

Lancelot reached under the table and grasped the fingers of one of the hands resting limply on her lap. She slid a glance his way beneath lowered lashes. Shadows darkened her eyes and doubts carved lines into her face. He squeezed her hand in a weak attempt at comfort. Still, he believed they would sort this mess out.

"Very peculiar indeed, druid," Vivien mused. "The Grail should have wiped away all magical enchantment, like with Lancelot. Although . . . perhaps the Grail's healing properties could not affect a more powerful enchantment."

"But what could be more powerful than the Grail?" Merlin asked.

"The magic of a goddess, obviously." Vivien huffed in irritation. Lancelot knew this look. His foster mother grew weary of mortals. But she continued when Merlin dipped his head for her to explain further. "Such as the goddess Danu. If Princess Fionnabhair Allán is the Gwenevere, then perhaps her mother placed a spell upon her that even the Grail could not break."

Merlin's eyes flashed gold as he turned toward Arthur. "I am telling you, Your Majesty, our answers lie in the Otherworld. With the court of the Túatha dé Danann."

Arthur sighed, taking a sip of wine. Servants were bringing out trays of food now, filling the room with the smell of spices and fresh bread. "I fear you are right. But we still do not have a way to travel there quickly."

"You seek the Otherworld?" Vivien asked, eyebrow arched. "As I already shared, you will not find Danu there. A steward holds court in her name. Though, I fear that after years of her absence, Danu would scarcely recognize the place."

"Answers from Danu would be a bonus," Merlin said, "but I have advised Arthur that the Cauldron of Plenty may be able to help feed the people while the curse lingers, as well as aid us if Morgana's armies lay siege."

"The Cauldron is rumored to have healing properties, as well," Vivien remarked, though somewhat distracted. She sniffed at the leg of lamb placed onto her trencher and wrinkled her nose. Lancelot resisted the urge to roll his eyes. His foster mother's focus was like a butterfly, flitting and fluttering about endlessly.

"If the rumors prove true," Arthur said, "that would be a helpful fact. Only, we don't have the time. With an army approaching, I cannot leave my keep."

"Can the Lady of the Lake assist?" Galahad suggested. "She did transport herself and Lancelot here by magical means, did she not?"

"Of course," Vivien purred, looking at Galahad with an appraising eye as she licked sauce from her fingertip. "But my power transports you between locations on the mortal plane. You would still need a key to enter the Otherworld."

"They have such a key," Merlin said. "Carved from the tusk of the Twrch Trwyth."

"And you mention this now?" Vivien nibbled on a bannock, melodramatically peering up at the rafters of the Great Hall, as though in great thought. "Then," she added after swallowing, "I could see you there, Little Dragon King. Entering the Otherworld would be as simple as stepping through a door."

"Truly?" Arthur set his goblet of wine down and leaned toward her. "Your assistance would help us greatly. This Cauldron, if the magical properties are true, could solve several of our problems efficiently."

"Which only leaves us with several other problems to contend with," Percival said cheerfully around a bite of chicken leg. Vivien grinned at the younger man and then side-eyed Lancelot. She knew. His foster mother sensed Lancelot's tether to Percival. How? He wasn't sure.

"Quite right, Percival." Arthur's gaze darkened. "Fionna, I should like you to accompany me. The Otherworld might hold answers for you as well."

Fionna's head snapped up and she stared at Arthur, eyes wide and unblinking, as though a startled deer. "As ye wish, Yer Majesty," she managed.

"If I may," Vivien interjected, practically cooing. "I would not take Fionna, if I were you."

"Why not?" Lancelot asked. His foster mother was always scheming and maneuvering, and he didn't trust the glimmer in her eyes.

"Do you mortals ever listen? As I said, the steward who rules over the court of the Túatha dé Danann has sworn fealty to Danu, but I fear over these years . . . her allegiances may have shifted."

"You didn't share this latter piece of information, mother," Lancelot muttered.

"No? Well, then listen now." Vivien's hand fluttered through the air as she giggled before turning solemn once more. "There could be faeries at court who are no longer friends of Danu. If Fionna is the Gwenevere, and if Danu placed a géis to shield her daughter's true nature, then she had reasons for doing so. Delivering Fionna to those who may be hostile toward her could prove dangerous."

Arthur's brow furrowed.

"Lady Vivien speaks sense," Merlin said. "Until we can untangle the truth of Fionna's heritage, and her powers, she is safest within your keep."

Fionna swept a heated gaze across the table, the fire in her finally rekindling. "I am no wilting maiden who needs protection. I am safe so long as I have my sword at my side and my knives in their sheaths," she snapped. Then she took a long, slow breath, seeming to re-center herself. "But I am happy to remain here, if everyone thinks it best. I have tasks to attend to here, anyway." She hurried on. "Ye know . . . assisting in the defense of Caerleon. I have the most knowledge of the Uí Tuírtri battle styles and tactics."

"Of course," Arthur said. "Merlin didn't mean to imply you couldn't protect yourself. Right Merlin?" Arthur raised an eyebrow, to which Merlin nodded in apology to Fionna.

Vivien ignored it all, continuing. "May I suggest . . . young, virile Galahad?" She turned to the brawny knight. "Elathia, Danu's regent, has a weakness for handsome mortals of his *persuasion*. His presence could prove useful."

"I will seize any advantage." Arthur sent a sly look to the knight in question. "What say you, young, virile Galahad?"

"Travel to the Otherworld as faerie bait?" Galahad sighed, blowing a loose strand of hair out of his face. "Of course, Your Majesty. Sounds like romping fun."

"Then it is settled. Galahad shall come with me. Lancelot, you are reappointed as my second-in-command. Percival and Fionna will assist in defending the keep and leading our men. Merlin, keep searching for cures or clues to Fionna's condition."

Percival hoisted his glass. "To the next mad adventure that will likely get us all killed."

Lancelot laughed darkly. "I'll drink to that."

They talked plans and strategy late into the night, as the dishes grew cold and the wine dwindled. Arthur was understandably hesitant to leave his keep with an imminent threat on the horizon; so, Lancelot forgave him his over-managing, his insistence of going twice over every piece of their defensive plans and fortifications.

Vivien and Merlin spoke of the Otherworld and what Arthur and Galahad might expect there, as well as speculated on the mystery of Fionna's condition. The night ended with many theories but no answers.

Fionna had grown quieter and more introspective until she finally excused herself, pleading exhaustion.

Indecision warred within Lancelot as Fionna's lithe form disappeared into the dark shadows of the corridor. There was much he wanted to say to her. There was time, but . . . he didn't want to wait. He needed to clear the air—now.

Lancelot stood. "Excuse me as well," he said, then strode after her. He didn't want another day to pass without telling her how he felt.

"Fionna," he called after her.

But she didn't slow. If anything, she sped up.

"Fionna!" He broke into a jog, catching up with her as she neared the hallway that led to her room in the North wing. He grabbed her arm and gently swung her around to face him. "Fi, speak to me."

Tears glittered on her white lashes and slipped down her cheeks.

Alarmed, he towed her into a darkened servant's hallway and away from prying eyes. "Why do you cry?"

She pinched her face up, her eyes closed, fighting the tears. "I betrayed my father and sister to stay here in Caerleon. Aideen is married to a bastard, the foulest man I've ever known. Because of me." She jabbed her thumb at her chest. "Because I forgot my duty and threw aside my honor to follow my heart. I acted like a foolish lass, one who put love over family. And now . . . that love was false!" Her voice cracked, and she clapped a hand over her mouth. "Every moment was false. Yer feelings, all of them, they were magic. A cruel faerie joke. Well the joke's on me."

Lancelot took her face in his hands, wiping her tears with his thumbs. Even with her face red and puffy, her nose streaming, she was beautiful. The most beautiful and powerful woman he had ever known. "If it was all a cruel faerie joke, and you no longer wear the enchanted necklace, then why do I still love you?"

She stepped out of his embrace and threw her shoulders back, head lifted high, her silver eyes rippling with anger. "Do not mock me."

"You think so little of me?"

"Ye once asked to know my love and then ye pushed me away. My heart cannot bear another game, Lancelot du Lac. No more lies."

Lancelot advanced toward her in such a way that she had no choice but to back up against the stone wall. "The only *lie* I want to know with you is the fiery, passionate truth between our bodies. Our souls."

"Is this your cock speaking or yer heart?"

"Both."

A furious laugh escaped her flushed lips. "Oh please, woo me more with your pretty words, prince."

The snappish reply was meant as an insult, but he glimpsed the challenge in her daggered gaze—a test. From the very first day, their every spark was born of weaponized words. Sparring wit and emotions and stubbornness. Her steel was his equal—in moments such as these and with real swords in hand.

Placing his forearm on the stone wall by her face, he leaned in close and whispered, "What I feel for you is more real than the ground beneath my feet. Than the air I breathe." Her breath pulsed hot on his lips, her breasts rising and falling in a seething tempo. With a devilish smile, he moved toward her ear and continued in moonlit whispers. "The love I feel for you was not born of magic. You were the only spark needed to kindle this blaze. And there is no man or magic who can tear it from me."

A disbelieving sob escaped Fionna, and her body tensed against more tears. She fisted the front of his tunic, her red-rimmed eyes locked onto his lips. "Ye wish for passion-filled *lies*?"

"Only if those *lies* seal the truth of us, princess."

A single tear rolled across her mouth as a raging heat billowed between their bodies.

"Show me."

Lancelot smirked. "Is this your cock speaking or your heart?"

"Both."

A soft laugh escaped him as he pulled her mouth to his.

Chapter Ten

Fionna

His mouth collided with mine, his fury begging me to meet his ferocity. Darkness had always danced between us. And I welcomed his grief as I fought my own. Lancelot was a flinted passion, a Winter Solstice's bonfire—cold when distanced yet breathtakingly hot when close Unlike Galahad's honeyed sensuality, Arthur's tender romance, and Percival's laughing kisses, the man who pressed me to a stone wall in a dark, rarely-used hallway was seductive wickedness and hidden moonlight. In a word: dangerous.

His lips left mine to explore my neck as his hand slid up the silk skirt of my gown. Calloused fingertips caressed my thigh, moving higher and higher. Determined. Then a single teasing finger paced a line between my sex and my slit when he discovered that I wasn't wearing any undergarments.

I couldn't breathe, my chest gasping for air at the fire of his touch.

"You want pretty words?" Lancelot murmured into the skin of my neck.

Gripping the back of my thigh, he yanked my leg up and around his waist, while his other hand pushed the neckline of my bodice down my arm until my breast sprang free. Rippling folds of my plum-hued silken skirt fell toward my stomach and exposed me further.

"I will claim your body first." He rocked his hip into me and I shuddered. The lightning strike of his bulging cock against my throbbing clit thundered through my core. My breast bounced with the rolling movement and he lowered his head, flicking his tongue against my nipple. "Gods woman, you taste sweet . . ." His murmured words trailed away as he took my breast into his mouth.

I stifled a sharp cry of pleasure as his teeth nibbled on me, his tongue roughly sucking my pebbled tip before releasing my breast to the night's chill.

He dragged his lips back to mine, whispering, "I want your anger," before seizing my mouth once more in a bruising kiss.

Heady, I pushed him back and leveled a glare. "My body isn't enough for ye? Goddess above, ye arrogant, infuriating boar."

The side of Lancelot's mouth tipped up. Still holding my thigh around his waist, he stroked my exposed skin with his hardening cock. Continuing to do so even as he began unlacing his breeches.

"I want *all* of you, Fionnabhair Allán," he said, and then I felt the crown of his smooth skin sliding across my swollen sex. "Your pain." The fingers of his free hand snaked up my torso to my breast and pinched my nipple. Molten iron pooled between my legs as his cock teased my body into submission simultaneously, sliding back and forth, back and forth.

I moaned, clawing at the front of his tunic, unable to contain the aching pang of pleasure. Furious and ecstatic that he could play my body as expertly as a bard plucks the strings of his harp.

"Your grief," he whispered next, softly kissing my jaw, my cheek, and each eyelid.

His tongue swirled patterns down my throat, as if he were writing his name on my skin. The very thought stoked the bonfire in my pulse and sparked embers flew into my veins.

"And I want your passion."

Lancelot bit down where my neck and collarbone met as he thrust his cock into me—deep, hard. I sucked in a sharp, ragged breath. Gods above, he felt incredible. And he didn't move, allowing me to feel the thick size of him as he stretched and filled me. Starlit waves of pleasure rushed between my legs, intense and leaving me breathless. An orgasm was building. But I wasn't ready yet, wanting more. *Needing* more.

Heat flared where his teeth gripped my skin, a feral pain that ignited a wildness in me. A soft whimper escaped my lips. This is how the fae claimed their lovers, I had heard once. A thought that left me wanting to become animal, to crave every forbidden carnal delight. To furiously take his body as he raged into mine.

And rage he did.

Grabbing my other leg, he hoisted me up––his shaft still buried to the hilt inside me––and then he pressed me harder against the stones digging into my back. I was now completely at his mercy, my legs dangling in the crook of his arms and spread wide for his taking. His hips crashed into mine.

I groaned, angering when I felt the hard length of him slide away, leaving me bare and empty. My hands loosened their grip on his tunic to clutch the soft, black curls around his head. Our eyes met, mouths parted in heaving breaths as his muscled, unyielding body crashed into mine again and again, filling me and leaving me, his hips grinding into mine with each thrust.

"Tell me you want me," he whispered between stirred breaths.

Those words pierced my heart as I understood. This was the dark pain he protected. The love he sought and feared to never know.

"I want ye."

His breath caught as his eyes fluttered closed. "Say it again."

"I want ye, Lancelot du Lac."

"Again," he breathed.

"I want ye all my days," I whispered before touching my mouth to his in a sweet, gentle kiss.

With our lips connected and his cock still buried inside me, Lancelot pulled away from the wall and carried me a few steps toward the stairs, where he softly laid my body down across the steps. He knelt on the stones, straddling my hips. Moonlight from a nearby latticed window dusted him in silvers and blues. My Winter Prince, all fire and ice. Breathtakingly gorgeous, with frosted blue eyes peering at me through curling black strands that fell over his flushed cheeks and swollen lips. Reaching behind his back, he pulled his tunic over his head and then flung the garment to the side.

Fingers of light caressed his muscled chest and torso, and I drank in the sight of him. He was tall and lean and well-built, with veins roping around his forearms and ink dancing across his skin in swirls and ancient patterns. The length of his cock glistened from our passion. Jealous of the moon's intimate knowledge of this man's body, I reached up and brushed my fingertips along the tattoos. "What do they mean?" I asked.

"Runes," Lancelot whispered back. "Ones that mark me as a faerie prince of the Túatha dé Danann."

"Ye are, truly?" My gaze locked with his. "I always thought 'faerie' was in jest or to mark yer upbringing."

"I am a prince of two realms, mortal and immortal, though not one of power or consequence in either. Any I have is only by the good favor of others." He angled his head away, as if in shame.

I cupped his cheek and drew him to me until our lips touched. "Ye have power over me, Lance. And . . ." I swallowed back the rising emotion. "And I not only love ye, I *choose* ye."

A tear slipped down his cheek and he hoarsely whispered, "I promise you, Fi . . . I promise to never intentionally hurt you again or push you away. I'm sorry. I'm so very sorry."

"Claim my heart, Lancelot. I am yers."

"And Arthur's?"

I smiled. "Aye, I'm Arthur's and Galahad's and Percival's. Just as yer heart also belongs to Percival."

He bit his bottom lip, a look both shy and sensual. "You don't mind my affection for Percival?"

"No, ye belong to each other too. But this moment is ours, only ye and me." The energy between us surged again, and another tear rolled down Lancelot's cheek. My hand traveled down his jaw and neck to his chest, over his pounding heart. "I *want* ye."

His eyes closed once more as he shuddered under the weighted truth of my confession.

"You've claimed my body," I said, running my hands across the beautiful, olive-toned skin of his chest. "Now lie with my heart."

And there, on the stairs, we joined once more. This time every moment slow, each touch to savor the beauty and wonder of the other, each whisper shared as though our souls entwined intimately too. This man made me so mad—both in fury and in adoration for him. But most of all, he humbled me. For I knew his heart wasn't a gift he gave easily or often, if ever until now. Nor did I doubt him: his love wasn't born of magic but freely given.

Delirious with pleasure and utterly drunk on his kisses, I yielded completely to him as I whispered over and over, "I want ye."

Chapter Eleven

Galahad

Galahad wasn't eager to reenter the Otherworld. But he was a knight, and a knight went where his king commanded.

His sleep had been fitful the night before, filled with images of faerie maidens with sharp ears and even sharper teeth. Through his dreams they tormented him, stabbing Arthur, twisting into Fionna's lithe form and back again, taunting him and his peasant origins, laughing at his mortal attempts to fight back.

Finally, he rose before dawn, stumbling toward the stable yard to pound at a straw man until sweat coated his entire body and the sun had risen. Until his dreams grew hazy and his body sore.

He then bathed and changed into a fresh tunic, letting his damp hair fall about his shoulders to dry. He was to meet Arthur, Merlin, and Vivien in Arthur's study, where the Lady of the Lake would open a portal. The familiar corridors of the keep comforted his troubled thoughts, as did motion. Moving always helped calm his agitation.

Before turning down another hallway, he crossed paths with Fionna. "My lady," he nodded to her. She looked like she had known little sleep as well—purpled shadows smudged the fair skin under her eyes. But her eyes, though worried, were strangely bright and alert. "Here to see us off?"

"I don't like this plan," she said, grabbing his hand and pulling him to a stop.

"What's to like?" Galahad turned to her. "But we must. For Caerleon."

"I know." She gnawed the inside of her lip in that adorable way of hers. "Promise ye will be careful. Don't do anything gát."

"I can make no such promises. They don't call me gallant Galahad for nothing."

Fionna snorted. "No one calls ye *that*." A smile hinted at the corner of her lips. "Yer nickname is chipmunk."

"Then I have little to concern myself with other than gathering for the winter. Perhaps I can find an acorn here?" He pulled her into his arms, burying his nose into the crook of her neck, kissing the soft skin there. "Or here?" He nosed up to her ear as she squirmed in his arms.

"Galahad!" she gasped, shrieking in laughter.

Someone cleared their throat and they flew apart, Fionna's face going as red as a huckleberry in spring.

Vivien and Merlin stood nearby—Merlin amused and Vivien with a mischievous and oddly curious glint in her dark blue gaze.

"They are a spirited bunch," Vivien remarked.

"You have no idea, Lady," Merlin replied.

"Are we ready?" Arthur strode down the hall between them and then ushered them into his study. He seemed full of nervous energy as well.

"We are, Little Dragon King," Vivien said.

Galahad nodded, pushing his hair back from his face and straightening his tunic. Play time was over.

Fionna watched from the corner, her arms twisted before her. "Arthur . . ." she hurried forward and pulled him into an embrace. He buried his face in her hair, just as Galahad had done moments before. "Be careful," she whispered.

Galahad observed the feelings within him, studying them with careful scrutiny. There was a hint of jealousy there, but it was fading. His king was a good man who deserved Fionna's love. Arthur's affections for her were clearly genuine and ran deep. Just as his own did. In his own way, Galahad was . . . happy for Arthur and Fionna.

Just as he was happy when he was with her. There was an unease there too. But that was understandable. Arthur had declared that Fionna would make her choice, which they would all respect, but kings weren't known for sharing. Would Arthur someday claim Fionna as his and his only?

He shook off the thought. His worries about Fionna would have to wait. He needed all his wits about him for where he and Arthur were heading.

Vivien stood before the fireplace, waving a hand, whispering words he couldn't hear, and no doubt would not understand, even if he could. The air before her appeared to shimmer, and smoke billowed from the nothingness before them, forming a sort of door.

"You have the key?" Merlin asked.

Arthur patted the pouch dangling from his belt. "We will be able to return. I am taking the adder stone too, just in case something is not as it seems."

"Wise. The door will only respond to you alone. When you're back through, Merlin has the means to banish the portal." Vivien cocked her head and grinned until her canines showed. "Good luck Little Dragon King. I hope you find what you seek."

"Thank you for your wisdom and aid, My Lady," Arthur said with an incline of his head. "Come Galahad. Let us plunge once more into the unknown."

Stepping through the door was like stepping into a dream. They exited into a dark forest glen illuminated by faerie light. Tall trees soared above them, blocking out the sky, if there even was one to see. What stars adorned the midnight tapestry of the Otherworld's sky? He knew not. Glowing purple fireflies winked in the air and lush flowers bloomed all around them, dripping nectar that glowed with magic.

"We stay together," Arthur said, stepping over one of the many vines that climbed around them like living things.

They followed the path of light as it joined with a tinkling river. A fish jumped in the water beside them, brilliant in shades of magenta and silver. Its brethren seemed to glow within the water, giving off more preternatural light.

"A beautiful place, that is for sure," Arthur said.

"When it comes to faeries—the more beautiful they seem, the more dangerous they are," Galahad quietly commented.

"What a remarkable sentiment," a melodic female voice said. "Is the same true of mortal men?"

Arthur's and Galahad's hands flew to their sword hilts as a female emerged onto the path before them. She wore a draping dress of the deepest purple, and her hair, through light like Fionna's, was a shade of violet Galahad had never seen on any creature, human or fae. She was exquisitely beautiful, her face round and perfectly symmetrical, her figure generously proportioned. *Dangerous*, he reminded himself.

"I am King Arthur Pendragon and this is my sworn knight, Sir Galahad of Swansea. We seek the regent, Elathia," Arthur said, dropping his hands to his side.

"You have found her," Elathia said, a secret smile curving on her face. She stepped closer to Galahad, her bright violet eyes examining him from toe to nose. He stood his ground against the obvious attentions. Vivien had said the faerie enjoyed the company of mortals. That was why he was here. Bait. He tried to ignore the fact that it never ended well for the bait.

"Come. Let us speak," she purred.

They followed Elathia down the path to a clearing. Before them, a massive rock face rose up amongst the trees, the stone's surface encrusted with glowing crystals in a rainbow of hues. Rivulets of water, shimmering in a prism of light, dripped down the face, gathering in a sparkling pool that fed the river they had passed. It was an impressive backdrop to the throne of vines and branches that sat below on a gentle mound of grass and moss.

As Elathia settled herself onto the throne, white blossoms—bright with vibrant magic—burst open around her, silhouetting her form. Galahad swallowed thickly. This faerie was not one to trifle with. The casual display of such magic demonstrated that as much as Vivien's warnings.

Other faeries drifted into the clearing, females with dresses of mesmerizing fabrics, handsome males with swords at their sides. Goblins and hobgoblins, brownies, and red caps. Even a monstrous creature with grey mottled skin and tentacles for arms that Galahad couldn't even begin to identify. It was as if it had crawled out of a sea abyss or deep crevices of the earth—like a Fomorian. But he knew that was ridiculous. Fomorians were mortal enemies of the Túatha dé Danann. Such a creature wouldn't peacefully grace this court. Still, Galahad shifted uncomfortably as the fae-born crowd silently filled in the ranks around Elathia. There was no way they could fight all these faeries, if things turned ugly.

"What brings you here, mortals?" Elathia asked.

"My land is ailing under a curse. My people begin to die of starvation. They cannot drink from the streams," Arthur said. "We seek the Cauldron of Plenty to feed them. If you could just loan this relic to me for a time, I would return it to you when the business is done. You have my word."

Elathia laughed, a sweet sound. "The Cauldron is one of the four relics of the Túatha dé Danann. It is not 'loaned' out for use. Danu did not appoint me as regent over her kingdom to simply allow mortal kings to walk out with our most precious treasures."

Arthur ground his teeth. "Is there nothing I can say to change your mind? I am trustworthy. Appointed as king over all of Briton by the Lady of the Lake herself."

"Your mortal kingship means little here," Elathia scoffed.

"Perhaps a feat of strength, to prove my worth—"

"My answer is no," she snapped.

Arthur inclined his head stiffly. "I apologize for wasting your time. Thank you for your hospitality." He turned on his heel, motioning to Galahad. Arthur's shoulders were hunched. His king was clearly furious, but Galahad saw little that they could do. If the faerie wasn't inclined to help them—

Galahad's feet stuck in the ground, and he fell forward onto his knees.

Arthur spun around too. Excalibur pointed out straight behind him, as if pinned by thin air.

"I did not excuse you," Elathia's voice cracked like a whip, and then she stood, stalking across the grass toward them.

"What is the meaning of this?" Arthur asked, his voice low and hard. "We came here in good faith. We have not wronged you."

"But you have something that belongs to us . . ." Elathia said, halting at their side. She reached out and stroked the length of Excalibur's sheath with one graceful violet-hued fingernail. Then she stroked that same finger down Galahad's arm, tracing the ripples of his muscles. He held back a shiver. Her sharp nail felt more like a claw. ". . . And something we want."

"Explain yourself," Arthur barked, drawing himself up to his full height.

"You're free to go, Little Dragon King," she said with glee, "but the sword and the knight stay."

Chapter Twelve

Arthur

The heat of anger burst through Arthur like greedy flames through dry tinder. How dare this faerie think to hold them here against their wills. They had done nothing to earn her ire, save the misfortune of being born mortal. He turned to her, wanting nothing more than to lay Excalibur's sweet edge across her milky-white throat. To *make* her listen.

"Excalibur is *my* blade," he practically growled, "given to me by the Lady of the Lake, appointing me with the blessing of your sovereign, the goddess Danu. The sword stays with me. And as for my knight Galahad, he is a free man, belonging only to himself. But he has sworn himself into my service. He stays with me too."

Galahad crossed his arms over his chest.

Elathia grinned, licking the points of her fangs. "You do not seem so impressive to be crowned king over all Briton. Indeed, you cannot even defeat a simple holding spell. Perhaps Danu made a mistake."

"Perhaps we should ask her," Arthur countered.

"Alas, she has not been seen for many years." Elathia didn't even appear upset over this. Rather, a secret smile curved her face.

"I'm not leaving here without my sword and my fellow," Arthur insisted.

"Then it seems we are at an impasse," she snapped back, stepping forward, and draping one hand over Galahad's shoulder. The other reached up to lift a tendril of his golden hair, examining the strands with interest.

Galahad stiffened beneath her touch, his mouth fixed in a firm line.

"We shall have to find a way to while away the hours," she murmured, her eyes making a leisurely assessment of Galahad's form and profile. Then she giggled, a sound of malicious joy that seemed innate to all faeries. The one that always sent crawling fingers of ice up Arthur's spine. He pressed his resolve further.

"Your actions here go against the will of your goddess," Arthur said, trying to draw her attention away from Galahad. "They will not be without consequence."

Elathia scoffed, and the faeries who had gathered around laughed, a harsh and raucous sound. "If you are the darling of Danu, perhaps you should prove yourself so." She cocked her head and locked her predatory violet gaze onto him.

"What do you propose?" Arthur asked carefully.

"If you are sovereign-blessed as you say, then you should pull the sword from the Stone of Knowledge. For surely, if the Sword of Light belongs to you, Excalibur will yield to your touch like an eager lover." She stepped close to Arthur now, running her finger along Excalibur's cross-guard. She smelled of berries and nightshade, of the lusciousness of death. "Prove your worth, Little Dragon King."

Galahad's deep blue eyes rounded with concern. "Your Majesty," he said, his voice low and careful, ripe with words unspoken. Arthur knew the thoughts racing through Galahad's mind, for they raged through his as well. Do not make a deal with faeries. It is a trick. They cannot be trusted. All of these cautions were true, but what better choice did he have? He and Galahad had no magic. They had only their convictions and the courage to face these mad creatures head on.

Arthur nodded. "If I allow you to drive Excalibur into this stone you speak of, and if I pull my blade back out, you will allow us to freely leave? With the sword?"

"I will allow you to leave with the sword." She smiled. "Your friend however—"

"I cannot abide by these terms," Arthur barked.

But Galahad held up a hand. "Free my feet, and I would offer my own wager, fair Elathia."

Arthur's eyes widened, but Elathia appeared intrigued. She waved her hand, and Galahad stepped forward.

"I do not find the company of a beautiful faerie to be distasteful," Galahad purred, taking her hand, and laying a soft kiss upon her long, delicate fingers. "To the contrary. Think of the pleasures we could enjoy together, if I were to stay of my own free will."

What the hell was Galahad doing? Arthur wanted to protest, to order him to silence, but the warning flash in Galahad's eye told him to stay steady. To trust him.

"Go on," Elathia said, her gleaming eyes fixed on Galahad.

"If Arthur pulls the sword from the stone, we leave with Excalibur *and* the Cauldron of Plenty." Her face darkened but Galahad pulled the female toward him, twisting her body so her back hit his broad chest. One of his arms snaked around her waist, the other splaying across her ribcage just below her breasts. He murmured into her ear, "If Arthur fails, then I stay behind of my own free will, and I will devote myself to your desires." He lay a soft kiss on the crook of her neck and her tongue flicked out, dampening her lips.

"An intriguing wager." Elathia pulled herself from Galahad's grasp and spun on her heel to face them both. She threw back her shoulders, haughtiness falling over her like a heavy rain. But the heaving of her bosom revealed the truth—she was affected by Galahad's seduction. Gods, Arthur himself had practically been moved by the display. Galahad was masterful.

"Your offer is one I accept," she said. To Arthur, she held out her hand and said, "The sword."

Arthur ground his teeth as he turned the jeweled hilt toward the faerie, offering her his beloved blade. Every fiber of his being shouted against the action, shouted at the wrongness. He was not supposed to be parted from the sword.

Elathia took Excalibur from him, a smirk on her face. "Follow me, mortals."

"What the hell was *that*," Arthur hissed as they joined the silent train of faeries who gathered in Elathia's wake.

"If you don't retrieve that sword from the stone, we're both stuck here," Galahad whispered back. "So, I figured I had better make it mean something when you do."

Arthur pressed his lips together. "A fool thing, to freely bind yourself to her. A brave thing, but a fool thing."

"Only if you don't pull the sword," Galahad countered. "And you'll pull the sword, right?"

"I had bloody better," Arthur muttered. Doubt reared its head, a monster dark and vicious. Vivien had granted him Excalibur, but so much had gone wrong since then. Morgana, the curses, a stolen Excalibur, now an invasion from Ireland. What if Danu was rethinking her blessing? What if all he had proven in the last years of his kingship was that he wasn't worthy?

"Watch for tricks," Galahad said. "With faeries, things are never as they seem."

Arthur nodded, swallowing back his nerves. He was either worthy or he wasn't. Today he would find out the truth, whether he was ready for the answer or not.

They climbed a harrowing path up the rock face to the left of the waterfall, following Elathia and the others. When they summited the craggy steps, they found themselves in a grotto aside a crystalline pool. Tall trees bowed around the clearing, their leaves the blues and greens of gemstones, glittering with dew. A white owl swept across the space of the lake, alighting on another tree branch. The bird, known as the bride of death, drew Arthur's eye for a moment, but his gaze and his thoughts—his very future—quickly came to rest on the boulder perched in the center of the lake. Glowing toadstools floated along the surface of the lake in a path leading to the stone—a path Elathia now walked, graceful as a queen. She took the two steps up to the top of the boulder, and then, with a movement of her lips, raised Excalibur and plunged the tip into the granite below. The sword's blade was buried halfway to the hilt, its red ruby pommel winking at him in the low light.

Elathia turned, her eyes bright with delight. "Come Little Dragon King, show us what you are made of."

Galahad squeezed Arthur's arm as Arthur pushed forward, past the prying faerie eyes. Arthur kept his gaze straight forward, his features impassive. He could do this. Claim his birthright. His kingship. The honor was his already. The familiar weight of Excalibur had hung at his hip for years. This sacred blade belonged to him, and he belonged to it.

Arthur balanced across the strange toadstools and took a step onto the boulder. The stone shivered beneath him, and then a deep voice called out, "Whoso pulleth out this sword from this stone shall be king born of all Briton." Arthur's heart raced in his chest at the words. He looked back at Elathia—had the stone's magic been her doing? He could not be certain. She clutched her hands before her chest, a smile on her face as though she were giddy about the day's turn of events.

Anger roared within Arthur once again. It was time to end this. He took a steadying breath and reached for the sword. And— his hands passed right through the pommel.

He lurched forward as the unexpected absence of the sword unbalanced him. He caught himself on the rough rock, sweeping his hand at Excalibur's hilt. His fingers passed straight through the pommel again, as if the sword were a ghost.

"Uh oh, looks like the sword is playing hide and seek," Elathia crooned behind him, giggling. Her faerie court laughed, the sound mocking and harsh to his ears.

He looked back at Galahad and noted how his knight's face had drained of blood. His stomach churning, Arthur turned back to the sword, his anger shifting to fear. A faerie trick. Why had he expected Elathia to fight fair? How could he pull the sword out, if he couldn't even touch it?

Arthur's mind raced for a solution, even as another part of him spun horrible scenarios out like cloth from a loom. Him and Galahad, stuck here indefinitely. Caerleon—a sick and blackened land. Fionna, Lancelot, and Percival, speared on Uí Tuírtri blades. No, gods, this future could not be. But what could he do, when he couldn't even see what was real?

A thought blazed bright and clear through him, and he plunged his hand into his pocket. His fingers closed around the adder stone, Percival's bloody magic rock. Instantly, the scene before him transformed. Excalibur's hilt stuck out from the stone, but a foot behind where he had been reaching. She had cast a simple glamor over the stone, making it look as if she had plunged Excalibur into the stone somewhere else.

Arthur smiled grimly as he reached out and seized the real sword's hilt. And began to pull.

Chapter Thirteen

Percival

A knock echoed against Percival's chamber door, and he flew across the wooden floor. He paused for a moment with his hand on the iron ring handle, taking a deep breath to steady himself. He pulled the door open, schooling his face into what he hoped was an expression of suave nonchalance. "Come in, lass."

Fionna strode into the room like she owned the place, spinning on her heel to face him. When she saw him, a burst of laughter escaped her rosy lips. "What are ye wearing?"

Percival looked down at himself, at the black tunic and dark breeches he had donned. "What? Are we not infiltrating an enemy camp? I wanted to look the part."

She crossed her arms before her. "Ye know it's near high noon. Don't you think someone might get a wee bit suspicious if you walk out into the sunshine like yer off to the god of the Underworld's own funeral? Change."

Percival's cheeks heated, but he covered his embarrassment with a grin. "Lass, if ye wanted to get me naked, there was no need to come up with such a contrivance. Ye need only ask, ye ken?"

Now it was her turn to flush. "We don't know how long Arthur and Galahad will be gone." She strode to the window, turning her back to provide him privacy. "We must be quick."

"Understood," Percival said, unbuckling his sword belt and pulling off his tunic. He grabbed another from the chest at the end of his bed, one boasting a deep green hue, and then pulled the garment over his head. He caught Fionna's silver eyes, peering over her shoulder, before she whipped her gaze back toward the window. He hardened at the reality of her—here in his room. "Why dove," he crossed to stand beside her, brushing a few of her braids over her shoulder. "Did I catch ye peeking?"

"I don't know what yer talking about," she said, though her neck arched as if she appreciated the soft brush of his fingers on her neck. "My eyes are firmly affixed on our task. We must find the enemy camp and acquaint ourselves with its layout."

"So, we can rescue yer father," Percival finished.

She nodded, her lush lips set in a thin line of determination.

"Fionna, ye know what we attempt is likely a dangerous folly that could get one or both of us killed. If the others discovered our—"

"Which is why they won't," Fionna said. "Not until we return with my father safely in hand. And the answers he holds. I know what Arthur would say . . . Lancelot . . . it's why I only trust ye with this."

"I will do everything in my power to prove that trust is not misplaced." He nodded. "Lead the way, My Lady."

Their clandestine mission painted the palace in a new light. Every servant they passed made his heart leap into his chest, as if they could see his very thoughts, discern his secret purpose. "I feel as if I might jump out of my own skin at the slightest surprise," Percival murmured. "Is this what it was like for ye those first days, when ye were set upon your mission to take Excalibur?"

"This, and a thousand times worse," she replied. "I only hope that I see the chance to drive my sword through O'Lynn's gut before this is all done."

"Och, I hope ye get that chance too," Percival said, as they crossed the open space to the stable. And caught sight of Lancelot coming toward them. "Dark and stormy, headed our way," Percival murmured.

"Curses," Fionna muttered, though she arranged her features

in greeting.

Something had shifted in Lancelot, and though the change was subtle, Percival knew his sword-brother's moods and mannerisms well enough to recognize the difference. The tense shadow that had draped over him since Morgana had lifted. Once again, his eyes were bright and sharp, his chiseled profile held high. He wore a tunic as blue as the sky, the neckline unlaced to reveal the lean muscle there, the pattern of ink across his skin that longed to be traced by gentle fingertips. And skies above, he wanted to explore those dark swirls and patterns. Percival swallowed and brought his mind back to the present. Lancelot was a cursed man no more. Arthur's proud second-in-command had returned to them, and just in time.

"You look as if you're heading somewhere." Lancelot stopped before them, his keen eyes locked onto Fionna. "Out of the keep?"

Percival looked to Fionna, for the lie that would roll smoothly off her tongue. But she seemed at a loss for words. "We—" she managed, clearing her throat.

Percival jumped in, his mind whirring. "Fionna wanted to take Zephyr for a short ride. To . . . test her leg. I thought to accompany her. We're, um, going to inspect the wall, to ensure there are no areas ripe for a breach."

Lancelot's gaze flit back and forth between them. "Wise idea," he finally said, slowly drawing out the words. "We haven't inspected the wall yet. Be careful though. Reports put O'Lynn's men on our southern shore, perhaps less than an hour's ride. There could be scouts."

"We'll be watchful," Fionna said, a grim smile on her lips.

"See me when you return," Lancelot said. "Some of the men who have come in from the villages are willing to fight. I could use your aid in outfitting them as well as putting them through a few rounds of basic training."

"Of course," Percival said brightly, pulling Fionna past. "We're at yer disposal."

Lancelot arched an eyebrow but let them pass.

"Och dove, I thought ye were a better liar than that," Percival whispered.

She shook her head wearily. "I've had enough lies for a lifetime. I think they're all spent."

"Ye'll have little need of them when this is all done."

"I hope yer right."

Percival and Fionna rode through the blighted countryside in silence, tense and alert. Lancelot's warning was fair. Caerleon wasn't safe anymore. There could be enemies at any turn. As they rode closer to the gray waters of the Severn Sea, Percival felt as if a hand seized his chest, squeezing tighter with each step. Surely, they were upon the invaders by now.

Fionna reigned in Zephyr, looking ahead with a peculiar expression. A grassy hill topped with a thicket of trees arose to the left, and the road curved around the slope, disappearing into the distance. She nodded up to the left. "We should have a good vantage point from up there. Let us get off the road and see if we can spot the enemy."

Percival wasted no time directing Kit with his knees to head up the hill. "I feel something," Percival said. "Perhaps it's my imagination, but it's . . . cloying. Almost a strange thickness in the air too."

Fionna nodded. "I feel it too. It feels like—"

"Magic," they said together, sharing a disquieted look.

They trekked around the shadowed-side of the hill, to avoid being spotted. Once arriving at the hill's backside, they walked into overgrown trees and across a blanket of thick ferns and mossy ground. A scattering of trees showed blackened signs of the curse's blight, but mostly they were surrounded by greenery.

"Let's dismount and leave the horses here," Fionna said. "I don't want a stray whinny alerting anyone to our position. The horses should be well-hidden."

Percival nodded and dismounted. They tied their horses to a tree and crept toward the front edge of the hill. Toward a view he had hoped never to see on Caerleon's fair lands. An invading army.

From the shadow of the canopy, the O'Lynn camp was stretched out before them. Hundreds of tents hugged the circumference of a small port town, one that looked overtaken by the enemy. Flags of blue and yellow with a snarling wolf fluttered in the breeze.

Fionna growled beside him, as though she were ready to surge down the hill, sword bared.

"Patience, dove. We must be smart about this. Now, do ye have any idea where yer father might be held?" Looking down below, their task suddenly seemed even more of a fool's errand. To bumble about amongst thousands of hostile warriors, searching for one man . . .

"O'Lynn is a warrior," Fionna said. "But he likes his comfort. He has injuries that pain him. He will have taken up residence in the grandest home in the village."

"The inn then," Percival said, gesturing at a three-story timbered building perched below. "Full larder, warm fire, comfy beds."

"He would keep his prisoners close by. Would a town like this have a gaol?"

Percival shook his head. "Nae. Only the stocks here."

"Then, he would keep him somewhere easily closed off. Out of the way."

Percival wracked his brain. "Like a cellar?"

Fionna's eyes lit up. "Would there be a cellar beneath the inn?"

"Aye."

"The cellar beneath the inn, then. That's where we'll find my father."

It seemed a thin thread indeed to stake their lives on. "Fionna—" he began.

"Let's head back to the horses," she said, striding into the trees.

He followed. "I know he's yer father . . . but if we defeat O'Lynn, we'll free him soon enough. Perhaps we should wait."

"Ye heard what Vivien shared. My father may be the only one with answers about my mother. Whether . . ." she trailed off.

"Whether ye are borne of a goddess," Percival finished.

She gave a curt nod. "If I truly have some power, then we may need my magic to defeat O'Lynn and Morgana. We can't wait."

"I ken, lass. But to walk into the middle of an enemy camp—" Zephyr and Kit whickered in greeting as they emerged back into the clearing where they had left them.

Fionna rounded on him, her face a twist of emotions. "I shouldn't have asked this of ye, Percy. I took advantage of yer feelings for me, for I knew ye wouldn't say no. But I can't ask ye to risk yerself. Ye should go back to Caerleon. I'll do this alone."

Percival stepped in closer, taking her face gently between his hands. "If ye think that the only reason I'm here is because ye tricked me, then ye ken me less than I thought. And if ye think I could leave ye here to go in alone . . . well, then ye don't ken me at all."

She tried to look down, but he held her face gently, tilting her chin back so she was forced to meet his eyes. "I am here, dove, because yer cause is just, *and* because I love ye. Ye don't have to carry these burdens alone anymore. I will help ye find the truth of yer past, just as ye helped me find mine."

Her chin quivered as she pressed her lips together. She closed her eyes, her white eyelashes brushing her soft cheeks. "I don't know how to thank ye," Fionna eventually said. And then her eyes snapped opened, and a different light glowed in them—a gleam he had seen only once before. "That's not true. I do know how to thank ye."

Then she surged against him and pressed her lips to his. A crow startled into flight from a branch above them—the last thing he saw before losing himself completely to her kiss.

Interlude

Morgana

The crow glided over the forest surrounding Caerleon, wings aloft with giddiness over finding a male and female who belonged to the Little Dragon King. Alone.

Just over the crest of maples, birch, and evergreens, an encampment came into view. Hide tents surrounded a small village. Smoke curled from thatched, lime-washed homes as well as from the inn and several fire circles dotting the premises. In the distance, longboats moored up the banks of the River Usk and against Caerleon's coastline along the Severin Sea.

Landing between a cluster of ferns and a moss-draped tree, the crow called upon the shadows of the forest and the blood-thirsty prayers of the nearby warmongers. Leaves and fallen lichen swirled around her until her female form materialized beneath a canopy of sun-dappled green maples. She then eased from the forest's edge and into the encampment. Dirt and sea grimed warriors—men and women both—stopped what they were doing to watch her swaying body walk past. Her skin fairly glowed in the pale sunlight, her face and clothing unblemished from travel or camp set-up.

The guard before O'Lynn's tent moved to block Morgana, but only for half a heartbeat. Bowing his head, he stepped aside and allowed her to enter. Incense wafted to her nose as she stepped through the flaps and into the lantern lit space. In the corner, the older man glanced up from where he sliced an apple from a crudely made corner table beside his cot. A cot occupied by the Allán waif, Aideen. Dark circles bruised her seasick gaze and Morgana smiled.

"Feeding your pet?" she asked O'Lynn.

"She must earn her food," he muttered under his breath as he went back to slicing a chunk of apple. "So far, the lass continues to displease me."

"Poor man," Morgana cooed. "I bear news that will surely please you."

At that, he looked up and arched an eyebrow. "Do ye now?"

"The witch is just over the hill with that Fisher whelp."

The younger woman gasped before she whispered, "Fionnabhair . . ."

"Yes," Morgana hissed, drawing out the sound. "Your sister is in the woods with a young lover. Did you honestly believe she would come and rescue you?" Morgana laughed low in her throat. "Poor lamb. Your hope is a foolish waste of the energy you barely can spare. Especially as your name is not the one leaving your sister's mouth in a breathless gasp right now."

O'Lynn pushed from his chair, throwing Aideen a glare, before marching to the tent's opening. When alone, Morgan sat on the edge of the cot and tilted her head. "He is a beautiful lad, the Fisher King. Copper hair, dark earthen eyes framed by long lashes, a boyish smile, and a fine, muscular body. Just two years older than you, I believe. And he loves her. The stench of his pheromones perfumed the trees and moss." Aideen turned her head toward the tent's wall, blinking back the forming tears. "And she fancies herself in love with him too. All of them. Including the abomination of a king, Arthur Pendragon. All this emotion, all this falling in love while you waste away beneath the hateful hand of your husband."

"Lies," Aideen spat. "All ye speak are lies."

"Then why do you cry?" Morgana arched to a stand, satisfied with the girl's roiling pulse and seething breaths.

O'Lynn stomped into the tent with a handsome man at his side. "This is Níall, one of my finest warriors. He'll take one of my fiercest fianna to kill her."

Morgana flashed a delighted glance at Aideen's teeth-bared expression as the girl strained against her chains in fury, and then she gracefully slinked toward Níall, examining the warrior. "The witch is a capable warrior," she said to O'Lynn. "Sending a fiann crashing through the forest will only serve to alert her and send her scampering back into the safety of Caerleon's keep. He should go alone. Or perhaps with one other." To the warrior, she said, "Come upon her quickly and with stealth, while she is otherwise engaged. This is how you shall end her."

"Very well," O'Lynn said grudgingly. His obedience training was coming along nicely. "Tell him exactly where ye last saw the witch and he'll run her through and then dump her carcass before King Arthur's gates."

"Follow the crow, she will guide you."

Chapter Fourteen

Fionna

Sunshine poured into my body as Percival tugged me closer, deepening his kiss. His warmth permeated every part of me with a bubbling urge to frolic and tease and laugh. But instead, my body yielded completely to the dancing rhythm of his lips and the gentle hands that roamed my back.

Until he lost his balance and jerked out of our embrace.

I yelped as he fell into a bush only to laugh a heartbeat later when Kit nodded his head up and down before nickering his displeasure. Percival's horse nudged him through the leafy boughs with his nose, stamping an impatient hoof.

"Aye, I see ye. Dinna fash yerself." Percival brushed dead leaves and twigs from his breeches and hair as he climbed out of the underbrush. Kit nickered again, and Percival rolled his eyes. "Ye know ye're the only one for me." Percival blocked Kit's view with a hand and then winked at me. I bit my bottom lip to stifle my snicker. "Here," he cooed and offered up an apple from his saddle bag. Kit lipped the apple, then wuffed at Percival's cheek, before taking the apple from his hand, turning his attention to his treat.

"The stallion fancies ye," I taunted in a sing-song voice. "A jealous male, if ever I saw one."

"A wee too leggy for my taste." Percival flashed me a cheeky grin. "Smothering hen too. A lad needs his freedom."

"Leggy?" I pretended to be outraged. "With such criticisms, I wonder what ye must think of me."

Percival stepped close—a good head taller than me, no less—and narrowed his eyes as he slowly inspected my legs, arms, torso, and face. "Open yer mouth and show me yer teeth." Not expecting this request, my mouth parted in shock and Percival's lips twitched. "A little wider. Cannae see the back."

Realizing my mouth was agape, I clamped my jaw shut and then smacked him across the upper arm. "Ye brute!" His laughter filled the woods around us and my heart soared at the rascally sound. Still, I placed fisted hands on my hips and glared at him. But he laughed only more. So, I picked up a handful of leaves from the forest floor and threw them at his face.

A leaf fluttered directly into his mouth, to my wicked delight. He sputtered, spitting brittle pieces out while batting at the others hitting his face, hair, and chest.

Now I laughed. "Yer lucky I didn't knock ye back onto yer sorry arse."

"Och, ye'll pay for this, dove," he declared, then pounced at me.

I spun away with a shriek, but not fast enough. He grabbed my arm and pulled me to him until his mouth collided with mine in a triumphant kiss. Gods, his lips. They were Otherworldly and full of impish magic. But I couldn't give into his attempts at distraction, even if his very touch was bliss. Which encouraged an idea. A plan that would be too easy, for I knew he felt the same as me. And, as expected, he deepened his luscious kiss and melted against my body, just enough that I could place my leg between his and then kick his heel out from underneath him. Percival's arms flew out in surprise, a waterfall of leaves splashing into the air as he landed with a satisfying *thwump*.

And then I ran.

I charged into the forest, ripping through ferns and undergrowth, unable to contain my glee. But I didn't get far. Percival hooked me around the waist and yanked me to a stop. An embarrassingly girlish squeal escaped me as we tumbled to the ground in a fit of laughter, his body settling atop mine.

Silken, copper strands curtained around my face as our mirth faded into soft smiles. His dark brown eyes crinkling with affection. My fingertips tracing along his jaw and then across his bottom lip. My chest heaved for breath and I wanted to moan with the arousing feel of my hardened nipples brushing against my chestplate. Memories of his stomach muscles, limned in candlelight, and the way he stroked himself as Galahad pleasured me teased my growing need.

Part of me knew this was foolish to give in to our carnal urges at this moment—that we were exposed here, so close to our enemy's camp. But the wood was thick and gnarled, and I felt safe here, with the tall trees standing sentinel over us. We had seen no signs of Uí Tuírtri scouts coming this way while we watched the camp. And we had hours left until dark. I could think of no better way to pass the time.

So, I tucked strands of chin-length hair behind his ear, then kissed him. Long. Slow. Every sensation languorous and yearning.

Pulling away, he caught his breath and whispered, "I ache for ye."

"Make me yers," I whispered back.

A crooked smile flitted across his lips. "Why did we wear so much armor?"

"Protection against me, of course."

"Aye, ye weaken me senseless."

"Let's remedy that."

"My weakness for ye?"

"No," I said with a roll of my eyes. "The armor."

From my position beneath him, I began unfastening his leather chest piece. Then I unlaced the bracers tightened at each wrist. I ran my fingers along his well-sculpted arm—an archer's forearm—calling back images of him on horseback while shooting from his longbow, his burnished hair tossed about in the wind. Heat kindled in my belly at the feel of his hardened body. Slowly, I moved up his abdomen and pectorals to his collarbone, where I unclasped the leather armor around his neck.

I would be his first, the one to awaken his body to a form of pleasure unlike any other. A part of me wanted to roll him over to gain control. To ride him until his every muscle tensed and shuddered with release. Until he moaned and clawed at the dirt and painted my bare skin with the earth stained on his fingertips. But this moment was his to control, his to navigate and discover. And mine to enjoy. For he chose me, and I would not disappoint the man who gifted me with his laughter and his heart.

His innocence.

He smiled sweetly, dipping down for a kiss. "I've waited my whole life for ye. I would search for the Grail and fight monsters all over again, just to prove myself worthy of yer love."

"Percy . . ." My heart clenched at his confession. "Ye have always been worthy of my love. There is naught to earn, ye silly goose."

"Sure, but I'm not made of tree trunks like Galahad or an experienced lover like Lancelot or as dreamy as Arthur."

"Dreamy?"

He quietly laughed. "Ye think he is, admit it."

"Sir Percival of Caer Benic, Fisher King and Grail Prince, the only matter I'll discuss right now is how much I fancy ye." I tried to hold a straight face, my voice even as I added, "Which is unmeasurably more than Kit."

"I dunno," he replied, a silly grin in place. "We have history."

"Kit has good taste in men. For a horse."

"He doesn't like to share my attentions."

I arched an eyebrow and flirtatiously whispered, "I would share ye. Perhaps, next time, I'll roll on the forest floor with ye and Lancelot together."

Percival shivered, his eyes shuttering for a wild heartbeat as his hand traveled southward to the bulge pressing against the laces of his breeches. "Och, I might end before we begin, if ye keep up this talk."

"Then no more talk."

I placed my hand over his, massaging his cock by moving his fingers over his own body. He moaned, increasing the friction. With my other hand, I cupped his hip and dragged him back and forth against my sex, pressing his hardening length to our joined hands. Long copper lashes brushed along his cheeks as more soft moans escaped his mouth. Unable to take my eyes off every flutter of pleasure coloring his face, I slipped my fingers beneath his and then gently stroked up and down his throbbing cock. His eyes snapped open, his breath hitching. This was the first time someone had touched him in this way. And I wanted nothing but the feel of skin and sweat and pleasure-laden breaths between us.

But I was still in armor.

Removing my hand, I began unfastening my chestplate. At first, he frowned until he saw what I was doing and then he began to help. In a matter of minutes, we had both undressed, reveling in the feel of each other's nakedness.

I sighed and sank into the feathery moss as Percival explored the curves of my breasts. Goddess save me, his lips—full, soft, and playful. Made for kissing. My pulse trilled when his mouth met mine once more, his kiss gently reverent yet gloriously fevered.

I had never longed for a man like him before, one who was as seductive as he was boyishly innocent. But he had captivated me from first sight, his masculine beauty the kind that made maidens jealous and men take notice. And men did, often. I had caught Lancelot shooting dark, possessive glares at several interested men during our travels. Percival, as usual, was unaware of his own bewitching attractiveness, or how his magnetism drew people to him. His guileless affect only added to his allure.

Arthur, Galahad, and Lancelot were intense lovers—emotional and serious, always. Intimacy was more a race to release the building energy between our attraction. But, with Percival, my body felt young and untouched. As though this was also my first time with a man. Every breath, every caress, every soft, enthralling sound of pleasure, was filled with wonder and beauty, as if I were falling in love with him all over again. And again. Losing myself to an endless cycle of discovery and reverie.

My heart halted a beat.

I loved Percival. *Loved* him, truly, and had for a long time, I realized. From the beginning, he has been my champion and my haven. I could talk to him about anything and he always provided the words and humor and acceptance I needed to remain strong. Nor has he ever felt intimidated by my sex or my battle prowess, unlike the other men. Rather, he was almost always the first to offer his support and forgiveness.

A sob tightened my throat as joy warmed my chest. What did I ever do to deserve such a man? Tears threatened to spill, but I pushed them back by smiling into our kiss.

"What, lass?" he asked, smiling back, caressing my cheek.

"Ye make me so happy," I whispered. "I love ye, Percy."

He kissed me sweetly. "I love ye too. Until my dying breath." His words bolstered me, filling me with tangible relief. The necklace was gone, but Percival's love remained. His love, too—like Lancelot's—had been true.

I gripped his hip tighter, lifting my thighs off the ground to deepen the sensations from our rocking rhythm. His head fell back with a rumbling moan. I could watch him savor every delicious sensation forever. And I longed to memorize the aroused, soft look of him when his body joined mine.

Releasing his hip, my hand tugged on his cock, my palm sliding up and down his velvety shaft. Skies, he was long. And hard. His Adam's apple bobbed and a hot, heaving breath rushed from his body. The muscles across his chest and shoulders rippled and his stomach flexed. The heat of anticipation curled through me as I guided him to my opening.

Percival pushed in slowly, gasping for breath. Pleasure tensed every muscle in his face, a rosy hue warming his neck and cheeks. With mouth parted, lips swollen, and every muscle tight with need, his hips began to move. Unsure at first, but then he found a rhythm and I moaned with the wondrous feel of him.

"Gods," he breathed.

His eyes pinched shut as he thrust harder, his hips rolling in the most erotic grinding motion I had ever felt. A move that liquified the blazing heat in my core. I felt as though magic swirled in my veins each time we joined. The feeling was so incredibly intense, I sank my fingers into the loamy soil beneath my body just to ground myself. The landscape of muscles across his blushed body tensed into defined lines as his shaft slid in and out, the soft skin and fiery curls of his pelvis rubbing along my clit with each smooth, sensual pumping motion.

The earth cradled my floating body. Vibrations tingled across the skin pressed into the moss, ferns, and leaves. Percival increased his rocking motions, the thighs touching mine flexing with each thrusting arc of his narrow hips. I explored the undulating ribbed muscles of his stomach as he ground into me—deep, hard—his balls slapping my sensitive skin, my swollen clit groaning with each caress. I grabbed his arse with both hands and dragged him harder across my pelvis until a lance of pleasure arrested the wild beat of my heart. I felt myself shattering into a million scintillating beams of light. I wanted to keep shattering until I was nothing but glittering ash.

Tilting my hips and spreading my legs wider, my fingernails digging into his soft flesh, I pulled him tight to me and held him there. I became rippling, spasming sensation. My core tightened around the length of him until his thick, hard body ignited my every nerve ending.

The ground began to gently tremor. I cried out as a soft rush of energy surged through me, my body becoming all the elements, the moon and stars, and the sun's golden fire.

"Oh gods," he moaned loudly. "Oh gods, oh gods . . ." His body stiffened despite the desperate, crazed rhythm of his pounding hips. Goddess, the way he moved. He was sensual grace and erotic bliss. His frenzied moans faded into breathy grunts until he cried out, "Fuck!" Followed by, "Foos yer doos!"

I almost orgasmed again, watching him peak. He was mesmerizing.

Wait.

I stilled, my brows furrowing as I pushed up on my elbows. "Foos yer doos?"

His eyes opened on an embarrassed smile, his cheeks reddening. "Uh, aye," he said, nodding his head comically, as though his awkward slip was intentional. "It means, 'how are yer pigeons.' In Doric, that is. It's the Gaelic language we speak where I'm from. Our way of asking, 'how are ye?'"

I stared at him for one more confused heartbeat before falling back to the moss in a fit of laughter. "My pigeons are cooing at present. Ye've made them quite happy." I laughed again, unable to help myself. "Foos yer doos?"

A silly, lopsided grin stretched across his handsome face. "Aye, peck'n away, peck'n away." Then he rolled his hips once more, before flashing another cheeky grin.

"Kiss me, ye fool man."

"Anything ye want, dove."

His lips returned to mine, both of us trying to hold back our sputtering laughter.

And then I heard a human sound nearby. A throat cleared, and I stilled. "Don't move," a man with a gravelly voice said in Gaelic—Irish Gaelic.

Chapter Fifteen

Fionna

Percival's head snapped up from where he was kissing my breasts. His eyes rounded as the tip of the man's blade came to rest just below Percival's Adam's apple.

My eyes darted to-and-fro, surveying the scene quickly. The man with the gravelly voice was as tall as Percival, and well-muscled, with dark brown hair braided down his back. Though he wore a thick beard, he was young. Younger than I. And quite convinced of his superiority, his immortality. He would be impetuous. Stupid and cocky. Another warrior circled us too, perhaps ten years older than me.

I grabbed the edge of my cloak and pulled the wool over my naked form as best as I could, not wishing to give these men—these Uí Tuírtri warriors—any more sight of me than they had already enjoyed. Which appeared, from the one man's lewd grin, and the other's quiet intensity, was everything.

"Enjoying the afternoon, were ye?" the other said. His voice was as low and quiet as his placid features, but his tone held a hint of mockery. Fairer than his companion, twisting tattoos ran up arms that were lean with muscle and sinew. His dark brown leather armor was well-cared and oiled, but the nicks showed how he had seen many battles. Bright blue eyes examined each of us, picking us apart piece by piece. Goosebumps rose on my skin as he watched me. A hunter, catching the scent of prey. Here was the more dangerous man of the two.

Our weapons were beyond arm's reach, buried beneath the hastily discarded pile of our clothes and armor. I could get to my sword, but not before the man speared Percival through. What idiots we had been, utter and complete fools! To get so wrapped up in each other when Uí Tuírtri camped mere leagues away. I wanted to rail at the tall trees—at the forest creatures—for not warning us. But I knew it was no one's fault but my own.

"My lady and I were enjoying a private retreat in the country," Percival said, his voice managing to sound imperious, regal. Like a king.

I wanted to cringe, to tell him that nobility would only get him speared more quickly here. Better to be common, low born. Beneath notice. Though, without clothes on, we were unrecognizable—perhaps the only blessing of being found naked by enemy soldiers. I prayed this small silver lining at least bought us a few moments before they spotted my Dál nAraidi armor and the birch tree ogham rune of clann Allán etched into my sword's hilt.

"Methinks your fair lady is in need of more of a man than ye." The younger man stepped closer, trailing his blade's edge to rest on the side of Percival's throat while gazing at me.

My hand itched for my sword, for my knives. To crush this man who looked at a woman and saw only a thing to have. To take.

"We have no quarrel with ye," Percival replied in Gaelic, his brown eyes flashing angrily. "But I will not allow ye to mistreat my lady in word or deed."

Gravelly-voice laughed, a cruel, mocking sound. "Hear that Níall? He won't *let us.*"

Percival stiffened at the taunt, and then the other man—Níall—spoke. His words were soft as he stepped forward. "Haven't ye heard? The Uí Tuírtri rule these lands now. Not yer bastard-born king. And we take what we want." His gaze flicked back to me.

Percival growled, his muscled form tense, as if ready to spring.

"Don't feel left out," gravelly-voice said, looking over his shoulder at Níall with a smirk. "Ye're pretty enough. We have some lads back at camp who would love a turn with ye."

The moment the warrior looked away, Percival surged forward. He knocked the warrior's sword aside, barreling into his chest like a storied Greek wrestler.

I scrambled for my blade, the protection of my cloak forgotten. I seized my sword belt and whirled, only to see Níall club Percival over the back of his head with the hilt of his sword.

Percival crumpled in on himself, his strong form now limp.

A sharp gasp escaped from my lips as the younger warrior shoved Percival off him with a roar while jumping back onto his feet. Spitting on the ground beside Percival's body, he pulled his sword from its sheath. And coiled back, preparing to stab Percival through.

"Wait," Níall barked, putting a hand out. The gravelly-voiced warrior lowered his sword slightly, waiting for his superior's instructions.

Níall's eyes were fixed upon me. Upon the sword belt in my hand. Upon my naked form. My skin crawled beneath his assessment, and my rage burned brighter within me.

"Drop the sword belt, princess," Níall cooed. "Ye don't want to hurt yerself." The word buffeted me like a gusting, biting wind. Did this man know who I was? Or was princess merely a term he used to ridicule? Indecision wracked me. I wished for nothing more than the chance to spear these men through. But Percival was unconscious. At their mercy. It would only take one vicious thrust and my sweet Percival would be torn from this world forever. I would endure whatever I must in order to save him.

"Drop yer blade and I will spare him," Níall said, and the decision was made for me, even though I didn't know if I could trust his word. I could only pray that they were too intent upon their sport of claiming me to dispatch him.

I let the leather slip from my clammy fingers. And I kept my face slack, letting him see what he wanted to see. The poor, helpless maiden, ripe for the plucking. Let him be blind to the truth. That even without a blade, I was not helpless.

"Watch him," Níall said, striding toward me. He crossed the distance between us in three strides and then loomed over me. Even knowing myself, knowing my skill, I was momentarily struck still with a sense of vulnerability I had never felt before—being bared before my enemy. My pulse pounded in my ears, drowning out the other clannsman's words, most likely complaints of having to go second.

My hands crept up on their own accord to cover my nakedness, a gesture which only made Níall grin. "Ye are a rare beauty, lass," he said, his eyes glittering. "I shall enjoy ye until my balls are empty. And then again as payment for all my men who were cut down by clann Allán."

When his last word finished, he gripped me, leaving me no time to process his comment. Or that he knew who I was. His hand fisted in my hair, yanking me back down to the earth where Percival and I had just shared the most beautiful gesture of love. Pain bit into my scalp, into my skin where the weight of the warrior settled upon me. The sharp buckles of his armor dug scratches into my body. But I ignored it all: the foul stench of sour ale on his breath, the sea's grime still on his skin, the vile feeling of his rough hands pawing at me. For I was focused on the one point where I knew I would find my salvation.

There was one thing clann Uí Tuírtri and Allán shared, and that was the design of our armor. And the sheaths for our knives. My hand reached around the man as he struggled to unlace his breeches, far too intent upon his task to pay attention to the creature he was about to violate. And so, he moved far too slow to stop me as I grabbed the knife sheathed at his hip, the one I plunged directly into his spine.

He stiffened atop me and, with a scream, I shoved at his bulk, jerking the bloodied knife out with the movement. But he was a hardened Dál nAraidi warrior, and such men don't die easily.

He lunged at me. One large hand closed around my throat while the other clamped around the wrist that held his knife, arresting my movement before I was able to stab the sharp point into his eye.

We grappled, but he was strong. I wheezed in air, struggling to draw breath. Then the hand around my windpipe squeezed even harder. His other hand gripped my wrist until I thought the delicate bones might snap from the pressure. I let out a garbled scream of frustration as the knife dropped from my numb fingers.

"Ye bitch," the other warrior was screaming now.

He thundered toward me, his sword blade gleaming. I tried to wrench my body to the side, but I was unable to move much. The older warrior held me fast and sure. *Oh goddess.* The darkness of unconsciousness began to claim me. I wasn't going to be able to fight my way out of this situation. And, this time, there was no pregnant pause giving me a chance to consider my life, my choices. Or the men I loved who I would leave behind. There was only one quicksilver realization—I was going to die.

But . . . I didn't feel the sword pierce me through. Not when I expected it. Instead, the sound of blades clashing met my ears. My attacker—distracted by whatever new challenge had presented itself and weakened from my inflicted wound—loosened his grip on me. In a vicious blow, I twisted my arm up and brought my elbow down onto the forearm holding my throat. His grip on my burning throat broke. I gasped large breaths of precious air, trying not to grimace with pain.

Without wasting another beat of my still-living heart, I lunged toward my sword. My hand closed around its hilt, the supple leather in my palm as welcome a feeling as I had ever known. I pulled my blade from its hilt and, with a smooth, powerful arc, severed Níall's head from his shoulders.

Instinct had my sword up before me and my body crouched in a defensive position, even as my mind tried to catch up with what had happened. My eyes locked onto the younger Uí Tuírtri warrior, now slumping to the ground. Dead.

And then I focused on the blessed vision of Lancelot standing behind him, sweat dripping down his face, bloody sword in hand.

Chapter Sixteen

Lancelot

Lancelot's chest heaved as he surveyed the scene before him—his mind barely able to comprehend the horror. How close he had come to losing Fionna. Percival.

"Percival," Fionna cried out, running to the young knight's prone form, caring little for her nakedness.

"What happened?" Lancelot leaned down to wipe the blood from his sword on a patch of moss.

She gently rolled Percival onto his back. The copper-haired knight moaned. Fionna deflated in relief and scrubbed at her face with shaking hands, before murmuring, "The Uí Tuírtri caught us unaware."

"I can see that," Lancelot snapped.

He sheathed his sword and then knelt next to Percival, probing gently at the clot of blood that was forming on his temple. One of the warriors must have hit him with something blunt. The wound didn't look too bad. Percival was already stirring. Good. Because now he could level both to the ground for their foolishness.

"The real question is," he began, "what in the bloody hell were you two doing out here?"

"We came to rescue my father." She raised her chin a notch.

"Naked?" Lancelot shot back.

"We . . . had some time to kill." She dropped her gaze to a cluster of ferns near her bare foot, crossing her arms beneath her supple breasts. It took all of Lancelot's focus to keep his attention on the lecture she deserved, rather than the beauty of her lean form.

"So, you thought you would just enjoy yourselves, here within a stone's throw of the might of Morgana's and O'Lynn's invading army? My gods Fionna, you're smarter than this. I would expect this idiocy from a green warrior, but not seasoned ones like you and Percival."

Heat suffused her face. "The Grail Quest is over . . ."

Lancelot's anger softened ever so much at that. Of course, a virile young man like Percival would be eager to take advantage of his new-found freedom.

She narrowed her eyes to slits. "I don't need this from ye," she hissed, pushing to her feet. "It's not like ye've never made a mistake."

"I paid for my mistakes." Lancelot followed her while she gathered up her clothes, her armor. "I pay for them still."

"So did we." Fionna dramatically motioned at Percival, and a shadow crossed over her face that gave Lancelot pause. He looked back at the two corpses, then Fionna, who now stalked behind a tree with a bundle of clothes and boots and armor in hand. "They didn't—" he cut himself off. Burning anger filled him at the very thought of those unclean animals defiling their Fionna. His Fionna.

She turned from the copse of trees. "No." Her voice was hard. "But not for lack of trying."

Percival groaned and Lancelot turned back to him, grateful for the distraction. He couldn't bear the thought of what the Uí Tuítri had tried to do to her. What they might have done if Lancelot hadn't trusted his gut and followed after Fionna and Percival's hoofprints.

Lancelot knelt at Percival's side as his sword-brother's eyes began to flutter open. His copper lashes were long and as soft as silk, dusting the sun-kissed apples of his cheeks. Percival's muscled body was stretched out before him, and though Lancelot shoved the thought to the back of his mind, a part of him appreciated what a fine body it was. Full of the coiled energy of youth and health.

Percival sat up with a curse and then groaned again, his hand flying to his injured temple. "Fionna," Percival cried out, his eyes wild and unfocused while attempting to surge up to his feet.

"Easy." Lancelot grabbed Percival's shoulder to hold him down gently but firmly. "She's safe. The men are gone."

"They were going—" Percival sucked in a sharp breath, unable to finish, seemingly lost in the horrible moment.

"It's okay. We stopped them. They're dead."

Percival looked at him, his eyes clearing as he registered Lancelot's presence. "Crabapple? How are ye here?"

Lancelot's mouth twisted in a smile at the name. What had once infuriated him, he was coming to regard with . . . fondness?

"Something struck me as off about your and Fionna's explanation. I had a bad feeling. I went to find you beside the wall, and you were nowhere to be found. I followed your tracks."

Percival sprang at Lancelot, pulling him into a crushing embrace. "Thank ye, Lancelot. If you hadn't followed . . ." The words were choked.

Despite his surprise, he wrapped his arms around Percival's strong back, gently rubbing a circle between his shoulder blades. Percival's skin flushed with heat beneath his touch. "It's all right. All is well."

Percival clung to him for a moment longer, before pulling back slowly. But he lingered, leaning his forehead against Lancelot's with a heavy sigh, one hand pressed to Lancelot's chest.

Lancelot's own hand settled behind Percival's neck, tangled in the soft strands of his hair. He had known other men before. But he had never yearned for another man like he desired Percival. A man who owned his heart. A man he never once believed could be his, even though he flirted and teased. And, for years, a man whom Lancelot secretly ached to touch in this way.

The moment on the stairs at the Castle of Maidens rushed back to him, and his pulse quickened. Heady with the enchanted feast, and silly with wine, he had kissed Percival. It had seemed a moment of levity at the time, silliness. They were all growing so close, their lives and stories becoming more intertwined by the day. But now, with Percival's sweet citrus smell washing over him, their lips mere inches apart . . .

"You have to be more careful," Lancelot whispered hoarsely. "Arthur would never forgive me, if I let anything happen to you."

Percival looked up then, his brown eyes filled with something that Lancelot thought he recognized as disappointment. "Right. Arthur," Percival said. He touched his wound and winced, before examining the blood on his fingertips.

"Not . . . just Arthur," Lancelot choked out, looking away.

"What do ye mean?" Percival whispered back.

"I would miss you Percival." Lancelot swallowed thickly, his breath coming in quick. Fionna had helped him pull down the walls used to shield his heart, and the remnants were still crumbling. No more running. No more hiding. "You bring light into the shadows of my life. Your jokes, and your stupid nicknames, your smile and laugh . . . they warm me."

Percival reached out a trembling hand and tilted Lancelot's chin, forcing Lancelot to meet his eyes. "I still remember the first moment I saw ye and Arthur ride into the forest, where I lived with my mother. The first time I had seen men in years. Arthur was majestic on his horse, every bit a king. But it was ye I couldn't take my eyes away from. I still can't."

Lancelot smiled. "I remember. You were so . . . *beautiful.* Gangly as hell, but you've always been the most beautiful man I know."

Percival laid his hand against Lancelot's breastplate. Warmth filled Lancelot's chest, radiating out from where Percival touched him. The gesture was an invitation—one which Lancelot wasn't going to squander, despite the lecture he had just given Fionna. Lancelot closed the gap between them.

Their mouths touched tentatively at first—curious and light. But a kindling spark quickly caught flame and the roar of heat blazed hot between them. Percival mouth was warm and sweet, his tongue soft as velvet. Unable to help himself, Lancelot tugged Percival closer until their chests pressed together. The younger man moaned. A sound that aroused Lancelot instantly, the hardening bulge in his breeches growing even tighter. Percival's hands moved up Lancelot's chest to cup his face. Percival's thumb traced along his cheekbone, his jaw, softly brushing along his stubble.

The forest was fading from Lancelot's awareness. All he knew was their tongues intertwined, their mouths moving in a fevered rhythm, their breaths mixing, their bodies caressing each other's in delicious strokes. And, in this stolen moment, Lancelot swore that Percival's heartbeat galloped in tandem beside his own trembling pulse.

A gentle, feminine throat-clearing sounded behind them, and Lancelot pulled back, more than a little reluctantly. Percival peered up at Fionna with a silly grin, his eyes almost sleepy.

"Ye appear to be well, Percy," Fionna said, a hint of a smile brightening her otherwise stoic expression. She stood, clothed and armored once more, a few feet from them.

"Aye, I will be," Percival replied. "My head is pounding, but Lancelot relieved my discomfort fer a spell. He's better than bitter willow bark tea."

Lancelot arched a humored eyebrow. "You may sip from my cup any time you wish."

Percival coughed, and then pushed to his feet, suddenly shy. "I should dress." As he stood, Lancelot took in his beautiful body, including the cock as hard and as throbbing as his own. Then, with a look that seemed to say that what had started in this grove would be continued—Percival grabbed his things and began dressing.

Lancelot pretended to inspect the surrounding woods, feeling a bit sheepish as he said to Fionna, "We need to get the hell out of here. We don't know when O'Lynn plans to move."

"Not until morning, surely," Fionna said. "And we can't leave yet. We haven't rescued my father."

Lancelot eyes rounded slowly, incredulity dawning. "Surely you're not still intent upon that mad plan."

Fionna stiffened. "I wasn't aware saving a king of Tara and one of the only two family members I have left in this world was mad. If we retrieve him, we'll manage to remove one of O'Lynn's major bargaining chips."

"It's too dangerous." Lancelot arched an eyebrow. "That army is two thousand strong. And we don't even know where they're keeping him."

"We have a strong suspicion." Percival had his pants and boots on now and was pulling his tunic over his head. "And Fionna knows how they organize their camps and keep watch. We'll be in and out like ghosts."

"No . . ." Lancelot drawled the word out, long and slow. He couldn't believe how they persisted in carrying out such a dangerous task. "Caerleon needs you back in the keep. Arthur does. *Your King*. What happens if our king comes back and finds you two captured? Talk about handing O'Lynn a bargaining chip!"

"Then we won't get captured," Fionna said.

"I forbid it, soldier," Lancelot snapped.

"Good thing no one asked you," Fionna shot back, squaring her stance to face his.

Lancelot took a step toward Fionna and leaned in close to her face. "I am second-in-command of the knights of Caerleon. And you are a knight of Caerleon, last I checked. Unless you betrayed our king *again* while I wasn't looking."

Percival winced at that, and Fionna narrowed her eyes to slits.

Lancelot knew as soon as the comment escaped his lips that it was a bridge too far. But why couldn't she understand? He had just witnessed her near-violation and murder by two foul Irishmen! And now she wanted to walk into a camp of *thousands*?

Percival finished buckling on his sword belt. "Perhaps this isn't the best place for a shouting match."

"Agreed. We go back to the keep," Lancelot gritted out.

"I'm not going," Fionna said, her grit matching his. "I feel him within my reach. I'm not giving up on my father."

Lancelot closed his eyes, willing patience. How to convince her? How to make her see sense? Why was it even so important to her? He understood that he might not have the closest connection to family, and of course she worried for her father, but he had been a prisoner for months. Why now? Fionna was normally so pragmatic. He breathed out slowly. He didn't want to fight with her anymore. He didn't want that to be their relationship.

"Why . . . why is this so important to you?"

Fionna and Percival exchanged a glance.

She took in a deep breath and let it out slowly. "Because of what Merlin and Vivien shared. That my father is the *only* person who can tell me about my mother. Whether I really do possess a strange sort of power." She hurried on. "If we are to war against the might of O'Lynn's clann and Tintagel, if there's a way my power could help . . . we need to know. *I need* to know."

Lancelot chewed on his bottom lip, his gaze flicking from Fionna to Percival. Percival nodded imperceptibly at him, his expression asking Lancelot to understand. This was why the other knight was here. He had seen the importance of Fionna's mission. What the information could mean for them all. It wasn't just a personal quest for a family reunion. If Fionna was a Gwenevere, if she was sovereign blessed, then her joining with Arthur would secure his kingship in a time when he desperately needed it. And if she was a Gwenevere, she had power. Perhaps even surpassing that of Morgana and her sisters.

Rescuing Fionna's father could be the difference between winning and losing this war. Between losing all they held dear or saving it. Lancelot muttered a curse. Damn it. They would have to infiltrate their enemy's camp and rescue a king.

Chapter Seventeen

Fionna

Lancelot was weakening—the indecision playing across his face. I pulled in a breath, not wanting to say something that might cause him to dig in his heels—again. After my and Lancelot's wild intimacy, I was now truly beginning to understand our dark second-in-command.

He was entirely too much like me.

"Fine," Lancelot said with a hiss of exasperation, raking a hand through his curls. "We'll rescue him."

"Thank ye!"

I hardly recognized the delighted squeal that escaped my mouth as I threw my arms around his neck. My gratitude was palpable. I felt unsteady and filled with the adrenaline of our near miss, and Lancelot's solid presence grounded me. He would be the needed counterpoint to Percival's optimism and my desperation. Together, the three of us could pull this off.

Lancelot squeezed my torso, burying his nose in my hair. His fresh scent and warmth permeated my being, and my body reacted, need blooming low and hot. I was still turned on after watching him and Percival kiss with barely restrained passion. Gods, I almost joined them, if not for the feel of my freshly dressed armor and boots and the corpses' bloody mess nearby. But it was easy to forget the dead with the relief of being alive and relatively uninjured. The rush of emotions was overwhelming. I couldn't fault Lancelot's slip in kissing Percival after his high-and-mighty speech.

I pulled back reluctantly, pressing a kiss to his cheek, doubting that I could control myself if I fastened my lips to his. Memories of our coupling in the hallway and on the stairs heated my cheeks, setting my blood to racing again. I glanced at Percival, who was once again exploring the goose egg on his temple with gentle fingers. What was it about these knights that robbed me of my good sense? When I was around them, I was little more than a wild woman buffeted by the winds of her desires—the demands of her body. And her heart. She was diametrically opposed to the warrior—the brutal fighter that I had cultivated so carefully over these years. And yet . . . I wanted to be both. I was both. Surely there was a way to reconcile these parts of myself.

I shoved my troubled thoughts aside, together with the fear that throbbed at the sight of the dead Uí Tuítri bodies on the ground. How close Percival and I had come . . .

"Percival," I said softly, clearing my throat. "Will ye be up to a fight, if it comes down to it?" I walked over to him and brushed the strands of his copper hair back gently, examining the wound. The injury wasn't too bad. Thankfully, it wasn't bleeding any longer. The bruise was concerning, though. Especially as he had been rendered unconscious.

"Aye, I'm feeling much better, dove." A sly smile crossed Percival's face at my nearness, and I fought an answering smile. His was the languid look of a man who had known a woman for the first time, and my heart was gladdened to see such a blissful expression. He continued, "Better than I've felt in some time, actually." He reached out to stroke my cheek and I pushed off his chest, turning. We didn't have time to go down that road again.

"He can fight."

"So, what's the plan?" Lancelot asked.

I filled him in quickly on our rough plan, wincing at the parts I knew sounded shaky and full of holes. I expected Lancelot to scoff and tear the plan to shreds. But he merely nodded. As if he were in for a pinch, in for a pound.

"We will wear the armor of these men." Lancelot gestured to

the two dead warriors. "Fionna's armor looks similar so long as no one looks closely. It's your hair that will draw attention."

Dusk had fallen over the camp below us, and fires and torches were winking to life like will-o-the-wisps.

"I'll keep my hood up," I said. "Unless ye have a better idea, *Faerie Prince*."

"You're the *Gwenevere*," he shot back, and I scowled, opening my mouth with a crude retort on the tip of my tongue.

"Shall we get changed?" Percival popped in-between us, cheerful as ever.

Lancelot grunted stiffly.

We dragged the two warriors deeper into the shelter of the trees, pulling off their armor and cloaks. I vacillated between watching the quiet camp and watching them don the attire of my enemies—a mix of unease and gratitude swirling within me. The dark leather armor didn't suit them, these brash knights of Caerleon. These two princes. I didn't know when it had happened, but something had shifted within me. The boiled leather of the Dál nAraidi looked crude to my eye, the dark burnished buckles dim. I had grown used to the bright color and shining beauty and finery of Caerleon and Arthur's court.

I swallowed back a forming knot in my throat. Every thought of seeing my father again made my stomach clench. Would he see the changes in me and scorn them? I had set out for Caerleon to save him and Aideen, to save the life I had built for myself and the clann that I loved. And, somehow in the process, Caerleon had changed me. Arthur and his knights had changed me. I had found a new family.

"Ready?" Percival asked quietly, stepping up beside me.

I softly smiled, grateful for the distraction.

Lancelot flanked us, his cut profile shadowed by his hood. "Swift and silent as a wraith. If we are identified, we must abort. There is no way we can fight our way out of this camp. It is stealth, or nothing at all."

"Agreed," I whispered. As much as I wanted to protest, Lancelot spoke sense. Arthur needed us alive even more than I needed my father. An all-out fight was a risk we couldn't take.

We padded down the hillside, our cloaks swathed around us to keep the light from glinting off our buckles or swords. The tents stretched around the village like a vast sea. I shoved aside the part of me that needed to count, needed to assess. So many had come to pluck the ripe fruit that was Gwent. To take what wasn't theirs.

We paused in the shadow of a massive oak as two sentries strolled by, their words carried off into the night air. The guards didn't seem particularly concerned with security. *That* could work in our favor.

Lancelot motioned us forward as the man passed, and we darted across the stretch to the nearest tents, pausing between two. "We stay out of sight. If we're spotted, act like we belong."

Percival and I grunted our assent. Part of me prickled at Lancelot seizing control of this mission, but I knew that was foolish. He was second-in-command. And if it was the price of him being here, it was a price I was happy to pay.

My heart galloped like Zephyr in an open field as we snaked between tents and cookfires, making our way into the outskirts of the village. The familiar sounds of a Dál nAraidi camp should have soothed me, but they set me more on edge. I wiped my palms on my breeches, cursing silently to myself. Give me a fair fight any day. But I was not cut out for sneaking around like a silent assassin.

My nerves were frayed to a single thread by the time we reached the village center, where the proud inn stood. Candlelight poured out the leadened window panes, together with the sounds of carousing. The Uí Tuírtri were clearly enjoying Caerleon's bounty. Hopefully they were now well into their cups.

One warrior stood guard before the cellar doors, and I smiled grimly. Percival and my deduction had been correct. Someone was in there. I turned to Lancelot to find him already moving, silent and quick as the wraith he had prompted us to be. In a few heartbeats, Lancelot had run up behind the man and slit his throat, catching his body and then dragging him into the dark shadows of a nearby alley.

Percival raised an eyebrow and we darted out to help, grabbing the deceased's legs and carrying him out of sight. The man's eyes were open as his lifeblood poured out, but I considered him little.

This man was guarding my father. Perhaps starving him. Beating him. He deserved no quarter.

I fumbled along the man's belt with numb fingers until I was rewarded with a ring of keys.

Rising as one, we poked our heads out of the shadow of the inn and surveyed the square. Two Uí Tuítri warriors were strolling across the dirt expanse, horns of ale in hand. I exchanged a wide-eyed glance with Lancelot. Would they notice how the guard was missing?

But the warriors passed through with a loud guffaw of laughter, and I let out a breath, my lungs burning for air.

"Now," Lancelot said.

We darted out into the open square, and I felt as exposed as I had while standing naked before those foul Uí Tuítri bastards. My hands shook as I tried one key and then another. The key's jangling sound seemed deafening in my ears, and I cringed. Any moment, I swore the inn's front door would crash open with a cry.

One of the keys slipped into the lock and turned with a click. I hauled open the door and Lancelot and Percival hurried inside as I urged them on.

I followed, pulling a knife from my belt as I heaved the door shut behind us with a muffled *thunk*.

As the door closed, we were swallowed completely in darkness. My senses roared to life as I gripped the dagger tightly. The smell of earth washed over me, the leeching cool of being underground pebbling my skin. We hadn't considered this. We didn't truly know what would await us in the dark.

"Who goes there?" A thin voice called out. "Is this a new game?" *That voice.* Recognition roared within me. Followed by relief.

"Father?" I called out, taking a blind step forward.

"Fionnabhair?" His voice—my father's voice. Alive. Here.

A sob escaped me, and I sheathed my knife, shuffling forward.

"Fionna," Lancelot hissed. He reached for my shoulder, but I shied away until his grip slipped from me.

"Da," I said, my hands out before me, reaching for the familiar form I longed to touch again, the wiry beard, the strong shoulders.

And then another hand made contact and cold, gnarled fingers twined with mine. We crashed together like a wave against the rocky shore, and hot tears spilled past my self-control to roll down my face. My senses told me he was thin and weak and dirty—but none of it mattered. He was my Da. He was alive. And he was *here*.

Chapter Eighteen

Arthur

The path from Elathia's throne back to Vivien's portal had transformed. Gone were the gentle scenes of faerie lights and fantastical flowers. Their path was now overgrown with thorns and gnarled brambles. Though it seemed Elathia was holding true to her side of Galahad's bet—letting Arthur, Galahad and the Cauldron of Plenty leave her court—she clearly wasn't pleased about it. And, therefore, didn't intend to let them go easily.

Arthur and Galahad navigated through the tangle of rambling limbs, ignoring the thorns tearing at their tunics and rending sharp slices across their arms and chests. Though no words passed between them, it was clear a similar sense of urgency gripped them both. They needed to get the hell out of here before Elathia changed her mind.

Galahad clutched the Cauldron of Plenty to his broad chest, as if it were the most precious possession he had ever held. For perhaps it was. This strange silver bowl—the shrunken cauldron—was the very relic that would save Caerleon. And Arthur's kingship. If they could only get through these cursed thorns!

Arthur was about pull Excalibur from its sheath and set to work like a common woodsman when the dense thicket cleared.

"Thank the gods," Galahad said.

"I'm not sure the gods have sway here anymore," Arthur muttered. "We go together," Arthur added. He grabbed Galahad's wrist and then they pushed through the portal Vivien had created.

And landed back into the Great Hall at Caerleon.

Arthur leaned over in physical relief, his hand on his stomach.

"The portal closed," Galahad said, heaving a sigh while running a hand through his long, wild strands. "Just like Vivien said. They can't follow us."

"We did it." Arthur laughed. "I can't believe we bloody did it." He turned to Galahad. "You bold son of a bitch. I can't believe you bet yourself."

"Well, I knew you weren't leaving Excalibur, and I wasn't leaving you." Galahad grinned. "So, I figured we might as well get comfortable."

"Did you see the look on Elathia's face when I crossed back over the lake with Excalibur?" The faerie had practically spit at him, pointing her finger like a spear. "*A bet well made. Now take the Cauldron and go.*"

Galahad guffawed. "I thought she had downed a tankard of vinegar! She was *not* pleased with you, Your Majesty. Not one bit."

Arthur laughed, reveling in how the tension drained from him each time he did so. They were back. They had the Cauldron. And with this relic, their chances of defeating O'Lynn and Morgana's army increased tenfold. Allowed them to feed Caerleon until they could figure out how to cure the curse for good too. "Shall we go find the others?"

"I'll make sure to regale Fionna with tales of your brave deeds." Galahad grinned again.

"And I yours," Arthur said, clapping Galahad on the back.

But the others were nowhere to be found. Not Lancelot, nor Percival, or Fionna.

Arthur and Galahad finally found Merlin. The druid stood atop one of the keep's towers with eyes glowing in the darkness.

"You have returned," Merlin said. He raised an eyebrow. "And with the Cauldron of Plenty, though smaller than I expected. I see Danu's steward is friendly to our cause."

"Not exactly." Arthur exchanged a wry look with Galahad.

"We have a bit of a tale to tell. Do you know where my other knights are?"

Merlin nodded out into the darkness. "They return anon."

Arthur frowned, squinting into the night. "They're not here? But I left instructions—"

"I suspect they have a tale to tell as well," Merlin interrupted.

"How fares the keep?" Galahad asked, ever the diplomat.

"Preparations for war are coming along well. But, if I may—" Merlin reached out a hand for the Bowl "—we need provisions. I will set up in the Great Hall. Galahad, please have all manner of food available brought to me?"

Galahad handed over the Cauldron stiffly, nodding. Arthur understood. After what he had almost sacrificed to gain this relic, he must feel a bit attached.

Hoofbeats reached Arthur's ears, and he leaned over the wall to identify the riders. Fionna and her dappled mare Zephyr came into view first, their white and silver hair and coat appearing like a specter in a distance. But . . . there was someone behind her on the horse. A man.

A story to tell indeed. "Come," Arthur said. "Let us meet them."

Arthur and Galahad were standing in the courtyard when the keep's thick doors were cranked open. Fionna, Lancelot, and Percival rode in. Guilty expressions colored their faces when they spotted Arthur and Galahad.

"You've returned," Lancelot said carefully, swinging down from Cheval.

"You, too, have returned," Arthur said dryly. "Though from where, I'm uncertain—"

"This was my idea," Fionna hastily interjected, swinging down from her own horse. Lancelot was crossing to help the man dismount behind her. When the older man's feet touched the ground, his knees buckled, and it was only Lancelot's strong grip that kept him from falling.

Fionna crossed to the older man's side and drew his arm around her shoulders gently, and with reverence. Together, Fionna and Lancelot helped the man forward, to stand before Arthur.

"Arthur, meet my father. His Majesty, Brin Allán, King of

Tara, Chieftain of Clann Allán."

Arthur's eyes widened. Fionna's father! How in the ten hells . . .

The man shrugged off Lancelot and Fionna's help and drew himself up to his full height. He was dirty and clearly malnourished, but there was a well of strength there that Arthur recognized. The man was as tall as he, and broad of shoulder, with a warrior's carriage. He looked to have a handsome face beneath the dirt and beard, the crinkled lines around his brown eyes speaking of laughter and kindness, in a time long past. "Forget all the formalities. I haven't been king of a pile of cow shit since O'Lynn took me. Call me Brin, lad." He held out a hand to Arthur.

Arthur laughed, and then took his hand, shaking it. This man was Fionna's father. This man, if Arthur had his way, would be his father-in-law. He was struck by the importance of this moment. "I see where Fionna gets her fire."

"Och, between her and her sister, it's a wonder the lasses didn't burn my keep down."

"Da," Fionna chided, but her eyes shone with happy tears, her face rapt.

"Welcome to Caerleon, Brin. I suspect you have need of food and a hot bath, though in what order, you may choose."

"Thank ye for yer hospitality, King Pendragon."

"Please, call me Arthur."

Brin inclined his head. "Arthur. If it's all the same to ye, I would like to drink an ale, catch up with my daughter, then plan how we're going to beat the shit out of O'Lynn and that faerie bitch at his side."

"Hear, hear," Lancelot murmured.

Arthur grinned. "Brin Allán, you are welcome indeed."

Fionna

I didn't want to break contact with him. My father. I held tight under his arm as we walked slowly toward a chamber next to mine, where Arthur's servants were already arranging a meal, a hot bath, and a change of clothes.

"I'm gonna lose my fingers if ye keep squeezing so tight." He looked at me sideways, a hint of mirth in his eyes.

"Sorry," I said ruefully, only loosening my grip slightly. "I think I'm still in shock that ye're actually here."

"Ye and me both, my duckling. When I heard yer voice in the dark . . ." he trailed off, his eyes growing distant. "I was sure it was another of that witch's foul tricks."

The mention of Morgana set my pulse pounding. "Did she mistreat ye? Did he?"

"No more than ye might expect. There was mocking and humiliation, and drunken nights where the Uí Tuítri thought I would make a fine punching bag. A man comes into this world naked and without pride. I supposed it was too much to expect that I would depart for the Otherworld any different."

"And a woman?" I asked softly, but he never answered me. We had reached the chamber next to mine and walked through the open door slowly as servant hurried about making his room ready. I took all the activity in, afraid to ask the question on my lips. "How is Aideen? Did . . ." I didn't know what to ask. Visions of my vibrant, sweet sister at the mercy of those monsters colored my vision blood red.

Brin sighed heavily. "They held her apart from the men, thank the gods. She got the taunts and the jabs twice as bad as me. As much as I hate to say it, O'Lynn taking her as a bride might be the best thing that could have happened to her."

"How could ye say such a vile thing?" I snapped. "The man's a foul brute!"

"Aye, but she's his now. And, thus, off limits. She'll be treated with respect, cared for. As much as I hate the thought of that man's hands on her, Aideen is strong. A woman can endure one man's unwelcome advances for a time. Without losing herself."

The servants poured the last of the steaming bathwater into the copper tub and curtseyed their leave. "Spoken like a man who's never had to endure such advances," I muttered under my breath, thinking of the Uí Tuírtri warrior scrambling atop me, believing he was entitled to my body. I didn't know what trauma Aideen would have suffered in O'Lynn's hands. But I prayed Brin was right. That she was strong enough to endure it.

"Let me help ye," I said as he took unsteady steps toward the bath.

"Help me by grabbing that ale I asked for," he replied gruffly, pulling his impossibly-dingy shirt over his head, before leaning one hand on the tub's rim.

The sight of his back stole my breath. Beneath the film of dirt and grime, his skin was crisscrossed with dark bruises and scabbed cuts. His once muscled form had shriveled from malnourishment. For the first time, he looked not like a King of Tara, the proud Brin Allán who had helped Brian Boru, then High King of Ireland, subdue the Norsemen out of the Kingdom of Dublin in the Battle of Clontarf. Now he looked like an old man. "Oh Da." The words slipped from my lips, and he stiffened.

"I don't need yer goggling, I need that ale!" he barked, and I turned to the tray of food the servants had left, giving him some privacy to finish undressing.

When I turned back with his blessed ale, he had slipped into the tub, a look of bliss on his face. I handed him the drink and he took a long swig, before releasing a satisfied sound.

"By the goddess," he murmured. "Thought I might never feel such pleasures again. A hot bath, a good ale. The sight of my beautiful Fionnabhair." He looked up at me, and I thought I glimpsed a flicker of emotion within his eyes, before the warrior's shield slid down once again.

"Do you want me to leave ye?" I asked, though I had a list of questions as long as my arm that I was desperate to ask him.

"Nay, don't leave, daughter," he said. "I've need of ye yet. Pull up that stool." So, I did, pulling a stool up beside the tub and perching upon it. "Hold this," he said, and I held his ale while he ducked under the water all the way, running his hand through his matted hair. The bathwater was already gritty and gray.

He came up for air and took his ale back. "Get me one of those chicken legs, eh?" He nodded back toward the tray of food.

"I see why ye want me here," I said but my words were gentle, and I retrieved the requested chicken leg for him.

"Not just that," he said. "I want to hear yer story. Why the hell ye're—why we're—in Briton. How ye became a knight of Caerleon. How ye came to live in this fine keep with the favor of a High King." He waved the leg around.

"How about a trade?" I offered. "Because I have questions for ye too. Ye ask one, I ask one."

He inclined his head. "Start talkin'. And while ye do, grab me a piece of that bread."

As he munched on the bread, I told him of Morgana and her sister's hatred for Arthur and Lancelot, as well as their three curses. O'Lynn's deal with me—to steal Excalibur from Arthur in exchange for their lives. I told him how I failed—how the knights stopped me on the road to Brunanburh in Northern Wales. But how they spared my life. Because they had learned I was a key to finding the Blessed Grail.

"And them sparing ye had nothing to do with how they all look at ye like lovesick whelps?" My father asked, now gnawing through a piece of roast venison.

My cheeks heated. "We have . . . come to care for one another.

It played a part." I was reluctant to share the extent of how. Not that I thought he would judge me for loving four men—having multiple lovers, especially among warriors, was as common as clover in Ireland—but for fear that he would judge me for putting my heart over his and Aideen's safety. Their very lives, even. For how could he not? I cursed myself for this predicament daily.

"So," he said, "somehow, we bumbled into the middle of a faerie war, and that idiot O'Lynn is merely a piece on the game board?"

I nodded. "That's a fair summary." I sighed. "I suppose I'm a piece too."

My father shook his head. "You were. But you've made yourself indispensable to these knights of Caerleon and their king. You will be a queen soon enough."

My blush deepened as my father voiced my secret hope. But also, if it was indeed true that I was a Gwenevere, then he already knew I would become queen one day. A queen destined to save a king.

"My turn," I said, voicing the question that had been crystalizing in my mind for weeks. I was grateful that I could speak the words without wavering. "Who is my mother?"

My father froze with the ale horn halfway to his mouth. He lowered his drink slowly, his brown eyes penetrating my own. "I always knew we would visit this topic someday." He swallowed. "First, know that my wife Catríona loved ye. She loved ye like her own daughter."

A numbness overtook me at his words. Catríona Allán wasn't my mother.

"It was, eh, twenty-one years ago now. I was riding through the woods near Aghanravel. Beautiful spring day. The buds were bright on the trees, birds flitting about. I came upon a woman. As beautiful as a field of wildflowers. Hair brown as loamy soil, skin soft as cotton-grass. Just standing there in the middle of the forest, wearing this gown of white. No horse, no possessions, just standing there. Like she was waiting for me. I stopped to see if she needed assistance. Things were fairly peaceful then, but still, there were dangers that could face such a fair maiden alone. She told me her name was Danu, and that she was waiting for me."

I hissed in a breath. "The goddess?"

He nodded. "I couldn't tumble off my horse and onto my knees fast enough. I begged her pardon and offered myself to aid her in whatever way she needed. She told me . . . she needed a daughter. Mind ye, I wasn't a young stag in my prime anymore."

My mouth parched like the poisoned land as he continued his tale. "I loved Catríona with all my heart. She was my wife before the law, but also my soul's lover. But when a goddess makes requests, ye serve. I laid with Danu in that very bed of wildflowers. When we were done, she thanked me, and was on her way. I told Catríona everything that evening, falling on my knees in apology. She pardoned me, so long as I forgive her should she lay with a handsome god who presented himself to her in request." A smile ghosted his lips. "I don't think she really believed me. Not until nine months later, when Danu appeared at our doorstep with a bundle in hand." He met my eyes. "That bundle was ye, a daughter she had named Fionnabhair."

"The White Fae," I whispered to myself as the heat of tears fell down my numb face. "Ye never told me . . ."

He shook his head. "She swore us to secrecy. The goddess shared how her enemies were moving against her, and that the child would be key in defeating them. A Gwenevere, as the Cymru call her." My heart nearly stopped beating. "But also, that the foretold White Enchantress needed to remain hidden. So, she placed a géis over you in protection against all forms of enchantment, and to disguise yer true demi-goddess form, as well as yer magical powers."

"A géis?" I asked, my mind struggling to process. "Who were her enemies?"

He shook his head. "I don't know, my duckling. No one ever came for ye. Not yer mother or those who opposed her. But if Morgana tried to pit ye against her enemy King Arthur by forcing ye to steal Excalibur, I suspect the secret might be out and that he is also the foretold High King who needs such a queen."

Chapter Twenty

Galahad

The mood that hung over the knights at breakfast was a strange one. Arthur was absent, seeing to Merlin's work with the Cauldron of Plenty. Lancelot and Percival were far too quiet for comfort. Well, Percival was far too quiet. Silence from crabapple was not out of character.

But the two kept exchanging pregnant glances that told Galahad that something had passed between both men last night. Had the tension between them boiled over into something more? But no . . . it wasn't quite the type of the secret smile he would expect if the two had spent a night together.

"Out with it," Galahad finally said, setting his tankard down with a thunk. "You two are as bad at keeping secrets as the maids when doing the washing together. What are you hiding?"

Fionna and her father appeared in the doorway, her father much changed from his condition last night. He was bathed, shaved, and clothed in a fresh tunic and pants. He still looked gaunt and shadow-eyed, but there was more spirit in him than before.

Fionna was the one who answered Galahad's question, even as she ushered her father to a spot at Galahad's side. "Our rescue last night didn't go entirely according to plan."

"What do you mean?" Galahad furrowed his brow.

"Our presence wasn't . . . unnoticed," she replied. "We killed two Uí Tuírtri warriors. I think one was a man of some importance."

"So, come daybreak—" Percival said.

"They'll know we poked the bear," Galahad finished.

Lancelot grimaced.

"The man Fionna spoke of, Níall. He was one of O'Lynn's oldest friends and most trusted leaders," Brin said.

"Ah, you didn't just poke a bear. You stirred the hornet's nest." Galahad let out a muffled curse. Even with the cauldron, the keep's fortifications and preparations weren't complete. They couldn't afford an all-out assault.

"In our defense, they were going to attack anyway," Percival said. "It's not like we turned an ally into an enemy."

"His Majesty will need to be told," Galahad said, sliding a look Brin's way. Honorific titles were needed now that they were in the presence of a foreign king.

"I'll tell him," Lancelot said at the same time as Fionna said, "Let me handle that."

The two exchanged an irritated glance.

"No one needs to tell me anything," Arthur appeared in the doorway, his face pinched. Galahad and his fellow knights rose to their feet and bowed their heads in respect. Arthur lifted a hand in appreciation then gestured to their chairs. "A messenger just arrived," he said as they returned to their seats. "O'Lynn is on the move. And burning everything he passes."

Curses of dismay rounded the table. "The villages should be mostly empty, Your Majesty," Galahad said.

Arthur nodded grimly. "It's a small consolation. But those homes, crops, livestock? Caerleon will need them if we are to have anything to harvest, and homes for our people to return to. We must stop what we can."

"So, we ride," Lancelot said, a determined smile crossing his face, perhaps grateful for a foe of flesh and blood rather than mist and magic. "I won't mind facing those Uí Tuítri bastards again. And showing Morgana that the might of Caerleon is not to be trifled with."

Arthur frowned, narrowing his eyes slightly while running a hand through his hair. Galahad knew that look of stern consideration: Arthur the strategist.

"Would O'Lynn move all of his forces out?" Arthur turned to Fionna. "Would he himself be among them? Morgana?"

She shook her head. "If they're just razing and burning, O'Lynn will likely be sitting back, fat and happy. Real battle, however? He would ride out among his warriors. But this . . . we will likely find him in his camp. Morgana too, if she is with him."

"We will split up, then," Arthur said. "Sir Percival, I'll send you with a force to meet the raiders. Harry them, draw them out, pick off the stragglers. Do not *fully* engage. Just distract them so they don't return. Lady Fionna, Sir Galahad, and I will take another force into their camp. We'll bring Merlin too. I'm sick to death of being on the defensive. It's time to take the offense to O'Lynn and Morgana. See how they like being blindsided by magical attacks for a change."

"Will Merlin fight?" Fionna asked. "I didn't know he used his magic in battle."

"Merlin was quite a fighter in his youth," Arthur said. "He will fight."

"And what of me, my King?" Lancelot asked.

"The most sacred task falls to you," Arthur said. "I need you to see to the defenses of Caerleon. You must hold this keep, whatever comes."

"Hold the keep?" Lancelot was incredulous. "Perhaps you've forgotten, Your Majesty, but it's not the king's role to be on the front lines. Let me win this battle for you. I gladly offer my services as your champion. You need not risk yourself."

"Dál nAraidi clann chieftains ride to battle at the front of their hordes," Brin said. "If King Arthur Pendragon does not go, even for a raid, it will be seen as a sign of weakness. Practically an admission of defeat."

"Says the king who was captured in battle by his enemies," Lancelot shot back.

Fionna's eyes narrowed at Lancelot's slight, though Galahad had to admit, it was a fair point by their second-in-command. Brin arched a humored eyebrow and smirked at their dark knight's fire, before glancing at his daughter, who just rolled her eyes back at her father.

Galahad lifted a hand to his mouth to hide a humored smile of his own. Fionna and Lancelot were too much alike at times, there were really only two acceptable reactions. Irritation or humor.

"I will not do anything rash," Arthur reassured. "Sir Galahad and Lady Fionna will be by my side. But I must see. I must take this man's measure. If we can cripple him and Morgana today, it could buy us the time Caerleon needs to figure out how to break this final curse."

"And to awaken my magic," Fionna added.

"What magic?" Galahad asked.

Fionna exchanged a glance with her father. "I had a chance to speak with my father last night. It turns out . . . Danu is my mother."

Silence fell over the room.

"I bloody knew ye were a goddess!" Percival finally said, slapping his knee with a laugh. "Any man could see that ye are no ordinary woman." The way Percival purred the words, and how Fionna's ears turned pink as a smile crept onto her face . . .

Galahad's eyes widened. The Grail Quest was over . . . had Percival claimed more than Fionna's heart?

"Indeed," Lancelot murmured. "If you are the daughter of Danu, then you are a Gwenevere. The first in a millennia. I told you, Fionna. The third curse didn't lie. Morgana said I would love a white enchantress. And here you are."

Fionna's cheeks reddened to a pretty hue and Galahad swung his head to take in the smug grin twisting Lancelot's mouth. The way his eyes rested on her, as if she were his. As if he knew every hidden place and secret whisper of Fionna's beautiful body. "Odin's beard, woman!" Galahad cried out, looking from Lancelot to Percival to Fionna. "We were gone for less than a day!"

Arthur frowned. "What are you talking about?"

Fionna full-on flushed now, as scarlet as a ripe cherry. "Stay on topic, *Sir*," she said pointedly to Galahad, then chanced a furtive glance her father's direction. "The important detail to discuss is how I do indeed possess magic, but my access has been locked up by Danu within a géis. To protect me from her enemies."

"A géis," Lancelot practically spat. "My foster mother thought as much."

"Danu's enemies?" It was Galahad's turn to exchange a look with Arthur. "The faerie we encountered in Danu's court was not . . . friendly. I think it's possible that Danu's enemies have already come home to roost."

"What enemies does an earth-goddess have?" Percival asked.

"The Fomorians," Arthur said slowly. "The curse over the land reminded us of their dark magic. Danu saw fit to hide her child from someone . . . and the Fomorians are the ancient enemy of the Túatha dé Danann." Arthur turned to Lancelot. "Can a Fomorian shift into the form of another faerie?"

"Why do you ask?"

"Well," Arthur drawled out, as if deep in thought. "I wonder if a Fomorian took on the shape of the faerie Danu had planned to appoint as regent in her absence? I cannot imagine she would just appoint anyone, let alone a Fomorian."

"Possible, I suppose," Lancelot answered. "Faeries can shift into animals or make themselves appear more human. Fomorians are beastly and quite ugly. Only halflings, a child of Danu and a child of Domnu, possess humanoid fae beauty."

Galahad ran a finger along the rim of his tankard. "Elathia, Danu's regent, was beautiful."

Lancelot curled his lip in disgust. "Bloody faeries."

"But if the Fomorians have returned from the sea's abyss," Arthur considered, "perhaps we have bigger concerns than O'Lynn and Morgana. We will consider all these things with Merlin when we return. Lady Fionna, I will see that the druid gives all his attention to breaking this géis over you." Their king swept his gaze across the table. "We will not solve this mystery over breakfast. Not when we have a battle to win."

Brin lifted his tankard into the air. "Aye, victory will be ours, Pendragon."

Breakfast was forgotten as they scrambled to rally their soldiers and prepared to ride out.

Lancelot scowled darkly but obeyed his king's command.

Several hours later, Galahad found himself mounted on his charger, riding through the countryside between Fionna, Arthur, and Merlin.

"What can you tell us about their war strategy?" Arthur asked Fionna.

"If we ride upon them quickly, they'll fight like banshees to defend their turf," Fionna answered. "In a more traditional engagement, they would try to strike fear into our hearts with war cries and horns. For those who have never heard a Dál nAraidi force crying out, it can be terrifying indeed. Then the foot soldiers and lightly-armored horsemen would charge us, to break our ranks. But, if we're able to hold rank, they will likely flee. Then the foreign Gaels will attack."

"The foreign Gaels?" Galahad asked. "You mean intermarried Gaelic Norsemen?"

"Aye, I do. They fight with the Danish axes ye're familiar with, together with our own Irish bows and darts. The foreign Gaels will hit us with the force of Odin's hammer," Fionna said, giving Galahad a weak smile.

"So," Arthur began, nodding thoughtfully, "we must ensure they don't have a chance to reach their mounts or weapons."

"There's no honor among Dál nAraidi, Your Majesty," Fionna stressed. "Such an attack won't surprise them much. O'Lynn's warriors will rally a defense quickly."

As Fionna spoke, they crested a forested hill and the Uí Tuírtri camp came into view below them. Galahad tightened his grip on his horse's reins. Thousands of warriors swarmed Caerleon's green rolling hills and the valley the peaks cradled. In the far distance, black smoke plumed into the sky where a village burned.

Arthur reined Llamrei to a stop, and the others reined their mounts in on either side. They had a force of a hundred men behind them.

"Merlin, can you create a cover for us?" Arthur asked.

Merlin nodded, and then closed his eyes, whispering into the air. A fog began to coat the ground, wisping down the hill before them.

"We push into the town." Arthur's words were hard. "Find O'Lynn and Morgana. And end them."

"And rescue my sister," Fionna added softly.

"So, it comes to this," Merlin said, his cambion eyes flashing.

"It has always been coming to this," Arthur said. "Ever since my half-sister set her sights on my kingdom." And with that, he kicked his heels into Llamrei's side and trotted down the hill and into the rising mist.

Galahad flashed a shared glance with Fionna before kicking his own charger forward, the clop of his horse's hooves muffled by the soft grass.

Uncertainty dogged Galahad's mind. But he shoved his misgivings aside, finding his clarity. His calm. And his blood sang a fierce battle cry to the elements as Fionna rode at his side, her white-blonde braids fluttering behind her.

For glory. For Arthur. For Caerleon.

Chapter Twenty-One

Arthur

The mist shrouded their approach. Tents eventually emerged like silent sentinels inside the curtain of thick fog. A warrior materialized before Arthur and Llamrei, and Arthur ran him through the neck with Excalibur before he could make a sound.

Galahad, Fionna, and Merlin had fanned out from him during their descent into the war camp. Though he couldn't see them in the whiteness, the hushed grunts, rustle of armor, and quiet clang of slaughter reassured Arthur that they were still close by.

He had instructed the soldiers who followed to burn what they passed. It grieved Arthur to do so, but allowing O'Lynn access to food and shelter felt like aiding his enemy. Arthur would rebuild the villages for his people and provide care within his keep's walls until they could return to their new homes.

Men's voices swam through the fog before him. He could make out the words in an Irish lilt that reminded him of Fionna's. "It isn't natural," one man said.

"Aye. Bloody faerie magic," another replied.

It was another moment before he saw them, before he saw that they were too many to take by surprise. But he would kill as many as he could before they raised the alarm.

One tall, thin man cried out as Arthur surged forward, spearing him through the chest.

Around the fire, the others scrambled for their weapons as Arthur and Llamrei leaped over the fire pit, Llamrei's sharp hooves trampling one of the men. Arthur dispatched the other two quickly, but it was too late. The cry had been heard.

Arthur felt a strange elation rise within him as he urged his horse forward, his blood crying out for battle. He was tired of O'Lynn taking from him, of Morgana taking from him. He was ready to take from someone else.

Shouts sounded to his left, where he knew Fionna was making her way through the mist as well.

Arthur focused before him, hacking and stabbing, a brutal harvest of Uí Tuírtri warriors caught unawares. It would have made Arthur's stomach curl, if not for the cruelties these men had already visited upon his people. Anglo-Saxon holy men shared of a god who insisted that a man was to turn the other cheek when insulted. Arthur snorted as he swung Excalibur, severing a man's head from his shoulders. Perhaps turning the other cheek worked in the Holy Roman Empire. But not in Gaelic lands. Here, a king stood his ground. And here in Briton, the Pendragon breathed fire and vanquished the enemies who invaded his realm.

Arthur had reached one of the little houses on the outskirts of the village, having made his way through the forest of hide tents. The sound of cracking flames and the smell of burning wood and fur followed close on their heels. They wouldn't be able to return this way. But, in her mission to retrieve her father, Fionna had identified another retreat route to the east toward Caerleon.

Arthur smiled grimly when a great wind buffeted against him, and the fog began to lift. "Morgana." He spit his half-sister's name like a curse. There would be no more easy killing from here on out.

His companions came into view as the mist began to lessen. Fionna and Zephyr, their pale forms flecked with sprays of blood; Galahad with his battle axe hewing a man nearly in two. And Merlin, shooting gouts of flame, burning the men before him where they stood. An endless sea of soldiers from Caerleon also now faced the tide of Irish clann warriors before them.

Arthur and his trusted circle halted on the outskirts of the village, though the main street was wide and open. And he could see into the village square, where a force of men were rallying. Banners were being lofted and flapped in the unnatural wind, bearing the sigil of clan Uí Tuírtri.

"To me!" Arthur called, and the others drew close around him.

"We punch through," Arthur said, "and see if we can find O'Lynn."

"I think we have found him," Fionna said, nodding toward the village square. A tall man swathed in furs was walking out of the village inn with a willowy woman in black at his side.

"Charge!" Arthur shouted, and his soldiers thundered forward, crashing into the bristling line of clannsmen before them.

Arthur fought furiously, hacking and slicing with Excalibur, but the crowd of warriors before O'Lynn and Morgana grew thicker. The clann leader was hanging back—comfortable. Letting Caerleon break itself against the rock that was a three-man-thick line of Irish warriors.

As Arthur stabbed a man who tried to slice Llamrei's side, his horse danced back, out of the way of another who took the man's place. Arthur felt his anger surge. "You hide like a child! Afraid to face me!" Arthur bellowed at O'Lynn.

"Just letting you tire yourself," O'Lynn shouted back. "I need not lift a finger. For I have Tintagel at my side!" He gestured at Morgana, and Arthur's faerie half-sister raised her clawed fingertips.

The sky around them darkened as hundreds—thousands—of crows descended upon them as if materialized from a black, gaping hole beside the suddenly shadowed sun. Sweat dripped into Arthur's eyes and he blinked back the stinging pain. Even without the momentary hazy eyesight, he struggled to take in what he was seeing. And then the swirling black vision in the sky shifted form into offensive positions. He barely had time to shout for his warriors to take cover before the birds swooped upon them in a hungry cloud, wings flapping, claws scraping, beaks pecking at exposed flesh, especially at ears and eyes.

"Merlin!" Arthur screamed, holding his sword arm up to shield his face from the attack.

A shock wave shot across the battle field, jarring Arthur to his bones. His eyes rounded at the foreign sensation, his heart in this throat. Then, crows fell from the sky, a dark rain that hammered trees, roofs, and armor alike. People from both camps lifted shields or ducked as Morgana shrieked, screaming over and over, "My crows!"

When the thumping, thundering sounds abated, Arthur swept a calculating gaze across the village to take in the damage. Smoke from the nearby fires ribboned around piles of black, feathered bodies as far as the eye could see. Easily thousands of birds littered the ground, flapping helplessly and cawing in pain beside writhing soldiers who covered their mutilated eye sockets while crying out. The sounds of torment was enough to make his ears weep.

He straightened his position atop Llamrei and grit his teeth until his jaw ached, meeting Morgana's wrathful gaze head-on. Snarling, he shouted, "Is that the best you can do, Queen of Darkness?"

Morgana narrowed her violet eyes, and then glanced to her left, beyond where he could see.

Two more fae females appeared at her side, stepping up before the inn beside her.

Arthur's blood turned cold. Morgause and Elaine. *Here.* His two eldest half-sisters. The ones who had treated him far more cruelly while growing up. The sisters who taught Morgana that he, their bastard-born brother, the product of their father's planned murder and mother's rape, deserved only eternal punishment for being an abomination in their eyes. And for bearing the title Pendragon, High King of Briton.

The onslaught was sudden and furious. A bolt of lightning crashed from a clear blue sky, striking the ground just inches from Arthur. His steed reared in fright, screaming as Arthur struggled to stay on her back.

The other sisters were muttering now while writing runes into the air. More lightning strikes hit. Some of Arthur's soldiers were not as lucky as he, and the men and horses were tossed into the sky. Claps of thunder shook his eardrums, deafening him. He swallowed his sorrow as more men he knew, men with wives and children, fell to their death atop the possessed crows. All because of him, because he was born from Uther Pendragon's line. Perhaps this was the true curse poisoning his life. He slid a glance toward Fionna, unable to bear his shame.

But that latter thought was ripped from his attention as a new fear took hold.

The ground began to rumble, and the very dirt they stood upon began to crack. A fissure appeared between Arthur and Fionna, and his eyes grew large as it snaked wider, opening into a chasm below. Men fell into the depths, screaming, and still the ground shook.

Terror clawed up from his gut as he screamed until his throat turned raw, scorched with grief. "Merlin!" Arthur looked around frantically. He caught his druid's eyes. Time seemed to slow for several beats of his heart as the man's horse danced back from a widening crack. Merlin eventually shook his head, even as he mouthed words, his hands dancing before him. Whatever spell the sisters wielded, it was too strong for Merlin to break.

They would be destroyed.

"Retreat!" Arthur cried out, and spun Llamrei, kicking her flanks hard. They leapt over a chasm, just barely clearing the wide expanse. *Fionna. Galahad.* Arthur peered over his shoulder to see Fionna and Zephyr dodging out of the way of a lightning strike. The sudden movement of the ground together with the strike sent Zephyr sideways, and the horse and rider crashed to the ground.

"Fionna!" Arthur kicked Llamrei forward, but his mare fought him, not wanting to return to the chaos of lightning strikes and cracking earth.

Zephyr scrambled to her feet, and spooked, galloped toward Galahad.

"Zephyr!" Fionna screamed.

Galahad turned, spurring his mount toward the fleeing mare.

With Fionna's attention pinned onto her horse, she didn't see the crack now slithering between her planted feet.

Arthur spurred Llamrei on, his heart about to pound out of his chest. "Fionna," he cried out at her again. "Watch out!"

She spun toward him, the horror in her eyes growing as she realized how the ground was about to give way beneath her. Arthur leaned over his saddle, stretching his arm out for her as far as he could reach. Praying it was far enough.

Fionna leapt for him as he passed. Their wrists locked. Pain groaned through him as her weight almost pulled his arm from its socket. But he had her. And the momentum of their movement helped swing her across Llamrei's rump just as the ground caved in beneath the spot where she had stood only moments earlier.

"Hold on," Arthur cried out over his shoulder.

Llamrei leapt over another fissure, and Fionna nearly slid off his horse's back. But when Llamrei's hooves connected with solid ground, Fionna stumbled to the ground. She then sprinted for Zephyr and sprang back into the saddle.

Arthur's warriors were streaming past them now. But something felt wrong. Warriors who hadn't been speared by lightning or lost to the unnatural depths of the earth were now riding for Caerleon with fresh terror gripping their sweaty dirt- and blood-smudged faces. He whipped his head back toward the war-sacked village and sucked in a ragged breath. A host of mounted Uí Tuírtri were pouring out from the west and around the village. They had taken advantage of the pitched battle, using the time to saddle their mounts and make an assault.

"Ride for the keep," Arthur shouted above the melee as he dug his heels into poor Llamrei's side once again. She surged into a gallop, flowing into the stream of riders thundering back toward the barracks within his walled fortress. He gave Llamrei her head and prayed, to whatever deity might be listening, that she would be fast enough.

Chapter Twenty-Two

Fionna

We made it into the keep a hair's breadth before the horde on our tail.

"Close the gate!" Arthur screamed, and soldiers scrambled to slam the huge oaken doors shut behind us. They heaved the cross-guard into place as a shuddering weight smashed against the outside.

I quickly surveyed the damage done to our group. We had lost perhaps a third of the warriors we had brought with us, between the fighting in the camp and the wild ride home. Dirt and sweat coated each soldier. But Arthur . . . Arthur appeared as though he dug his way free from the Underworld. "Percival," I gasped, my breast heaving from the frantic flight. But fear seized the very air from my lungs. I didn't see the copper hair of my sweet knight. "Has Sir Percival returned with his men?" I called out to the guards.

"Aye," a man answered from the courtyard. "They returned a candle mark ago."

My shoulders slumped in relief, even as another cry went up outside the gates, followed by another shuddering crash.

"They're trying to hack through the gate," Galahad said, wiping the sweat from his face. Grime smudged across his cheek and forehead. "It'll take them till Samhain at this rate."

"Get archers up on those walls," Arthur barked. "I don't want the gate compromised. Take those men down."

Soldiers scrambled to obey. I slid off Zephyr and then patted her heaving, lathered flank.

"Druid," I called out. My eyes darted around until I found Merlin amongst the tumult of men and horses in the courtyard. "We have work to do."

Merlin nodded grimly, dismounting from his own horse and motioning to me.

"What do you plan to do?" Arthur asked, stepping before me. His crown was askew, and his face was flecked with blood and dirt, his eyes red with restrained emotion. But he had never looked more handsome than he did now. A man, despite our near-defeat, in full command of the world around him. A king.

"We have one magic-wielder against three," I explained. "However strong yer walls are, they cannot hold against Morgana and her sisters, if their full magic is brought to bear. Danu told my father I have latent power within my blood. Merlin and I must find it."

Arthur nodded, looking away. As though hiding the building emotion—the fear, the grief. "This is your most precious task."

I cupped his cheek and whispered, "Arthur . . ."

He appeared as though he wanted to lean into my touch. Instead he stepped back with a sad smile and said, "See it done," before spinning on his heel and marching away.

A groom took Zephyr's reins as I stared after Arthur's retreating form. Then I hurried after Merlin as he angled his way through the thick crowd of villagers who led the injured to the Great Hall.

My body was exhausted from the fight and the ride, but my mind was alive with excitement and nerves. If I were honest with myself, there was trepidation there too. I had always been happy with Fionnabhair Allán. Being the daughter of a Dál nAraidi woman—a good wife and mother. Being a warrior, fighting with my fiann. I had been happy being me. And I had been happy in Caerleon too. With Arthur and my knights. Each man had awakened a passion and carnal femininity that had slumbered deep within me. I felt as though I needed nothing else—no power or might or divinity. I needed nothing but time on this green earth with the men

I loved. But my enemies—Arthur's enemies—would take even that from me. So, I would surrender myself to the unknown. Would I be happy with the woman who emerged? If my father's tale proved true, I would be a Gwenevere. An enchantress, a goddess. But would I still be me?

"Be at ease, Fionna," Merlin said as we reached the living area of his cave. "This has been a part of you all along. If anything, you will be more you than before."

"Do yer powers extend even to reading thoughts?" I muttered, for I knew I hadn't spoken my fears aloud.

"My powers extend to human nature. And your worry is written plain on your face."

"What do ye plan to do?" I asked. Dwelling on my misgivings wouldn't help me. Arthur needed an enchantress at his side, and so I would yield myself. For Arthur, I would yield my life, my very soul. How small a sacrifice was my identity?

"Your true essence is locked deep inside you," Merlin said, pulling bottles off his shelf and returning to his desk, where a mortar and pestle sat. "The human mind is like . . . a turtle."

"A turtle?" I scoffed.

"Floating in the water. You can see the eyes. That is the conscious mind, what we use to think and reason and process. But beneath the surface is something much larger. More powerful. I think this is where your powers lie. I will give you a potion to take you deep within yourself. I hope you can find your way to the answers."

"And if I can't?" I asked.

"Then we'll try something else," Merlin said. "Until we find what works."

Merlin poured the potion into a mug of ale, and then handed the clay cup to me. I downed the contents in one swallow, before coughing and hacking. "Awful!"

"Magic doesn't usually taste good." The druid took my arm and led me to the chairs beside his fireplace. "Sit," he said, and I dropped into a seat upon the fur cover. A fire burst to life before me in the hearth, and I jumped.

Merlin sat beside me. "You may see strange things in your mind. Visions. A guide may appear. Ask him to show you the way to the géis. Whatever happens, focus only on finding the géis. Your mind will take you there."

The room swam as a flush of heat consumed me. "I feel . . . strange," I murmured.

Merlin took the cup from me. "Close your eyes. Let the magic take you."

I did as he instructed, and another wave of heat battered against my tingling body, warming my skin, until I felt as though I were suffocating in my armor. I reached up to start unbuckling my leathers, but Merlin's hand grasp mine. "Your conscious mind will do everything it can to try and keep you from journeying deep. It's uncomfortable with the unknown. Focus inside. The feelings will pass."

I huffed in frustration but tried to do as I was told. It was dark behind my eyelids, but the darkness swam, as if alive. Moving. The darkness began to materialize—to take form. I hissed in a breath as I watched in disbelief. A forest. It was as if I were standing in a shadowy forest. On the ground before me, a form emerged, soft gray against the mossy earth. A dove.

"Are you my guide?" I asked.

The dove hopped once on the ground. I took that for a yes.

Bending at the knees, I hunched down and asked, "Can you lead me to the géis?"

The dove flitted into the air, whizzing into the forest.

"Wait!" I cried out, running after the bird.

I darted beneath branches and bounded over fallen logs, all the time wondering what in the goddess's name this place represented. And knowing that I was moving farther away from where I had started. Deeper into the unknown.

The dove flew quickly for this type of bird. Stranger still, I could move fast as well, keeping up with my winged guide. I slowed to a stop before the dove now sitting on a branch before me, expecting a need to catch my breath. But there was no breath here. My lungs didn't rise and fall with life-giving motions.

Bothered by this realization, I peered past the dove. Ahead of where we paused, a ring of trees circled inside a clearing. The landscape reminded me of the faerie ring where we had found the standing stone pointing us toward Caer Benic. But no monolith lay inside the ring. Instead, a woman stared at me. A woman trapped in a cage made of vines.

And the woman was *me*.

"Impossible," came my garbled cry. I ran forward and threw myself against the bars, wrapping my fingers around the iron. The woman within looked at me with sullen, downcast eyes, a frown dipping her mouth. But she did not speak. I pressed my face to the space between the bars, my eyes drinking in her strange form. For she was *me*. But not. This me was fae. She had delicate tapered ears and skin as white and as smooth as a first-fallen snow. I knew that men found me beautiful, but this version—she was ethereal. The animal movements of her head, the glow around the pure white hair, pulled back in elaborate braids . . . she was a dream.

"How do I free ye?" I tugged on the bars to test their strength.

"A worthy question."

I whirled, grasping for a dagger at my waist that was no longer there.

Another faerie stood before me. No, not a faerie. A goddess. She wore a dress of shimmering green and gold, the colors of spring and summer and autumn woven together in a majestic cloth finer than any mortal hand could create. Her cascading tresses were the green of the forest, interwoven with vines of ivy. Her skin was pale and glistened with dew, like a cloud. Her tilted eyes were a startling blue that raged like the sea, calm like a glassy lake, with a fluid gaze that rested on me like the gentle pool of a river.

I fell to one knee, my fingertips burying in the earth. "Goddess Danu," I said, my mind racing. I didn't know if she was a figment of my mind, but I didn't want to risk offending her on the chance she was more. Real.

"Rise my daughter," she said. Her words were the soft touch of a new lamb's wool.

I rose to shaky feet, meeting her gaze. There were so many things I wanted to say to her. To ask. Why my father. Why me. Where had she been. But . . . there was only one question that mattered right now. "Can ye . . ." I stumbled over my words. "Can ye help me break the géis?"

She glided forward, wrapping her own slender fingers around the bars and tugging. Flames alit in her hands, and I shied back. But they quickly snuffed out.

She stepped away, shaking her head. A look of pinched frustration flit across her face, an expression that appeared very out of place. "I cannot," she admitted.

"But ye placed it upon me, did ye not?" I asked. "Can ye not undo yer magic?"

"My enemies have trapped me in a remote corner of the Otherworld. It stretches me thin as the Otherworld's mist to even be here. If I were here in my full force, yes, I could undo the géis. It seems I have protected you too well. Even from myself."

"The Fomorians did this to ye, didn't they," I said. "They have returned."

She nodded. "They have. They take my court, they take my land. They will take Arthur's sovereignty and all of Briton, if you let them. They use Morgana and her sisters like pawns, playing upon their petty vengeances."

"Is there a way to break ye free?" I asked. "We need yer help defeating them."

"Perhaps when your power is fully restored, you could break my prison."

"But my power cannot be restarted until ye are free," I said slowly, now seeing the knot fate had tied us into.

"There might be another way," Danu said.

"Tell me," I asked eagerly.

"Arthur. You and he are destined for each other. He is the sovereign-blessed king of all Briton, you the goddess who will bestow the final blessing upon him."

"How?" I asked. "Tell me how and I will do it."

"Your love, and your joining. You must love Arthur, and you must marry him. And when you lay with him, perhaps there will be power enough to break even my spell."

$\mathbf{I}$nterlude

Morgana

The crow hopped into the herb-incensed cave. Above, crystals glittered in the flickering firelight as though twinkling stars in a midnight, moonless sky. Magic swelled in this place, filling even the crevices in the stone walls and the insect burrows in the ground. A magic the crow knew well. The familiar smoke- and flame-scrying fireplace and soothing, hypnotic tones of the ancient druid within called to the crow's own druidic and fae magic.

Not wanting to be noticed, the crow surrounded herself with the shifting shadows and whispered druid incantations. Her feathers ruffled in the swirling wind and then her lashes snapped open as she tucked black strands behind her ear and away from her face.

Morgana chanced a look around a natural wall in the cave before the narrow passage opened into Merlin's den. The druid sat beside the witch, his eyes glowing bright gold and his pupils narrowed to reptilian slits. The hearth leapt with flames that danced in the shape of fae creatures. The court of the Túatha dé Danann, perhaps? In this trance, he would unlikely sense her presence, and Morgana relaxed a notch.

Perspiration dripped down the witch's face. Her hands gripped the arms of the chair until her knuckles turned white and fingertips purple. Silver-dusted lashes rested on her flushed cheeks as she sifted through magic and subconscious thoughts to the deepest part of herself. Morgana knew the ogham runes Merlin spoke over the witch's ensorcelled form.

An invitation to Danu, the mother goddess, to find her daughter.

A plea to break a géis.

A request to open and flood the witch with her fae-born powers.

Morgana's lip curled in disgust. She had suspected Fionnabhair Allán as fae-born for years—even suspected she might be a Gwenevere—ever since she encountered the warrior in training after her first bloods. As the crow, Morgana sat above a branch and watched, curious. The witch had always contained a strange smell that was *other*. One that perfumed sweetly of earthen white magic—but not one she had encountered before. A subtle scent like heather and hawthorn and the faint fragrance of an apple blossom.

The air grew thick and Morgana narrowed her eyes just as the witch regained consciousness.

"Steady," Merlin said, placing a hand on her arm as she coughed and wiped at her eyes. "Did you find Danu?"

"Aye," the witch said, a bit breathless. "My mother couldn't unlock the géis. But she did have an idea of how I might be able to do so."

"Excellent. Tell me as we walk back to the keep and find Arthur."

The witch stood and then met Merlin's gaze. "There's more. The Fomorians have taken over Danu's court."

"Ah," the druid said. "As we suspected. Come, let us tell the king."

Morgana quickly backed out of the cave and into the night in a flight of feather-light footsteps. She needed to share this news with her sisters quickly. Before the witch regained her powers. If she was the daughter of Danu, Morgana and her sisters would need to devise a more powerful plan than the one currently in place. A far stronger magic was now needed. A far stronger Fomorian ally too.

The whispers of the desperate and dying circled Morgana in a rush of leaves and shadows and wind. Blinking her black eyes, the crow hopped onto a mossy rock and watched as the witch and druid left the cave and wandered up the path toward the keep.

Elathia had promised them aid in defeating her half-brother and securing his kingdom. But so far, the regent had done little. It was time to call in a favor. When Caerleon came for them again, they would be ready. With a weapon strong enough to defeat even a Gwenevere.

Chapter Twenty-Three

Arthur

'Lynn's army had arrived at the keep. The maelstrom of warriors outside was deafening. Horns, shouts and war cries, horses whinnying.

Arthur took the stairs two by two, vaulting up to the top of the keep's wall where Percival, Galahad, and Lancelot grimly surveyed the scene below.

"How many?" Arthur asked, blowing out a breath.

"All of them," Lancelot replied. "Plus three dark faeries. We need Merlin up here. *Now.*"

"He's with Fionna, trying to break the géis. We must not disturb them unless it is absolutely necessary," Arthur replied.

"It's beginning to feel absolutely necessary, ye ken." Percival's normally cheerful face was grave.

"They're not showing signs of a full-on assault." Galahad scratched at the dirt-caked sweat in his beard. "It seems they plan to intimidate."

"They don't need to assault us," Lancelot said. "They can just sit there scratching their balls and starve us out."

Arthur smiled. For once he had a counter to Lancelot's dark assessment. "They don't know we have the Cauldron of Plenty. They'll starve before we do."

"But will the curse continue to worsen?" Lancelot asked.

"One problem at a time, Lance," Arthur said. "Our focus now must be on defending the keep and watching for any tricks they might be trying to play. And we must buy Fionna and Merlin time to discover what has been hidden."

The soldiers below were falling silent, a pregnant hush falling over the landscape. The horde of warriors parted as O'Lynn walked forward with Morgana at his side.

Fionna's father Brin was slowly ascending the stairs, and then halted next to Arthur. "It's a fine fortress you have here," he said softly, his eyes fixed on the mass below.

"But?" Arthur asked, his eyes not leaving his enemies' form.

"But I know a thing or two about the calm before the storm, lad. And a great storm is about to break upon yer shores, Arthur Pendragon. I'm sorry for my part in it."

"My father set this into action long ago with his greed and treachery. No apologies necessary." Hot tears burned the back of Arthur's eyes as he grit out, "This war is now mine to finish as Uther's bastard prince."

As much as Arthur had wanted to be different, to avoid his father's bloody legacy, the battle had still found him. Here he was, unwittingly pitted against the Túatha dé Danann. The name Pendragon carried the might of a dynasty, but also all the blood that had been spilled. Yet . . . perhaps there could be another way. If Uther Pendragon stood upon this wall, he would vow to crush the army below him like an insect beneath his boot. If war was Uther's way, could not diplomacy be Arthur's? Surely there was some way to solve this through negotiations. And, if not, talking could buy Fionna and Merlin the time they needed to break the géis.

"O'Lynn," Arthur shouted, his voice carrying on the wind. "Before we suffer even more of a grievous loss of life, I would treat with you. To see if we can reach a peace between us!"

Lancelot and the other knights looked at him sharply but said nothing. In this, Arthur was king, and they obeyed.

"Peace?" O'Lynn hollered back. The scoffing tone of his voice was clear even at this distance.

But then Morgana leaned in, whispering in his ear.

What Arthur would give to be a fly buzzing about that conversation. To know what schemes she concocted, even now.

"We agree to a meeting," O'Lynn shouted. "Tomorrow at daybreak. Before yer gates."

"We each bring a delegation of four," Arthur shouted. "No more."

"Agreed," O'Lynn replied.

Arthur heaved a sigh, and then turned to Lancelot.

"You do not think there can be peace with Morgana, do you?" Lancelot was incredulous.

"Likely not. But I just bought Lady Fionna another night."

"If I may," Brin said. "Do not let yer guard down. It would be like the Uí Tuírtri to mount a sneak offensive while yer not looking."

"A wise caution, Your Majesty," Arthur said. "Lancelot, I want soldiers patrolling every crack of these walls."

Lancelot nodded. "Who will you bring?"

"Merlin and Lady Fionna." Arthur considered. He wanted Lancelot and Galahad here, commanding his troops. The soldiers were most familiar with them, and they would keep cool heads if anything went wrong. "Sir Percival, bring that adder stone of yours. You will be the fourth. We will have advanced warning, if Morgana tries anything."

"Aye," Percival said eagerly.

Arthur turned. "I'm going to see how things are going for Merlin and Fionna. Hopefully they've made some progress." He turned and hurried down the stairs, his mind racing. What could he offer Morgana and her sisters that would appease them? Presently, they wanted nothing short of his kingdom, perhaps his very life. He would not yield to their vengeful whims willingly.

"Arthur!"

Arthur recoiled as he almost smashed into Fionna. Merlin was following close behind. He let out a rueful grin. "Apologies," Arthur said. "I was not paying attention to where I was going."

"Ye have much on your mind," Fionna said. Her silver eyes were shining, and her color was high. Did they have a breakthrough? "We could hear the shouts and war cries from Merlin's cave."

"The enemies are at our gates," Arthur said. "Please tell me you have made some progress."

Fionna glanced sideways at Merlin, who stepped up beside her. "We have and we have not. Fionna did make contact with Danu. The goddess was not able to lift the géis. But, she gave us an idea for how to help Fionna break free."

"Excellent!" Arthur said. "Let's do what is necessary. What are we waiting for?"

"It is not so simple a thing," Fionna said, ducking her chin and shifting her focus to her boots.

"Perhaps I will leave you two to talk," Merlin said, and then he swooped off towards the wall.

Fionna studied the dirt beneath her, where she was toeing the ground with her boot. Her lips thinned into a straight line as an uncharacteristic spark of doubt glittered in her distracted silvered gaze. Then, in typical Fionna fashion, she lifted her head and straightened her shoulders, her eyes peering ahead as if a sentry on guard.

Arthur's heart stuttered in his chest. To see Fionna so uncertain was a strange vision indeed. He took her chin gently in his hand, tilting her face so she met his eyes. "Whatever this challenge is, we will meet it together."

She licked her lips, her eyes flicking from his. "That's the thing, My King. Danu shared how the only way for us to break the géis is"––She sucked in a ragged breath and then the words tumbled out––"for ye and I to wed. And join together."

Arthur felt rooted to the earth as her words sank in. He and Fionna, wed? The very thought made him lightheaded with joy. He wished for nothing else in his heart of hearts––but . . . she seemed so uncertain.

"You do not seem pleased at this turn of events," Arthur said carefully. "Do you not wish to wed?"

She tore her chin from his fingers, looking away. Tears glittered in her eyes. "I wish it more than anything in this world," she admitted softly. "But I don't know if this is what ye want. I would not have you take me as a wife out of obligation, nor crown me queen consort of Caerleon if ye wish for a different political alliance."

I wish it more than anything in this world.

Her words melted into his very essence, setting his soul aflame with light and fire and desire. Fionna wanted to marry him. To have Fionna at his side, in his bed, all the days of his life—such an outcome could only be a delirious dream. "Princess Fionnabhair," he whispered, his voice cracking with emotion. "I too wish to marry you more than anything in this world."

"Truly?" She looked at him with breathless hope. "A king is to seek his future queen's hand, is he not? And ye had not asked—"

"We've been a little busy," Arthur said, his eyebrows shooting up. "And since when did Fionna Allán see fit to be bound by the constraints of Welsh societal tradition?"

A smile grew on her face, and it was as if the sun broke from behind the clouds, bathing him in its warm glow. "So . . . we're to be married?"

Arthur nodded, feeling his own grin stretch across his face until his cheeks wanted to cry out from the might of it. "We shall marry." He swooped her up into his arms and spun her around and around until he was drunk on dizziness. "We're getting married!" he shouted to the heavens and all who were listening. For in the history of mankind, he thought a man had never been happier than he in this very moment.

Chapter Twenty-Four

Fionna

The world spun beneath me as Arthur twirled me around and around, until I was dizzy with the headiness of our moment.

Arthur placed me down gently and then his lips were on mine as I staggered into his chest, anchoring myself in his strong stance, his firm foundation. His kiss set my head spinning all the more—insistent and full of promise. My toes curled at the thought of a night with Arthur—the only one of my knights I had not lain with. As though, deep down, I knew to save this special moment for last.

At the thought of my other knights, my elation dimmed.

Someone nearby cleared their throat, and I seized upon the distraction, breaking off the kiss. It was Merlin.

"Congratulations," the druid said, nodding at us. His unlined face was impassive as ever, but something about him seemed . . . pleased. "There are arrangements to be made. Shall we convene in three candle-marks time in the Great Hall?"

"Perfect," Arthur said, his arm about my shoulders. "We'll rally what we can for a ceremony. You will preside?"

Merlin inclined his head. "It would be my honor, Your Majesty."

My father, Percival, and Galahad were crossing the courtyard to join us.

"Is it true?" Brin asked. "I heard ye hollering. Is my darling daughter to be wed?"

I nodded, and my father crossed the distance between us, pulling me into his arms. "Congratulations, lass," he whispered in my ear. "May yer years be filled with happiness."

I fought the lump in my throat as I pulled back, as my father shook Arthur's hand, offering him kind words. But my eyes were locked onto Percival and Galahad, the sad smiles on their faces. Percival stepped up first, pulling me into an embrace. I breathed in the citrus scent of him, the warm aura of sunshine that washed over me. "I suppose I always knew he'd take the prize, dove," Percival said, attempting a shaky smile. "But it was fun to play. And . . . and I will still love ye until my dying breath."

Tears shimmered in my eyes, as a blizzard of emotions buffeted me. This wasn't right. To feel happy and so full of sorrow at the same time. Did marrying Arthur truly mean giving up these other extraordinary men? Resigning them to sadness and want? Galahad embraced me next, and a sob wracked my body, despite my every effort to hold in my emotions. My big knight enveloped me, as warm as a hearth fire and as strong as an oak tree. To never again see the golden stretch of Galahad's skin, tawny beneath my pale fingers . . .

"Be strong," Galahad whispered in my ear. "It is a knight's duty to sacrifice for their king. And no one deserves yer love more than Arthur."

His words emboldened me. He was right. I did love Arthur deeply, and I had never known a king or a man worthier of devotion. So why did my heart cry out for more?

"Lancelot?" I asked.

"He's watching the wall," Percival said. I looked up and spotted his dark curls against the fading dusk. He looked away as our eyes met, turning back to the army below. It would be too much to exchange these regrets with him.

I hastily wiped a threatening tear and turned with a bright smile toward Arthur. My king. My soon-to-be husband. Arthur caught the look on my face and his gaze flicked to Percival and

Galahad, his own smile dimming.

"I need a dress!" I said, and hurried toward my chamber, away from the prying eyes of these men who saw and understood too much.

aerleon's servants did an admirable job of readying the keep for a wedding, given the hostile army camping at our gate and the limited time to prepare for the festivities. Several serving girls rallied to my aid, drawing a bath for me in record time. After scrubbing the blood and grime of war from my body, they helped me wash and then braid my hair in an intricate crown atop my head with half of my waist-length hair cascading down my back. Another found a gown, a resplendent thing in dark red trimmed in gold—the colors of my king's banner–the swooping neckline and cuffs beaded with tiny pearls. I hardly felt ready when the time came for me to walk to the Great Hall. My stomach flipped with nerves.

My father waited outside my room, clad in a fresh tunic. "I thought ye might like an escort." He offered me his arm.

"I'm so glad ye're here Da," I said, hitching my elbow through his. "If only Aideen could be here too."

"We'll get her back." Brin patted my hand.

"Aye, we will."

"Perhaps ye have one thing to thank that bastard O'Lynn for," my father continued. "I would be captured a hundred times if it meant you would end up here, where ye were meant to be. Happy."

"It would be nice for me to be happy *without* ye having to be captured and tortured . . ." I smiled.

"If wishes were horses, beggars would ride," he said.

We rounded the corner, and Arthur stood, waiting nervously by the door. He had bathed and changed too, and now looked devastatingly handsome in a tunic of dark red—a similar shade to my gown—the hems trimmed with gold. His polished oak-leaf crown sat atop his brows, one now arching as he gaze roved over my face.

"Might I have a minute with Fionna, Your Majesty?" Arthur asked, his eyes never leaving mine. "Before we go in."

"Ye're the king," Brin said, and gave me a kiss on the cheek, before slipping through the double doors.

Arthur took my hands, looking me up and down reverently. "You look as beautiful as the sunrise."

I smiled. "You'll do too."

Arthur took in a deep breath, ignoring my attempts at humor. "I have been thinking. It does not seem right for our happiness to come at the expense of my brothers'. Lancelot, Galahad, Percival . . . they love you as much as I. And I know you love them too. We are family, all of us together."

I softened, stroking his cheek, feeling the smooth skin of his fresh shave. "Never was there a more generous man than ye, Arthur Pendragon. It is one of the many reasons I love ye." An idea was churning in my mind, a dream I kept locked tight in the deepest recesses of my heart. A way that all of us might be together. If Arthur was open. And his words warmed me that he might be. But Arthur deserved a wedding. A bride. A queen. Just as I had moments with each of my knights, my king deserved a moment all to himself. "I choose all of ye, it's true. Ye each own a piece of my heart. But let us think only on the piece you hold tonight. Ye and me. I would have us focus on our joy. To celebrate our love. There will be time to discuss a different future, with all of us together, as one." I hoped.

Arthur nodded, exhaling. "I would like that very much."

"Shall we?" I held out my hand, and Arthur took it, threading his fingers through mine.

"We shall."

The servants had managed to find bouquets of wildflowers and bows of greenery to festoon around the tables nearby where Merlin stood. Candles flickered on stands behind him while unlit tapers rested in the hands of those who gathered. The room crowded with people, nobles and villagers alike, who had been ushered inside the safety of the keep's walls from O'Lynn's ravaging. In the front row stood my knights, even Lancelot. I swallowed, trying to catch his eye, but he looked straight ahead, his rugged face stoic. I tucked thoughts of them aside, as carefully as a baby bird. I had meant what I said. Arthur deserved my undivided attention at our wedding.

Merlin raised his hands above his head and said, "Let us form a circle and bless this place."

I joined hands with Percival and Arthur, who joined hands with the other knights and nobles until we formed a circle. The remaining crowd stood at our backs as we watched Merlin lift a bundle of burning sage and meadowsweet.

The druid paced the perimeter of the circle, saying, "Elements of the north, come. Elements of the east, you are welcome. Elements of the south, join us. Elements of the west, attend us now. Gods and goddesses, we invite you to witness and bless the sacred union between Arthur Pendragon, High King of Briton, to Fionnabhair Allán, the Gwenevere, daughter of Danu, and earth- and sovereignty-goddess."

Murmurs rumbled around the circle, curious eyes glancing my way. But I ignored them all.

Merlin reached for the Blessed Grail on the table behind him and then dipped his fingers into the enchanted bowl. "We cleanse this circle of any wickedness and impurity." Lifting his fingers from the water, he flicked droplets across the stone floors as he paced round and round. "May only goodness and health flow from these stones and dance in this air." When complete, he set the Grail back onto the table and then approached me and Arthur. "Come, My King and his faerie bride. Step into the circle's center and open your hearts to the Earth and all her blessings. She smiles upon your union this day." The rings around Merlin's eyes flashed gold as his pupils narrowed to slits. "Yes, she has many riches in store for you both."

Arthur led me to the center, weaving his fingers with mine. His chest rose and fell in a quick rhythm, much like my own. An energy was present, one that flowed through my veins, my muscles, tingling, dripping sweet like honey until the very sensation coated me completely.

Merlin next grabbed a candle from the stand behind him and lit Lancelot's candle, who then lit Galahad's, then Percival's and so forth until the circle illuminated with tiny, sinewy flames. The image was magic itself. The amber glow painted me and Arthur in flickering shadows and light. Dressed in the Pendragon red, we appeared as though fire-breathing dragons. Mighty. Immortal. And fierce.

With a ceremonial hemp cord, Merlin began tying a knot over my and Arthur's clasped hand, his lips moving in ancient incantations and blessings. Arthur's green eyes met mine and held me captive. He was the blazing hearth fire of home, a soothing cool breeze in summer, a sturdy oak rooted deep in the earth, and a warm rainfall in spring. But most of all, he was my king and I was his land. And, from this point forward, I possessed power over his kingship as well as the health of his people. A power he granted me willingly.

My knees threatened to buckle, my legs wobbly. Even as Arthur spoke his vows and I spoke mine. Even when Merlin removed the corded knot from our hands. And when Arthur placed a crown of golden holly leaves and berries upon my brows. Together, we ruled the seasons, all the elements, light and darkness and, through our consummation, fertility for the land and her people.

The bright, tingling power surged through me and my head grew faint at the Otherworldly feel of Arthur's mouth pressing against mine. "My Queen," he whispered across my lips, claiming the breath in my lungs and the very beat of my heart. Ribbons of smoke twirled and writhed upward from the many candles now snuffed out in people's hands.

The crowd cheered around us. Then the knights and nobles rushed toward us in a crushing embrace.

I floated on wings of ebullience through the quick, makeshift feast. Nodding when I should and answering questions as they crossed my path. But my head was full of Arthur. An energy was building within me. The same energy that entered me in the circle's center. I thought I would burst as my heart cried out to know his pulse intimately. Then he grabbed my hand, a boyish smile on those very lips I wanted to taste again, and he led me out of the Great Hall and toward the gardens.

Chapter Twenty-Five

Fionna

Waning sunlight haloed Arthur in billowing golds and corals. The evening wind toyed with his shortened strands and carried to me the verdant scents of an oak forest, freshly cut apples, and spiced wine. I wanted to bury my nose against his skin and breathe deeply.

He led me past the kitchen garden to a seam in the timbered wall nearby. From the naked eye, the hidden opening appeared as though solid beams of hewn wood. A continuing wall. But, once through the opening, a new world spread out before me, one I had never encountered in all my explorations. "Beautiful," I said under my breath.

Slowing to a stop, Arthur cupped my face, his eyes searching mine. "I love you, Fionnabhair Allán," he whispered. "With your permission, I would know you completely."

"Yes," I breathed. "Ye have my permission, Arthur Pendragon."

His eyes shuttered as he drew in a giddy breath. "We should be alone here. Safe from both prying eyes and invading armies." He gestured to the wild garden around us, secluded by several trees and a partial timber wall jutting out from the keep, but protected by the outlaying defensive wall. Flowers in every color of the rainbow blanketed the ground and climbed trellises all around us, as though a storied faerie garden. "This was my mother's favorite spot when she wished to hide." His smile dimmed. "But I would be glad to build new memories here with you. Happy ones."

I placed my hand on his chest and he looked away, brows furrowed, though he continued to cradle my face in his hands. "I am sorry we cannot journey into the forest alone," Arthur said.

Danu had explained to me that the best chance of awakening my powers would be found if we lay together upon the earth itself. "I care not where we make love," I replied. "Only that my heart can finally know the beating rhythm of yers."

He returned his gaze to mine in a single, soft blink. "Then, My Queen," he whispered, "marry me to the land and make me your king."

We couldn't shed our clothes fast enough. Though, at the same time, we wanted to relish each new flash of skin. He untied my gown from behind until the bodice slipped down my arms and gathered at my breasts. The silk caressed my body and I shivered with delight, anticipating Arthur's touch. His lips pressed to my shoulder. Then his mouth traveled to my neck, until he nibbled on my ear lobe.

"Not even the beauty of the moon compares to you," he whispered in my ear. His warm breath pulsed onto my skin and my eyes fluttered closed. "Nor do the stars in the night sky hold a flickering candle to the soft lines and curves of your body."

Pleasure rushed through me at his poetic words and the sultry gravel of voice.

"Your breasts," he continued, his hands cupping the soft mounds and encouraging my gown to pool at my feet. "Your skin, and goddess above, your hips . . . they hold a spell over me." He stepped away from my back and turned me gently but firmly to face him. And, when his lips brushed along mine, he whispered, "And your mouth. You taste like an orchard in bloom. I want to savor your every kiss."

My fingers trailed down the freckles of his muscled chest as his lips captured mine. His skin was deliciously warm and drew me closer until my breasts pressed into the hard, ribbed lines of his torso. I ached to be surrounded by him, to drown in the heat of his passion. His arms wrapped around my waist as his hands splayed across the toned lines of my back as our kiss deepened.

His touch humbled me—reverent and soft—as if I were the most fragile thing he had ever held. And perhaps I was, for I knew I claimed not only his heart, but his land. I owned him completely now, and there was no going back. Other marriages may handfast for a year and a day, but not ours. We were forever bound before the gods and elements.

Gently, he lowered me beneath him in the swaying wildflowers. The moss and grass cradled my trembling body. The energy wanted release. Wanted *him*.

His fingers tenderly brushed strands of flyaway hair from my face as his eyes drank me in. "I am so in love with you," he said. "I am lost in this feeling."

"Come find me, then," I said in playful reply.

A shy smile played across his lips. This boyish side of him always pulled on my heartstrings. We were a king and a queen, a ruler and a demi-goddess. But this moment, as I took in his rising blush, cherished each freckle on his face, felt the way his fingers grazed along my side, past my hip, to my thigh, we were just a boy and a girl. In the face of our enemies and tribulations, it was easy to forget that I was only twenty years old and he just two and twenty. But here, our kingdoms and duties and powers fell away until our breath formed the wind fluttering the leaves above us and our bodies became the very earth we lay upon.

He slid into me as we kissed, and I gasped as the building power swirling within me released into him. He sucked in a deep breath, his eyes closing with the feel me. All of me. The ground beneath us tremored, similar to my experience with Percival. And, for a single sand of time, I thought of this, how both Percival and Arthur were sovereign-blessed kings, and how I had joined with them both and only when the earth lay beneath my back.

Then we began to move, all else forgotten but Arthur. His strong arms embraced me as his hips ground into mine. I could feel the sculpted muscles of his chest, his stomach, the way the muscles of his back rolled beneath my fingertips. He was beautiful, a breathtaking dance of passion and love, infused with the headiest romance

I have ever known. Even the way his body moved was poetry.

His lips kissed down my throat and then dragged back to mine. "I want to become the sun in your hands," he whispered. "To burn . . . to know total destruction."

My breath stirred for an intoxicating beat of my heart. And then I rolled him over until he was pressed into the moss and grass. Wildflowers swayed around my head and the wind fingered through the long tresses rippling down my back. The sun sank behind the walls and trees and brushed the sky in streaks of lavender and indigo.

Our eyes locked as my hips began to roll against his. "Burn, My King," I said, and his arms fell over his head as pleasure rippled through us both in glittering waves of bliss. Light and sensation filled my body as I watched this gorgeous, powerful man surrender to me. Bearing his neck and leaving his body vulnerable. I understood his demonstration of submission and tears pricked at my eyes. He would lay his life down before me to destroy and make whole.

"Arthur . . ." I moaned his name when the earth rose up to consume me. I was every blade of grass, the breaking dawn, the life-giving soil. Glistening dew drops rolled down my body like twinkling stars. My fingernails dug into his pectorals as he heaved for breath, his lips flushed with arousal. His fingers gripped my arse, pulling me tighter against him. Deeper. With every thrust of his hips, I died. With every roll of mine, I was reborn.

The swirling, tingling energy—I could now name the sensation. Thousands of roots curled through me and anchored me to the earth in sensual touches. Unfurling leaves of feral light shimmered along my self-control until every scintillating beam bloomed in my core. I turned to fire, ablaze with the feel of Arthur's body tangling with mine. He was an oak tree and I was his life-giving energy, our limbs the rambling roots burying deep into the soil of our future.

In this place, we were a mighty force. Armies blew away before us in a hot gust of fury. The ground healed and brightened to every vibrant shade imaginable. Our love was immovable. Our destiny unshakable.

Arthur cried out first, his body arching in muscled spasms of pleasure. I cried out next as my body became moonlight—silvered, crystallized dust and the throbbing illumination of an entire star-flecked sky. We remained still, basking in the glow of our love-making. Even as his seed dripped from my thighs and anointed the ground.

His eyes fluttered open and then he stared at me in hazy bliss. I had married my king to the land.

My hand fluttered up to feel the curve of my ear. It was human as always—no sharp faerie point. And though I had felt a taste of the earthen magic brewing inside of me when we joined, it had drained from me with our climax. I now felt the same as before. A warrior princess from across the Irish Sea who held the heart of a king and his three knights. Sated and languid with the love of a king, but not magic. Not . . . godlike. Disappointment welled within me. Perhaps I wasn't the Gwenevere and my vision of Danu had been induced by desperation alone.

I looked around the garden and frowned. No change. Same as when I drank from the Grail at the Red Spring. Same as when I joined with Percival in the forest, even though the earth trembled beneath me.

Arthur caressed my cheek. "My wife . . ."

Tears gathered on my eyelashes and spilled down my cheeks. "It didn't work," I said through the lump growing in my throat.

"Fionna," he whispered softly. "You are all I have ever wanted. Anything else you bring to our union is a bonus. But you . . . you are more than enough. You're my every heartbeat. My very breath."

He wiped away a tear with his thumb and then gathered me to him. There, in this hidden garden, Arthur held me as I wept, our bodies entangled, my head pressed into the crook of his neck. I had once stolen his sword and risked his kingship. Now, I represented the very land he ruled. And I was still broken.

Chapter Twenty-Six

Lancelot

The stench of burning feathers carried on the wind. An insufferable scent. O'Lynn's war camp must have burned dead crows and their fallen throughout the entire night.

But the reeking haze in the air wasn't what truly bothered Lancelot.

The keep felt different this morning. Lancelot felt different. As if a weight hung around his neck, a heavy shroud cloaking his body and blocking out the air and light. Was it the enemies surrounding them, pressing at their walls with oppressive presence? Or was it the fact that Fionna was wed. She was his queen. And she was Arthur's. And queens didn't deign to fraternize with mere knights. Even if they were exiled French faerie princes.

Last night, as the delicate circlet of holly leaves was placed on her brow, Fionna had looked more beautiful than he had ever seen her. And more distant. She had tried to catch his eye a dozen times, as she stood in the circle at the ceremony, as she sipped from a golden goblet at the hasty feast. He couldn't bring himself to meet those silver pools. To see in them all that could have been. And would never be. Was it better to taste heaven's sweet essence and then have it ripped from you, or to never know? Lancelot thought he preferred the latter. It was ironic, in a way. In the end, Morgana's curse wasn't even necessary. Fate saw fit to rob Lancelot of the only woman he had ever truly loved. His Gwenevere.

He trudged outside to meet the others where they were to gather before the gates. It was time for Arthur to treat with O'Lynn and Morgana. A risk, but a risk worth taking if it bought Fionna enough time to break the géis and unlock her powers.

At the gates, she was the only one waiting. Gone was the gauzy dress of last night, the one that hugged every lithe curve. She was back in her boiled-leather armor, her swords at her hips, her hair braided in a long tail down her back. She turned as he approached, as if she felt his very presence.

"Lancelot," she murmured, her hand drifting to her heart as she gazed upon him.

"My queen," he said, bowing deeply at the waist.

"Don't do that," she crooned. The space between them felt as wide as the waters separating Britannia from the mainland.

He muttered, "It's only proper."

"Since when are *ye* concerned with propriety?" she asked. "Ye don't fawn over Arthur like *that*. Nothing has changed. I'm still me."

"Everything has changed," he replied.

His words were flint, lighting the fire in her eyes. She stepped toward him, and he stepped back. "It changes nothing about how I feel for ye."

"I'm sure your husband would have something to say about that." Lancelot knew his words were unfair. Especially as he knew why they had wed so suddenly, with so little discussion. But he couldn't help it. Two days ago, he had been buried to the hilt in this enthralling woman, his heart soaring as though he had never flown before. And now she was wed to another.

To Arthur. His brother.

Percival and Galahad approached, and Lancelot seized upon the distraction. "You ready Percy?" he asked, but Percival ignored him, approaching Fionna and pulling her into an embrace. "Congratulations, dove," he said, and Fionna leaned into him, burying her face in his chest.

Lancelot exchanged a look with Galahad as his chest tightened with envy. How did Percival do that? Make affection look so easy.

Let the twists of fate fall from his shoulders like water off a duck's back? Perhaps Percival's love for Fionna was purer than his own. A love little concerned with propriety or jealousy or competition. Unconditional. That was Percival. And one of the reasons his own heart desired this man for himself as well.

They broke off their embrace and turned, Percival still with his arm slung around Fionna's shoulder. "To answer your question, crabapple, I am indeed ready. Adder stone in hand. Well, in pocket," he finished.

"How do ye feel?" Galahad asked Fionna. His words were careful—formal—with none of the sultry banter they'd carried in the past. Their big knight was holding himself back from their new queen as well. "Different? Powerful?" Fionna and Merlin had explained how Danu thought marrying Arthur and laying with him might be the only way to break the géis that blocked her from embodying her full Gwenevere powers.

Fionna shrugged, brushing a strand of hair back from her forehead. "The same, honestly. Like me. I'm not sure what I was expecting . . . but I don't feel anything new." Her lips tilted in a frown and she shifted on her feet, clearing her throat.

"Maybe there's a delayed reaction," Percival suggested.

"Or perhaps your magic requires a threat to activate," Galahad offered. "Your powers will appear when the time is right. Like the Grail Sword."

"Perhaps," Fionna said. "I just wish Danu could have helped me. Helped us. She got me into this, seems like she should be the one to get me out."

"Goddesses," Percival quipped. "Can't live with 'em, can't live without 'em."

"I just hope we're all living at the end of this," Galahad remarked.

Arthur and Merlin crossed the courtyard to join them. Arthur's color was high, his eyes sparkled with vigor as he met Fionna's. Lancelot supposed wedding and bedding the woman of your dreams, who also happened to be a demi-goddess in disguise, would do that to a man.

"It's time," Arthur said, pulling his gaze away from Fionna and taking them all in. "We'll see if we can find a way through this mess. Perhaps diplomacy isn't dead."

"Be careful," Lancelot found himself saying. "Keep your eyes on her."

Arthur slid him wary look and nodded. There was no confusing who he meant.

Galahad and Lancelot stood ram-rod straight as the other four strode toward the wide oaken gates.

"Open the gates," Arthur called out, and soldiers manning the gates hopped into action, retracting the big oaken bars.

"I can't shake the feeling that this is a terrible idea," Galahad said quietly, his eyes locked onto the four figures filing through the narrowly opened doors. "Even death's ash clings to the air."

Lancelot frowned, his brows furrowing deeply. "My observation as well."

Lancelot paced stiffly through the keep. Last night he had checked on the soldiers in the barracks, secured the positions of the men along the wall. Weapons were oiled and sharpened, and bundles of arrows were stacked neatly next to jugs of oil. The Great Hall had been returned to its role as makeshift medical ward and hospital, with supplies piled and ready for any coming battle. Merlin had spent the evening making food in the Cauldron of Plenty, which, though some remarkable turn of druidic magic, had transformed to a cauldron large enough for a man to sit inside. Sacks of grain, piles of potatoes, squash, and figs, even jugs of ale all came out of this remarkable cauldron, filling their larders and stores. They were as ready as they could be for a siege or a battle.

But, still, Lancelot felt jumpy and uneasy. He had passed the unsettled feeling off as lingering effects from Fionna's wedding. But, if he were being honest with himself, that wasn't the reason. Something niggled at him, as if he had left a candle burning unsupervised in his chamber or forgotten something necessary.

His feet carried him into the hallways, through the back of the keep and toward the rear gate that led to the path down to Merlin's cave. Though they normally kept the gate open, the secret door in the keep's wall was invisible from the outside when the doors were closed, vanishing into just another stretch of formidable stone and timber. It was the only other way into the keep beside the front gate. And, unless a person knew it was there, they would never find the opening.

A lightning bolt of realization struck him. "Idiot!" he shouted at himself, so loud he startled a passing serving woman. In all his concern over rescuing Fionna and Percival from their own fool rescue plan, followed by Fionna's Gwenevere powers, and the wedding, he had completely forgotten that Morgana apprenticed to Merlin. She knew about this secret door. She knew exactly where to find it too.

Lancelot broke into a run, his boots flying on the stone floors. They needed to reinforce the door. They needed to station men at the entrance in case O'Lynn attempted an assault. O'Lynn and Morgana would, without question, take advantage of a distraction created by peace negotiations to break in the back door.

He burst out of the main keep, barreling across the narrow courtyard to the back wall. He took the stairs two at a time, shouldering past surprised servants. Morning fog still clung to the ground outside the keep, not an uncommon sight in this marine climate. He hung over the edge of the wall, squinting into the mist. Then at the figures he saw moving there. A silent host, bristling with weapons. Readying to invade the keep.

Chapter Twenty-Seven

Percival

Percival ercival gripped the adder stone tightly in his pocket, its jagged edge cutting into his palm. He didn't know what they would find when they stepped outside the gates, but he suspected it would only be trouble.

No one waited for them on the stone path outside the main gates as Percival, Arthur, Fionna, and Merlin walked slowly to the agreed upon spot to meet O'Lynn. In the distance, three horses approached.

Percival tried to keep his gaze fixed ahead on the horses trotting toward them, but he found his eyes gravitating toward Fionna. Her shoulders were tight; the muscles in her fine jaw were working furiously. She seemed like a notched bowstring waiting to be released.

It hadn't been fair to Fionna—the wedding night she had enjoyed. A ceremony hurried through with enemies at the door. She deserved joy and she deserved a celebration unlike Caerleon had ever seen. She deserved a languished morning naked in the sheets. He swallowed at the memory of her lean body beneath his, the silk of her skin. She deserved the very world.

He wasn't sure why Fionna's marriage to Arthur hadn't hit him like it had his sword brothers. Perhaps because he had known it was inevitable. This was the finale they had been dancing toward this entire time, was it not? Her marriage didn't have to change things. The wedding hadn't changed Fionna's heart, he was certain of that. Nor his. In his and Fionna's Gaelic worlds, lovers outside of marriage were a normal affair and permitted before their laws. And intimacy between warriors was also common, even between noble-titled warriors such as princes and queens. Especially as, unlike Wales and Briton, women were equal among the men and permitted as fellow warriors. So, Percival would keep pushing his luck until his king told him to back off.

The horses were growing nearer, and Percival could make out the riders. Two he recognized, two he did not.

"O'Lynn," Fionna spat.

"Morgana," Merlin said, the gold rings in his eyes flashing with magic.

A dark warrior with a shaved head and a long, black beard rode the last horse. Behind him was a beautiful young woman near his own age, with curls the color of chestnut.

Fionna hissed in a breath next to him, her eyes fixed onto the young woman. "Aideen," she breathed.

Percival and Arthur both looked at her sharply before looking back with a more appraising eye. So, this was Fionna's sister—O'Lynn's new, unwilling bride.

The group reined in their horses about fifty yards from where Percival, Arthur, Fionna, and Merlin stood.

Morgana slid gracefully from her black mare. Her dress was of the deepest blue and showed far more of her pale bosom then Percival imagined was proper. Atop her dark locks sat a sort of crown fashioned of antlers. It reminded Percival of Fionna's stag helm from the day she had earned her place as their fifth knight.

This crown made him uneasy, though. The black-painted bones whispered of dark magic and even darker nights.

The bald warrior before Aideen helped her from the horse and onto the dirt road. It was then that Percival noticed a thin collar around her neck, threaded with a chain the warrior held firmly in his meaty fist.

Fionna must have seen it too, because her swords rang in the crisp morning air as she pulled them from their scabbards. "I'll run the bastard through," she grit between clenched teeth.

Arthur held Excalibur before her, blocking her from O'Lynn's party. "Easy Fionna," Arthur said. It was the voice of a king speaking to his knight, not a husband to his new bride. "He brought Aideen to provoke you. Do not play into his hands."

Fionna mumbled a curse but gave a sharp nod.

Arthur dropped Excalibur, but Percival noticed Fionna did not re-sheathe her swords.

The last to dismount and swagger up to them was Donal O'Lynn himself. The tall broad man was burly, with dark hair and a thick beard. He wore a gold torque about his neck. His boiled leather armor resembled Fionna's, the only thing that set him apart was the emerald green cape that was draped about his shoulders . . . that and the cocky-arse smile on his face.

Percival had never even met the man and he already wanted to slice him through. He couldn't imagine what restraint Fionna must be exercising.

"Arthur Pendragon," the man drawled in his Irish brogue.

"Donal O'Lynn," Arthur replied.

"Aren't ye going to welcome us to Caerleon, one king to another?"

"You have no need of a welcome. I've already seen how you've made yourself quite at home."

A smile spread across O'Lynn's face before he released a low laugh. "Such a fine land," he said. "Shame it's cursed."

Arthur pursed his lips. "Yes well, you need not concern yourself with that small detail. We have a remedy well in hand."

"Does not appear you do, *brother*," Morgana said. Her voice slithered like cold fingers up Percival's spine.

"We are here to discuss the terms of a possible peace between our people," Arthur said, his tone as hard as granite. "You have brought a hostile army to my shores. You have burned and ravaged my villages. But . . . the inevitable clash between our warriors would result in a great loss of life. I am willing to grant you this one chance to reach an accord between us. What is it that you want?"

"Straight to the point," O'Lynn said. "There are a few things I want, lad. That fancy sword of yers . . ."

Arthur's lips tightened into a straight line.

"All yer lands, the keys to this fine keep of yers . . . and that witch at yer side." He nodded toward Fionna.

"This is a peace negotiation," Fionna spat. "And yer request for me is an insult." Her face was furious, her silver eyes flashing between O'Lynn and where Aideen stood demurely with that horrible collar around her neck.

O'Lynn's thumbs were hooked in his belt loops, as if he were having the time of his life.

Arthur held up a hand and Fionna fell silent. "I'm afraid the possession of my wife is not part of our negotiations."

Morgana's eyes widened, and Percival thought he saw something there—something like fear. But the emotion was gone as quickly as it appeared.

O'Lynn's smile slipped but he recovered quickly. "Seems we've both tasted the nectar of the Allán women. Though, I admit, I found the vintage a bit sour."

"Captivity can do that to a woman," Fionna gritted out. "Perhaps if ye could find one ye didn't have to chain—"

But Arthur looked at her, and she fell silent, her fuming rage palpable. "Let me tell you what my terms will be," Arthur said. His composure hadn't slipped a hair's breadth the entire time. Percival had to admit, he was impressed. Arthur continued. "You turn over Aideen to us, and then you leave these shores, never to return. You take no more aggressive action toward Clann Allán and you never conspire with my half-sister or her two sisters again. Those are my terms. What say you?"

O'Lynn smiled deepened as his eyes glittered wickedly. "Appears we will be unable to reach an accord, Pendragon."

The gate creaked open behind them and Percival dared a glance over his shoulder.

Lancelot slipped through the doors, hurrying toward them.

"What is this?" O'Lynn said.

"Peace," Arthur said, holding up a hand. "There must be a matter of some importance. He means you no harm."

"I'll be the judge that. The agreement was four, Pendragon, and here I see five."

Lancelot whispered in Arthur's ear even as O'Lynn bellowed at him.

Percival watched as Arthur's face darkened, turning stormy. He whipped his head back to the party before them. "My second tells me that there are Uí Tuírtri warriors surrounding our keep even now. You have broken the terms of this engagement." Arthur pulled Excalibur from its sheath. And the sound vibrated through Percival's very chest.

Following suit, Percival pulled out his blade, not sure what would happen next. Would Arthur engage? Or retreat to the keep?

But something very unexpected happened, something that robbed all thoughts of battle from his mind. Darkness fell over their party as thick as pitch. Cries of alarm arose from both Arthur and Lancelot.

But with the adder stone in Percival's hand, he peered through a strange bubble of daylight. Morgana's hands were up, the darkness oozing from her like squid ink.

O'Lynn hurried to his horse. He was fleeing.

Relief washed over Percival. They would not come to blows. Not yet anyway.

Then, in the bubble of light, he caught sight of something that chilled the blood raging through his veins.

Fionna—blind as a bat, bathed in unnatural darkness—sprinted across the distance between them and O'Lynn. Toward her sister.

"Fionna!" Percival couldn't help the cry that escaped from his mouth. For the warrior who held Aideen's chain had pulled a knife from his belt, a blade as long as his forearm, and swung the knife wildly before him. And Fionna was running straight toward the warrior.

Fionna connected with her sister. Their hands grasped at each other, the women crashing together with the force of a lifetime of sisterhood ripped apart.

Percival sprinted toward Fionna even as the warrior who held Aideen's chain stabbed blindly. But it was too late.

The warrior brought his wicked dagger down—into Fiona's back.

She stiffened in surprise, her mouth opening in a silent scream, her body going rigid in Aideen's arms.

Percival was crossing the distance, but his legs were too slow.

The warrior pulled the knife out and stabbed again. And again.

Aideen screamed her sister's name. Tears coursed down her face.

Percival rammed the man through to the hilt with his sword in the strange darkness, a roar of fury bellowing from him.

"Percival?" Fionna said as she staggered backward into his arms.

"Fionna!" Aideen cried out, but O'Lynn moved his horse between them, and it was all Percival could do to get a grip under Fionna's back and knees and haul her up into his arms.

He turned and lunged toward the keep, Fionna's blood slick on his fingers. Her eyelids fluttered.

It all happened in a few split heartbeats of time—the few measures it took Merlin to counteract Morgana's strange darkness.

Daylight flared once again and Percival blinked at the brightness, almost running into Arthur. His king's eyes went wide at the sight of Fionna in Percival's arms. Fionna bleeding. And dying.

Galahad

Galahad jogged back from the barracks, breathless from rallying the soldiers to defend the keep. Longbow archers were arrayed along the wall above the secret western gate while men boarded up the doors, barricading the narrow corridor with furniture, stray stones, anything they could find.

Galahad had an uneasy feeling in his chest—a tightness. As if in a moment, everything could change. He was eager to return to the courtyard and make sure their king was all right. And their queen. He shoved aside all the emotions that word bubbled to the surface. Fionna was their queen. Arthur's wife. And that was that. A man didn't lie with another man's wife. Certainly not his king's. This was strict code within the Norse village where he'd been raised, and one he took seriously.

The gates were creaking open now and the figures retreating through sent a lance of fear straight to his heart. In Percival's arms was Fionna. Bleeding and unconscious.

"Fetch the chirurgeon, and her father!" Galahad bellowed at a servant, who startled like a skittish deer before running back toward the keep.

"What happened?" Galahad asked as he met them.

Arthur's face was haggard, as if his king had aged a lifetime, while Lancelot's face was more furious than he had ever seen. Even Merlin wore an expression of shock and doubt, more emotion than Galahad had ever witnessed from the stoic druid. Percival appeared as though the only one determined, his arms firmly fixed beneath the body of their fifth knight and queen.

"She went for Aideen," Percival said, his voice breaking. "And was stabbed."

"Her sister was there?" Galahad asked, mouth falling open. What kind of man would flaunt a prisoner at a peace meeting?

"Later," Arthur snarled. "Let's get her inside."

"The Great Hall," Galahad said. "It's been set up as a medical ward." He received his first real look at Fionna as he hurried beside them, and his mouth went dry. Her face was as pale as death, except for the crimson flecks that dotted her lips. Her wound must be grievous indeed. Was she even still breathing?

"Merlin?" Arthur asked as they raced through the halls, as fast as they could go without Percival jostling Fionna too much. "Can you sustain her with your magic?"

"I am trying," Merlin said. The lines furrowing about his mouth and brow deepened. "She is weakening. Perhaps with the herbs in my cave—"

"The cave is cut off," Galahad said. "There's no way."

Merlin grimaced. "I will do what I can."

"Do everything, man," Arthur snapped. "If you have to lend her your own life essence, you do it."

"Of course, my king."

"Set her down here," Galahad said, knocking a bowl and a pile of linens off a table to clear a space.

Percival set her down gently, and when he stepped back, wiping his hair back from his forehead, Galahad saw that his hands—his leathers—were drenched in blood. "My gods," Galahad whispered. Swallowing back his fear, he placed a trembling finger to her wrist, hoping to still feel a pulse.

"She was stabbed in the back," Percival managed as he hiccupped back a sob. His crimson hand hovered before his mouth, his eyes not leaving her. "Three wounds."

Galahad leaned an ear down over her mouth, trying to listen

over the thunder of his heart. To feel some faint whisper of breath. Some sign of life. Something more than the silence he was feeling in her wrist. The absence of movement where a pulse should be. From his vantage with his head crooked, Merlin was in his line of sight. The druid met his eyes and pursed his lips into a thin line. And infinitesimal nod. No. No. Merlin was confirming what the signs were telling Galahad, the ones his mind was refusing to accept.

Galahad slowly straightened, placing Fionna's arm back down at her side, curling his fingers around hers. When he spoke, the words were a rasping whisper. "I'm . . . I'm sorry, Arthur. She—" He sucked in a sharp breath. "She's gone."

Fionnabhair Allán was dead.

Silence settled upon them, thick and deafening. Percival's bloody hand still fluttered before his mouth, while Lancelot looked as white as Fionna, as if he himself had been struck by a mortal blow. Arthur's eyes were wide and wild, and he only shook his head, over and over, his breath coming in tight and quick.

The light that was their Fionna had dimmed and snuffed out.

Galahad looked at her, part of him needing to double check. Wanting to be wrong. Fionna was tough as nails, unyielding as the winter wind. It would take something far more than a blade to wound her. To rip her from this world.

A keening note ripped from Arthur's lips and he fell upon her body, grasping her limp hand in his own, pressing his forehead to her breast. "My queen. My love," he mumbled, and then the sobs came, wracking his body, tearing open the wound Galahad was so valiantly trying to hold together—with little more than determination and duty. For this was Arthur's time to mourn. She was his wife. But Arthur's grief sang to a note in Galahad's own soul that he couldn't fight. Tears began to fall, hot and salty, gathering in his beard.

Percival rubbed at his face, her blood streaking down his eyes and cheeks. He muttered, "I didn't reach her in time. Oh gods—" His body began to shake as his own tears streamed through Fionna's blood. "I couldn't save her," he sputtered through his grief. "I couldn't save her. I'll . . . I'll never forgive myself." Lancelot turned

Percival away from the awful sight and then the two men clung to each other. Percival buried his head into Lancelot's shoulders, their dark knight becoming a solid rock against the tide of sorrow. But an ember of volatile grief flickered in Lancelot's steeled eyes and, when the vengeance emerged, Galahad knew that O'Lynn would never know what dark, violent power of wrath sliced him and Morgana through.

Arthur gripped Fionna's body to his, her head lolling off his arm. Every part of Arthur shook as he openly wept, apologizing over and over again to her corpse. Silver eyes stared absently at Galahad.

Galahad turned, a shudder of sorrow clawing down his spine. He was unable to bear the sight of Fionna's perfectly still body any longer. Hushed stillness where vibrancy and life had been only moments before. Her body looked frail and small without the vitality of Fionna's essence. His king's keening sobs pierced the remainder of Galahad's resolve. He wiped tears from his cheek with the back of his hand, knowing it was useless, for more quickly followed. His eyes darted from object to object, anything to distract him from his reality. Anything to dull the pain. Skipping past Merlin, Galahad's gaze fell upon the Cauldron of Plenty, sitting quietly in the corner of the Great Hall, forgotten by all including the shocked servants who stood about, their eyes wide with the sight of their king's wild grief.

The Cauldron of Plenty. Hadn't Merlin and Vivien shared how the Cauldron was rumored to be so powerful that it could even raise the dead?

A spark flared within the cold corners of Galahad's heartbreak.

He strode over to Merlin and seized the druid's arm, spinning him around and pointing at the Cauldron with a desperate finger. "Could it work?" He gripped Merlin's muscular bicep tighter, clinging to this last vestige of hope. For a different future.

Merlin's eyes rounded. "By the gods, it just might."

Galahad staggered back, wiping away his tears. Purpose and hope surged through him bright as a sunrise.

"Arthur," Merlin barked. "The Cauldron. The relic resurrects. Bring her here."

Arthur lifted his head, his eyes clouded and hazy. "She is gone," Arthur whispered, then spat, "Do not toy with me, druid."

Merlin clapped his hands, and it seemed the very thing to break Arthur free of his fog. "We have a chance to save her! Bring her body here!"

Blinking back his tears, Arthur scooped up Fionna and strode across the room.

"What magic is this?" Lancelot asked as he and Percival pulled apart.

"The Cauldron of Plenty is a powerful relic of the gods," Galahad said. "It's rumored to be able to resurrect the dead, remember?"

Percival's eyes lit up. "Och, what are we waiting for?! Do it!"

"We are doing it," Merlin snapped. He was helping Arthur lower Fionna's body into the cauldron. She disappeared into the black bowl as their hands released her body. Galahad and the others crowded closer. Fionna's body was curled into the fetal position on the bottom of the cauldron.

"You four," Merlin said. "Arrange yourselves around the cauldron." He stepped back and allowed each of them to form a circle around the relic. "Lancelot and Percival, you switch." Merlin said.

"What are you doing?" Galahad asked.

"Something I thought when we were first searching for a fifth knight, but the idea has only just crystallized in my mind. There is preternatural strength in your connection. The five elements. Fire," he pointed to Lancelot. "Earth," to Arthur, "Air," to Percival, "and water" to Galahad. "Fionna is the aether, the fifth element that binds you. I will draw on your essence while working the cauldron. It will strengthen the spell, and hopefully pull her soul back into her body."

"What must we do?" Lancelot asked.

"Just be willing," Merlin said. He pushed up his sleeves and closed his eyes. He then began chanting in a voice that raised the fine hairs on the back of Galahad's neck. Magic made him uneasy, but for Fionna, he would endure anything. A wind rose, even in the closed room, fluttering the tendrils of Galahad's hair. Merlin's words seemed to course through him, mingling with his blood until they were galloping through his veins, filling him with a tingling feeling unlike any sensation he had ever known.

The timbre of Merlin's voice rose, and the interior of the cauldron started to glow with lavender light. Galahad was shocked to see that the eyes of his fellow knights started to glow as well, as if their life force was bolstering the magic of the cauldron. Arthur's eyes glowed the vibrant green of grass in the summer sun; Lancelot's as red as the embers of a hearth fire. Percival's brown eyes now glowed silver, like Fionna's sometimes seemed too. The wind picked up and Merlin was shouting now, his arms raised.

Galahad held up his hand before his face and his palm reflected a blue glow, no doubt from his own eyes. He set aside his shock and focused on the cauldron, willing his energy, his life, his love, into that dark space. Into Fionna. Take all of me, Galahad thought. Take whatever you need, Fionna. I am yours. I would give my life a thousand times over, if it meant you could live.

A great bolt of lightning snaked from the ceiling into the cauldron's bowl, and Galahad threw up his hands against the brightness of the image. A crack of thunder followed, as deafening as the fall of a great oak.

Then silence.

Galahad slowly lowered his hands, straightening.

Merlin's shoulders sagged, but he was nodding. Footsteps raced behind them and Arthur turned. From the corner of Galahad's eye, he could see Brin Allán slow before them, his face bloodless, his shoulders shaking.

Ignoring everyone around him, Galahad peeked over the edge of the cauldron. Into the black space. Breathless with anticipation. With fear and hope.

And he started like a hare before a wolf as a pale hand reached out from the darkness and clapped onto the rim of the cauldron.

Chapter Twenty-Nine

Arthur

Arthur dared not hope. True, Merlin had said that the Cauldron of Plenty had the power to resurrect the dead. But the lands of Briton were littered with objects with supposed supernatural powers. These claims were not always true. Yet as Merlin spoke in words of power, Arthur could not deny that he felt magic pulsing through him—emanating from him—and mingling with power from the others. And then, as quickly as the magic had begun, the whirlwind ended, leaving only Arthur and the ragged edges of his heart. Fionna was dead. His love. *His wife*. Why did the fates see fit to torment him so? To find love only to have it ripped from him—

A hand emerged from the recesses of the cauldron, gripping the lip. His hope flared to life like a shooting star blazing across the moonless night sky.

The others had jumped back at the unexpected movement.

Percival had his hand to his chest. "Merlin's balls," he practically yelped.

From the corner of his vision, Arthur could see his druid look sideways at the knight. But Arthur's gaze was fixed only on the cauldron. On the figure emerging from the mist within.

"Fionna?" Galahad murmured softly, stepping forward.

Then it was Arthur's turn to press a hand to his chest, as if he could keep his beating heart from galloping away. For the figure was Fionna. But also . . . not. Beside him, Brin whispered his daughter's name with reverence.

As she climbed to her feet, Arthur recognized the familiar. Fionna still wore her boiled armor stained with her lifeblood. Her silver-white hair was braided as it had been. But . . . a bright white light emanated from her once-silver eyes, and her skin glowed like milk in the moonlight. Her ears were also tapered to delicate points.

"Galahad?" Fionna asked, turning to him, blinking the light away. The glow died, leaving only her feather-soft lashes and her quicksilver eyes.

"Fionna!" Galahad closed the distance between them, wrapping her in his arms.

Percival whooped with joy, jumping a foot in the air. He dashed forward, embracing Fionna too, even while Galahad's arms remained around her, his golden locks splayed across her shoulder.

Across from him, Lancelot was shaking his head in disbelief, leaning forward, his hands on his knees.

Brin crossed the distance and joined the celebration of limbs and laughter, taking his daughter's face in his hands before openly weeping at the sight of her.

Arthur observed it all through his tears, even as a sweet rush of relief stirred him with force enough to weaken his knees. Fionna was alive. Fionna was . . . fae.

Brin, Galahad, and Percival broke off their embrace, stepping back while wiping tears from their eyes. Lancelot straightened and nodded as their eyes met.

Then Fionna turned to him. Arthur's stomach flipped. Gods, he was nervous! Fionna had always been beautiful, even unnaturally so. But now . . . She was radiant. Ethereal. Otherworldly. She was the moon. She was the snow in winter. The spread wings of a hundred swans in flight. An earth goddess. A Gwenevere. Who was he to deign to love her? Let alone be wed to her. Lay with her—

"Is my husband just going to stand there like a daft imbecile?" Fionna put her hands on her hips. "Or are ye going to embrace me?"

A startled bark of laughter escaped him, even as his cheeks reddened.

"It isn't every day I come back from the dead," she continued, stepping out of the cauldron and toward him. "I would think some congratulations are in order."

Yes, she was the first Gwenevere in a thousand years. A white enchantress of tremendous power. But she was also Fionna. His wife. And you didn't keep Fionna waiting. Arthur stepped forward, taking her face gently in his hands. Her skin was as soft as goose down and he could swear it glittered faintly beneath his dirty fingers.

She met his eyes and smiled. "Now kiss me, ye idiot."

Arthur smiled too, and drew her mouth to his, tasting the first thaw of spring, the wild whortleberries in summer. She tasted like eternity. And possibility. And also, distinctly, like his Fionna.

"Is it just me or does fae Fionna seem feistier than human Fionna?" Percival mused to himself as Arthur broke off the kiss.

"Not sure that's possible," Galahad replied. "You can only contain so much feisty in one body."

"One human body, aye," Percival countered. "But her body is fae now. The normal rules don't apply."

"You two are idiots," Lancelot said, but his words were light.

Fionna tucked herself under Arthur's arm, acknowledging each of them in turn. "Thank ye. And Merlin." She turned to the druid. "Thank ye most of all. For bringing me back from the darkness."

"I owe ye all a life debt, twice over now," Brin said.

"Da . . ."

"Brin," Arthur began, "Your Majesty, there is no debt to be paid."

"But—"

Arthur placed a hand on the older man's shoulder. "Peace. Let us talk no more of death and debts."

Fionna smiled at her father. "For our connection runs far deeper than death. As my foot touched the Underworld, I still felt a tether to yer heart," she said first to Galahad, "And yers," to Percival, "and yers," to Lancelot." Her eyes softened and rested on Arthur, and she whispered, "And yers, My King."

Merlin inclined his head. His hands were tucked in his robes. "Indeed, it was your connection to each knight that saved you. I was just the conduit for the magic to work."

Fionna's eyes went thoughtful at that, and she exchanged a look with Arthur.

"So, is it safe to assume that the géis is broken?" Lancelot asked. "You look different. Do you feel different? Powerful?"

"I do feel different," Fionna said. "I can sense things. Like . . . I'm connected to it all. I can feel the sickness in the land. And as for power . . ." she closed her eyes. "There is something there. A well. I am not sure how to access it though." She furrowed her brow, and a gust of cold wind curled past, making Arthur shiver.

"Is that . . ." Galahad pointed to something in the air between them.

"A snowflake," Lancelot said, incredulous, stepping closer.

"Where?" Fionna asked, opening her eyes. The snowflake vanished as the room re-warmed.

"Morgana and her sisters will tremble before the might of your snowflake." Percival nodded with mock seriousness.

Fionna reached out and cuffed him gently. "Just wait until the snowflake brings friends."

Lancelot gaped at Fionna, a strange look for his friend. "I can't believe it," he eventually pushed out in a breathy whisper.

"What?" Arthur asked.

"Morgana's curse. She said that I would love a Gwenevere as pure as the driven snow. I always thought it meant Fionna's fair coloring. But what if it was more? Fae don't have the ability to lie, but they speak in riddles and poetry. Perhaps Morgana foresaw how this Gwenevere's magic would have the ability to affect the weather. To bring snowfall, even in the heat of summer."

"Wait, so Fionna can't lie?" Percival grinned. "Whose manhood is lar——"

"She's only half fae," Galahad said, taking his turn to cuff Percival.

"Merlin," Lancelot turned to the druid. "Do you think you could teach Fionna how to wield her magic, so she could bring blizzard-like conditions?"

"Possibly," Merlin answered. "We'll need some time, however."

"How much time?" Arthur asked. "Because Morgana and O'Lynn won't give us much."

"Magic usually cannot be learned in an afternoon. But since it is in Fionna's very essence, I suspect she will be a quick study," Merlin said.

An idea was coming to life in Arthur's mind. "What's the status of O'Lynn's armies?" He asked.

Lancelot replied. "A soldier came and told me that the men behind the keep's wall had retreated. They were hoping for a stealth attack, not a drawn-out engagement. When O'Lynn learned we knew of his treachery, he must have pulled them back."

"But the reprieve will be short," Arthur said. "Tomorrow, at the latest, they will engage. They won't sit around too much longer."

"Aye, yer king speaks truth," Brin added.

"It's a big army to feed," Galahad said. "And with the sickness in the land, they won't be able to rely on foraging."

"Finally, something works to our advantage," Arthur murmured. "If Fionna can summon a blizzard, I want to bring the battle to them. Do you think you can manage it?"

Fionna nodded, a grim smile on her face. "To trounce Morgana and O'Lynn? I'll be ready."

Arthur took her hand, threading his fingers though hers and squeezing. "Good. I grow tired of Morgana's games. I grow tired of O'Lynn's soldiers darkening my doorstep. Ready the soldiers for battle. We attack tonight."

Fionna

I was inundated with sensation. Merlin and I couldn't risk being caught unawares in his cave, so we ducked into a back corner of the library, where my knights had received strict orders to leave us alone.

But even here, in this hushed dusty place, I was overwhelmed. With my new fae senses, I felt like I was coming up from a lifetime underwater. Every fiber of Merlin's robes, every whorl of his tattoos, I could see them more clearly than I knew was possible. The smell of crisp, aging pages and old leather threatened to submerge me. So potent were the scents in the air that I could taste each one on my tongue. My ears perked at the sounds of a moth's wings brushing against a leather spine one row over. My ears—I couldn't help but feel them again, the delicate tapered points. Was this the true me? It didn't feel like me. It felt like stepping into someone else's body. I hoped this sensory saturation would settle in time.

But nothing was more foreign than the feel of magic. My skin felt alive with it—everywhere, tingling all around me. In the Great Hall, I hadn't understood how Arthur and each of the knights felt so different, so strange to me. Yet, familiar . . . like an old lullaby you had forgotten until you heard the familiar, comforting melody on someone else's lips. Now, I think, I was beginning to understand.

"Your Majesty. Did you hear me?" Merlin snapped his fingers

in front of me, and I jerked to attention. "Magic is a lot to take in," he continued, his tone softening. "If these studies are too much, tell Arthur. You should not be expected to have mastered all the lessons in a few hours."

I squared my shoulders. "They're depending on me. Caerleon is. If I don't master my magic, people will die. There's no real choice."

"Then pay attention." The words were harsh, but his face held kindness. Understanding.

"Start again." I sighed, focusing on him. My sight zoomed in until I could see every pore. I shook my head, struggling to adjust.

"You know of the five elements," Merlin began again. "They are the basic building blocks of all life. They are also the fundamental essence of magic. To manipulate matter, you must understand its component parts."

I nodded sagely. I think I was following.

"Druids use aids to access these parts, to mold them as we will. Spells, herbs, other ingredients that will aid our manipulation. You, however, have those elements within you. You need no help to utilize them."

"Like the snowflake in the Great Hall," I said.

"Exactly. Anything you might want to change or create is all just a matter of fitting the elements together in different combinations and patterns. Most fae have an affinity to one or more of the elements. You, Fionna, are almost all aether."

"Great," I said, pausing to take in his words. "What does that mean?"

"Aether is space. The space between elements, where the spark of life itself begins and lives."

I pursed my lips together. "I don't know how that translates to magic."

Merlin considered, leaning back. "Imagine that performing a spell is like . . . planting a garden. You need the seed, the air for the sprout to breath, water, and the warmth of the sun. But you also need a place to plant it. Fertile soil. That is aether. That is *you*, Fionna."

That did make some sense. Though, the concept brought me

no closer to doing actual magic.

"Let us try. You seem like the type where action may be preferable to theory," Merlin said. "Close your eyes."

I did as instructed and, almost immediately, a new sensation filled me. A light tug on my awareness.

"You must first find where within you your magic resides," Merlin said.

I knew that's what this feeling was. The moment I yielded to the tug, it was like I was pulled sideways within my own essence, into a place of infinite darkness. But it was not a fearful darkness. It was just . . . empty. Waiting.

"This inner place may feel like—"

"I'm there," I said, cutting Merlin off.

A pause. "Very well. Now you must locate the other elements. Bring them into this space, and then use your will to mold them into what you wish them to be."

"And that will . . . make things happen? Magic?"

"Indeed. This is the law of correspondences. One of the immutable laws of the universe. As within, so without."

I was already reaching out, feeling for the elements. This was harder, I didn't know them like I knew aether. Like I knew myself.

But then, my consciousness brushed against something familiar, and realization flared within me. This feeling—this essence—it was one I knew. It felt like . . . Arthur. Like hearth and home, the smell of fresh churned soil, and fresh-baked bread. Earth.

I reached for the other elements eagerly, already knowing what I would find. I was familiar with them, the feel and taste and touch of them were written on my heart, on my very soul. I knew these elements as I knew my knights.

I found air next, the feel of Zephyr galloping beneath me, the wind whipping my hair about my face. Trees fluttering in the breeze, bearing the scent of berries and green grass and the sound of laughter. Percival.

Then water. The strength and stamina that was Galahad, a raging river carving its way through the rocks and soil until after a patient millennia, all had yielded to the current's curving path. It was the strange feel of buoyancy as I floated on my back in a lake, face upturned to the heavens, supported by everything and nothing all at once.

Lastly there was fire. The heat and smell of a bonfire raging beneath the wide-open sky, the warmth of the embers shining in Lancelot's eyes. The feel of the sun as it filtered through a green forest, dappling my face with its sweet kisses. *Fire*, I thought. *I would know you anywhere.*

Tears trickled down my face as I pulled the elements to me, molding them in this space. Each unique—each essential for life. Every bit of flora and fauna that graced the earth, every man, woman, and child. Without all four, the world would fall to dust.

And, so would I.

I opened my eyes and found that my tears were joined by a warm deluge. Rain poured from the air above us, dripping down me and Merlin in rivulets. A surprised laugh escaped me as I put my hands up, blinking against the droplets.

"I think Arthur might appreciate it if you did not drown his entire library." A hint of a smile flitted across Merlin's lips.

Chagrined, I retreated into the space within myself, pulling the elements apart, wishing them well on their journeys back to their source.

When I opened my eyes again, the rain had stopped.

Merlin wiped his face, flicking the water to the ground. "Well. I think it's safe to say you have the source of your magic."

I surged to my feet, my heart soaring within me. "Aye. Aye, I have."

Chapter Thirty-One

Percival

Arthur had bid his knights to meet in his study when their tasks were complete. So, Percival found his feet bearing him that direction, though his mind was elsewhere. With Fionna. The morning's events seemed a strange dream. She had died. And come to life as a shining goddess, her appearance reflecting the wonder that Percival already knew was within.

It had taken all of them to bring her back. Merlin had set them around the Cauldron, and Percival had felt the magic tug on him, pull from him. He had known all along—the curse over the land, the blessed five, the Grail—from the very beginning they were tied and tangled together in a web of magic and emotion that could never be unknotted.

Percival stopped outside the door to Arthur's study, rallying his courage. He needed to tell his king. Fionna belonged to all of them, and herself. Percival wanted to marry her too. If she would have him.

His heart stuttered nervously as he stepped into the study. Lancelot, Galahad, and Arthur were gathered around Arthur's desk and standing over what looked like a crude map.

Their dark knight was leaning over the table and pointing at the paper in a way that displayed the formed muscles of his legs and finely-shaped arse. Percival jerked his eyes upward as he realized where they lingered, his face heating. A man could objectively admire the fine form of another man, no? *Never mind*, his mind whispered. His admiration for Lancelot was anything but objective.

"Ah, Percival," Arthur said. "The armory has provided the extra arrows we need?"

Percival nodded. "The bower discovered a few extra bundles of arrows inside a dusty chest in the corner of the armory. He placed them beside the cauldron for Merlin when he finishes with Fionna."

"Excellent," Arthur said. "I think we're all set here too." He put his hands on his hips. "How do we think our Fionna is doing?"

"Yer Fionna is faring well," Fionna said, striding into the room, her eyes shining like incandescent pearls.

Percival took a step back, despite himself. Fionna had always exuded force and confidence, but now . . . her very presence made him want to fall to a knee before her. She was *majestic*.

"You have accessed your magic?" Arthur asked.

She smiled. "Merlin is a wonderful teacher. And I am an apt pupil, if I do say so myself."

"And a humble one at that," Lancelot quipped.

"The battle plans are set," Galahad said. "If you're ready, we can attack at nightfall."

"I'm . . . almost ready," she said. "There is something I must attend to before we ride for battle. My King, may I speak with ye privately for a moment?"

Arthur nodded, and the two crossed the room to a corner, whispering in hushed tones.

Percival swaggered to the table and examined the map, wishing with every fiber of his being that he could look over his shoulder and lip-read what was going on in that corner. For he had something he needed to say too. But he wasn't sure if now was the right time.

Lancelot had no such compunctions. He was watching Arthur and Fionna with hawk eyes.

"And the three of us on the outside," Galahad rumbled softly. "How it ever shall be."

Percival looked up at that, unaccustomed to such moroseness

from Galahad. He supposed losing the woman you love could do that to a man. In a way, she had died twice to them.

"It should not be so," Percival said. "I have not given up hope."

Lancelot reached out to cuff him, and Percival grabbed his wrist before he made contact, stopping his hand mid-air. Their eyes locked and Lancelot slowly raised an eyebrow. "Look who's all grown up," he murmured.

"I am," Percival said, perhaps a bit forcefully. "And I plan on asking for Fionna's hand. The worst he can say is no."

"The worst he can do is execute you or throw you out on your ear." Lancelot eyes darkened, and a muscle pulsed along his jaw. Then he dropped his voice for Percival alone. "And I . . . I can't lose—"

"This is Arthur we're talking about," Galahad said quietly, interrupting. "He would never."

A throat cleared and the three of them snapped to attention. Fionna stood before them, Arthur a few paces behind.

"It's not every day a woman dies and comes back to life," she began. "And it makes a person realize a thing or two about what's important. When I felt the knife pierce my back, my mind was filled with the woeful thought of leaving Arthur. But more than that. I was filled with sorrow over the thought of leaving each of ye."

"And we ye, dove," Percival whispered.

She took in a long, shaky breath, and then lifted her chin. "The fact is, I love ye. Each of ye. And I think, despite the necklace's charms, that ye each love me. Truly."

"Ye know I do," Percival said.

"There's no other," Galahad agreed, resignation written across his handsome face.

Lancelot nodded slowly. "As much as I've tried to fight it, my heart is yours."

"When I tried to access my magic, I realized something. We are tied together, us five. By honor, and duty, and respect. By love. But by more than that. There is magic deep in each of us, in each of ye. It sings in yer blood, in yer very soul. I knew the magic, because I know each of ye intimately. The gods, or fate, or chance .

. . something brought us five together. And fused us together with unbreakable bonds. Bonds of love."

"What are you saying, Fionna?" Lancelot asked. His face was hard. "You're married to our king and now our queen."

"Aye." She turned and reached a hand back to Arthur. He grasped hers and squeezed. "Arthur is my husband." She twisted back and met each of our eyes. "But in Ireland, a woman may take more than one husband." She dropped Arthur's hand and approached Galahad until she stood before his immense bulk. "Sir Galjorheledanik of Swansea—"

"You finally learned to pronounce my Norse name," Galahad said, a smile crossing his face.

She laughed. "I did. Galahad, I claim ye. I would have ye as my husband, if ye would pledge yerself to me."

Percival hissed in a breath. Truly? Was this truly happening?

Galahad looked at Arthur with cautious expectancy. "This isn't Ireland."

Arthur merely nodded his assent.

With a huzzah, Galahad pulled Fionna into a bear hug, spinning her around before claiming her mouth with a kiss. Then the big man began laughing and, Percival swore, tears formed in Galahad's eyes.

Percival watched with breathless excitement. For he was next.

"Sir Percival of Caer Benic, His Majesty, the Fisher King," she said, as Galahad put her down on somewhat shaky legs. Looking at her in that moment, Percival thought his heart might swell to bursting. "I claim ye, pigeon. Would—"

"Aye lass, I willingly join yer harem of husbands. Now kiss me already," Percival said, grinning as he dipped her back. In the background he could hear the other knights' laughter, but Fionna filled his awareness. Her lips and tongue now buzzed with power and magic, hitting him in a heady wave. He lifted her back up, breaking their kiss. Joining with the Gwenevere would be an . . . invigorating experience.

Then it hit him. She called him "pigeon." He slid her a sly smile and she winked.

Fionna turned to Lancelot next. His jaw was set, his fists

clenched at his side. As if he couldn't dare believe such good fortune would come his way. "Sir Lancelot du Lac, Prince of two worlds," Fionna murmured, reaching a hand up to caress his chiseled cheek. "I claim ye. Will ye marry me, and let me show ye how much I want ye all the days of yer life?"

"My King?" Lancelot raised his eyes to look at Arthur across the room. "Are you sure this is what you desire? Our brotherhood means too much—"

"Peace," Arthur said, stepping forward to put a hand on Lancelot's shoulder, closing the circle beside Fionna. "I was thinking of this harem of husbands, as Percival put it, far before Fionna brought the idea to me. It has been my honor to share my kingship and my hearth with such fine brothers as you all. I can think of no one else whom I would want as *family*."

Fionna turned back to Lancelot, who was blinking back emotion. Then, in one powerful move, he seized Fionna by the arse and lifted her up astride his waist, spinning slowly while their lips met. As they joined in a kiss, an energy filled the air, lighting the circle with power that heated Percival's blood. Fionna broke off the kiss and, with her legs still wrapped around Lancelot, leaned back to kiss Arthur, claiming their king with her lips.

Galahad reached out with a reverent hand to brush a stray braid from her arched throat, and Fionna responded by pulling back from Arthur. Their Gwenevere's eyes were alight with desire and love and magic, and she leaned forward to kiss Galahad once more.

As she did, Percival met Lancelot's eye and saw such a grin of genuine happiness there that it nearly took his breath. He wrapped one arm around Lancelot's shoulder, pulling him close. "Joy suits ye, brother," Percival murmured, and Lancelot turned his head until their faces nearly touched. Something passed between them, different from Fionna's magic. A tingling, a knowing that Percival recognized, a current of magic. The same one he experienced the first time he first glimpsed Lancelot riding through the forest. A recognition of kinship. And love.

"I learn from the best," Lancelot murmured softly, and then leaned in for a kiss.

Chapter Thirty-Two

Lancelot

Soldiers filled the dark courtyard. Rows and rows of armed warriors waited silently for the gates to open, for their king's command. Lancelot shifted, scrunching his toes in his boots to keep them warm. Though it was nearing midsummer, his breath fogged the air, the chill cutting through his leathers to rest deep in his core. Where their enemy slept, in the quiet camp beyond, a steady snow began to fall.

Fionna had taken to magic like she had to everything—effortlessly. She stood atop the keep's wall like a white sentinel, her eyes closed, her form barely visible in the low light. It was a full moon tonight, but the heavy clouds Fionna had summoned blotted out all but the faintest glow of Cerridwen's light.

"A good night for a dark deed," Lancelot said under his breath.

Arthur, standing at his side, glanced his way. "I fear our course lacks honor. Attacking under cover of dark. Is this the coward's way?"

"Our enemy has no honor," Lancelot said. "O'Lynn wouldn't hesitate for a second to take Caerleon by stealth or trickery. And don't get me started on Morgana. Remember the Castle of Maidens?"

Arthur's hand floated to his side where he had been wounded by the faerie spear. "How could I forget."

"This is the best way. And will result in the least loss of life, on both sides. You know that."

"I do," Arthur sighed. "It's only that sometimes I wonder if chivalry is dying."

"Let's stay alive to save it then," Lancelot said, clapping Arthur on the shoulder. "And secure Fionna a wedding gift in the process."

"Eh?" Arthur raised an eyebrow.

"Her sister's freedom."

Arthur's eyes narrowed and his jaw set. "I think it's time to be on the move. Fionna's magic has chilled the summer's dawn for an hour now. The snow will muffle our movements and reduce visibility. Let's just hope the Uí Tuírtri don't know we're coming until we're already upon them."

Their king gave the signal and the gate squeaked ominously as the oaken doors opened. Fionna left her post and descended the stairs, making her way to where a groom held Zephyr's reins.

The sight of her set Lancelot's heart on fire like a young lad. Part of him still couldn't believe that Fionna was going to be his wife. He kept expecting to wake up from a dream. But here she was.

Joy. Bliss.

He tried to channel Percival's endless optimism, but all he could think of was that now that she had bound herself to him, he had something to lose. And there were about two thousand things that stood between all their happiness—two thousand Uí Tuírtri blades.

"Ye look like ye ate something sour," Fionna remarked, leading Zephyr to stand beside Cheval.

"Just promise me you'll be careful," Lancelot said, trying to memorize every feature of her transformed, elfin face.

"Ye forget, Lance. I'm immortal now." She swung into the saddle as the last word left her mouth.

"Only half immortal," Lancelot muttered.

"I'll be careful," she said. "Promise."

"Good." He mounted his own horse and then leaned in close. "Because I want to take that new faerie body of yours for a ride it won't ever forget."

He was rewarded with the sight of Fionna blushing up to her

hairline as he kicked Cheval into a trot.

The farther they rode from the keep, the thicker the snow fell. The plan was simple. Sneak in while clearing a silent path through the clannsmen in their way. Find O'Lynn and kill him, before demanding the rest of the clann surrender. Cut off the snake's head and the body will die.

Lancelot shivered and pulled his cloak tighter about him as a gust of freezing wind, swirling with fat snowflakes, hit him. The gust's icy fingers trailed down the collar of his armor. He tried to think of the wind as Fionna. Fionna caressing his skin, warming him, her soft touch drifting down his chest, down farther to the line of dark hair beneath his navel . . . His cock stirred painfully against his armor and he tried, unsuccessfully, to adjust himself. Never mind. Bad idea. The snow was just snow.

The creak of leather and the soft snorts of horses were stolen away by the storm. Lancelot and his soldiers were nearly upon the first sentries when men emerged from the snow. But Percival and Galahad's arrows were quicker than the men's cries, taking the soldiers in the throat before they could raise the alarm.

Tents appeared in the distance, and the soldiers fanned out to sneak inside and dispatch the inhabitants. Brutal work, to kill a man in his bed. And as Arthur said, lacking in honor. But Caerleon's warriors needed to ensure their avenue of retreat wasn't cut off, if the alarm was roused. The cruelty would save more lives in the long run.

A cookfire appeared out of the snowstorm, and two dark forms huddled close. Lancelot wasted no time in spearing the nearest man through.

He gurgled a cry, and the other man shouted before Lancelot spurred Cheval forward and stabbed him through.

The world around them silenced in a deafening hush. Lancelot's breath was loud in his ears.

The dark forms of soldiers nearby froze where they stood. All tilted ears to the wind, waiting to hear if another had picked up the cry. But there was no sound.

Lancelot blew out a soft, shaky breath, adjusting his grip on his sword.

Close. Too close.

They had only entered the main ring of village buildings.

He nudged Cheval with his heels, motioning forward with his hand.

Then the snow began to lessen.

And, as they made their way closer, the snow stopped. The air hung heavy against him, like an inhaled breath. All around, the warriors of Caerleon halted too, suddenly exposed in the night air.

Lancelot turned to Fionna, who he could now make out a dozen yards away. He motioned to the sky in an inquiring way.

She shook her head, her jaw set. She hadn't stopped the storm. Which meant that someone else had.

An arrow zinged through the air, catching a soldier next to him in the shoulder. The man toppled backwards off his horse.

"Charge!" Lancelot cried out, slapping Cheval's rump with the flat of his blade. The stallion leaped beneath him, as another arrow whizzed by his head. The arrow's shaft and fletching were so close, he could feel the arrow's movement in the air.

Uí Tuírtri warriors poured out of buildings with guttural cries of rage. The men and women were unarmored, without the normal bristling assortment of weapons each warrior held. Caerleon had taken them by surprise. Still, the warriors were fierce.

A woman ran screaming at him with an axe held high above her. Lancelot swung his sword, slicing her across the chest. Cheval barreled into another warrior before him, and Lancelot felt the man go down beneath his horse's hooves.

The village center loomed before them as more warriors poured out of houses and buildings, blocking their path.

"To me!" Lancelot shouted above the melee, spurring Cheval forward, toward the enemy. Galahad and Percival, together with a dozen of their best soldiers, funneled into the wide main street, forming a cavalry charge into the thick of invading warriors.

A calming battle focus settled over Lancelot, and his vision narrowed. In this heightened state, he easily parried two fast blows from a warrior with bared teeth, dispatching the man with a powerful blow.

Lancelot's task was clear. Punch a hole through these men,

allowing Arthur and Fionna to ride in their wake into the center of town. To attend to their mission.

To find and to kill O'Lynn.

Chapter Thirty-Three

Arthur

The fighting was thick. Little by little Arthur's warriors gained ground, hacking and slicing their way through men and women and beasts.

Excalibur's hilt was slick in Arthur's hand from the snow and sweat and blood. But as many soldiers as they felled, it seemed as though more took their place.

This was the part of their plan that had been a risk—a terrible, terrible risk. Two thousand Uí Tuírtri warriors slept in this camp. Caerleon had invaded O'Lynn's war camp with less than a thousand-armed men. If the entire force was roused from sleep and then surrounded them . . . Caerleon would be destroyed. Their plan depended on finding and killing O'Lynn quickly. Then demoralizing the rest of his men. But the time ticked by, time filled with clashing blades and ringing metal and screams of dying men. Time they could ill afford.

Fear began to bubble up in Arthur. "Fionna!" he shouted, taking advantage of a moment within the onslaught to find his fae warrior. "We must move forward! To the inn!"

She nodded before twisting her body out of the way of a dagger thrown at her by a snarling woman. Fionna spurred Zephyr and charged the woman, reaching down and disabling her with a skillful blow of her blade. She tried to close her eyes to focus on her magic. But another warrior came at her and she was forced to rein Zephyr back, dancing out of the way of his blow. She needed time and space to perform whatever magic she attempted.

Arthur roared his fury and dug his heels into Llamrei's side. Together, her hooves and his blade cut a path forward, until they flanked Fionna just yards from the steps of the inn.

"There are too many," Arthur yelled over the maelstrom of weapons and warriors. "We must find O'Lynn."

"He must be in there." Fionna gestured toward the inn with her head and then swung off Zephyr.

Arthur slid off Llamrei's back and then caught her hand. "And if he isn't?"

"He is," she said, her breast heaving. A glow wreathed around her in the darkness, as if she were a celestial body reflecting the light of the moon. "Cover me." She closed her eyes and, within a couple thunderous heartbeats, the ground beneath their feet began to shift. Boulders jutted up from the ground in a semi-circle, forming a defensive perimeter.

Llamrei reared, screaming, her eyes wild, and Arthur had to leap up to catch her reins.

Enemy warriors shouted in fear, scrambling out of the way, their eyes growing owlish with fear of Fionna's powerful magic.

Her eyelashes fluttered open when she finished. The land around the inn was now protected by craggy rocks as tall as a man's chest. Warriors would be able to crawl over them, but the stones would slow them down.

Fionna swiveled toward him, her jaw set. "O'Lynn."

"O'Lynn!" Arthur's eyes widened as the front door of the inn exploded outward, kicked by a powerful blow. O'Lynn emerged from the opening. The man wore full Dál nAraidi armor, the leather oiled and gleaming, and a dark helm atop his head. One hand gripped a huge battle axe, his eyes glowing like malevolent embers from inside his headgear.

"Speak of the wretched man and he appears," Fionna spat.

"That's not a very nice thing to say about yer kin. We're family now, Fionnabhair." O'Lynn reached inside the door and jerked something toward him. A chain.

A cry went out as a woman stumbled into him, falling to her knees on the splintered remains of the inn's door. Aideen. O'Lynn shoved a fist into her hair and then jerked her back to her feet. Aideen yelped in pain and Fionna stepped forward, hissing.

Fury rose within Arthur. He could taste Fionna's matching anger on the air—like the energy before a storm. Fionna was about to do something stupid, or reckless, or both. Though, he couldn't blame her. If his mother or Fionna were paraded before him in a similar fashion, he might behave the same despite his training as a warrior. Still . . .

"Hold Fionna," Arthur said quietly as O'Lynn pulled Aideen back against his body, laying the blade of the huge axe against her exposed throat. The young woman's eyes brimmed with tears as they widened, as if silently pleading.

"I'm afraid ye've made a miscalculation, Pendragon," O'Lynn gloated. "For yer force is surrounded, and if ye don't surrender, I'll spill the blood of this woman before ye without a second thought. How'd ye like to see yer sister die, Fionna?"

Arthur feared Fionna's rage would boil over into a tempest unlike any they had ever seen, so he hurried on. "You won't do that, O'Lynn."

"Why not?" he sneered.

"Because then you would lose your only bargaining chip, leaving you defenseless."

"I'm hardly defenseless, ye pompous Welsh bastard! I was slitting heads with this axe when yer mother was still wiping yer arse!"

"Yet we found you inside that inn, rather than on the battlefield with your men."

O'Lynn's eyes glittered dangerously.

Arthur continued. "Let's end this without further bloodshed. Single combat. For the future of Caerleon."

The axe blade lowered slightly, and Aideen took in a shuddering breath. "Aye. Single combat. Ye and me."

"No," Fionna said. "Ye and me."

Part of Arthur railed against it, but he knew that he could not deprive Fionna of her vengeance. She was as good as, or a better fighter, than he.

"Ye would have yer bitch fight for ye? The gelding of Caerleon, eh?" O'Lynn scoffed.

"Fionna is many things," Arthur said, his voice ringing clear and true. "She is my wife. She is a warrior. A princess of Tara, heir to Clann Allán, queen of Caerleon and overqueen of Gwent. She is the most powerful sorceress in a millennia. The fae-born daughter of the goddess Danu. But of all things, she is a free woman, beholden to no man, not even a king. She makes her own choices. And it will give me great pleasure to watch her spear you through like a mewling pig."

O'Lynn growled at that while tossing Aideen hard to the inn's threshold. Then he opened his arms before him and held his great axe out as he took a step forward. "Daughter of Danu or no, I'll enjoy killing ye more than ye can know," he spat at Fionna.

"The feeling is mutual," Fionna replied, also stepping forward, her twin swords bared.

Arthur held his breath—unable to move in the pregnant moment before the two warriors charged each other. Before the clash began.

But he could never have predicted what happened next. Aideen Allán, rising like a vengeful wraith with a wicked blade in one hand. Where she had been hiding it, Arthur didn't know. But he recognized the skill she wielded as she leaped onto O'Lynn's back, her arms clinging to his neck. As she drove the dagger deep into his exposed windpipe—all the way to the hilt.

O'Lynn froze, seemingly unable to comprehend what was happening. Aideen pulled the dagger out and drove the blade in again, this time angling the point up, into the man's chin.

Arthur closed his eyes against the violence of it, the lethal precision of those blows.

Fionna had no such compunctions. A gasp of delight escaped from her and she ran forward, scrambling over the boulder separating them from O'Lynn and Aideen.

Aideen then crumbled to the ground and Fionna grabbed her hand, pulling her out of the way of O'Lynn's blade.

The man dropped to his knees. With a *thunk*, his axe fell to the ground as his hands flew to his throat. As if he could hold in his lifeblood with only his fingertips.

Fionna darted forward and seized his helmet, wrenching it off his head before retreating to where her sister stood. Face bared, O'Lynn's wound was even more horrendous, his face draining of blood. Always his eyes remained on the two women who stood before him, brimming with hate.

"A wedding gift," Aideen said. Her shoulders were squared, her back straight. "Courtesy of Clann Allán."

O'Lynn fell face first to the ground—dead.

Aideen's hand flew to her mouth as she let out a sob. Matching tears coursed down Fionna's cheeks as she pulled her sister into a tight embrace, murmuring into her hair, rocking her gently.

Arthur turned to where the battle still raged outside the ring of protective boulders. It was time to end this war. He summited a boulder and faced the soldiers.

"Men of Clann Uí Tuírtri!" he bellowed. "Your chieftain is dead! Lay down your weapons and you will be permitted to leave these shores and return to your homes! Keep fighting and Caerleon will show no mercy! Every last warrior will be slaughtered!"

Arthur would never execute men who had surrendered, but he thought O'Lynn's warriors could use the added incentive.

In the distance, Arthur watched as a man raised his hands in the middle of a fight with Galahad, dropping his sword. The muffled sound of the weapon hitting the dirt was repeated all around the village and camp as enemy fighters began to drop their weapons.

Relief flooded Arthur. By the gods, they had done it. They had won.

The earth beneath their feet rumbled once again and he lost his balance. As he hit the ground, the boulders around them slowly began to sink into the earth. Arthur whipped his head Fionna's direction with a raised eyebrow. But her face was stricken.

"It's not me," she said.

The sea of fighters parted as a woman in a black dress and flapping violet cloak strode toward them. Morgana. Her pale purple eyes were baleful as she spoke, her voice echoing over the hushed silence. "I'm sorry brother, but we're not done here. Not even close."

Chapter Thirty-Four

Fionna

The air crackled between us. I sensed more than saw the moment before Morgana struck. The bolt of lightning shot from her hand, streaking toward me like a viper.

I dodged out of the way, rolling to my feet while summoning the elements to me. I welcomed each one into the void within me. The sky above Morgana darkened right before ripping open. Then a hailstorm erupted, dumping sheets of solid ice upon the Queen of Darkness. The hail was so thick, I couldn't see if the ice stones had smothered her or not.

Until another bolt of lightning struck my side out of nowhere. I fell to my hip, hitting the ground hard. My teeth clamped together as pain exploded through me. I struggled to my feet, ignoring how my very skin felt raw, ignoring the throbbing that I hoped didn't signal a serious wound. But I had no time to consider. My eyes focused on where Morgana's crow form flapped into the air.

I blew a jet of air at her, tumbling the crow out of the sky.

She turned back into a female, mere heartbeats before her fae form collided with compacted grass and dirt. Afraid to lose my momentary advantage, I summoned earth and water to me, liquefying the ground beneath her into a pool of quicksand. Morgana shrieked as she began sinking into the muck, her knees, then her thighs, as the mud lapped at her fine gown.

Panic flashed in her eyes while she struggled to free herself, her hands now mired in the sludge. I prepared and released my own lightning strike, but my bolt missed her as an invisible force jerked her up, pulling her body out of the quicksand. Morgana's eyes widened—it wasn't her doing this.

I whipped my head to peer over my shoulder as I spun on my heels, and my eyes narrowed when two more faeries approached from an alley between the houses. A brunette in a scarlet dress and her fair sister in gold. Elaine and Morgause.

Morgana pulled swirls of magic to her, spinning her dress into a new form, ridding herself of the heavy, sticky mud.

I shot a gout of flame at her during her wardrobe change. But Elaine deflected my attack with green fire of her own. The combined flames, an eerie blend of red and green, crashed against a nearby building and whooshed up the thatch roof.

I sent water at the blaze while pulling the air from around the building. The situation would only get worse if the village started to burn too.

"Fionna!" Arthur shouted. He and my knights were pressed against the inn, watching the magical combat with fear tightening their faces into frowns and scowls.

A chill scraped down my spine in a violent strike as the air around me shifted to a rapidly plunging cold. A bitter cold that threatened to freeze the blood in my veins. My breath puffed from me in quick foggy bursts as I struggled to summon fire to warm myself. Limbs stiff, I returned focus toward the alley and grit my chattering teeth. It appeared the sisters had taken advantage of my distraction.

I was one, and they were three. I needed to do something quickly to end this fight before they wore me down. Or before I made a mistake. My magic was new to me while they had cast spells since childhood. I might be more powerful, but they were more skilled.

I summoned the wind to me, spinning the air into a cyclone the size of which frightened even me. My braids whipped at my face, stinging me as they thrashed like serpents. I tossed the storm at the sisters and they scattered, sprinting for the cover of a nearby building. I wanted the cyclone to chase after them. But I hesitated to destroy the building. The structure could contain innocents who were also sheltering from the madness on the battlefield. So, I let the storm dissipate.

In my peripheral vision, I glimpsed my knights again. Arthur pointed behind me. Then I saw my name on his lips. But I couldn't hear his voice over the rumble that shook beneath me, as if the ground itself began to rebel. The sisters were working a spell. And it was a powerful one.

I fell to the earth and sharp pebbles scraped my palms. I tried to pull apart whatever spell they were weaving, but the magic wouldn't yield to me. Sweat beaded my brow. Something was brewing. Something strong.

Morgana and her sisters huddled together, chanting in unison. Energy surrounded them. Then the landscape rended before me—a thunderous rip in the earth—releasing a white-hot jet of flame that surged hungrily for the sky.

I dove out of the way, covering my head as a shower of embers rained upon me.

"Gwenevere," I heard Morgana shout. "Let's see how your magic fares against the power of Domnu's children!"

My heart stuttered in my chest.

Domnu . . . the sire of the Fomorians. The ancient enemy of Danu, my goddess—my mother. A gripping urge to run from this place seized me, but I held firm. I was the only one who could stand between whatever came out of that chasm and my knights. The rest of Caerleon. I would lay down my life for the ones I loved . . . no matter what happened here. Even if this fight demanded all of me.

Still, my resolve was tested when a giant rock and amber hand, streaked with flaming embers, crashed against the lip of the chasm. My pulse skidded to a stop. A horrific, fearsome beast was clawing topside from below. The hand alone was as tall as I was.

I scrambled back as the other hand appeared. Then the face—if I could call the gruesome monstrosity atop its shoulders a face. The creature had vaguely humanoid features—two eyes that reflected the chaos of Dubnos, the great abyss, above an opening that could perhaps be described as a mouth, one filled with blue and white licking flames.

My eyes flicked to the dark faerie sisters as my mind worked for a solution, for a way to end this beast. The Morrígan were intent, their eyes wide, their figures stiff. As if summoning this monster wasted every bit of their energy. Apparently, they were willing to destroy Caerleon rather than allow Arthur to continue sitting on the throne.

The fire beast pulled itself from the chasm and stood. And when it roared, I thought my eardrums might blow. Screams sounded behind me as soldiers from both camps blended together in a unified mass of terrified, fleeing humanity.

The beast took a step and flattened a nearby wagon. The ground shook as it moved. The creature fixed its fathomless eyes in the distance, drawn to the movement of the fleeing people.

"Fomorian!" I shouted while waving my arms, foolishly drawing its attention back to me. I knew not how to defeat this thing. Water perhaps? Ice? I summoned a rain cloud, as big and black and as heavy as I could create. I opened the deluge above the beast and it roared in pain as steam rose from its glowing magma-formed body. Boiling water rolled down its crags and crevices to the soil in near-vaporous rivulets.

Yet, the creature didn't stop.

I struggled to turn the water to ice, perhaps to freeze the fire beast within a glacial cocoon. But the beast was too strong. It writhed and broke apart the ice as soon I could crystalize the water. The Fomorian was just too hot.

The monster took two steps toward me and kicked out with its flaming foot.

I threw myself back, falling onto my arse and scrambling back out of its way. My hands scrabbled in the clover and weeds poking through cracks in the cobbles of the village square.

A jolt of understanding crashed into me. This creature was unnatural. It crawled out from the earth's deep, and back to the earth it needed to return.

My knights were moving behind the roiling heat of the beast, trying to sneak around the square toward Morgana and her sisters. Perhaps my knights could get to the dark enchantresses and incapacitate them, as the sisters were still intent upon the creature.

I needed to slay this monster from the abyss. No more thoughts or second guesses. Instinct took over and I reached down, past bedrock, to the earth's deep, feeling within the bubbling rivers of fire for the dormant life that lay there. Danu's power—the power of green things. Trees and grass and the wild creatures of the earth. I reached within and I summoned the powers of my goddess.

I invited the roots from the sacred trees—oak and ash and yew. My magic cried out for them to come to me. And come they did, exploding out of the ground like powerful warrior druids crackling with nature's endlessly looping energy. The gnarled roots wrapped around the flame monster like coiled tendrils of rope. Treed tentacles lashed at where the beast stood, and then sank trunked fingers back into the soil and began to grow, even as the beast thrashed violently, striking at the rambling limbs to free itself.

The vines and roots grew larger, until the creature's legs looked like two thick tree trunks wrapped in ivy. Up and up the tree grew, forming all around the fire creature. Bark and wood grew faster, hardening around the beast. The monster's arms were now stiff, and its torso was quickly enveloped until only its head remained free. White and blue fire blazed from its grotesque mouth as the beast roared in a promise of vengeance.

But Danu's power was stronger. My power.

What was meant as a scream of hatred became a hissing death rattle. The unnatural fire snuffed out, cooling the remnant traces of reds and oranges to grays and blues. Ribbons of smoke curled from the monster's mouth and danced upward toward the sky. The tree trunks continued to grow despite the creature's violent transfiguration from life to death to rebirth. Limbs, branches, and flower buds exploded outward and around the beast's rocky surface. And then leaves—forming a broad green canopy over the beast.

I felt the tree settle as the leaves shivered out into existence, before growing still with contentment.

I slumped onto my elbows and gazed up in awe at the sight before me. A massive oak tree stood in the middle of the town square, its limbs stretching wide, shielding the buildings from the light of the stars. With intricately knotted roots, the tree looked as if it had lived there for a thousand years—at least. But rendered in the gnarled bark, one could almost make out a face, and the twisted, frozen scream of a Fomorian fire beast.

Chapter Thirty-Five

Galahad

alahad seized a faerie from behind, laying his blade across her pale throat. The blonde faerie—Elaine he thought she was—stiffened beneath him. Next to her, Lancelot seized Morgana as Percival rested his blade on Morgause's fine collarbone. The sisters had been so intent upon fighting Fionna's efforts with the fire beast, that the knights had no trouble sneaking up on them.

A screech erupted from Morgana as she glared at Lancelot with baleful eyes. But even she must see that the battle was lost. O'Lynn was dead. The Uí Tuírtri were scattered. And the faerie sisters' magic had been routed by Danu's and Fionna's power. The Gwenevere.

Fionna pushed to a stand, staggering toward them. She looked dead on her feet, even her ethereal faerie countenance drawn and exhausted.

"You have trapped our magic!" Morgana screamed at Fionna as their queen approached. "Give it back!"

Fionna shook her head wearily, but she managed to straighten her spine, throwing her shoulders back as she faced the sisters of Tintagel. "Ye have done nothing but harry my king and this land. Why should I return yer power?"

"Because we are part of the balance," Elaine, the faerie Galahad held, growled. "I admit my sisters and I got carried away these past months in our anger at the Little Dragon King—"

"You have been angry with me since my birth, of which I had no control over," Arthur gritted between clenched teeth. "The punishment must stop. Let us be better than Uther Pendragon."

Elaine considered his words. "Yes, brother. Let us be better than that vile man." She flicked a look at Morgause, then said, "We will swear to never do harm to you or any you love, if the White Enchantress will merely give us our power back."

Morgause nodded in agreement. "Without our magic, we will die. To secure its return, we will gladly make you such a promise."

"Even you?" Lancelot asked Morgana.

She bared her canines at Lancelot with a snarling glare but finally relented and gave a curt nod.

Arthur approached, his hand resting on Excalibur. "You will each swear." Arthur put an arm around Fionna's waist and she sagged against him gratefully. Gods, she might collapse any moment. "Each of you swear on your sisters' lives that you will never again interfere or harm or seek to harm myself, my knights, my wife, or the kingdom of Caerleon and its people. If you do, Fionna will return your magic to you." He looked at her with a raised eyebrow, and Fionna murmured her agreement.

Galahad had no idea how Fionna had trapped the faeries' magic, or even if she could release it. But he supposed that was why he was here, holding a simple sword while Fionna performed great works of magic.

Each of the sisters said a vow on the lives of the others and, when they finished, Fionna closed her eyes. The trunk of the great tree Fionna had created shivered and moved, and a small hole appeared. One that looked as though an owl might nest there. Then, out of the hole flowed a stream of shimmering light that fell upon each of the sisters.

Galahad held himself still against the burning impulse to release the magical creature beneath him. But as the returned power settled upon her, he felt his limbs go limp. She stepped out of his hold as Morgana turned into a crow and flapped out of Lancelot's arms and flew away.

Relief washed over Galahad as strength flooded back into his arms.

Morgause and Elaine stepped together, turning to face them. "We apologize, brother," Elaine said. "For all that has been done to you and your land. Let this be the turning point in relations between us."

Arthur nodded. "No more animosity. After all, we are family."

"Indeed," Morgause said, and a misty portal opened behind them. They stepped through and were gone.

Fionna swayed against Arthur. Her eyes slid closed right before she fell toward the ground. Arthur caught her deftly, swinging her up into his arms.

Galahad wiped his sword, returning the blade to its sheath. His hair was a tangled mess around his face, sweat and dirt coating him from head to toe. Yet, he felt better than he had felt in ages. He had just watched Fionna battle a demon monster from Hel, turning it into the most beautiful oak tree that he had ever seen. But that was their fifth knight.

Her eyes fluttered as they walked toward their horses. "Is she all right?" Arthur asked him.

Galahad lifted her wrist, feeling for her pulse. "I believe so. Her strength is likely depleted from the battle."

"I can't imagine how much energy it takes turn a fire monster into a tree," Percival added.

"We won't hear the end of this," Lancelot quipped. "Every time we do something she doesn't like or if we don't appreciate her, she'll say . . . 'remember that time when I defeated three powerful sorceresses, and you all sat around with your thumbs up your arses?'"

Arthur chuckled. "I for one would be happy to take such abuse."

Lancelot smiled, and it was clear that he would too.

"Let's get back to Caerleon," Arthur said.

Lancelot strode away to find a commander to relay instructions to. The wounded would be brought home, while the remaining soldiers were to oversee the orderly return of the Irish warriors to their boats. From the Uí Tuírtri's shocked and weary faces, Galahad didn't think they would be putting up much more of a fight. But it was always best to be careful with such things.

Arthur tapped Llamrei's leg, and then mounted. Galahad and Percival helped to secure Fionna in the saddle before him. Her head lolled down, her braids hanging white against Llamrei's black coat.

"I can't believe the battle with my sisters is finally over," Arthur said as they made their way out of city and back to toward the keep.

"Looks like it isnae completely over, ye ken," Percival said. He pointed to a patch of brown grass where the curse still showed.

Arthur frowned. "I should have insisted Morgana and her sisters remove the curse over the land."

Galahad knew that he should be concerned, but with everything that just happened—that they had just survived—he felt deep within that the land would heal in time. "I'm sure if we make a special request to Elaine and Morgause, we will be able to get the curse lifted."

Arthur considered Galahad's suggestion, then said, "I think they will be far more inclined to work with us."

"Or perhaps Fionna, with her newfound powers, will be able to break the final part of the curse," Galahad replied. "Once she has time to consult with Danu."

"Curses and goddesses. Can we talk about what's really important?" Percival asked.

"What?" Lancelot asked, as he trotted up to join them.

"The wedding! Arthur's already married to Fionna, but I'm not."

They all laughed at their younger knight. Typical Percival.

"So eager?" Lancelot asked.

"Och, do ye blame me?" Percival asked. "She was beautiful and fierce and intimidating *before* she was fae, before she was a Gwenevere. But now . . ." His eyes fell upon Fionna's sleeping form. "I cannae believe I would be lucky enough to be with her. I want to lock her down before she changes her mind."

"You think her feelings are so changeable?" Lancelot said. "You find yourself so unworthy of love?"

"All I know is that if there's one thing men do best, it's screw up their relationships with women," Percival said quietly, then blew out a long, slow breath. "I would rather marry the lass before that happens."

Galahad laughed. "I must admit, I wouldn't mind holding the wedding sooner rather than later." He raised an eyebrow at Arthur.

"It's only fair," Arthur agreed. "We can make all the arrangements, so when she regains her strength, we will be ready."

As the keep appeared over the horizon, the large, wooden gates standing tall before the rising sun, Galahad felt his spirit soar up to meet the dawn. He was to be married. And he couldn't wait.

Chapter Thirty-Six

Arthur had decided the ceremony should take place in the library. This was a small affair, just for them. Servants had adorned the shelves and tables with boughs of greenery threaded with tiny white flowers. Arthur and Merlin stood before the leaded glass window, waiting for the others to arrive.

This time, instead of the groom, Arthur would serve as a in witness. To watch joyfully as Merlin, his oldest friend, joined matrimony the woman he loved with the three men he loved like brothers. Brin and Aideen Allán would also bear witness. Together with the gods.

After the battle against Morgana and her sisters, Fionna had slept for a day and a night. Her sister Aideen had barely left her side. When Fionna awoke, after eating enough for three people, she had expressed her eagerness to hold the ceremony. To make their bonds of love more permanent. And then, once wed, and with the help of Merlin, she wanted to break Danu free and reclaim the Otherworld from the Fomorians. Life was certainly an adventure with Fionna.

Arthur's throat grew tight as his sword brothers entered the library.

Galahad—broad and strong as the oak Fionna had raised in the village. His honey-blond hair was washed and brushed, dusting the shoulders of the green linen tunic he wore.

Percival—his eyes bright, his grin wider than Arthur had ever seen it, wearing a tunic of rust with bronze accents.

And then there was Lancelot, with his signature black curls and blue tunic. But he had changed too—he wore a look of ease and happiness that made Arthur want to weep with joy.

Arthur smiled at Merlin as each of the men took their places. The druid softly smiled in reply, the gold ring around his eyes flashing. Arthur knew that his old friend understood what this ceremony meant to him. To have found a family to love, who loved him in return.

alahad watched with bated breath as Fionna appeared in the hallway. She glided through the doors like the goddess she was, her father on one arm, her sister on the other.

She was everything to him. And she had honored Galahad by choosing him—an honor more powerful than he had ever imagined possible. He was the oldest son of a Norse blacksmith, and he was about to marry the daughter of a goddess and a king. But more than that. He was marrying Fionna. The woman he loved.

A smile spread across her face as she moved toward them. Her dress was the glittering silver of a moonlit reflection dusting a lake. In her hands, she held a bouquet of heather, hawthorn, and other greenery. At her brow was a circlet of holly leaves, similar in style to Arthur's oak leaf crown.

This woman set his blood racing in a way he had never known. He wanted every moment with her, again and again. To taste her skin, to feel her silken touch, to hear her laugh. To see her perhaps, one day, swell with child. Every moment with Fionna would be a treasure. And he could think of no one better to share it with than these men whom he had come to respect and to love in kind.

It was all Percival could do to keep himself from jumping up and down. He had never been so excited as he was when Fionna reached their cluster in the library's front. She embraced her father, then her sister, squeezing them each tightly. He knew how much their nearness meant to her, to have her family safe at last. And here to witness her vows.

Fionna took her place across from Merlin. They were a circle. Percival stood across from Arthur, Lancelot across from Galahad. Percival winked at Fionna, and she winked back.

"I admit," Merlin said, clearing his throat, "since living at Tintagel in Cornwall and now Wales with Uther's line, I have not presided over a wedding as found in the other Gaelic lands. But," Merlin paused a heartbeat then continued, "I can think of nothing more fitting than a number such as this. Five is the sacred number of elements on this earth. Each of you brings something unique and powerful. When joined together, the elements create all manner of wonders. I see this in you five. In a way," Merlin said with a humored smile, "we owe Morgana a debt of gratitude, for bringing Fionna into our lives."

Lancelot snorted at that.

But it wasn't untrue. Percival thought on all that had happened in the past months since Fionna had arrived so suddenly, besting every knight in the kingdom at the tourney. The Grail Quest. Seizing his Fisher King heritage. Defeating Morgana and drinking the blood of the land. Lancelot's kisses and touch. . . Throwing off his vow of chastity—finally! Life would always be interesting with her.

He longed to see what adventures unfolded next. And he longed to share them with her. His eyes flicked to Lancelot. And his brothers.

ancelot couldn't take his eyes off Fionna. Nor could he believe that in the next few moments she would be his. Truly his. He kept expecting another catastrophe to arrive. The roof to cave in, a stray spell to explode. But there was nothing but the perfect sweet smile on her face. The fresh herbal smell of the flowers in her hands and strung around the library. The brightness of Percival at his side, Galahad's steady presence, Arthur's beaming smile.

Growing up on the Isle of Man, he swore that he would never marry a faerie. Lay with them, dally with them—sure. Use them as they used him. But never marry one. He had declared this vow again after the foolishness of Morgana.

But here, today, he knew deep in his heart and soul that marrying the Gwenevere was the right decision. He had come home in Caerleon. He had come home in Arthur, and he had come home in Fionna. Here was a family who inspired him, who challenged him, who filled him with passion. He glanced sideways at Percival and then Fionna. A family who accepted him for who he was. He was meant to be here. And as Merlin began to speak, asking each of them for their vows, Lancelot couldn't say the words fast enough to bind his life to these warriors at his side. This king, these knights, this goddess. They were who he wanted in his life. Forever and always.

struggled with the tears threatening to fall as each warrior in the circle said our promises to each other. I wanted to give each of my men a moment . . . to show my knights how much they each meant to me. They were my friends, my compatriots, my trusted allies, my equals. They were the sun and the moon and the stars above. Each man held a piece of my soul and my heart and, together, they lit me afire—a burning inferno that would never be quenched.

After I had slept, eaten my fill, and bathed . . . I ached to celebrate our triumphs. We had seized upon the slimmest of chances and made it ours. Through our ingenuity and our hope and our trust in one another, we were victorious.

I wanted nothing so much as my wedding night with these beautiful men, and my eternity after. I wanted no more worry over curses. I wanted no more talk of politics or faeries or goddesses. I only wanted skin and lips and the coiling desire within me sated by the men I loved.

As I spoke my vows and sighed into each kiss, my body, mind, and soul trilled with the possibility of what the future would hold for me.

Chapter Thirty-Seven

The horses' hooves clopped softly through the swaying grass and over the moss-blanketed earth. The warm night wrapped around me as we journeyed toward the forest across the Usk River that held a pond Arthur oft visited. The same pool in which the Lady of the Lake had appeared—offering Arthur Excalibur and a new destiny.

A cool breeze fluttered wisps of my hair across my eyes. I tucked them behind my ears and back beneath my hooded cloak. We were sneaking away from the keep and didn't want to draw any attention. Only Merlin and a few of Arthur's most trusted officers knew of our whereabouts this night.

Our honeymoon night.

I followed behind Arthur and Llamrei as his black mare plunged into the river. Water lapped at the toe of my boots in inky waves. Behind me, Galahad, Lancelot, and Percival splashed into the same shallow section of river atop their chargers. The energy between us swirled in comfortable silence, our hearts full of the promise of passion to come. The love we would share. A new consummation for each of us, since I had transformed into my fae form and become the Gwenevere. I was not only Arthur's faerie bride, but my fellow knights' as well.

Zephyr nickered as we crossed the line between light and

shadows and entered the forest. A few heartbeats later, the trees opened to reveal a circled patch of stars. Beneath the indigo sky, a small pond shimmered in dusted moonlight. A silver-misted waterfall hushed the leaves' lullaby in the breeze as a creek spilled over an outcropping of large rocks covered in ferns and moss. But, as enchanting as this place was, the curse visibly lingered. Black fingers of death had left their marks on tree trunks. Brown, brittle ferns dotted between healthy, new growth. I dismounted and considered the swirls of yellow moss cutting through the green.

Merlin speculated that, similar to the Blessed Grail, my magic would fully heal Caerleon and Briton as I joined with each man. Marrying the sovereign-blessed king—Arthur—to the land once more as his Gwenevere wouldn't be enough, as Galahad, Lancelot, and Percival still carried a piece of Arthur's sovereignty from being knighted with Excalibur. It was strangely fitting. Our magic and love were interlocked in an endlessly looping knot. In this Otherworldly place, we would know if our joining healed the land—this time truly.

We busied with unpacking our bedrolls and supplies for the night. Percival scoured the underbrush for kindling and logs to burn and then began a fire. Lancelot placed jugs of wine and pewter chalices near a basket of cheeses, pear tarts, and other delicious samplings from the keep's kitchens. Arthur removed Llamrei's saddle as I unbuckled Zephyr's.

Galahad passed by me after gathering all our saddles and tack to lay across a log within a stone's throw from our camp.

I began untying my cloak when a pair of arms wrapped around my waist. Galahad nuzzled my neck with bearded kisses before spinning me around to face him. "Join me for a dip?"

"Is the water safe?" I asked.

"Aye, lass," Percival said nearby. "We tested the pond earlier today."

Lancelot sidled up beside me with a chalice of honeyed wine. "The waters here are protected by The Lady of the Lake. But we weren't sure if the curse had also destroyed Vivien's magic."

Zephyr moved behind me and I turned to find Arthur leading the horses to a copse where they could graze. Our eyes touched as he lifted a soft smile before returning to his task. I enjoyed a long sip of mead and then re-focused on my knights. And frowned.

Galahad's glorious mane of hair was up in a messy knot, his typical style for weaponry practice or battle. Handing my now empty chalice back to Lancelot, I stood on tip-toes, reached above Galahad, and pulled the leather strip. Wavy strands fell around his face and shoulders in a rippling cascade of gold. I sighed in contentment at the sight. My fingers tangled in his silky hair as I tugged him closer, closer, closer still. Our bodies collided in a sensual dance of lips, arms, fingers, and hips. His kisses tasted better than bridal mead. Lifting his tunic up and over his head, my mouth explored the expanse of his muscled chest. Tasting the ambrosial saltiness of his skin while drowning myself in his honeyed scent of sweet hay, leather, and sex. And I wanted more.

Lancelot pressed to my back as he gathered my waist-length, un-braided hair and draped all my tresses—glowing white under the moonlight—over my shoulder. His quickened breath pulsed hot on my neck as he finished untying my cloak, and my lids fluttered closed. The wool fell to the forest floor around my booted feet. Then his hands cradled my throat as he tipped my head back to nibble my earlobe and kiss my neck before his fingertips brushed down my chest to palm my breasts.

I heard a soft splash and opened my eyes. Percival waded into the dark waters, and I bit down on a forming smile. Moonlight touched the play of muscle and sinew on his back. And gods, his tight arse. I want to feel his soft flesh in my hands as he thrust into me. Memories of our time together came rushing back and I grew impatient with each remembered touch.

Percival peered over his shoulder and winked at me before diving in, resurfacing in the middle of the pond with a shake of his head. Droplets sprinkled the water surface around his glistening body as he grinned.

"Come in, dove," he shouted. "I'm waiting for ye."

Galahad rolled his eyes with a quiet laugh. "The lad has the patience of a frolicking goat."

"Do you blame him?" Lancelot asked as his hands traveled farther down to the laces of my riding breeches. "Fionna, naked . . .

and wet."

"Mmmm," Galahad murmured in agreement.

Both men made quick work of undressing me until I stood before them bare, heat coiling between my thighs in anticipation. Especially as Galahad slowly pulled off his breeches, providing me a feast of muscle and skin and sultry, knowing smiles. As Galahad undressed, Lancelot kissed my shoulder, the shell of my ear—even the sensitive point—while his calloused fingers played against my nipples. I knew his eyes were upon Galahad and enjoying the show as well. How could he not? Galahad was the most godlike man I had ever seen. And he was mine.

Lancelot gently pushed me toward Galahad once the giant of a man stood before me naked. Then I heard my dark knight begin to undress.

I placed my hands onto Galahad's ribbed torso right as he scooped me up, one arm beneath my knees, the other beneath my arms. My plan to melt into his warmth quickly dissolved, however, when he ran for the pond. I shrieked, to my horror, and screamed again when he splashed in and tossed me toward the center of the pond. Galahad's roar of laughter followed me through the air, the rumbling vibrations even traveling through the water to mock me when I submerged into the obsidian depths.

I gasped for breath when I surfaced, a growl low in my throat. That man would pay. The infernal knight was still laughing. So much so, he didn't notice me. My lips curled in vengeance before I dipped back into the water to swim toward where he stood. In a few strokes, I had reached him and pinched his calf—hard—until my nails dug into his skin. Caught off guard, he lifted his foot and I could hear him boom a swear word, providing me an opportunity to yank his other leg out from underneath him. The great knight fell into the shallow depths with a giant splash. Before he could surface, I pounced on him, our limbs tangling in a wrestling match. I could hear the garbled sounds of Arthur, Lancelot, and Percival cheering for me.

Both Galahad and I shot up into the air, laughter streaming from us in rivulets. But I refused to give him quarter and shoved him back hard with a foot to his stomach. He fell again, to the boisterous humor of everyone, especially Arthur. Sprawled out in the pond, his knees and shoulders poking out as though in a bath, Galahad arched an eyebrow at me.

"Surrender," I mock-demanded.

"A draw." The man grinned at me in challenge. "You can't best me, Fionna."

"Keep up these sweet nothings and I'll make ye wait until morning," I cooed, my hands firmly planted on my exposed hips. The men laughed again.

"Make him kneel before you and beg," Lancelot called out. "No mercy!"

Arthur gifted me another soft smile as he and Lancelot waded into the water—in a location safe from Galahad and my antics.

"You can't resist me," Galahad said, ignoring the others, while swimming toward where I stood. "You've never able to resist me." Droplets raced down his body as he slowly rose from the water, and goddess help me. I couldn't help the stab of jealousy I felt toward each rolling drop of water for knowing every divine part of him so intimately.

"I think she's resisting ye, ye big oaf," Percival called out from near the waterfall. Galahad's playful glare shot daggers over my shoulder at the younger man.

Taking Percival's lead, I pushed back into the water. My eyes remained fixed on Galahad while I treaded away from him, the we're-not-finished smirk on his face matching mine. Percival came up from behind and tugged me through the waterfall as our limbs tangled together. The alcove was small. Just big enough for two, maybe three, bodies. Maidenhair ferns sprouted from crevices in the rocks and mist shrouded our forms.

"Ye are so beautiful," Percival said. "Especially when ye take down Norse giants."

A smile twitched my lips as I wrapped my legs around his waist and wiggled over his hardened cock. "Oh aye? Ye find that sexy do ye?"

"Och, to fall to a goddess in battle . . ." He whispered, affected by my touch, his eyes blinking closed for a slow heartbeat of time.

I brushed a wet strand of copper hair off his cheek. "Be my first tonight, husband," I whispered back.

A triumphant grin brightened his face. "Slay me, then, fair goddess-wife. But gentler than ye handled Galahad. I'm already weak for ye."

Laughter bubbled from my chest. "Ye fool man."

Percival found Fionna's mouth with his. That first taste of her lips nearly slayed him. Her laughter had filled his heart to brimming until he overflowed with wondrous sensations. They remained locked in a slow, passionate kiss as they gradually floated back toward shore. Her legs were still wrapped around his waist and hovered just above his growing cock. From the corner of his eye, he could see the other men watch them.

Cupping her arse, Percival emerged from the water and carried her toward where the fire now blazed in a hypnotic rhythm. Gently, he lay her on the spongy moss by his bedroll, remembering that she needed to remain connected to the earth to marry them each to the land. Light flickered across her damp skin and reflected in her silver eyes.

"I love ye, Percy," she whispered while studying his face.

He brushed her cheek with the back of his fingers. "Ye own my heart, dove." Then Percival slid into her waiting body in one smooth motion. A ragged breath left her mouth as he whispered across her swollen lips, "I am yers, always."

"Make me coo, pigeon," she teased, and he released a low chuckle.

Stealing a kiss first, Percival pushed up on his arms and then rolled his hips. He wanted his pelvis to dance across hers and grind to the rhythm of their drumming pulse. A satisfied moan filled his ears, rewarding his efforts. Encouraged, he increased his tempo while dipping down to take her breast into his mouth. Feeling her soft flesh and the hardened tip of her nipple bounce against his tongue elicited a moan of his own. How could one woman hold so many delights?

Percival pulled away from her breasts and drew in an excited breath as he lowered before Fionna's tumbling swirl of long, white hair. His prince. Firelight caressed the handsome planes of Lancelot's face, turning his dampened black locks to dark bronze. Shadows outlined his muscled body and tattoos, and Percival was riveted. Ice-blue eyes, framed by long, black lashes, fastened to the sway of Percival's hips as he arced into each thrust. Licking his lips, Lancelot lifted his gaze to Percival's. Lust and longing and heat softened every beloved feature on the man's face as he stroked up and down the length of his thick shaft. Percival bit his bottom lip as he slowed and emphasized his grinding motions for Lancelot's viewing pleasure.

Fionna reached out and gripped Percival's arse as she turned her head toward Lancelot and flicked her tongue across the crown of his glorious cock. With a deep moan, Lancelot leaned into her touch until her parted lips slid down his shaft. Then Lancelot began rolling his hips, his cock moving in and out of her mouth as his heavy-lidded gaze locked onto Percival's. Like a moth to flame, Percival stretched toward Lancelot until their mouths crashed in a burst of passion—his own length buried deep into Fionna's core, Lancelot's between her soft, warm lips.

A flurry of pleasure overcame Percival in a blizzard of wild sensations. Lancelot bit down on Percival's lower lip and every muscle in Percival's body stiffened as a heady rush cut through his, Fionna's, and Lancelot sensual haze. His head grew light. His legs began to shake.

Fionna's nails dug into his arse and dragged him harder against her.

Percival cried out as his body pulsed in hot, breathless waves into Fionna. And he swore he could feel the earth move beneath them as she cried out in release with him.

Lancelot pulled out of Fionna's mouth before he peaked. Percival still filled her, his head thrown back in a groan as his body shook. Around them, an invisible but palpable energy flit from rock to tree to the wild grass, graceful and whisper-soft like butterfly wings. The velvety moss beneath their bodies deepened in color and thickened as Lancelot stretched out beside Fionna, until his skin pressed to hers.

She was ethereal under moonlight, silver dusting the hard lines and soft curves of her toned body. Lancelot knotted his fingers into her hair as he captured her wicked mouth with his. Gods, that mouth had the power to destroy him. Those plump, berry-red lips too. Her tongue teased his in a playful flick. And, for a quavering heartbeat, he could taste himself. Hungry for more, he deepened his kiss until their tongues twined in a seductive cadence of give and take.

Percival rolled off Fionna to his back and lay beside her, one arm behind his head, his muscled chest rising and falling in deep, sated breaths. Lancelot pushed to a seat and pulled Fionna up with him. An impish smile flashed across her face as she straddled his hips, lowering—achingly slow—onto the heat of his throbbing cock.

"Do ye want pretty words?" she whispered to him.

His answering reply was sliding her up the long length of his shaft and pushing her back down until he was buried to the hilt.

With a moan, she wrapped her legs around his waist. "I want yer passion," she whispered into the crook of his shoulder as she kissed his tattoos. And then her hips began to writhe. A hard, up and down motion that sent his head spinning until he was dizzy.

"And I want yer pain."

Then, to his surprise, she bit him, where she had been feathering soft kisses a moment before. The points of her short canines broke his skin and sank into him as she lapped at the wound. Fire rolled across his shoulder and curled into his chest. Her tongue then flicked at the bite to soothe the wound.

She had bloody claimed him as her mate!

In the way of the fae!

"Oh gods," Percival whispered at their side. He had nearly forgotten about the young man in his delirium.

Overwhelmed with emotion, Lancelot tangled his fingers back into her hair and yanked her lips to his in a bruising kiss. They collided in a heat so intense, he felt the steeled remnants of every bit of grief melting away. She was an inferno of passion and pleasure and he wanted to burn to ash with every searing touch of her body.

"Tell me ye want me," she whispered into their kiss.

He smiled. "I want you."

"Tell me again."

"I want you all my days," he replied in a heady whisper.

Fionna grabbed his shoulders and shoved him down toward the moss. But, before his head touched the forest floor, he rolled her onto her back. Then he pushed into her in a single, quick thrust. And again. Each pump of his hips as hard and fast as his pounding pulse. She traced her fingers along the swirls and knots inked onto his chest and shoulders.

"I want yer strength, Prince Lancelot du Lac. My husband." Her eyes flicked to his.

His breath caught as he blinked back the hot tears gathering behind his eyelids. "I want your strength, Fionnabhair Allán. My Gwenevere." He lowered and softly tasted her lips and whispered, "My faerie wife."

In a rush of breath, his heart emptied into the moon-touched magic of their kiss as the heat of his body emptied into hers. The ground beneath her gently quaked and Lancelot orgasmed again, moaning her name to the night sky and the stars above.

In the wake of release, lichens bloomed on the trunks of neighboring trees and across stones. Spectral ribbons of mist slithered across the pond and rolled onto the banks, where reeds and water irises sprouted and then speared up into the blue, shimmering air.

alahad bided his time by staring into the fire and drinking mead. Lancelot and Percival had been caressing the tantalizing curves of Fionna's naked form following their intimacies—one man before her, the other behind. Galahad wanted her to rest before enjoying him next, especially after their bout earlier this evening in the pond. A corner of his mouth quirked up. Gods, he loved it when she stormed in fury at him.

"Thinking of my victory over ye?"

She now stood before him. A soft glow illuminated the pale skin of her luscious body in the firelight.

He grinned, slow and lazy. "I demand a re-match, Lady."

"Do ye, now?"

Galahad fell back onto his bedroll as Arthur snorted nearby. Their king had also imbibed in a few chalices of honeyed wine. "Are you afraid you'll lose?" Galahad teased.

Fionna knelt between his legs with a mischievous glint in her eyes. And then she began kissing his calf, behind his knees, and up his thighs. At his groin, she lifted her head and met his shuttered gaze. "I hear fear in yer voice, fair Knight."

He boomed with laughter at her attempts of intimidation. As his humor faded into the dark air, she licked up the hard length of his cock, and his quieting laugh quickly dissolved into an appreciative moan.

"Ye want more?" she asked.

"What's your price?"

"Beg me." Her eyes were bright with mirth.

Lancelot grunted with approval on the other side of the fire circle.

Galahad pushed up onto his elbows and arched an eyebrow her direction. "I might need another sample of your ardor first."

"Like this?" She swirled her tongue across the crown of his cock and all the breath in his lungs expelled on the airy wings of pleasure.

He whispered, "Yes, My Queen," as his back pressed into his bedroll once more.

"Now beg me, warrior." Her warm breath caressed his shaft and he shivered.

"Own my body," he half-whispered. "Make me yours. Please."

Satisfied with his desperate entreaty, her mouth slid down his throbbing length. Heat curled in his belly as her tongue carved her name along the sensitive underside. He heaved for much needed breath and then clutched fistfuls of her hair, guiding her head up and down, up and down. Slowly, he thrust into her mouth, his hips wanting to increase in speed. But she pulled away from his aching body before he could, and the fires of Hel danced in her eyes.

"What is your plea?" she purred.

"Gods, woman," Galahad groaned. "You're cruel."

"I can be crueler." Fionna leaned back and tilted her head. Long, white strands of hair fell over her shoulders and draped across her pert breasts. She then cupped his balls and gently tugged as she massaged each one between her fingers. "Tell me, warrior. What do you desire?"

"Destroy me," he growled. "No mercy, My Queen."

Biting her lower lip, she crawled up his body until she reached the patch of hair just below his navel. Then she flicked out her tongue and licked the rippling muscles across his abs, up his ribbed torso, to his pectorals where the tip of her wicked tongue and the sharp edges of her teeth tortured his hardened nipples. His hips bucked with need. His hands clawing for her waist. Amused, she lowered her lips to his with a little laugh as her wet sex rubbed along his cock. Their mouths crashed together in a single sword strike. The spark of her metal against his ignited their bodies into motion.

Forget being dominated. His entire being strained against the urge to fight back, to disregard the unspoken rules of this battle. Until he did. Flipping Fionna onto her stomach, Galahad lifted her hips and sank his cock into her—deep, hard. A low growl rumbled from his chest as his pelvis grinded into her arse, his fingers gripping her soft flesh. She moaned—loud. Then again, louder this time before crying out. Her body spasmed and tightened around his cock. Gods, the scent of her arousal, the way her breasts bounced. It was enough to drive a man to madness.

Gently, he wrapped an arm around her waist and pulled her against him, sliding his hand between her legs to massage her swollen nub. Her head fell back onto his shoulder and he claimed her parted lips as he rocked into their joined bodies. Blood hammered the anvils in his ears. Sweat dripped down his face. His muscles flexed and stiffened as pleasure flooded his veins.

"Fionna . . ." he breathed, her name a prayer on his lips. "Oh gods."

She fell back onto her hands as his seed dripped down her thighs and onto the moss and leaf-littered forest floor, even though he remained buried deep. Brittle ferns brightened to vibrant greens and wildflowers bloomed all around their camp in a rainbow of colors as a rush of energy flooded his body, making the hairs on his arms rise.

Bending over her arched spine, he caressed the silky skin of her sides and stomach as he kissed her back, whispering, "I love you, wife." Then he collapsed onto his bedroll.

She curled up against him and rested her head on his chest. "I love you, husband." Kissing the salt from his skin, she then murmured, "I won this bout."

Galahad burst into laughter, unable to contain himself.

Arthur sighed in contentment as he swept a gaze across the fire circle. Galahad snored atop his bedroll, Fionna in his arms. Arthur chuckled to himself. He swore the large Norseman fell asleep within seconds of finishing.

On the other side of the flickering flames, Lancelot had pinned Percival's hands above his head and passionately kissed the younger knight as their bodies rubbed together in slow, erotic strokes. Their soft moans filled the night air and Arthur smiled. This wasn't the first time he had seen male warriors make love. It was a common affair among Celtic soldiers. His heart soared for his foster brother. Percival would be good for Lancelot, in more ways than one.

Arthur was about to curl up in his furs for the night when he noticed Fionna stirring. She sat up and stretched her arms, first taking in Lancelot and Percival, then him. Their eyes connected, and she smiled. A heartbeat later, she lowered next to him and pulled his fur blankets up and over both of their bodies until only their faces were exposed to the night.

"How do you fare, My Queen?" Arthur softly asked.

"I have never known such happiness until this day," she whispered back.

"Nor I." Arthur kissed her forehead. "Rest, Fionna."

"Not yet." She leaned up on her elbow. "I have not joined with ye."

The corners of his mouth tipped up as he caressed the curve of her cheek with his knuckles. "I would not ask intimacies from you after you have given yourself to the others."

"But the curse—"

"Can wait until morning or later tomorrow, even. Taking advantage of your body when you must be spent doesn't sit well with me."

"And if I want ye?" She brushed a finger along his bottom lip in feather-light touches.

He swallowed. "Fionna . . ."

"Arthur Pendragon," she whispered as her fingertips left his mouth to rest over his heart, "ye are the most beautiful man I have ever known."

Moved, he leaned in and kissed her lips, a sweet, chaste embrace. "Fionnabhair Allán. My wife. My Queen. My Gwenevere." His hand wandered up her face and he traced along her ear to the point. "I am so very much in love with you."

"Allow me to show ye the depth of my love?" she asked.

He studied the silver pool of her eyes before granting his consent in a single, breathy word. "Yes." Then he added, "But only if you promise me this is truly what you want right now."

Fionna kissed his throat and then buried her face into his neck, whispering, "Ye are always what I want, Arthur."

A blush warmed his face at her confession.

"And," she whispered into his chest as she kissed his skin, "I adore your freckles."

"Ugh," he said with a shy laugh. "Those infernal things."

"Beautiful, My King. Ye are beautiful, inside and out."

She positioned the furs over her back as her waterfall of hair curtained around their faces. Then she pressed her mouth to his, sliding onto his hardened cock. They remained in this place for several heartbeats—their lips dancing to a melody only their hearts knew while their bodies sighed with bliss at being one. Slowly, she began to move, and he shuddered with pleasure at the feel of her hips rocking back and forth across his.

Arthur cradled her curving hips and deepened their kiss. Her skin was unbelievably soft for a warrior. He drank in the feel of her body coupling with his, her heather scent, and the love that passed between them swelling in his heart. For him, there was no woman who could compare. No love as bright and pure.

He peered up at the star-flecked sky as her mouth roamed the expanse of his muscled chest. To think, their story could have ended far differently. Many outcomes and many possibilities. But, in the end, she chose him. She chose all of them—Lancelot, Percival, Galahad. His Gwenevere, created just for them and they for her.

My head grew faint at the enormity of Arthur's love for me, shown in his gentle touches, the reverent brush of his lips across mine, and the way he sighed—not only in pleasure, but in contentment. I made this man happy, a king who had known only heartache and injustice.

His body was perfection. Freckles spilled across his skin as though stars in the night sky. The sound of his breathy moans aroused me further. His warm lips captured mine in a languid kiss, as slow and sensual as the undulating rhythm of our hips.

As I pulled away, he surprised me with a delicate flower he had plucked from beside where we lay, tucking the violet behind my ear. My heart fluttered wildly as I realized—it was Arthur who had placed the bouquet of wildflowers upon my bedroll during our trip to Chester. Flowers I had kept in my saddle bag and then later pressed into a book as a keepsake.

Beneath the fur blankets, his hands traveled up the length of my back and sank into my hair, tugging my lips back to his. The building heat between my thighs trembled into a long, thundering spasm.

"I love ye," I whispered, kissing his jaw, his cheek, his flushed lips. "I love ye so much."

Gently, he rolled away from the fire and toward the moss, until my back pressed into the earth and the moon bathed me in silver, the fur blankets all forgotten. Wildflowers covered our bodies from sight and framed my king against a backdrop of midnight blues. His body slid in and out of mine, his breath warming my bare skin.

"My fierce Fionna . . ." he whispered. "My love." And then his face tensed as his muscles stiffened, a powerful moan escaping his parted lips.

The ground beneath me quaked, as though the earth and stones and water cried out in reply. Trees swayed a lover's dance as the black fingers of death disappeared to reveal strong, healthy bark. More wildflowers and ferns sprang up from the ground, and Arthur and I quickly returned to his bedroll in laughter. I squealed as he covered our heads with the fur blankets, our happy smiles turning into happy kisses, his body gathering mine close to his. Pulling the blankets off our faces, I laughed again, soaking in the sight of our land, whole and hale.

Beside us, Galahad continued to snore, his arms and legs spread out languidly. Lancelot and Percival returned our grins as we took in our surroundings. The land was healed. Truly healed.

Mere months ago, I was a warrior princess tasked with travelling across the Irish Sea to steal a faerie sword from a king. That king now claimed me as his queen, as did these knights who fought beside me proudly. Men who helped me unearth the secrets of my life—of me.

I snuggled into the crook of Arthur's arm and shoulder as he tucked his other hand behind his head. His heart raced beneath me, and I couldn't help the grin that stretched wide across my face. I stared out into the forest, lost to reverie, as his breaths evened and as he fell into a deep, restful sleep. From the sounds of our camp, Lancelot and Percival slumbered too. A yawn escaped my mouth and I buried deeper into Arthur's warmth. But, before my eyes fluttered closed, lulled by the bliss of making love to my knights, my king, I watched as a lily grew along the forest's edge. A white lily that glowed in the shadows beneath the goddess moon.

The End

Historical Notes

Greetings, readers! This is your *Knights of Caerleon* lore keeper, Jesikah Sundin. This final book was an interesting tale to undertake as it was more about our twist on Celtic mythology and less about historical notations. But, as we've discussed in the previous *Historical Notes*, Arthurian Lore is a blend of Roman/Celtic history and Celtic mythology that is assimilated by and regurgitated into something new with each generation. Think of it like perpetually making new meals out of leftovers. That is the collection of Arthurian Cycle stories. Speaking of, if you've missed the *Historical Notes* for the first two books, you can read up on all the juicy details here:

1) <u>Who Was Arthur Pendragon?</u>

2) <u>Who is the Real Gwenevere in Arthurian Lore?</u>

And now onto the fun and somewhat controversial origins of Lancelot, Galahad, Percival, Morgana, and Donal O'Lynn. I'm leaving Merlin out of this line-up as his history is just waaaaay too long and complicated and dates to when the Milesians came to Ireland (later known as the Túatha dé Danann).

LANCELOT

Arthur Pendragon had existed for centuries before "the greatest swordsmen in the world" arrived on the scene and stole the entire show. And, yes, this is what Lancelot was known as, because obviously only *the best knights* come from France *sticks French tongue out at the rest of the uncivilized world* We can thank the French poet Chrétien de Troyes for this hunky knight, who created Lancelot in *Le Chevalier de la Charrette*, a collection of poems between 1180 – 1240 A.D., which was finished by Godefroy de Lagny after Troyes died. The sole purpose of Lancelot was at the behest of the Countess Marie de Champagne, daughter of Louis VII of France and Eleanor of Aquitaine, to illustrate the pros and cons of "courtly love." Lancelot's famous adulterous affair with Queen Guinevere being the ultimate offense and why kingdoms *obviously* fall *French evil eye to young noblewomen checking out all the hot knights* *J'accuse!* In the French courts, Lancelot took center stage and forced Arthur to become a side-character. As in our story, Lancelot is the natural born son of King Ban of Benoic (Benwick) but raised by Vivien, Lady of the Lake, hence his romantic name: Lancelot du Lac.

GALAHAD

The bastard-born son of Lancelot du Lac and Elaine of Corbenic (Caer Benic . . . yeah, Percival's origins. There's a reason for this. I'll explain in a bit). As with many medieval stories (especially French ones), the woman tricks the man to sleep with them *side-eyes trickster Eve archetypes* and then arrives sometime later with the news, "Surprise! You have a son and he's destined for great things." *side-eyes Christ archetypes, to redeem the fall of man because of Eve archetypes* And poor Lancelot is no stranger to the trickery of fair maids, as many a young Frenchmen experienced back then. Apparently. And, thus, "Galahad the Chaste" was born. Yeah, "The Chaste." His holy virgin status allowed him to finish the Grail Quest, where his father had failed because Lancelot shagged the queen. Plus, the stories of "Sir Percival"— who had no relation to their beloved Lancelot, whatsoever—was boring the French courts, and so they wanted a new Grail hero.

Claire and I decided to make Galahad a Welsh-born Norseman from the Danish seaport village of Swansea, as you know. And definitely not chaste! But we did give a nod to his origins in book 2 when Lancelot says that if he ever has a son, he'll name him Galahad in his sword-brother's honor.

PERCIVAL

AKA "the original Galahad" that entertained the courtly-love thirsty French of the 12th and 13th centuries before Galahad was born. The earliest "Percival" mention is also by Chrétien de Troyes in his unfinished *Percival, the Story of the Grail* (around 1190 A.D.). Known as "Percival the Chaste," son of Elaine of Corbenic (Caer Benic) and sometimes the oldest son of King Pellinore, he eventually finds the Holy Grail and becomes the Fisher King. Some stories have him dying a virgin after claiming the Grail, sadly. Poor, pigeon . . . Eventually, Percival was kicked to the curb for "Galahad the Chaste," son of Lancelot du Lac. But scholars believe Troyes was inspired by Peredur of sub-Roman Celtic Mythology. Peredur is also found in Arthurian "histories" by 11th century Welsh author, Geoffrey of Monmouth and, later, in the old orated Welsh tales that were written down in the *Mabinogion*, including the famous "Peredur the Son of Efrawc," which we leaned on heavily for Grail Quest adventures in *The Third Curse*.

AND since our series revolves around so much Grail lore, we decided to go with the original Grail Quest characters: Arthur, Lancelot, Percival, and Galahad . . . but refashioned by our clever fairy tale re-telling brains, if I do say so myself *high-fives Claire*

MORGAN LA FEY

Her origins are as misty as the Otherworld, especially as her name is linked to the Celtic Morrígu (aka The Morrígan), the goddess of war and death, and one of the three sisters in the triple goddess head, The Morrígana. In Irish mythology, she would shapeshift into a crow, shriek over the battle field, and collect the heads of fallen soldiers as trophies. Um . . . that's some creepy shit. The Celts were dark, though. And not afraid to die, or apparently have their heads collected by a shape-shifting sídhe. But, I digress . . . The name Morgan (male) / Morgain (female) means "water nymph" in Breton (Celtic Cornish / Welsh)—which makes sense, since most Celtic deities were water born. But Morgan being a strictly male Celtic name was lost in translation with the French and, thus, they crowned The Morrígan, Morgan la Fey. Despite her circling carri-on crow form, she wasn't a feared goddess. Rather, The Morrígan was also revered as the patron goddess of art and beauty, because that totally makes sense given her decorating tastes.

Interestingly enough, in most Arthurian tales, she's not evil. That's more of a neo-pagan / modern fairy tale view of her. In the original Arthurian Cycle stories, she had two older sisters (Morgause and Elaine *points to The Morrígana explanation*), and she loved her half-brother and even brought Arthur to Avalon for healing when he was mortally wounded in the Battle of Camlann. Still, Claire and I went with the more modern take on Morgana. Because evil is fun. And she was such a fun, sexy villainess to write.

DONAL O'LYNN

Clann O'Lynn are a real, historic clan from Ulster, y'all. And, they are possible descendants of Colla Uias, the famed 4th century High King of Ireland. The Irish Gaelic version of their name is Ó Fhloinn (which I think is pretty) and they were part of the Tuírtri area of Northern Ireland (now incorporated into Antrim), and originally hailed from Lough Insholin in Londonderry, which means "Lake of the O'Lynn Island." Savvy? Cool. So, eventually they conquered and inhabited most of County Antrim sometime in the 12th century—even Fionna's area in the Glens of Antrim. And they ruled this region until the 15th century when the Mac-Donnells swept in. See what I did there? Donal O'Lynn . . . Mac-Donnells defeated the O'Lynn . . . he was his own worst enemy. #HistoryGeekGirlHumor. Now, I'll be honest . . . the 12th century is a hazy date. O'Lynn was a prominent clan in the area and their expansion/settlement into Antrim might be earlier, like when we set our story: the mid-1000's. If you're an O'Lynn of Antrim, let me know! And, we hope you didn't mind us making a fictional descendant a villain. Your ancestry tied so well into our *Ulster Cy-*

cle-inspired Fionnabhair. Bad guys are cool, right?

THE FOUR ANCIENT ARTIFACTS OF IRELAND

Also called "The Four Magical Treasures of the Túatha dé Danann." The more you dive into Celtic and Irish mythology, the more items in British Isles fairy tales and folklore begin to make sense. Especially in Arthurian Legend tales. Here's a quick overview without getting too detailed with the mythological stories behind each artifact (and I'm presenting them out of order, sorry Irish scholars):

THE SWORD OF LIGHT "Shining Sword" (Sword of King Nuada of the Túatha dé Danann) was a weapon that symbolized and "illuminated" truth, justice, law, and punishment to Ireland's enemies during conflict.

Arthurian Treasure: Excalibur

LIA FÁIL "Stone of Destiny," also known as the Stone of Scone and the "Talking Stone," was originally on the Hill of Tara and where the ancient Kings of Ireland were coronated. But only after the stone roared, which it would only do if the rightful king stood upon it. The Lia Fáil was eventually brought over to England by Edward the 1st in 1297 and is now the Coronation Stone in Westminster Abbey.

Arthurian Treasure: The Stone, as in The Sword in The Stone.

SWORD OF LUGH "Invincible Spear" or the "Spear of Victory" belonged to the Celtic sun god, Lugh of the Long Arms. The longer the spear was held, the hotter it would become. And, its perfect targeting powers also thirsted for blood. So much so, it wept blood. This spear is later used in Grail stories and connected to the spear that pierced the side of Jesus of Nazareth during his crucifixion (the son of god vs the sun god).

Arthurian Treasure: The spear that wept blood during the Grail Maiden's odd and fantastical Grail procession, and the spear that maimed the Fisher King.

THE CAULDRON OF THE DAGDA is a magical vessel that could heal through food and drink to whomever deserved such blessings. And raise the dead too, just for kicks and giggles. The food and drink never ended, either . . . as the cauldron was bottomless. Hence the saying, "bottomless pit" to describe those who are always hungry and pack in their meals.

Arthurian Treasure: The Holy Grail. A grail (graal / sangrael) a small, common household bowl (aka cauldron), which later became synonymous with the bowl used by Jesus during the Last Supper (Cup of Christ) and the vessel Joseph of Arimathea used to catch the blood that spilled from Christ's pierced side. If you drank from the Grail, you would be healed of all your ailments and injuries and, perhaps, even gain immortality (think communal wine and bread).

And, for fun (yeah, this is fun to me), I want to address a few misconceptions about hygiene in the Middle Ages as well as homosexuality within Celtic cultures, especially among warriors. As a refresher: Celtic culture in this context are the people of Ireland, Scotland, and Briton (Cornwall, Wales, and parts of western Scotland). The Norse are the Vikings, from the Nordic/Scandinavian lands as well as those who settled in the British Isles.

DID PEOPLE BATHE REGULARLY IN THE MEDIEVAL ERA?

Yes! Big, emphatic YES. In fact, in Celtic, Norse, and Mediterranean cultures, good hygiene was part of daily life. The movies consistently paint dirty, grimy peasants with blackening teeth and shiny-faced nobles with perfect smiles (remnants of Victorian classist culture). According to the <u>Medievalist</u>, there are extensive medical texts waxing poetic the benefits of bathing—for the common and noble man alike. They even understood that washing your hands and face before meals was essential for better health. By the medieval era, bathing culture across the Isles was a thing, hence all the funny tapestries and art depicting people in tubs.

And this well-known poem, dating back to the 1300's:

Hey! rub-a-dub, ho! rub-a-dub, three maids in a tub,
And who do you think were there?
The butcher, the baker, the candlestick-maker,
And all of them gone to the fair.

"Three men in a tub" who "were out to sea" was a change made in the late-1700's to be "safe for children." Which begs the question: what was this poem really about? You're gonna love this. *clears throat* Men of industry who were going to the village fair to see a peep show of naked, young maidens bathing each other in a tub. Sexy times!

DID CELTIC CULTURES ACCEPT HOMOSEXUALITY?

They didn't even bat an eye at two men as lovers, or two women for that matter. Sexuality wasn't a complex issue to the Celts. Partly because marriage in Celtic cultures was for childbearing only. Brehon Law (ancient Irish law that existed through the 17th century and that bled into other Gaelic lands) permitted married couples to have lovers outside of their handfasting vows. And why this allowance? The Celts saw marriage as a necessity for politics and clan building, but lovers were for the soul. And so, many had lovers, including same-sex partners. But homosexuality was observed most among the warriors. It was so common, <u>Warrior Lovers</u> became a well-noted thing, even causing the <u>non-homophobic Greeks to raise an eyebrow</u>. This changed in the late-Middle Ages with Christianization, however. Now, open sexuality was ONLY among the Celts. The Norse didn't practice homosexuality as a culture. Like today, the Nordic land's equivalent to "gay" was an insult to a man's masculinity.

WAS MEDICAL KNOWLEDGE ONLY RESTRICTED TO HERBAL LORE?

Uh, no. Some of the best artifacts from the Middle Ages are all the fantastic medical texts. So. Many. Medical. Texts. Their illustrations are wonderfully entertaining too. Medieval people practiced all manner of surgeries, even cesarean births. And the believed cures for various ailments or concerns (like wrinkling skin) are sometimes hysterical. They even washed their hands before medical procedures. Modern scientists are now looking back at the texts and folklore from the Middle Ages as they're finding interesting leads to medical discoveries, such as the <u>"healing soil" in Ireland</u> once used by druids, which was recently documented as effective treatment for four of the six world's superbugs.

Whew! We did it. We covered all the major Celtic culture and Arthurian Lore tie-ins.

But as this is fiction, and fantasy fiction no less, there are some historical inaccuracies. *J'accuse!* Heh. The biggest one? At no time, that we know of, did a war camp from Clan O'Lynn travel to southern Wales. We bent history for our plot. Sorry-not-sorry. As mentioned above, Galahad was the son of Lancelot du Lac and Percival was "The Chaste" before Lancelot and his son stole the Grail Quest show. The small, nameless villages mentioned outside of Caerleon are from the fictional realm inside my and Claire's heads. The village Inn is also a fast-forward into history, as medieval inns didn't appear until the 14th century. The UK does not have chipmunks (I feel sorry for you, UK friends. They're sooooo cute!). Still, we used this nickname for Galahad because it just felt perfect. If you can suspend belief for faerie magic, then pretending adorable, chubby-cheeked chipmunks roam the UK shouldn't be too hard a task. And I'm sure there are other historical inaccuracies too, though I tried to keep proper details intact for the most part.

All errors that may exist while trying to represent Celtic and Welsh culture, mythology, geography, and Arthurian Legend elements are entirely mine. I am a storyteller, weaving together information that builds and forms worlds in our imaginations. In the famous words of Nennius, a 9th century Celtic monk, "I have made a heap of all that I could find."

Your *Knights of Caerleon* lore keeper,

Jesikah Sundin

Author Thanks

Thank you, Readers for giving our Arthurian Legend reverse harem tale a try. We hope you enjoyed Fionna and her brave knights! Please leave a review on Amazon, Goodreads, or wherever else online you talk books. Reviews will help other readers find our book and is a wonderful way to thank an author for entertaining you.

Writing a book takes a village! And, in this case . . . an international one :-)

Our hearty thanks to Gareth Thomson of North Lanarkshire, Scotland for helping us craft Percival's lyrical language. We had so much fun pouring over the list of words and slang you so wonderfully provided us.

And, our eternal gratitude to fellow author Dierdre Reidy of Dublin, Ireland for reading a beta copy of The First Knight to provide feedback on the Irish elements in our story, including the language.

We also appreciate Deborah Woods of Norway for

her insight into Scandinavian culture to help shape Galahad into the loveable Norseman that he is, and Katie Kent of Seattle, U.S. for assisting us with our druid research (as she's in druidic bardic studies) as well as lending us the book, "Arthurian Magic" by John & Caitlin Matthews.

Audiobooks are now available from Tantor Media and narrated by the amazingly talented Cornell Collins and Gabrielle Baker. THEY ARE SO GOOD!!!

All right . . . time to get back to writing :-)

Happy reading!

Claire Luana & Jesikah Sundin

More Books

Claire Luana & Jesikah Sundin

THE KNIGHTS OF CAERLEON
The Fifth Knight, book 1
The Third Curse, book 2
The First Gwenevere, book 3

Claire Luana

MOONBURNER CYCLE
Moonburner, book 1
Sunburner, book 2
Starburner, book 3
Burning Fate, prequel

THE CONFECTIONER'S GUILD
The Confectioner's Guild, book 1
The Confectioner's Truth, book 2
The Confectioner's Coup, book 3
The Confectioner's Exile, prequel

THE FAERIE RACE
Co-authored with J.A. Armitage

The Sorcery Trials, book 1
The Elemental Trials, book 2
The Doomsday Trials, book 3

STANDALONES

Orion's Kiss

Jesikah Sundin

THE BIODOME CHRONICLES
Legacy, book 1
Elements, book 2
Transitions: Novella Collection, book 2.5
Gamemaster, book 3

THE EALDSPELL CYCLE
Æroreh, book 1

CLAIRE LUANA grew up reading everything she could get her hands on and writing every chance she could. Eventually, adulthood won out, and she turned her writing talents to more scholarly pursuits, going to work as a commercial litigation attorney.

While continuing to practice law, Claire decided to return to her roots and try her hand once again at creative writing. She has written and published the Moonburner Cycle and the forthcoming Confectioner Chronicles, a trilogy about magical food. She is currently working on the Knights of Caerleon trilogy, an Arthurian Legend fantasy romance series, which she is co-writing with Jesikah Sundin. She lives in Seattle, Washington with her husband and two dogs. In her (little) remaining spare time, she loves to hike, travel, binge-watch CW shows, and of course, fall into a good book.

www.claireluana.com

JESIKAH SUNDIN is a multi-award win-ning Ecopunk SciFi and Forest Fantasy writer mom of three nerdlets and devoted wife to a gam-er geek. In addition to her family, she shares her home in Monroe, Washington with a red-foot-ed tortoise and a collection of seatbelt purses. She is addicted to coffee, laughing, and Dr. Martens shoes ... Oh! And the forest is her happy place.

www.jesikahsundin.com
www.jesikahsundin.com/moontreebooks